The MAGE WARS

A VALDEMAR OMNIBUS

Available now from Mercedes Lackey and Titan Books

The MAGE WARS

MERCEDES LACKEY
& LARRY DIXON

TITAN BOOKS

The Mage Wars Omnibus
Print edition ISBN: 9781783296149
E-book edition ISBN: 9781785653568

Published by Titan Books
A division of Titan Publishing Group Ltd
144 Southwark Street, London
SE1 0UP

First edition: September 2016
2 4 6 8 10 9 7 5 3 1

Printed and bound in Great Britain by CPI Group Ltd.

The MAGE WARS

A VALDEMAR OMNIBUS

THE BLACK GRYPHON

A VALDEMAR OMNIBUS

BOOK ONE
OF THE MAGE WARS

Dedicated to Mel White, Coyote Woman
A legend in the hearts of all who know her

CHAPTER ONE

*S*ilence.

Cold wind played against Skandranon's nares—a cold wind as frigid as the hearts of the killers below. Their hearts pumped blood unlike any other creatures'; black, thick blood, warmed when their commanders willed it—only when they flew, only when they hunted, only when they killed.

Their blood was cold, and yet it ran warmer than their masters'. This much Skandranon Rashkae knew; he had fought their masters since he was a fledgling himself. They were cruel and cunning, these makaar, and yet the worst aspects of these manufactured horrors paled before the cruelty of their creators.

Silence. Stay still. Quiet.

Skandranon remained motionless, crouched, feathers compressed tight to his body. He was silent to more than hearing; that silence was but one of the powers that had made his master and friend so powerful, although it was the power that had given him his name—Urtho, the Mage of Silence. Urtho's champions had invisibility against magical sight—to mind-scanning, to detection spells, to magical scrying. The enemies of his monarchy had spent much of their resources on foiling that edge—to no avail, it seemed—and now concentrated on more direct methods of destroying Urtho's hold on the verdant central-land's riches.

Skan kept his wings folded, the leading edge of each wing tucked under the soft black feathers at the sides of his chest. It was important to be quiet, head down, even this far from the encampment. The journey here had been one of long soars and kiting, and although he was in his best physical shape ever, flight muscles protested even yet. Better now to rest and watch. The chill wind rippled against his coat of feathers. This day had turned out unseasonably cold, which hadn't helped him any—except that it kept the makaar willing to make only the most necessary flights.

He watched them sleeping restlessly, twitching in their dreaming. Did they know how transient, how fleeting, they were? How their creators built them, bred them, refined them, letting the bad stock die out by assigning them to the border? Did they know their masters designed them with short lives so the generations would cycle quicker, reveal the defects more conveniently?

They were, despite their horrifying appearances and deadly claws, quite pitiful. They'd never know the caress of a caring lover—they would only know the heat of imposed breeding. They knew their lot was the searing pain of a torture-weapon if they failed. They never lay in the sun with a friend, or dashed in the air with their wingmates…

They'd never risk their lives to do something because they felt it was *right.* Perhaps that was the greatest pity of all; they could not be broken because they had no honor to compromise, no will to subvert.

The makaar and the gryphons were a study in contrasts, despite the darker mages' obvious attempts to mimic the Mage of Silence's handiwork. If gryphons were sinuous, graceful storms, makaar were blustering squalls. The gryphons were bold, intelligent, crafty; the makaar were conditioned to blind obedience. And one need only ask Skandranon which was the more attractive; he'd likely answer "I am."

Vain bird. You'll make a lovely skin on a commander's wall.

Skandranon breathed deeply behind the line of trees atop the hill; before him was the Pass of Stelvi. The coming army had stormed it, at the cost of but a few hundred of their soldiers compared to the thousand of Urtho's garrison. Further down the pass was the split valley which once supported a thriving trade-town. Laisfaar was now the army's quarters, and the surviving townsfolk made into servants no better off than slaves. In the other fork of the valley the commanders had stationed the army's supplies and creatures, including the sleeping makaar.

They might as well sleep; they did not need to fear sorcerous spying. The army's mages had shielded the area from magical scrying, and none of Urtho's many attempts to search the valley by spell had worked. That had left the need for study by stealth—risky at best, suicidal at worst.

Skandranon had, of course, volunteered.

Fly proudly to your doom laughing, vain bird, the best of the best; more suitors than sense, more wealth than wisdom, sharp claws ready to dig your own funeral pit…

His meeting with Urtho had been brief by choice. The offer was made to send guards and mages; Skandranon declined. Urtho offered to bolster his defensive spells, as he had done so many times before; it was declined as well. What Skan asked for was enhancement of his magical senses—his magesight had been losing sharpness of late due to disuse. Urtho had smiled and granted it, and Skandranon left immediately from the Tower itself, leaping broad-winged onto the wind's shivering back.

That was three dozen leagues and four meals ago; a long time to cover such a distance. It was a tactical disaster for his side that the enemy's army had advanced this close to Urtho's Tower; now it appeared they were prepared to march on the Tower itself. The layout of the encampments showed three separate cadres of troops; the makaar had been assigned equally to two of them. And between those two was the weapons-master's coach, staked firmly and blanketed, flanked by two canvas-covered wagons.

Hold a moment, now. With a town nearby—hearths and comfortable bedding— the weapons-master is staying in a tent?

Each side in this war had Seers and Diviners, whose powers could throw secret plans, however perfectly laid, awry. A Seer waking with a premonition of an assassination could thwart the attempt, for instance. The night before Stelvi Pass was taken, a Seer's vision told of a horrible new weapon that would devastate the garrison Urtho had placed there. It was something magical, the woman had said, but was in the hands of common soldiers. That warning alone was enough to make the gryphon wary, and had made him determined to explore this valley.

In a war of mages, the limited number of Adepts and Masters made tactical planning easier—you could study your opponents, guess their resources, even identify them by their strategies without ever seeing the commander himself. What alarmed Skandranon was the idea that the power of a mage could be put in the hands of untrained people—those who did not have the innate powers or learned skills of a mage. The units that could be fielded with such weapons would be an unwelcome variable, difficult to guard against if at all. A Master could ride onto a battlefield and call on his own powers, unleashing firebolts, lightning, hurricanes of killing wind—but he was still but one man, and could be eliminated. But soldiers who could do that would be devastating, even if the weapons were employed but once each. And if an Adept had discovered a way for the weapons to draw on power from magical nodes—

That was too horrifying to think of further. Skandranon had faced the

Adept commander of all the troops below, the Kiyamvir Ma'ar, twenty months ago. He had volunteered for that mission, too, and had limped home wing-broken, stricken with nightmares. He had seen his wingmates skinned by the Adept's spells, feathered coats peeled back in strips by the Adept's will alone in full daylight, despite Skan's attempts to counterspell. The nightmares had left him, now, but the memory made him determined to protect Urtho's people from the Kiyamvir's merciless rule.

Skandranon's eyes focused on the town of Laisfaar. Urtho's garrison had not all been human; there had been hertasi, a few tervardi, and three families of gryphons. His eyes searched the ramparts, noted the wisps of smoke of fires still burning since the attack. There were the aeries of the gryphons; the ramps for visitors, the sunning beds, the fledglings' nests…

…the bloodstains, the burned feathers, the glistening ribcage…

All the usual atrocities. Damn them.

She had been alive until very recently; she had escaped the worst of it by dying of shock and bloodloss. The makaar had no love for gryphons, and their masters gave them a still-living one after a battle as a reward. Often it was a terrified fledgling, like this gray-shafted gryphon had been. The rest of the garrison's gryphons had doubtless been wing-cut, caged, and sent to the Kiyamvir for his pleasures by now. Skandranon knew well that, unless Ma'ar was distracted by his business of conquest, there would be nothing left of them to rescue by day's end.

If he could, Skandranon would insure the captives would not last that long. Crippled as they would likely be, he couldn't help them escape; but he could possibly end their ordeal.

But before that, he had a larger duty to attend to.

Now he moved, slinking belly-flat to the ground, catlike; one slow step at a time, feeling his way through the underbrush with such delicate care that not even a leaf rustled. The weapons-master's wagons had plenty of guards, but not even the weapons-master could control terrain. The mountains themselves provided brush-filled ravines for Skandranon to creep through, and escarpments that overlooked the wagons. The encampment was guarded from attack from above by makaar, but only over the immediate vicinity of the camp. It was guarded from penetration from below by the foot-soldiers, but only outside the camp itself. No one had guarded against the possibility of someone flying into the area of the camp, behind the sentry-lines, then landing and proceeding on foot to the center of the camp.

No one could have, except a gryphon. No one would have, except Skandranon. The omission of a defense against gryphon spying told him volumes about the military commanders who led this force. The Kiyamvir would reprimand them well for such a mistake—but then, Ma'ar was the only one of their side who understood the gryphons' abilities. Most commanders simply assumed gryphons and makaar were alike, and planned defenses accordingly.

So, Skandranon stayed in the shadows, moving quietly, as unlike a makaar as possible.

Time meant nothing to him; he was quite prepared to spend all night creeping into place. Even in the most strictly ruled of armies, discipline slackens after a victory. Soldiers are weary and need rest; victory makes them careless. Skan had timed his movements to coincide with that period of carelessness.

He noted no sentries within the bounds of the camp itself; his sharp hearing brought him no hint that the commanders prowled about, as they were wont to do before a battle. Doubtless, the commanders were as weary as the soldiers, and slept just as deeply.

He spent his moments waiting committing details to memory; even if he died, if his body was somehow recovered, Urtho could still sift his last memories for information. That would only work if he died swiftly, though. Otherwise, the memories could be overcome by sensory input; thus the immediate torture of gryphon captives. Daring rescues had occurred before, and once retrieved, the gryphons' bodies were tremendous sources of information.

That could also be a clue to where the rest of the gryphon families were; it was also not unheard of to use captives as bait for rescue-traps. Captives' minds were often stripped of the will to resist, and prisoners forced to give information to the enemy. This was why Skandranon held a horrible power—a spell of death keyed to gryphons—for mercy.

And he hoped with every drop of blood that he would never be required to use it again.

Halfway to his goal, he froze, as he heard footsteps approaching the stand of tall grasses where he lay hidden. The cover that had seemed adequate a moment earlier seemed all too thin now—

Clever bird, hiding in grass. Better hope the wind doesn't blow—

But the footsteps stumbled, and Skan held his breath, not wanting to betray his position by breathing steam into the cold air. He froze in mid-step, right foreclaw held a mere thumb-length above the ground.

He could not see the human who approached without turning his head, which he would not do. He could only wait and listen.

The footsteps stopped; there was a muffled curse, and the sound of hands fumbling with cloth—

Then, clear and unmistakable, the sound of a thin stream of water hitting the matted grasses.

The human grunted, yawned; the sound of trousers being hitched up followed. The footsteps stumbled away again.

Skandranon unfroze, and lowered his claw to the ground.

There were no other incidents as he made his way up the escarpment and slid under the shelter of a knot of wild plum bushes to wait until dawn. He could feel the beetles and spiders of the thicket exploring their newly arrived piece of landscape as the minutes went by. Despite the impulse to yelp and swat them, though, he stayed still. Their irritation provided a blessing in a way; something to feel, to keep his senses alert after nightfall.

Skandranon's tentative plan was to wait until darkness, then sneak out to explore the camp. Other warriors suspected his stealthiness was a result of Urtho's magicking, although the elder denied it, citing the gryphon's near-obsessive interest in dancing-movements. He had often watched Skandranon mimicking human, tervardi, and hertasi performers in private. Skandranon had trained himself with a dedication he would never admit except as a boast, applying that knowledge to flight, to lovemaking, and to combat. That, in truth, was what made him quieter than a whisper of wind; no spells or tricks, just practiced grace.

Silence alone is not enough. Urtho has learned that the hard way—we've lost border-towns for half a generation, and only now begun doing more than simply defending our borders. Eh, well, Urtho had never intended to become Archmage. He's more suited to crafting silver and carving figures than deploying armies.

Such a pity that a man so kindhearted would be pressed into the role of a warlord... but better he than a heartless man.

And I'd certainly rather be off making little gryphlets.

That would have to wait until the world became a safer place to raise young, though. For now, Skandranon waited... until a shriek from the town rang out, echoing off the walls of the valley.

Only practiced self-control kept him from leaping into the air, claws stretched to rend and tear.

One at least still lives. I'm coming, friend, I'm coming... just hold on a little longer. Just a little.

Feh, I can't wait any longer.

Skandranon stood and surveyed the layout of the encampment again; he'd heard screams like that too many times in his life. Not again. He spread his wings half-open, and leapt, down towards the weapons-master's wagons, depending on speed to be his ally. Knifelike wind whistled against his nares, chilling his sinuses, sharpening his mind. All the sights and sounds of the world intensified when he was in motion, sizes and details of shapes all taken into account for the entire span of his vision.

Snatch and fly, that's your plan, isn't it, damned foolish bird? You're going to die the hero they all call you, for what? Because you couldn't stand another moment of another gryphon's pain? Couldn't wait any longer.

The wagons rushed closer in his sight, and their magical alarms blazed into light, waiting like barbed snares to be triggered. Were they traps too, besides being alarms? Would they trap him? Were they the bait, not the tortured gryphon?

Would it matter? You're too damned predictable, Skan, too sensitive, couldn't stand to wait. She'd die anyway, you know it, by the time you'd have gone in. Why do it?

Colors and textures rushed past him in three dimensions, as he dove ever closer to the wagons.

It's because you're not bright enough, stupid gryphon. Stupid, stupid gryphon.

Well, death is inevitable anyway, so dying for the right reason is…

Just as final.

Stupid gryphon.

Too late for reconsideration, though. The wagon alarm-fields loomed nearer and Skan had to risk a spell to disarm them—the easiest was one which made them detect another place nearby, instead of the place they were supposed to protect. He focused on them, released the flow into them, diverted their field away to an open part of the camp… and they did not sound. Now his troubles stemmed from the soldiers who might still be outside—and the makaar. He might be invisible to the alarms, but he was still pitch black to anyone's vision. A soldier of Ma'ar's army would not wonder at a shadow that moved through the sky—he'd call an alert.

He half-hoped for detection, since he would likely have the quarry before any spells could be leveled against him. Once discovered, he would not have to skulk about any longer… he could blaze away with a detection-spell to find the gryphon whose scream he heard earlier. Otherwise there would be delicate searching around, for… who knew how long. Of course, discovery also brought such pesky distractions as arrows and firebolts and snares and spells...

He backwinged and landed, kicking up clods of dirt next to the wagon, and his head darted side to side, looking for spotters. None yet, but that would change all too quickly. Two steps to the back of the wagon, then under it—*no one ever guards the bottoms of things, only sides and doors*—and he began prying at the wagon's floorboards, next to the struts and axles, where the mud, water, and friction of traveling always rots the wood. He was curled up under the wagon completely, on his back, tail tucked between his legs, wings folded in against his ribs, hind claws holding the wingtips. He didn't dare rip at the canvas of the wagon's bonnet—past experience had shown that apparently flimsy defenses were often imbued with alarm-spells. His claws glowed faintly with the disruption-spell he was using, and the wood shriveled above where his claws slowly raked, silent from the sound-muffling of his cupped wings.

The enemy's wagons traditionally had an aisle down the middle, and that was where Skandranon was working... another four cuts, five, six, and he'd be able to pull the boards down under the blanket of a silence-spell. Then he'd get a look inside at their coveted prize...

He began mentally reciting the silence-spell, calling up the energy from inside himself and releasing it around the wagon. He was careful to mold it just short of touching the wagon itself, building it up from the ground. The wagon's defenses might yet be sensitive to the touch of just such a spell. It was hard to tell anymore, so many variables, so many new traps...

He hoped that the mages under Ma'ar's command did not sweep the camp for magic at work. Things were going so well, so far. Skan reached up, claws digging firmly into the crossbrace, cracked through it, and the entire aisle section fell to the ground, inches in front of his beak...

...and Skandranon found himself face to face with a *very* upset, recently awakened weapons-master, who was drawing *something*—surely a weapon—up from beneath his bedding. The weapon pointed at the gryphon, and started changing...

Skan's right claw shot out and struck the human's scalp and squeezed, finding flesh yielding. His thumb pierced the man's eye-socket, and inside the envelope of silence, a gurgling scream faded into the wet sounds of Skan withdrawing his talons from the kill.

The man's hands twitched and dropped the weapon, which was pointing at Skandranon still. It was a polished rod, wrapped in leather, with a glowing, spiked tip revealed where the leather ended. It rolled from the dead man's fingers and fell to the ground, and the tip withdrew into the rod.

On your back, underneath a wagon, in an enemy camp, you kill a weapons-master one-handed? No one will ever believe it. Ever. That was too close, too close, stupid gryphon.

Someone will come by soon, Skan. Move. Get the whatever-it-is and get away. That's all you need to do. Get away.

Skan released his wingtips and pulled himself across the body of the slain human, keelbone scraping against the ragged edge of sundered wood. His wing-edges caught, pinning him in the opening, and he wheezed with the effort of pulling himself through too small an opening. It was dim inside. Only the waning light from outside leaking through the canvas-openings provided any light. Around him, stacked in open cases, waited glistening objects, the same as the weapons-master had held, each the size of his foreclaws.

Each far more deadly than his claws, he was sure.

They must be some entirely new kind of arm, and he needed no spellcasting to know their magical origin. They exuded magic, their collective power making his feathers crawl like being in the heart of a lightning-storm a-brewing. Now to grab one, and leave! Skan reached towards the cases, almost touching one of them, when his inner voice screamed *No!*

The weapons-master had one, he was guarding these, these may all be trapped...

A hair-thin crackle of reddish energy arced between the weapons and his extended foreclaw, confirming his fears.

Then there may be only one that isn't trapped...

He moved slowly, wings folded so tight it hurt, up onto his haunches, then back down to all fours, until he faced the rear of the wagon. Then he reached down through the shattered floorboards, groping for the slain master's weapon. It didn't make sense to Skan that the man would trap his own weapon, even if he was a mage; weapons-masters as a rule tended to be terribly impressed with themselves, and thought they could handle anything themselves. *Too bad, so sad, first mistake and last. What's that, stupid bird, you're getting cocky because you've lasted this long? More to do, and every second is borrowed time.*

At last came the feel of the rod, warm to his touch despite the thickness of his scaled skin. He reared back, eyes closed to the thinnest of slits, concentrating on not touching the racks of trapped arms. He transferred his prize to his mouth, clenching it tightly above his tongue, and fell forward across the gaping entrance he'd made, stretching across it towards the untied flap of the wagon bonnet.

All right. What's the worst that could happen? I touch the canvas, and the entire wagon goes up with all the energy in these things. That'd be just like Ma'ar: if he can't have them, no one else can... I'd better count on it.

Skandranon bunched up his leg muscles, preparing for a massive leap through the exit, when he heard bootsteps outside, and a moment later, a shadowy figure opened the flap, cursing in the enemy's tongue.

Now. Now!

In the same instant, the figure opened the canvas, and the gryphon leapt. Skan used the man's shoulders as a vault, crushing the man's face against the back of the wagon from his momentum. He snapped his wings open, catching the edges, as the human crumpled underneath him. Then a deafening sound exploded around them as the wagon's massive final trap was set off—a crimson circle of fire spread across the ground, incinerating the human, catching the other wagon. A thrashing body was engulfed in the flame arcing from it as Skandranon gained altitude.

The makaar roused.

End of your charmed life, gryphon. At least now you can cast freely before you die... find her, wherever she is, accomplish that at least—

Skan's wings rowed at the air, clutching for distance from the camp. There was one thing yet to do, before his conscience would let him leave. Somewhere—his mind searched through the camp and town for where—there was one of his own kind being killed, slowly...

He searched, and found her tortured mind as he crested the ridge. It felt as if her body had been lanced deep by thousands of needles, cut on by a hundred mad surgeons, broken by mallets, yet still she lived. There was a wrenching moment as Skan's mind reeled from the backlash of what had been done to her, and he felt his wings fold involuntarily.

:*Kill me,*: she screamed, -.*stop them, something anything!*:

.*Open up to me,*: Skan sent to her, -.*open up to me and trust—there will be pain at first, then all will be dark. You'll fly again, as Urtho wills...*

She halted her scream as she recognized the code-sign for the death-spell. No one had made a move to block it yet—

He pulled back from her for a bare second, trying to steady himself in his flight. He reached out again, riding the wind, then unleashed the spell, caught her mind, pulled it free of her body for one gut-wrenching second. The spell struck home and stopped her heart.

I am sorry, so sorry... you will fly again after the dark... Then he released her spirit to the winds.

Somewhere in the captured inn, a bound and wing-cut body convulsed, then lay still. Above the valley, Skandranon raced away desperately, unable to cry out for her, as seven makaar surged skyward to destroy him.

At last, the General slept.

Amberdrake started to rise, then sank back down to his seat on the side of the General's bed as Corani woke convulsively, with a tiny gasp. The anguish was still there, filling the room, palpable even to the weakest Empath. For an Empath as strong as Amberdrake, the impact of Corani's pain was a blow to the heart.

Amberdrake waited for the General to speak, while radiating warmth and reassurance, concentrating on the soothing scents still flavoring the air as a vehicle for that reassurance; the gentle hint of amber incense, the chamomile in the oils he had used in his massage, the jessamine covering the taste of sleep-herbs in the tea he'd given Corani. He ignored the throbbing pain in his own temples, his tension-knotted stomach, and the terrible sense of foreboding that had come upon him at the General's summons. His feelings did not matter; he was a kestra'chern, and his client—more patient than client, as was often the case—needed him. He must be the strong one, the rock to rest against. He did not know Corani well; that was all to the good. Often men of power found it easier to unburden themselves to a stranger than to a friend.

The General's suite was in Urtho's keep and not in a tent in the camp; easy enough here to pull heavy curtains to shut out the light and the world with it, to burn dim, scented lamps that invoked a feeling of disassociation from the armed camp beyond the keep. The General himself had not summoned Amberdrake; the few times he had called to the camp for a kestra'chern, it had been Riannon Silkedre he had wanted—slightly inferior to Amberdrake in skill, an accomplished and well-respected female. No, one of Urtho's aides had come to the tent— quietly, with his livery hidden beneath a cloak, which said more about the aide's visit than the boy himself did.

Urtho was still closeted with his General when Amberdrake arrived, but when he finally returned to his quarters, he did not seem surprised to see Amberdrake there. He was clearly distraught, and yet it had taken Amberdrake hours and every bit of his skill to persuade him to unburden himself.

And he knew why Urtho had chosen him and not Riannon. There were times when it was easier for a man to reveal his pain to a man— and Amberdrake was utterly trustworthy. Whatever was revealed to him remained with him, forever. He was many things to many people; tonight, he had been something of a Healer, something of a priest, something of a simple, noncommittal ear.

"You must be disappointed," the General said into the lamplit dimness, his voice resigned. "You must think I'm a weakling now."

That was what Corani *said;* Amberdrake, being what he was, heard what Corani *meant.*

He was really saying, "I must disgust you for falling apart like this, for looking so poorly composed," and "You must despise me and think me unworthy of my position."

"No," Amberdrake replied simply, to both the spoken and unspoken assertions. He did not want to think what the General's collapse meant to him, personally; he *must not* think of it. Must not remember the messengers that roused the camp last night; the premonitions that had awakened the more sensitive and marginally Gifted among the Healers and kestra'chern from nightmares of blood and fire against the outline of the mountains. Must not think of the fact that Corani's family came from Laisfaar at Stelvi Pass, and that while his sons had posts with the army here, his wife and all his relatives were back *there.* There, where Skandranon had gone. He and Gesten did not know why, or for what reason; Amberdrake only knew that he had gone off without a farewell.

"No," Amberdrake repeated, taking the General's outflung hand before Corani could reclaim it and massaging the palm and fingers carefully. The muscles felt cramped and tight; Corani's hand was cold. "How could I be that stupid? You are human and mortal; we are the sum of our weak moments and our strong. Everyone has a moment they must break at; this one was yours. It is no shame to need help, and know it."

Somewhere, deep inside, he wondered if it was also *his.* There was pressure building inside him that threatened to break free at any moment. He was not so self-confident that he thought he could do without help. The question was, would there be any there for him? Too many battered spirits to mend—too many bruised bodies to comfort—the resources of Healers and kestra'chern alike were stretched and overstretched. That he was near the end of his reserves made little difference.

Far too many of his clients had gone out to battle and had not returned. And Skan had been due back this morning; it had been near sunset when the aide left him in Corani's quarters. Skan was never overdue.

But for now, this moment, he must put his own strain aside. None of that must show—he shouldn't let it break his concentration or his focus. Corani came first; Corani must be comforted enough, given enough reinforcing, as if he was a crumbling wall, that he could function and come to heal. Something had gone wrong, terribly wrong, at Stelvi Pass. Corani had not told him what, but Amberdrake knew, with dreadful certainty. Stelvi Pass had been overrun; Laisfaar, and Corani's family with it, was no more. It would be better for them to be dead than in Ma'ar's hands unless they'd hidden their identities and vanished into the general population. And that was unlikely.

Corani accepted this, as wise generals accepted all facts. Corani had accepted Amberdrake's comforting as well. For the moment, anyway. That was another of Amberdrake's abilities; it bought time. Time to bring distance, time to heal. "My sons—"

"I think that Urtho has seen to them as well," Amberdrake replied quickly. Urtho would have seen to everything; it was his way.

Skan-

Quickly, he suppressed the thought, and the anguish it caused.

The drugs in the General's tea took effect; in the dim light, Corani struggled to keep his eyes open, eyes still red and swollen from weeping. The General had fought those tears; fought to keep them properly held inside with the determination that had made him the leader he was. Amberdrake had fought his determination with a will of his own that was no less stubborn. "It's time to sleep," Amberdrake said quietly.

Corani blinked, but held him with an assessing gaze. "I'm not certain what I expected when I saw you here," he said finally. "Based on Riannon—"

"What Riannon gave you was what you needed then," Amberdrake replied, gently touching the General's cheek. "What I do is what you need now. Sometimes neither is what the recipient expects." He laid a soothing hand on Corani's forehead. "That is what a kestra'chern does, after all; gives you what you need."

"And not necessarily what I want," Corani said quickly.

Amberdrake shook his head. "No, General. Not necessarily what you *think* you want. Your heart knows what you want, but often your head

21

has some other idea. It is the task of the kestra'chern to ask your heart, and not your head, what you need, and answer that need."

Corani nodded, his eyelids drooping.

"You are a strong man and a good leader, General Corani," Amberdrake continued. "But no man can be in two places at the same time. You could not be here, and there as well. You cannot anticipate everything the enemy will do, nor where he will strike. The war thinks its own way. You are not answerable for the entire army. You did what you could, and you did it well."

The muscles of Corani's throat tightened visibly as he fought for control. Amberdrake sensed tears being forced down. Corani was on the verge of more than tears; he was on the verge of a breakdown. This would accomplish nothing, worse than nothing. The man needed rest, and with Amberdrake's hand resting on his forehead, he was open to Amberdrake's will.

"You must sleep," Kestra'chern Amberdrake said, imposing a mental command on top of the drugs. Corani closed his eyes, and this time he did not reawaken when Amberdrake rose to go.

Gesten would be where he had been since dawn: at the landing-field, waiting for Skandranon to return. Amberdrake left the keep, slipping unobtrusively out into the scarlet of a spectacular sunset. The landing-field was not that far away, and Amberdrake decided to head there, rather than returning straight back to his tent.

Depression weighed heavily on his heart, a depression that was not relieved at the sight of Gesten alone on the field, patiently making preparations to wait out the night-watch.

Amberdrake held his peace for a moment, then spoke.

"He's not coming back this time," Amberdrake said quietly.

His hertasi companion, Gesten, looked up at him with his expressive eyes and exhaled through his nostrils. He held his pebble-scaled snout shut for a long minute. "He'll come. He always does," Gesten finally said. "Somehow."

Amberdrake wished with all his heart that the little hertasi would be right this time. Skandranon had flown from the Tower two days before, and Stelvi Pass was less than a day away, flying; he had never been delayed by so much before. Gesten was going about the task of building a watch-fire for their friend, laying out colored smoke-pots amidst the kindling. It might be a useless gesture, but it was all he could really do right now, with dawn so far away. Light up a pattern of blue and white to welcome the flyer home, let him know from afar that safety was close… Amberdrake tried to help, but he was so awkward, and his heart wasn't in it. How odd, that one so graceful in his calling could be so clumsy outside it.

"Urtho has called a council." That much was common knowledge; no harm in telling the hertasi now. "Two gryphons came streaking in from Laisfaar straight to the Tower, and two hours after that, Urtho sent a message ordering me to tend General Corani."

Gesten nodded, apparently taking Amberdrake's meaning—that Corani needed the peculiar skills of a kestra'chern. The General had been permanently assigned to the Pass, until Urtho needed him more than his home district did. For the last week he'd been at the Tower, pleading with Urtho for some special protection for Stelvi Pass and the town. That much was common knowledge too.

"What can you tell me?" Gesten knew very well that there was only so much Amberdrake could reveal to him. "What did Corani need?"

Amberdrake paused, searching for the right word.

"He needed sympathy, Gesten," he said as he laid down a stack of oily fire-fuel logs. "Something happened in the Tower that he didn't want to talk about; and I can only assume that from the way he acted, the news was the worst. Kept talking about blind spots—he was near to a breakdown. That's not like him. And now… Skandranon is late." Amberdrake smoothed his silk caftan, brushing the wood-chips away. He felt worry-lines creasing a face even his enemies called handsome, but he was too depressed to even care.

He absently pulled his long hair back from where it had fallen astray. "I don't think he's coming back this time. I can feel it in my gut…"

Gesten picked up a firelog and pointed it up at Amberdrake. "He *will* be back, I feel it in *my* gut, Drake, and I won't put up with your whining about "poor Skan." He always comes back. *Always.* Understand? And I'll be here, with this watchfire, until either he comes back or this army runs out of firelogs."

Amberdrake stepped back, thoroughly chastised, and more than a little surprised at the vehemence of the normally quiet lizard's speech. Gesten stood pointing the stick at him for a moment further, then spit at the air and threw it on the growing stack of kindling.

"I'm sorry, Gesten." Though he meant he was sorry about angering the hertasi, Gesten would probably take it some other way. "It's just that… you know how I feel about him."

"Feh. I know. Everyone knows. You seem to be the only one who doesn't know." The hertasi opened the latch on the firebox and withdrew a coal with blackened tongs. His tail lashed as he spoke. "You worry about everything, Drake, and you don't listen to yourself talking. There is no one in Urtho's service who is better than him. No one else more likely to come back." Gesten dropped the coal into the folds of cotton batting and woodchips between the two firepots. "Even if he doesn't come back he'll have died the way he wanted to."

Amberdrake bit his lip. Gesten thought he was right, as usual; nothing would dissuade him. Nothing Amberdrake *could* tell him would persuade him that the situation was hopeless; only the things Amberdrake could not tell him would do that. And he was right: Skan had died the way he wanted to. "I'll—keep quiet, until we know."

"Damned right you will. Now go back to your tent. You can manage your clients without me tonight." Gesten turned his attention to lighting the center fire, then the blue and white smoke-pots blazed into light. Amberdrake walked in the cooling night air towards the Tower and the semi-mobile city that clustered around it, stopping once to look back at the lonely figure who'd wait for all eternity if need be for the black gryphon's return. His heart, already heavy, was a burden almost too great to bear with the added weight of tears he dared not shed.

Oh, not now, I don't need this…

Skandranon struggled against gravity and rough air, jaws clenched tightly on his prize. His heart was beating hard enough to burst from his chest, and the chase had barely begun—the makaar behind him were gaining, and he was only now past the ridge. As if it weren't enough that makaar were quicker than gryphons, they possessed better endurance. All they had to do was cut him off, and fly him in circles…

That was clearly what they intended to do. His advantage was his ability to gain and lose altitude more quickly than they. With cleverness, he could make them *react*, not act. At least they weren't terribly well organized—it wasn't as though Kili was leading them—

Skandranon twisted his head to assess his pursuers, and spotted an all-too-familiar black and white crest—Kili, the old makaar leader Skan had taunted numerous times. Kili, who had almost trapped him once before, with a much smaller force aflight, was streaking to a pitch a thousand feet above the other six, screaming commands.

Three gray-patched makaar canted wings back and swept into a shallow dive, gaining on him all the faster by trading height for speed. Their trajectory took them below and past him a few seconds later— and they were followed by another three. He tried to watch them all, eyes darting from one to the other, as they split off and rejoined. Why head below him, when altitude was so important against a gryphon?

Altitude—damn!

Instinct took over even as he realized Kili's gambit. He folded his right wing completely, rolling sideways in midair as the elder makaar streaked past him by a featherlength. A shrill scream of rage rang in his ears as Kili missed, and Skan threw himself out of the roll by snapping his wing open again and spiraling nose-first towards the earth—and the six makaar there.

That bastard! *He had the audacity to* learn *from me!*

Skan clamped his wings tightly and plummeted through the massed makaar below him, seeing the claws and razor-edged beaks of the surprised makaar as a blur as he shot past. He followed dead on the tail of Kili. The chances of surviving that move were slim—he'd gambled on his swiftness, and the makaar did no more damage than removing a few covert feathers.

Distance for speed—let's see if they can follow this.

Kili was so very close ahead that Skan was tempted to strike at him, but he couldn't afford to be distracted from his primary objective— to survive and escape. Already, the two flights of makaar behind him stroked rapidly to pursue, crying out in rage. He passed the makaar leader, who predictably took a swipe at him and lost precious speed, and Kili's recovery was further fouled by the wind turbulence of his passing underlings. The six rowed past Kili, gaining on Skandranon as he coursed back towards Laisfaar.

Stupid gryphon, the point is to get away *from this place!*

The barrier range swept inexorably closer. Skandranon narrowed his concentration to the rockface before him, and studied the erosion-channels cut into the stone by ages past. His breath turned ragged through his nares as he struggled against fatigue. From the edge of his vision, he saw the other makaar winging through the Pass, cutting an arc towards the pursuit.

They'll see my wings flare, and assume I'm braking to turn or climb—

Skan cupped his wings as he streaked in a straight line for the sheer cliff-face, feeling but not seeing the bloodthirsty makaar gaining on him from behind. The barrier stone filled his vision as he executed his desperate move: he folded his wings until their leading edges curled under him with a clap and his straining body rolled into a tumbler's somersault. He plummeted in a descending arc as lift abandoned him and momentum hurled him towards unforgiving stone.

Gravity reversed itself; his head snapped into his chest as he fell. Numbly, detachedly, he realized the new, tiny pain in his chest was where the sharp tip of his beak had pierced it. Disorientation took him. All he could do was keep his jaws closed as his world went black, and wonder how many bones this last trick of his would break.

Follow through—do it, bird, do it—

He stretched his hindlegs out, and fanned his tail. Wind rushed against the lay of his feathers as he hurtled backwards.

In the next instant, he was surrounded by shocked makaar, three above, three below, whose attention was locked on him instead of the rock rushing to strike them from the sky.

It's going to work—lucky, stupid gryphon—

The dizzying sensations of gravity's pull, momentum's throw, and the rushing of blood mixed with the sound of six makaars' screams and the crunch of their bodies against stone. Skandranon's feet touched the unforgiving rock behind him—and he pushed off.

The strange maneuver stabilized his tumble; gave him the chance to spread his wings in a snap and break his fall, turn it from a fall into a dive.

Only the ground was *awfully* close...

Pull up, stupid bird, pull up!

Wings straining, heart racing, he skimmed the rock at the bottom of the cliff, so close that his wingtips brushed it, using his momentum to send himself shooting skyward again, past the spreading stain on the rock that was all that was left of his first pursuers.

Now get out *of here, idiot!*

He reversed his course, away from the Pass, back towards home and safety—and looked down.

At several hundred crossbows.

Of course, they couldn't see him, except, perhaps, as a fleeting shadow. But they knew he was up there, and they only had to fill the sky with arrow with bolts and rocks, and one or more of them would probably hit him. A quick glance to either side showed that he'd been flanked by the two new flights of makaar; they hemmed him in, and had several gryphon-lengths' worth of altitude on him. Kili was not in sight; he was probably up above, somewhere, waiting.

His only chance lay in speed. If he could just get past the archers before they let fly—

Too late.

From below came a whirring sound; the air around him filled with a deadly reverse-rain of crossbow-bolts and slung shot. He pulled in his wings in a vain attempt to narrow the target-area.

At first, he didn't feel pain, only impact. Out of the corner of his eye, he saw a mist of his own blood as his right wing came forward on the downstroke.

Then it crumpled.

Then it hurt.

He tumbled again, only nominally under control, shrieking incoherently around his beakful of stolen weapon.

He shuddered under the impact of two more hits; the pain came quickly this time, but he forced himself to ignore it. Once again, he tumbled out of control, and this time there was no handy cliff to push off of.

He pulled in his left wing and rolled over completely; righted himself, still falling. He dared not try and brake completely; the injured wing wouldn't take it. Instead, he extended just enough of both to turn the fall into another steep dive, angled away from the battle and towards friendly territory.

Just after his wings flared, he saw Kili whistle past where he had been.

A little farther—a little farther—

The ground was coming up awfully fast.

He was over Urtho's territory now, on the other side of the enemy lines, but he could not, dared not, flare his wings completely. His dive was a steep, fast one, but it was still a dive. The ground had never looked so inviting. Or so hard.

Ah sketi, *this is going to hurt—*

CHAPTER TWO

Amberdrake could not sleep; weary as he was, there was no point in lying awake and watching the inside of his eyelids. He wrapped a blanket around his shoulders and made his way down the dark aisles between the tent-rows to the landing-field.

As he came out into the open, away from the lights of the camp, he saw that the sky to the west was a haze of silvery light from the setting moon; it could not be long now, a few hours at most, until dawn. Gesten waited patiently beside his fire, as he had waited all night. Amberdrake had left the last of his clients to join the little lizard, but Gesten was clearly not in any mood to talk.

The hertasi tended to be silent when something affected his emotions. Amberdrake shared that tendency. In his case, it was due to long self-training; for both of them, it was to preserve the illusion of immutable and eternal stability.

It was Amberdrake's duty to convey an impression of serene concern—for Amberdrake's clients were always damaged in some way these days. Sympathy worked better than empathy, more often than not.

Clients didn't *want* to know their kestra'chern had problems of his own.

Since he couldn't be rid of them, he mustn't let them show, not even for a moment. It was part of the burden of his avocation, and though he'd come to accept it, it still caused a dull ache like a sympathy pain.

Sympathy pain. Yes, that was exactly what it was like.

The depression had worsened with every rumor, every bit of camp-gossip. Skan had never been this late in returning from a mission; even Gesten must know by now that he wasn't coming back. He had always joked about how Skan always rushed back at top speed from a mission; that he couldn't be back to his rewards and admiration fast enough.

By now the news had leaked out of a terrible disaster at Stelvi Pass, worse than any defeat Urtho's forces had faced before. The reaction was not panic, but Amberdrake wondered if there was anyone in the ranks who guessed at what he already knew: that the garrison had been overrun and wiped out completely. As the night grew colder, so did Amberdrake's heart, and wrapping his body in a spiral-knit blanket over his silks didn't help at all.

Gesten still hadn't spoken. Finally he could bear it no longer. Without a word, he left his place beside the watch-fire and walked away into the darkness, looking back over his shoulder at the little spot of light and the patient figure hunched beside it. His heart ached, and his throat threatened to close with tears he feared to shed—feared, because once they began, he was not certain he would be able to stop them. Tears for Gesten—and for Skan. Wherever *he* was.

Waiting out in the darkness for someone who—wasn't going to

come home—wasn't going to accomplish anything. The war went on, for its own reasons, no matter who grieved. Amberdrake, like so many Kaled'a'in, had long been thinking of the war as a being of its own, with its own needs, plans, and hungers. Those who chose to obey its will, and those who found themselves swept along in its path, had to go on living and pursuing their dreams, even if it did feel as if they were constantly trying to bail a leaky boat with their bare hands. The skills Amberdrake possessed would be needed regardless of whether the war raged on or ebbed—people would always feel pain, loneliness, instability, doubt, strain. He had long ago resigned himself to the responsibility of caring for those who needed him. No—caring for those who needed his *skills*. They didn't necessarily need him, they needed his skills. It was *that* realization, too, that chilled his heart, and had caused him to leave the smoky-white pyre.

Gesten had only his duties to Amberdrake and to the Black Gryphon, and Amberdrake could do without him for a while. Gesten clearly intended to keep his watch no matter what Amberdrake required of him. Amberdrake, on the other hand, always had his duties. And right now he felt terribly, horribly *lonely.* After all, once you've given up a large slice of yourself to someone and they're suddenly *gone*—how else *could* you feel? He'd never had a magical bond to the Black Gryphon, nothing that would let him know with absolute certainty if Skandranon was alive or dead. So he only had his reasoning and the known facts, and they pointed to the loss of a friend. A trusted one.

He neared the camp.

He entered the lighted areas of the camp, fixed a frozen, slight smile on his face and checked his walk to ensure it conveyed the proper confidence, and the other more subtle cues of his profession. There were few folk awake at this time of the night—or rather, morning—but those few needed to be reassured if they saw him. A frowning Healer was a bad omen; an unhappy kestra'chern often meant that one of his clients had confided something so grave that it threatened the kestra'chern's proverbial stability—and since Amberdrake was both those things, anything other than serenity would add fuel to the rumors already flooding the camp. And for *Amberdrake* to be upset would further inflame the rumors. He could never forget who and what he was, so long as he was in a public place.

Even though his face ached and felt stiff from the pleasant expression he had forced upon it.

Urtho kept an orderly camp; with tents laid out in rows, every fifth row lighted by a lantern on a perching-pole, anyone who happened to see Amberdrake would be able to read his expression clearly. It must look as if nothing had changed in the past few hours.

And yet, before he could do anyone else any good, he was going to have to deal with his own sorrows, his own fears and pain. He knew that as well as he knew the rest of it.

He strode into the Healers' bivouac, his steps faltering only once. There was a distant part of him that felt ashamed at that little faltering step. He attributed that feeling to his tumultuous state of mind—hadn't he soothingly spoken to others that there was no shame in such things? Still...

Help was not far off, if he asked for it. It was his right, of course. He was entitled to counsel and Healing, and all of his own profession's skills he wished. He had taken comfort in such ways before, and given it hundreds of times. And though a small internal voice might echo words of weakness from the walls of his mind—tell him to just hold it in, not to succumb to the strain—he was not too proud to ask for that help. Not at this point, not when he was a mass of raw nerves and trembling on the edge of a breakdown. He had seen the signs of such things too often not to recognize them in himself.

In tents and shacks he passed, small lanterns or lightstones illuminated solitary figures. They carved surgical instruments or sewed torn clothing and bandages. The surreal acoustics of the still night made an old Healer's work-time whistling seem louder than it should be, as he cut and assembled arm-slings by lantern light, apparently oblivious to the world outside his opened tent. On perches by the surgery-tent, messenger-birds slept with their heads tucked under soft-feathered wings, with kyree sleeping soundly in front of them. The soft jingling of hanging harness and tackle sounded like windchimes from a tranquil garden. How odd that in the middle of upheavals, such poignant moments still occurred.

Healer Tamsin and his lover and apprentice, Lady Cinnabar, were on night-duty for the next ten days or so. He should be able to find them inside the surgery-tent. There past the Healers' and surgeons' tents, on the little rise ahead of him called "Healer's Hill", stood the common tents being used for infirmaries and treatment-centers. Several of the tents had been used, in happier days, to hold Kaled'a'in celebrations, and had the capacity of housing a hundred or more. Their colors had been allowed to discreetly fade over the years, since their current uses were anything but festive.

Lights in the central tent, and shadows moving inside it, told him that *someone*, at least, was there. He pushed aside the flap and moved quietly inside, and found Tamsin and Cinnabar bandaging a middle-aged land-scout, surrounded by tables bearing the debris of a thorough patching-job. A mercenary; Amberdrake caught sight of the badge on his shoulder and recognized the wolf-head of Pedron's Wolves. Urtho was very careful about the mercenaries he hired, and the Wolves had a particularly good reputation. Even the gryphons spoke well of them.

Even Skan had spoken well of—

Sketi, *Drake, you're fixated. It's a downward spiral, and it's got to be broken— before you are.*

He sagged against a tent-brace and hid his face in the shadows as he lost control over his expression. He wanted to be within sensing distance, but he also didn't want to be obtrusive. He shielded as much of his grief as he could, but these were fellow Healers, Empaths—and the closest friends he had.

Next to Gesten and Skan…

Tamsin didn't look his way, but Amberdrake sensed his attention, and in the next moment he said to the mercenary, "You'll do well enough, fire-eater. What you need now is some rest. Limit your activity to complaining for a few days. Here's your green chit for days off." He signed the wooden square in silver-ink and handed it off. "Three days, and six more at light duty."

Now Tamsin looked up, as if noticing Amberdrake for the first time, and added quietly, "I think I have a friend in need of a little help himself at the moment."

The mere looked up, caught sight of Amberdrake standing in the shadows, and grunted. "Thankee, Master Tamsin. I 'spect you'll send me the charge, eh?"

Tamsin laughed at the tired old joke, and the mercenary shuffled off, passing Amberdrake with a nod, and pushed through the tent-flap into the warm dark beyond. Amberdrake laid himself down on the cot the scout had just vacated, disregarding the binding of the silk caftan against his body as he rolled over. He threw his arm over his eyes, hand bunched into a fist. A fist was a sign superstitiously avoided among Healers as being bad luck, but his mind was not on wards and omens. He heard the sounds of hands being washed and toweled dry, and instruments being laid back in trays. Minutes passed without a word, and the after-Healing cleanup was concluded. He heard a curtain being drawn around them for privacy.

"The rumors about Stelvi are true—truth's probably worse than you've heard," he said to the waiting silence. "And Skandranon didn't make it back."

He felt one hand touch his cheek, lightly; felt someone else take his hand. Both touches released the flood of grief he had pent up within him, and lost in the dark waters of mourning, he couldn't tell which of the two was touching him. Focus wavered in his mind. It didn't matter which of the two touched him where; what mattered was that they did. He welcomed them both.

Tears threaded their way down his face, soaking the hair at his temples. The knot in his throat choked further speech.

"Don't mourn for one who might still be alive," Tamsin chided gently. "Wait until you know..."

But they both knew that if Skandranon were able, he'd have made it back by now, or he'd have somehow sent a message. Tamsin made a swallowing sound, as if he had stopped himself before he said anything stupid.

"I think it's the fact that we don't know, Lady Cinnabar said, as Amberdrake fought for control. "Drake, we love him too, you know—but we've seen too many times when people we've given up as lost made it back. Skandranon—"

"Has never failed a mission in his *life*," Amberdrake cried, half in anger, half in grief. "If he didn't—if he couldn't... "

The rest was lost in tears, as he finally stopped trying to control himself and simply let himself weep. The cot creaked as two weights settled beside him; one of them kissed his forehead, the other embraced him, and he buried his face in the proffered shoulder as a wave of compassion and reassurance spread from both of them.

"This is too much!" he sobbed bitterly, as whoever was holding him rocked him a little, like a child. "Waiting here, waiting to see who comes back in pieces—who doesn't come back at all. Not being *there* when they're hurt and dying."

"We know," Tamsin murmured, a world of sorrow in his own voice. "We know."

"But you don't know the rest of it—rewarding the ones who survive, when inside I cry for the ones who didn't... "

There was nothing they *could* say to that.

"I'm *sick* of detaching myself!" he burst out, in another flood of tears. "They come to me to forget *their* pain, but when am I allowed to mourn?"

There was no spoken answer for that, since they *were* the answer. They simply held him while he wept, held him and tried to give him the little comfort they had. Finally, after he had cried himself out in their arms, he was able to talk a little more calmly.

"Drake, you've heard it all before," Cinnabar said, as Tamsin got up to retrieve a damp cloth for Amberdrake. "But I'll tell you again; we are here to help you, just as you help others. You've been bearing up through all this better than anyone else. No one has ever seen you lose control, but you don't have to be superhuman."

"I know that," he said, exhausted by his bout of emotion. "Gods, that's exactly what I just got through saying to someone else tonight. But I've never felt like this before. It's *Skandranon* this time—he was my constant. I always knew he'd be all right; it was safe to love him because I never thought I'd lose him. He never comes back with anything worse than a lost tailfeather."

Cinnabar smoothed Amberdrake's damp hair back from his forehead with the cool cloth, cool as winter skies, as the ache in his heart struck him once again. "Now—just losing *him*—I can't bear it. It hurts too much."

Early-morning sounds, muffled by the cloth and canvas of the tent, punctuated the talk. Wasn't it too early, yet, for all of that? Maybe time had simply gotten away from them. Maybe that was the next lesson in all of this—that no matter how Amberdrake felt, all would still go on without him. Still...

Tamsin settled on the other side of him as Cinnabar captured his hands in hers.

"There's nothing I can say that you don't already know," Tamsin said quietly. "You have a harder task than we—a double burden. We have flesh to make whole again; you have hearts and minds to heal as well. The only comfort I can offer is to say you aren't alone. We hurt too. Skan is our friend, and he—"

The noise outside didn't settle to the dull murmurs of daybreak; instead it kept rising.

It sounded, in fact, as if a small riot was approaching the surgery-tent. A pang of *what have I done now?* struck Amberdrake in his self-pitying state, but left when reason returned a heartbeat later.

Amberdrake pushed the cloth away from his eyes and sat up—just as a pain-filled shriek ripped through the pre-dawn air, shattering his eardrums, and ensuring that all three Healers had their full attention taken by the noise outside.

"What in—" Tamsin leapt to his feet, Cinnabar beside him, just as the tent-flap flew open and the mob shoved its way inside.

In the center of the mob was an unholy mating of gryphon and brush-pile, all liberally mired in mud. Amberdrake would not have recognized it as Skandranon, except for the black feathers and the incredible vocabulary of half-delirious curse-words.

He rolled off the cot and to his feet, as Gesten directed the litter-team—for there was a litter under all that mess—to get what was left of the gryphon up onto one of the surgery tables. The hertasi looked around for a Healer; spotted Tamsin and Cinnabar, and Amberdrake behind them.

"You'll do. Here!" Gesten snapped.

Gods, if he ran the army...

But the three Healers had begun their work before he spoke; Tamsin getting the clattering trays of surgical instruments, Cinnabar calling for their assistants, and Amberdrake pushing aside the litter-bearers to get at the injured gryphon, heedless of anything else.

Amberdrake touched the Black Gryphon, and felt Skandranon's pain as if it screamed through his own nerves, striking him like a hammer-blow to the forehead. This was the drawback of working on so close a friend. He shielded somewhat, automatically, but that pain also told him what was wrong, and he dared not block it all out.

As Cinnabar's assistants scraped and washed the mud from the tangled flesh and cut branches away from broken limbs, Amberdrake took Skandranon's pain deeper into himself, warning the others when they were going to cause more damage by moving something. He could feel his mouth agape as he sucked in halting breaths; felt his eyes wide in double-Sight, his mind split between seeing the physical and Seeing inside. It seemed an eternity before they got Skandranon's body free of the remains of the tree he'd crashed into, another eternity before they got him washed down so that they could see the external injuries clearly.

Wordlessly, the other two left the wings to Amberdrake and concentrated on Skan's legs and body. Amberdrake was one of the few in camp who knew the gryphons' anatomy well enough to Heal wings to be flight-worthy again. Muscle, tendon, bone, vein, all were dependent on each other in living bodies—yet in an avian's body this seemed doubly true. Alter *this*, and balance and weight distribution and control surface and a hundred other things would change…

The right wing had a crossbow-wound, still bleeding sluggishly. The left was broken in several places. Amberdrake directed Gesten to put pressure on the bleeding bolt-wound. Gryphon wing-bones tended to knit almost as soon as they broke, like a bird's, and the sooner he got to the breaks, the less likely that he would have to rebreak anything to set it properly.

Skandranon whimpered a little and coughed, until a fourth Healer, still sleepy-eyed and robed from bed, came to stand at his head, and with one hand on either side of the huge beak, willed the gryphon into slumber. Skandranon's throat gurgled as his beak parted.

The wing-muscles relaxed, and Amberdrake went to work.

He eased the shattered fragments of each broken bone together, then held them in place with his bare hands while his mind forced the bits and pieces into the right order and prodded them into the process of knitting, all the while drawing away the fluids that built up around the damage. When the bone started healing, he called for splints and bandages, wrapped the section of wing tightly, and went on to the next, pausing only to wipe the drying blood from his hands before it caked so thick it interfered.

"Drake?" Gesten said, barely making a stir in his concentration.

"What?" he asked shortly, all of his attention focused on getting the final bone to draw together.

"I think you'd better hurry." That was all the hertasi said, but it was enough. He left the splinting of the final bone and the binding of the wing as a whole to one of the assistants, and came around to Gesten's side of the table.

He knew with a glance why Gesten had called him; the sheer dead weight of the injured wing was so great that the bolt-wound was tearing open, and the great wing-vein was perilously close to the site of the wound. A fracture under that pressure could simply break wide open and sever the vein as it went.

Quickly, he directed Gesten under the gryphon's wing, to take some of the strain off, and reached out to hold the wound closed, careful not to pinch. He closed his eyes and concentrated, Seeing the injury with his inner sight, bringing together the torn muscle-fibers, rejoining bleeding veins, goading it all into the process of Healing at a rate a thousand times faster than it would naturally, and providing the energy the body required to do so from within himself. Infection threatened; he burned it away, ruthlessly. He strengthened the rest of the muscles, taking some of the strain off the injured ones. When they threatened to cramp, a finger's touch soothed them. He found smaller broken bones, wounds and cuts he had not noticed in Healing the larger ones. He dealt with them all, searching out dangerous blood-clots and filtering them from the bloodstream, until the wings had been wrapped in a binding of energies that would allow Skandranon to fly again, in time.

Skandranon moaned and coughed weakly, as if something was caught in his throat. His breathing steadied as the fourth Healer pushed him back into slumber, but he was taken by a fit of coughing again that caused everyone near to hold onto him tightly. Amberdrake was peripherally aware of Tamsin putting his arm down Skandranon's gullet while an assistant held the beak open with a metal bar, and then the badly wounded gryphon wheezed, shook, and fell into deep sleep again.

The assistants administered fortifying herbal and mineral infusions of all kinds into the gryphon while Amberdrake set Skandranon's fractured forearms and splinted his foreclaws.

Finally, it was over, and he swayed away from the table, letting the assistants do their mechanical labor of bandaging and bracing. He saw then that Tamsin and Cinnabar had already finished; Cinnabar instructed the litter-bearers where to take Skan, and Tamsin had disappeared. The early-morning sun shone brightly through the walls of the tent, making them glow with a warm amber light.

The tables and floors were a disaster. Blood—*how could a flyer hold so much blood?* he thought—and cut-away feathers pasted bits of bark and leaves to the floor. On the table, a length of a crossbow-bolt lay amid the other debris, next to something that was relatively clean—a leather-wrapped handle of some kind, perhaps a broken sword. *That must have been what was blocking his throat,* Amberdrake thought numbly. *How would it get there...?*

Amberdrake blinked once, and staggered back.

"No you don't!" Gesten left Skandranon's side to go to Amberdrake's, getting under the kestra'chern's arm and bracing him upright. "It's bed for you, Drake. Skan's going to be fine—but you'd better get lying flat before you pass out!"

"I think you're right," Amberdrake murmured, actually finding a chuckle somewhere. *Skan's going to be all right. He made it back.* That was all that really mattered, after all. The cold place inside him had warmed; the emptiness refilled. *Skan made it back.*

With Gesten's help, he tottered off down the slight slope to the kestra'cherns' portion of the camp, just beyond the Healers'. He was so tired, he hardly noticed when he was guided into his own tent, except that the bright light of the morning sun dimmed, and the cool, fresh air took on a tinge of incense and body-scent. That was when he pulled away from Gesten, staggered to his bed, and collapsed across it. He managed after a moment to get himself lying the right way, but after that, he knew nothing more.

Amberdrake felt Skandranon's pain and frustration even as he awoke. Even after—how many?—hours of needed oblivion, there was a dull ache in Amberdrake's body in all the places he'd helped Heal in Skandranon's body the night before. In all the places that Amberdrake *didn't* have a direct analog to—the wings and tail, especially the wings—there was an ache. It was an aftershock effect that Healers knew well and had to live with; in the case of the wing-pain, it bunched in Amberdrake's shoulder-blades and upper arms, like a bruised muscle cramping to the bone.

Amberdrake had awakened feeling as if he had run for days carrying a full pack; as if he had worked for two days without a rest—in short, as if he had served his full roster of clients, then Healed a gravely injured gryphon.

Gesten—loyal, competent Gesten—had drawn the sleeping-curtains to block as much light as possible from reaching the exhausted kestra'chern, and was no doubt away from the tent clearing Amberdrake's schedule of responsibilities.

Amberdrake pulled the blankets from himself and stood up, steadying himself on a ring set into the overbuilt bed-frame. He washed quickly and gulped down a meal of meat-strips and flatbread, and then pulled on the caftan and belt Gesten had laid out for him. By his clothes was a roster-sheet of appointments for the day; all but one had been crossed out, and that one was not due for another two hours.

Amberdrake stepped out from the spell-quieted canvas of his multi-roomed tent into the afternoon daylight of the camp. Messenger-birds shot past, brightly colored, calling their descending chittering cry, while smoke from cook-fires scented the air they flew through. Three laughing children ran by, wearing the green and yellow ribbons of their parents' cadre, chased by a playful kyree with a bright red ball in its mouth. This was the way that life should be. Amberdrake stretched, then ran a hand across his chin and cheeks as he squinted in the light; time to shave again, before serving that client. A thorough general grooming was in order after he insured that Skandranon was healing properly. Being immaculately groomed always made him feel better.

He threaded his way through the shacks, forges, and service huts to the great tent where he'd left the Black Gryphon languishing that morning. In the daytime, the camp was far more inviting, despite the tension that was apparent everywhere you looked.

Assistant Healers and surgery aides surged past Amberdrake as he stepped inside, all intent on taking care of small administrative tasks and stocking supply shelves while the luxury of time was theirs. Casualties could course in as an overwhelming wave at any moment, so any spare minutes had to be spent in preparation. The war hadn't left the Healers much time to rest; they (and the grave-diggers, body-burners, and clergy) had few hours of leisure time. That was the nature of a war, after all. It ate spirits and bodies. It fed like any other creature.

War forced individuals and species together in ways no peacetime situation would duplicate, and some of the oddest friendships—even loves—came out of that. Amberdrake's affection for Gesten was natural, given the long association that hertasi had with the Kaled'a'in. Only the war and the needs of the fighters for support personnel had prevented Amberdrake from acquiring an entire troop of the little lizard-folk. As it was, he had to share Gesten's services with Skandranon.

But the bond between himself and the Black Gryphon—that was something that would never have occurred in peaceful times. The gryphons were literally unnatural—creations of Urtho, the Mage of Silence—and they would never have been found near the rolling plains that the nomadic Kaled'a'in called home. At least, not in Amberdrake's lifetime. He had heard Urtho mention some kind of vague plans he'd had, of planting them in little aeries in some of the wilder parts of the mountains, creating yet another population of non-human intelligences, as Urtho's predecessors had done with the hertasi and the kyree. But that plan, of course, had come to nothing with the onset of war among the Great Mages.

Urtho had tried to stay out of the conflict, with the result that the conflict had come to him. Amberdrake wondered if he sometimes berated himself for waiting. There had probably been a point early in Ma'ar's career when Urtho could have defeated him easily, had he not held his hand. But who could have known that war would have come to roost in Ma'ar's willful head? Urtho couldn't be blamed for not bottling up the Kiyamvir long ago.

There were little joys amid all the pain, and some of those joys could come from the bindings of affection that just sprang up, like wildflowers in a battlefield.

Amberdrake sighed a little. He loved Skan as much as if he and the gryphon had been raised in the same nest, in the same home, but he wondered now if Skan felt anything more than simple friendship. It was hard to read the gryphon; the raptorial features reflected emotion in far more subtle ways than, say, a kyree's mobile face. And Skan was— well, Skan. He often kept his deepest feelings to himself, covering them with jokes and pranks—or complaints and feigned irritation. If he felt affection for someone, he was just as likely to mock him as praise him.

Caring for the gryphon certainly had its drawbacks.

Amberdrake made his way quietly and unobtrusively through the rows of smaller tents housing the recovering wounded. There was a special section for gryphons: an array of tents with reinforced frames, built to be used for traction, to keep any of the gryphons' four limbs or two wings immobile.

He spotted Gesten leaving one of the tents just as the hertasi saw him. Gesten looked uncommonly cheerful, all things considered; his eyes twinkled with good humor and he carried his tail high.

"His Royal Highness has one demon of a headache, and he says he's too nauseous to eat," Gesten reported. "Cinnabar says that's because he's got a concussion, and His Highness irritated his throat with the thingummy he stuffed into his crop, and since I couldn't get him to eat anything, she wants you to try."

Amberdrake nodded. "What was that thing he tried to swallow?" he asked. "It kept intruding on my dreams last night."

Gesten ducked his head in a shrug. "Some magical weapon Urtho sent him after," the hertasi said, indifferently. "There was a big fuss over it after I got you to bed—half the mages in the Tower came looking for it when Himself found out Skan had been carried in. One of 'em woke Tamsin and tried to dress him down for not reporting it right away."

Amberdrake noticed the careful use of the word "tried." "I take it that Tamsin gave him an earful?"

Gesten chuckled happily and bobbed his head. "It was a pleasure and a privilege to hear," he said with satisfaction. "It was *almost* as good as you do when someone gets to you."

"Hmm." Amberdrake shook his head. "So, it was some kind of mage-weapon—well, I suppose we'll never know the whole truth of the matter." It occurred to him that this "weapon," whatever it was, may have been the reason that Laisfaar had been taken. Or it might have been the single factor that made their loss possible, which made it imperative for Skan to have found one and gotten it back so that Urtho's mages could create a counter-agent.

If Skan knew that, he wouldn't reveal it. The less anyone knew, the better, really. It was terribly easy for a spy to move through Urtho's camp—precisely because Urtho's people as a whole were far less ruthless than their counterparts on Ma'ar's side of the conflict. And camp gossip, as he had seen last night, spread as quickly as flame in oil-soaked tinder.

Amberdrake had long since resigned himself to the fact that he was going to overhear and accidentally see a million tantalizing details that would never make sense. That, too, was in the nature of his avocation.

"Anyway, if you can get His Grumpiness—"

"I heard that," came a low growl from behind the tent flap.

"—His Contrariness to eat something, I can get the place ready for your next client," Gesten concluded smoothly.

Amberdrake chuckled. "I think I can manage. For one thing, now that I know his throat is irritated, I can do something about that."

"Don't strain yourself," Gesten warned, as he pulled back the tent-flap to go inside. "He isn't your only charge. And *he* isn't even *paying.*"

That last had to have been added for Skandranon's benefit. The gryphon only raised his chin off his bandaged forearms a moment, and said with immense dignity and a touch of ill-temper, "I ssshould think thisss sssort of thing came underrr the heading of 'jussst rewarrrd for a missssion sssatisssfactorilly completed.'"

"I would agree with you," Amberdrake said absently, noting that Skandranon was pointedly rolling his sibilants for "emphasssisss." Skandranon's diction was as crisp as any human's, when he wanted it to be. Amberdrake extended his finely honed senses and found nothing more amiss than healing bones, healing wounds, and—yes, a healing concussion.

"How's the head?" he asked conversationally, letting his awareness sink into the area of Skan's throat and crop, soothing the irritation caused by the foreign object Skan had (inadvertently?) swallowed. It was something of a truism that a gryphon could not store anything in the crop that was bigger than he could successfully swallow, but that did not mean that the object in question would be a *comfortable* thing to store. Particularly if it was as angular and unyielding as Amberdrake thought he remembered.

"The head isss missserable, thank you," the gryphon replied with irritation. "I ssshould think you could do sssomething about it."

"Sorry, Skan," Amberdrake replied apologetically. "I wish I could— but I'm not a specialist in that kind of injury. I could do more harm than good by messing about with your head."

He exerted a touch of Healing energy—being careful not to overextend himself; he hadn't needed Gesten's warning on that score. He'd run himself into the ground once already; if he did it again, he was asking for trouble, and it generally took two or more Healers to fix what a stupid Healer did to himself. In a moment, the heat that meant "soreness and irritation" to Amberdrake faded and died from Skan's throat, and the gryphon swallowed experimentally.

"Well, I suppose you aren't going to go away unless I eat something," Skan said, without a sign of any kind of gratitude. "So I'd better do it and get you out of here so I can sleep."

Amberdrake didn't make any comments, he simply held out hand-sized pieces of fresh, red meat for Skan to swallow whole. Like all gryphons, Skan preferred his food to be fresh-killed, as fresh as possible, although he could and would eat dried or prepared food, and actually enjoyed breads and pastries. Gesten had left a large bowl of the meat-chunks; Amberdrake didn't stop handing them to the gryphon until the bowl was empty, even though Skan looked as if he would have liked to take a piece of Amberdrake's hand with his meal.

Amberdrake tried not to let his feelings get hurt. He'd seen this kind of thing often enough in other cases, of those who had been extremely active and had been forced by injuries to depend even a little on others. Skan had been completely immobilized by his injuries, and couldn't even use his forelegs. Add to that the pounding of his concussion-headache, and he really wasn't behaving too badly, all things considered.

But on the other hand, Amberdrake was a friend, and Skan was treating him in ways that he wouldn't have inflicted on an indentured servant.

Some of this must have shown in Amberdrake's expression for, just as the last strip of raw meat went down Skan's throat, Gesten returned, took one look at the two of them, and proceeded to give Skan a lecture on gratitude.

"You'd *think* that the smartest gryphon in Urtho's army would have a mudcake's sense, wouldn't you?" he railed. "You'd think that same gryphon might recall Amberdrake putting his wings together for him until Drake fell over with exhaustion! You'd think that same gryphon might possibly remember that Drake would be feeling phantom-pain this afternoon from all that Healing. But *no*..." Gesten snorted. "That takes common sense, and common courtesy. So when Drake isn't sitting here right by the tent, waiting for a certain gryphon to wake up, that gryphon pouts and thinks nobody loves him, and then acts like a spoiled brat when Drake does show up *even before he's had a shave.*"

Skan couldn't possibly have looked worse, but his ear-tufts, which had been lying fairly close to his head, now flattened against his skull. And the gryphon looked distinctly chagrined.

And penitent.

Silence followed Gesten's lecture, as the hertasi gave Skan his "you messed up" glare, and Skan sighed.

"Drake," the gryphon said softly. "I am sssorry. I have been—verrry rrrude. I—"

Amberdrake knew this mood. Skan was likely to keep apologizing for the next candlemark—and perversely, getting more irritating and irritable with every word of apology.

"Skan, it's all right," Amberdrake said hastily. "You haven't been any ruder than some of my clients, after all. I'm used to it." He managed a weak chuckle. "I'm a pretty rotten patient myself when I'm sick—just ask Gesten."

The hertasi rolled his eyes, but said nothing.

"So don't worry. We're just glad you're back, however many pieces you came back in." Amberdrake slid his hand in among the neck-feathers and scratched places where he knew Skan had not been able to reach—and would not for some time.

The gryphon sighed, and put his head back down on his bandaged and splinted forelegs. "You arrre too patient, Drrrake."

"Actually, if I don't get him moving, he's going to be too *late,*" Gesten interjected, apparently mollified by the apology. "You've got a client, kestra'chern. And you're going to have to make up for the fact that you had to cancel out all your morning appointments."

"Right." Amberdrake gave Skan's neck a final scratch, and stood up, brushing out the folds of his robe. "And I'd better shave and clean up first. How much time have I got?"

"Not much, for the grooming you need," Gesten replied. "You'd better put some speed on it."

A little later, Amberdrake wondered why he'd bothered. This was not one of his usual clients, and he had not known what to expect, but he could have been a wooden simulacrum for all the man looked at him.

He was a mercenary mage, one of the hire-ons that Urtho had taken as his own allies and apprentices proved inadequate to take on all the mages that Ma'ar controlled. While he was probably a handsome man, it was difficult to tell that at the moment. His expression was as rigid and unreadable as a mask, and his needs were, to be blunt, basic.

In fact, if he wanted what he *said* he wanted, he need not have come to Amberdrake for it. He could have gone to any of the first- or second-rank kestra'chern in the cadre, and have spent a great deal less money. The illusion of grace and luxury, relaxation, pampering—and the inevitable: a kestra'chern was not a bed-mate-for-hire, although plenty of people had that impression, this mage included. If that was all he wanted, there were plenty of sources for that, including, if the man were up to it, actually winning the respect of someone.

Amberdrake was tempted to send him away for just that reason; this was, in its way, as insulting as ordering a master cook to make oatmeal.

But as he had told the General, as every kestra'chern must, he had learned over the years that what a client asked for might not be what he wanted—and what he wanted might not even be something he understood. That was what made him the expert he was.

When a few, quiet questions elicited nothing more than a growled order to "just do your job," Amberdrake stood up, and surveyed the man from a position of superior height.

"I can't do my job to your satisfaction if you're a mass of tension," he countered sternly. "And what's more, I can't do it to *my* satisfaction. Now, why don't we just start with a simple massage?"

He nodded at the padded table on the brighter side of the chamber, and the mage reluctantly rose, and even more reluctantly took his place on it.

Gesten appeared as if Amberdrake had called him, and deftly stripped the man down and put out the oils. Amberdrake chose one scented with chamomile and infused with herbs that induced relaxation, then began with the mage's shoulders. With a Healer's hands, he sought out and released knots of tension—and, as always, the release of tension released information on the source of the tension.

"It's Winterhart," the man said, with irritation. "She's started pulling away from me, and damned if I know why! I just don't understand her anymore, but I told her that if *she* wasn't willing to give me satisfaction, I could and damned well would go elsewhere for it."

Amberdrake surmised from the feelings associated with the woman's name that "Winterhart" was this fellow's lover—or at least, he thought she was. Odd, for that kind of name was usually worn by one of the Kaled'a'in, and yet he seldom saw Kaled'a'in associating intimately with those of other races.

"So why did you come here?" Amberdrake asked, prodding a little at the knot of tangled emotions as he prodded at the knotted muscles. "Why not someone—less expensive?"

The man grunted. "Because the whole army knows your name," he replied. "Everyone in our section will know I came here this afternoon and there won't be any question why."

Very tangled emotions, he mused. Because although the top layer was a desire to hurt by going publicly to a notorious—or famed, depending on your views—kestra'chern, underneath was a peculiar and twisted desire to flatter. As if by going only to the best and most expensive, he was trying to say to Winterhart that nothing but the best would remotely be a substitute for her.

And another layer—in doing so he equated her to a paid companion, thereby once again insulting her by counting her outside his personal, deeper emotional life. Still, there was that backhanded flattery. Amberdrake was not a bed-mate for hire, he was a kestra'chern, a profession which was held in high regard by Urtho and most of the command-circle. Among the Kaled'a'in, he was the next thing to a Goddess-touched priest. The word itself had connotations of divine insight and soul-healing, and of friendship. So, then, there was wishful thinking—or again, the desire to impress this "Winterhart," whoever she was.

There were more mysteries than answers no matter where he turned these days.

"You do know that what happens in this tent depends upon what I decide is best for you, don't you?" he asked, just to set the record straight. If all the man wanted was exhausting exercise, let him go elsewhere for it.

Amberdrake was massaging the man's feet, using pressure and heat to ease twinges all through the body, without resorting to any actual Healing powers. Amberdrake had detractors who thought he worked *less* because of his power to Heal flesh and soothe nerves. His predecessors had used purely physical, learned skills—like this massage—for generations, driven by sharp senses and a clear mind. In his role as kestra'chern, he used his Healing gifts only when more "conventional" skills were ineffective. Still, one *did* complement the other, and he would use the whole of his abilities if a client warranted it. So far, though, this mere hadn't warranted it; he hadn't even warranted the kind of services he would get from a perchi. This was still at the level of banter-and-pose.

"Well… urrgh… I'd heard that." He said it as if he hadn't quite believed.

"If you aren't satisfied with that, I can suggest the name of a perchi or two, accustomed to those of rank," Amberdrake ventured. There was no point in having the man angry; he was paying for expensive treatment, and if he felt he hadn't gotten his money's worth, he might attempt to make trouble.

"What you do… ah… isn't important now, is it?" the mage replied shrewdly. "It's what Winterhart thought you did. You *are* required to keep this confidential, that much I know, so I'll let her use her imagination. It'll probably be more colorful anyway."

Amberdrake was tempted at that point to send the man away. He was right; what he was planning was also very cruel to his lover.

Assuming she didn't deserve it; she might. He could have no way of knowing.

Amberdrake sighed. There was still his professional pride. He decided to give the man his money's worth—and to make certain that, as it progressed, as little of it as possible was what the client had anticipated.

CHAPTER THREE

"I hope that's all for tonight, Gesten," Amberdrake said, as the curtain dropped behind him. He rubbed the side of his nose with his knuckle and sighed. "I'm exhausted. That last client wanted a soft-hammer-massage and an argument. Roster indicated a gentle counseling session."

"That's all you've got for the night," Gesten replied, a bit smugly. "The last two made up for all the clients you canceled this morning, since they were straight-pay and not reward-chits. I'd have warned you if I'd known about the last. He didn't say anything about the hammers; I'd have had them warmed and ready for you if I'd known. He was pretty closed-mouthed."

"I'm not complaining. You'd probably have sent him elsewhere if he *had* said anything; I'm certain he would have made it into an insult somehow." Amberdrake didn't elaborate. The last two clients had been, to be charitable, annoying. And since Gesten always discreetly monitored the workroom, he was probably well aware of that. The hertasi simply laid out a clean sleeping-robe, simple and unadorned (unlike the robes Amberdrake wore for his clients), and uncovered a plate of army-bread and cheese. Few delicacies appeared in the hands of Urtho's folk these days, even for those who could afford them; the ones Amberdrake got his hands on he reserved for his clients, who often responded well to gustatory pampering. Rumor had it that Urtho himself had given up his favorite treats. One thing there was no shortage of, at least, was water. There was a hot bath waiting in the corner, steam rising invitingly from the frame-and-skin tub.

"Thank you, Gesten," he said with genuine appreciation.

Amberdrake stripped off his sweat-dampened silks and slipped into the bath, wincing a little at the heat. He was going to look as if he'd been boiled in few minutes, but it would be worth it to relax his muscles. He recalled, as from a distant past, that before they had packed up their families and herds and moved here, the Kaled'a'in had created hot springs where they settled, if there were none there already. But much had changed; mage-created hot springs required an enormous expenditure of magical energy, and that was now a luxury no one could afford.

The war tried to eat up everything in its path. For Amberdrake and those who supported the warriors, it was the war they fought, not the army, spells, and makaar. This was the way many of the warriors saw it, too—saw war as a natural enemy, to be dealt with firmly and then put behind you. But war's devouring power was why Urtho had tried to avoid it for so long—why he had successfully avoided it until it came to his very doorstep. Folk from northern climes referred to the people of the South as "civilized"; it had little to do with their technologies and powers, but far more with their philosophy—and they were as pragmatic as they might be idealistic. When Ma'ar's army threatened at the border, opposition was there to meet it.

That was why Amberdrake's services, which in peacetime would have been divided between the wealthiest of outsiders and the needs of his own people, had been volunteered to be the reward for heroes...

And as the very expensive indulgence for those whose egos demanded the best.

That thought brought him uncomfortably right back to that mere mage, a man whose cold soul he had been unable to warm. Most of the mages in Urtho's forces were there because they felt Urtho's cause was right, or because they honored Urtho as one of the greatest Adepts ever born and hoped to be able to learn from him as they helped to defend his land. Or simply because they hated Ma'ar, or their own lands or overlords had been destroyed by the rapacious conqueror. Few fought in this army simply for the money.

This man, Conn Levas, was one. He had few friends, few interests outside his own skill and power. He was, in fact, one of the most monofocused people Amberdrake had ever seen; a narcissist of a high degree. Everything for him was centered around how he could increase his personal wealth and prestige. To him, the war was a convenient way to do that. Urtho was the master to serve because Urtho gave his mages much more autonomy and better rewards than Ma'ar.

Still, it was that kind of focus that made the hunting beasts of the world so successful, so perhaps he shouldn't be faulted for it. But how a Kaled'a'in woman had ever become his lover, Amberdrake could not guess.

Levas had at least admitted that his own coldness was a part of why this Winterhart was disenchanted with him. Amberdrake had the feeling that such an admission that *anything* was due to personal fault was a major concession.

Disenchanted... now there was a thought. Could this mage have worked a beglamorment on the woman? He couldn't have used a stronger spell, since other mages would have noticed, but a beglamorment, at the right time, would have made him what she most wanted to see. She could have found her way into his bed long before she realized he wasn't what she had thought. To have a Kaled'a'in lover was considered a coup by some meres in Urtho's forces; to have a Healer as a lover even more so. She might represent just another symbol of success to be acquired. And—Why was he worrying about *her?* He didn't even know her, only that her name sounded Kaled'a'in. She might not be Kaled'a'in at all; there were others who took on colorful names or were given them at birth. For that matter, why was he worrying about Conn Levas? The man had gotten good and ample service for his money. He was unlikely to return, given his uneasiness at Amberdrake's probing questions; Amberdrake knew the mere had been disturbed at how much he had revealed. Well. The service he'd rendered was easily enough, even by kestra'chern's standards. Still...

If you worry about every man and woman in the army, you'll tie yourself up in knots for no good reason, he told himself. *You're making up things out of nothing, then worrying about them. You've never even seen this Healer Winterhart. Why work yourself into a headache?*

Oh, he knew why he was worrying about them; it was to keep from worrying about Skan.

As if he didn't have enough to worry about already.

Skandranon was grateful to be alive, even more grateful to have gotten his mission completed successfully, and *entirely* grateful to have been put back together. He'd been assured—repeatedly—that he would be able to fly again. But he was in constant pain, his head pounded horribly, and on top of all of it, having to be *that* grateful made him want to bite.

This was very bad of him, and he knew it, which made him want to bite even more. He only liked to be bad on his *own* terms. If only he could have someone show up to see him who deserved a good, scathing dressing-down—the fool who had assured Urtho that Stelvi Pass had been in no danger, for instance, or the idiot who had issued the orders that grounded the gryphons between specific missions. Even the imbecile cook who had first sent him raw fish for breakfast instead of good, red meat, then had made it worse by sending yesterday's stew instead of fresh, still-bleeding meat. But the only people who came near him were those he was supposed to be *grateful* to—how *annoying!*—Gesten and Drake, Tamsin and Cinnabar, the members of his wing, and the scouts and meres who had risked their lives to get him home. After Gesten's lecture, he made doubly sure to convey his proper gratitude to them...

But he still wanted to bite—so he did. The camp could find another pillow somewhere.

Now if only his beak didn't hurt; there was a persistent sting from small scratches around his nares, and an itch across his cere, and his sinuses felt like—

Like you hit something hard after a prolonged plummet, bird.

It didn't help that he was forced to lie in a completely unnatural position, forelegs stretched in front of him, hindlegs stretched straight under him and bound by splints, unable to get comfortable. He knew Healers could fuse the bones of a mage-bred creature like himself in a single session of concentrated Healing. He also knew that there was plenty of pain on the front lines, and people in real danger of dying if they didn't get to a Healer, and that such a session was fairly low on the list of priorities.

That didn't help.

But much to his surprise, late in the afternoon, Tamsin and Cinnabar made an appearance at his tent—and from the implements their hertasi was carrying, this was no social-call. Tamsin was in his usual simple green breeches and shirt, his short-cropped blond hair and beard in stark contrast to many of the other Healers, who usually let their hair grow long and went clean-shaven. And he could not have made a better foil for the graceful and tall Lady Cinnabar; he was as stocky and muscled as a wrestler. Cinnabar, of course, was as elegant as if she had just come from holding court, her scarlet gown cut to mid-calf, showing scarlet leather boots and slender ankles, her sleeves cut tight, displaying her graceful arms without an unseemly show of flesh. Skandranon had heard that by human standards she was not beautiful, not even handsome, but her strong-nosed face, so like a proud falcon, seemed attractive enough to him. She even had a crest; her hair was cut short on the sides and top so that it stood up, and flowed in a braided tail down her back. Lovely.

Both of them looked relatively rested and full of energy. Skan's hopes rose. Were they—

"All right, old bird," Tamsin said cheerfully, as he held the tent-flap open for the laden hertasi. "We need to do something about those legs so you can get a proper rest. Think you're up to it?"

"Do you think I would sssay otherwissse?" Skan countered. "I would do anything!"

"Anything?" Cinnabar replied archly. Then, at Tamsin's eloquently raised eyebrow, she added hastily, "No, don't answer. You are the most insatiable creature I have ever met!"

Skan wanted to leer, but couldn't manage it. "Pleassse," he near-whimpered instead.

By near-sunset, after much effort on their part and pain and cooperative effort on his, the fractured bones of his forelegs fused, and the hindlegs healed enough that the splints could come off and he could carefully walk a few steps. He could attend to his personal needs—which was just as well, since so far as he knew, no one had come up with the equivalent of a chamber-pot for a gryphon. He would be able to feed himself, and since Cinnabar had blessedly done something about the headache, he was ravenous. Now he could lie back down in a much more comfortable position to listen to his bowels rumble.

Cinnabar looked as serene and composed now as when they had started; Tamsin was clearly tired, but just as cheerful. That should do you, old bird," he said, slapping Skan on the. flank. "Dinner first, or visitor?"

"Both," Skan replied. "If it isss sssomeone who cannot bearrr to watch a gryphon eat, let him come back laterrr. And if it isss sssomeone I do not want to sssee, *he* will be the dinner."

He would not be eating little chunks of meat tonight; no, Cinnabar and Tamsin knew gryphons, and unless that idiot cook mistakenly countermanded their orders, there would be a nice fat haunch of something fresh-killed and bloody, something Skan could tear into and take out some of his frustrations on. Maybe even half a deer or ox—he was quite hungry enough to eat either.

A silver-brocaded hertasi signaled from beside the canvas doorway, and the other hertasi disappeared as if they had evaporated. A moment later, the tent-flap was pushed aside, to reveal a beloved and unique personage.

"I should think I can bear to watch a gryphon eat," said Urtho, the Mage of Silence.

He swept into the room with a single step; he said nothing more, but projected a soothing *presence* into the damp, warm room. It was impossible to tell Urtho's real age; he could be sixty or six hundred. For as long as Skan had known him, Urtho had looked the same, an eternal image of genius. Tall and thin, storklike, with a waist-length fall of curly silver-gray hair, huge gray eyes, a nose as prominent as Lady Cinnabar's and a lantern jaw kept scrupulously clean-shaven, he did not look like the finest of Adept-class mages. He did not look like any kind of mage. He looked more like a scribe, or perhaps a silversmith or retired acrobat.

Skan thought there might be Kaled'a'in blood in Urtho's veins. That might well be true, given his nose and the long-standing association he had with them. But if that was true, no one had ever confirmed it in Skan's hearing.

Urtho held the flap open for two hertasi bringing in the forequarters of a deer; both front legs, shoulders, and the chest, hide and all. No head though, but perhaps that was a bit much to ask. Humans were so queasy when it came to delivering a gryphon's dinner with head intact, never mind that the head was delicious. Well, humans were queasy about a great many silly things. Skan seized the prize in his foreclaws as soon as the hertasi had laid it in front of him, and tore off a mouthful of meat and hide before acknowledging the commander of one of the two largest armies that Velgarth had ever seen.

He tossed his head, and swallowed the bite whole. Like the raptors the Kaled'a'in bred, he needed the hair and stringy hide to clean his crop. "Join me for dinner?" he offered.

Urtho laughed. "Is that like a falcon offering to meet a mouse for lunch?" Tamsin and Cinnabar both bowed respectfully and made a somewhat hasty exit. Urtho's power tended to overawe people who didn't know him well. He nodded to them both, took one of the two seats the Healers had left, and settled himself down onto it.

Skandranon tore off another mouthful of meat; it tasted wonderful, rich and salt-sweet. He swallowed, feeling the striations of the blood-slick muscles slither against his throat, down into his crop. He flicked an ear and cocked his head at his leader. Their gazes met, and tales sped between them in the flicker of their eyes.

"Well, old man, I sssurvived afterrr all. I hope you have *it*."

Urtho nodded casually. "So you did. And you were right when you insisted you were the one to go. You did very well, Skan, and yes, I have it. Even though you tried to swallow it whole."

"I wasss the only one ssstupid enough to trrry, you mean," Skan replied, trying not to preen with pride. He scissored another bite out of his meal.

"I seem to recall that you not only volunteered, you insisted." Urtho made it a statement, and a bit of a challenge. Skan simply grunted.

"Perhapsss," he suggested teasingly, after a moment, "your memorrry isss faulty."

Somewhat to his surprise, Urtho sighed. "It is," he said wearily. "I've been forgetting a great deal lately. Kelethen has been most impatient with me."

"You have much to rrrememberrr," Skan pointed out quickly. "Kelethen isss asss fusssy asss any other herrrtasssi. You should tell him that if he isss upssset, he can jussst keep an appointment calendar, asss if you werrre a kessstra'cherrrn."

"Sometimes I feel like a kestra'chern," Urtho told him ruefully. "Expected to please everyone and generally pleasing—"

"Almossst everrryone." Skan interrupted. "Besssidesss, sssomeone hasss to lead, and I am too busy. What arrre you doing down herrre, anyway? Isssn't there a weapon to invessstigate, a Passs to retake? I am only one ssstupid grrryphon, afterrr all."

"True." Urtho sighed again. "But you are a very special stupid gryphon; I was concerned and I wanted to see that you were doing as well as the Healers claimed. The weapon has been dealt with, counter-attack on the Pass is in the hands of the commanders; there is little I can do from here now that it has been launched."

Urtho's face was a little thinner, and Skan guessed he had not been sleeping or eating much in the past few days. He could sympathize with the mage for wishing to escape from his Tower for a little. Still… "I hope that sssomeone knowsss where you are."

"Kelethen does. I wish that this was over, or better still, had never begun."

Skandranon wiped his beak against the fur and cast his eyes supportively to Urtho. "Urtho. It isss begun and continuesss. We fly thessse windsss together. You did not cause the windsss to become a sssstorm."

"I would say that I had done nothing to cause this, but the simple fact of our existence was enough to trigger this assault from Ma'ar. I've studied him. Even as a young man, he wanted power, far more than he wanted anything else, and he enjoyed having power *over* people." Urtho shook his head, as if he simply could not understand anyone with that kind of mind. "Whatever he had, it was never enough. It was a kind of hunger with him, but one that could not be sated. There could only be one master of the world, and that one must be Ma'ar."

"Insssane," Skan replied.

"Not exactly," Urtho said, surprising the gryphon. "Not insane as we know the meaning of the word. But his sanity holds nothing but himself, if that makes any sense."

"No," Skan said, shortly. He could not even begin to imagine anyone with a mind like that, and what he had seen of Ma'ar and Ma'ar's creations did not convince him that the Mage of Black Fire was anything but evil *and* insane.

"I would help him if I could," Urtho said softly.

"*What?*" Skan squawked, every feather on end with surprise. He felt very nearly the same as he had when he'd hit the ground; breath knocked out of him and too stunned to even think.

"I would," Urtho insisted. "If he would even stop to think about all the harm he has caused and come to me, I would help him. But he will not. He cannot. Not and still be Ma'ar." He shook his head. "His obsessions are like mine, Skandranon. I understand him far better than he understands me. He thinks I am soft enough that at some point, I will surrender because so many have died and more will die. He thinks I don't realize that the killing would not end just because we had surrendered. I don't think he has the barest idea what we will do to stop him." There was no mistaking the grim determination in Urtho's voice.

Skan relaxed; for a moment he had thought that the latest turn of the conflict might have unhinged the mage.

"He isss a mad dog," Skan said brusquely. "You do not try to help a mad dog, you ssslay it."

"Harsh words, my child." Urtho frowned a little, although by now he should have been well aware of the gryphon's raptorial and somewhat bloodthirsty nature.

Skan thought of the tortured gryphons at Stelvi Pass, and hissed. "Not harsssh enough. I did not tell you what they did to the Ssstelvi Wing. Everrrything you have everrr hearrrd of. All of them, down to the nessstlingsss, and worssse than wasss done to my flight."

Urtho turned pale, and Skan instantly regretted what he had blurted out. Urtho had never wedded, and had no children, and he considered all of his intelligent creations to be his children, but that was especially true of the gryphons.

An awkward silence loomed between them for a moment, and Skan cursed his habit of blurting out the first thing he thought. *Stupid bird; you might think before you say something, once in a while. It would be a distinct improvement.*

During the silence, the camp-sounds seemed particularly loud and intrusive: people shouting to one another, and somewhere nearby, the hammering of metal on metal. Skan continued eating, his hunger overcoming his manners, as he thought of a way to apologize.

"I am sorry, Urtho," he said, finally. "I am hungry, hurt, and a very irritable and stupid bird. Think of me as being in molt."

"You're right, Skan," Urtho said, finally. "You're right. Despite what I just said, I sometimes don't think of what Ma'ar is capable of. It stretches my imagination and willpower to think like Ma'ar, and it isn't something I—enjoy."

Skandranon had no reply for that; perhaps there was no possible reply. He simply swallowed another beakful of meat.

"Well, thanks to you, those new weapons of his will no longer threaten us," the mage continued, changing the subject. "And what I really came here for, my friend, was to discover what you want as your reward. You more than deserve one. Offspring, perhaps? You certainly have a high potential, and any female in the wings would be happy to oblige you. I would like to see the Rashkae line continued."

The offer of the reward did not surprise Skan, but what Urtho had called him—"my friend"—certainly did. And yet, the simple words should not have been such a revelation. Urtho had spent many hours talking to him, not as commander to subordinate, nor as master to servant, nor even as creator to creation—but as equal to equal. Skandranon alone of the gryphons was privileged to come and go at will from Urtho's Tower, and to interrupt the mage at any time of the day or night.

"I will think about it," Skan replied. "At the moment, I should be verrry glad merrrely to be healed and flying again."

Urtho nodded. "As you will. I'm sure you'll think of something. Just please be mindful of our limited resources! And the impossibility of transporting massive libraries wherever you go!"

Skan gryphon-grinned; Urtho had not forgotten his love of books. "I am sure I shall think of sssomething."

Urtho showed no disposition to rise and go his way, however, so Skan simply continued eating while the greatest single power in their entire army spoke of camp gossip. And it was in the midst of this that Commander Loren found them.

No doors to knock on existed in a tent, of course, but the ostentatious clearing of a throat outside the closed flap told Skan that there was a visitor, and one whose voice he did not recognize. Skan instinctively bristled, all his reactions trying to force his body into readiness to protect Urtho, even though he was in no shape to do so.

Urtho did recognize the voice, of course; it was one of those traits of his that Skan could only marvel at, that he knew every leader in his huge army well enough to recognize their voices. Urtho's memory was remarkable and reputedly utterly reliable, so much so that forgetting even minor things upset him.

"You might as well come in, Loren," Urtho said immediately. "If it's all that important that you tracked me down."

When Commander Loren pushed aside the tent-flap, Skandranon recognized the brick-like face and body, although he could not have put the proper name to the man. Loren was neither outstandingly good in deploying the gryphons assigned to him, nor outstandingly poor at it. Only one or the other would have made a gryphon take notice of him.

So Loren's first words made Skan raise his head from the remains of his meal in surprise.

"I need you to reward a gryphon, Lord Urtho," Loren said apologetically, "and I would never have troubled you when you had so obviously gone to the effort of losing your aides, except that I didn't want this one to slip through the cracks."

"Obviously, this gryphon has done something exceptional..." Urtho paused significantly.

"Very." Loren's beefy face reddened with pride. "She was on patrol in what was supposed to have been a safe sector, and discovered and eliminated three makaar."

Three makaar? Skan was impressed. "Who isss flying with herrr?" he asked. "I ssshould like to know who ssset them up for herrr." Setting someone up for a triple kill took almost as much skill and more courage than actually making the kills.

"That's just it, Black Gryphon," Loren said, face practically glowing. "She did it by herself. Alone. It was supposed to be a safe area; as thin as my patrols are spread, we thought it was reasonable to fly safe areas in singles instead of pairs, to give the younger or smaller gryphons experience without risking them too much. Her name is Zhaneel."

To destroy three makaar was remarkable; to destroy three at once was uncommon even among experienced frontliners. *Who is this "Zhaneel?"* he thought, beak agape with surprise. *And why have I never heard of her before this?*

Urtho's surprise was just as great as Skan's, from the dumbfounded look on his face, and that was astonishing in itself. The gryphons were his favorite creations, and he knew and kept track of every promising youngster. Yet he did not appear to know of this one.

"You mussst bring herrr herrre," Skan said imperiously, before Urtho could speak.

Loren looked to Urtho for permission first. When the mage nodded, he pushed back the tent-flap and stalked out into the sunset-reddened dust and activity of the camp.

He returned much more quickly than Skan would have expected, though not too soon for the gryphon's impatient nature. He had bolted the last of his meal and called the hertasi to come take the remains away and light the lamps before they arrived, partially to be able to devote all of his attention to the visitors, and partially out of a wish to be seen at his best, limited though that "best" might be at the moment. He hardly presented a gallant sight, swathed still in bandages, propped up by pillows, and without having had a proper bath in days. Still, Gesten had groomed him as best he could manage, and it did not do to be presented to a brave lady with the leavings of a greedy meal in front of him.

You just want to look good for the lady, vain bird. As if you want to be sure that you could add her to your harem if you wanted; like a collector of figurines lusting after yet another little statue.

Still, he didn't want her to think that he was some kind of ragged-tailed hooligan. The gods only knew what she'd heard about him; Drake and Gesten wouldn't repeat half of the stories they *said* they'd heard about him. But then again, he had only their word for the fact that they'd heard these stories at all...

It was a good thing that this was a relatively large tent, made for two gryphons as patients and only holding Skan at the moment; once Commander Loren brought his young gryphon in, things became just a little crowded.

"This is Zhaneel, my lords," Loren said formally. "Lord Urtho, Skandranon, this is young Zhaneel, who today disposed of three makaar single-handedly."

While Urtho made the usual congratulatory speech, Skandranon kept very quiet and examined Zhaneel. She was small, and lightly built, with a deep keelbone but narrow chest. Her ear-tufts were compact and dainty, her feathers very smooth, and she had no neck-ruff at all. In color she was a light brown with a dusty-gold edge to her primaries; like most gryphons except the unassigned, her primary feathers had been bleached, then dipped in the colors of her wing—in this case, red and gold. On her head and face, she had malar-stripes of a slightly darker brown, and eye-markings flowing down her cheeks, like soft-edged tear-tracks.

While Loren and Urtho spoke, she kept her head down and turned to the side, as if she was shy or embarrassed—the gryphonic equivalent of blushing. Was she simply shy, or was she truly uncomfortable in their presence? Most of the gryphons that Skan knew might have been subdued in the presence of their overlord and creator, but they wouldn't have acted like this.

When Loren finally coaxed her to speak, her voice was low and soft, and she spoke in simple sentences with a great deal of hissing and trilling—and yet it was not because she was stupid. A stupid gryphon would not have been able to do what she had done. It was as if she simply could not get the words past her shyness.

"It wasss nothing," she insisted. "I only fly high, verrry high. Sssaferrr it isss. Makaarrr cannot fly ssso high. I sssee them, thrrrée, below me."

Skan could readily picture it in his mind's eye; especially if she was flying as high as he thought she was. Those tapering wings—surely with wings like those the aspect ratio would be remarkable, and the narrow leading edge would complement the long primaries. The makaar would have been halfway between her and the earth; she would have been invisible to them.

"Too farrr to rrreturrrn to rrreport, it wasss," she continued. "They would be gone when warrriorrrsss came. They mussst have been looking for sssomething. Sssent. They would have found it, and gone."

Now Skan nodded. "True," he rumbled, and Zhaneel started at the sound of his voice. "Quite true. Your duty was to try to stop them."

Her hissing had made him conscious of his own speech; normally he only hissed and trilled when he was under stress or very, very relaxed, among friends. When he chose, he could speak as well as any human, and he chose to do so now. Perhaps it would comfort her.

"But how did you kill them?" Urtho persisted.

She ducked her head. "I wasss high. They could not sssee me. I ssstooped on them; hit the leader. Like thisss…"

She held up one foreclaw, fisted.

"I ssstruck hisss head; he fell from the sssky, and died."

No doubt; coming from the height Zhaneel had been at, she must have broken the leader's neck on impact, and the ground finished him.

"I followed him down; the othersss pursssued, but I climbed again, too fassst for them to follow." She pantomimed with her foreclaw, and Skan saw then what he had not noticed before—a reason she may not have struck to slash, or bind to her quarry as he would have. Her talons were actually very short; her "toes" long and flexible, very like stubby human fingers. A slash would only have angered the makaar unless she had managed against all odds to slash the major artery in the neck.

"I go high again, verrry high; the two follow, but cannot go ssso high. I turrrn, dive, hit the lead asss he fliesss to meet me." She sat back on her hindquarters and mimed that meeting with both of her odd foreclaws; how the makaar struggled to gain height, how she had come at him head-on, angling her dive at the last possible moment to strike the top of his head with her closed fists.

"He wasss ssstunned; he fell, brrroke hisss neck when he hit. I follow him down, to be sssure, then turrrn dive into climb again." She would not look at any of the three of them, keeping her eyes fixed on some invisible point on the ground. "The thirrrd one, he isss afrraid now, he trrries to rrrun. I go high again, asss high asss I can, and dive. He isss fassst, but my dive isss fassster. I hit him. He fallsss." She ducked her head. "It isss overrr. It isss nothing ssspecial."

Nothing special—except that these were tactics few, if any, gryphons had tried before. Spectacularly successful tactics, too, if Zhaneel's experience was anything to go by. Most gryphons, when they fought makaar, closed for the kill, binding to the prey's back and bringing it down, or slashing with talons in passing strikes. Hawk and eagle tactics, not falcon. Zhaneel had fought as would a very hungry—or very brave—falcon, when taking a goose or very large duck, prey that would outweigh her twofold or more: knocking the prey out of the sky, and *not* using her talons.

"Zhaneel, your act of courage has probably saved any number of our people, and no few of your own kind," Urtho said, as these thoughts passed through Skan's mind. "I am quite impressed, and quite pleased that Commander Loren thought to bring you to my attention personally. At the very least, my dear child, I am going to present you with the reward you richly deserve."

With that, he reached into a pocket and pulled out one of the reward-tokens he used instead of medals or decorations. Urtho felt medals were fairly useless; he rewarded bravery directly.

This particular token was the highest possible: a square of gold with a sword stamped on one side and a many-rayed sun-in-glory on the other. He slipped this into the tiny pouch Zhaneel wore around her neck, an accessory that most gryphons not on duty wore. She could trade that particular token for virtually anything in the camp, from a fine tent to the exclusive services for a month of her very own hertasi. Or she could save it and add it to others, to obtain other luxuries. Skan simply kept a running account with Gesten, whose services he shared with Amberdrake. Before he had left on this last mission, he had been quite a few months ahead, and Gesten would be a very wealthy hertasi when the war was over.

"But child, I am curious," Urtho continued, his eyes fixed on her, as Loren beamed his approval and the young gryphon stammered her thanks. "Who are your parents? Who trained you besides them?"

"My parentsss arrre no morrre," she replied. "They died when I wasss jussst fledged and I have no sssiblingsss."

Urtho's disappointment was clear even to Skan; there would be no more like Zhaneel unless she mated. But before he could persist in finding out how she had been trained, since her parents had obviously been unable to give her that training, one of his aides burst into the tent without so much as an "excuse me."

"Lord Urtho! The counter-attack at Stelvi Pass—"

That was all the boy needed to say; Urtho was off, following him at an undignified run that belied his silver hair, out into the lamplight, and from then into the darkness.

This was not the first time Urtho had left Skan holding the line, and it probably would not be the last. Skandranon knew what to do, and summoning as much dignity and aplomb as his injuries permitted, he proceeded to deal with the situation.

"Lord Commander, thank you for bringing Zhaneel here," he said, raising his head and then bowing it slightly to Loren. "Once again, you have gone beyond mere duty, and if Urtho had not been forced to leave, he would have told you so himself."

He hoped that Loren would take that as a hint, and so he did. "Thank you, Black Gryphon," he replied, then continued, with an honesty that was not necessarily common among the commanders, "It has taken me a while to learn the best way to employ fighters other than human, but I hope that Zhaneel's success is a harbinger of more such victories to come. Now, if you will excuse me, news from Stelvi Pass is going to affect all of us, and I must go at once."

He turned to Zhaneel. "Scout Zhaneel, you are officially on reward-leave for the next two days. I will inform your wing-leader, and I hope you can enjoy your well-earned rest."

Loren turned and pushed aside the tent-flap, following Urtho into the night, though at a more dignified fast walk.

Skan had hoped that the departure of the humans would relax the youngster, but she was clearly still terrified. It was a bit disconcerting. No one had ever been terrified of him before, not among those on Urtho's side, least of all one of his own kind, and an attractive lady at that. He would have expected flirtatiousness, not fear.

He fluffed his feathers and let his eyelids droop a little, hoping his posture of relaxation would make her relax in turn. A good theory, but unfortunately, it didn't work.

"Since Urtho has been called away, I must ask the rest of the questions he wanted to ask you," Skan told her, in a very low, coaxing voice. "Believe me, it is not that we wish to make you uncomfortable, but we need to know these things to improve the training of the next batch of fledglings."

She bobbed her head stiffly, but gave no indication of relaxing. "It wasss no grrreat deed," she insisted. "I did not clossse and fight prrroperly. No one can learrrn prrroperrr fighting frrrom thisss."

Skan had heard any number of "modest" protestations in his time, and had made a few of them himself, but this didn't seem to be the kind of modesty that covered the very opposite. On the contrary, Zhaneel apparently believed what she was saying: that she had done nothing of note.

"Not all gryphons are large and powerful enough to close with makaar," he reminded her gently. "And for even those, it is not always wise to try, particularly when there is more than one of them. Who trained you to strike like a falcon?"

"N-n-no one," she stammered. "I did thisss becaussse I *cannot* fight like a prrroperrr grrryphon, becaussse I am too sssmall and weak to be a prrroperrr grrryphon."

Small, perhaps, but she was certainly not weak, and Skan would far rather have brains on his side than brawn. He'd seen too many muscle-bound specimens close with makaar, believing themselves invincible, and had to go to their rescue when they found out otherwise. Whoever, whatever her trainer was, Skan was just about ready to put the being on report. This little female had emerged from training that should have given her confidence in her own abilities, with a load of self-doubt. She would have been useless except for her own courage, determination, and sense of responsibility. It was also fairly obvious that this self-doubt carried right on down to how she felt about her physical appearance. She held herself as if she was certain there was nothing attractive about her—in fact, as if she thought she was a horrid freak.

Didn't he recall some of the fledglings in training baiting a smaller one a while ago, about a year or two? It could have been...

Yes, he remembered now, as Zhaneel continued to protest that what she had done was less than nothing, unworthy of reward. Three or four, all nest-brothers by the look of them, surrounded the smaller one and had been name-calling and insulting the little one. The object of their taunting could have been Zhaneel; he only remembered that he had broken it up when the trainer did not appear to intervene, and that the youngster was small, awkward, adolescent. Considering the way she was trying to disappear into the tent-canvas now, it would not be surprising that—if it had been her—he did not remember her.

But that had been some time ago, and the only reason he remembered it was because the appropriate authority had not stepped in to handle the problem, and the noise had gotten on his nerves. There was a certain amount of competition among the youngsters; gryphons were still not a "finished" race, and those who could not succeed in training, Urtho took for the less demanding jobs of messenger and camp-helper. These were, of course, never permitted to breed.

But if that youngster had been Zhaneel, by completing her training she had proved herself. Now, Zhaneel was a working member of a wing, and entitled to the same care and protection Skan himself got. There should be no reason why she should continue to suffer these feelings of inferiority. There would be a Trondi'irn assigned to her wing, whose job was to see to everything but serious injuries, whose duty was to know every gryphon in the wings assigned to him by name and peculiarity. So why hadn't the Trondi'irn noticed Zhaneel's problems?

Well, there was someone who *would* take notice of her mental state, do something about it himself, and then see to it that the Trondi'irn in question would get an earful afterwards.

"If you have no plans for your token, you might take it to Amberdrake," he suggested casually. "He's the best there is."

Drake will have her feeling better in no time—and by the time he and Gesten get done massaging, grooming, and adorning her, she'll be so elegant that she'll have half her wing at her feet. That *should make her feel better about herself.* That was one of the many things a truly talented kestra'chern and his or her assistants did—spending hours, sometimes more, taking an ordinary creature and transforming her (or him) into the most stunning example of her race possible within her physical limitations. Most gryphons went to a kestra'chern before a mating-flight, though few could afford the services of one like Amberdrake.

"That is simply a suggestion, of course," he added. "You may already have something in mind."

"N-no," she said. She seemed a bit stunned, though whether it was the suggestion itself or that Skan had made it, he couldn't tell. "If you think it isss a good thing to do. I have neverrr had a token beforrre…"

"Well, this is likely to be only the first of many tokens for you. You might as well spend this one on something you are going to enjoy," Skan told her. "You won't regret going to Drake, I promise you."

She seemed to take that as a dismissal, although it had not been meant as one, and stammered her thanks, backing out of the tent before Skan could ask her to stay. He thought about calling her back, but it was already dark, and she probably had things she wanted to do.

He wondered about Urtho's interest in her; it had been something more than the usual interest in a successful fighter. It was as if something about either the gryphon herself or the way she had fought and brought back a memory that Urtho had forgotten for more pressing concerns.

But now that the visitors had left, and darkness had crept over the camp, not even the lamps could keep Skan awake. His pain was bearable; he could lie down in relative comfort, and he had a full crop. Urtho had that mysterious weapon, and in any case, there was nothing for Skan to do until he healed. Sleep seemed in order, and there were no mysteries so pressing that they could not wait until tomorrow.

He shifted himself around on his cushions until he found the best possible position. He put his head down on his forelegs and yawned once—and that was the last thing he remembered doing or thinking until the Healers woke him at dawn.

CHAPTER FOUR

Gesten had rearranged Amberdrake's schedule to include Skan as a regular "patient" for the next several days. Amberdrake discovered the change when he checked the roster the next morning. He didn't bother to comment on it; he knew that Gesten's reply would be sardonic. Dear Gesten, whom he'd hired on so long ago, liked to think he fostered a heartless image, constantly spitting barbed comments and double-entendres. Even though the little hertasi failed utterly at posing as a bossy ogre, Amberdrake was not going to tell him so, directly or by implication. So often the gruffness a person showed the world was a defense, meant to protect the ones they loved. That was how it was with Gesten. It was also how it was with Skandranon, and when Amberdrake wasn't indulging himself in self-pity, he was well aware of that.

And Skan was first on the day's roster, with a generous amount of time allotted to him. Amberdrake could visit him, add his own touch to the Healing meld, and spend some time simply enjoying Skan's company before returning to work at the tent.

This was interesting; his schedule was bracketed by gryphons today. The first patient was Skan, and the last a gryphon named "Zhaneel." A female, according to the log, with a gold-square token. He'd have to make certain Gesten had the bleaches and dyes ready; she might want a feather-tip job in addition to whatever other pampering and primping she desired. Amberdrake's other talents often obscured this one, and few knew he had ended his apprenticeship at the ancient trade of kestra'chern as a feather-painter, and he still enjoyed doing it. Skan, of course, wouldn't let him practice on *his* feathers, no matter how Amberdrake tried to assure him that it would be a subtle pattern, sophisticated and elegant. No, the Black Gryphon was the *Black* Gryphon, and black he would remain. Skan had made it clear time and time again that the only dye to touch *his* feathers was the stark black he himself had chosen.

But female gryphons, to whom nature and Urtho had given fairly drab coloration, tended to be very fond of painted feathers. In peacetime they had sometimes sported patterned feathers as gaudy as a Kaled'a'in weaving or a messenger-bird's bright plumes—now they had to confine themselves to something that made them less of a target. *If she's got goshawk-coloring, perhaps I can persuade her into something in blue and gray,* he mused. *That way she'd have the advantage of sky-camouflage when she was flying, but up close she would be dappled in fishbone patterns and ribbons.*

That would be a pleasant way to end the day.

He washed and shaved, tied his hair back, then donned a plain linen tunic and breeches to stroll over to the mess-tent for breakfast. He could eat in his quarters, and often did when he was pressed for time or tired, but he preferred to share at least one meal with the other kestra'chern. Experience and observation had taught him that if the top-ranked kestra'chern acted no differently than the rest, there would be less acrimony and jealousy, both of which could lead to unpleasantness and outright sabotage. He was careful to dress plainly when off-duty, shared his knowledge and experience freely, and when forced to cancel appointments, did his best to see that the canceled clients had been distributed fairly among the others. Thanks to this, the rest of the kestra'chern tended to regard him as their unofficial leader and spokesperson. He had mixed feelings about *that,* but it was probably better that he was in that position, rather than someone else. He was the only Kaled'a'in among them, the other Kaled'a'in kestra'chern choosing to work among the Healers and save their other skills for their own people. No other working kestra'chern in the camp had as much training as Amberdrake, and when the Kaled'a'in had moved to Urtho's Tower and the question of what his job should be had come up, he had felt no hesitation. He made, at best, an ordinary Healer, and to operate under the constraints of a Healer would have made him feel as if he worked with half his fingers gone. It was best to do what he was truly good at.

Breakfast was unusually quiet; Amberdrake's companions were tired and subdued. Like the rest of the army. After all, the kestra'chern were by no means immune to what had happened at Stelvi Pass. Even if none of them had friends or acquaintances there, the fighters themselves would, inevitably, bring their troubles to the anonymous comfort of those whose business was pleasure and support.

No one seemed in any mood for conversation on a personal level; no one looked at Amberdrake with the desperate eyes of someone who has taken on more pain than he or she could handle, nor asked Amberdrake for advice in affairs of their own hearts. At first, he simply ate his breakfast in quiet, kept the conversation light, intending to leave with a quiet greeting for everyone.

One of the junior kestra'chern inquired about Corani, and was met with a brief, sharp glance from Amberdrake. This served as an impetus for several other kestra'chern at the table to start talking about the news from Stelvi Pass, Laisfaar, and the Tower, each adding their own slices of information. They had likely as not gleaned it from their clients as from camp gossip. As long as no one revealed the identities of the clients, many of them thought, putting the pieces of the puzzle together in the confidence of other kestra'chern was something of a challenge to all concerned. It was done all the time, and Amberdrake knew it, and although it was a source of some of the kestra'cherns' hidden power, he didn't entirely approve of this free sharing of basically private knowledge. Still, the war made its own rules, and they fought the war itself, and not the army of the enemy. Perhaps this *technical* transgression of kestra'chern protocol could yield valuable insights. So he told himself.

Regardless of Amberdrake's private mullings about the talk, it went on unabated, and he found himself offering up the occasional "It may well be" and "From what I know, unlikely" comments, which helped lay in more pieces of the puzzle. When he felt it was time to go, he directed the discussion back towards client care and techniques, then slipped out unobtrusively.

When he reached the Black Gryphon's tent, Skan was awake, and evidently in a much better mood this morning. Skan had looked him up and down in mock-amazement. "Tchah, the kestra'chern has lost his commission? All your fine plumage is gone, strutting-bird!"

"Heh, dressing to match the job."

"It seems likely you turned in here mistakenly on the way to the horse-stalls, then," Skandranon replied smoothly. Yes, he was definitely feeling better. Yesterday he would have growled.

"Has anyone looked at your wings?" Amberdrake asked.

"Not since you did," Skan told him. His pronunciation was much improved from yesterday, too. He hissed his sibilants only a little, hardly enough to notice. "All who have come have said it was best left to the expert."

"They're probably right, but lacking an expert, I'll have to do," Amberdrake said absently, running his hand just above the surface of the splinted and bandaged right wing. He extended his awareness down into the wing itself, into the muscle, tendon, and bone. "You're doing all right, though. Bear with me for a minute, here, I need to probe some more."

He shifted from simple awareness into true Healing with a deft twist of his mind. Carefully, for if he sped the Healing of the bones too much, they would not heal properly but would remain weak, as the bones of a very old person might be after setting. He sent energy to the torn muscle, to the tiny arteries and veins that had been savaged, and then, delicately, to the bones.

Finally he pulled his awareness away and came back to himself, shaking his head a little to clear it of the shared pain. "I'd leave the bandages on for now," he continued. "It's going to take another couple of days of work to mend those wings, and a couple of weeks to strengthen them enough that you can use them. Keeping them bandaged like that keeps them from being strained. I hope you have feathers saved from your last molts; we're going to have to imp a lot of broken secondaries and primaries. That's one thing we can't do for you: grow new feathers."

"You're the Healer," Skan replied philosophically. Then he looked sheepishly at Amberdrake out of the corner of his eye. "I have to apologize to you, Drake. Again, I mean. The apology I gave you yesterday wasn't exactly sincere." He took a deep breath and let it out slowly. "I treated you badly yesterday. It wasn't fair, and it wasn't right. My only defense is that I was in pain, and I'm not at my best when I hurt."

Amberdrake snorted. "Not at your best? Skan, you could give a makaar lessons in surly!" But he smiled, and scratched Skan's eartufts, while the gryphon feigned indignation. "That's all right; I'm not a good patient either, you know. It's just a good thing I'm not hurt or sick very often, or I'd probably lose Gesten."

"Not Gesten; he enjoys suffering. He enjoys letting you know he's suffering even more," Skan replied wickedly—and accurately. "What's happening out there? Nobody tells me anything; they're afraid I might not want to heal up."

"Ma'ar's forces threw back our counter-attack," Amberdrake told him, knowing that if he didn't, Skan would find some other way of getting the information. "We've lost the Pass, for now at least, unless Urtho can come up with some way of dislodging them."

Skan shook his massive head and sighed. "I can't see how, Drake. Stelvi was built well, as impregnable as possible, with water supplies in every part of the fortress. That was part of the reason why no one took an attack there seriously." He stared at the canvas wall of his tent, as if by sheer force of will he could see beyond it to the Pass. "So it's to be another retreat, then. Eventually abandoning the Tower, if this goes on."

Amberdrake nodded. "I'm afraid so."

"Damn them." Skan glared at the tent-wall until Amberdrake was afraid he might burn a hole in it. Then he shook his head, and when he turned back to Amberdrake, his eyes were clear, although wrinkles betrayed a deep and abiding anger burning at the bottom of them. "Has Ma'ar given us any new and unpleasant surprises?"

It was Amberdrake's turn to shake his head, but this time it was with relief. "Like that mage-shot he pelted us with last month? Not that I've heard, and I heard most of the rumors three times over between my tent and ours."

"Good." Skan had been tense; now he relaxed a bit. Amberdrake would have given a month's pay to know what had prompted that question—and knew very well that Skan would never tell him. He could surmise that there had been some kind of new weapon in use by Ma'ar's army—and that Skan had neutralized it, somehow. He could surmise it, but Skan would never reveal the truth of the matter.

"So, wicked one, what have you been up to while I have been wallowing at my ease in a nest of pillows?" Skan asked, quickly changing the subject before Amberdrake had a chance to ask him anyway. "Any new and interesting clients?"

"One new one yesterday, who I *hope* is never going to come back," Amberdrake told him. "A more unpleasant man I have never met, and a mercenary mage on top of that."

He told Skan all there was to tell about Conn Levas, without revealing the man's name or divulging anything that might identify him—not even the fact that the man's lover might be Kaled'a'in. He didn't often break client-confidentiality, and even then it would only be to a superior, like Artis Camlodon, the Chief Healer, or to Urtho, himself, should he ever find himself in that exalted being's presence. Few people overawed Amberdrake—he had seen too many of the great and powerful unclothed both physically and spiritually, but Urtho always left him feeling as if his mouth was hanging wide open. The blazing intellect, the aura of controlled and absolute power, and the overwhelming competence of the man added up to the kind of charisma that left Amberdrake weak in the knees. What he looked like didn't matter; Amberdrake invariably saw the Mage of Silence with a kestra'chern's eyes—the eyes of one who saw past the surface, always.

Still, Amberdrake found himself telling Skan more than he would have told anyone else, and Skan listened with every indication of interest. It was marvelous, simply having a friend to talk to this way, and they both exulted in it behind their calm and rehearsed exteriors.

"I feel sorry for that one's lover," Skan said, finally. "Very sorry, actually. She seems more important as a possession than as a person to him."

"That was more-or-less the conclusion I came to," Amberdrake admitted. "What was worse, though, was that I was supposed to be dealing with my client's problems, and I found myself wishing there was a way I could have a good long talk with his lover instead. That wasn't very professional of me, I suppose, but then again, he wouldn't *let* me help him."

"Then more fool he," Skan said scornfully, "to pay good money and then refuse to take what it purchased."

Trust Skan to put the situation into the simplest possible terms! Amberdrake had to smile. "Thank you, Skandranon Rashkae, you'll make me a perchi yet. Should I simply become a baker, and save myself some worry?"

"You would find another way to take on the army's burdens as a baker. Each little slice of bread would have a soldier's very life and spirits slathered upon it," Skan snorted.

Amberdrake laughed in response—it was, after all, a good return volley. "I suppose that in the grand context of an entire army, one mage's emotional problems aren't too high on the list of things I need to worry about."

Skan chuckled. "That is a reasonable statement. More reasonable than the fretting. You've spent more time with me than you should have. Your other clients will be unhappy if they find out."

"Then they won't find out." Amberdrake got up to leave. "This is going to be a very interesting day; I'm going to begin and end with a gryphon. It's the first time something like that has ever happened."

"I thought I was your only gryphon client," Skan mock-chided. "I may become jealous!"

"Don't bother, old bird," Amberdrake told him. "This is just a once-only, a reward. I'm not sure why this gryphon chose me when she could have had the same treatment from an apprentice at a fraction of the fee, but it will be a nice change from emotionally damaged fighters and deservedly traumatized mages."

Skan snorted approval at the small insult of Conn Levas. He had long maintained that Amberdrake was too gracious. "I may still be jealous."

Amberdrake smoothed his unwrinkled tunic as a mocking gesture. "She's a young female, I believe, and if you're *very* good, I might introduce you to her after Gesten and I finish prettying her. Not that you'll be in any shape to seduce her, but you might be able to persuade her you'll be worth keeping in mind when you heal!"

Skan wore a very peculiar expression; as if he tried to hold back something. He seethed with amusement. Amberdrake couldn't for a moment imagine why, though; the female gryphon hadn't been listed as being from any wing Skan had ever flown with, and was several years his junior besides. Whatever his secret was, though, he managed to keep it behind his beak. Amberdrake waited for him to betray himself, but he said only, "I should like very much to meet this young lady once you've been with her."

"I'll see what I can do," Amberdrake said. And since Skan didn't seem disposed to reveal anything, he finally waved goodbye and went back to his scheduled work.

Very much like to see her, indeed… Vain bird, he's probably planning his post-mating dinner with her already.

Amberdrake sat wiping thick oil from his hands with a rag, when Gesten reminded him of his last client for the day. It had been a day marked by trauma and pain, from the emotional trauma of a young Healer who had seen one too many die, to the pain of a horseback skirmisher who'd had three beasts shot out from under her at the attempt to retake Stelvi Pass. She had had so many wrenched and displaced vertebrae from falls that Amberdrake almost sent her to the Healers instead, regardless of what she said she wanted. But she swore to him that she had rather have "the best kestra'chern in the world" put her spine back in place than any

Healer, and seemed thrilled to be with him, as if she spoke to a great dancer or singer. She'd sworn that she could bear the pain he would have to put her through to do so.

The reason? An admirable one; she'd felt that the Healers were overburdened, and that they would feel obliged to pain-block her, which would add to their burden. Yes, she'd known that the Healers would treat her for nothing, and that his services cost a high-ranking reward-chit. No, she hadn't cared. "I've got a pile of these things already, so I'm saving them up for a better commission once the war's dead," she'd said gruffly. "Urtho's aides brought me a new horse—Kaled'a'in-bred at that. I've got a new tent. I don't crave pretties. I look like a horse myself, so fancy clothing on me would look like barding on a mule. So what else am I going to spend a chit on? Besides, this way I get an attractive man to put his hands all over me. That, I can use."

So he manipulated her vertebrae as she stifled her gasps of pain, until her gasps turned to ones of sheer relief. He was so impressed at her courage and sense that he'd had Gesten prepare a hot soaking tub for her, with aromatic oils in it. He had her soak until her muscles completely relaxed, then he gave her the massage she had paid for, rubbing her down gently until she was just dozing. Then he did for her what he would not do for Conn Levas. They were good hours.

She had left his tent, smiling and exhausted. He sat back while Gesten cleaned up and prepared for the last client of the day, smiling just as widely as she had. Once in a while, he got a client who was worthy of his skills in every way—that skirmisher was just such a one, and it had been a privilege to serve her. Odd; both she and Conn Levas were mercenaries, and yet they were so unlike each other. Ah, well, experience had shown that the only thing similar about most soldiers was the uniform they wore.

"That was a fine lady," Gesten observed, as he expertly put away the oils and stowed the massage table. "I think I ought to go over and suggest she spend one of those "useless" chits of hers on a makeover with us. I don't see any reason why she has to keep on looking like a wild mare. She's lean enough to be elegant, and if she'd just let me do something with her hair…"

"That's a good idea, if you want to," Amberdrake agreed. "I'd take the exotic approach with her—you know, she could carry off some of the Kaled'a'in costumes quite impressively. Maybe with a cat-stripe paint-pattern across her shoulders—"

"That's what I like about you, Drake," Gesten interrupted cheerfully. "You always see the potential. Think you can exercise that one more time today? That gryphon Zhaneel will be here shortly."

"Gryphon?" Amberdrake replied, momentarily confused. Then he hit his head with the heel of his hand. "Right! I nearly forgot! My mind is still muddled from this day. I'm just tired. Did you—"

"I've got the oils and the satin-cords and the beads and feather-paint," Gesten said, snorting a little. "As if I'd forget! Listen, I'd like to go over and put Skan to bed if you don't mind. Do you think you can handle this youngster alone?"

It was Amberdrake's turn to snort. "As if I hadn't been taking care of gryphons all by myself long before *you* came looking for *some fool* to hire you! Of course I can."

"All right then, fool-who-hired-me," Gesten replied, giving him back as good an insult as he'd gotten. "I'll go make sure that featherhead up on the hill gets his sleep, then I'll see to it you don't drown yourself in the tub when I get back."

Gesten indicated a bright but battered wheeled storage-chest with a nod of his snout. "Everything you need is in there, and I replaced whatever had dried out or was too old to use. If I do say so myself, I don't think there's a kestra'chern in the army with a better stock of 'gryphon pretties'. By the time you get done, she should be stunning. Provided you can do *your* job."

He whisked through the curtain before Amberdrake could make a rejoinder. Amberdrake just laughed, and took his time getting out of his chair. He changed into a utilitarian pair of loose linen breeches and baggy shirt, tying a sash about the latter. He would not need any fancy robes with this client; instead, he needed clothing he could work in, clothing that could be splashed with dye and not take harm. Over that he wore his receiving-robe, with its intricate designs.

Amberdrake stepped outside the tent to take in some of the camp's relatively fresh air before the client arrived. "Small" feathers—the size of a hand—drifted by in the breeze, discards from some gryphon's vigorous preening, no doubt. Activity in the camp had stepped up a bit from earlier that day; it seemed that the rumors had fed a packing-frenzy. The children that he'd seen before were engaged in tying blankets and packs, with the help of two kyree tugging with their teeth. He saw adults mending wagon-covers and double-checking the wheels of carts. Further beyond that, a set of soldiers and an Apprentice mage—who looked to be Vikteren, one of Amberdrake's social acquaintances—leveled and tested a hovering-sled. The large sleds floated half a man-height above the ground—although they could be raised higher—and were mainly used for troops' supplies. A few of the kestra'chern, Amberdrake included, had bought one for use in moving their own gear, rather than relying on the army to do so for them.

Next to them, the horse-skirmisher he'd cared for earlier—who was moving much more freely than before he'd begun—was keeping a number of her fellow warriors enthralled with some great tale. Or if not great, certainly one that called for a substantial amount of gesturing.

Maybe she's talking about me… ? That would be good if she was. Let them know I treat the lower ranks as well as I do their commanders.

Hidden back behind the cluster of humans, though, was a mere wisp of a gryphon—a fledgling, judging by her size, or a sub-adult. She—yes, definitely a female—was eavesdropping on whatever it was the horse-skirmisher was saying. How strange—normally, gryphons simply walked into conversations they wanted to be a part of, invited or not.

Then Amberdrake's attention was taken by a flight of messenger-birds winging past, darts of living paint flittering across the sky. Their bounding flight carried them and their messages towards the Tower; with luck, they carried news that the war's hunger was sated for a while.

Amberdrake turned back inside, and set about finger-weaving feather-shaft adornments for his next client. It would be so relaxing, for a change.

Zhaneel, when she arrived, turned out to be the little gryphon he'd seen lurking behind the warriors earlier. She was a very pretty thing, in a quiet way; lean and fit, with long wings and feathers that laid very close to her body. He'd walked out from the back room of the tent with a handful of finger-woven satin cords, and found her in the receiving area, hesitantly nosing around the cushions and boxes.

She's never been to a kestra'chern before, I can tell that right now. Nervous, expectant, unsure of herself.

He cleared his throat gently, and she started. "Welcome, Zhaneel," he said in a soft but commanding voice. "My name is Amberdrake. I am honored to serve you." He executed the sweeping, graceful bow that customarily accompanied the greeting and ended it down on one knee, so that he would not be looming over her. His receiving-robe gathered around him in glossy folds as he knelt, a shimmering contrast to the work-clothes underneath it.

Her eyes darted across his entire body as he bent forward to touch one of her forelegs, as was also customary. It was in this first touch that an experienced kestra'chern could tell the way the session was going to go. Involuntary reactions mixed with postures and poses, hopeful or desperate projections, all would be caught by a sensitive kestra'chern in good form. One did not have to be an Empath to read body-language; that was a skill taught to every kestra'chern during his or her apprenticeship.

In this case, the signals were decidedly odd. Zhaneel slicked her feathers down and turned her head until her delicate beak touched the wrist-joint of her folded wing. A soft, sibilant voice came from that beak, in as near to a whisper as gryphons could manage.

"The Black Grrryphon sssent me to you. You are my k-kessstrrra'cherrrn." Then her head dipped and her wings, fluttered near her body, spread ever so slightly.

"Yes. I am the kestra'chern that will serve you, Zhaneel, as you requested, and as your reward for bravery. I will adorn, comfort and help you, and give you the attentions you may deserve and the insight you may need." Amberdrake raised his other hand and touched the remaining foreleg, reading her physical reactions clearly while another part of his mind reasoned out what to do about it.

She's practically seething with sexual tension… definitely worked herself up into a frenzy somehow over the past candlemark. Well, I know what that usually means. Some feather-work and oils should increase this unique beauty of hers, so her lover will be especially pleased by her after our session. Still…

Still, this sleek little creature wasn't coming across like the usual gryphon client to be prepared for a special tryst. There was anticipation, and an electric desire, but there didn't seem to be any *confidence* in the outcome of the night, nor the sense of certainty that gryphons were so well known for. And no gryphon went for an expensive tryst-grooming unless they were *positive* they had a partner waiting for them!

Zhaneel looked directly at him suddenly and stepped forward, causing Amberdrake to rebalance himself—and then she kept moving forward. Amberdrake fell backwards as Zhaneel straddled him. Her long wings spread to either side of them, with her tail up and neck feathers roused. Her beaked face was nearly touching his nose when she asked, "You will give me pleasssurrre, Amberrrdrrrake?"

Oh gods… that explains what…

He stared at her beak—remembered the size of gryphon talons—

and felt himself blanch. "Zhaneel, no—wait—you'll hurt me," he begged. "Please let me up!"

Skandranon marked his page with a discarded feather and stretched, looking back to where Gesten meticulously brushed and treated his back just above his tail. Urtho had sent down a book by an explorer who had been in his employ from before the war had started, and the heavy tome was filled with small notes written in the margins, observations and anecdotes by others that the book had been loaned to. Urtho had sent it by messenger-kyree to make up for his hasty departure earlier; yet another small gesture that told the Black Gryphon of his status in Urtho's eyes. Gesten had been there for at least two candlemarks, quietly putting all of the details right for Skandranon: cutting, sanding, and rounding partially snapped feathers, rubbing in soothing gels around strained feather-shafts. Without saying a dozen words, he'd moved Skandranon—who was twice the weight of most human men—into easier positions for tending tiny skin-cuts the Healers hadn't gotten. He had sanded down the chips in Skan's beak, filling in near-invisible cracks with cement, and coping his overgrowing talons. He then moved on to a deep and thorough combing, removing all the tiny snags and remaining bits of burr and twig from Skan's black coat.

Skan was in good shape—much better than even this morning, he mused—and in little pain, thanks to one of Lady Cinnabar's clever abilities, a trick with shunting pain away. She was a delight to know, even peripherally,. and seemed to have the sort of personality he'd like to find in a gryphon mate one day.

Skan counted himself fortunate that he'd lived this long. Ah, but taking a mate? Seriously considering the possibility of fathering young had been reduced to a worn pastime over his years of service, one that at some times felt like his only reason for persevering, and at others like an impossible fantasy from a laugh-singer's tale. The concern was not one of merely finding sex. He had no lack of lovers; there were few gryphons who wouldn't be ecstatic to raise their tails to him, but still, they were at best casual friends, and none of them fertile. Mmm, but there were those that had been so sweet, so warm…

He shifted the way he laid; thinking about lovers was causing his belly to tighten with longing. He'd never been embarrassed about his virility before, and felt no pangs of such now, but his healing state kept poking reminders at him about how limited his movement really *was*.

Gesten didn't miss a stroke while grooming Skan's flank and tail, although he surely noticed the outward signs of Skan's line of thought. There seemed to be very little the little hertasi missed; but, as with other topics that came up around him daily, Gesten's best comment was not to comment at all.

Tchah, by now little Zhaneel is settled in warm and comfortable with Amberdrake. Amberdrake knows how to make everything right. He's such a good kestra'chern—so clever, so graceful, so intelligent. I'm proud to know him; I'm glad I sent her to him.

I'm going to kill Skandranon for this. Amberdrake fumed as he faced away from Zhaneel. Surely that mindless, oversexed, bug-bitten, arrogant mass of black feathers had given Zhaneel the impression that Amberdrake was going to make love to her somehow. This was an unforgivably cruel joke on Skan's part! After this situation was handled, Amberdrake resolved to go over and give Skan a verbal flaying, asleep, injured, or in whatever condition he happened to be.

Zhaneel had disentangled herself from him only a moment before, and was now watching his every move for some cue to resume, her head bobbing up and down and hindclaws clenching.

Amberdrake wiped a palm across his face and turned back to speak to her pointedly. "Zhaneel, I can't be the kind of lover you want. You and I aren't physically compatible. I just can't…"

A moment passed.

An unmistakable, inexplicable look of horror transformed Zhaneel's entire demeanor from one of desperate desire to one of emotional devastation. She let out a gurgling cry, and suddenly bolted through the opened tent-flap and into the darker and more private inner room.

Skandranon finished the annotated chapter on social organization among the southeastern tribes, and luxuriated in the attention Gesten was giving his recently battered crest.

By now she must feel like the most beautiful and capable gryphon in the entire world! Amberdrake always knows how to say exactly the right thing to make someone feel good. He's given me so many compliments, and he's hardly ever wrong. Maybe once I'm recovered, he can give me a tryst-grooming, and we can talk about how much good my suggestion did Zhaneel.

The Black Gryphon sighed and settled down for a nap, smug in the knowledge that all was right with the world as far as Zhaneel and Amberdrake were concerned.

Amberdrake found Zhaneel curled into a ball in the furthest corner of the tent, shivering, her head tucked under her wings. It was a saddening, unnerving thing for Drake to see; this was the gryphon equivalent of wracking sobs, as bad as any he'd seen in mourning or after nightmares. Surging, palpable waves of shame pounded at him; feelings of self-blame hissed in his mental "ears" the closer he got to her. He braced himself to receive a backlash and reached out to touch her quivering body.

Instead of the expected strike, she didn't acknowledge his presence at all. Nothing. Yet, with the touch, a staggering rush of sickening emotions blinded Amberdrake for the span of a heartbeat.

She hates *herself. She genuinely hates herself, for gods' sake. Self-doubt, self-pity, an overwhelming sense of worthlessness, of loss. From a gryphon! This I could expect from a human, but from a gryphon? They're all convinced that Urtho created them as an improvement on all other races! Who or whatever made her this way was long in building. If it* can *be stopped, it has to stop now. If I can change her, it has to start* now.

He spoke quietly, soothingly. "Zhaneel?"

She whimpered, the barest whisper of sound.

"Shh, little one, I am here for you'. Please listen. Please listen. I'll make you feel better, I promise it. I am here for you." He moved in closer and folded his robed body across hers, to comfort her, as he had other distressed gryphons, with the sensation of protective, caring wings wrapped over them. He could feel her underneath him, body temperature high, breathing fast and there, yes, her eyes tightly shut. Her delicate ear-tufts folded back tight to her head. Drake stroked her neck feathers and spoke more reassuring words, keeping his voice steady and deep, speaking "into" her, and held her as her shuddering subsided.

The sexual anticipation earlier can help some, at least… Amberdrake swam through Zhaneel's nerves with his Healing powers, found her pleasure-centers, and gently stimulated them while he soothed her with his words. Gryphons' bodies held stores of specialized fluids, elements, in various glands and repositories, and the delicate touch of an experienced Healer could release them at the right time. A careful nudge *there* and a feather-light stimulation *so,* and the "rewarding" sensation following a mating coursed through her veins; in a small amount, by no means as great as the euphoria following a real mating, but definitely there. It had the desired effect; she slowly went from quivering to a state of relaxation—physically, at least—and uncurled from her ball after what felt like a harrowing eternity. All the while, Amberdrake reassured her, and spoke encouragements. It didn't cure any of her problems, no, that could come later, but her gradual relaxation at least opened a doorway towards a cure.

A candlemark must have passed since her arrival before she spoke again. It was a time in which her kestra'chern held her and scratched her ear-tufts, all the while carefully touching her mind and soaking in the feelings she unknowingly projected into him. He could not help thinking that it was a good thing she had chosen him, rather than a kestra'chern with no Empathic or Healing abilities. Anyone else would have had to send for her Trondi'irn—and an apprentice would have been as terrified and traumatized as she.

"Zhaneel," he said urgently, "you must tell me *why* I distressed you so. I had no intention of hurting you."

She shivered all over. "You… kessstra'cherrrn. Think I am m-misssborrrn too. No desssirrre, neverrr…" She hunched her shoulders and hung her head, deep in purest misery. "Should have died," she cried softly, "not worth raisssing, ssshould have died. Trrried."

Amberdrake didn't hesitate a moment; strange how, after waiting in silence for so long, a moment's delay in a reply could cause damage. "No, lovely child, you misunderstood me entirely! You're far from misborn, Zhaneel. You were made by Urtho as his proudest creation. And you are lovely to me."

She uncoiled some more, and nervously looked at him with one eye. "But you sssaid—no lover. Physssically. Not even you want me…"

He rubbed his cheek against hers, as a gryphon-sib would do, and replied quickly. "Zhaneel, no, little one! I said I *can*-not, not that I would not if I could. I am only a human. Thin skin, and smaller than you. We wouldn't fit, you and I, our sizes and bodies are too different. And you'd tear me up trying." He allowed a small chuckle. "Dearheart, believe me, if I were a gryphon, you and I would be in the sky together the moment after I saw you."

She opened both eyes and blinked, twice, as if the dry observation that humans were perhaps a third the size of a gryphon—in every salient way—hadn't even occurred to her.

Some people think a kestra'chern can do anything!

"Never learned how mating goes. Parents died. Left me, left me alone." Zhaneel slumped down, her beak touching the floor. "Misborn, wings too long and pointy, too long for body, head too big, too round, no ear-tufts at *all!*" she cried out, shivering. "That's why they left me, why they flew and died. I was misborn, and they were ashamed."

Amberdrake scratched her head, fingers disappearing into the deep, soft down-feathers, and projected more calm into her, soothing her, lest she ball herself up again and never uncurl. "I just can't believe that, Zhaneel. You are lovely and strong. Your parents must surely have treasured you, and looked forward to seeing you fly."

Apparently, a flood-gate had been released when she had first started speaking. She continued to pour out her feelings. "Not enough talon to hurt even mites—"

Amberdrake surveyed the outstretched forefoot dubiously. The talons looked plenty long to him.

"—freakish, misborn, should have *died,*" she whispered hoarsely. "No one wants Zhaneel in wing. No one. No one wants Zhaneel as mate. Worthless."

Amberdrake lifted her head up—a more difficult task than he tried to make it appear—and caressed her briefly around the nares, then held up the forgotten reward-square.

"If you're so worthless, then how did you earn this? They don't give these away for digging latrines, sky-lady. Only the bravest receive this kind of reward."

His left arm was complaining bitterly about supporting the weight of her head, when she finally lifted it herself and blinked. Then she looked down.

"Not brave," she insisted faintly.

Amberdrake smiled gently. "Why don't you tell me how you earned it, and let me be the judge of that? I would sincerely like to hear, Zhaneel. Join me. I'll make you a fine strong tea." He stood up creakily and gestured for her to come with him; she rose, took three hesitant steps towards his bed, and then sat beside it.

"No one would accept me into their wing. But I wanted to fly for Urtho. So I—I just moved into a wing. Kelreesha Trondaar's wing."

Ah. Interesting, the same wing that merc-mage Conn Levas is attached to. Amberdrake prodded the coals in the ever-burning brazier, then set a copper kettle of water on it. "And then…?"

"I flew patrols. The back patrols—the ones fledglings fly in relays." Her voice broke at that. The duty she described was humiliating for an adult gryphon, usually reserved for punishment because of its length and uneventfulness, and for training fledglings in procedure. "It gave me—time away from the camp. Time to fly. Can fly the circuit faster than anyone else."

Amberdrake dropped herb-packed cloth pouches into the kettle, and spoke gently. "Faster than any other gryphon; that is wonderful in itself. How much faster, Zhaneel?"

"A third faster. I fly the circuit alone." Amberdrake raised an eyebrow in surprise and appreciation. "I was at fifth-cloud height," she continued. *Half again higher than other gryphons fly on patrol—even more interesting...* "And I found makaar. There were three, leaving our territory. They had to be stopped somehow, they must have been spying. But I can't Mindspeak well—I couldn't call for help. So I dove on them and fought them. It didn't matter if I died stopping them."

Amberdrake's thoughts ran quickly, despite the practiced, impassive expression on his face. *She means that. She means that if she died trying, that was as well as living. It's plain why she said she wasn't brave. She was suicidal. And she wanted her death to* mean *something.* He took a deep breath and smoothed back his hair.

"Zhaneel—I've known many warriors, many shaman and priests and High Mages. So many of them have felt inadequate, and I've spoken to them, as I am to you, dear sky-lady. When warriors feel afraid they lack something, it is only because they are forgetful. They have forgotten how capable they truly are." He settled down on the bed beside her, and caressed her brow as she listened. "If you were anyone besides Zhaneel—lovely, powerful, sleek Zhaneel—you would have gone for help, or flown away frightened, or attacked the makaar and failed. You succeeded wholly because of who and what you are, and by the power of your mind as well as your body. That is no small thing, given that *some* gryphons I know have no more brains than an ox."

Again, he held up the token and gently touched it to her beak. "And now you have this, given by Urtho's own hand. Do you know how rare that is?" She shook her head, human-like, indicating she didn't. "It's very rare, Zhaneel, very unusual. It shows that you are exceptionally *good*, dear one, and not a freak. Not misborn. *And far* from worthless."

"Doesn't matter," she croaked. "Everyone thinks I am."

"Everyone didn't stop three makaar, and everyone didn't get this token." He shook his head, certain that he had her attention now. "Sometimes 'everyone' can be wrong, too. Didn't 'everyone' say that Stelvi Pass was impregnable?"

Her ear-tufts rose just a little, and she bobbed her beak once in cautious agreement.

He considered her; her build, her very look. "You are different, Zhaneel, just as I am different from my own people. And when I came here, I felt a little like you do—no, a lot like you do. I was scorned simply because of who I was, and what I do. The Healers wouldn't accept me because I was kestra'chern. The kestra'chern were wary of me because I could Heal. Yet as I saw them dance away from me, I studied the moves of their dance." Amberdrake smiled again, as Zhaneel relaxed some more and gazed at him, an enraptured raptor listening to a storyteller. "They would look at me and I was a mirror. They could see parts of themselves in me, layers and shards of their own lives they'd tucked away in their sleeves. When I spoke, the Healers knew I had that kestra'chern insight, and they felt threatened. And the other kestra'chern distrusted my station and Healing abilities. Yet through it all, there I was. Still myself, Zhaneel, just as you are still you. Those who push you down fear you. They are jealous of you. And you are stronger than you know."

Zhaneel fidgeted, uneasy under his care-filled eyes. "Not strong, sir."

He shook his head, and chuckled again. "Nah, sky-lady. Please don't call me 'sir.' I am only Amberdrake—a friend. Ah." He stood and moved gracefully to the tea-kettle, and poured two cups, one large, one small, as he spoke. "If you were not strong, I would never have met you, Zhaneel. You would have been dead and forgotten, not honored by the Mage of Silence himself. And *not* noticed by the Black Gryphon."

Zhaneel turned her head aside, and her nares flushed in embarrassment. *Ah, so she's as impressed with Skandranon as he is by himself. I'm still going to skin him later, but I'll certainly use his image to Zhaneel's advantage.*

"Let me tell you of Skandranon, Zhaneel," he began. "*They* make fun of Skandranon, too. He is called a glory-hound, reckless, arrogant, petulant, and some say he has the manners of a hungry fledgling. Still, he is there, doing what he is best at. *They* are jealous of him, too— mainly because he actually *does* what *they* only talk about doing. Actions define strength. And you, sky-lady, fly faster and farther than *they* do, and can strike down three makaar alone."

She blushed again, and once more he wondered what went wrong in her childhood. Where were her teachers, her parents? The simple things he told her should have been the most basic concepts that a young gryphlet was raised on. *Normally,* though, was the key word. Amberdrake had seen a thousand souls laid bare, and knew well that what most called "normal" was anything but reality. He also felt the warmth in his chest and belly, and the simmering heat in his mind, that told him that the hunt was good this time—that this young Zhaneel was going to survive.

"Always, I hear how *they* have said this or that, and yet, I have never come face-to-face with one of *them*. Who are *they* anyway?" he asked—rhetorically, since he did not truly expect her to answer. "What gives them a monopoly on truth? Why are they any more expert than you or I?"

Another few steps, and he presented her with the larger cup. He marveled at the deftness with which she grasped the cup, with a single foreclaw—no—with a single *hand*. And she followed his gaze.

"No claws to speak of. Have to wear war-claws like silly kyree," she murmured, and looked down again.

"Tchah, no. That's no defect, sky-lady. See my arms and legs, my muscles? They match my body well, as the parts of your body match well. Now see my hands, and their proportion to my arms." Her sight fixed on his hands.

And her eyes widened, as she realized what she was seeing. "Your hands—are like mine."

"Yes! Very similar. All the Powers made me this way." He nodded his approval. "And Urtho created you, with exactly *this* shape to your foreclaws, your body, your wings. Do you believe that Urtho would be so incompetent as to create an ugly, mismatched creature?"

That went against the most basic of gryphonic tenants; even Zhaneel would not believe that. "No!"

He smiled; now he had her. "Of course, we all know that Urtho would not. He has always been thorough and detailed, with a vision unmatched by any Adept in history. No, I believe, Zhaneel, that you are something new. Sleek and small, fast—like a falcon. The others, they all have the shapes of broad-winged birds, of hawks and eagles—but you are something very different. Not a gryphon at all, but something new—gryphon and falcon. *Gryfalcon.*"

Her eyes sparkled with wonder, and she caught her breath, still holding the cup of steaming tea. She spoke the word that Amberdrake had just made up, testing it on her tongue as she would try a sweet apple or cold winter wine. "Gryfalcon."

This was going so much better than a candlemark ago. Amberdrake took a sip of his cup of tea, and luxuriated in the play of flavors—rich and bitter, sweet and acidic, each in turn. Complex blends that suited the mood of a complex problem.

Outside the tent, dusk had darkened to night as they talked further, and Zhaneel had told him, in words that faltered, of her parents' fate. They had both been killed on what should have been a low-risk mission; once again, the war had hungered, and had fed as all things must feed. Zhaneel had been left alone, a fledgling cared for thereafter by a succession of foster-parents and Trondi'irn who felt no particular affection for her. One by one, they changed or disappeared, and the memories of her parents became a soft-edged memory of nurturing acceptance, a memory so distant it came to seem like a dream or a tale, having nothing to do with her reality.

It was the *contrast* between the fledgling's memories of loving care and the sub-adult's reality of indifference that had suffocated her in the cold box of self-hate.

Conversely, however, the same thing had kept her from killing herself.

The knowledge, only half-aware, that when she was still in the downy coat of a fledgling she was *loved*, had given her soul the broad feathers it needed. There were no specific images now, and no remembered words; there was only the sensation that yes, with certainty, they had trilled their affection as she drowsed and taught her when she awoke. Brief as that time had been, it had given her an underlying strength, and a reason to endure.

By the time their cups were empty, most of the night had passed by, and they had wandered into mutual observations. Zhaneel asked about the life of a kestra'chern. He'd wondered aloud, once he knew the subject would not alarm her, where she had gotten her idea that Amberdrake would be her lover.

Her nares flushed. "The horse-rider was telling the others about you, and I listened. I didn't understand some of it, but I thought it was because she was a human." She ducked her head a little as her nares flushed deeper. "I thought, this must be what you do with all who come to you. I thought, this was why Great Skandranon had told me to come to you when I was given the reward."

He clenched his jaw for a moment. *I might have known Skan was at the bottom of this! No wonder he was acting so—so smug!* But a confrontation with Skan would have to wait. Now, all unknowing, she had given him another opening to bolster her self-esteem.

"Skan sent you here?" He blinked as if he was surprised, but continued quickly, before she could burst into frantic protest that he really *had,* as if he might doubt her truthfulness. "Do you realize just how impressed he must have been with you, Zhaneel? Why, it was only two days ago he was brought in, injured—he is still not healed, and he has made it very clear to me, his friend, that he does not wish to be troubled with inconsequential things. And yet he thought enough of your proper reward to send you to me! How much time did he spend with you?"

"I—do not know… half a candlemark, perhaps?" she said, doubtfully.

"Half a candlemark?" Amberdrake chuckled. "I cannot think of any other he has spent so much time with, other than his Healers. Truly, he must have found you fascinating!"

"Oh," she replied faintly, and her nares flushed again. "Perhaps he was bored?" she suggested, just as faintly.

Amberdrake laughed at that. "If he was bored, he would have sent you elsewhere. Skan's cures for boredom are reading, sleep, and teasing his friends, in that order. No, I think he must have found you very interesting."

By now, from her body-language and her voice, it was fairly obvious to him that Zhaneel had—at the very least—a substantial infatuation with the Black Gryphon.

"He doesn't pay that kind of attention to just anyone," he continued smoothly. "If he noticed you, it is because you are noteworthy."

She perked up for a moment, then her ear-tufts flattened again. "If he noticed me, it wasss sssurely to sssee how freakish I am."

"How different you are—not freakish," he admonished. "Skandranon is not one to be afraid of what is different."

"Am I—" She hesitated, and he sensed that she was about to say something very daring, for her. "Am I—different enough that he might recall me? Notice me again?"

Amberdrake pretended to think. "I take it that you want him to do more than simply take notice of you?"

She ducked her head, very shyly. "Yesss," she breathed. "Oh ycsss…"

"Well, Zhaneel, Skan is not easily impressed. You would have to be something very special to hold his interest. You would have to do more than simply take out a couple of makaar once." That was a daring thing to say to her, but fortunately she did not take it badly; she only looked at him eagerly, as if hoping he could give her the answers she needed. "I know him very well; if you want Skan, Zhaneel, you will have to impress him enough that he wants you—enough to make him ask you to join his wing." Before she could lose courage, he leaned forward, and said, with every bit of skill and empathy that he possessed, "You can do this, Zhaneel. I know you can. I believe in you."

Her eyes grew bright, and her ear-tufts perked completely up. "I could—I could entrrrap the makaar..." She paused as he shook his head slightly. "Perhaps if I made of myself a target, outflew them to ambush?" Again he shook his head. Both her ideas were far too impulsive—and suicidal.

"It will have to be something that only you can do, Zhaneel," he suggested. "You don't have to make a hero of yourself every day—you don't have to have an immediate result, either. But whatever you do must be something only *you* can do—just as the way you killed those three makaar was done in a way only you could have performed. Perhaps something that Urtho or Skan said to you could help you think of something..."

She sat, deep in thought, while Amberdrake got himself a second cup of tea. Finally she spoke.

"Urrrtho asked me what training I had, and he was disappointed that no one had given me any special attentions." She looked up at him intently, and he gave her an encouraging nod. "Skandranon also seemed surprised that I had no special training. And if I cannot fly and fight as the others do—perhaps—perhaps I should train myself?" Again she looked to him, and he nodded enthusiastically. "Perhaps I should ask for—for courses, such as they put the young humans across, only for flying..."

"That is a *good* plan, sky-lady," he told her firmly. "It is one that will benefit not only you, but others who are also small and light. And as you become skilled, you will definitely attract Skan's attention."

But now she had turned her attention to his hands, and then to her own foreclaws.

"Amberdrrrake, I have hands, like humans—I can do human things, can I not?" She flexed her hands, first one, then the other, as if testing their mobility. "Perhaps I can use a weapon—or—perhaps I can *fly* to help wounded!" Her beak parted in excitement, and Amberdrake had to work to suppress his own excitement. The idea of a gryphon-Healer, even the kind of field-Healer who could only splint bones and bandage wounds—*that* was enough to make him want to jump up and put the plan into motion immediately. How many fighters had bled their lives out simply because no one could reach them? The mobility of a gryphon would save so many of those otherwise lost lives...

"This is going to take time, Zhaneel," he cautioned, repeating the words to himself as well as her. "All of it is going to take time to learn, more time to practice. But it is a *wonderful* idea. I will help you all I can, I swear it!"

Zhaneel listened to his cautions, then bobbed her head gravely. "One weapon," she declared. "I shall learn one weapon. Crossbow; it ssseems easy enough to massster. And I shall learn the simple healing that the green-bands know."

By "green-bands," she meant the squires and serjeants who wore a green arm-band and acted as rough field-Healers, who knew the basics. Enough to patch someone up long enough for them to get to a real Healer.

Enough to save lives.

"And I would be honored to teach you that Healing, my sky-lady," Amberdrake said softly.

"And…" She dropped her voice to a shy whisper. "And Skandranon will notice me?"

Amberdrake chuckled. "Oh, yes, my lady. He won't be able to help himself. You will be one of the few things that he does notice, I think."

She cocked her head to one side. "Few things?" she asked curiously.

He shook his head, and shrugged. "Oh, sometimes I think he is so obsessed with topping his last escapade that he does not notice much of anything, including his friends."

She continued to stare at him quizzically, and finally said, "He notices. He loves you. The whole camp knows this."

That was not what he had expected to hear, and for once, he was taken by surprise. "He—what?" Amberdrake replied. He thought for a moment that he had misheard her, but she repeated her statement.

"He loves you, as if you were a nest-mate," she insisted. "Perhaps he does not say so, but all the camp knows that Amberdrake and Skandranon might as well have come from a single mother."

As his mouth dropped open a little, she gurgled—a gryphon-giggle, and the first sound of happiness he had heard from her yet. "I heard this—I heard him tell some of the captains that you were a being of great integrrrity!"

"You what?" he said, trying to picture Skan doing anything of the sort.

"I heard him," she said firmly; and with coaxing, the story emerged. She had—once again—been eavesdropping when she shouldn't have. Some of the mercenary captains had been bandying about the names and reputations of several of the perchi and kestra'chern, and Amberdrake's name had come up just as Skan passed by. That would have been enough to attract his attention, but one of the captains had called out to him, tauntingly, asking him to verify what they had heard "since you know him so well."

And Skan had, indeed, defended Amberdrake's problematical honor, at the cost of some ridicule, which Skan hated worse than cold water.

"So," Zhaneel concluded. "You see."

Amberdrake did see—and he was rather overwhelmed at this evidence of affection, affection that he had hoped for, but had not really believed in. A kestra'chern had so few friends—so few of those more than the merest of superficial acquaintances...

He blinked; finding his eyes stinging a little.

"Amberdrake," she said into the silence. "You are a Healer."

He blinked his eyes clear and returned her grave stare, expecting a return to the earlier topic of discussion. "Of course, sky-lady."

But she turned the tables on him. "And when you are hurt, who heals the Healer?"

Has she suddenly turned into Gesten, or Tamsin, to sense my feelings before I know them? he thought, startled again. But he chuckled, to cover his confusion, and replied, "My lady, I am not likely to be needing the services of a Healer, after all. I do not ply my various trades on the battlefield."

She snorted, in a way that sounded very like Skan, but she said nothing more. And just at that moment, the sentries called midnight, and they both blinked in surprise.

Half the night has gone—but why am I surprised? It almost feels like half a year.

"You should take some rest, lady," he said, taking the half-forgotten token and putting it back in her pouch. She started to protest; he placed a hand on her beak to stop her. "It is in my discretion what my fee is. You keep this. If you have some difficulty convincing your wing-leader that you need special training and equipment, you could use that to deal with him. And when you find someone worthy of you, then come to me with it, and I shall turn you from simply lovely into the most breathtaking creature ever to fly."

Her nares flushed again, but this time with pleasure. She started to leave, then paused on the threshold.

Tugging a hand-sized covert-feather loose, she gravely handed it to him. "And when you need—anything—you bring *me* this. Healer."

Then she was gone, leaving him with a slate-gray feather in his hand,

and a great deal to think about. He let down the entrance-flap, closing his tent against the night and any observers, and ran the feather between the fingers of his right hand.

Who heals the Healer...?

CHAPTER FIVE

"Well, great hero," Tamsin said dryly, pushing his way through the tent-flap, "I see you have a tent-mate now. Did they discover you weren't a General, and you weren't supposed to have private quarters?"

Skan chuckled; it was amazing how much better a tiny improvement in his condition made him feel. Not great, but less like snapping someone's head off, anyway. "No, they decided that I must be lonely, but instead of giving me a lithe young female, they sent this disgusting heap of tattered feathers. Meet Aubri. Be careful not to step in him."

The other gryphon in the tent, swathed in bandages covering burns, raised one lazy eyebrow and snorted. "I thought I was being punished. I was put in here with you, featherhead." He raised his head from his foreclaws and regarded Tamsin and Cinnabar with a long-suffering gaze. "I'll have you know," he continued, in mock-aggravation, "he whistles in his sleep."

"So do you," Skan countered. "I dreamed I was being attacked by a giant tone-deaf songbird, and woke up to discover it was you. Maybe it was yourself you heard, loud enough to wake yourself up!"

"I *don't* think so," Aubri countered, then put his head back down on his foreclaws and pretended to sleep.

Skan chuckled again. "I like him," he confided to Tamsin in an easily overheard feigned whisper, "but don't let him know. He'll get arrogant enough to be mistaken for me."

A single snort of derision was all that came from the "sleeping" Aubri.

"Well, you know why we are here," Cinnabar told him, coming up behind her lover and giving him a greeting that was more than half a caress.

"Yesss," Skan said. "You are here to pretend to tend to my hurts, while you put your hands all over each other. Tchah! You lifebonded types! Always all over each other! Bad enough that as humans you are always in season..."

"And you are not?" Aubri rumbled from the background.

"What?" Skan asked. "Did I hear something?"

"No," Aubri replied. "I am asleep. You heard nothing."

"Ah, good." Skan returned his attention to the two humans who were doing their best not to break into laughter. "As I said, bad enough that you are always in season—but you lifebonded types are always preening each other. It's enough to give an honest gryphon sugar-sickness."

"Then Skandranon is in no danger, for he is hardly honest," came the rumble.

Skan shook his head sadly. "What did I tell you? The lout not only whistles in his sleep, he mumbles nonsense as well. Perhaps most of his injuries were to his rump, since that is surely where his brain resides."

"He's upset I'm not succumbing to his imagined 'charisma'," Aubri grumbled, raising his head. "And upset I beat him in his fledgling-baiting 'logic puzzles'."

"You have no logic to use. Lucky guesses, all of them. I beat Urtho with them." Skandranon looked back to the Healers, chagrined.

Cinnabar moved to the gryphon's left, hands moving expertly over his wing and flank. "Gesten did a fine job with you, I see—you look very fit. You'll soon be in good enough shape to dazzle all the potential mates you like, Skan. Are you finally going to take a mate?"

Skandranon flicked his wings suddenly and stabbed a glare at her, which was much harsher than he'd really intended. He felt his nares darkening—how *maddening* to be constantly asked that! As if they had placed bets on who and when and how!

Cinnabar bit her lip and backed off, pretending—pretense that was just a little too obvious—to search for something in her belt packs. Tamsin broke the tension by clearing his throat and pulling Skan's head towards him.

"Here now, Skan, let me look at your eyes."

"He'll just think you're in love with him," Aubri snickered.

Before Skan could make any retort, Tamsin clamped Skandranon's beak closed with one hand and stabbed a Look at him. This was serious business. Gryphons could judge relative distance and speed from each eye independently, and could clearly compare minute details of objects directly ahead. The paper texture of the book Skandranon had been studying, for instance, had been in sharp relief to him, even the furrows left by the pen. Like many other parts of a gryphon's body, though, the eyes were used to judge the health of the rest of the body. Tamsin leaned in until his face was barely inches away from the lens of Skandranon's right eye, becoming an encompassing blur which filled most of his wide field of vision. "You're dilating well. Not as scratchy as I'd expect. No problems with focus? Good depth perception from each eye?"

"With Aubri, therrre's little depth to ssstudy," Skandranon said dryly. "But yes, all seems to be well enough. I want to be back in action immediately."

"There'll be plenty of action for you, warrior, and that surely means we'll see you back in surgery soon enough," Cinnabar joked. "By now, Ma'ar's troops have stopped wagering on you. They know that sooner or later, every one of them will get a chance to shoot at you."

Skandranon stood, feeling more lively than before, and mantled in indignation. In walked an opportunity for mischief. "They haven't killed me yet! Have they, Jewel?"

A laden and bewildered hertasi looked at Skan wide-eyed, having just come in bearing rolls of blankets for Aubri. "N... no?" she said, with a nervous glance at the Healers.

This, of course, was a favorite trick of the Black Gryphon's—getting people involved in his arguments, whether they liked it or not, or whether they had any knowledge of the subject at hand. Always fun! Especially when the topic of discussion was *him*, and it had turned unflattering. "There, you see? Jewel knows. This was just a temporary setback, and I'll be back to save Urtho's army in no time at all." He puffed up his chest feathers and struck an heroic pose.

"Oh, *save* me from him!" came Aubri's plaintive cry. Tamsin and Cinnabar broke up in laughter, while Jewel scurried about positioning the rolls of blankets for Aubri's comfort, still bewildered by the whole scene. Skan, of course, continued to play to his audience.

"He's unaccustomed to being near greatness." Skan gave Aubri a lofty, and condescending, sidelong glance.

"I'm unaccustomed to drowning in such *sketi*. I can't stand him asleep or awake!" Aubri moaned. "Healers, could you *please* either still his tongue or eliminate my hearing? Something? Anything?"

"Tchah! Blind fledgling," Skandranon retorted. "I am forced to take up company with the unappreciative. It's worse than physical wounds, I tell you honestly."

Jewel paused for a heartbeat, took in the tableau of laughing and posturing, and evidently decided that folding fresh bandages for Aubri was the right thing to do. She fell into doing so with religious fervor on the far side of the tent. Lady Cinnabar recovered from her laughter and flashed her wide grin at Skandranon, as Tamsin tweaked Skan's tail. Tamsin then wiped his hands as if he'd just finished a day's work, and shot a satisfied look at his lover.

"I'd say our labor is done here, Lady. He's as good as he'll ever be."

"What a sad thought," Aubri muttered.

"Oh, please," Skan countered. "I have capacities I've—"

"Boasted about for years," Aubri inserted quickly. "And never fulfilled."

Skan decided that a quick change of subject was in order. "Are you two keeping an eye on our Lord and Master?" he asked. "When Urtho visited me, I thought he looked underfed."

"It hasn't been easy, but I've been making certain he gets at least a bite or two out of every meal brought him," Cinnabar replied with a sigh. "And his hertasi have been bringing him meals every two candlemarks or so. Still, no sooner does he settle down to eat than more bad news comes from the front lines, and off he goes again, food forgotten."

"He's giving more than he can afford to," Skan told her, sitting down and becoming serious for a moment. "He never wanted to be a warlord. He isn't suited to it."

"He's doing well enough—we're all still alive," Cinnabar offered. "The only reason he's in charge is because the King folded up. And all the King's men, the gutless lot."

Aubri's eyes twinkled. "She only says that because it's true."

But Skan stuck his tongue out in distaste. "She's being charitable, Aubri. When Ma'ar first swept down, the border lands burned up like kindling. All the Barons were terrified, and the King's best efforts couldn't hold them together. It all fell apart, and we had only Urtho to turn to. No one else had any knowledge of what we faced. Cinnabar's family and a few others stood against the Kingdom's dissolution; the rest fled like frightened hens, and just about as witless."

"We remembered that we serve our subjects, the ones who ran served themselves, and left their people crying in their wake," Cinnabar added. "We don't know what happened to most of them. Some had their faces changed. Some went mad or died. Most are still in hiding. Urtho doesn't blame them even now—he told the King that Ma'ar sent a spell of fear into them. However," she said while rebraiding a lock of hair, "it seems not all of us were affected."

A shadow fell across the tent-flap threshold, and was followed a second later by a severe-looking, impeccably uniformed woman stepping through. Her brown hair was short-cut but for three thin braids trailing down her back, each as long as a human's forearm, all of which laid in mathematical precision along her smooth neck. As she stepped in, her hazel eyes flicked from human to gryphon to hertasi in that order; she then flowed like icy water towards Aubri. Or rather, she would have flowed, had she not been trying to cover a limp. Skan stared at her; to intrude uninvited into a tent was not only rude, it was dangerous when the tent contained injured gryphons. Yet Aubri did not look surprised or even affronted, only resigned.

"May we help you?" Tamsin asked, openly astonished that the woman had not offered so much as a common greeting.

The woman did not even look at him. "No, thank you, Healer. I am here to tend to this gryphon."

"And you arrre…?" Skandranon rumbled, his tone dangerous. She either did not catch the nuance, or ignored it.

"His Trondi'irn, Winterhart, of Sixth Wing East," she replied crisply—not to Skan, but towards Tamsin, as if Skan did not matter. "His name is Aubri, and he has suffered burns from an enemy attack," she supplied.

Oh, how nice of her. She's provided us with details of the obvious, as if we had no minds of our own or eyes to see with. How she honors us! Except that she was paying no attention to the nonhumans, only the humans, Tamsin and Cinnabar. *What does this arrogant wench think she is? Urtho's chosen bride?*

But the woman was not finished. "I've also come to reassign you, hertasi Jewel. Your services are required in food preparation with Sixth Wing East. Report there immediately."

Jewel gulped and blinked, then nodded.

Winterhart drew a short but obviously sharp silver blade from her glossy belt and cut one of Aubri's bandages free, looking over the blistered skin underneath.

"I don't think—" Tamsin began. The woman cut him off, as Jewel scurried out of the tent.

"Aubri doesn't require her any longer," she said curtly, "and the Sixth is shorthanded."

Skan ignored the rudeness this time, for Winterhart had caught his attention. "Sssixth Wing—that of Zhaneel?" he asked.

The woman looked at him as if affronted that he had spoken to her, but she answered anyway. "Yes. That is an extraordinary case, though. She surprised us all by somehow distinguishing herself." Winterhart's shrug dismissed Zhaneel and her accomplishments as trivial. "Rather odd. We've never had a cull in our ranks before."

Skandranon's eyes blazed and he found himself lunging towards the woman. "*Cull?*"

Tamsin and Cinnabar held onto both of Skandranon's wings. He repeated his incredulous question. "*Cull?*"

Winterhart ignored both his obvious anger and his question. Instead, she rebandaged Aubri and held her hands over his burns.

Even Skan knew better than to interrupt a Healing-trance, but it took him several long moments to get his anger back under control. "Cull, indeed!" he snorted to Tamsin, indignantly. "Young Zhaneel is no more a cull than I am! These idiots in Sixth Wing don't know how to train anyone who isn't a muscle-bound broadwing, that's their problem! Cull!"

Tamsin made soothing noises, which Skan ignored. Instead, he watched Winterhart closely. The fact that this cold-hearted *thing* was Zhaneel's Trondi'irn explained a great deal about why no one had tended to the youngster's obvious emotional trauma and low level of self-esteem. Winterhart simply did not *care* about emotional trauma or self-esteem. She treated her gryphon-charges like so many catapults; seeing that they were war-ready and properly repaired, and ignoring anything that was not purely physical. Zhaneel needed someone like Cinnabar, or like Amberdrake, not like this… walking icicle.

But she was giving Aubri the full measure of her Healing powers; at least she was not stingy in that respect. And she was good, very good, provided that the patient didn't give a hung-claw about bedside manner or Empathy. Aubri was clearly used to treatment like this; he simply absorbed the Healing quietly, and made neither comment nor complaint when she had finished.

But for the rest of her duties—those, she scanted on. She did not see that Aubri was comfortable. She did not inquire as to any other injuries he might have, other than the obvious. She did not ask him if there was anything he needed. She simply gave Tamsin and Cinnabar another curt nod, ignored Skan altogether, and left.

No one said a word.

"Well!" Cinnabar said into the silence. "If that is the quality of Healers these days, I should have Urtho look into where that—woman— got her training!"

Tamsin nodded gravely, but Cinnabar's expression suddenly turned thoughtful.

"Odd," she muttered. "I could have sworn I'd seen her before, but where?"

But a moment later, she shook her head, and turned to Aubri and said, "I'll have one of my personal hertasi come to see to your needs, until we can get Jewel back for you. Is there anything I can do for you now?"

Aubri's ear-tufts pricked up in surprise. "Ah—no, thank you, my lady," he replied, struggling to hide his amazement. "I'm really quite comfortable, actually."

"Well, if there is, make sure someone sends me word." Having disposed of the problem, Cinnabar turned back to Skan. "Do you think you can keep your temper in check when *that one* comes back?" she asked. "If you can't I'll have Aubri moved so you won't have to encounter her again."

"I won't promissse," Skan rumbled, "but I will trrry." It was a measure of his anger that he was hissing his sibilants and rolling his r's again.

"I won't ask more of you than that," Cinnabar replied, her eyes bright with anger as she glanced at the still-waving tent-flap. "It is all I could expect from myself."

Tamsin mumbled something; perhaps he had forgotten that a gryphon's hearing was as acute as his eyesight. It would have been inaudible to a human, but Skan heard him quite distinctly.

"I *must* speak with Amberdrake about that one…"

Tamsin chewed his lower lip for a moment, his brow wrinkled a little with worry, and then sighed. "Well, greatest of the sky-warriors," he said lightly, with a teasing glance to the side, "I think *you* won't have any real need for us in the next few hours, so we'll go tend to those with greater hurts and smaller egos."

Skan pretended to be offended, and Aubri snorted his amusement; Cinnabar lost some of her anger as her lover took her hand and led her out.

Ai'bri settled back down, wincing a little as burns rubbed against bandages. Skan arranged himself in his own nest of cushions with a care to his healing bones, and watched his tent-mate with anticipation, hoping for another battle of wits. But the Healing had tired Aubri considerably, and the easing of some of his pain had only left an opening for his exhaustion to move in, assassin-like, to strike him down. Before either of them had a chance to think of anything to say, Aubri's eyes had closed, and he was whistling.

Skan snorted. "Told you," he whispered to the sleeping gryphon.

At least the poor thing was finally *getting* some sleep. Skan was only too well aware that Aubri's sleep had been scant last night, and punctuated by long intervals of wakeful, pain-filled restlessness. Skan had wondered then why his tent-mate's Trondi'irn hadn't come to ensure that the gryphon at least got some sleep—well, now he knew why.

Because this "Winterhart" doesn't care for us. We're just weapons to her; weapons that have the convenient feature of being able to find their own targets. All she cares for is how quickly she can get us repaired and back on the front line again. She might as well be fletching arrows.

Winterhart wasn't the only person in Urtho's forces to think that way; unfortunately, two of Urtho's commanders, General Shaiknam of the Sixth and his next-in-command, Commander Garber, had the same attitude. Urtho's most marvelous creations meant the same as a horse or a hawk, or a hound to them. If a gryphon didn't do *precisely* as ordered, no matter if the orders flew in the face of good sense, there was hell to pay. Obviously, Shaiknam picked underlings who had that same humanocentric attitude.

Skan put his chin down on his foreclaws and brooded. It wasn't often he had his beak so thoroughly rubbed in the fact that he was *incredibly* lucky to have Amberdrake as his Trondi'irn and Tamsin and Cinnabar as his assigned Healers-of-choice.

And if anything ever happened to Amberdrake?

I could end up with another cold, unfeeling rock like Winterhart. And I would have no say in the matter… just as I have no say in when I may sire young, which commander I must serve, nor any way to change battle-plans if the commander does not wish a gryphon's viewpoint.

The gryphons found themselves treated, as often as not, as exactly what Shaiknam and his ilk thought them to be: stupid animals, deployable decoys, with no will, intelligence, or souls of their own.

The more he brooded, the more bitter his thoughts became. Thanks to Amberdrake, he had led a relatively indulged life, insofar as it was possible for any of the Urtho's combatants to be sheltered. But Zhaneel was an example of how a perfectly good gryphon could be turned into a self-deprecating mess, simply by neglect.

Because too many of Urtho's folk—and sometimes even Urtho!—treat us as if we aren't intelligent beings. We're things. We have no autonomy.

From where he lay, he had no trouble reading the titles on the spines of the books Urtho had loaned to him. Biographies and diaries, mostly— all humans, of course—and all great leaders, or leaders Skan considered to be great. Did Urtho have any notion how Skan studied those books, those men and women, and what they did to inspire those who followed them? How he searched for the spark, the secret, the words that turned mere followers into devotees? Or did he think that Skan read them as pure entertainment?

Make your motivations secret to the enemy, fool them into false planning, use their force against them, lead them onto harsh ground, hold true to the beliefs of your followers and show them the ways they may become like you. Lead by example. Those weren't fictions on a page, they were a way of life for those who had become legends in the past. *Urtho knew half of these writers. A quarter of them worked for him when he created us. One he served.*

Urtho had learned from all of them; and now, so did Skandranon. So *why* must things remain the same?

Amberdrake came conscious to the smell of simmering bitteralm-and-cream. Gesten bustled about with fluid efficiency as the kestra'chern awoke, whistling jaunty hertasi tunes while he folded towels and polished brass, pausing only to check the bitteralm pot on the brazier between tasks. Amberdrake couldn't help thinking of morning-wrens greeting the dawn, like the hertasi tale of how the sun had to be coaxed from slumber each day with music.

Amberdrake rolled over and slid sideways, stretching his legs underneath the glossy red and silver satin cover that Urtho had sent to him upon his graduation from apprenticeship. He curled up around a body-pillow and hoped that Gesten wouldn't realize he was awake, but it was too late. The hertasi pulled back a corner of the blanket and offered a cup.

"Morning and daylight, kestra'chern. Much to be done, as always."

Amberdrake blinked and mumbled something that could have been interpreted as rude, if it had been intelligible. Gesten was as unimpressed by it as he'd been the last hundred times, and proceeded to prop up pillows behind the Healer's head. "There's hot bread and sliced kilsie waiting outside. We have three clients today. Losita has pulled muscles and can't take her usual clients, so I accepted one of hers for us. Should not take long. And before you ask, nothing has gone wrong with Skandranon, he is fine, and sends his best regards."

Amberdrake took a sip of the hot, frothy bitteralm-and-cream, and smiled at Gesten. What would any kestra'chern do without hertasi, and what would he do without Gesten? "So things are back to normal."

"As normal as ever in a war. Tchah," the hertasi spat, and flicked his tail. "New orders are down from Shaiknam and his second, Garber. 'All hertasi of convalescing personnel are to be reassigned to more important tasks, according to the judgment of the ranking human officer.'" He thumped his tail against the bed-frame. "I don't think Urtho knows. It's the most stupid thing I've heard in years—we aren't tools to be traded around! Hertasi know their charges. It takes time to learn someone! And to send off a hertasi when their charge is in pain—it's unthinkable. Worse, it's rude."

Amberdrake finished his cupful and thought for a moment. Gesten apparently expected him to do something about this—an assumption that was confirmed when Gesten produced Amberdrake's full wardrobe for the day, laid out his sandals, and stood with his arms crossed, impatiently tapping his foot.

"So, just how *did* you manage to get yourself bunged up?" Skandranon asked his erstwhile companion, when they had both finished the hearty breakfast that Gesten brought them at dawn. Somehow—possibly from Cinnabar, or one of Cinnabar's hertasi—the little fellow had learned that Aubri was without an attendant, and had simply added one more gryphon to his roster of duties. Hence, the double breakfast: a lovely fat sheep shared out between them. *With* the head, which Skan had courteously offered to Aubri, and which Aubri had accepted and had Gesten deftly split, so that each of them could share the dainty.

Aubri had been profuse with his thanks, and Skan had quietly kept his requests to an absolute minimum so that Gesten could concentrate on Aubri. By the time Gesten left, Aubri was cradled in a soft nest of feather-beds that put no pressure on his burns, and the tell-tale signs of a gryphon in pain were all but gone.

"How was I hurt?" Aubri asked. "Huh. Partly stupidity. We were flying scout for Shaiknam's grunts; we had one report of fire-throwers coming up from behind the enemy lines, but only one. And you know Shaiknam."

Skan snorted derision. "Indeed. One report is not enough for him."

"Especially when it comes from a nonhuman." Aubri growled "Needless to say, one report was certainly enough for *us*, but he ignored it. He didn't even bother to send out a second scout for a follow-up on the report."

The broadwing grunted a little and flexed his talons, as if he'd like to set them into the hide of a certain commander. Skan didn't blame him.

"Anyway," Aubri continued after a moment, "I was just in from my last flight and officially off-duty, so he couldn't order me on one of his fool's errands, and I figured I was fresh enough to go have a look-see for myself. And I found the fire-throwers, all right."

"With your tail, I see," Skan said dryly.

Aubri snorted laughter, as Tamsin arrived, with Cinnabar and two of the Lady's personal hertasi. "At least Shaiknam believed the evidence of his eyes and nose, when I came in smoking and practically crushed him!" Aubri chuckled. "You should have seen his face! I set fire to his tent when I landed, and I only wish I could have seen how much of it burned."

"Not as much as you or I would like, Aubri," Tamsin said. "By the way, flaming hero, we've had you reassigned for the duration of *this* injury, anyway. You're our patient now, and if Her Royalness Winterhart comes giving you orders, you tell her to report to *me* first."

Skan blinked in surprise; it wasn't often that Tamsin made room in his overcrowded schedule for a patient from another wing and another commander. Winterhart must have truly angered him yesterday!

"Tchah, Shaiknam should be set down to scrub pots a while," Cinnabar added, wrinkling her elegant nose in distaste. "My family has known his since our grandfathers were children, and it is a pity that anyone ever gave the cream-faced goose any vestige of authority. The only thing he truly has a talent for is losing interest in one project after another."

"And spending someone else's money," Tamsin reminded her.

She shook her head, and brushed her hair back over her shoulders. "That was for peace-time," she corrected him. "Now he simply trades upon his father's reputation, rather than spending his father's gold on one incomplete project after another." She began telling off some of them on graceful fingers, as Skan and Aubri listened with pricked-up ears. "There was the theater-company he abandoned, with the play into rehearsals, the scenery half-built, and the costumes half-made. They struggled on to produce the play, no thanks to him, but since it was written by one of his friends with more hair than wit, it did not fare well and the company disbanded quickly. Then he set himself up as a publisher, but once again, when the tasks proved to entail more than an hour or so of work at a time, he lost interest, and left half-a-dozen writers wondering what would ever become of their works. Then there was the pleasure-garden he planned—oh, Amberdrake knows the tale of *that* better than I—but it was the same old story. The garden languishes weed-filled and half-finished, and a number of talented folk who had turned down other offers of employment to take up with him ended up scrabbling after work and taking second and third place to those with less talent but more perception when it came to dealing with Shaiknam and his enthusiasms."

"His father was Urtho's first and greatest general," Tamsin told the two fascinated gryphons, "and I have heard the man with my own ears say that he is certain he is heir to all of his father's genius. As if wisdom and experience could be inherited!"

Skan laughed aloud at that. "I would say that Shaiknam is living proof that intelligence can skip entire generations."

Cinnabar's lips twitched, and her eyes gleamed with amusement. "Well, as proof that the so-observant Skandranon is right, this is the latest of Shaiknam's orders—that 'hertasi of convalescing personnel are to be immediately reassigned to tasks of more immediate importance.' That is why I brought Calla and Rio; right, little friends?"

She looked down fondly on the two hertasi, who gave her toothy grins. "Let some fool from Sixth Wing East come in here and try ordering *us* about," said Rio, who, like his fellow, was clearly clad in the personal colors of Lady Cinnabar's retinue. "We'll send him out of here with boxed ears."

"You'll have to share us, though," added Calla. "The Lady is seeing how many injured there are from Shaiknam's command, and we're to tend them all, if we can. You don't mind?"

"Mind?" Aubri replied, clearly surprised, pleased, and a little embarrassed. "How could I mind? I didn't expect *any* help! I can only thank you, and know that thanks are inadequate..."

But both Lady Cinnabar and Rio waved away any thanks. "My friends have been itching to do *something* besides tend to my nonexistent needs," she replied. "If my family had not insisted that I take a retinue due my rank, they would not be here at all."

"For which we are grateful," Rio butted in. "And grateful to be able to do something useful. So, we will return when we know how many patients there are, and see what it is you will be needing from us. Eh?"

Aubri nodded, speechless for once.

"It isn't surprising that Shaiknam would have someone like that Winterhart woman as a Trondi'irn," Tamsin observed, checking Skan's healing bones as Cinnabar and her two helpers rebandaged Aubri's burns with soothing creams and paddings.

Aubri let out his breath in a hiss of pain, but replied, "It's typical of him. She won't stand up to him at all; that's why he picked her. Honestly,

I don't think there's a Trondi'irn in the army that would put up with his *sketi*, other than her. But she's just like him: thinks we're nothing more than self-reproducing field-pieces. We're like fire-throwers, only better, because we repair ourselves if you leave us alone long enough. *Very* efficient, is Winterhart."

"Efficient enough to requisition Jewel as soon as she knew you were down," Skan observed.

Aubri snorted. "Surprised she left Jewel with me as long as she did. Maybe she just didn't notice I was gone. She's been *quite* efficient about that new order."

"Who actually issued that particular chunk of offal?" Tamsin demanded in disgust.

"Garber. Shaiknam's second. In case you don't know him, he's by-the-book, and every inch an *officer.*" Aubri's tone made it very clear what he thought of *officers* like Garber.

"So in the meantime, those who have been injured in the front line—where, presumably, Shaiknam and Garber never go—are supposed to do without those who might serve as their hands and make their recovery more comfortable." Lady Cinnabar's cold voice only told Skan that there was a great deal of heat within. The angrier she became, the chillier her voice. "We'll just see about that."

Skan quickly bent his head to keep from betraying his glee. Lady Cinnabar rarely *used* that rank of hers—she was one of Urtho's most trusted advisors when she chose to actually give that advice—but when she did, mountains moved, oceans parted, and strong men trembled until she was safely satisfied. If it had only been a case of one-on-one combat, Urtho could have sent the Lady in against Ma'ar and been secure in the knowledge that Cinnabar would return from the combat with not a single hair disarranged and Ma'ar would be on all fours, following at her heels, begging for her mercy.

But she never, ever, forgot courtesy, even when most angry. She bade Aubri and Skan a polite farewell, instructed Calla and Rio to stay with Tamsin to review the rest of the patients from Shaiknam's command, and only then stalked off.

Tamsin chuckled; Skan joined him. Aubri stared at the two of them in wonder.

"What has gotten into *you* two?" he asked finally, eaten up with curiosity.

Skan exchanged a knowing look with Tamsin, a look which only sent him into further convulsions of laugher. Skan answered for the both of them.

"Lady Cinnabar has Urtho's ear in a way that no one else does," he explained. "I think she's a combination of younger sister and respected teacher. And when she's angry—aiee, she can melt glass! She won't be satisfied with simply talking with Urtho and getting a change in those orders, she'll insist on seeing Garber *and* Shaiknam and delivering a choice lecture in person. By the time she is done, you won't be the only one nursing a scorched tail!"

CHAPTER SIX

Since Gesten was obviously not going to be satisfied until after he *had* done something about the situation with Shaiknam, Amberdrake put off his own breakfast until after he had a chance to schedule a conference with Urtho. He had hoped to simply slip in and have a quiet chat with the wizard, but that was not in the stars; Urtho was chin-deep in advisors long before Amberdrake arrived at his Tower, and it was obvious that there were other matters far more pressing—or disastrous—than the assignment of a handful of hertasi.

The situation would probably be taken care of, at least in the short term, as soon as senior Healers Lady Cinnabar and Tamsin got wind of it. It could easily be dealt with permanently later, when Urtho had a moment of leisure to spare and Amberdrake could have that quiet word with the mage. Provided, of course, that Lady Cinnabar *herself* did not save him the effort and broach the subject to her kinsman. That was only reasonable. But Gesten was not noted for taking a reasonable view when it came to things *he* considered important, so Amberdrake avoided a confrontation by avoiding *him*. Instead of returning to his tent for a solitary breakfast, he went to the mess-tent shared by all the kestra'chern. The food would be exactly the same there as he always had when he was alone; Gesten generally fetched it directly from the mess-cooks. And even though he enjoyed the peace of a meal by himself, it was part of his duty as the highest-ranking kestra'chern to spend as much time in casual company with the others as possible. While the kestra'chern had nothing like a regular organization, it fell upon Amberdrake to see that no one was overburdened, that those who needed help got it, and to keep this corps of support troops functioning as smoothly as the rest of the army. They were all Healers, after all, and not just "of a sort." They had a real impact on the combat-troops.

A delicate undertaking, being "leader" of a group with no leaders—and not a position he would have chosen if it had not been forced upon him.

Whatever was going on that had Urtho up to his eyebrows in work hadn't yet worked its way down to the underlings, it seemed. The tent hadn't more than a half-dozen kestra'chern seated at their makeshift tables of scrap wood, sipping bitteralm and conversing over bread and porridge. That wasn't unusual; kestra'chern were not early risers, given that they generally worked late into the night. No one seemed overly tense or upset. They all greeted Amberdrake with varying degrees of respect and warmth, and went back to their conversations. Amberdrake got himself another cup of bitteralm and a slice of bread and a hard-boiled egg, and took a seat near enough to all of them that he could listen in without being obtrusive.

Two of the women had been having a particularly intense conversation; soon after Amberdrake seated himself, it grew increasingly heated. He knew both of them, and neither were Kaled'a'in; one was a robust redhead called, incongruously enough, Lily. The other, named Jaseen, was a thin, ethereal, fragile-looking blonde who could probably have taken any man in the infantry and broken him in half without working up a sweat.

It was Jaseen who was the angriest, it seemed, and all over a client that had been reassigned to Lily. Amberdrake bent his head over his cup and listened, as her voice rose from a whisper to something a great deal more—public.

"I don't care where he's been assigned or who did it!" she hissed. "You don't have the background to handle him, and I do—"

"You don't have the skill!" Lily interrupted rudely. "And I do! That was why he was reassigned to me—"

"Oh really?" Jaseen replied, her voice dripping with sweet acidity. "I suppose that now the ability to drive a man into exhausted collapse is called a *skill* and counts more than experience!"

Lily sprang to her feet, both hands clenched into fists, and her face flushed. "Superior skill in anything is nothing to be ashamed of!" she cried.

"Tell her, Lily," urged one of the bystanders, as another rose from his seat and moved to Jaseen's side.

They're taking sides. It's time for me to stop this! Amberdrake got up quickly...

And just in time; Lily pulled her arm back to deliver a slap to Jaseen's cheek. Amberdrake moved quickly as a striking snake and grabbed her wrist before she could complete the blow.

"What are the two of you doing?" he not-quite-shouted, bringing the argument to a sudden halt. All parties involved stared at him in shock; they had clearly forgotten that he was there.

He let go of Lily's wrist; her cheeks scarlet with shame, she hid both hands behind her back. He looked from her to Jaseen and back again, making no secret of his disapproval.

"I know that the tension has gotten to everyone, but this is no way to handle it! You two are acting precisely as our critics *expect* us to act!" he accused. "Don't you think that you're both being utterly childish? Bad enough that the two of you started this—but in *public*, in a common mess-tent! The Healers use this tent, and what would one of them have thought if he had come in here to find you two brawling over a client like a pair of—of…" He shook his head, unable to force himself to say the word.

Now it wasn't only Lily who was flushing; Jaseen and the two who had taken sides in the argument had turned scarlet with humiliation as well.

Now that he had their attention, he would need to engage in a verbal dance as intricate as anything woven by a priest or a seasoned diplomat. Somehow he must chide both of them without touching on the tragedies that had made them kestra'chern in the first place.

No one knows hurt and heartache like a kestra'chern, his teachers had said, *Because no one feels more pain than their own. Not so with us.* There were tragic stories behind every pair of doe-soft eyes and tears behind all the comely smiles in this camp, and no one knew that better than Amberdrake.

"Neither of you has ever lacked for clients," he scolded. "It is not as if you are not well-sought-after! And if you hear anyone rating you like athletes, I want to hear about it! You both have the same rank; you differ only in your strongest characteristics. This client you argued about—he has specific needs. Jaseen, *what* comes first—your own pride, or the client's well-being?"

At all costs he must never say the word "poison" around Jaseen—she had spent three years imprisoned for poisoning her lover, only to be freed when his brother confessed that *he* had done it. By then, the "tender" ministrations of the guards had left her a changed woman.

She hid behind the curtain of her hair, but her blushes were still clearly visible. "The client," she replied, her voice choked with shame.

"Exactly," he said sternly. "That is what we are all here for. And what is the second rule, Lily?"

Lily had trained as a fighter—and had served in Urtho's army. Injured, and left for dead, the experience had shattered her nerves, and the injuries themselves left her unfit to face combat again. Lily had been treated as a hopeless cripple, destroyed in both nerve and body, until she fought her way back to what she was now. She looked him in the eyes, but her face was so scarlet that it matched her hair. "The client receives what he *needs*, not what he wants."

"And you may—if, in your sacred judgment, and not merely your *opinion*—deliver what he wants *after* he gets what he needs," Amberdrake told them both.

Jaseen sniffed a little, and looked up at him to see if she'd had any effect on him with that sniffle of self-pity. Amberdrake's expression must have told her that she wasn't winning any points, for she slowly raised her head and brushed her hair back, although her red face was a match for Lily's.

"Jaseen. Just now it was my judgment, as it was the judgment of your old client's Healer, that he needed a little less cosseting and a little more spine." He leveled his gaze right into her eyes so that she could not look away. "You are quite good at sympathy, but your chief failing is that you don't know when to stop giving it. Sympathy can be addictive, and can kill strong men as surely as a diet of nothing but sugar."

She whispered something inaudible, but he was good enough at lip-reading to know she had said only, "Yes, Amberdrake." He turned to Lily.

"It was *your* job to challenge him. I hope that you did—I will only know after his Healer talks to me. And by 'challenging' him, I don't necessarily mean physically. You could even have challenged him by making him *earn* what he got from you." The fact that she avoided his gaze told him she hadn't exactly done that. "We aren't even primarily bed-mates," he reminded both of them sternly. "That's what makes us something more than—what our critics claim we are."

Both these women had mended from their past shatterings—he knew that, every kestra'chern in this encampment knew that. If they hadn't been, they simply wouldn't be here. They'd been given guidance in reassembling themselves from the splintered pasts fate had left them, and were obliged by that training to help others as much as they had helped themselves. Amberdrake would not permit incompetence— and although he was not officially a "leader," he had that much power among the kestra'chern without needing the title. In his experience, true leaders seldom had or needed flamboyant titles.

Jaseen and Lily bowed their heads, their blushes fading. "Yes, Amberdrake," Lily murmured. "You are right, of course. But it's easy to forget, sometimes, with the way we're treated…"

"People treat you as what they wish you were, and that is not always what you are," he said gently, reminding them both of their pasts. "You must always remember what you *are*. Always. And always believe in each other."

Jaseen nodded wordlessly.

He raised his voice slightly so the rest of the observers could hear better. "Whatever the kestra'chern have been in the past, we are now something very important to these warriors. The war may turn upon what we do. We are the rest after the battle, and the blanket to warm them when they shiver. We are comfort in the darkness when death has become far *too* personal; we are the listeners who hear without judgment. We are priest and lover, companion and stranger. We are all the family many of them have, and something so foreign they can say *anything* to us. They need us, as they need their rations, their weapons, their Healers. Keep that always in mind, no matter how you are treated."

Both of them stood taller and straighter, and looked him right in the eyes. Several of the others nodded in agreement with his words, he noted with satisfaction.

"Now, let's get back to the business of living," he told them. "You are both too sensible to quarrel over this." He summoned an infectious grin for the two recent quarrelers and the others, and it caught all around. "We could be spending our time complaining about the seasons. Or the weather. Something productive, something useful."

With that he turned back to his own neglected breakfast, to leave the two of them to patch things up on their own. Or not—but they were both responsible adults, and he was fairly certain they would behave sensibly.

They whispered tensely for a few moments, then took themselves elsewhere. Well, that was fine—and even if they were foolish enough to continue the quarrel, so long as they did so privately, Amberdrake didn't care…

I'm slipping, he thought, as he held out his cup for a hertasi to refill, and rewarded the little lizard with a weak smile. *I would have cared, a while ago. I would have stayed with those two until I was certain they had reconciled their argument. Now, I'm too tired to make all the world happy.*

Too tired, or, perhaps, just too practical. He used to think that everyone could be friends with everyone else, if only people took the time to talk about their differences. Now it was enough for him if they kept their differences out of the working relationships, and got the job done.

I'm settling for less these days, I suppose. I just pray there isn't less out there to settle for. Right now he couldn't have said if this lack of energy was a good thing, or a bad one. It just *was,* and he harbored his resources for those times when they were really needed. For his clients, for Urtho, for Skan—if he spent every last bit of energy he had, he'd wind up clumsy at the wrong time, or weak when the next emergency arose. That—

"Are you Amberdrake?"

The harsh query snapped him out of his reverie, and he looked up, a little startled. A young man stood over him, a Healer by his green robes, and a new one, by the pristine condition of the fabric. The scowl he wore did nothing to improve his face—a most unlikely Healer, who stood awkwardly, held himself in clumsy tension, whose big, blunt-fingered hands would have been more at home wrapped around the handle of an ax or guiding a plow. His carrot-colored hair was cut to a short fuzz, and his blocky face, well-sprinkled with freckles, was clean-shaven, but sunburned. Not the sort one thought of as a Healer.

Well, then, but neither was I...

"Are you Amberdrake?" the youngster demanded again, those heavy hands clenched into fists. "They said you were."

Amberdrake didn't bother to ask who "they" were; he saw no reason to deny his own identity. "I am, sir," he said instead, with careful courtesy. "What may I do for you? I must warn you, my client list is fairly long and if you had hoped to make an appointment—"

"*Make* an appointment?" the boy exploded. "Not a chance—I want you to take my patient *off* that so-called 'client list' of yours! What in the name of all that's holy did you think you were doing, taking a man that's just out of his bed and..."

The young Healer continued on in the same vein for some time; Amberdrake simply waited for him to run out of breath, as his own anger smoldered dangerously. The fool was obviously harboring the usual expectations of what a kestra'chern was, and compounding that error by thinking it was *Amberdrake* who had solicited his patient for some exotic amorous activity.

All without ever *asking* anyone about Amberdrake, his clients, or how he got them. *One word in the Healers' compound would have gotten him all the right answers,* Amberdrake thought, clenching his jaw so hard his teeth hurt. *One word, and he'd have known clients come to me, not the other way around... and that "his" patient has been sent to me for therapeutic massage by a senior Healer. But no—no, he'd much rather nurse his own home-grown prejudices than go looking for the truth!*

When the boy finally stopped shouting, Amberdrake stood. His eyes were on a level with the Healer's but the outrage in them made the boy take an involuntary step backwards.

But Amberdrake only smiled—a smile that Gesten and Tamsin would have recognized. They then would have gleefully begun taking bets on how few words it would take Amberdrake to verbally flay the poor fool.

"You're new to Urtho's camp, aren't you?" he said softly, a sentence that had come to represent insult among Urtho's troops. It implied every pejorative ever invented to describe someone who was hopelessly ignorant, impossibly inexperienced—*dry-seed, greenie, wet-behind-the-ears, clod-hopper, milk-fed, dunce, country-cousin*—and was generally used to begin a dressing-down of one kind or another.

The boy had been with the troops long enough to recognize the phrase when he heard it. He flushed and opened his mouth, but Amberdrake cut him off before he could begin.

"I'll make allowances for a new recruit," he said acidly. "But I suggest that you never address another kestra'chern in the tones you just used with me—not if you want to avoid getting yourself a lecture from your senior Healer and possibly find yourself beaten well enough your own skills wouldn't help you. Did you even bother to *ask* why 'your' patient was sent to me? For your information, 'your' patient was assigned to me by Senior Healer M'laud for therapeutic massage, and I had to *seriously* juggle my overcrowded schedule to fit him in. I am doing *you* a favor; the man needs treatments that you have not been trained to give. If you had tried, you probably would have injured him. *If* you had bothered to *ask* your senior Healer why he had scheduled this patient for other treatments, instead of barging in here to insult and embarrass me, you would have been told exactly that."

The boy's mouth hung open and his ears reddened. His eyes were flat and expressionless, he had been taken so much by surprise.

"Furthermore," Amberdrake continued, warming to his subject, "if you had taken the time to ask your senior Healer why anyone would send a patient down the Hill here to the kestra'chern for treatment, you would have learned that we are considered by all the *senior* Healers to *be* Healers with skills on a par with their own—and that there are some things that you, with all your training, will never be able to supply that a kestra'chern can. Our preliminary training is identical to yours— with the exception that most kestra'chern don't have the luxury of Healing Gifts to rely on. We have to do our job with patience, Words, and physical effort. Healing means more than mending the *body*, young man—it means mending the heart, the mind, and the spirit as well, or the body is useless. That doesn't make us better or worse than you. Just different. Just as there are times when you heal what we cannot, so there are times when *we* can mend what *you* cannot. You would do well to learn that, and quickly. Inexperience can be overcome, ignorance be enlightened, but prejudice will destroy you." He allowed his anger to show now, a little. "This war is not forgiving of fools."

The Healer took another involuntary step back, his eyes wide and blind with confusion.

Amberdrake nodded, stiffly. "I will see your former patient at the arranged time, and if you wish to overrule it I will speak with Urtho personally about the matter. The word of Healer M'laud should take precedence over your objections."

And with that, he turned and left the tent, too angry to wait and see if the boy managed to stammer out an apology, and in no mood to accept it if he did.

He returned to his tent, knowing that it would be empty while Gesten made his own rounds up on Healer's Hill. That was good; he didn't really want anyone around at the moment. He needed to cool down; to temper his own reaction with reason.

He shoved the tent-flap aside and tied it closed—clear warning to anyone looking for him that he did not want to be disturbed. Once inside, he took several deep breaths, and considered his next action for a moment, letting the faintly perfumed "twilight" within the tent walls soothe him.

There were things he could do while he thought: plenty of things he normally left to Gesten. Mending, for one. Gesten would be only too pleased to discover that chore no longer waiting his attention.

Fine. He passed into the inner chamber of the tent, where no client ever came, to his own bed and the minor chaos that Gesten had not been able to clean up yet. *Clothing needing mending is in the sage-hamper.* He gathered up a number of articles with popped seams and trim that had

106

parted company with the main body of the garment; fetched the supply of needles and thread out from its hiding place. He settled himself in a pile of cushions where the light was good, and began replacing a sleeve with fine, precise stitches.

The Chirurgeons that had been his teachers had admired those stitches, once upon a time.

No one knows hurt and heartache like a kestra'chern, because no one has felt it like a kestra'chern. If he had told the boy that, would the young idiot have believed it?

What if I had told him a story—"Once on a time, there was a Kaled'a'in family, living far from the camps of their kin…"

His family, who, with several others, had accepted the burden of living far from the Clans, in the land once named Tantara and a city called Therium. They had accepted the burden of living so far away so that the Kaled'a'in would have agents there. His family had become accustomed to the ways of cities after living there for several generations, and had adopted many of the habits and thoughts of those dwelling within them. They became a Kaled'a'in family who had taken on so many of those characteristics that it would have been difficult to tell them from the natives except for their coloring—unmistakably Kaled'a'in, with black hair, deep amber skin, and blue, blue eyes.

Once upon a time, this was a family who had seen the potential for great Empathic and Healing power in one of their youngest sons. And rather than sending him back to the Clans to learn the "old-fashioned" ways of the Kaled'a'in Healers, had instead sent him farther away, to the capital of the neighboring country of Predain, to learn "modern medicine."

He took a sudden sharp breath at the renewed pain of that long-ago separation. It never went away—it simply became duller, a bit easier to endure with passing time.

They thought they were doing the right thing. Everyone told me how important it was to learn the most modern methods.

Everyone told me how important it was to use the Gifts that I had been born with. I was only thirteen, I had to believe them. The only problem was that the College of Chirurgeons was so "modern" it didn't believe in Empathy, Healing, or any other Gift. The Chirurgeons only believed in what they could see, weigh, and measure; in what anyone with training could do, and "not just those with some so-called mystical Gifts."

The Predain College of Chirurgeons *did* provide a good, solid grounding in the kinds of Healing that were performed without any arcane Gifts at all. Amberdrake was taught surgical techniques, the compounding of medicines from herbs and minerals, bone-setting, diagnoses, and more. And if he had been living at home, he *might* even have come to enjoy it.

But he was not at home. Surrounded by the sick and injured, sent far away from anyone who understood him—in his first year he was the butt of unkind jokes and tricks from his fellow classmates, who called him "barbarian," and he was constantly falling ill. The Gift of Empathy was no Gift at all, when there were too many sick and dying people to shut out. And the Chirurgeons that were his teachers only made him sicker, misdiagnosing him and dosing him for illnesses he didn't even have.

And on top of it all, he was lonely, with no more than a handful of people his own age willing even to be decent to him. Sick at heart and sick in spirit, little wonder he was sick in reality as well.

He had been so sick that he didn't realize how things had changed outside the College—had no inkling of how a mage named Ma'ar had raised an army of followers and supporters in his quest for mundane, rather than arcane, power. He heard of Ma'ar only in the context of "Ma'ar says" when one of his less-friendly classmates found some way to persecute him, and felt the need to justify that persecution.

From those chance-fallen quotes, he knew only that Ma'ar was a would-be warrior and philosopher who had united dozens of warring tribes under his fist, making them part of his "Superior Breed." Proponents of superior-breed theories had come and gone before, attracted a few fanatics, then faded away after breaking a few windows. All the teachers said so when he asked them…

I saw no reason to disbelieve them. Amberdrake took his tiny, careful stitches, concentrating his will on them, as if by mending up his sleeve he could mend up his past.

He had paid no real attention to things happening outside the College. He didn't realize that Ma'ar had been made Prime Minister to the King of Predain. He was too sunk in depression to pay much attention when the King died without an heir, leaving Ma'ar the titular ruler of Predain. *King* Ma'ar, the warrior-king.

But he certainly noticed the changes that followed.

Kaled'a'in and other "foreigners" throughout Predain were suddenly subject to more and more restrictions—where they could go, what they could do, even what they were permitted to wear. Inside the College or out of it, wherever he went he was the subject of taunts, and once or twice, even physical attacks.

By then, the teachers at the college were apologetic, even fearful of what was going on in the greater world; they protected him in their own way, but the best they could do was to confine him to the College and its grounds. And they were bewildered; they had paid no attention to "Ma'ar and his ruffians" and now it was too late to do anything about them. Intellectual problems they understood, but a problem requiring direct action left them baffled and helpless.

And in that, how unlike Urtho they were!

The restrictions from outside continued, turning him into a prisoner within the walls of the College. He stopped getting letters from his family. He was no longer allowed to send letters to them.

I was only fifteen! How should I know what to do?

Then he heard the rumors from the town, overheard from other students frightened for themselves. Ma'ar's men were "deporting" the "foreigners" and taking them away, and no one knew where. Ill, terrified, and in a panic, he had done the only thing he could think of when the rumors said Ma'ar's men were coming to the College to sift through the ranks of students and teachers alike for more "decadent foreigners."

He ran away that very night—with only the clothes on his back, the little money he had with him, and the food he could steal from the College kitchen. In the dead of winter, he fled across country, hiding by day, traveling by night, stealing to eat, all the way back to Therium. He spent almost a week in a fevered delirium, acting more like a crazed animal than the moody but bright young Healer-student he was. He was captured by town police twice, and escaped from them the first time by violence, the second time by trickery.

Before he was halfway home, his town-shoes had split apart, leaving his feet frozen and numb while he slogged across the barren countryside. He had stolen new shoes from farmhouse steps, and heard more of the rumors himself as he eavesdropped on conversations in taverns and kitchens. Then, from many of his hiding places, he saw the reality. Ma'ar was eliminating anyone who opposed his rule—and anyone who might oppose war with the neighboring lands. He had mastered the army, and augmented it with officers chosen from the ranks of his followers. Ma'ar intended to strike before his neighbors had any warning of his intentions.

Ma'ar was making himself an emperor.

And at home, indeed, as the students had said—all the "foreigners" were being rounded up and taken away. Sick with fear and guilt, Amberdrake hid in the daylight hours, once in an abandoned house with a broken-down door. Ma'ar's troopers had been there first, and when night came, he took whatever food he found there and continued his flight.

Looting the bones of the lost. May they forgive me.

It would have been a difficult journey for an adult with money and some resources, with experience. It was a nightmare for Amberdrake. The bulk of his journey lay across farmlands, forests, grazing lands. Mostly, he went hungry, and slept in ditches and under piles of brush. Small wonder that when he stumbled at last into Therium, he burned with fever again and was weak and nauseous with starvation.

I came home. And I found an empty house, in a city that was in a panic. Ma'ar's troops were a day behind me.

No one knew what had become of his family. No one cared what became of him.

He found the neighbors preparing to evacuate, piling their wagon high with their possessions. They had no time for him, these folk who had called themselves "friends," and who had known him all his life.

I begged them to tell me where my family was—I went to my knees and begged with tears pouring down my face. I knelt there in the mud and horse dung and falling snow and pleaded with them. They called me vile names—and when I got to my feet...

Old sorrow, bitter sorrow, choked him again, blinded his eyes until he had to stop taking his tiny stitches and wait for the tears to clear.

I never knew till then what "alone" truly meant. Father, Mother, Firemare, Starsinger, little Zephyr—gone, all gone—Uncle Silverhorn, Stargem, Windsteed, Brightbird...

He had flung himself at the false neighbors, and they had shoved him away, and then raised the horse whip to him. One blow was all it took, and the world and sky disappeared for Amberdrake. He awoke bleeding, at least a candlemark later, with a welt across his chest as thick as his hand. Half-mad with terror and grief, he staggered on into the snow.

He fell against the side of another wagon full of escapees.

The wagon belonging to kestra'chern Silver Veil, and her household and apprentices.

He forced his hands to remain steady. *This is the past. I cannot change it. I did what I could, I tried my best, and how was I to know what Ma'ar would do when older and wiser folk than I did not?*

Silver Veil did not send her servants to drive him away; although by now he hardly knew what was happening to him. In pain, freezing and burning by turns, he barely recalled being taken up into the moving wagon, falling into soft darkness.

In that darkness he remained for a very long time...

His hands shook, and he put the mending down for a moment, closed his eyes, and performed a breathing exercise to calm himself—one that the Silver Veil herself had taught him, in fact.

He had heard of her, in rude whispers, before he had been sent away. As little boys on the verge of puberty always did, his gang of friends spoke about her and boasted how they would seek her out when they were older and had money. She was as beautiful as a statue carved by a master sculptor, slim as a boy, graceful as a gazelle. She took her name from her hair, a platinum fall of silk that she had never cut, that trailed on the ground behind her when she let it fall loose. He had always thought she was simply a courtesan, more exotic and expensive than most, but only that.

It took living within her household to learn differently.

She tended him through his illness, she and her household. He posed as one of her apprentices as they made their way to some place safer—and then, after a time, it was no longer a pose.

The Silver Veil did her best to shelter her own from the horrors of that flight, but there was no way to shelter them from all of it. She had no Gifts, but she had an uncanny sense for finding safe routes—unfortunately, many of those lay through places Ma'ar's troops had lately passed through.

Ma'ar's forces were not kind to the defeated; they were even less kind to those who had resisted them. Amberdrake still woke in the night, sometimes, shaking and drenched with sweat, from terrible dreams of seeing whole families impaled on stakes to die. Nearly as terrible was the one time they had been forced to hide while Ma'ar's picked men—and his makaar—force-marched a seemingly endless column of captives past them. Amberdrake had watched in shock from fear and dread, searching each haggard face for signs of his own kin.

Was it a blessing he had not seen anyone he knew, or a curse?

The Silver Veil plied her trade as they fled—sometimes for a fee, but just as often for nothing, for the sake of those who needed her. And sometimes, as a bribe, to get her household through one of Ma'ar's checkpoints. The apprentices, Amberdrake among them, tried to spare her that as much as possible, offering themselves in her place. Often as not, the offer was accepted, for there was something about Silver Veil that intimidated many of Ma'ar's officers. She was too serene, too intelligent, too sophisticated for them. It was by no means unusual to find that the man they needed to bribe preferred something less—refined—than anything Silver Veil offered.

And finally, as spring crept cautiously out of hiding, they came out into lands that were in friendly hands. But when the Silver Veil reviewed her options, she learned that they were fewer than she had hoped. Soon she knew that she must seek a road that would take her away from the likeliest direction his family had taken—that is, back to Ka'venusho, the land of the Kaled'a'in.

And once again, she provided for young Amberdrake—she found another kestra'chern to take him as an apprentice and be his protector; one who would be willing to go with him to Ka'venusho. This time, the kestra'chern was old, mostly retired—and unlike the Silver Veil, Lorshallen shared with Amberdrake the Gifts of Healing and Empathy. The Silver Veil took a tear-filled leave of him and his new mentor, and she and her household fled on into the south. One of the apprentices claimed that she had a place waiting for her in the train of one of the Shaman-Kings there, in a land where winter never came. Amberdrake hoped so; he had never heard anything more of her.

The war encroached, as the Silver Veil had known it would, and Amberdrake and his new mentor Lorshallen fled before it.

Lorshallen taught everything he knew about his ancient art; Amberdrake learned it all with a fierce desire to master each and every discipline. All the things that the Chirurgeons had not believed in, he mastered under Lorshallen's hands. And he, in his turn, taught Lorshallen the things that they *had* known. The Silver Veil had completed his erotic education and had done her best to heal his body; Lorshallen completed his education as a Healer and had done his best to heal Amberdrake's mind and heart.

Eventually, they came to the Clans, and Amberdrake briefly, took his place among his own people, an honored place, for the Kaled'a'in knew the value of a kestra'chern, particularly one as highly trained as Amberdrake, and they respected the pain he had gone through. The Kaled'a'in had a deep belief that no pain was meaningless—something always came of it. He knew that tales of what he had gone through were whispered around cook-fires, although such a thing was never even hinted at to him. Those in pain could look for strength to someone who had suffered more than they.

Always, he searched for word of his family—and his people

understood, for to a Kaled'a'in, the Clan is all. The Clan he settled among, k'leshya, did their best, sending out messages to all the rest, looking into every rumor of refugees, searching always for word of kestra'chern Amberdrake's lost family.

And they never found it. In a nation of close-knit families, I remain alone, always alone... There will be no brother to share man-talk with, no sister to comfort for her first broken heart. No father to nod with pride at my accomplishment, no mother to come to for advice. No cousins to ask me to stand as kin-next at a naming ceremony for a child. And when I die, it will be to go alone into that last great darkness...

I have lost so much that sometimes I think I am nothing inside but one hollow husk, an emptiness that nothing will ever fill. Still, I try to bail in more and more hope, in hopes that the sorrow will seep out.

When the call came for volunteers from the Mage of Silence, Amberdrake answered at once. At least he would no longer be surrounded by Clans and families to which he would never belong, but by others torn from their homes and roots. And he would fight Ma'ar, in his own way, with his own skills.

Eventually, all of the Clans came to settle at the base of Urtho's Tower, but by then he had already carved his place among the kestra'chern.

He shook his head and bit his lip. Gesten might think he was blind to the workings of his own mind, but *he* knew why he felt the way he did about Skan. The Black Gryphon and Gesten had become the closest thing he had to a family, now.

And the closest thing I am ever likely to have, now.

When—best say, *if*—a kestra'chern ever found a mate, it was nearly always someone from within the ranks of the kestra'chern. No one else would understand; no one else would ever be able to tolerate sharing a mate with others. But for such a pairing to work, it had to be between equals. The altercation between Jaseen and Lily had only shown how easily quarrels could spring up over a client. And if one kestra'chern in a pairing was of a higher rank than another, such quarrels—and, even deadlier, jealousy—were more than likely, they were inevitable. Beneath the surface of every kestra'chern Amberdrake had ever met was a lurking fear of inadequacy. So unless both in a pairing were equal...

The lesser would eventually come to envy and fear the greater. And fear that his or her own skills would not be enough to hold the partner.

Amberdrake was the equal of no kestra'chern here; that was an established fact. And it meant even temporary liaisons must be approached with great caution.

Which left him even more alone.

Even more alone—no. This is ridiculous. If I were a client, I'd be told to stop feeling sorry for myself and concentrate on something that would make me feel good. Or at least stop me from being engulfed by the past.

The sleeve was done; he picked up a second garment and began sewing a fringe of tiny beads back in place. Thousands of tiny beads had been strung into a heavy, glittering fall of color, in luxurious imitation of a Kaled'a'in dancing costume where the fringe would be made of dyed leather. It was a task exacting enough to require quite a bit of concentration and, with gratitude, he lost himself in it.

Until someone scratched at the tied flap of the tent-door, and he looked up in startlement. The silhouetted shadow on the beige of the canvas was human, and not that of a hertasi.

Now what? he wondered, but put his mending down and rose to answer it.

He was a little disconcerted to find yet *another* young Healer—another stranger, and another newcomer—waiting uneasily for him to answer the summons.

"Are you—ah—Amberdrake?" the youngster asked, blushing furiously. "The—ah—kes-kes-kes—"

"Yes, I am Kestra'chern Amberdrake," he replied, with a sigh. "How may I help you?"

The youngster—barely out of a scrawny, gawky adolescence, and not yet grown into the slender and graceful adult Amberdrake saw signs he would become—stared down at his shoes. "I ah—have a patient, and—my senior Healer said my patient needs to see you and if I wanted to know why—I, ah, should ask you myself."

"And who is your senior Healer?" Amberdrake asked, a little more sharply than he had intended.

"M'laud," came the barely audible reply.

At that, Amberdrake came very near to destroying the poor lad with a bray of laughter. After having sent *one* of M'laud's juniors up the hill with his tail on fire, the senior Healer had evidently decided to teach his juniors about kestra'chern directly.

But he kept control of himself, and when the lad looked up, it was to see a very serene countenance, a mask that would have done the Silver Veil herself proud.

"Come in, please," Amberdrake said calmly. "I think you are probably laboring under a great many misconceptions, and I would be most happy to dispel those for you."

When he held the tent-flap wide and gestured, the boy had no choice but to come inside. Amberdrake noted with amusement how the youngster stared around him, while trying not to look as if he was doing so.

What does he expect to see? Never mind, I think I can guess.

"Take a seat, please," he said, gesturing to a hassock at a comfortable distance from the cushion he took for himself. "I take it that you are afraid that I am going to hurt your patient. Is that true?" At the boy's stiff nod, he smiled. "I take it also that you have never had the services of a kestra'chern yourself?"

"Of *course* not!" the young Healer blurted with indignation—then realized how rude that was, and winced. But Amberdrake only chuckled.

"Young man—what is your name, anyway?"

"Lanz," came the gurgled reply.

"Lanz—by now, I should think that M'laud has made you aware that the preliminary training for Healers and kestra'chern is practically identical. And I *know*—I began my training as a Healer." Amberdrake raised his eyebrow at the boy, who gaped at him.

"But why didn't you—I mean—why a *kestra'chern?*" Lanz blurted again.

"You sound as if you were saying, 'why a chunk of dung?' do you realize that?" Amberdrake countered. "When you consider that the Kaled'a'in rank the kestra'chern with shaman, that's not only rude, that's likely to get you smacked, at least by anyone in the Clans!"

Lanz hung his head and said something too smothered to hear, but his ears and neck turned as scarlet as Amberdrake's favorite robe.

I seem to be making a great many people blush, today. Another Gift? "Lanz, most of the reasons I became a kestra'chern are too complicated to go into for the most part—but I can tell you the only simple one. I am also Empathic, too strong an Empath to be of any use as a conventional Healer." Amberdrake nodded as Lanz looked up cautiously from beneath a fringe of dark hair. "That doesn't mean I became this because I am afflicted by some horrible mental curse—but as a kestra'chern, well, I never see those who are so badly injured that their physical pain overwhelms everything else. But I *can* use my Gifts and my training to Heal the deeper and more subtle pains, injuries of mind, body, and heart they may not even be aware they have."

"But not all kestra'chern are Healers," Lanz said doubtfully. "Or Empaths…"

Amberdrake smiled. "That is true. Most of them are not. And those who have no Gifts must work the harder to learn how to read the languages of body and tone; to see the subtle signals of things that the Gifted can read directly." As Lanz's blushes faded, he allowed himself a chuckle. "My friend, there is one thing that the kestra'chern have learned over the centuries: people who believe they are coming to someone only for an hour or two of pleasure are *far* more likely to unburden themselves than people who are confronted with a Healer or other figure of authority. If we honey-coat the Healing with a bit of enjoyment, of physical pleasure, where's the harm: Now—is your patient the last one on my roster tonight?"

"I think so." Lanz sat up a little straighter now, and he had lost some of the tension in his body that had told Amberdrake the boy was afraid of him.

"M'laud sent me a briefing on her. The reason she is coming to me is that she is under some kind of great inner tension that M'laud has been unable to release, as well as some severe battlefield trauma, and that is making it impossible for her damaged body to heal." Lanz's face lit up—and Amberdrake decided that *he* must have thought her failure to heal was *his* fault. "M'laud suspects that she suffered some kind of abuse in her childhood, which is the real root of her problems—essentially, she is unconsciously punishing herself for being such a bad person that she deserved abuse." He sighed and shook his head. "I know that this makes no sense, but this is something that kestra'chern in particular see and hear all the time. And it is not something you have any chance of dealing with, for I greatly doubt you would ever get her to trust you enough. Not because you are not trustworthy, but simply because of her own problems. You have other responsibilities to take your time, and you are less experienced with this kind of problem than I. I am a stranger, and it is often easier to say terrible things to a stranger than it is to someone who has known you, for the stranger will not pre-judge. I will not be anywhere near the front lines, *ever,* and thus she will know that I have no chance of being cut down by the enemy—I become safe to think of as a friend, because she knows she will not lose me."

Lanz shifted a little in his seat, looking rather doubtful, and Amberdrake decided to overwhelm him, just a little. "Here—I'll prove it to you," he said, in an authoritative voice.

And he told off the litany of all the formal training he'd had, first with the Chirurgeons, then the Silver Veil, and finally Lorshallen. It took rather a long time, and before he was finished, Lanz's eyes had glazed over and it looked to Amberdrake as if the poor boy's head was in quite a spin.

"You see?" he finished. "If you've had *half* that training, I'd call you a good Healer."

"I never knew," the youngster said in a daze, "and when Karly came up the Hill from talking to you…"

"Karly? The red-head?" Amberdrake threw back his head and laughed.

Shyly, Lanz joined the laughter. "I heard that one of the other senior Healers said, 'I hope he has a regular bed-mate, because after talking to Amberdrake the way he did, there isn't a kestra'chern in all of the camp who'll take him for any price!' I suppose he was awfully rude to you."

"Rude?!" Amberdrake replied. "That doesn't begin to describe him! Still, Karly needn't worry. We're *obligated* to take those in need, and I can't imagine anyone more in need of—our services—than he is!"

Lanz smiled shyly. "And—Karly's rather thick," he offered. "After talking to you—you being so kind and all—well, if you take any of my patients, I think I'm going to be awfully grateful, and kind of flattered."

This time Amberdrake's smile was as much full of surprise as pleasure. "Thank you, Lanz. I will take that as a very high compliment. Can I offer you anything?"

The boy blinked shyly. "I don't suppose a cup of bitteralm would delay me much—and could you tell me a little more about some of the others down here?"

Amberdrake rose, and Lanz rose with him. "Why not come with me to the mess-tent and see for yourself?" he asked.

"I think I will!" Lanz replied, as if he was surprised by his own response.

By such little victories are wars and hearts won, Amberdrake thought with a wry pleasure, as he led the way.

CHAPTER SEVEN

Zhaneel flexed her talons, digging them into the wood of her enormous block-perch. She checked over her harness again—wire-scissors, bolts, spikes, rope-knife, pre-knotted ties, all sized for her large, stubby "hands"—and stared out over the obstacle-course she herself had set up.

The course covered several acres by now, built mainly in erosion-trenches and brook-cut hollows that were of little value to anyone in Urtho's camp, dotted with fallen trees and sandstone boulders. To get from here to the end of it, she would have to fly, dodge, crawl, and even swim. There were water hazards, fire hazards, missiles lobbed by catapult—

And now, magic.

She had already gotten the help of Amberdrake's hertasi, Gesten, in this endeavor. He'd been there. from the very beginning; somehow he had known, perhaps through Amberdrake, what she was going to attempt. He had never asked her *why.* He simply showed up unasked, acted as her hands, then found three others to aid him in setting up the course and in triggering the hazards. At first, no one had paid any attention to what she was doing, but gradually her runs attracted a small audience. This had bothered her, until the day when, after several unsuccessful tries at passing a hazard of simulated crossbow-bolts, she made it through untouched and the tiny group applauded wildly.

That was when she realized that they were *not* there to make fun of her, but to cheer her on.

She had honestly not known what to make of that; it bewildered her. Why should anyone take an interest in *her?*

Then again, she had never been able to effectively figure out why hertasi and humans did most things…

But today, she had a larger audience than ever before, and she knew precisely *why* this time. Word had spread that her obstacle course included magic.

She hadn't planned on including magical traps; those took effort and much energy, and she had never for a moment believed that there was any mage in the entire camp willing to devote so much as a candlemark of practice-time to helping her. Or so she had thought, until a few days ago.

A young mage, a Journeyman named Vikteren approached *her* for help. He needed spell-components. *Still-living* spell-components, which were not at all interested in becoming components of anything.

Zhaneel's speed and agility were what caught his attention; speed and agility were precisely what he lacked in going after starlings, rabbits, and other small, swift creatures. So they struck a bargain: she would hunt for him, and he would provide her with magical obstacles.

He had been doing so for several days now—and he had told her yesterday, grinning, that he was very impressed. Actually, what he had said was, "You're *good*, gryphon! Very *damned* good!"

So, much to her shock and amazement, had the gryphons' trainer, Taran Shire. The day after Vikteren began helping her, Taran showed up on the sidelines. Now, along with the young Journeyman, the seasoned trainer joined her every day, working with her on his own time.

She tried to put her audience out of her mind, although that was far from easy—her own kind were out there, other gryphons, those from other wings as well as her own. And what was more, some of those same gryphons had taken to training on the course and leaving her tokens of appreciation.

Every time she made a pass on the course, people cheered her efforts, from hertasi to humans, from gryphons to a lone kyree who seemed to find her fascinating. Now, they waited for her to start yet again.

A white and red striped flag midway down the course went up and waved twice, and she launched from the block. This was a rescue mission—to free a captured gryphon. The details had been kept secret, at her request, so she had only a general idea what to expect. One thing she knew for certain—Vikteren and the hertasi planned to make her work harder than ever before.

The first danger came only twelve wing-strokes after starting—a sudden gust of wind from her right. It hit her hard and pushed her towards a downed tree's spidery limbs—an easy place to lose feathers and find lacerations. She reacted by rolling in midair and grounding, folding her wings in tight while she clutched at stones and brush. The wind gusts ceased, and Zhaneel leapt over a ravine, to the cheers of the audience.

She crept into the next erosion-channel, popping her head up to look for danger every few seconds. A quick bolt of fire shot towards the ravine from behind a boulder, and was followed by a huge fire-ball that roared like a sustained lightning-strike. It burned slowly through the ravine, catching the underbrush afire. She heard the audience gasp even over the roar, as Zhaneel scrambled out of their line of sight, disappearing from their view. She knew what was in their minds. *Had the game gone too far?*

But she couldn't worry about them. They'd see her soon enough...

She popped up again at the far end of the adjoining erosion-cut. She leapt to the sandstone boulder with a growl, and drew her rope-knife on the surprised mage hiding behind it. *Hah! Hello, Vikteren.*

"You die!" she sang out, and Vikteren grinned and fell backwards.

"I'm dead *here,*" he reminded her as he stood up and brushed off his robes. "See you further on, maybe."

"You might not see me at all, dead body!" she laughed, then sheathed the knife. There was a mission to accomplish, a gryphon to rescue, and the adventure had barely begun.

Amberdrake felt like a proud and anxious father as he watched the young gryphon waiting on her block-perch. Every line and quivering muscle betrayed her tension and her concentration. He had arrived after she took her position, but still managed to commandeer a place in the front beside Skan. The Black Gryphon had recovered from his injuries nicely, although he was still officially convalescing on the orders of Lady Cinnabar. He was keeping an uncharacteristically low profile, however—as if he was afraid his presence would distract the young female at some crucial moment.

Well, it might. The youngster had been patently overawed by the Black Gryphon; if she knew he was watching, she might well lose her concentration.

Skan's tail twitched impatiently, but as Amberdrake put a comradely hand on his shoulder, he gave Amberdrake a sideways gryph-grin, before riveting his attention on the distant gray and buff figure of Zhaneel.

At the end of the course, a flag dropped. Zhaneel left the block with a leap, followed by an audible *snap* of wings opening.

Amberdrake had never seen a gryphon run an obstacle-course before, though he'd heard from Gesten that Skan had been out here to watch for the past three days in a row. He hadn't been able to imagine what kinds of obstacles *could* be put in front of a gryphon, whose aerial nature made ordinary obstacles ridiculous. He was impressed, both with Zhaneel's ability to create the course, and her ability to run it.

More to the point, so was Skan.

He gasped with the others when it appeared, briefly, that a rolling fireball had accidentally engulfed her; he hadn't realized that there would be some hazards on this course that were *real,* and not just illusions. He sighed with relief when she reappeared, and cheered when she "killed" someone, a Journeyman mage by his clothing.

Skan remained absolutely motionless, except for the very end of his tail, which flopped and twitched like a fish on land. Like a cat, the end of his tail betrayed his mental state.

Well, every other gryphon in the audience was watching her closely too; gryphons were by nature impressed with any kind of fancy flying. It was part of courtship and mating, after all. But none of the others had quite the same rapt intensity in their gaze as Skan did.

In point of fact, he looked as much stunned as enraptured, rather as if he'd been hit in the back of the head with a club.

Amberdrake smothered a chuckle when he realized that Skan's eyes had glazed over. Poor Black Gryphon! He was used to impressing, not *being* impressed!

Zhaneel neatly dodged a set of ambushes; crossbow-bolts, dropping nets, and an illusion of fighters. "She's good, isn't she," he said, feeling incredibly proud of her. She wasn't just good, she was smooth. She integrated her movements, flowing from flight to ground and back again seamlessly.

"She's beautiful," Skan rumbled absently. "Just—beautiful…"

His beak gaped a little, and Amberdrake had to choke back another laugh. So, the great Black Gryphon was a little bit *more* than simply impressed, was he? Well, fancy flying *was* the gryphonic equivalent of erotic dance.

"Skan," he muttered under his breath, "You're going to embarrass both of us. That tongue looks really stupid sticking out of the corner of your beak."

Skandranon hadn't realized that he was making his interest in Zhaneel *quite* so obvious.

"Pull it in, Skan," Amberdrake muttered insistently. And annoyingly, but that was the privilege of an old friend. Better him than anyone else, though. There were plenty of other folk who enjoyed a chance to get a jab in; why give them more fuel for their fires?

More to the point, such teasing might be turned against Zhaneel, and he already knew that her fragile self-esteem would not survive it. He wasn't even certain she'd recognize teasing if she encountered it.

One of the Second Wing West gryphons, a female named Lyosha, sidled up beside him and preened his neck-ruff briefly. It was a common enough sort of greeting between gryphons—one which could lead to further intimacies, or simply be accepted as a greeting and nothing more. He and Lyosha had flown spirals together before, and she was obviously hoping the greeting would lead to the former, but he was not interested this time. Not with Zhaneel dancing her pattern with danger before his eyes.

"Lyosha," he said simply, acknowledging her presence in a friendly manner, but offering nothing more. "This is fascinating."

Lyosha gave his feathers one last nibble, then subsided with a sigh. "True enough," she replied with resignation. "I'm tempted to start running this course myself. It's enough to set a gryphon's tail afire!"

He ignored the hint, and coughed politely. "Well," he said, his eyes never leaving Zhaneel, "if she's not careful, the tail that's afire may be *hers.*"

And let Lyosha make of that what she will...

Zhaneel slunk over a decaying tree-trunk towards four upright sacks of hay. The sacks had been clustered around a burning campfire and wore discarded uniforms. A sign next to them read, "Off-duty. Talking. Eating." Next to them was a mid-sized tent and pickets for four horses, but no horses were there.

Tent is big enough to hold ten. Four here, four horses gone, may mean eight. Four still out or on mission. Ma'ar squads are eight and one officer, but officers get separate tents. Where is the officer, then, and the others?

Zhaneel drew her hand-crossbow. A tug with her beak, and it was cocked for a bolt to be laid in the track. She pulled one from her harness and laid it in, ready to fire.

Use the cover you have available. Steady with solid object.

She lowered herself behind the trunk and braced the hand-crossbow on the crumbling bark—and fired. The shaft hit the sack on the far left, and she hastily drew a second bolt while recocking the weapon with her beak. The second shot hit the next sack dead center and pitched it forward into the fire. She then snapped the hand-crossbow onto its tension-buckle and leapt over the tree-trunk to maul the remaining two sacks of hay.

That was when the barrage began.

The tree-line to her left erupted with slung stones as the hidden miniature siege engines on the right shredded their foliage. Zhaneel power-stroked high into the air and avoided major damage, although some of the stones stung her on the feet and flank. That put her in the open for the fan of firebolts from the hillside, where she saw her objective—a gryphon. A *real* gryphon, under a wire net, staked out in a very unflattering position.

Oh no! I hadn't asked for that!

So Vikteren's promised surprise was that she wouldn't be rescuing a bundle of cloth called a "gryphon"—she would have to deal with an actual one! But if Vikteren had gotten the cooperation of a gryphon as a prisoner, then what else could he have—

A whistling flash from the sky was her only warning. Two broadwings—from Fourth Wing West, by their wingtip markings—stooped down on her. They trailed white ribbons from their hind legs—sparring markers. *Simulated makaar!*

So be it!

Amberdrake's hand tightened on Skan's shoulder, and he felt Skan's muscles tense up underneath his fingers. The two "makaar" swooped down on Zhaneel from above, and he could not see any way that she could escape them.

He couldn't, but she most clearly did!

She ducked—and *rolled,* so that the "makaar" missed her by a scant talon-length; as they shot past her, she leapt up into the air behind them. By luck or incredible timing, she snagged the trailing white streamer of one, and ripped it off.

The "dead makaar" spat out a good-natured curse and a laugh, then obligingly kited out of the way of combat. It was a good thing he did so, because Zhaneel had shot skyward, gaining altitude and speed, and was just about to turn to make a second attack run. The second broadwing had tried to pursue her, but his heavy body was just not capable of keeping up with her. If her objective had simply been to survive this course, she would already have won.

But it wasn't, of course. She still had to "free the trapped gryphon," and get both of them off the course "alive." The trapped one was Skan's old tent-mate Aubri, whose injuries still had him on the "recovering" list, and who would not be able to move very quickly. Again, that was a reflection of reality; any gryphon held captive would be injured, perhaps seriously, and his speed and movement would be severely limited.

Aubri had volunteered for the ignominious position he was currently in, partly out of boredom, partly out of a wish to help Zhaneel, and partly because it pleased him to irk their commander in every way possible. And Zhaneel's success in these special training bouts must be irking the very devil out of their commander, who could hardly encompass the notion that a gryphon might have a mind of her own, and must be in knots over one who had *ideas* of her own.

Zhaneel wheeled and started her dive. The "makaar," who had been trying vainly to pursue her, suddenly realized that although he would be more than a match for her in a straight-on combat, he was never going to be able to take her on in strike-and-run tactics.

And she was not going to let *him* close.

He turned, heading for a place that Amberdrake suspected held that young mage—would Zhaneel see it, too?

Or would she be so involved in the immediate enemy that she would forget there were others on this course?

Like a falcon stooping on her prey, her wings folded tightly along her back, and she held her talons up against her body—but unlike the broadwings, who held their talons ready to strike and bind, hers were fisted. She had learned how to knock her foes out of the sky once, and now it was second nature to her—was she so caught up in the euphoria of combat that the "kill" was all she saw?

Skan held his breath as Zhaneel dropped down out of the sky. He was certain she had forgotten the Journeyman mage, but he certainly had not forgotten her—and the best place for him was somewhere near the staked-out "prisoner." She might get her immediate foe, but Vikteren would certainly get *her*...

But as the broadwing pumped frantically to evade her, she shot past him completely, ignoring him!

Instead, she stooped on an insignificant-looking mound of shrubbery, leveled out into a shallow curve, and buffeted it with fists and wings until the illusion of brush dissolved and Vikteren tumbled out of the way, laughing.

"All right!" he called, scrubbing dust out of his eyes with his fists. "Holy Kreeshta, you've got me already! Give me a moment, will you?"

"You die twice, mage!" she cried, as she leapt skyward again. She looked around for the second "makaar," but the broadwing had followed the example of most makaar left to face a gryphon alone and had fled the scene, his ribbon and his "life" intact. Of course, unlike a real makaar, he would remain unpunished for such desertion.

Skan rumbled approval deep in his chest as she landed as close to the staked-out and netted "prisoner" as possible—which, in her case, was practically on top of him. There were probably traps all around her, but she avoided setting any of them off, simply by dint of remaining within the narrow margins that humans would have used while restraining the prisoner. A broadwing couldn't have pulled this off; nor could a broadwing have used foreclaws as cleverly as she did, snipping the wire net free with special scissors, then cutting the ropes holding Aubri down with a heavy knife she had already used once to good effect.

Oh, clever, clever, little gryphon! he applauded mentally. *Now, how do you guard the back of the injured one? That will be the real test.*

124

* * *

Zhaneel's gaze darted all over Aubri. "Can you fly?" she asked impatiently.

"No. Can't move any faster than a broke-legged horse, either. And my wounds are real, hey?"

Zhaneel spat a curse away from Aubri and looked around for anything she could use. Within a few wing-lengths there were tree limbs, and she had the lengths of rope she'd just cut, as well as the remains of the wire net. She grasped the lengths of rope readily available, coiled them up and held them to her keel.

"Two questions," she said. "How far can you jump, and can you hold a pole steady?"

Aubri narrowed his eyes, obviously trying to second-guess what this odd rescuer had in mind. He also, just as obviously, gave up. "Could leap... maybe twice my length, if I had to. But I wouldn't enjoy it. And I can hold a pole steady. I still feel strong enough to chew makaar."

"Good. Stay here." She parted her beak in what was meant to be a reassuring smile, then bunched her legs up and concentrated. She leapt high into the air with her burden of cord. At the zenith of her jump, she power-stroked out of Aubri's immediate area towards the tree limbs nearby.

Conventional gryphon-traps were usually built to fire sideways across a broad area, the kind she had been stung by at the fake-soldiers' camp. Magical ones were often designed to detect a low flyer approaching, shoot high up, blossom, and spread while falling. They could kill or maim at any point after they deployed. Since Vikteren—a mage—was involved, she had every reason to assume she would be facing both types.

So, the best way to sweep for traps is... to not be near them at all!

Within a few minutes, she had what she needed. A long branch, snapped off with her beak and trimmed of snags, for Aubri to hold. At its narrowest end, it forked for two claw-lengths, and she had carved indentations for the two branches that were now tied across it. They were firmly in place.

Now to deliver my little nesting-gift.

A few minutes' more work, and the long pieces of rope were one very long length of rope—inelegant, but effective! Zhaneel used four of her pre-knotted ties to bind up the foliage and small branches she had trimmed scant minutes earlier to one end of the rope. She bobbed her head, measuring the range to Aubri and the "safe" ceiling she had flown at already without triggering traps, then took wing, the loose end of the rope clutched tightly in her hindclaws.

Magical gryphon-traps are triggered by something living flying over their kill range, but not always. Can sometimes be triggered by anything—have to go high!

Zhaneel circled up, straining only for altitude—and it was *work*, hard work, because the higher she went, the heavier the burden of the rope became. Finally there was a shudder as the bundles of foliage lifted. She angled away from the still-perplexed Aubri, carrying the rope higher and higher until the bundles below were above what she had determined to be safe. Then, she turned her struggle for altitude into an exhausting dive from the far side of the clearing, towards where the tied branches were. She judged, hoped—and let go.

The bunches of foliage sailed down, directly for the hapless Aubri. Behind them, the rope coiled and twisted wildly, gaining on the clusters of branches that had more wind-resistance than the rope. While Zhaneel surged back up into the sky, the green leaves and twigs struck Aubri's wings and back. It was surely uncomfortable, but easily less painful than anything a makaar would have done to a captive gryphon. Amid indignant curses from the "captive," the rope fell in a snaky line across the clearing. As hoped, no traps triggered immediately from the rope's impact.

Next trick.

She landed and collected her thoughts, taking deep breaths. Aubri glared at her indignantly, but voiced no ill thoughts towards his "rescuer" for the moment. She waved a reassurance to him, looped the rope around the fork of the branch-affair she'd made earlier, and tied it off.

Several heartbeats later, she was in the air again, with two stripped branches clipped to the back of her harness. She followed the air-path she knew was safe and dropped straight down to land next to Aubri.

"I assume you have a good reason for pelting me with salad?" he rumbled.

"I'm sorry. But I have a plan to get you out safely. Hold this…" she muttered while unclipping the branches from her back. "They scratch! There. Now. Lay sideways and curl up. Hold these sticks up, one in hindclaws, one in foreclaws. So both are that way." She indicated the direction the rope lay. "Be patient."

Aubri sighed. "Where would I go? My life is yours."

Zhaneel pulled the wire-mesh until it faced as Aubri did, and used two more ties to anchor it to the two sticks. Then understanding dawned in Aubri's eyes as she fastened the foliage bundles to the net.

"A shield."

"Yes. Not a big one, but could help us." She smiled and nibbled his crest reassuringly. "Now, let me down there in the hollow of your belly, where the rope goes under the net."

Aubri complied, fascinated. After settling herself in, Zhaneel reeled the rope in claw-over-claw until the heavy branches tied to the other end ground their way towards the two gryphons.

"Searching for ground traps," Zhaneel muttered. "If one goes, hold tight to the sticks! Let me protect your belly." *Only makes sense—he can't fly, so I am as good as ground-bound. If I can shield him from a fatal injury by taking an injury myself, we will still both be alive to return home.*

A deep thudding sounded, like a massive crossbow cord releasing, and a hail of stones showered much of the clearing. Both gryphons squinted their eyes while pebbles struck the greenery protecting them, then resumed pulling. Two ground panels lurched open and drove stakes into the ground nearby. A few minutes later, Zhaneel could reach out and grasp the quarry herself.

Last trick.

She patiently explained to Aubri what she was doing as she worked, and allowed herself a moment of satisfaction when she was done. The crowd watching had approved of the way she'd triggered the ground traps, and waited, enraptured, wondering what she would do next. Zhaneel knew they saw her raise the canopy she had just finished, made of wire net, foliage and branches, above Aubri.

"You *must* hold this steady, understand? Must!"

Aubri nodded. "Y'got me this far, skydancer."

Zhaneel's nares blushed red and she leapt straight up, gaining altitude madly. When she had reached twice the height she counted as "safe," she rolled over on her back, straightened, and folded her wings in tight, hurtling faster than any crossbow bolt. Her shadow streaked across the ground below as she flattened the dive. She felt the wind cut across her body and saw the landscape become a blur as she shot across the clearing, scant wing-lengths above the ground, following the same path in the air that her sweep earlier had done on the surface.

Behind her, she could hear fire-balls erupting, and saw flashes of yellow light. Moments later, she traded speed for altitude and pulled up, to see sparks raining down on the entire clearing—and Aubri's shield.

The improvised shield held and protected him from harm.

With the first victory cry she had ever uttered, she closed on him to lead him from his captivity.

Winterhart grimaced as the audience began cheering. Someone jostled her, jarring her back and sending a jab of pain down her right leg, further souring her mood.

Garber had ordered her to come here, orders she hadn't much liked and wasn't sure she agreed with. Right now, though, she wasn't very fond of gryphons; it was a gryphon that had injured her back.

Be fair. It wasn't her fault. She'd been having backaches and ignoring them—after all, who *didn't* have a headache or a backache by day's end around here? She had been restraining an hysterical and delirious broadwing with severe lacerations; she'd lashed out with both hind feet and sent Winterhart twisting and tumbling sideways. She hadn't broken anything, but her back spasmed as soon as she got up, and it had been getting worse, not better, with time.

She was a Healer; she *knew* she should be seeing another Healer, or should at least stay in bed, flat, for a while. She was even fairly certain that she knew what was wrong. But there were no Healers and no time to spare, so she simply hadn't mentioned it to anyone. She moved as little as possible, said she had "sprained" her back, and used that as an excuse not to do things that made it hurt worse. But she was in constant pain; there were only two positions she could take that allowed the pain to stop, and neither of them were appropriate for getting any work done. It was *embarrassing.* A Healer should be able to keep herself in one piece. This was altogether too much like a display of incompetence.

The pain wasn't doing much for her temper, and getting jostled and making it worse didn't help.

Damn Garber. He's right, but for all the wrong reasons.

She'd been watching Zhaneel herself for several days, since she'd gotten wind of this "obstacle-course" business, and long before dimwitted Garber had any notion that it was going on. Even before today she'd found herself torn between two violently conflicting opinions.

On the one hand—she had to admire the little gryphon; obviously unsuited for combat, she had found ways to *make* herself suited to it. She had been pushing herself, finding her absolute limits, turning handicaps into benefits. The number of things she'd had to work out for herself to overcome her own deficiencies was incredible, and the ingenious ways she had done so were amazing. It was difficult to believe that this was the little runt Garber saw no use for at all.

But on the other hand, Zhaneel was exhausting herself completely with these so-called "training sessions"; no one had ever *authorized* her to do what she was doing, which made them quasi-legal at best. But that could be ignored—what could not be ignored was the fact that she had led other gryphons into trying her unorthodox tactics, with very mixed results.

Zhaneel herself had come out of these sessions with pulled muscles; she hadn't come to Winterhart for any help, but that made no difference. The gryphon had been hurt, and she was the one who had invented the course and the training. Winterhart was afraid that one of the others was very likely to be seriously injured trying some of her nonsense.

Even if the other gryphons didn't manage to hurt themselves on this course, the fact still remained that they burned off energy and resources they *might* need later, where it counted. Out on the front lines. The war escalated, resources diminished. Although it was not common knowledge, Urtho's forces had lost ground, a little more every day. There was a new breed of makaar in the air now, and they took a toll on the gryphons. If the gryphons wasted their energy or strained themselves on this obstacle-course of Zhaneel's, they might not have that little extra they needed to survive an encounter with these new makaar.

Garber, of course, only knew that the gryphon cull was doing things he hadn't ordered, not so much flouting his authority as ignoring it. No gryphon in Sixth Wing was allowed to think for itself; the very idea was preposterous. He was already aching with humiliation at the lecture the Lady Cinnabar had delivered—on Urtho's behalf—concerning the reassignment of injured gryphons' hertasi. Winterhart had not been present, but several who had overheard the Lady had indicated she had been less than flattering concerning Garber's intelligence and ability to make a sound decision. Then came news of Zhaneel, creating some unorthodox training program, encouraging others to join her in it, completely bypassing Garber's authority. This could not be permitted, so he had sent the gryphon's Trondi'irn—the lowest-ranking officer in the Wing, she acidly reminded herself—to dress her down for it. Never mind that it was a *successful* program so far. That was hardly the point.

Winterhart threaded through the crowd, more uneasy with every passing moment. She did not like confrontations. She particularly disliked them when there was a possible audience involved.

But she had direct orders. She also had an exact speech, delivered to her by Garber's aide-de-camp, and duly memorized. Presumably the commander did not trust her to deliver a proper dressing-down... or perhaps he was as contemptuous of her intelligence as he was of the gryphons'.

Abruptly, she found herself in a clear space, and practically nose-to-beak with the runt.

Zhaneel blinked in surprise, and backed up a pace or so. "Winterrrharrrt," she said blankly. "What do you herrre?"

That was all the opening that Winterhart required. "It is more to the point to ask you what *you* are doing here, gryphon," she said coldly. "You are here without orders, you have commandeered equipment and personnel that you have no right to, and you have subverted other gryphons inside and outside of your wing into not only aiding you, but following in your ill-conceived plans. Your commander is highly displeased. What have you to say for yourself?"

She expected Zhaneel to behave as she always had: to cower a little, stammer an apology, and creep off to her aerie, forgetting and abandoning her ridiculous "training program." She had readied a magnanimous acceptance of that apology before she was halfway through her speech. Something that would make her look a little less like Garber's mouthpiece...

"I?" the cull replied—and every hair and feather on her body bristled. She drew herself up to her full, if substandard, height, and looked down her beak at the Trondi'irn with eyes full of rage. "I?" she repeated, raising her voice. "How isss it that I am to blame becaussse the commanderrr of Sssixth Wing hasss no morrre imagination than a mud-turrrtle? How isss it that it isss *my* fault that therrre isss only *one* trrraining progrrram for all, no matter the cirrrcumssstancesss, norrr if they change? What isss it that I am doing *wrrrong?* What isss it that I am doing that I should be accusssed of doing wrrrong?" Her voice rose to full volume, and the audience, which had begun to disperse, regrouped in anticipation of another sort of spectacle. It was clear in an instant that they would *not* be siding with Winterhart.

"I do *nothing* wrrrong!" Zhaneel shouted. "I do what *should* have been done, that no one carrred to do! And you, my Trrrondi'irrrn, *you* should have ssseen that it needed doing!"

By now the audience had surrounded the two of them, leaving Winterhart no route of escape. She couldn't help herself, she flushed with profound embarrassment.

"You had no orders and no permission—" she began.

"Orrrderrrsss?" the gryphon replied with shrill incredulity. "I am on leave time! Thessse who help me arrre off-duty! What need have we of orrrderrrsss, of perrrmisssssionsss? Arrre we to requessst leave to *pissss* now?"

Growls from behind her, a little laughter on all sides, and nods and angry looks on the faces she could see—her face burned painfully.

"*We arrre off-duty,*" the gryphon repeated. "When hasss Garrrberrr the rrright to decrrree what we do off-duty?"

"He doesn't," Winterhart admitted, reluctantly. "But he gave me the orders—"

Before she could say anything more, a huge, black-dyed gryphon with no regimental marks pushed through the crowd and faced her with challenge in every line of him. "Then why," rumbled the infamous Skandranon, the Black Gryphon, "don't you tell that overbearing half-fledged idiot that his orders are a pile of steaming mutes? You're a Trondi'irn, you have that right *and* duty for your gryphons."

She stared at him. She had never heard the Black Gryphon speak before—at least, not more than a word or two. When he had shared a tent on Healer's Hill with her gryphon Aubri, he had not spoken more than a word or two in her presence at most. He was either asleep, or ignoring her. She had no idea he was so articulate, with so little gryphonic accent. Hearing that clear, clipped voice coming from that beak—it was such a shock, she addressed him as she would have another human.

"I couldn't do that!" she exclaimed, automatically. "He's my superior!"

But the Black Gryphon only shrugged. "In what way? I don't see why you shouldn't tell him he's being hopelessly thick," he replied. "I tell *my* superiors when they're idiots often enough. I generally tell them they couldn't tell their crest from their tailfeathers on a daily basis. And that includes Urtho."

Urtho? This—this creation, this construct, talked back to *Urtho?* She was aghast, appalled, and tried to put some of that into words, but all that came out was, "B-but that's n-not the way things are *done!*" She'd stammered, which made it sound all the stupider.

Skandranon only snorted his contempt, as equally contemptuous laughter erupted around the circle. "That's not the way *you* do things, maybe," the Black Gryphon replied. "It seems to me that the main problem we have is that there are too many officers thinking that books and noble birth give you all the answers you need—and too many order-takers who *believe* them without question." He took a step or two closer to her, looming over her, and staring down his beak at her. "Amuse me. Bring me up on charges. You didn't even think for yourself when

Garber handed you that scoop of manure to deliver here. Didn't it ever occur to you that the real reason you were told to lecture this young lady was *not* that she was doing anything wrong, but because she was doing something Garber and Shaiknam didn't think of—or steal—first? It must gall them both that what they would call a 'mere beast' has been more clever than they were. Without asking for permission. Without being *told*, Trondi'irn."

Winterhart opened her mouth to say something—and could not think of anything to say. Certainly she could not refute what the gryphon had just said—hadn't she been thinking it herself? And she could not bring herself to defend Garber, not when his aide had been condescending to the point of insulting when he had delivered those orders. All she could do was to stand there with her mouth hanging open, looking stupid and shamed.

It was Zhaneel who salvaged what little was left of the situation. "Trrrondi'irrrrn," she said crisply, "I will have worrrdsss with you. In prrrivate. Now."

Winterhart took the escape, narrow as it was, and nodded.

After all, there was nothing else she could do but follow.

But then, wasn't she used to that, by now?

CHAPTER EIGHT

Amberdrake managed to get Skan out of earshot of most of the camp before the Black Gryphon exploded, pulling him deeply into the heart of the obstacle-course and into a little sheltered area with a tree or two for shade and a rock to sit on. He counted himself lucky, at that; this obstacle-course of Zhaneel's was large enough for privacy even at the level of shouting Skan was capable of. Large gryphons had large lungs.

The course should be safe enough with all the traps sprung, and now that the "show" was over, anyone who might happen to overhear Skan's outburst was likely to be sympathetic, anyway. Up until today there hadn't been anyone unfriendly among the spectators.

Zhaneel's first "show" had been utterly eclipsed by her second; standing up for her rights to that officious Trondi'irn, Winterhart. It was nothing anyone had expected, given Zhaneel's diffident manner up until this moment.

She must just have been pushed too far. Not surprising. That woman would have pushed me over the edge.

Even the Sixth Wing trainer had been disgusted with the woman, and even more disgusted with Garber. If everyone who said they would actually *did* lodge a protest with Urtho—bypassing Shaiknam altogether—Garber would go down on record as the commander most disliked, *ever*. Even the humans had been appalled by the precedent that would be set if this action was not met with immediate protest, a precedent that permitted a commanding officer to decree what could and could not be done during off-duty hours.

Well, the woman had at least enough conscience left that she was embarrassed by those orders she was supposed to deliver. That's about all I can say in her behalf. If first impressions are important, I can't say she's made a very good one on me.

Trondi'irn should have enough fortitude to stand up for her charges, not roll over and show her belly every time the commander issues some stupid order. And wasn't she the one Gesten told me about, that ordered the hertasi to be reassigned? Can't she do anything but parrot whatever Garber wants?

Amberdrake took a seat on the sun-warmed rock, and let Skan wear himself out venting his anger. He was annoyed with the woman, and *very* put out with her commander. But Skandranon was enraged enough to have chewed up swords and then spit out tacks. It was better for him to show that anger to Amberdrake than sweep into camp and get himself in trouble. It wouldn't have been the first time that his beak had dug him a hole big enough to fall into.

"*This* is what I mean!" Skan foamed, striding back and forth, wings flipping impatiently. His talons tore up the ground with every step he took, leaving long furrows in the crumbling earth. "This is *exactly* what I've been trying to tell you! Now you see it for yourself—this whole sorry business! We gryphons are *constantly* being ordered about by humans who know and care nothing about us! We get chewed up trying to keep them alive, and they won't let us figure out ways to keep *ourselves* alive! Damned idiots can't tell their helms from the privy, and *they're* trying to tell *us* what to do! And now they're ordering us around when we're *off-duty*, and the dung-heads think it's their *right* and *privilege!*"

There was more, much more, in the same vein. Amberdrake simply remained where he was on his rock, nodded, looked somber, and made appropriately soothing noises from time to time. He wished there was something else he could do, but right now, all he could provide Skan with was a sympathetic ear. He was, himself, too angry to do Skan any good. If he tried to calm the gryphon through logic games, he'd only let his own anger out. Besides, Skan didn't want to be calmed, he wanted a target.

The trouble was, Skan was right on all counts; Amberdrake had seen it time and time again. And it wasn't as if the gryphons had any choice—they couldn't simply pack up and leave their creator, no matter how onerous conditions got. They were, in a sense, enslaved to their creator, for only Urtho held the secret of their fertility. Without that, they could not reproduce. Without that, if they left, they would be the last of their kind.

Skan knew that, better than anyone else, since every time he returned from a mission, intact or otherwise, someone asked him when he was going to pick a mate and father a brood. It was a constant irritant to him; he never forgot it, no matter how cavalier he might seem about it. And yet, he had never once brought it up to Urtho directly.

Why? I don't know. Maybe he's afraid to, for all his boasting that he speaks to Urtho as an equal. Maybe he keeps thinking that Urtho will realize what an injustice has been done on his own...

Amberdrake wished there was some legitimate way that he could calm his friend down; by now Skan had worked himself up into a full gryphonic rage-display—crest up, hackles up, wings mantling, tearing the thin sod to shreds with his talons. He agreed with the Black Gryphon more with every moment. How could he calm Skan down when he himself wanted to carefully and clinically take Garber and Shaiknam apart on Skan and Zhaneel's behalf?

Not just their behalf, either. How long before they try that sketi on the other troops? Or before they try to command the exclusive services of one or more Healers, or even kestra'chern? If they're willing to break the rules once, how many more times will they break them? And then when they make *the rules, who can oppose them?*

He'd thought that Skan's display had cleared the area—no one really wanted to get too near a gryphon in that state, especially not when the gryphon was Skandranon. He'd never actually hurt anyone—but when he was this angry, he got malicious enjoyment out of coming within a feather's-width of doing so. But after listening to Skan for a quarter-candlemark, Amberdrake spotted someone else storming up over the rough ground towards them, short Journeyman's robes marking him as a mage, and carrot-colored hair identifying him as Vikteren.

He's heading straight for us. Good gods, what now? Another disaster?

"Gods!" the young mage shouted as Skan paused for breath. "I would have the *hide* off that fatuous, fat-brained idiot, if only I knew how to make it hurt enough!"

"Garber?" Amberdrake asked mildly.

"Gods! *And* Shaiknam!" Vikteren said bitterly, dropping his voice below a shout. The young mage snatched up a fallen branch as he reached them, and began methodically breaking it into smaller and smaller pieces. "Ant-hills and honey spring to mind—and harp-strings, delicate organs, and rocks! I thought this bigoted business with poor Zhaneel was bad enough—but now…!"

He struggled with the press of his emotions; clearly his rage was hot enough to choke him, and even Skan lowered his hackles and cocked his head to one side, distracted from his own state of rage in seeing Vikteren's. The youngster was one of the coolest heads in the mage-corps; he prided himself on his control under all circumstances. Whatever had happened to break that control must have been dreadful indeed.

"What happened?" Amberdrake asked anxiously, projecting calm now, as he had not with Skan. Not much—but enough to keep the young mage from exploding with temper.

Vikteren took several long, calculated breaths, closing his eyes, as his flush faded to something less apoplectic. "I heard Skan just now, and I have to tell you both that it isn't just his non-human troops that Shaiknam's been using up. He's been decimating everyone with the same abandon. I just talked to the mages from Sixth Command. We almost lost *all* of Sixth Crimson this morning, the mage included, because Shaiknam led them into an ambush that he'd been *told* was an ambush by his scouts. Ividian covered their retreat; he *died* covering that retreat, and it was all that saved them. Ividian *died!* And Shaiknam reprimanded the entire company for 'unauthorized maneuvers'! And I'm not just livid because Ividian was my friend—Shaiknam killed three more mages today, and he has the brass to claim it was *by accident.*"

Amberdrake let out his breath in a hiss, his gut clenched and his skin suddenly cold. The loss of any portion of Sixth Crimson was terrible—and the loss of their mage dreadful. And all through prideful stupidity, like all of Shaiknam's losses.

But what Vikteren had just implied was more than stupidity, he had very nearly said that Shaiknam had murdered the other three mages lost. "How," he asked carefully, "do you kill a mage by accident?"

Vikteren's face flushed crimson again. "He forced them—ordered them—to exhaust themselves to unconsciousness. Then he *left them there*, where they fell. Ignored them. Got them no aid at all, not even a blanket to cover them. They died of power-drain shock where they lay. He said that there was so much going on at the time that he "just forgot" they were there, but I heard someone say that he ordered them to be left alone, said if they were such powerful and mighty mages they could fix themselves. Called them weaklings. Said they needed to be taught a lesson."

Amberdrake and Skan both growled. That *was* more like murder-by-neglect. A mage worked to unconsciousness needed to be treated immediately, or he would die. Every commander knew that. Even Shaiknam.

There was no excuse. None.

"Shaiknam's a petty man, a *stupid* man—the trouble is he gives petty orders that do a lot of damage," Vikteren finished, his scarlet flush of anger slowly fading. "He has no compassion, no sense of anything outside of his own importance, no perspective at all. He used those three up just so he could recoup the losses he took on the retreat—*just* so that he wouldn't look bad! That was the *only* reason he ordered them to attack; they fought there against ordinary troops, there was no need for mage-weaponry!"

Vikteren took another deep breath and dropped the splinters still clenched in his hands. "I came to tell you two that there's going to be a meeting of all the mages tonight. We're going to tell Urtho that none of us are going to serve under Shaiknam or any other abusive commander, ever again. We're tired of being treated like arbalests and catapults. I'm going to have a few things to say at that meeting, and before I'm done, you'd better believe they're going to follow my vote!"

"But *you* won't have a vote," Amberdrake protested. "You're just an apprentice—well, a Journeyman, but—"

But Vikteren snorted. "Hah! I'm not a Journeyman, I'm a full Master mage at the least—but my master never passed me up. He saw who was in charge, and snarled the status on purpose so I'd work back here and not get sent out on the lines to get killed by a fool. He saved my life today, that's how I feel. I could be a Master if I wanted to get slaughtered, and every mage in the army knows it."

Amberdrake glanced over at Skan, who nodded slightly. One Master mage could always pick out another. Well, that was certainly interesting, but not particularly relevant to their situation.

But Vikteren wasn't finished. "Dammit, Amberdrake! We're not makaar, we're not slaves, and we're not replaced with a snap of the fingers! We're going to demand autonomy, and a say in how we're deployed, and I came to tell you that all the mages I've talked to think you gryphons ought to do the same! Maybe if both parties gang up on Urtho at once, he'll be more inclined to take us seriously!"

Skan's hackles went up again, and his claws contracted in the turf with a tearing noise. "We are *not* going to gang up on Urtho! He is my friend. Still—we might as well be stinking makaar," he rumbled. "While Urtho is the only one who can make our matings fertile, he holds all of us bound to him." Then in a hiss, "Much as I care for him, I could *hate* him for that."

Vikteren started. "What are you talking about?" he asked, obviously taken aback. "I've never heard of anything of the sort—"

"Let me," Amberdrake said hastily, before Skan roused back to his full rage. "Vikteren, it's because they're constructs. Urtho alone knows the controls—what triggers fertility, and what doesn't. Gryphons that survive a certain number of missions are the only ones permitted to raise a brood. There's some things only Urtho knows that trigger fertility, and they are different for male and female gryphons; both have to have something secret and specific done to them before their mating results in offspring—plus they have to make an aerial courtship display. Only if all three of those things happen do you have a fertile coupling."

"We can go through the motions of breeding as much as we like," Skan said tonelessly. "But without that knowledge, or that component that Urtho keeps to himself, it's strictly recreational." He shook his massive head. "Not only is it slavery, or worse than slavery, it's *dangerous*. There are never more than a tenth of us fertile at any one time. All it would take is one spell from Ma'ar—or for Urtho to die—and our race would die! You can't have a viable breeding population with only a tenth of the adults fertile! Even the breeders of hounds know that…"

"But why?" Vikteren said, bewildered. "Why does he hold that over you?"

Skan sighed gustily. "I have no idea. None. We don't *need* to be controlled. Do you know how much we revere him? We'd continue to serve him the way the kyree do. We'd do it because he is *right*, and because we respect and care for him, not because he controls our destiny. We'd probably serve him better if he *didn't* control us like that. Damn! If he doesn't give it to us, maybe we ought to *steal* it."

"So—steal it? The spell, or whatever it is?" Vikteren said slowly. "That's not a bad idea." Amberdrake stared at him, not believing the mage had said anything so audacious even though the words had come out of his mouth.

"What good would that do?" Amberdrake asked. "If you need a mage to make it work…"

Skan closed his eyes for a moment, as if Vikteren's words had caused a series of thoughts to cascade. "About half of the gryphons are apprentice-level mages, or better," he rumbled. "We are magical by nature. We wouldn't need a mage to cooperate with us. I'm a full Master, for instance."

"Even if you lacked for mages among yourselves, you'd find plenty of volunteers with the human mages," Vikteren insisted. "Do it, Skan! You're right! If he won't give it to you, steal the damn spell! And if you're a Master, then make the change permanent! Don't put up with being manipulated like this!"

Amberdrake found himself agreeing, much to his own surprise.

Think of the families sundered by Ma'ar. They, who did not deserve such horrors, and now these gryphons you know and love cannot have families at all unless their lord wills it.

"Take your freedom, Skan," Amberdrake whispered. "Steal the spell, and teach it to everyone you trust."

Skandranon backwinged in place, then pulled himself up to his full, magnificent height.

The brisk wind from the Black Gryphon's wings sent Vikteren's hair into his face, and kicked up a bit of dust that made Amberdrake squint for a moment.

"Stealing a spell from Urtho though..." Vikteren's eyes lit up with a manic glee. "You know that'd be nearly impossible? Not working the spell itself, that would be pretty simple, fertility spells nearly always are. No, it's the stealing part that would be hard. Getting into Urtho's Tower, getting past all the protections..."

From the look on Vikteren's face, he relished that very challenge and impossibility.

"It would not be impossible for *me,*" Skan replied, his crest-feathers rising arrogantly.

But Amberdrake shook his head. "Be realistic, Skan—you've always flown directly to Urtho's balcony when you went to see him. You have no idea what safeguards are in that Tower, many of them built only for human hands. It would be impossible for you. But not for us."

"Us?" Skan asked, eying them both. Vikteren nodded gleefully, seconding Amberdrake.

"Exactly," the kestra'chern said with immense satisfaction, feeling as if the weight of a hundred gryphons was lifted off him. "Us."

* * *

In the end, the "us" also included Tamsin and Cinnabar. After a brief discussion, the means of bypassing all those special protections turned out to be absurdly easy.

Cinnabar crafted a message to be sent to Urtho *just* before Urtho was to meet with the leader of the mages' delegation. She claimed that there were some problems she and Tamsin were encountering with gryphon anatomy—not even a lie!—and that she and he needed to consult the records on the gryphons' development so that they could tell what Urtho used for a "model."

She did not specify who she would have with her, only that she needed some "help."

"Urtho keeps records on everything he's ever done," she said, as they waited in her tent for the reply. She sat as calmly and quietly as if they were all her guests for an evening of quiet social chat, and not gathered to perform what could, by some standards, be considered a major theft. Her hands were folded in her lap, and she leaned into Tamsin's shoulder, wearing an enigmatic little smile. Her pale green robes were as smooth and cool as tinted porcelain; beside her lover, she looked like an expensive doll propped next to a peasant-child's rag-toy. "I know he has extensive records on how he put your race together, and what he modeled you on. I specified 'internal problems,' which could be anything in the gut, and that's difficult stuff to muck about with when you don't know what you're doing. It isn't enough to be a Healer familiar with raptors in order to be successful with gryphons, even though that is *how* I became a default Healer to your people, Skan. You aren't all, or even mostly, raptorial. I'm counting on his being preoccupied with this mages' meeting; he should simply give us access to the Tower rather than taking the time to explain things to us in person."

"A pity about the timing on that," Skan observed dispassionately. "Vikteren did want to be here, and he has some—ah—unusual talents for a mage. He could have been very useful. Still, he will surely keep Urtho's attention at the meeting." The Black Gryphon lay along one side of the tent on Cinnabar's expensive carpet of crimson and gold, where the furniture had been cleared away for him. Until he moved or spoke, he looked like an expensive piece of sculpture, brought in to match the carpet. Or, perhaps, like a very expensive and odd couch.

Amberdrake chuckled. "Well, he'll be here in spirit, anyway," he said, patting his pocket where the bespelled lock-breaker Vikteren had loaned him resided. "It's just as well, given that we've been huddled together like conspirators for the whole afternoon. This way, if anyone has seen us all together, they can assume we won't do anything without him, and won't be watching us."

Tamsin laughed, and reached across Cinnabar for a cup of hot tea. "You've heard too many adventure-tales, kestra'chern," he mocked. "Who would be watching us? And why? Even if Urtho catches us, the worst he'll do is dress us down. It's not as if we were trying to take over his Power Stone or something. We are not even particularly important personages in this camp."

Skan raised his hackles at that. "Speak for yourself, Tamsin!" he responded sharply. Tamsin only laughed, and Cinnabar smiled a little wider.

Before a verbal sparring match could begin, one of Cinnabar's hertasi scratched at the tent-flap, then let herself in, handing the Lady a sealed envelope. Cinnabar opened it, read the contents, and nodded with satisfaction.

"As I thought," she said, to no one in particular. "Urtho is so caught up with the mages that he didn't even ask me what the complaint is. He's leaving orders to pass us into the Tower. We have relatively free access to the gryphon records; he warned me that some things have some magical protections on them, and that if I want to see them, I'll have to ask him."

"Which of course we will not," Amberdrake said. "Since we have other means of getting at them."

"So, you see, we didn't need all that skulking and going in through windows that you three wanted to do," Cinnabar replied, with just a hint of reproach in her voice.

"Lady, don't include me in that!" Amberdrake protested. "It was Tamsin, Skan and Vikteren that wanted to go breaking into the Tower! I knew better!"

"Of course you did," Tamsin muttered under his breath, as they all rose to go. "And *you* never collected ropes and equipment for securing prisoners. I don't even want to know why you conveniently had all that stuff on hand!"

Amberdrake raised an eyebrow and pretended not to hear him, and simply rose with all of the dignity that years of practise could grant.

They all walked very calmly into the Tower, a massive and yet curiously graceful structure of smooth, sculpted stone. They gave a friendly nod to the guard on duty, and received one in return; very clearly he was expecting them. They didn't even need to make up some excuse for

Amberdrake and Skan being with them—the guard didn't bother to ask why they were there.

There were no fences; the Tower didn't need them. It probably didn't need a human guard, either, but such things made mere mortals feel a little more comfortable around a mage like Urtho. The entrance was recessed into the Tower wall, and the door opened for them at the guard's touch. They passed out of the darkness and into a lighted antechamber bare of all furnishings, with a mosaic of stone inlaid on the floor. Three doors led out of it; Cinnabar had been here before and she led the way.

Ah, bless the mages, Amberdrake thought yet again. *If it hadn't been for them...*

Then again, perhaps Lady Cinnabar would have found another excuse. She was a woman of remarkable resources, the Lady was.

The area where Urtho kept his records on the gryphons was several floors up, but all of them were fit enough that they didn't much mind the climb. The circular staircase was wide enough for Skan, and other than the fact that it was lit by mage-lights, seemed completely ordinary. It was constructed entirely of the native stone of the area, planed smooth, and fitted together so closely that the joins looked hardly wider than the blade of a knife.

However, as they reached the floor they wanted, a gently curved door opened itself as they approached. All the other doors they had passed remained securely closed, with no visible means of opening them. They passed through that open door into an area of halls and cubicles, all lined floor-to-ceiling with books.

It certainly looked as if this was the right place. Amberdrake wondered how Urtho kept the air moving and fresh in a place like this; there was no more than a hint of dust in the air, no mold, and no moisture. If he stood very still, there *was* a gentle, steady current of air running past him, but where it came from and where it went he simply couldn't tell.

This place, too, glowed with mage-lights; a wise precaution with so many flammable books around.

Interesting that Cinnabar herself said we ought to simply take the secret without confronting Urtho. She knows him better than any of us. I wish I knew why she'd come to that conclusion, but she must have some reason to think he would have refused to give his hold over the gryphons away.

As a kestra'chern, Amberdrake's curiosity had been aroused by that. He could think of many possible motivations, but he would have liked to know which of them was the most likely.

So while Tamsin and Cinnabar perused the index to the record room to find the books on the gryphons' reproductive system, he browsed through the notations written on the spines of the books in search of clues.

He didn't find any, unfortunately. The notations were all strictly impersonal, mostly dates or specific keywords to the contents. *Eggs, raptor, failure-rate,* said one. *Breeding records, Kaled'a'in bondbirds.*

So he had a hand in that as well? Or did he just study what my people did?

Next to it, *Breeding records, Kaled'a'in horses.*

Amberdrake had to chuckle at that. Just one book? Then Urtho had no real idea of what the Kaled'a'in were up to with their horse-herds. Unless, of course, this was a very limited study of what they did with the war-horse breed.

That might be his only interest, but even so, Amberdrake doubted that the Kaled'a'in horse-masters had parted with their inmost secrets even for the mighty Urtho, Mage of Silence and their titular liege-lord. Kaled'a'in Healers and mages together worked on both the war-horses and the bondbirds—and while the results with the raptors might be the more obvious, the ones with the horses were far more spectacular, though never to the naked eye.

The raptors had been given increased intelligence and curiosity, the ability to speak mind-to-mind with humans, and the ability to flock-bond to each other and to the humans who raised them. To compensate for the increased mass of brain-tissue, and to make them more effective as fighting-partners, they were larger than their wild counterparts.

But the horses had been changed in far more subtle ways. Bone density had been increased, hoof strength increased, in some cases extra muscles had been created that simply didn't exist in a "normal" horse. The digestion had been changed; the war-horses could forage where few other horses could feed, taking nourishment from such unlikely sources as thistle and dead or dried plants, like a goat or a wild sheep. As with the raptors, the intelligence had been increased, but one thing had been utterly changed.

The war-horses were no longer herd beasts. They were pack animals. Their behavior was no longer that of a horse, but like a dog. Properly trained, there was nothing they would not do for their riders—and unlike a horse, the rider could count on his mount to continue a command after the rider was out of sight. "Guard," for instance. Or "Go home."

Very few people knew this, or the amount of work it took to change a *behavior* set rather than a simple physical characteristic. Did Urtho?

He was reaching for the book when Cinnabar called him. Regretfully, he pulled his hand back. Another mystery that would remain unsolved, at least for now.

"We've found the book we want," Tamsin said, as he followed Cinnabar's voice into yet another book-lined cubicle. "Very nicely annotated in the index, with the fact that it contains the fertility formula. He refers to it as that, by the way, rather than an actual 'spell,' so Cinnabar and I are assuming that only a small part of it actually requires magic."

"That's good news for the gryphons, then," Skan said with interest, padding in from the opposite direction as Amberdrake.

"If it only requires a little magic, most should be able to do it for themselves."

"As we expected, however, the book is mage-locked," Cinnabar interrupted, gesturing to a large leather-bound volume securely fastened with leather and metal straps. There were no visible locks, but then there wouldn't be, not with a volume that was mage-locked.

But, thanks to Vikteren, that was not going to be a problem.

The "lock-picks" didn't look like anything of the sort; rather, they looked like a set of inscribed beads of various sorts. "Urtho only uses about a dozen different spells to hold his ordinary magic-books," Vikteren had said. "There aren't more than a hundred common spells of that sort in existence. Of course, there's always a chance he used something entirely new, but why? Most people don't know more than two or three mage-lock spells, even at the Master level. The chances that he'd use something esoteric for a relatively common book that he's going to *want* to consult easily are pretty remote."

Amberdrake had looked over the string of beads curiously. "So how many counter-spells are there here?" he'd asked.

"Seventy-six," Vikteren had replied with a grin. "My Master is a Lock-master among his other talents. I paid attention. You never know when you may need to get into something."

"Or out of it," Amberdrake had remarked sardonically. But he'd taken the "picks."

Now it was just a matter of trying the beads against the place where all the straps met, one at a time. Vikteren had strung them in order— from the most common to the least, and that was how Amberdrake would use them. All it would take would be patience.

He didn't need to try more than a dozen, however; as he took the bead away and fingered up the next, the straps suddenly parted company, unfolding neatly down onto the stand, and leaving the book ready for perusal.

Cinnabar exclaimed with satisfaction, and flipped the cover open. "Ah, Urtho," she said with a chuckle. "Just as methodical as always. Indexed as neatly as a scribe's copy, and here's what we want on page five hundred and two…"

She and Tamsin leafed through the pages rapidly, and soon copied the relevant formula down. They planned to make two copies, just in case they were discovered; they would turn over one, but not the second, unless Urtho somehow *knew* that they'd made it.

Suddenly, Skan's head snapped up, alarm in his eyes, his crest-feathers erect and quivering.

"What is it?" Amberdrake whispered, afraid to make a sound. Was there a guard coming?

"There's—another gryphon up here!" Skan muttered, his head weaving back and forth a little, his eyes slightly glazed with concentration. "It's in the next room, but there's something wrong, something odd…"

Before Amberdrake could stop him, the Black Gryphon had snatched the lock-pick beads out of his hand. He turned and trotted down the hall to a doorway barely visible at the end of it.

Tamsin and Cinnabar became so engrossed in their copying that they didn't even notice Skan's abrupt departure. It was left to Amberdrake to chase after him and snatch the beads out of his talons as he shoved them in a bundle against the door-lock.

"What are you trying to do?" he hissed, as the gryphon turned to look at him with reproach. "Do you *want* us to be discovered?"

"I…" Skan shook his head. "I just felt as if there was—something I should do about that other gryphon. It felt important. It felt as if I needed to get in there quickly."

Amberdrake did *not* make the scathing retort he wanted to. "And what if that was the point?" he asked, instead. "What if there is some kind of trap in there and this feeling of yours is the bait? We both know how tricky Urtho is! That's exactly the kind of thing he'd do!"

"He wouldn't be mad—at least not for long," Skan replied weakly. "I could talk him down."

"Until he figured out that we had taken his precious fertility formula!"

Amberdrake retorted. "Now will you be sensible? Did you actually unlock that door?"

"I thought I heard a click," the Black Gryphon told him, with uncharacteristic meekness. "But I don't know, I could have heard the beads clicking together."

These were meant to unlock books, not doors—maybe nothing happened. "Look, Skan, whatever it is behind that door, it can wait until you have a chance to ask Urtho yourself. If he wants you to know, he'll tell you. You were supposed to be here, after all, and you can say you sensed another gryphon—then you can ask him what was going on. He'll probably tell you."

"Just like he's told me the fertility formula?" the gryphon replied scornfully, sounding *much* more like his usual self. He walked beside Amberdrake with his usual unnerving lack of sound. "Oh please..."

"We're done!" Tamsin grinned. "We copied legitimate information to cover the notes on the fertility formula, if we meet Urtho on the way out and he asks. Let's get out of here. I'd rather not try and bluff him."

"Right." Amberdrake said. "Come on, Skan. You can solve mysteries later."

He stuffed the "picks" into a deep pocket, one full of other miscellaneous junk of the kind a kestra'chern often collected: bits of trim, loose beads, a heavy neck-chain, the odd token or two. He hoped that among all that junk the beads would appear insignificant. And hopefully Urtho, if they met him, would not check him over for magic.

He hurried down the hall to join the others, assuming Skan followed. The mage-lights extinguished in his wake, leaving darkness and silence behind him.

CHAPTER NINE

Skan pushed the unlocked door open the tiniest bit. *Stupid gryphon. Stupid, stupid gryphon. Going to get yourself into trouble again. This time with your own side!* Skan shoved the door open a little more, carefully, listening, watching for moving shadows as he opened the portal, taking a huge breath of air and testing it for scents other than dust. His bump of curiosity was eating him alive. His weaker bump of caution was screaming at him to turn around and join the others on the staircase. As always, his bump of curiosity won.

Metal doors, and I wonder why? Never mind, Urtho's not going to like this, stupid gryphon. He puts locks on things for a reason.

Yes, but what could that reason be? Why would paternal, kindly Urtho hide something that called to him like a gryphon—only not quite? What if it was something important, and out-of-keeping with Urtho's kind-hearted image? What if Urtho was as bad as Ma'ar beneath that absent-minded and gentle exterior? After all, hadn't the Mage of Silence been withholding the fertility secret all this time? What if he was hiding something sinister?

Stupid and paranoid, gryphon. Maybe you addled your brains when you struck the too-hard earth. It's been known to happen.

Still. Just because you were paranoid, that did not mean your fears had no foundation. What if Urtho had no intention of giving the gryphons their fertility and their autonomy because he already had their replacement waiting in the wings, so to speak?

Some kind of super-gryphon, but one that wouldn't do such an inconvenient thing as begin to think for itself and hold its own opinions. A prettier sort of makaar?

Stupid, stupid gryphon. And if you find out that's really the case, what then? Take the chance that Urtho won't know and stay to tell the others, or fly away before he can catch you? If so, to where?

The door moved, slowly, a talon-width at a time. Then, suddenly, it swung open very quickly indeed, all at once, as if he had triggered something.

For a moment, he looked into darkness, overwhelmed by a wash of gryphon "presence," so strong that surely, surely it must be from *many* gryphons.

Then the lights came up, albeit dim ones that left the far walls in shadow-shrouded obscurity, and he found himself staring at—

Gryphon-ghosts!

That was his first thought; they hung in midair, floated, and he could see right through them. *They* were the source of most of the light in the room. Wasn't that the way ghosts were supposed to look? Surely they must be the source of the "presence" that had hit him so strongly!

But then he saw that they didn't move at all, they didn't even breathe; they stared into nothingness, with a peculiar lack of expression. *Not dead... but lifeless,* he thought. *As if they never lived in the first place.*

And as he continued to stare, it occurred to him that it wasn't only their *surface* that he saw, it was their insides too! Every detail of their anatomy, in fact. If he concentrated on *stomach* when he stared at one, there would be the stomach, eerily see-through, suspended inside the transparent gryphon.

Fascinated now, if a trifle revolted, he stepped inside, and the door closed softly behind him.

They hung at about knee-height to a human above the floor, so that one could, if he chose, crawl under them to view the detail from below. Each one differed from the one next to it, some in trivial ways, some very drastically. Here was a rufous broadwing, like Aubri; there a dark gray gos-type, with the goshawk's mad red eyes, blazingly life-like even in the lifeless face. There was the compact-bodied suntail that was best at flying cover...

They're all types. I'm looking at types of gryphons! All of them, every kind I've ever seen! We aren't just one race, we're many races! Why did I never see that before? Is that why Urtho keeps the fertility secret to himself? Is he trying to keep the types pure?

Dazed with the revelation, he wandered past another three of the transparent models, to find himself beak-to-beak with—

Zhaneel!

Only it wasn't Zhaneel at all, it was a creature with no personality. But there was her general build, her coloration and configuration.

He looked back along the line of gryphons, following them up to where he stood, and the Zhaneel-type. Back and forth he looked, a thought slowly forming in his mind. There was something about this line of gryphons, something that had struck an unconscious chord. What was it? Of course. The types closest to the door represented more numerous populations than the ones nearest him, and as far as he knew of the Zhaneel-type there was only Zhaneel...

Because she is the first?

That was it! This was a visual record of Urtho's entire breeding program! Zhaneel *wasn't* a freak, she wasn't malformed, she was the very first of an entirely new gryphon *type!*

Now all those questions Urtho asked her, about her parents, her siblings, her training, they begin to make sense! Surely her parents knew that she was a new type—and if they had lived, they would have seen to it that she got special training for her special skills! But with them gone, she was left to flounder, and Urtho cannot remember everything...

As Urtho himself had reminded Skan. He could not remember everything, and evidently he had forgotten that one, solitary gryphon of a new falcon type—

Amberdrake called her—a gryfalcon!

—who survived, was alone and needed an eye kept on her. Skan had been angry with the mage, and now he was furious. How could he have *done* that to her? Surely he knew what lay ahead of her when she didn't look anything like the others! Surely he knew how the gryphons felt about runts, sports, the "misborn."

But there was the war. How could he remember? He could only trust to his trainers to be clever and see that she was not some misborn freak, but something entirely new. It is as much their fault as his, if not more. His anger faded, he sighed, and rounded the image of the gryfalcon.

And he looked upon his own feet, his own chest, his face. His own beak, eyes, and crest, lifeless, mutely staring through the living Skandranon.

The shock was a little less, this time. He was quicker to see that it was no more him than the other was Zhaneel. Still, the shock was of an entirely different sort; he was perfectly well able to think of the other gryphons as the end result of a breeding program, and even think of Zhaneel that way—but it was profoundly harder to think of himself in those terms.

It was, in fact, uncomfortable enough that he had to remind himself to resume breathing.

But as he studied the model, he took some comfort in noting that his proportions were rather better than its were. Especially in some specific areas.

And I'm definitely handsomer. Better-feathered. Smoother-muscled. Longer—
:FEAR-ALARM-ANGER!:

The emotion hit him like a catapult-boulder, and before he could even get his mental "feet" underneath him, something physical hit him from behind. It hurtled out of a place he had subconsciously noted was a doorframe, but had dismissed because there were no lights on the other side.

The strike sent his feet slipping out from under him, causing him to fall sideways through the image of himself. He tumbled into a wall, and his dancer's grace was not helping him in the least at the moment. Whatever wanted his hide was only about half his size, and it smelled like gryphon—

—only not *quite* like gryphon. It was muskier, earthier...

But this was no time to start contemplating scents! Whatever this was, it jumped him again and kicked his beak sideways into the wall. Only reflexes kept him from being blinded by the next slash—and then the assault began again.

This thing—is like a wildcat! Too small to take me, and too crazy to know better. It just might hurt me bad. I don't like being hurt bad!

And if this is something of Urtho's—oh damn and blast, I have to stop it without hurting it!

A scratch across his cere carried up over his eyes and sent blood down into them. He was momentarily blinded, but blinked the haze away and rolled. He gathered his hindlegs under him, ignored the pain of the bites and claw-marks for a moment, then tucked both of his feet under its belly and heaved.

It tumbled into the other wall, without any sign of control, as if parts of it got tangled up with the rest of it. But it was game, that much was for certain; as soon as it stopped rolling, it sprang to its feet again and faced him, claws up and hissing.

It *was* a gryphon.

It was what Zhaneel had misnamed herself, something that the gryphons referred to as a "misborn." It was actually about a quarter of Skan's size, not half. Its head was small in proportion to its size, and very narrow, more like a true raptor's head than a gryphon or gryfalcon's broader cranium. The wings were far too long for its body, and they dragged the floor so badly that the ends of the primaries had been rubbed off by the constant friction.

In coloration, it was a dusty gray and buff. It was *that* which made Skan realize why it looked slightly familiar.

It was a misborn—of Zhaneel's type.

It was at that moment that it finally penetrated that the creature wasn't hissing—it was trying, and failing, to produce a true gryphonic scream of challenge.

He blinked again, clearing the blood from his eyes with the flight membranes. The powerful telepathic "presence" of *gryphon*, a presence so strong he had thought that it must come from several of his kind, was all emanating from this single small creature that valiantly tried to howl defiance at him.

The mental hammering of alarm-fear-rage had come, and was still coming, from it.

Skan had reared instinctively into a fighting stance while his mind was putting all this together. The misborn looked up at him—four times larger than it was.

Its eyes widened for a moment, and it cringed.

But in the next second, it had gone back into a defensive posture.

The intensity of its mental radiations increased, and Skan dropped back a little. It wasn't consciously attacking him with those thoughts, but they were strong. Very strong.

The moment he dropped back, it glanced to the side and scrambled away, into the new room. Lights came on in there as it entered, leaping up onto a table with incredible speed considering how clumsy it was. It scattered books and instruments in all directions with its too-long wings, and reared up again from the advantage of this greater height.

"Bad! Bad!" the thing hissed. "Go away!"

Skan forced himself to relax, and got down out of his fighting posture. The bites and claw-marks stung, but his injuries weren't *that* bad, no worse than he got when playing with a rowdy bunch of fledglings. This poor little thing was obviously scared witless.

"What—ah—who are you?" he asked carefully. It *did* have enough language to tell him to go away; surely it would understand him.

"Go away!" it hissed again, feinting with a claw. "Go away! Where is he? Did you hurt him?"

It reared up again into a ridiculous parody of full battle display, and it was clear that its anger was overwhelming its fear. But why was it so frightened and angry? And who was 'he'? "I hurt you!" it tried to shriek. "I hurt you! I will!"

Skan was completely bewildered, and he could only hope that there was some kind of sense behind all this. If the creature was completely mad, he would have to render it unconscious or trap it before he could make his own escape, and he really didn't want to hurt it.

Urtho be damned; it would be like hurting a cat defending its litter. This creature doesn't know what I am and that I don't intend any harm—and unless I can get that through to it, I don't think it's going to stop attacking me.

"Hurt who?" he asked. "I haven't hurt anyone; I haven't even *seen* anyone here! Hurt who? Urtho? Who are you?"

He put his ear-tufts and hackles flat, and gryph-grinned, trying to look as friendly as possible. Evidently it worked, for the little creature stared at him for a moment, then suddenly sat down on the shredded desk-blotter. It came out of its battle-posture, instantly deflating, and wiped its foreclaws free of Skandranon's blood. "Not bad?" it asked plaintively, its anger gone completely. "Not hurt Father? Where *is* Father?"

Father? What on earth can this creature mean? Surely no other gryphons have ever been up here; no one could keep a secret like this for long! No, of course there haven't been any gryphons here, otherwise this little thing would recognize me for one.

He looked around at the room for clues who "Father" was, but there weren't any; just the table with odd bits of equipment and a few books and papers, an old cabinet that looked mostly empty, and a sink. In fact, it looked more like a Healer's examination room than anything.

"No," he said persuasively. "I'm not bad. I haven't hurt anyone. I just opened up a door and came inside." He edged a little closer to the creature as it relaxed. "Who is Father? Who are you?"

"Father is Father," the creature replied, as if stating the obvious for a very slow child. "Father calls me Kechara."

Skan moved right over to the table and sat beside it, which put him just about beak-to-beak with the little one. "Tell me about your father, Kechara," he said softly. "Everything you can. All right? There are a lot of people where I come from, and I need you to tell me what Father looks like so I know which person he is."

Kechara (which meant "beloved" or "darling" in Kaled'a'in) was a female, as near as he could tell. It might have been more appropriate to say that Kechara was a neuter, for she had none of the outward sexual characteristics of a female gryphon. That peculiar muskiness of hers was not a sexual musk, just an odd and very primitive scent.

"Father comes here, Father goes," Kechara told him. "Father bring me treats. Father brings toys, plays with me. He not here for a while, and I play."

"What does Father look like, Kechara?" Skan asked.

The little creature wrinkled up its brow with intense thought. "Two legs, not four," it said hesitantly. "No wings, no feathers. No beak. Has— long stuff, not grown, not feathers, over legs and body. Skin, smooth skin, here—" it pawed its face. "—long crest-hair here—" it ran its paws down where the scalp would be on a human. "And Father makes pretty cries, when he comes, so I know he here. Cries like songbirds, and he dances with me."

That clinched it; the only person that would come into this area that whistled was Urtho. Oddly enough, Skan had noticed that most mages couldn't whistle. Vikteren and Urtho were the only exceptions in this camp.

"How long have you been here?" he asked, trying to get some sense of how long Urtho had concealed the creature here.

But it just stared at him blankly, and when he rephrased the question several times, Kechara could only say that there was nothing else *but* here, for her. Only Father went somewhere else.

Which meant that Urtho had confined this poor thing to this section of his Tower for her entire life. There were places Urtho had taken her where she could look out through windows, which was how she had seen and heard songbirds, but that was the closest she had come to the outdoors.

For a scant heartbeat, Skan was outraged. But after attempting a few more questions with Kechara, he understood why Urtho had thought it better to keep her here.

She couldn't possibly function in normal gryphon society without protectors. She couldn't *do* anything productive. Zhaneel had been made fun of as she grew up, and she was marvelous. This poor thing would be tormented if there wasn't always someone watching out for her. Zhaneel was highly intelligent, resilient, and capable of remarkable things; this little one wouldn't even know how to defend herself without risking injuring herself.

She seemed to be very much on the same level of intelligence as some of Urtho's enhanced animals, and the biggest difference between her and one of those animals was that she had a rudimentary ability to speak: She didn't seem to have much of a concept of time, either. She never actually lost track of the conversation, but sometimes there was a long wait between when he asked a question and she answered it, a wait usually punctuated by a short game of chase-her-shadow.

Then again, that might not be a lack of intelligence, that might be because she hasn't had anyone to model her behavior on but Urtho. The winds only know he's done the same thing.

He coaxed her down off the table, and into taking a short walk with him, since she seemed very restless and kept fidgeting when he talked with her. After that, the conversation seemed to flow a little better; she bounded ahead or lagged back with him as he strolled through the gallery of "models." She paid them no attention whatsoever, which didn't much surprise him. She must be as used to them by now as he was to the messenger-birds or Amberdrake's eye-blinding clothing.

But suddenly, as they drew opposite the "Skandranon" type of model, she looked from it to him and back again, as if she could not believe her eyes. She blinked, shook her head, and looked again.

"That *you!*" she said, as if she'd had a major revelation.

"Oh, it does look something like me," he replied casually. "Just a bit." He left it at that, and she promptly seemed to forget about it.

A moment later, she made a dash into another room, and once again, the lights came up as she entered. She headed straight for a bowl sitting beside what must have been her bed, a nicely made nest of bound straw lined with soft, silky material. There was a box with a pile of brightly colored objects in it: toys, probably. The top ones looked like the normal sorts of balls and blocks that young gryphlets were given to play with as nestlings, before they fledged. She grabbed for a clawful of something brown and moist—then, like a child suddenly remembering its manners, she shyly offered him some of it—her food, presumably. It did not look like much, and Skan declined, although Kechara wolfed it down with every evidence of enjoyment.

I can't tell how old she is, he thought, watching her eat. She did manage that fairly well; gryphons were not the daintiest of eaters at the best of times. *She has no idea of the passage of time, she can't see the rising and setting of the sun from in here. She eats when she's hungry, sleeps when she's tired, and Urtho comes and goes at unpredictable intervals. But if I were to guess—misborns don't tend to live very long, and I'd guess she's near the end of her "normal" lifespan.*

The notion revolted him as much as the food had. All her life had been spent in close confinement, never feeling the free wind, only seldom seeing the sky, the sun, the moon and the stars.

When she was bred for the skies, and only accident and bad fortune made her the way she is, and not like Zhaneel—

—or like—me...

He ground his beak a little in frustration. Then there was the other side of the rock. How could she live outside? Maybe that was precisely why she was in here, because she *couldn't* live outside the Tower. Misborn were also notoriously delicate, prone to disease, weaknesses of the lungs and other organs.

Maybe only living here in complete shelter made it possible for her to live at all.

This may be kindness, but it has a bitter taste.

He noticed that all of his earlier bleeding had stopped, and that reminded him of his own internal time-sense. He was surprised at how long he had been in here with her. "I must go, Kechara," he said at the first break in conversation. Such as it was.

She blinked at him for a moment. Then she asked him something completely unexpected. "You come back?" she asked hopefully. "You come play again?" And she looked up at him with wide and pleading eyes.

Oh, high winds and rock-slides! She may not know the emotion for what it is, but she's lonely. What can I tell her?

He ground his beak for a moment, then told her the truth. "I don't know, Kechara. I have to talk to Father first. He makes the rules, you know."

She nodded, as if she could accept that. "I ask Father too," she said decisively. "I tell him I need you to play with me."

Then, as he paused at the door, she reared up on her haunches and spread her forelegs wide. It was such a *weird* posture that at first Skan could not even begin to imagine what she was up. to…

But then he understood. She was waiting for a hug, a human hug. The kind she always got from "Father" when he left her.

That simple gesture told Skan all he needed to know; whatever Urtho's motives were in keeping this little thing here, they were meant to be kindly, and he gave her all the affection he could.

It was awkward, but somehow Skan managed. Then he gave her a real gryphonic gesture of parting, a little preening of her neck-hackles.

It would have been much worse if she had put up some kind of a fuss about his leaving, but she didn't; she simply waved a talon in farewell, and turned and trotted back to her nest-room, presumably to play by herself.

She's learned that fussing doesn't change anything, he decided, as he walked stunned through the book-rooms and touched the door to the staircase to open it. *She's learned that people come and go in her life without her having any control over where and when they do it. Poor thing. Poor little thing.*

The lights dimmed behind him as he made his way down the stairs; slowly, for staircases were difficult for gryphons to descend, although climbing them was no real problem. When he got to the bottom, he was very tempted to try one of the other doors in the antechamber…

Stupid gryphon! Don't tempt your luck. You'll be in enough trouble with Urtho as soon as you bring up Kechara.

Oh dear. That made another problem. *How do you bring up Kechara without revealing you got into a locked room? And if you got into a locked room, how much else would he guess you got into?*

The guard nodded to him as he left, and grinned. "Damned hard for you critters to manage staircases, eh?" he said, as Skan realized that some of his injuries from the spat with Kechara must *surely* be visible.

And he hadn't come in with fresh scratches on him.

But the guard had just offered him a fabulous excuse for his appearance, and he seized it with gratitude. "More than damned hard," he grumbled. "I must've slipped and fallen once for every dozen steps. And would the others wait? Hell no! They were in such a hurry to scuttle off with their Healer-stuff that they didn't even notice I was lagging!"

The guard laughed sympathetically and patted Skan on the shoulder.

"Know how you feel," he replied. "With this gimpy leg I can't even climb *one* staircase good anymore. Never much thought about how you critters managed until I got that crossbow-bolt through the calf."

Some chat might not be a bad cover at the moment, and I don't really have anywhere to go… Tamsin and Cinnabar will be deciphering the text they copied and putting it into terms we gryphons can use. They'll be so busy with that they wouldn't know if I was there or not.

"Kyree and hertasi can manage all right," he replied. "But us, the dyheli, the tervardi—staircases are hell, and other things are worse! You'd think with all the veterans hurt that can't walk that they'd put in some ramps. But *no.*"

The guard sighed. "Well, that's the way of the world; everybody sees it according to what *he* needs. If a man don't need a special way up the stairs, why, he don't think nobody else needs it, neither."

Skan snorted. "You figured that right, brother! And my bloody aching head agrees with you too!"

"Best run along and catch up with those Healer friends of yours, an' make 'em patch you up," the guard advised. "Maybe then they'll think twice before they rush off an' leave you alone!"

Skan laughed, and promised he would do that; the guard limped on his rounds with a friendly wave as Skan headed back towards camp, and Healer's Hill.

All right, I'd better get this all in order. We'll get the fertility spell straight; I'll pass it on to the rest. Then, once I know everyone has it—I'll come to Urtho and tell him what I did. That's when I bring up Kechara. That would take a few days at the best, and his conscience bothered him about leaving her alone in there for so long…

But she's been alone in there for all of her life. A few days, more or less, will make no difference.

There was an additional complication, however. What if Urtho made a visit to his—well—pet? If Kechara happened to mention Skan…

I'll have to hope that she doesn't. Or if she does, Urtho just thinks she's talking about the models.

Complications, complications.

Stupid gryphon. You're trying to do too much too fast. But doesn't it need to be done? If not you, then who?

The walk down to the camp was a long one. There weren't many people out at this time of night. Most of the ones still awake were entertaining themselves; the rest had duties, or were preparing their gear for combat tomorrow. It was a peculiar thing, this war between wizards; the front lines were immensely far away, and yet the combat-troops bivouacked here, below Urtho's stronghold, in the heart of his lands.

It was the Gates that made such things possible, the Gates, and the gryphons.

The first meant that Urtho could move large numbers of troops anywhere at a moment's notice. There were even permanent Gates with set destinations that did not require anything more than a simple activation-spell, something even an apprentice could manage. Because of this, Urtho's troops were highly mobile, and the problem of supply-lines was virtually negated.

Of course, that was true for Ma'ar's men as well. The defender had the advantage in a situation like this—a mage setting up a Gate had to *know* the place where he intended it to go, and Urtho or his mages knew every inch of the territory he was defending. Ma'ar's mage could only set up Gates where they had been, places that they *knew*, so Ma'ar's Gates would always be behind his lines.

There had even been one or two successful forays early on in the campaign where Urtho had infiltrated troops *behind* Ma'ar's. That, however, would only work once or twice before your enemy started setting watches for Gate-energies, and in order to blast the Gate as it was forming. This tended to cost your mage his life as the energies lashed him at a time when he was wide-open and vulnerable. That was why Urtho's forces didn't do that any more, and there wasn't a mage in the entire army who would obey an order to do so.

Not that Shaiknam hasn't tried. But only once.

The gryphons were the other factor that made this war-at-a-distance possible. They could cover immense stretches of territory aloft, and their incredibly keen vision allowed them to scout from distances so high that not even the makaar would challenge them, unless they were in the very rare situation where they were at a greater altitude than the incoming gryphon. Makaar were not built for the winds and the chill of high altitude; there were gryphons who were, though they were not the best fighters.

And there were gryphons built for long-distance scouting that had ways of overcoming their physical shortcomings that made them poor choices for combat. The one who it seemed could do it best was Zhaneel.

One gryphon, anyway. Maybe… one day, more.

As Skan took to the air for the brief flight to Healer's Hill, his sharp eyes picked out the glow of the tent shared by Tamsin and Cinnabar. *Hard at work already. They may even have it by the time I get there. Good.*

The Black Gryphon used a thermal to kite in that direction, appreciative that the night was so clear and calm. He noted that Amberdrake's tent was also aglow.

Hard at work, too? He chuckled. *Well, the night usually is when most of his work is done. He bears the hearts of many, mine included. He is there when he is needed, even this late at night. I shall not tease him about it.*

This *time!*

CHAPTER TEN

Amberdrake did not notice that Skan wasn't behind them on the stairs until they reached the outside of the Tower, beyond the antechamber. That was when he turned to say something to the Black Gryphon—

And the Black Gryphon wasn't there.

They were already beyond the immediate perimeter of the Tower. Amberdrake swore under his breath. It was too late to go back and get him; the doors probably wouldn't admit them a second time, and the guard would wonder what was going on when they returned, looking for Skan.

A light breeze blew at Amberdrake's back, and camp-sounds carried up from the tents below. It would be better to go back to his tent, go on with the plan, as if nothing was out of the ordinary. Gryphons had a hard time with staircases. With luck, the guard knew that. Maybe he would figure that Skan was still inching his way down, step by painful step.

Not that Skan had any trouble with staircases, spiral or otherwise. He was as graceful as a cat under any circumstances. It was the dancing that did it; Amberdrake had seen him climbing trees, eeling through brush and scaling the outside of tower-walls with equal ease and panache. But Amberdrake was one of the few people who knew that.

Amberdrake lingered in the shadows as Tamsin and Cinnabar hurried on ahead. He waited on the off-chance that his friend might simply be sauntering along as if time had no meaning. *He's been known to do that... "It's image," he says.*

Skan still did not appear. Whatever he was doing, it was not just a case of lagging behind. *Where the hell is that idiot featherhead?* he thought with irritation. *Caught up in his own reflection somewhere?*

Far more likely that he had found some book that had caught his eye, and was leafing through it, oblivious to the time. Amberdrake could only hope that it was something as innocent as a book that had detained him.

But time was running out, for Amberdrake at least. Wherever he was, whatever he was doing, the Black Gryphon would have to make his own excuses, and bail himself out of any trouble he got into. Amberdrake could not wait any longer. He had an appointment; a last-minute appointment set up by Urtho himself. This was not a client to keep waiting.

Especially not tonight. If he broke that appointment, or was even a tiny bit late for it, *someone* might put that together with Tamsin and Cinnabar's request, ask the guard who had been with them, and put two and two together and figure they had all been up to something. And that *someone* would probably be Urtho.

Skandranon was a big gryphon; he could take care of himself. If he had been asked, that is exactly what he would have said.

The way back to camp was as clear as the night sky, with no one in sight anywhere close. That meant there was no one to take note if he broke into a sprint and wonder why he was running—or at least not close enough to recognize a distant runner as kestra'chern Amberdrake. He took off at a lope, and didn't pause until he was just within sight of his own tent.

I'm in better shape than I thought, he thought, with pardonable pride, as he composed himself before making his "entrance," right on time. *I'm not even out of breath.*

Fortunately his hertasi assistant, Gesten, would have everything he needed for this client prepared for him ahead of time. It had been a very long time since Amberdrake had performed the simple chores that surrounded his profession—getting out the massage table, warming the oils, putting towels in the steamer, preparing incense. Simple chores, but time-consuming. Things it would be impossible to take care of before a client came, if the kestra'chern in question happened to be doing something he didn't want anyone to know about. For instance, in case a kestra'chern absolutely had to snoop around in the Great Mage's Tower.

Thank goodness for hertasi.

The client was not waiting, which could mean a number of things. She could simply be late; she might be a little reluctant to go to a kestra'chern—new clients often were, until they realized how little of a kestra'chern's work had to do with amorous dealings. That was fine;

it meant he had time to change into his work clothes in peace. He *could* have done a massage in his current Outfit, but he didn't want to. He had a reputation to uphold, and much of that reputation involved his appearance. Clients should see him at his very best, for that was what he always gave them.

So he pushed the draperies aside and slipped into his private quarters, quickly shed his clothing, and donned one of the three appropriate massage-costumes that Gesten had laid ready for him. Tunic and breeches again, but of very soft, thick, absorbent material in a deep crimson with vivid blue trim. The cut was more than loose enough to permit him to take whatever contortion was required to give his client relief from stressed or sore muscles. And in the soft lighting of the tent, it looked opulent, rich, *special.* That would make the client feel special as well.

He braided his long hair up out of the way, but fastened the ends of the braids with small chiming bells, which would whisper musically when he moved. He had found that the rhythmic chiming that followed the motions of the massage soothed his clients.

The new client still had not appeared when he moved back to the "business" side of the tent, so he double-checked on Gesten's preparations. Not that he had any doubt of Gesten's thoroughness, but it never hurt to check. The laws of the universe dictated that the one time he did *not* check, something would be missing.

The bottles of scented oil waited in their pan of warm water, and already nicely up to temperature. The hot stones had been set in the bottom of the towel-warming chest, and the steam that rose from the cracks in the upper portion, carrying with it the scent of warm, clean cloth, told him that all was in readiness there as well. The massage table had been unfolded and covered with a soft pad, of course, and a crimson chair was beside it in case the client was too stiff or sore to be able to get on it without assistance.

The wooden rollers were ready; so were the warming ointments for after the massage, in case the muscles needed herbal therapy. There was a pot of vero-grass tea steeping in case he needed to get her to relax beforehand.

And most importantly for a new and possibly shy client, all the other tools of his many trades had been packed away out of sight. Most of them, in fact, currently cluttered up his private quarters. The only hint that he might not be a simple Healer was the incense in the air, the opulent hangings, and the scattering of pillows around the floor.

He prowled the room anyway, rearranging the pillows, making *certain* that nothing had been left out by accident, checking the oils to be certain they hadn't gone the least tiny bit rancid. It was all energy-wasting, and he knew it, but the energy he was wasting was all from nerves, and it was his to waste if he chose.

He wouldn't have been here, now, if he'd had any other choice. He'd be waiting outside the tower for Skan, or lurking outside the mages' meeting.

I wish I knew what was going on at the meeting, he thought fretfully. *I wonder if the hertasi have anyone there? If they do, Gesten will know the results as soon as they get out. Maybe before. I hope so—but of course Vikteren will tell me whatever happened...*

Gods, I hope Skan got out of the Tower without tripping some alarm or other. I hope the guard doesn't figure he was up to something. I hope he wasn't up to something. He simply spotted a book he could not resist, I'm sure. I hope Tamsin and Cinnabar really can find a way to give the gryphons their fertility...

Mental nattering, really. Fretting over things he could not control and could not change was a habit of his. If he could change something, he did so; if he couldn't he fretted it to pieces in hopes of finding a way he *could* affect the situation.

Fortunately he didn't have time to work himself up over either the mages' meeting or Skan; Gesten finally poked his nose through the door-flap and motioned someone inside.

A female, but Amberdrake knew that already. But now he knew why Urtho had not specified *who* was coming, in making this appointment.

Stiff, severe posture, mathematically precise hair, with three thin braids down the back of her neck, pinched expression, perfectly pressed and creased utilitarian clothing—*Winterhart? Oh gods.*

His shoulder muscles tensed, and his head started aching. He stopped his lip from curling with distaste just in time and dropped his mask of impassiveness into place.

I am a professional. Urtho sent her to me, and the fee he included should quite cover the fact that she is a pain in the tail. I can take care of her without becoming the least involved. She is only here for physical therapy. I don't have to know her inmost secrets, I don't even have to speak more than a dozen words to her.

All that flashed through his mind, as he altered his expression into a carefully indifferent and businesslike smile. She was moving very stiffly, more so than he remembered, and it wasn't all because she was not happy to be here. What had the note Urtho sent said? *Back injury.* Interesting; she was far stiffer than even a back injury would account for.

I don't have to open up to her to know that she is as tense as a cocked catapult. It's written in every muscle. I can't work on her like that, and she is not going to relax…

Interesting; I don't think she recognizes me as having been with Skan. Maybe the dim light is working for me.

There was certainly no sign of recognition in her eyes—and then, there was recognition, but no sudden pulling back that would indicate she realized he had watched while Skan and Zhaneel made her look the fool.

Well, that tenseness was the reason there was vero-grass tea steeping. She wouldn't be the first client who had come to a kestra'chern too tense to get any benefit from the visit.

"You look thirsty," he said quickly, as she looked around suspiciously. "Please, do drink this tea before we begin. It will help you."

And, as a Trondi'irn should know, vero-grass was thick with minerals; someone with a back injury was in need of minerals.

She accepted the cup of tea dubiously, waved aside his offer of honey to sweeten it, and took a sip. Her eyes widened as she recognized what it was, but she said nothing, she simply gulped it down.

Grimly, he thought. *As if she was daring him to do his worst.*

Well, he wouldn't do his worst, he would do his *best,* and to hell with her and her opinions.

"I'd like you to disrobe, please," he said, taking the cup away from her and placing it out of the way. "And lie on the table."

Winterhart had not known until she stepped into this tent that Urtho had ordered her to the hands of a kestra'chern. But she knew Amberdrake by sight—it seemed that he was always messing about with the Healers and the gryphons in one way or another—and she knew what his profession was.

She had *thought* she was being sent to a minor, unGifted Healer for her back problems—on Urtho's direct orders, of course, and after that rather painful interview following the altercation with Zhaneel. How the mage had wormed the fact of her injury out of her, she had no idea.

Then again, she had told him any number of things that she hadn't intended to, and that was only one of them. At least the fact of the injury and the pain she was in had apparently saved her from a reprimand; Urtho evidently counted it as a reason for her irritation with the world in general and gryphons specifically.

When he had told her that—and that he was ordering her to get treatment that he himself would schedule—she had been resentful, but just a little relieved.

Now she was resentful, not at all relieved, angry—and truth to tell, more than a little frightened. Angry that Urtho had set her up like this without telling her. Resentful that he had interfered in her private life, arbitrarily assuming that there was something wrong with her sexual relations and setting her up with a kestra'chern.

And frightened of what could happen at the hands of this particular kestra'chern.

She had heard very embarrassing things about kestra'chern in general and this Amberdrake in particular, stories that would curl the hair of any well-born young woman with a sense of decency. Amberdrake had a reputation for things that were rather—*exotic.* Conn Levas had used the fact that he had gone to this particular kestra'chern to taunt her with her inadequacies, and the things *he* had said had gone on here were considerably more than exotic.

And worst of all, she had *no* clue what Urtho had ordered for her… treatment.

If anyone back in her wing found out she was here, she would never hear the end of it.

And her back *still* hurt! That was reason enough to wish herself elsewhere!

*The gods only know what's going to happen to my back if—if—*she found herself flushing and resented her own embarrassment. *A lot of arching would be very bad for my spine right now. And I doubt he has any notion of that.*

Her suspicions hardened into certainty when she recognized the taste of the vero-grass tea. It was a calmative, yes, but it also had a reputation for enhancing other things than calm. But it *was* a muscle-relaxant as well, and right now…

Right now, my back needs it badly enough that I'll drink the damned stuff, she thought grimly. *Maybe he thinks that if he drugs me enough, I'll be too limp to stop him. Huh. Not with this back. One cup of tea isn't going to do worse than take the edge off the pain.*

Then he looked at her as if he was sizing her up for purchase, and said, "Disrobe and get on the table, please."

She stared at him, utterly taken aback, as much by his clinical coldness as by the words. Wasn't there supposed to be some—well-*finesse* involved here?

She looked from Amberdrake, to the table, and back again. "You want me to *what?*" she asked, still stunned.

* * *

Amberdrake sighed with exasperation. What was wrong with the stupid woman? Couldn't she understand that in order to massage her he would have to have her unclothed and on the table? Surely she didn't think he could do anything with her standing in the middle of the room like a statue!

"You *are* who Urtho sent me, aren't you?" he asked, with just a touch of irony.

She swallowed, but with difficulty. "Yes…" she replied.

"And you *do* have a back injury, do you not?" he persisted. What was going on in her mind?

She answered with more reluctance than before. "Yes…"

He sighed with open exasperation, which seemed to annoy her. Well, good. Up until this moment, *he'd* been the one who was annoyed. Let *her* enjoy the sensation for a change. "Then please, lady, let me help you, as I was assigned to do. I cannot help you if you will not disrobe and get on the table."

"Help me *how?*" she replied sharply, her eyes darting this way and that. "I thought I was being sent to a Healer!"

He gritted his teeth so hard it hurt. "You have been sent to a Healer," he replied, allowing his tone to tell her that there was *no doubt* that he was exasperated. "Apparently you are not aware that a human cannot be effectively massaged through her clothing. If you would rather this were done by someone other than myself, you are quite free to leave. But *you* can explain to Urtho why you walked out on this rather expensive session. I perform my services in a professional manner, even with reluctant clients—and the services I intended to perform on you are entirely different from the ones I think you have imagined."

Beneath his calm, cool exterior he was seething, and his back teeth jammed so tightly together that it was a wonder they didn't split. *Another gods-be-dammed, pure-as-rain Healer. I should have known she'd react this way. Tamsin and Cinnabar were only too accurate in the way they described her. Bright Keros, how much more am I going to have to put up with this kind of nonsense? I'm besieged, truly I am!*

And as for Winterhart the Pure—well, from the pinched look on her face, I'd say she's certainly living down her reputation as the Princess of Prim and Proper.

She hadn't budged a thumb-length since he'd begun talking, and if his muscle-readings were correct, she was so tense that he was rather mildly surprised that her eyes weren't bulging out.

And it was all too obvious that she not only didn't believe he was a

Healer, she was certain it was just some kind of a ploy to take advantage of her.

As if I'd want to. I like my partners willing, thank you.

His headache worsened. Wonderful. It wasn't just *his* headache, it was coming from her as well. No wonder she had a pinched and sour look to her.

Now how do I convince her that I am a Healer? Chop off Gesten's hand and fuse it back on? I wonder if Her Majesty the Ice-Maiden here would even react to that! She and that steel-necked lover of hers deserve each other. If Urtho hadn't sent her to me, I'd invite her to take herself and her token back to her tent.

But outwardly, years of practise kept so much as a stray expression from crossing his face. "I am no threat to your—virtue—and I do assure you that you can relax. This is a massage table. I am to work on your back injury, and perhaps see if it is something that I can Heal. It is that simple." He patted the table, and smiled a cool and professional smile.

She shifted her weight uneasily, and moved ever so slightly away from the tent-flap and towards the table.

If that's the best she can do, we're going to be here all night before she gets on the damned table!

"Massage," he repeated, as if to a very simple child. "I am very good at it. Lady Cinnabar will not have anyone else work on her but me."

That earned him another couple of steps towards the table; he closed his eyes for just a moment, and counted to ten. She was turning what should have been a simple session into an ordeal for both of them!

"If you are body-shy with a stranger, I will turn my back while you disrobe. You may drape yourself with the sheet that is folded beside the table," he said; he pointed out the sheet to her, and turned away.

The sound of clothing rustling told him that he had finally convinced her of his sincerity, if not his expertise.

His head was absolutely pounding with shared pain; he shielded himself against her, and it finally ebbed a bit. That was a shame. He generally didn't need to shield himself against a fellow-Healer, and allowing his Empathy to remain wide-open generally got him some useful information. Remaining that way also improved his sensitivity to what was going on with injuries and pain and helped him block it; before a client even realized that something hurt, he would be able to correct the problem and move on.

Correct the problem. Well. Unfortunately, he could very well imagine why Urtho had sent the woman *here.* The few notes he had on her indicated some trauma in her life that she simply had not faced—something that she had done or that had been done to her. Trondi'irn were generally not so busy they disregarded their own health. There was the possibility she was punishing herself by leaving her conditions unattended, or worsening them in her mind. Oh, he had no doubt that there was a real, physical injury there as well—but the way she acted told him that this was not a healthy, well-adjusted woman. Urtho must have seen that too; here was the implied message in his sending her here.

You're supposed to Heal minds, so Heal this one.

What had Urtho said about her?

That she had abusive parents. But the signs are all wrong for them to have been physically abusive...

Urtho was known for having a very enlightened idea of what constituted "abuse."

No, this woman hadn't been mistreated or neglected physically. But emotionally—ah, there was the theory that fit the pattern.

I would bet a bolt of silk on cold, demanding parents, who expected perfection—and got it. Very little real affection in her life, and most of it delivered when she managed, somehow, to achieve the impossible goals her parents set. Yes, that fits the picture.

And now, she was as demanding of everyone else as her parents had been to her. More than that, she was as demanding of herself as they used to be.

Well, that was why she would have gotten involved with an arrogant manipulator like that mage in the first place. She doesn't see herself as "deserving" anyone who cares, so she picks someone who reminds her of what she grew up with. And then treats him the same, since she never learned to do otherwise.

He ran his fingers across his forehead as the creaking of the table behind him told him he had managed to convince her to trust him that far. *I can't undo decades of harm in a few candlemarks. Start with the easy stuff and release the pain. Then take it from there.*

Amberdrake turned back to find her on her stomach, draped from neck to knee with the sheet, as modest as a village maiden. He selected one of the oils—one with a lavender base; that would be clean and fresh enough to help convince her that he was not going to seduce her. Then, before she could react, he turned the sheet down with brisk efficiency worthy of Gesten, poured some of the oil in his hands to warm it, then rubbed his palms together. A moment later was kneading the muscles of her back and shoulders.

He had not been boasting; he was particularly good at massage. Lady Cinnabar *did* prefer his services to anyone else in or out of the camp. Slowly, as he worked the knots of tension out of her back and shoulders, he sensed other tension ebbing. His expertise at massage was convincing her that he was, at least in part, what he claimed to be.

Some of the barriers she was holding against him came down.

But he did not take immediate advantage of the altered situation.

No, my dear Icicle; I intend to show you that I am everything I said I was and a lot more besides.

You area challenge. And I never could resist a challenge. And Urtho, damn his hide, knows that.

When Winterhart realized that the man really did know what he was doing—at least insofar as massage was concerned—she let the fear ebb from her body. The more she relaxed, the more his hands seemed to be actually soothing away the pain in her poor back.

Odd. I always thought massage was supposed to be painful...

In fact, it was so soothing that she felt herself drifting away, not quite asleep, but certainly not quite awake. Several moments passed before she realized that the tingling sensation in her back really *was* something very familiar, after all. The difference was that she had never experienced it before as the recipient.

Her eyes opened wide, although she did not move. She didn't dare. The man was Healing her, and you didn't interrupt a Healing trance!

"Well, came the conversational voice from behind her. "You certainly have broken up your back in a most spectacular fashion."

He was *talking!* How could you trance and talk at the same time?

"Your main problem is with one of the pads between the vertebrae," the voice continued. "It's squashed rather messily. I'm putting back what I can; if I can get the inflammation down, that will clear the way to stop most of the pain you've been enduring."

"Oh," she replied weakly. "I'd thought perhaps that I had cracked a vertebra..."

"Oh, nothing nearly so exciting," the voice replied. "But this could have been worse. It is good that Urtho sent you to me when he did. Do you feel any tension here...?"

Winterhart felt a spot of cold amid the sea of warmth in her back. This man was amazing—the Healers she knew could activate the nerves in a specific point of the body, but never a specific sensation. By the time her training had been terminated, she could not activate a circle of nerves smaller than her thumb's width without causing the patient to feel heat, cold, pressure, and pain there all at once. And here this—this kestra'chern—was pinpointing the nerves in a tenth of that area, and making her feel only a chill. *Not* pain!

She could only grunt an affirmative, and let her defenses slip a little more. He knew what he was doing, and he felt so competent, so *good*...

Amberdrake let the fluids around the damage balance slower than absolutely necessary, partly out of caution but mostly to buy some more time.

This was not going to be as easy as he had thought.

Winterhart was like an onion; you peeled away one layer, thinking you had found the core, only to find just another layer. She had so many defenses that he was forced to wonder just what it was she thought she was defending herself *against*.

"How did you manage to do this?" he asked quietly, letting the soothing qualities he put into his voice lull her a little more. "This kind of injury doesn't usually happen all at once; didn't you notice anything wrong earlier?"

"Well, my back had been bothering me for a while," she replied with obvious reluctance, "but I never really thought about it. My fami—I've always had a little problem with my back, you know how it is, tensions always strike at your weakest point, right?"

"True," he replied, wondering why she had changed "my family" to "I." How would revealing a family history of back trouble reveal anything about her? "And your back is your weakest point, I take it?" He thought carefully before asking his next question; he didn't want to put her more on the defensive than she already was. "I suppose you must have seen how busy all the Healers were, and you decided just to ignore the pain. Not necessarily *wise*, but certainly considerate of you."

She grunted, and the skin on the back of her neck reddened a little. "I don't like to whine about things," she said. "Especially not things I can't change. So I kept my mouth shut and drank a lot of willow. Anyway, after the defensive at Polda, one of the Sixth Wing gryphons was brought in with some extensive lacerations to its underbelly, delirious, and when you tried to restrain it, it nearly went berserk."

Interesting. Resentment there. As if she somehow thought that the gryphon in question had been acting unreasonably.

"Who was it?" Amberdrake asked.

"What are you talking about?" she replied suspiciously.

"Who was the gryphon?" Amberdrake repeated mildly. "I knew about Aubri's burns, but I didn't know anything about a Sixth Wing gryphon with lacerations. I was wondering if it was Sheran; if it was, I'm not surprised she reacted badly to being restrained. She was one of the gryphons that Third Wing rescued just before Stelvi Pass. Ma'ar had them all in chains and was going to pinion them. We don't know what else he did to them, but we do know they had been tortured in some fairly sophisticated and sadistic ways."

There. Make her think of the gryphon in question as a personality, and not an "it." See what that unlocks.

"It could have been," Winterhart said, slowly, as if the notion startled her. "There was a lot of scar tissue I couldn't account for, and it was a female…"

Amberdrake probed the injury again, before he spoke. "Ma'ar saves some of his worst tortures for the gryphons. Urtho thinks it's because Ma'ar knows he thinks of them as his children, not as simply his 'creations'."

"I didn't know that." Silence for a while, as the flames of the lanterns overhead burned with faint hissing and crackling sounds. "I like animals; I was always good with horses and dogs. That was why I became a Trondi'irn."

"Gryphons—" He started to say, "Gryphons aren't animals," then stopped himself just in time.

"I thought gryphons were just animals, like the Kaled'a'in war-horses. I thought they only spoke like the messenger-birds… just mimicking without really understanding more than simple orders." She sighed; the muscles of her back heaved, and trembled a little beneath his hands, and he exerted his powers to keep them from going into a full and painful spasm. "I kept telling myself that, but it isn't true, they aren't just animals. But I hate to see anything in pain, and it's worse to see something that can think in a state like that gryphon was."

"Well," Amberdrake replied, choosing his words with care, "I've always thought it was worse to see an animal in pain than a creature like the hertasi, the gryphons, the kyree, or the tervardi injured. You can't explain to an animal that you are going to hurt it a little more *now* to make it feel better later. You *can* explain those things to a thinking creature, and chances are it will believe you and cooperate. And it has always been worse, for me, to see an animal die—especially one that is attached to you. They've come to think of you as a kind of god, and expect you to make everything better—and when you can't, it's shattering to have to betray that trust, even though you can't avoid it."

"You sound as if you've thought this sort of thing over quite a bit," she said, her voice sounding rather odd; very, very controlled. Over-controlled, in fact.

"It is my job," he reminded her with irony. "You would be amazed at the number of people who come to me after a dreadful battle with nightmares of seeing their favorite puppy dying on the battlefield. Part of what I do is to explain to them why they see the puppy, and not the friends they just lost. Only I don't explain it quite that clinically."

There wasn't much she could say to that, so after a few breaths, she returned to the safer topic. "Anyway, I was trying to treat the gryphon, and I'd gotten bent over in quite an odd position to stitch her up without tying her down, when she lashed out at me with both hindlegs. She sent me flying, and I landed badly. I got up, felt a little more pain but not much, and thought I was all right.

Good. The gryphon has gone from "it" to "she." That's progress anyway.

"But the pain kept getting worse instead of better, right?" he probed. "That's the sign you've done something to one of those spinal pads."

"I think that's one lesson I'm not likely to forget very soon," she countered, with irony as heavy as his had been. "But as you said, the Healers were all busy with injuries worse than mine, and I don't believe in whining about things as trivial as a backache."

"I would never call telling of extreme pain whining," was all he said.

She relaxed a little more; minutely, but visible to him.

"This is going to need more than one treatment," he continued. "If you can bring yourself to resort to a mere kestra'chern, that is."

The skin of her neck flushed again. "I—you are a better Healer than I am," she replied, with painful humility. She hadn't liked admitting that. "If you would be so kind—I know what your fees are for other things—but if you can spare the time…"

"To make certain that the Healer of my friends is in the best of health, I would forgo the fee a king would offer for my services," Amberdrake replied with dignity. "When you are in pain, you can't do your best work; you know that as well as I do. Skan is not the only gryphon friend I have, and I want my friends to have nothing less than the finest and most competent of care."

"Ah," she said weakly. "Ah, thank you."

He examined the injury again. "I've done all I can about this spinal pad right now," he told her truthfully. "I need to finish that massage, and then you can go. I think you'll feel some difference."

"I already do," she admitted.

He rubbed some fresh scented oil into the palms of his hands to warm it, and started soothing the muscles of her back he had not reached earlier. They had gone into spasms so often they had become as tense and tight as harp-wires, and as knotted as a child's first spun thread.

She gasped as the first of them released; quivered all over, in fact. Amberdrake was quite familiar with that reaction, but evidently she wasn't.

"Oh!" she exclaimed, and tensed again. "I—"

"It's quite all right, don't move," he ordered. "It's the natural reaction to releasing tensed muscles. Ignore it if you can, and try to enjoy it if you can't ignore it."

She didn't reply to that; interesting. The last commoner he'd made that particular remark to had said, with dangerous irony, "What, like rape?" It was a natural thought for the ordinary soldier, who all too often found him or herself in the position of victim.

But there was no tightening of Winterhart's neck-muscles, no tensing at all to indicate that thought had occurred to her.

Interesting. Very interesting. So whatever she is afraid of it isn't that. And she is not the "ordinary soul" she says that she is.

"If I hurt you, tell me," he said. "A good massage should not hurt—and in your case, if I start to hurt you, you'll tense up again, and undo everything I've done so far other than the real Healing."

"I will," she promised. "But it doesn't hurt. It just feels very odd. My m—the massages I've had in the past were never for injuries."

What other kinds of massages are there? She can't mean sexual. So for beauty treatments?

That would account for the superb state of her body. There were no blemishes, no signs of scarring anywhere. When the posturing and stiffness were gone from Winterhart's body, she was a magnificent sculpture of human beauty. She cared for her skin and hair scrupulously, filed her toenails, and had no calluses anywhere that he had seen, not even the calluses associated with riding or fighting.

Unusual, and definitely the marks of someone high-born, and he thought he knew all the humans of noble lineage who had ever lived near Urtho's Tower.

Perhaps she was from before I came here? But that would date back to the very beginning of the war.

"Do you get along with your commanders?" he asked, adding, "I need to know because if you don't, it is going to affect how your muscles will react—and I may need to ask you to resort to herbal muscle relaxants when you are around them."

She was silent for a very long time. "They think I am the proper subordinate. I suppose I used to be; that may be why my back went badly wrong all at once. I don't ever contradict them, even now. I suppose you'll think I'm a coward, but even though I don't agree with the way they treat the gryphons, I don't want to be stripped of my rank and sent away."

"You wouldn't be, if you took your case to Urtho," he pointed out. "As Trondi'irn, it is your job to countermand even the generals if you believe your charges are being mistreated."

"I can't do that." Her skin was cold; she was afraid. Of what? Of confrontation? Of going directly to Urtho?

"Besides," she continued hurriedly. "My l-lover is one of Shaiknam's mages; his name is Conn Levas. If I went to Urtho, I'd still be reassigned, and I don't want to be reassigned to some other wing than his."

Untrue! Her muscles proclaimed it, and Amberdrake's intuition agreed. The way she had stumbled over the word "lover," not as if she was ashamed to say it, but because she could hardly bear to give the man that title. Amberdrake remembered Conn Levas, the mage who had come to *him* in order to shame his lover. That lover was Winterhart. She and the mage might trade animal passions, but there was no love in that relationship. She didn't care that she might be reassigned someplace where he wasn't, precisely.

There is something deeper going on here. In some way, the man protects her. He must not know he is doing so, because if he did, he'd use it against her.

This was getting more and more complicated all the time.

"Well, I would say you aren't going to have to worry about that much longer," he said without thinking.

"What do you mean?" Her alarm was real, and very deep; she actually started.

He put a hand in the middle of her back and soothed the jerking muscles. "Only that thanks to Zhaneel, Urtho is already aware of the situation in Sixth Wing. You won't have to confront anyone now. I suspect he'll take care of things. He always does."

"Oh." She relaxed again.

Now what on earth set her off like that? It has to be something to do with whatever it is that she is afraid of.

What that could be, he had *no* clue. Perhaps he ought to try probing further back in her past—so far back that it would not seem like a threat.

"I learned all of my skills at Healing when I was a child," he said casually. "My parents sent me to a very odd school, one that did not admit the existence of a Healing Gift, nor of Empathy. I *did* learn quite a bit about Healing without the use of either—everything from massage to anatomy to herbal and mineral medicines. But I was also more or less trapped among very sick people with Empathy too strong to shut them out. I was miserable, and my parents didn't understand why when I wrote them letters begging to come home. They thought they were doing their best for me, and couldn't understand why I wasn't grateful."

"My parents were like that," she said, sounding sleepy. "They *knew* their children were exceptional, and they wouldn't accept anything less than perfection. They never understood why I wasn't fawningly grateful for all the opportunities they gave me."

I thought as much! Well, this is *something I can start on, right this moment.*

"Like my parents, yours surely thought they had your best interests at heart," he replied quickly. "Perhaps they were too young for children. Perhaps they simply didn't understand that a child is not a small copy of one's own self. Many people think that. They feel the child *must* have the same needs and interests they do, simply because it sprang from them. They have no notion that a child can be drastically different from its parents."

"So?" she replied, probably more harshly than she intended. "Does that excuse them?"

He let her think about that for a long time before he answered. "There are no excuses," he said at last, "but there are reasons. Reasons why we are what we are. Reasons why we do not have to stay that way. Even Ma'ar has reasons for what he does."

That turned the discussion into one of philosophy, and by the time he sent her away, he had come, grudgingly, not only to feel sorry for her, but even to like her a little.

But she was going to have to change, and she would have a hard time doing so all alone. He was going to have to help her. As she was, she was a danger, not only to herself, but possibly to everyone she came in contact with. No matter how she tried to hide it, she was unbalanced and afraid.

And fear was Ma'ar's best weapon.

CHAPTER ELEVEN

S kandranon cautiously pushed his way into Tamsin's work-tent with a careful talon, and the tail of a playful breeze followed him inside, teasing his crest feathers. As he had expected, Tamsin and Cinnabar mumbled to each other over their notes, oblivious to anything else going on. They made quite a pretty picture, with their heads so close they just touched, lamplight shining down on them, the table, and the precious stack of paper. Dark hair and bright shone beneath the lantern. They were a vision of peace. But pretty pictures were not precisely what he was after at the moment, and all peace was illusory as long as Ma'ar kept moving. And he knew that, despite his motivations, stealing this secret was a dangerous game to play.

But this secret would at least ensure the survival of his people, no matter what befell Urtho.

"Took you long enough to get here," Tamsin said without looking up, though Cinnabar gave him a wink and a wry grin. He wrote another word or two, then set aside the paper he had been scrawling on and raised his eyes to meet Skan's. "What did you do, stop to seduce a half-dozen gryphons on the way here?"

Skan's nares flushed, but he managed to keep his voice from betraying him. Half-a-dozen gryphons? Well—one female, and there certainly wasn't a seduction involved. And until he had a chance to think out a plan, he'd rather not discuss Kechara with anyone. "Not at all; I just stopped to look at something very interesting in the Tower. So, what have you discovered?"

By the gleam in Tamsin's eyes, it was good news, very good news. "That your so-called 'spell' isn't precisely that," Tamsin replied. "Enabling fertility in male and female gryphons takes a combination of things, and all of them are the sort of preparation that any gryphon could do without magical help, though a little magic makes it easier. Urtho just shrouds the whole procedure in mysticism, so that you *think* it's something powerfully magical. His notes detail what to do to make the most impressive effects for the least expenditure of energy. He's been bluffing you all, Skan."

Skan's head jerked up so quickly that he hit the top of the doorframe with it and blinked. He'd hoped for simple spells; he had *not* expected anything like this. "*What?*" he exclaimed.

Tamsin chuckled, and leaned back in his chair, lacing his fingers behind his head. "When he designed you, he wanted to have some automatic controls on your fertility, so he borrowed some things from a number of different beasties. Take the Great White Owl—the females don't lay fertile eggs unless their mate has stuffed them first with tundra-mice. The sudden increase in meat triggers their bodies to permit fertilization of the eggs; and the more meat, the more eggs they lay. Well, Urtho borrowed that for your females. The 'ritual' for the female gryphon is to fast for two days, then gorge on fresh meat just before the mating-flight. That gorging tells her instincts that there's food enough to support a family, just like with the tundra owls, and she becomes fertile."

"But…" Skan protested weakly. "We don't lay eggs. How can that—"

Tamsin ignored him. "He borrowed from the snow-tigers as well; they would have litters four times a year in a warmer climate, but they only have one because the male's body temperature is so high that his seed is sterile except in the winter. So Urtho designed you males so that your body temperature is normally so high that your seed is dormant, just like theirs. So *your* half of the 'ritual' is that business of sleeping and meditating in the cave for two days while the female fasts. That drops your body temperature enough that your seed becomes active. A very simple spell ensures that the male's temperature *stays* lower than normal until after the mating-flight is over. And this is the only bit of magic Urtho performs that actually accomplishes anything. It's such a minor spell that even an untrained Healer could do it—or there are drugs and infusions we could give you that have that effect, temporarily."

"Or you could sit on a chunk of ice," Cinnabar added gleefully, tossing her hair over her shoulder. Another breath of breeze entered the open tent-flap and made the flame of the lantern flicker for a moment.

"Thank you," Skan said with as much dignity as he could muster. "But I doubt I shall."

"Seriously though, that means that in the total absence of Healers or herbs, a male gryphon could keep his seed active simply by mating in the winter like a snow-tiger, or by sleeping for two days in a cave and then flying *very* high during the mating-flight, where the air is cold even in the summer," Tamsin said. Then he laughed. It had been a long time since Skan had heard the Healer laughing with such ease. It was a good sound. "But as hot-blooded as the Black Gryphon is, he may need to go to the northernmost edge of the world!"

Cinnabar joined her lover in laughter, and even Skandranon wheezed a slight chuckle. It had been a long time since Tamsin had researched anything that concerned creation, rather than destruction. For this brief time, perhaps he had been able to forget the war and all it meant. "Oh, and there's the mating-flight itself. The better the flight, the easier it is for—ah—everything to get together. Gets the blood and other things moving. And with a strenuous flight... there," he said, and proffered a sheet of notes, "the better the flight, the more likely that there will be more than one gryphlet conceived. But that's basically it."

Skan sat down heavily, right in the doorway. Hard to believe, after all the mystery, all the bitterness, that it could be so simple. "But that's *all?*" he asked, too surprised to feel elation yet.

That's it." Cinnabar shrugged, and idly braided a strand of hair. "The rest is simply Urtho's own indulgence in theatrics—which is considerable. He is quite an artist. Most of his notes were involved with that and only that. I promise you, though, that unless those guidelines are *strictly* adhered to, you gryphons will be sterile as always." She tilted her head to one side and regarded him with dark, thoughtful eyes. "He designed you very well, and I think you ought to know that his notes said precisely *why* he made you sterile unless elaborate preparations were made."

Skan waited for her to elaborate, but she was obviously enjoying herself in a peculiar way, and intended to make him *ask* why.

"Well, why did he?" the gryphon growled. Some of the anger he had felt at Urtho was back. "Not that I can't think of a number of reasons. We are supposed to be warriors, after all, and it's difficult to wreak destruction away from home while there are gryphlets in the nest to tend to."

"You have a flair for the dramatic yourself. 'Wreak destruction?'" Cinnabar teased.

Skandranon tried to ignore her. "He might not have wanted to discover himself neck-deep in fledglings. That would mean a strain on food supplies, and hungry gryphons could decimate wild game over a wide area. Also, we're his creations; he might have wanted more control over which pairings produced offspring."

That breeding program. He might have wanted nothing but pure "types." He wouldn't have wanted hybrids, I would imagine. Breeders usually don't.

"He might only have wanted the control over us that holding this 'secret' had." The bitterness he felt in discovering Kechara's plight and the records of the "breeding program" showed more than he liked. "So. Was I close?"

Cinnabar's expression was understanding, and her tone softened. She leaned forward, earnestly. "Skan, it was for none of those reasons. Here it is, in his own words—let me read it for you, and I think you might feel a little better about all of this."

She bent over the notes and read them quietly, aloud. "'Too often have I seen human parents who were too young, too unstable, or otherwise unfit or unready for children produce child after doomed, mistreated child. I will have none of this for these, my gryphons. By watching them, and then training others what to watch for, I can discover which pairings are loving and stable, which would-be parents have the patience and understanding to *be* parents. And in this way, perhaps my creations will have a happier start in life than most of the humans around them. While I may not be an expert in such things, I have at least learned how to observe the actions of others, and experience may give me an edge in judging which couples are ready for little ones. Those who desire children must not bring them into our dangerous world out of a wish for a replica of themselves, a creature to mold and control, a way to achieve what they could not, or the need for something that will offer unconditional love. For that, they must look elsewhere, and most likely into themselves.'"

Cinnabar paused, giving him a moment to absorb it all; then continued. "'The reasons for bearing young should simply be love and respect for the incipient child, and for the world they will be born into. If it took more effort to produce a child than the exercise of a moment's lust, perhaps there might be less misery in this world. Perhaps my gryphons will be happier creatures than their creator.'"

Cinnabar looked back up at him expectantly. Skan simply sat where he was, blinking, surrounded with silence. The sounds of the camp seemed very distant and somewhat removed from reality. Or, perhaps, eclipsed by a more important reality.

Skandranon's internal image of Urtho had undergone multiple drastic changes over the course of the evening. But this...

Elation—and a crazy joy—began to grow in him again. Simple, uncomplicated joy; the same joy that he'd had in his friendship with Urtho, and had thought he had lost. *This is more than I ever hoped to hear. A reason, a good one, a sound one. One even I can agree with. He wrote that in his own hand, to himself and no other. The whole secret makes sense. And look how even with all those precautions in place, a mistake can happen. One happened with Zhaneel; her parents died, and she was neglected by others who thought her to be misborn. I had no idea he had put such thought into this...*

"Urtho is—wiser than I thought," he said at last, his voice thick with emotion that he simply could not express. "He was right to guide us so."

"Oh, I dare say you all can do well enough on your own," Tamsin told him, with a twinkle in his eye. "If nothing else, all this takes considerable effort on the gryphons' part, and a pair will probably think carefully before all that effort."

Skandranon squinted his eyes shut tight and took a deep breath, then shook his body and flared his breast and back feathers. "There's no 'probably' about it," he told Tamsin, with some of his humor returning. "We can be as lazy as any other race. There *will* be more young, but not that many more, not at first. For one thing—with the war, there is rarely the leisure to make such extensive preparations."

Cinnabar smiled, and nodded her understanding. Tamsin sighed. "By the way," he said, "it's obvious from the notes that a male or female *can't* be overweight if they want to produce a youngster, and a mating-flight has to be *damned* impressive in order to get everything moving well enough that fertility is assured. If you don't put everything you've got into that flight, well, you won't get anything *out* of it except a bit of exercise." He raised his eyebrow suggestively.

"Sometimes exercise can be very beneficial," Skan replied, with dignity.

"Well," Lady Cinnabar replied, with a face so innocent that Skan knew she was intending to prod him. "You should know. I've heard you're probably the biggest expert in gryphon exercise that has ever lived."

"I?" Skan contrived to look *just* as innocent as she. He would never miss a chance to boast a little in good company. Anyone as well-known as he had detractors to belittle any and all of his traits; so it was up to him to say otherwise, wasn't it? "I suppose, since I am an expert dancer, attractive, and skilled in aerobatics, you might be correct about that."

Tamsin's shoulders shook with silent laughter; Cinnabar simply smiled serenely, and released the bit of hair she had been braiding. "I'd have been worried about you if you'd said otherwise, Skan," she said gravely a heartbeat later. "In all of this, it would be easy to lose yourself."

"I won't say that I am not feeling like a feather in a gale, my lady. But I have to maintain who and what I am. And since I *am* irresistible, it is only responsible for me to say so to reassure you all that I have not been overwhelmed.

"I owe you most *profound* thanks, my friends," he quickly continued, changing the subject before Cinnabar could ask him who he was supposedly irresistible *to*. "I could not have done this alone. And that is perhaps the first and last time you will have heard the Black Gryphon admit he could not do something."

"Indeed!" Tamsin's brows rose. "Quite a concession, your highness. We were going to ask for all your possessions as payment, but that concession is rarer than—"

Cinnabar elbowed her lover sharply. "He's serious, dolt," she scolded. "About the thanks, that is."

"So much so, that I cannot think how to properly repay you," Skan told her softly. "It will not only be me that owes you a tremendous debt, but all of us."

But Cinnabar only shook her head. "Don't think of it as *owing* anyone," she replied. The expression in her face was affectionate. "Think of it simply as a gift between friends. Perhaps the greatest gift that we could ever give you—and it was a privilege to do so, not a burden."

He regarded her with surprise. He had not known that she felt that way—oh, he had known that they were his friends, but he had never realized just how much that word could mean. "Why?" he asked, making no secret of his surprise.

Cinnabar looked thoughtful for a moment. "Tamsin, Amberdrake, and I are greater admirers of your folk than you know, I think. It is the same with nearly all the Trondi'irn as well. One cannot deal with gryphons without feeling that admiration; there is so much about you that is good."

Skan ground his beak, torn between pleasure and embarrassment. It was one thing for *him* to boast about gryphons in general and himself in particular—it was quite another thing to hear such effusive praise coming from the sweet lips of Lady Cinnabar, who had traveled the world, been entertained in the highest Courts, and seldom praised anything or anyone.

"Still, you are an *aggravating* lot," she continued, her expression lightening with mischief, "and an abundance of equally aggravating nestlings is exactly what you all deserve to teach you proper humility!"

Skan snorted and drew himself up to his full height, until his crest flattened against the canvas roof of the tent. "Indeed," he replied. "We shall be put in our place, if you would be so kind as to teach me that 'simple Healing spell' of yours, then tell me what herbs are needed. I will start circulating the information among the others."

"All ready, my friend." Tamsin flourished a neatly-lettered paper at him. "Memorize this, follow it through to the letter, and the joys of parenthood will be yours! And any other gryphon that you want to condemn to years of nestling-feeding, baby-chasing, and endless rounds of 'Whyyyyyyy?—'just give them this."

Skan took it from him, and quickly committed the contents to memory. As soon as he had finished reading he tucked the paper away in his neck-pouch for safe-keeping. "Have either of you heard anything from the mages yet?" he asked.

Both shook their heads. "I know I won't be able to sleep until I do," Tamsin said, in all seriousness. "What happens with the mages is very likely to affect what happens to you and the other nonhumans."

"I know." Skan tongued the point of his beak for a moment. "Well. I have a reasonable idea. Shall we lie in wait for Vikteren? He will want to know what happened to us as much as we want to know what happened to him."

Tamsin rose, and offered his hand to Cinnabar. "Let's go ambush the man."

They found Vikteren coming to look for them, on the path halfway between the Tower and Healer's Hill, weary and not terribly coherent. And in the end, it turned out that the resolution wasn't much of a resolution at all. Vikteren was exhausted by the time the meeting broke up, and all he would say to them when he met them was, "Well, we have a solution of sorts. Nobody's entirely happy, so I guess it must have been a good compromise."

That was enough for Tamsin and Cinnabar, particularly since Cinnabar knew she would hear Urtho's version soon enough, but not enough for Skan.

The young mage promised Skan an explanation after he had gotten some rest, and Skan made certain to assail him again the next day. When they headed for Zhaneel's obstacle-course, Vikteren was able to elaborate a little more on what had evidently turned out to be one of the most anarchic meetings ever perpetrated in Urtho's ranks. "There was a lot of complaining, a lot of yelling, a lot of talking, but I can pretty much boil it down in a couple of sentences. We bitched and moaned, named names, and pointed fingers. That took up most of the night. Urtho said the mages don't know strategy, so they're in no position to dictate it. But he agreed that we had some points, that there *were* certain leaders who acted as if troops were expendable, and that he would take care of it. And in the meantime, the mages were to retain their assignments, but now to report directly to that Kaled'a'in Adept Snowstar, who would report directly to him. That's where we left it." Vikteren shrugged. "Snowstar wasn't really pleased about being appointed like that, but he's the most organized Adept next to Urtho that I know, so I figure he's the logical choice. He has a huge staff of attendants to keep records, and a dozen messenger-birds. Anyway, the mages bitched about so little actually being done, but the generals bitched too, about giving up any of their power, so I guess we came out ahead."

"I would say you did." They settled down on a little rise in the shade. Skan had come here to watch Zhaneel again, but Vikteren was not participating in this run; she was supervising other gryphons on the obstacle-course. Vikteren was not up to helping her *and* all these others in what was still unofficial training.

Of course, according to rumor, that would change. Trainer Shire was pushing for it, and he had the backing of some of the mages, who saw this as an excellent place to train apprentices in combative magics. But until this training became official, anything Vikteren did here was going to be with strictly limited resources.

Neither of them knew what had gone on in Zhaneel's "little talk" with Winterhart, other than the fact that Zhaneel appeared much more confident—and that she had told Aubri that the Trondi'irn Winterhart actually "had a point" worth considering. The "point," it seemed, was that gryphons who were unsuited to *her* style of attack-and-evasion tried to emulate it, and that she and the trainer needed to supervise them before they hurt themselves. So now Zhaneel actually found herself in a position of authority, which had to be a unique experience for her.

It seemed to be doing her a great deal of good, at least from what Skan could see. He observed that there were a number of positive changes in her. She walked, stood, and even flew with more confidence, more energy. She looked others straight in the eyes, even humans, who she had formerly deferred to with abject humility. Her feathers were crisp and neatly preened, her coat shone with health.

In short, she was the most desirable creature he had ever laid eyes on in his life. However, he wasn't the only gryphon to make that particular observation.

It did *not* escape his notice that the other male gryphons exerted themselves—and posed—whenever she happened to look their way. It was also apparent that she was perfectly well aware of their interest.

It was enough to make him grind his beak in frustration.

She treated them all impartially, which was some relief, but she wasn't paying the least bit of attention to *him*, which was no relief at all. He was sitting quite prominently in the open, after all. He was always conspicuous to gryphons, especially in the daylight. Surely she saw him. Had she forgotten already how he had defended her to Winterhart?

"So, how are you coming with spreading your little secret around?" Vikteren asked, idly braiding grass-stems into a string.

"It spreads itself," Skan replied, watching as Zhaneel demonstrated a tuck-and-roll maneuver, and wondering if his poor flesh and bones had healed enough to permit him to join her pupils. His dancing-skills would surely help him in becoming a star pupil. What had become of that shy little gryfalcon who had so aroused his protective instincts? The instinct she aroused now was anything but just protective! "I told the eight wingleaders and their mates. They in turn told four more gryphons each, and so forth. As Tamsin said, it is an absurdly simple thing, once you know how much was simple misdirection. I expect that in three days, every gryphon here will know."

And that includes Zhaneel. But the information I want to give her—I must find a way to get her alone. I need to tell her what she really is.

"Has anyone asked how you came by this?" The young mage glanced at him sideways. "Or are you playing stupid?"

Skan laughed, and raised his ear-tufts. "I seldom need to *play* stupid! If anyone asks, I have half-a-dozen different tales to explain how I learned this information. None of them are true, and all of them are plausible. The greater truth is that this is so important to us all that no one is likely to question the origin, so long as Tamsin and Cinnabar can verify that it is accurate. And it is so important that I do not believe there is a single gryphon who will even tell his hertasi that he is privy to the secret. At least, not soon. No one wishes Urtho to learn that we have this knowledge until I am ready to tell him."

Vikteren raised both eyebrows. "So you're the victim—sorry, the volunteer who'll take him the bad news and get nailed to his workroom wall?"

Skandranon's nares flushed deep red. He could have done without hearing that. "Urtho is my friend. And right or wrong, it was my idea to steal the secret. I should be the one to face Urtho, and not a messenger.

The gryphons are all agreed that I will be the one to tell him that he no longer controls us through our wish for progeny. They believe I am the one who can best express this without causing him to react badly."

"You mean, they think he's less likely to remove portions of *your* hide than that of any other gryphon," Vikteren observed. "They're probably right."

"I can only hope," Skan muttered. "I can only hope."

Will Zhaneel know where the knowledge came from when it is passed to her? He sighed. *I wish I dared tell her myself...*

Amberdrake had taken to finding Zhaneel for a few moments every day just to talk, if he could; this evening was no exception, and this evening he had quite a bit of time free, for a change. That was just as well; all the recent improvement in her spirits and morale had triggered a partial molt, and she had a number of new blood-feathers with feather-sheaths that needed to be flaked and preened away. He hadn't done *that* for any gryphon except Skan since his days as an apprentice and a feather-painter. The simple task was oddly soothing. Feeling the hardness of the feather-shaft against the softness of the insulating down, the pulse of her heartbeat just under the deep red skin, and the incredible heat a gryphon's body generated, was always exhilarating.

"He was there again today," Zhaneel told Amberdrake, as he helped her groom her itching feathers. "I saw him. He looked thin."

Amberdrake did not need to ask who "he" was, and the kestra'chern smiled to think of the mighty Skandranon watching Zhaneel from afar like a lovesick brancher in a juvenile infatuation. "He is thin," Amberdrake replied. "That's partially because he's recovering from his injuries. We haven't been letting him exercise as much as he'd like; he always overstresses himself too soon after he's been hurt. But I think he might benefit from one of your classes; should I see if he's interested?"

Interested? He'll probably claw his way through anyone who stands in his way to get in!

"Oh..." Zhaneel's nares paled. "I... he..."

"Don't let him overawe you, my dear," Amberdrake said sharply. "He is *just* a gryphon, like any other. Yes, he is beautiful, but he has as many faults as he has virtues. *You* are an expert on these new tactics of yours. He is not." Amberdrake tapped her gently and playfully on the beak. "Furthermore, if you are interested in him, *don't show it.* He has females flinging themselves at him all the time. You need to establish yourself as different from them. Pretend you think of him with simple admiration for what he's done, but no more."

"I do not know…" She looked at him over her shoulder, doubtfully. "I do not know that I can do that. He is *Skandranon*. How can I not show…?" Her nares flushed with embarrassment.

"Why not?" he countered. "Zhaneel, you are every bit as good as he is. You know that; Trainer Shire and I have told you that daily. Haven't we?"

"Ye-es," she said slowly.

"So, just be yourself. It isn't as hard as you might think. Haven't you always been yourself with me? Let your respect show, and let him guess at the rest." Amberdrake carefully crumbled a bit of feather-sheath from around a newly emerging wing feather. "Try to think of him the way you think of all those admiring gryphons who are showing off for you on your obstacle course. You don't treat any of *them* specially."

She blinked at him in perplexity. Amberdrake sighed—lessons in the games-playing of love never went easily. It was a concept totally foreign to Zhaneel, but eventually she grasped it.

"The quail that escapes is always fatter than the one you catch," she observed. "I will try, if you think that will work."

"Since no one has ever succeeded in playing that particular game with Skan before, I suspect that it will," Amberdrake replied with amusement. "And what's more, I think it will serve him right. It will do him good to think that he suddenly *can't* have any lovely lady he wants. Should surprise him that there's one who is immune to all his charms."

He brushed Zhaneel's feathers down with a slightly oiled cloth, both to pick up the feather-sheath dust and to shine the feathers themselves. "There," he said, stepping back. "You look wonderful. Sleek, tough, competent, ready for anything."

Zhaneel bobbed her head with modest embarrassment. "Or anyone?"

He put his hand beneath her beak and raised it.

"I tell you again, you are a match for any gryphon that ever existed." He nodded approval as she lifted her head again. "Never forget that, and remember who told you. I am a kestra'chern. I *know.*"

"I shall try," she promised solemnly.

"Good." Amberdrake tossed the cloth into a pile of things for Gesten to clean up and sort, pulled the tent-flap aside, and gestured to her to walk beside him. "Care to take a stroll with me? I have time, if you do."

But she shook her head. "I would like this, but truly, I must go. I have a mission to fly in the morning." She glowed with pride. "A real mission, and not make-work for a misborn."

His heart plummeted. It had been so easy to think of those exercises of hers as mere games, and to forget that they were intended to make her fit for combat. It had been possible to pretend that she would never go where so many others had been lost. "A long one?" he asked, trying not to show his apprehension. There was no more reason to be apprehensive about her than about any other gryphon. Less so, in fact, for the makaar would not anticipate her moves as they could those of a gryphon with conventional training. Wasn't that what made Skan so successful, that the makaar couldn't anticipate what he would do next?

Nevertheless, a chill he knew only too well settled over him. *That is what makes Skan so much of a target as well. Eliminate him, and you strike a terrible blow at the gryphons as a whole, for it makes them more predictable.*

Once again, someone he knew and cared for would be going away, making herself into a *thing* the enemy could strike at and—

And this was a war, however he might like to forget the fact. It was Zhaneel's responsibility to obey her orders, wherever they took her—a responsibility she had been bred and trained for.

And she was so pleased, so happy about this assignment; so very proud that she had been entrusted with it. How could he spoil it with his own fears and nerves?

He couldn't, of course. So, as always, he tried to ignore the way his insides knotted up around a ball of ice in the pit of his stomach, and smiled and praised her, as he had smiled and praised every fighter he had sent out to this war. And despite the anxiety he felt, he did mean every word.

That was his duty, his responsibility. *Give them confidence; relax them. Make them forget the past if they must, and remind them of what their reasons for fighting are. Show them that they have a life beyond the fighting, a life worth saving.*

"It is a high-flight *mission*," Zhaneel continued, blissfully unaware of the way his heart ached, and the pain in his soul. "The place where Skandranon found those stick-things. I am to carry the thing that Urtho made, which undoes them, and fly a pattern while I make it work; the rest of Sixth Wing East is to rain them with smoke-boxes. Then the fighters come, under cover of the smoke."

So she would be above the general level of the fighting, presumably out of reach of any ground weapons. But makaar?

They'll have to fight their way through Sixth Wing to get to her, he reminded himself. *She's carrying one of Urtho's magic boxes, which makes her non-expendable. They'll protect her.*

If they can. If the makaar don't get through. If the magic really does work on those lightning-sticks.

If, if, if. Who commanded this mission, anyway? If it was General Shaiknam—then even carrying a precious magical artifact, Zhaneel was considered expendable by virtue of the fact that she was a gryphon.

"Urtho planned this," Zhaneel continued, thereby easing some of his unspoken fears. "He commands the mission, and General Sulma Farle is the field-commander. And I am to carry the magic thing, because I have true hands to make it work. If it is triggered too far away, it will not work, Urtho says."

Then fly high and well, warrior," Amberdrake told her, patting her shoulder with expertly simulated confidence. "I shall have fresh fish waiting for your return, and a victory feast."

Zhaneel's tiny ear-tufts rose at that. "Fresh fish?" she said, clicking her beak in anticipation. "Truly?" She adored fresh fish—by which she meant still *alive*—and liked it better when they wiggled as she swallowed them. Where she had acquired this particular taste, Amberdrake could not imagine; most gryphons preferred raw, red meat, and *none* but she liked their fish still living.

Maybe there's some osprey in her somewhere. Or there are some eagles that have a liking for fish. Or maybe it is only because it is Zhaneel. "Truly," he promised. "A victory feast between friends, though I shall have *my* fish nicely cooked."

Zhaneel made a little hiss of distaste to tease him, but readily agreed to the celebration.

What Amberdrake had not told her was that it was not going to be a victory dinner for two, but for four. Zhaneel, himself, Gesten—and Skandranon. Though he would not tell Skan, either. This should be very amusing, at the very least, and with luck it would come off well.

Now let her only survive this, he thought, as he saw her off to her roost for the night. *Let her only survive this...*

Zhaneel held the precious box between her foreclaws, although it was quite securely fastened to her elaborate harness by clips and straps so that it did not interfere with her flying in any way. Her orders from Urtho had been quite detailed and just as specific. She must come in very high, far above the rest of the Sixth Wing; she must then dive as steeply as she could, then level off at about treetop-height, making a fast pass above the heads of Ma'ar's troopers, and press the catch that opened the bottom of the box as she did so.

A spy had confirmed that lightning-sticks had been distributed to the fighters. Urtho had told her before she left—Urtho himself!—that the thing in the box was something like a lantern, and its "light" would make the lightning-sticks useless as the "light" fell on them. She would have to make several passes in order to be certain of getting most of the lightning-sticks, and each time he wanted her to come in from high above at great speed—hopefully so great that no one could train his weapons on her in time and no makaar would be swift enough to follow. Like a peregrine falcon on a flock of ducks—or a merlin harassing pigeons.

It would take several passes to be certain of most of the lightning-sticks, for the box was useless past a certain range. And even Urtho was not sure how many passes it would take to neutralize the bulk of them. It depended on how closely the troops had been packed together, and whether Ma'ar's mages had put shielding on the sticks themselves, or those who carried them.

It would likely be on the stick. Ma'ar would not care if the man survived, so long as the stick did.

The box would work through a shield; Urtho was confident of that. He'd warned her not to use any spells if she had them, saying the box was simply a thing that *negated* the controlling force on magic. It would negate the shield as well as the stick's power pent within. The trick was, he couldn't anticipate the effect of two spells being negated at the same time. He had used the only example of the stick that they had in making *certain* the box worked at a reasonable distance. Zhaneel had seen the effect of that—not much. A little light, and that was all.

But there were easily twenty *types* of shields, Urtho had said, and the troops could possibly be protected by a barrier-shield, a force deflector, a pain-bringer or a concussion field—the complex interaction of three spells could not be anticipated without knowing what *kind* of shield that Ma'ar would use.

Whatever it is, I do not think it will affect us. Unless it unleashes winds. That could happen. I must anticipate that. Or great light that might blind us; I must think of that as well.

They neared the target, and Zhaneel signaled her flight and took herself high up above the clouds, so high that the other gryphons of her wing were scarcely more than ranks of dots below her, even to her keen eyes. Wisps of clouds passed between her and them; the sun overhead scorched her outstretched wings and back, but the wind bit bitterly against her nares, her underbelly, and her foreclaws.

The precious box protected her chest from the wind, but the icy currents chilled her throat and her breath only warmed when it reached her lungs. Was she high enough? The air was very thin up here, and her lungs and wings burned with the effort of staying aloft.

But soon enough, she would be a spear from the heavens. They neared their objective, Laisfaar at the Pass of Stelvi. Zhaneel had never seen the town when it had been in Urtho's hands, but she had been told that the invaders had wrought terrible changes there.

They bring terrible change wherever they go; why should here be any different?

There had been gryphons here. Well, she knew well enough what Ma'ar's forces did to gryphons. They had assuredly done such terrible things to her own parents...

Reason enough to hate the creatures below. Reason enough to wish that what she carried might do terrible things to *them*.

It was time; she swept her wings back slowly.

There! There was the Pass, and below it, Ma'ar's troops, a moving blotch upon the land below her fellows of the wing. Black makaar labored up from their perches on the heights, a swarm of evil. They rose like biting flies to attack the oncoming forces, to pull the gryphons to the ground, where the men there could capture them in cruel wire-nets and stab them with terrible, biting spears.

The men below. Who have the lightning-sticks.

She folded her wings, and dropped like a stone from heaven, foreclaws clutched around the precious weapon the Mage of Silence had entrusted to her.

Faster, faster; the wind of her dive pressed against her as the earth rose up in her eyes, and it seemed as if the earth was trying to pull her down and swallow her. She narrowed her eyes and kept her wings pulled in tightly against her body, guiding herself with a tiny flick of a primary, a movement of the tail, even a single claw outstretched for a fraction of a heartbeat. The other gryphons could not spare an eye for her; she must watch out for *them*. She must avoid them as she lanced through the center of their formation; this would take timing of the most delicate kind, and the control of the best.

But not for nothing had she danced her dance of speed and skill against the imaginary enemies of her obstacle-course. Even as the makaar closed with the leaders, she shot arrow-swift straight past makaar and gryphon alike, unstoppable.

The ground rushed at her.

Now!

Zhaneel arched her neck and fanned her wings open, feeling them vibrate as if the mountains themselves pushed her towards the ground as she strained. By tree-top height she had changed her angle just enough to pull out of the dive, but she was still streaking almost as rapidly as her initial stooping dive. And her foreclaws tightened, opening the shutter on Urtho's magic box, as she skimmed over the heads of the fighters— who were nothing but so many uptilted heads and round, open mouths to her, passing below in a blur.

Her course took her straight for the cliff, and she headed for it unswervingly. These fighters did not seem to have the magic-sticks, but the ones between this lot and the cliff could—

An explosion of—not light, but actual fire! flashed up at her from below, startling her, causing her to veer and slow a trifle. What was that? Did Ma'ar have some new weapon to use against her?

Taking no chances, she aborted the run, closing the shutter and shooting skyward again, opening her wings as she pumped furiously, laboring back up above the clouds to her position of superiority.

Only then did she look down, to focus on the place where the fire had come from.

The ground there was littered with blackened bodies, most of them still afire, and they did not move—while the troops around that area tried to flee.

Slowly, the answer came to her. *Ma'ar shielded these new weapons of his, just as we thought he might. And Urtho said he could not tell what canceling two such spells would do... perhaps the shield holds just enough that it contains the force of the lightning-stick and turns it into a fire-ball.*

Savage joy filled her heart as she realized the havoc she could wreak among her enemies, and she folded her wings again.

This time they saw her coming; pointing, running, they tried to evade her. She knew what was in their minds. They thought that it was the box she carried that was the source of the attack on them, and not the properties of one of the weapons they themselves carried. Zhaneel quickly learned the range of the "light" as she purposefully pursued the fleeing men, rising into the sky only to descend again, leaving fire, death, and terror in her wake.

Her heart pounded with lust and excitement; the blood sang in her veins. Makaar tried to stop her, but she was too swift for them. Either they fell by the wayside, or they got too close to her, and she sent them tumbling injured out of the sky, slashed by one of her wicked hind-feet, to be finished off by one of the other gryphons. When they tried to set an ambush for her, the others broke it up. When makaar tried to get above her, the cold and thin air drove them back down, gasping for breath.

Again and again she made her runs, as flashes of orange and blossoming flames traced her path on the ground, and her fellow gryphons pursued the makaar pursuing her. But finally, there were no more of those explosions, and the makaar turned tail and ran, their numbers depleted to less than half of those that had risen to fight off the gryphons.

Zhaneel's instincts screamed at her to pursue the makaar, but she remembered her orders and fought the impulse, taking herself and her burden up into the clouds again, where the makaar could not go. Now was her moment of retreat, and the Sixth Wing's moment of glory. It was time for the other gryphons to detach the canisters on the harnesses around their shoulders and drop them, creating a pall of choking smoke to confuse the enemy. The few mages below would be trying to negate the "magical attack" of Urtho's box, not knowing it would simply negate any spell they threw at her. They would assume that the smoke was magical in nature as well, and waste precious time trying to destroy an "illusion" or cancel out a smoke-spell. By the time they realized that it was real smoke and called up winds to disperse it, it would be too late.

She would not be there to see the result. Urtho's orders were specific. *When there are no more fighters carrying lightning-sticks, return home.*

Perhaps Skandranon might have ignored those orders to fight makaar, but as Zhaneel reached her altitude again, the elation and battle-lust drained away, leaving her only weary and ready to drop and perch at the first possible moment. Her wings ached; holding them tight and steady against her dives, over and over again, had taken a toll of her muscles that not even preparation and strengthening on the obstacle-course had prepared her for. Her neck and back felt strained, and she longed for a high peak, where she could rest for just a moment...

No rest, not now. No telling who is watching, and one gryphon with a magic box is no match for Ma'ar or another Great Mage! And he will want you, little gryphon, for spoiling his lovely lightning-sticks and hurting his fighters. Fly fast, Zhaneel! If you are lucky, he will not track you!

Now fear, which battle-heat had kept away for so long, set hard, cold claws into her, and gave her wings new strength. How far could Ma'ar scry?

Would he know to look for one particular gryphon? Would he look high, or among the others? Would he look for one lone gryphon, retreating?

No way to tell, Zhaneel. The only escape is to fly, fly, fly away, back to Urtho and his shields, his mages!

Her wings pumped, her lungs labored, and she cast a look behind her.

Smoke rose above the battlefield, thick and white, obscuring everything to the rear. Under the cover of that smoke, Urtho's ground-fighters Gated in to retake Stelvi Pass.

And behind her, below her, just above the level of the smoke, were little dots of brown and gold, blue-gray and white, moving in her direction. The gryphons of Sixth Wing, *properly* deployed, turning to follow her home, their job done as well.

Ma'ar had more things to think about than one little gray gryphon swiftly winging her way back to his enemy's home. Urtho had sent enough troops to take Stelvi Pass *without* the devastating effect of the explosions Zhaneel had inadvertently set off. Now, the fighters of the Sixth would be encountering a demoralized and frightened enemy, as well as one confused by the smoke.

Her fear ebbed, and she slowed to let her fellows catch up with her. Yes, Ma'ar had more than enough on his hands at the moment; he would not waste scrying on her. Her task was over, but the reclaiming of Laisfaar had only begun. She and the others would learn the end of it with everyone else, and not until it was long over. But their chances were good, and the odds were with them to win this one.

And at the moment, that is enough.

CHAPTER TWELVE

Winterhart paused at the threshold of Amberdrake's tent, squinting out into the sunlight. Amberdrake dropped his hand down onto her shoulder, in a gesture meant to convey comfort and support.

"Remember," he said, "right now nothing that you or I will do can change the outcome of what's happening with the Sixth. If you did everything in your power to get each and every gryphon ready for this, then you have contributed enough. And if you have prepared for the worst case you can imagine, then you are ready for their return. No one could expect any more than that; only the gods have the ability to do more."

"I know, I mean, my head knows, but—" Winterhart began.

"Then listen to your head, and stop thinking you have to be superhuman." He patted her shoulder once, and then gave her a little nudge in the direction of the path to the gryphons' landing-field. "They'll be coming back soon, I think."

"Right. And—thank you, Amberdrake. For the advice as well as the massage." Winterhart smiled—wanly, but it was a real smile, and one of the few he had seen on her face. It was a start, at any rate.

She took herself off, and Amberdrake dropped the tent-flap as soon as Winterhart was out of sight, sighed, and retreated to the comforting surroundings of his private quarters. Once there, he flung himself down on his bed, and performed the little mental exercises that allowed him to relax each and every muscle in his back and neck without benefit of a massage.

Not that I wouldn't love one, but I don't have time to call in any favors right now. Not and still get my little "victory feast" together.

He still had his share to do, though the bulk of that preparation had fallen, as always, on the capable shoulders of Gesten. They had raided Amberdrake's hoard of tokens to prepare for this, but it had been Gesten who had done the truly impossible when it came to the feast itself. He had found a party of convalescing fighters willing and able to go hunting and fishing in exchange for those tokens, and now there was a prime raebuck waiting for Skan, a tub full of moon-trout for Zhaneel, and most precious of all, a covey of fat young quail as appetizers before the main course. Amberdrake could not recall the last time he had seen a quail in the camp, and he had purloined one of them for his meal without a blush. And for Gesten, the hunters had picked a basket full of the succulent sponge-mushrooms that the hertasi prized so much. It would, indeed, be a feast, and a welcome change for all of them from camp-rations. Skan had assured him any number of times that different creatures tasted differently, even to a carnivore that did not cook or season its meals, and that he and every other gryphon grew as tired of the taste of herd-beasts as any soldier grew of field-rations.

But before he could do anything, Winterhart had had a therapy session scheduled, the last one of the day before the feast. She was making progress, both physically and mentally, but with all of the Sixth Wing gone, Winterhart had nothing to do. And that meant that she started thinking...

She needs to think less, and act more. That was just one of her many, many problems. She thought too much, and there were times when she became paralyzed with indecision as one possibility after another occurred to her. Those were the times when she was most vulnerable to anyone who would come along and give her orders—for if she followed someone *else's* orders, she could not be blamed if something went wrong. Or so her insidious little circle of reasoning went.

She so seldom did anything on impulse that she literally could not recall the last time she had followed such a course.

Or so she says. Then again, given what I surmise of her upbringing, it probably is true.

Part of that was due in no small part to that lover of hers—better say, "bedmate," since love had very little to do with *that* relationship—the Sixth Wing mage, Conn Levas.

Amberdrake still had no more idea of how she had come to be involved with that selfish bastard than he did of how she had come by a Kaled'a'in name when she was no more Kaled'a'in than Lady Cinnabar was. Information about her past came in tiny bits, pieces that she let loose with extreme reluctance.

He had guesses, that was all. Everything about Winterhart that showed on the surface was an illusion, a mask intended to keep the observer from asking questions.

She was not Kaled'a'in, but she knew enough about them to choose an appropriate Kaled'a'in name—since most of the Trondi'irn *were* Kaled'a'in, having such a name would tend to keep a casual acquaintance (which was all she allowed) from asking why she had chosen such a service. That made him think she must have had exposure to the Kaled'a'in in the past.

She had parents who had expected the infinite of her, and would reward nothing less. Hence the self-expectation that she must be superhuman.

She had impeccable manners.

That, in and of itself, was interesting, for she tried to pretend as if she were nothing more than an ordinary Trondi'irn. Whatever their virtues, the Kaled'a'in did not cultivate the kind of manners that the elite of Urtho's land learned as a matter of course. She tried to act as much like Conn Levas and his ilk as she could. But it was an act, and it slipped when she was under stress. She had to *think*, to act "thoughtlessly." Insults did not fall easily from her lips, and she could not bring herself to curse under any circumstance whatsoever.

In short, whenever she did not think she was observed, or when she was under stress, she acted like a lady.

In a camp where it was often difficult to find the time to bathe thoroughly and regularly, she was immaculate at all times.

In an army where no one cared if your uniform was a little shabby, hers looked as if it had been newly issued, neatly pressed, pristine.

And far more to the point, she had "the manner born." She carried herself as if she never doubted her own authority, nor that she had the *right* to that authority.

To Amberdrake's mind, that spelled out only one thing.

Far from being the commoner she pretended to be, she was of noble birth, perhaps as high as Cinnabar's. That might be why she avoided Cinnabar's presence as much as possible. If the Lady ever got a good look at her, long enough for unconscious mannerisms to show through the Trondi'irn's carefully cultivated facade, Winterhart's ruse might well be over. One could change one's face, gain weight or lose it, alter clothing and hair with the exchange of a little coin, but habits and mannerisms often proved impossible to break.

Then again, Cinnabar is the soul of discretion. She might already have recognized Winterhart, and she's keeping quiet about it. If there was no compelling reason to unmask Winterhart, Cinnabar would probably let things stand.

Now that he came to think about it, ever since he had begun Winterhart's treatments, Lady Cinnabar had been very silent on the subject of that particular Trondi'irn. This despite Cinnabar's intervention at the time of the "hertasi incident'. The Healer had been as angry as anyone else over Winterhart's parroted orders, but since then she had not said a word about Winterhart even when others discussed something she had said or done. Perhaps Cinnabar recognized her, or perhaps not; in any event, the Lady was a powerful enough Empath as well as a Healer to realize, once she had been around the Trondi'irn for any length of time, how much of Winterhart's coldness was due to emotional damage and fear.

Little by little, she reveals herself to me, as she begins to trust me. But I think this may be the most difficult case I have ever dealt with. Zhaneel was simple in comparison; she only needed to learn how outstanding she was, and to be given a way to succeed on her own terms. Once she had those, she blossomed. Winterhart has so pent herself up that I do not even know who she truly is, only what the facade and the cracks in it tell me. Winterhart is afraid, every moment of her life, and she has yet to show me what she is afraid of.

Maybe that was why she had taken Conn Levas into her bed. The man was appallingly simple to understand.

Simply give him everything he wants, and he is happy to let you have an identity as "his woman." He is protection, of a sort, because he is so possessive about everything he thinks is his. He doesn't even know she isn't a Kaled'a'in. He thinks she is, just because of the name, that's how unobservant he is.

Then again, that was simply a reflection of what Amberdrake already knew. A mercenary mage, in this war only for the pay, would have to be unobservant. Anyone who could even *consider* being in the pay of Ma'ar would have to be completely amoral.

But Conn Levas was incidental to the puzzle. Amberdrake laid his forearm across his eyes for a moment, and tried to put the pieces he had so far into some kind of an arrangement. *When she joined the army, it had to be for a reason. I don't know what that reason is yet. But she joined it under a cloud of fear, terrified that her identity would be revealed, even though, since she is very intelligent, she must have chosen the profession of Trondi'irn because it was utterly unlike anything else she had been known for in her previous identity. She may also have taken that position because of another fear; the Trondi'irn do not normally go anywhere near the front lines. I know that fighting terrifies her. I know that she is horribly afraid of what Ma'ar and his mages can do.*

He had seen her in the grip of that fear himself, more than once, when the two of them had been together at a moment when news came in from the front lines. She controlled herself well, but there was always an instant when absolute terror painted her features with a different kind of mask than the facade of coldness she habitually wore.

So, when Conn Levas propositioned her, it must have seemed sent from the gods. Perhaps he even wooed, charmed her. I am certain that he has the ability to do just that, when he chooses. He had a position with Sixth Wing; so would she. He had an identity that no one questioned; so would she, as "his woman." No one would ask her anything personal. And she could do her job among the gryphons impersonally—after all, they were "obviously" nothing more than sophisticated animals. She could deal with them on terms that cost her nothing, other than a bit of energy.

That was where Zhaneel had inadvertently shaken up her world as much as Amberdrake had. The gryfalcon had forced Winterhart to accept the fact that the gryphons in her charge were *not* "sophisticated animals" with limited ability to ape human speech—for she had tried to convince herself that they were only something a little larger than a messenger-bird, but along the same lines.

But Zhaneel changed all that. Zhaneel showed her in no uncertain terms that these charges of hers were people. And she had an obligation to them, to see that they received treatment as such, with consideration, politeness, and decency. She had an obligation to act as their advocate to the commander of the Sixth Wing.

She was in every way as responsible for them as their commander was.

She had not wanted to know that; it was putting stresses on her that showed up when she came to get her treatments for her back from Amberdrake. So long as the gryphons had not been "people" to her, she had been able to cope. Now they were real to her, as they had not been before. Now she had to look at them and know there were personalities there behind the beaks and alien eyes, personalities like those of every human in the ranks. She was sending *people* off into the war to be swallowed up, and she could no longer ignore that fact.

She had begun to feel again, and, ironically, it was that very fact that was sending tremors through her relationship with her lover. As long as she had not been able to feel, she did not care what he did to her, said to her, or how he treated her. Now she did care, and she was no longer giving him the absolute deference he required. That much came through in the edited things that she told Amberdrake.

Circumstances have been keeping them separated quite a bit, but once this operation is over, he'll be back, wanting "his rights." She's not going to put up with his arrogance and indifference to her feelings anymore; she is bound to break off with him. I don't think she's been sleeping with him much even when he's in camp; maybe she's been finding reasons to avoid their tent. I wonder if I should see if he's been going to any of the perchi? Or should I stay out of it?

It was hard to tell; this was not the usual client–kestra'chern relationship, and had not been since the beginning. And of the two people in the relationship, only one was currently his client. How much interference was too much? When did "need to know" end and "snooping" begin?

And she was so profoundly damaged, so terribly brittle. A confrontation with Conn Levas would shatter her, for he would not hesitate to use the most hurtful things he could think of against her. Yet, under her fragility, there was a core of strength that *he* would like to have the privilege of calling on, from time to time. He needed a confidant as much as she did—and he had the feeling that once she sorted herself out, she would be able to fill that need better than anyone he knew. He sensed that he could trust her, and there were not many people that a kestra'chern *could* trust. All too often, the profession became a bone of contention, or a cause for derision. But somehow, he knew that

Winterhart would never do that to him; no matter what, she would keep the things she knew would hurt the most under the tightest control.

He *knew* that. Even though he couldn't have told why he was so certain about it.

This end of camp was very quiet, unusually so for the middle of the day. Off in the distance, he heard a sergeant bellowing orders, but here there was scarcely more than the chattering of messenger-birds and the occasional rattle of equipment. He guessed that most of the other kestra'chern had opted for a nap, in anticipation of being needed when the Sixth returned. *Well, all this thinking is not getting the dinner taken care of. And I do have my share of it to do!*

He was as relaxed as he was going to get, and the tension-headache that had threatened to bloom while he was counseling Winterhart had gone away.

He took his arm away from his eyes and rolled off the bed. Time to get to work. First thing: find out what was happening with the Sixth and the attempt to retake Stelvi Pass. If all went well, the first gryphons from Sixth Wing, Zhaneel leading, should be coming back about now. But there would be more than enough folk crowding the landing-field at the moment, and this was not supposed to be a mission whose purpose was widely known. No point in making a spectacle when someone might make some inferences.

So—find a messenger-bird, or appropriate one.

The birds were easy enough to come by most times; they swarmed the camp, and all you had to do to attract one was to scatter some of their favorite seed on the ground and wait. Amberdrake didn't need the services of a bird often, but he did have a small store of the succulent sunseeds handy, since people liked the savory seeds as well as the little birds did. And Amberdrake was no exception to that liking.

He had a bag in his quarters, next to the bed; he dug out a handful, and took the fat, striped seeds to the cleared area in front of the tent, where he scattered them in a patch of sunlight. A few moments later, he had his choice of a dozen birds, all patterned in every color imaginable. They pounced on the seeds with chortles and chirps, making a racket all out of proportion to their small size.

He watched them for a moment, trying to pick out a smart one, then chose a clever little fellow whose colors of red and black, with vivid blue streaks in its hackles, made him easy to see at a distance. He whistled to it and leaned down to extend his hand, sending it a little tendril of comforting thought to attract it. The bird hopped onto his outstretched hand with no sign of fear, and waited for his orders, cocking its head sideways to look at him.

While these were *not* the altered birds of prey favored by the Kaled'a'in, they were able to respond fairly well to limited mental commands. Amberdrake held the bird so that he could look directly into one bright bronze eye, and made his orders as simple as he could.

:Go to gryphon-field. Wait for gryphons. Look for this one -: He mentally sent an image of Zhaneel. *:Listen, return, and repeat what you heard.:*

That last was a fairly common order, when someone wanted to know what was going on in another part of the camp. The birds could recall and repeat several sentences, and the odds were good that at least one of those sentences would give some idea of what was happening at a distant location. And if it didn't—well you could send the bird back to eavesdrop some more.

The bird flew off, lumbering away rather like a beetle. They weren't strong flyers, and they were fairly noisy about it; their wings *whirred* with the effort of keeping their plump little bodies aloft, and they usually chirped or screeched as they flew. So if you didn't want anyone to know what you were about, you had plenty of warning before you actually saw a messenger-bird arrive to snoop. But many people made pets of specific birds, as much for their engaging personalities and clownish antics as for their usefulness, so you had to really go to an extraordinary amount of effort to avoid them.

There would, without a doubt, be hundreds of birds waiting at the gryphons' landing-field. Although it was supposed to be something of a secret that the Sixth Wing was going to try to retake Stelvi Pass, enough people knew that the area would look as if the birds had learned of a major sunseed spill there. That was the discreet way of learning about the outcome of something that was supposed to be a secret: send a bird to watch, rather than looking around yourself.

And I am nothing if not discreet.

Well, now that he had a winged informant aloft, it was time to get on with the dinner itself. The preparations on his part were fairly simple, since a dinner with gryphons was by necessity informal. He cleared the front of the tent of everything except the piles of pillows. He saved one each for himself and Gesten, and arranged the rest in two gryphon-sized "couches." On the rugs in front of these he placed waterproof tarpaulins—gryphons were not neat eaters.

The buck, the quail, and the tub of trout were behind the tent, and Gesten was seeing to the cooking of his mushrooms and Amberdrake's quail. He had hinted that he would see to a few more small, culinary surprises. So that much was taken care of.

Amberdrake changed into his Kaled'a'in festival clothing; the real thing this time, and not the fancy kestra'chern fakery. A silk shirt, leather tunic and tight breeches, both beaded and fringed, and knee-high fringed boots. It was amazing how comfortable the leathers and silks felt, and how simply shedding his "identity" of Amberdrake the Kestra'chern made him relax a little further.

I wonder if Winterhart has ever actually seen Kaled'a'in festival clothing—or if she is only familiar with what we would wear to blend in with folk from OutClan?

He was tying up his hair when the chattering of the messenger-bird brought him to the front of his tent.

He held up his hand, his eyes straining to spot the red dot of the bird against the bright sky. The little red and black creature whirred in, and backwinged to a landing on his finger, still chattering at a high rate of speed. He placed one hand on its back to calm it, and it fell silent for a moment.

As he took his hand away, it muttered to itself a little, then began repeating what it had heard. Although its voice was very much that of a bird, the cadences and accents were readily identifiable as individual people. Sometimes the clever little things could imitate a favorite person so well that you would swear the person it was imitating was there before you.

But the first thing that the bird produced was a series of crowd-noises, among which a few phrases were discernible.

"She's exhausted." "Get water!" "It isss all rrright—" this last obviously being Zhaneel.

Then the voice of Trainer Shire: "Zhaneel, I have a link to Urtho here, can you give him a quick report?"

The bird spoke again in Zhaneel's voice, her sibilants hissed and r's rolled, as much as Skan spoke when he was agitated or weary. "The box hasss worrrked. It made explosssionsss, and killed many, ssso the sssticksss mussst have been shielded. Therrre arrre injurrred grrryphonsss, but no dead. The sssmoke wasss sssprrreading when we rrreturrrned, and the fighterrrsss moving in. The rrressst follow me."

The bird imitated the sound of a cheering crowd with uncanny accuracy, Zhaneel saying that she was fine and would take care of herself, and the voice of Winterhart countermanding that, and ordering hertasi to be in readiness for injured gryphons coming in.

Amberdrake very nearly cheered himself; he gave the little bird his reward of fruit, and sent him off to rejoin his flock with such elation that he came close to giving the bird more fruit than it could carry away. He *did* kiss it, an endearment which the little clown accepted with a chortle, returning the caress with its mobile tongue.

Zhaneel would be along after she made her longer report to Urtho in person, rested, and cleaned herself up a bit. Skan was due before she arrived—Amberdrake had decided to get the Black Gryphon settled first. Skan did *not* know that Zhaneel was the guest of honor at this feast; he thought it was simply a whim of Amberdrake's.

In a short time the camp was alive with rumors, a steady hum of conversation coming from everywhere. Amberdrake knew that Skan, if he had not been at the landing-field, would surely be in the thick of things and have all the news by the time he arrived.

Gesten arrived even before Skan, pulling a laden cart. Amberdrake raised an eyebrow at that; he was not particularly concerned with the cost in tokens, but *where* in a war-camp had the hertasi found so much in the way of treats?

Never mind. Better not to ask. There were always those who had hoards of rarities and were willing to part with them for a price. And tokens for the kestra'chern were prized possessions. Eventually, in an irony that Amberdrake certainly appreciated, there was no doubt that a fair number of those tokens would find their way back to *his* coffers, anyway.

"Skan's on the way," Gesten said, as Amberdrake hurried to give him a hand. "I've got some real goodies in here. Hope he appreciates 'em."

"Save the best for Zhaneel; she deserves it," Amberdrake told him with amusement.

"Huh. Got a couple things for you, too, Drake. And don't tell me *you* don't need a treat; you've been wearing yourself out between that Winterhart, Zhaneel, and the Black Boy." Gesten pushed the cart to the back wall of the "public" room, and opened it up. "Look here—fresh nut-bread, *good* cheese, an' not that tasteless army stuff, a nice mess of vegetables, pastry, eels for Zhaneel, an' heart for Skan. Couldn't ask for better."

"I have to agree to that," Amberdrake replied, a little dazed. "I don't think I want to know where you got most of that."

"Legally," the hertasi said, turning up his snout saucily. "So none of your lip."

"What about lip?" Skan said, pushing aside the tent-flap. "Is Drake trying to give you excuses about why he can't have a proper meal for a change?"

"Oh, you know Drake," the hertasi replied before Amberdrake could even say a word in his own defense. "If no one else has something, he doesn't think he should have it either. Martyr, martyr, martyr."

"That is *not* true," Amberdrake replied, going straight over to the cart and popping a bit of pastry into his mouth to prove Gesten wrong. "It is only that I do not think that I should take advantage of my position to indulge myself alone."

"Oh?" Skan chuckled. "And what do you call this?"

"Indulging a client," Amberdrake told him promptly. "You *are* one of my clients, aren't you?"

"Well, yes—"

"And you *have* been undergoing a prolonged and painful convalescence, haven't you?"

"Well, yes—"

"And you *do* deserve a bit of indulgence, don't you?"

Skan coughed. "Well, I happen to—"

"There, you see?" Amberdrake turned to Gesten in triumph. "Moral indulgence!"

"My eye," the hertasi replied, chuckling, and began taking things out of the cart. Skan eyed the heart appreciatively, and moved a little nearer.

"Away from that, you!" Gesten slapped his beak. "That's your dessert. And stop drooling."

"I wasn't drooling!" Skan replied with indignation. "I never drool!"

It was on the tip of Amberdrake's tongue to say, "Not even over Zhaneel?" but that would spoil the surprise. So he winked at Gesten, and gave the hertasi a hand in unloading the gloriously laden cart, while Skan stood by and made helpful comments.

"I hope you weren't planning on eating right away," Amberdrake said, as Skan settled down on his pile of pillows. "This is a little early for me, and I'd rather appreciate good food with a good appetite."

"Oh, I can wait," the Black Gryphon replied lazily. "Besides, by now everyone knows about the operation at Stelvi and I expect you want to hear how the Sixth did."

"I'm sure you'd tell us even if we didn't care," Gesten sniped. "But since we do care, you might as well give us the benefit of your superior oration."

Skandranon pretended to be offended for just a moment, then tossed a pillow at him, which Gesten ducked expertly. "You cannot spoil my mood; I am feeling far too pleased. The Sixth has retaken the Pass. The messages are in from the mages, and the town is back in our hands." He continued at length, with as much detail as Amberdrake could have wished for, then concluded, "But I have saved the best for last." His eyes gleamed with malicious enjoyment. "General Shaiknam and Commander Garber have been placed on 'detached duty for medical reasons', and General Farle has been given the Sixth Wing as a reward for successfully commanding them in this operation—and for, I quote, 'appropriate and strategic use of the air forces' end quote."

"Meaning the gryphons," Amberdrake said with pleasure. "Including Zhaneel."

It was not his imagination: Skan's nostrils flared at the sound of her name, and his nares flushed a deep scarlet.

He was going to probe a little further, but a shadow fell upon the closed flap of the tent. "Ah, here is our fourth guest," he said instead, and rose and went to the door of the tent himself. "Lovely lady," he said, bowing and gesturing for Zhaneel to come in, "You brighten our company with your presence."

Zhaneel *was* looking very lovely, if rather tired; Winterhart must have helped her with her grooming. But then, since Zhaneel had been ordered to report directly to Urtho before she came here, the Trondi'irn would have taken pains to make her look especially good, at least to human eyes.

From the stunned expression on Skan's face, she looked especially good to gryphon eyes as well.

She stepped inside, and only then did she see who was waiting there. She froze in place, and Amberdrake put one hand on her shoulder to keep her from fleeing.

"You know Gesten, of course," he said quickly, "and this as you know is Skandranon—I do not believe you have actually been introduced, but as I recall, he gave you some good advice on the disposition of a valor-token."

Amberdrake had no difficulty in reading Skan's eyes. *I'll get you for this one, Drake.* Well, this was fair return for the false impression that Skan had given poor little Zhaneel—however well the whole affair had turned out, *he* owed *Skan* for that one.

"I took the liberty of adding him to your victory dinner, Zhaneel," he added. "I didn't think you would mind."

"No—" she replied faintly. "Of course not."

But to her credit, she did *not* bolt, she did not become tongue-tied—in fact, she recovered her poise in a much shorter time than he would have thought. She blinked once or twice, then moved forward into the room and took her place on the pile of pillows that Amberdrake pointed out to her.

Skan recovered some, but by no means all, of his aplomb. As the dinner progressed, he was much quieter than usual, leaving most of the conversation to Amberdrake and Gesten. Zhaneel managed to seem friendly towards Skan, and full of admiration, but not particularly overwhelmed by him—an attitude that clearly took him rather aback.

As darkness fell, and Gesten got up to light the lamps, she seemed to relax quite a bit. Of course, these were familiar surroundings to her by now, and perhaps that helped put her at ease. Before the dinner was over, Skan *did* manage to ask if she would accept him into one of her training classes, subject, of course, to Amberdrake's approval…

"He's my Healer, you know," Skan added hastily. "Best gryphon-Healer there is."

He fell silent then, as Amberdrake grinned. "Why thank you, Skan," the kestra'chern replied. "I personally think you're more than overdue for some retraining, if Zhaneel is willing to accept someone who's as likely to give her arguments as not."

"I should be pleased," she said with dignity, as her eyes caught the light of the lamps. "Skandranon is wise enough to know that one does not argue with the trainer on the field, I think."

Her nares were flushed, but in the dim light of the tent, only Amberdrake was near enough to notice. "Did you know that General Farle is being given command of the Sixth?" he asked, changing the subject. "Skan brought us the news."

"No!" she exclaimed, with delight and pleasure. "But that is excellent! Most excellent indeed! He is a good commander; most went according to plan, there were no missed commands, and when things happened outside of the plan, General Farle had an answer for them."

"That leaves Shaiknam and Garber at loose ends, though," Gesten put in, his voice full of concern. "I don't know, I just don't like thinking of those two with nothing to do but think about how they've been wronged."

"But they haven't been," Skandranon protested. "They retain their rank, they retain all their privileges; they simply do not have a command anymore."

"Which means they have no power," Gesten countered. "They have no prestige. They messed up, and everyone knows it. They've been shamed, they've lost face. That's a dangerous mood for a man like Shaiknam to be in."

Amberdrake only shrugged. "Dangerous if he still had any power, or any kind of following—but he doesn't, and thinking of him is spoiling my appetite. General Shaiknam will descend to his deserved obscurity with or without us, so let's forget him."

"I second that motion," Skan rumbled, and applied himself to his coveted heart, as Zhaneel ate her eels.

And yet, somehow, despite his own words, Amberdrake could not forget the General—

—or his well-deserved reputation for vindictiveness.

Skandranon ached in *every* muscle, and he needed *more* than a bath, he needed a soak to get the mud and muck out of his feathers. But that was not why he came looking for Amberdrake, hoping that his friend was between appointments. Drake wasn't in the "public" portion of his tent, but the disheveled state of the place told Skan that the kestra'chern *had* been there so short a time ago that Gesten hadn't had time to tidy up.

As it happened, luck was with him; Drake was lying on a heap of pillows in his own quarters, looking about the same way that Skan felt, when the gryphon poked his nose through the slit in the partition.

"Thunderheads!" Skan exclaimed. "Who've *you* been wrestling with? Or should I ask 'what' rather than 'who'? You look like you've been fighting the war by yourself!"

"Don't ask," Amberdrake sighed, levering himself up off the bed. "It isn't what you think. You don't look much better." The kestra'chern pulled sweaty hair out of his eyes, and regarded Skan with a certain weary amusement. "Zhaneel, I trust?"

Skan flung himself down on the rug right where he stood. "Yes," he replied, "but it isn't what you think. Unfortunately. It was a lesson." He groaned, as his weary muscles complained about just how weary they were. "I thought I might impress her. It was a bad idea. She decided that if I was that much better than the rest of the class, I could run *her* course along with *her.*"

Amberdrake passed a hand over his mouth.

Skan glowered. "You'd better not be laughing," he said accusingly.

Amberdrake gave him a look full of limpid innocence. "Now *why* would I be laughing?" he asked, guilelessly. "You look all in; you've obviously been pushing yourself just as hard as you could. Why would I laugh at that?"

Skan only glowered more. He couldn't put it into words, but he had the distinct feeling that Drake was behind all of this, somehow. Zhaneel, the lessons, the private lesson—all of it. "I have been pushing, and pushed, and I am *exhausted*. I need to borrow Gesten, Drake, or I'm never going to get the mud out of my coat and feathers. And I wish you'd let me steal your magic fingers for a bit." And he sighed, finally admitting his downfall "—and I need to talk to you."

Amberdrake nodded, as if he had expected as much. *Which, if he really is behind all this, shouldn't surprise me.*

"In private, I take it?" the kestra'chern asked. As if he didn't know.

"Very private," Skan confirmed, and flattened his ear-tufts to his skull in real misery. "Drake, it's Zhaneel. She's the one—*the* one. And I'm nothing more to her than one of her students."

"And just how do you figure that?" Amberdrake asked casually.

"Because she—I just don't impress her, no matter what I do!" Skan exclaimed in desperation. "It's driving me insane! I don't know what to do!"

"Let me see if I understand what you're saying correctly," Amberdrake replied, leaning back on one elbow. "You have decided that Zhaneel is your ideal mate, and you are upset because she isn't following you and draping herself all over you like every other gryphon you've wanted. Then, when you strut and puff and act in general like a peacock, she *still* isn't impressed. Is that it?"

Skan felt his nares flushing hotly. "I wouldn't put it *that* way!" he protested.

"I would," Gesten said, from behind him. The hertasi pushed his way in through the curtains past Skan. "Feh," he added, "you look like a used mop. If I were a female, I wouldn't have you either."

"*Drake!*" Skan cried.

"Gesten, that's enough," Amberdrake admonished. "Skan, has it ever once occurred to you to go and *talk* with the lady? Just talk? Not to try to impress her, but to find out what she's like, what she thinks is important, what kind of a person she is? Find out about *her* instead of talking about yourself?"

"Ah—" the gryphon stammered.

"Try it sometime," Amberdrake said, leaning back into his pillows. "You might be surprised at the results. Gesten, this used mop would like to know if you're willing to help him look more like a gryphon. I can go get a bath in the shower-tent for once; I look worse than I feel."

"If you want," Gesten said, dubiously. "I think you sprained something."

"Then I can get Cinnabar to unsprain it for me," Amberdrake said to the roof of the tent. "Go on, Skan needs your help more than I do at the moment, and we *are* supposed to be sharing your very excellent services."

"All right," the hertasi said with resignation. "Come on, Black Boy. But you'll have to put up with my massaging; Drake is no way going to be up to it."

Skan climbed to his feet with more groans. "Right now, I'd accept a massage from a makaar," he replied. "And I'd court the damned thing, if it would get the muck off me."

Gesten looked back over his shoulder and batted his eyes at Skan in a clever imitation of a flirtatious human. "Why Skan, I never guessed! Harboring an unfulfilled passion for little me?"

Skan only snorted, and followed the hertasi into the sunlight behind the tent. Gesten opened a box built into the side of the wagon that carried Amberdrake and all his gear when the entire army was on the move, and got out the brushes and special combs needed for grooming gryphons. "You really ought to go find a vacant tub and have a bath," the hertasi said, looking him over. "You're mage enough to heat the water so your muscles don't stiffen up in the cold."

"Once you brush me out, please," Skan pleaded. "If I go in like this, it'll be a mud bath."

"You have a point." The hertasi picked up one of the brushes and set to work with a will. Bits of dried, caked mud flew everywhere with the force of Gesten's vigorous strokes. "So besides you being infatuated with Zhaneel, and her having the good sense to see through you, what else is new out there?"

Skan ignored the first part of the question to answer the second. "What's new is that we may have the Pass, but Ma'ar isn't budging another toe-length." He shook his head, and leaned into Gesten's brush. "I don't know, Gesten. I can't tell if things look good for us, or bad."

"Neither can anyone else." Gesten put the brush down and picked up one with finer bristles. "Urtho don't know what to do, I hear. Ma'ar won't leave us be, and Urtho won't spend troops like Ma'ar does to get rid of him. That's the problem with an ethical commander; the guy who doesn't care how many of his men he kills has an edge."

Skan shook his head. "Too much for me, at least right now."

The hertasi snickered. "Yah. I know what's on your mind—what there is of it. Don't know how Drake thinks you're going to impress Zhaneel with it, since I haven't seen much evidence of a mind in you since I met you."

Skan did not rise to his teasing this time. "Gesten—" he said hesitantly, "do you really think she'd ever pay any attention to me if I did what Drake said? Nothing I've done has worked."

"So try it. Who knows?" Gesten slapped him on the shoulder, raising a cloud of dust. The man's job is the heart, you know. I figure he probably knows what he's talking about."

Skan considered that. Gesten was right. *And besides, I have to tell her what she is, what I learned in the Tower. Might as well kill two birds with the same stone, as they say.*

"But first, Skan," Gesten cautioned, "there's something that's *really* important you need to do."

Skan craned his neck around to look at him, the hertasi sounded so serious. "What is it?" he asked anxiously.

Gesten fixed him with a sobering gaze for a long moment, then said, with deadpan seriousness, "Skan—get a bath."

The hertasi made it all the way to the tent-flap before the flung brush caught up with him.

CHAPTER THIRTEEN

Zhaneel preened a talon thoughtfully, then looked down at her hand. *Hand,* and not a misshapen collection of foreclaws. She was not some kind of an accident. As Amberdrake had surmised, she was the living result of something that had been planned.

"So." She looked from the talon to Skandranon, and even though she managed to keep her expression calm and serene, her heart raced to have *him* here beside her, on her favorite rock overlooking the obstacle-course. "I am the first of a breed, you say? And you saw evidence of that in Urtho's Tower?"

Skan nodded; his great golden eyes fixed upon her as steadily as if he were the needle of a compass, and she were the Northern Cross. The sun shone down on his black feathers, bringing up the patterns in them that were normally concealed by the dye he used. "There seem to be about fifty different types altogether. Mostly broadwings, eagle-types. You are based on the only kind that looks really falcon-based. I don't know what Urtho had in mind to call your type, but I'd call you a gryfalcon."

"Gryfalcon." She rolled the word around on her tongue. It sounded even better when Skan had said it than when Amberdrake had come up with it. "And none of *this*—" she spread her foreclaws wide "—is accidental. I am simply the only one of my kind."

"Not that I saw. But Zhaneel…" He hesitated a long moment, and she looked at him curiously. From the tension in his body, he was trying to make up his mind about saying something more. "Zhaneel, you aren't precisely the only one of your type. Only the first *successful* gryfalcon." He ground his beak for a moment, then clearly made up his mind to continue. "There's—well, what we'd call a *real* misborn in the Tower, too. It looks as if she started out to be a gryfalcon, but something went wrong. She's distorted, like a child in her head, I think she's a neuter, and there are probably other things wrong with her as well."

Zhaneel's tiny ear-tufts rose. "In the Tower? But why—why would Urtho keep her there? I—" But then all of the slights and insults, the teasing and the bullying of her own childhood returned to her, and she *knew* why. "No. I see." Gryphons did not cry, but sadness made their throats tighten and triggered a need to utter a keening sound. She bowed her head, and stifled the urge to keen. *The poor, poor thing. Perhaps it is as well that it is like a child, for it cannot understand how cruel the world can be, and it will not mourn what it has never seen.* "Does it have a name, this poor little one?"

Skan nodded. "Urtho calls it 'Kechara', and it says that he visits and plays with it often. I don't think it is in any kind of pain or want."

"Kechara—beloved…" She took a deep breath, and her throat opened again. "Yes, that would be like Urtho, to care for the poor thing that was not quite what he wanted, to make it as happy as he could." She had come to understand their leader very well during the past several weeks. She wondered if Skandranon knew how often Urtho had taken the time to talk to her; Amberdrake knew, and several times things that Amberdrake had told her made her think that Urtho had been talking with him about her. "But what does this mean for us? I think that if we can, we should find a way to free Kechara. With two of us to protect her, she will not suffer taunts as I did, do you not think? With two of us, acting as her family…? We should not have younglings just yet, I think, but Kechara will serve as practise of a kind. Now that you have made it possible for us to do so, whether or not Urtho approves."

She cocked her head to one side, shyly. Skan gaped at her, looking extremely silly, as the sense of what she had just suggested penetrated to him.

He looked even sillier a moment later, but it was because he was giddy with elation. But then, so was she.

She above all knew how exhausted he must be after the workout of this afternoon, yet from somewhere he found the strength to follow as she leapt into the air, giving him a playful, come-hither look over her shoulder. And as the moon rose, she led him on a true courtship chase, a chase that ended when they caught each other, landing in the warm grass of a hillside far above Urtho's Tower.

As was the only way to end a courtship chase, after all.

This was the face of defeat. Chaos on the landing-field; shouting, and the screaming of gryphons hurt too badly to keep still. Healers and Trondi'irn from the Hill and every wing swarmed the site, somehow never getting in each other's way. Winterhart ignored it all as she held the bleeding gryphon in life by the barest of margins, holding the mangled body together with Gift and hands both, until a more Gifted Healer could reach her. She swore at and coaxed the poor creature by turns, stopping only to breathe and to scrub tears from her eyes by rubbing her cheek against her blood-stained shoulder.

"Don't you die on me, Feliss!" she scolded. "Not after all the work Zhaneel's put in on you! If you die, I swear, I'm going to have Urtho catch your spirit and put it in the body of a celibate Priestess of Kylan the Chaste! That'd teach you!"

Tears rose up again to blind and choke her; she wiped them away again, and ignored the way her own energy was running out of her the way Feliss' blood ran between her fingers. Gods, gods, it had been easier a few short weeks ago—before she had been forced to see these gryphons the way Amberdrake saw them. Before she had found herself caring for them, and about what happened to them. Before she learned to think of them as something more than a simple responsibility...

Before Amberdrake made her *like* them, and Zhaneel made her respect them.

Tears rose again, but there was no time now to wipe them away; she held on, grief-blinded, unable to see—

Until a Gift so much greater than hers that it dazzled her touched her, and used her as the conduit to bring the Healing to Feliss that she had not been able to give. Emerald-green Healing energy poured through her, and beneath her hands the gaping wounds closed, the flesh knit up, the bleeding stopped.

Winterhart closed her eyes, and concentrated only on *being* that conduit, on keeping Feliss' heartbeat strong, until the energy faded, blood no longer flowed through her fingers, and the heartbeat strengthened of itself. Only then did she open her eyes again.

Lady Cinnabar removed her long, aristocratic hands from where they rested atop Winterhart's, and looked deeply into the Trondi'irn's eyes. Winterhart was paralyzed, frozen in place like a terrified rabbit. She had been trying for weeks to avoid the Lady's presence, ever since the moment she'd thought she'd seen a flicker of recognition in Cinnabar's face.

Who would ever have thought that a song *would give me away?* She'd been humming, on her way back from a session with Amberdrake; her back felt normal for the first time in ages, Conn was still in the field and *not* in her bed, and she'd actually been cheerful enough to hum under her breath.

But she hadn't thought about what she was humming, until she passed Lady Cinnabar (hurriedly, and with her face a little averted), and the Lady turned to give her a penetrating stare.

Only then did she realize that she had been humming a song that had been all the rage at High King Leodhan's court—for the single week just before Ma'ar had challenged the King to defend his land. Like the nobles who had fled the challenge in terror, or simply melted away in abject fear, the song had vanished into obscurity. Only someone like Lady Cinnabar, who had been at the High King's Court at that time, would recognize it.

Only someone else who had been part of the Court for that brief period of time would have known it well enough to hum it.

Winterhart had seen Cinnabar's eyes narrow in speculation, just before she hurried away, hoping against hope that Cinnabar would decide that she was mistaken in what she thought she had heard.

But the Lady was more persistent than that, and Winterhart caught Cinnabar studying her at a distance, more than once. And she knew, because this was the one thing she had dreaded, that Cinnabar was the kind of person who knew enough about the woman she had once been, that the Lady would uncover her secret simply by catching her in habitual things no amount of control could change or eliminate.

And now—here the Lady was, staring into Winterhart's eyes, with the look on her face of one who has finally solved a perplexing little puzzle.

"You are a good channel, and you worked today to better effect than I have ever seen you work before," Cinnabar said mildly. "And your ability and encouragement kept this feathered one clinging to life. You are a better Trondi'im and Healer than you were a few weeks ago."

"Thank you," Winterhart said faintly, trying to look away from Cinnabar's strange, reddish-brown eyes, and failing.

"Altogether you are much improved; get rid of that Conn Levas creature, and stand upon your own worth, and you will be outstanding." Cinnabar's crisp words came to Winterhart as from a great distance. "He is not worthy of you, and you do not need him, Reanna."

And with that, she turned and moved on to the next patient, leaving Winterhart standing there, stunned.

Not just by the blunt advice, but by Cinnabar's last word.

Reanna.

Winterhart went on to her next patient in a daze; fortunately her hands knew what to do without needing any direction from her mind. Her mind ran in circles, like a mouse in a barrel.

Lady Cinnabar *knew.* Winterhart had been unmasked.

How long before the Lady told her kinsman Urtho that Reanna Laury—missing and presumed fled—was working in the ranks as a simple Trondi'irn? How long before everyone knew? How long before her shame was revealed to the entire army?

But before Winterhart could free herself from her paralysis, Cinnabar was back. "You and the rest can handle everything else from here on," the Healer said quietly. "I'm needed back up on the Hill. The gryphons are not the only injured. And Reanna—"

Winterhart started at the sound of her old name.

Cinnabar laid one cool hand on Winterhart's arm. "No one will know what I have just spoken, that you do not tell," the Healer said quietly. "If you choose to be only Winterhart, then Winterhart is all anyone will know. But I believe you should tell Amberdrake. He has some information that you should hear."

The Lady smiled her famous, dazzling smile.

"Sometimes being in the middle of a situation gives one a very skewed notion of what is actually going on. If I was a minnow in the middle of a school, I would not know *why* the school moved this way and that. I would only see that the rest of the school was in flight, and not what they fled. I would never know when they ran from a pike, or a shadow."

And with that rather obscure bit of observation, the Lady turned, and was gone.

Winterhart sat in her own, austere tent, and braided and rebraided a bit of leather; her nerves had completely eroded. In another few moments, she was scheduled for a treatment for her back—treatments she had come to look forward to. The kestra'chern Amberdrake was the easiest person to talk to that she had ever known—although the changes he had caused in her were not so easy to deal with.

But now—Cinnabar knew. And although she had said that she would not reveal Winterhart's secret, she had also said something else.

"I believe you should tell Amberdrake." Cinnabar's words haunted her. Who and what was this man, that she should tell *him* what she had not told anyone, the secret of her past that she would rather remained buried?

Why would Cinnabar say anything so outrageous?

And most of all—*why* did she want to follow the Lady's advice?

Oh gods—what am I going to do? What am I going to say?

She could say nothing, of course, but Amberdrake was skilled at reading all the nuances of the body, and he would know she was upset about something. He had a way of getting whatever he wanted to know out of a person, as easily as she could extract a thorn from the claw of her charges.

I could stop going to him. I could find someone else to handle the rest of the treatments.

But she was not just seeing him for her back, and she knew it. Not anymore. Amberdrake was the closest thing she had to a real friend in this place, and what was more, he was the only person she would ever consider telling all her secrets to.

So why not do it?

Because she didn't want to lose that friendship. If he heard what she was, how could he ever have any respect for her, ever again?

Then there was the rest of what Lady Cinnabar had said. *"Get rid of that Conn Levas creature and stand on your own."* Oh, Cinnabar was right about that; she and Conn were no more suited for each other than a bird and a fish. And dealing with Conn took more out of her than anyone ever guessed.

She had always known, whether or not Conn was aware of it, that her liaison with the mage was temporary. She had thought when she first accepted his invitation to "be his woman" that it would only last until

Ma'ar overran them all, and killed them. A matter of weeks, months at the most. But Urtho was a better leader than anyone had thought, and she found herself living long past the time when she had thought she would be dead.

Then she had decided that sooner or later Conn would grow tired of her, and get rid of her. But it seemed that either most women around the Sixth knew the mage for the kind of man he was—an overgrown child in many ways, with a child's tantrums and possessiveness—or else he perversely prized her. He made no move to be rid of her, for all his complaints of her coldness.

Then again, he was a master of manipulation, and one of the people he manipulated as easily as breathing was her. She didn't like unpleasantness; she hated a scene. She was easily embarrassed. He knew how to threaten, what to threaten her with, and when to turn from threats to charming cajolery.

On her part the relationship originally had been as cool and prearranged as any marriage of state. He supplied her with an identity, and she gave him what he wanted. They maintained their own separate gear and sleeping quarters; they shared nothing except company.

But you don't allow someone into your bed without getting some emotional baggage out of it. She was wise enough to admit that. And even though she would have been glad enough to be rid of him, as long as he claimed he had some feelings for her, and he needed her, she knew she would stay. Not until *he* walked away would she feel free of him.

Amberdrake had skillfully pried that out of her already—and in so doing, had made her face squarely what she had not been willing to admit until that moment. She didn't want Conn anymore, she heartily wished him out of her life, and the most he would ever be able to evoke in her was a mild pity. There was no passion there anymore, not even physical passion. Amberdrake gave her more pleasure than he did, without ever once venturing into the amorous or erotic. And now Cinnabar, saying she should be rid of him…

Cinnabar must think he's a drain on me, on my resources. I suppose he is. Every time he comes back from the front lines, there's a scene—I spend half the night trying to make him feel better, and I end up feeling worse. I find myself wishing that he would die out there, and then I'm torn up with guilt for ill-wishing him…

Oh, it was all too tangled. Amberdrake could help her sort it all out—but if she kept her appointment, Amberdrake would learn her secrets.

Her stomach hurt. Her stomach always hurt when she was like this.

Amberdrake knew everything that there was to know about herbal remedies; maybe he would have something for her stomach as well as her back, and if she just kept the subject on *that* she could avoid telling him anything important.

She put the bit of leather aside and got up off her bedroll, pushing aside the tent-flaps to emerge into the blue-gray of twilight.

Time to go. There was no place to run from it now. And no point in running.

Amberdrake knew the moment that Winterhart slipped through the tent door that there was something wrong. Even if he hadn't been an Empath, even if he was still an apprentice in the various arts of the kestra'chern, he'd have known it. She moved stiffly, her muscles taut with tension, and the little frown-line between her brows was much deeper than usual. Her eyes looked red and irritated, and she held her shoulders as if she expected a blow to come down out of the sky at any moment.

"Is Conn Levas back yet?" he asked casually, assuming that the mage was the reason for her tension.

But the startled look of surprise, as if that was the very last thing she had expected him to say, told him that the shot had gone far wide of the mark. Whatever was troubling her, it was not her erstwhile lover.

"No," she replied, and turned her back to him, modest as always, to disrobe so that he could work on her back. "No, the foot-troops are still out. They aren't doing well, though. I suppose you know that Ma'ar is pushing them out of the Pass again. The Sixth got hit badly, and the Fourth and Third sent in gryphons with carry-nets to evacuate the wounded. It was bad on the landing-field."

"So I'd heard." Skan was out there now; as the only gryphon who could keep up with Zhaneel, Urtho had assigned him to fly protective cover on her. No standard scouting raids for *them;* they only flew at Urtho's express orders, usually bearing one or more of his magic weapons or protections. The Black Gryphon had already given Amberdrake a terse account of the damage, before going out on a second sortie. "After a day like today, I'm not surprised that you're tense."

"And my stomach's in a knot," she said, wrapping herself in a loose robe, before she turned back to face him. Her expression mingled wry hope with resignation, as if she hated to admit that her body had failed her. "I don't suppose you have anything for that, do you?"

"Assuming you trust my intentions," he countered, trying to make a joke of it. "I'd prescribe an infusion of vero-grass, alem-lily root, and mallow. All of which I *do* have on hand. You aren't the only person who's come to me today with your muscles and stomach all in knots."

Her eyes widened a little, for all three herbs were very powerful, and had a deserved reputation for loosening the tongue and giving it free rein—and for loosening inhibitions as well. "I don't know," she replied hesitantly. "Then again, between the state of my back and my stomach, maybe I'd better."

He had made the same concoction often enough for himself that he could nod sympathetically as he went to his chest of herbs. He took measured amounts of each into a cup, poured in hot water, and left the medicine to steep. "Believe me, I know how you feel. As I said, I've had to resort to my own herbs more than once since this war started. I've been with Urtho's forces since—let me think—right after the High King collapsed, and Urtho more-or-less took over as leader."

She accepted the cup of bitter tea carefully, made a face as she tasted it, and drank it down all at once. "That's longer than I have," she remarked. "If you've been with Urtho that long, I suppose you must have seen quite a bit of the Court, then."

"Me? Hardly." He laughed, and could have *sworn* that she relaxed a little. "No, I was just one kestra'chern with the Kaled'a'in; all the Clans came in as fast as they could when Urtho called us in, and he didn't sort us out for several months after that. He just gave the Clan Chiefs his orders, and let them decide how to carry them out, while he tried to organize what was left of the defenses. At that point, no one knew what ranking I was qualified for—kestra'chern aren't given a rank among the Clans the way they are on the outside world. My rank and all that came later, as things got organized."

She arranged herself on the massage table, face-down. "The way that the Clans stood by him, though—you must have been disgusted at the way the nobles just panicked and deserted him."

He paused, a bottle of warm oil in his hand, at the odd tone in her voice. She surely knew that *he* knew she was no Kaled'a'in—but there was something about the way she had phrased that last that was sending little half-understood signals to him. And the direction the conversation had been going in...

Go slowly, go carefully with this, he thought. *There is more going on here than there appears to be. I think, if I am very careful, all my questions about her are about to be answered.*

"We stood by him because we were protected and never felt the fear," he replied, pouring a little oil in the palm of his hand and spreading it on her back. "We have our own mages, you know. Granted, we don't go about making much of the fact, and they only serve Kaled'a'in, but between the mages and the shaman, Ma'ar couldn't touch us—and there was no way that he could insinuate agents into our midst to bring us down. Not the way he did the High King and his Court."

The muscles under his hand jumped. "What do you mean by that?" she demanded, her voice sharp and anxious.

He soothed her back with his hands, and deliberately injected a soothing tone into his voice. "Well, Ma'ar has *always* been a master of opportunity, and he's never used a direct attack when an indirect one would work as well. Treachery, betrayal, manipulation—those are his favorite weapons. That was how he got control in his own land in the first place, and that is how he prefers to weaken other lands before he moves in to take them with his troops. He may be ruthless and heartless, but he never spends more than he has to in order to get what he wants."

"But what does that have to do with us?" she demanded harshly. "What does that have to do with the way those cowards simply *deserted* the High King, fled and left the Court and their own holdings in complete chaos?"

"Why, everything," he told her in mild surprise. "Ma'ar had a dozen agents in the Court, didn't you know that? Their job was to spread rumors, create dissension, make things as difficult as possible for the High King to get anything accomplished. I don't know their names, but Cinnabar does; she was instrumental in winkling them out and dealing with them after the King collapsed. But the major thing was that once Ma'ar believed that his agents had done everything they could to get the Court just below the boiling point, he sent one of them into the Palace with a little 'present' for the King and his supporters." His mouth twisted in distaste. "Treachery of the worst sort. Have you ever heard of something called a *dyrstaf*?"

"No," she said blankly.

"Skan could tell you more about it—he was there at the time, in Urtho's Tower, and he found out about everything pretty much as it happened. For that matter, so was Lady Cinnabar, but she's not a mage, and Skan is." He tried to recall everything that Cinnabar and Skan had told him. "It's a rather nasty little thing—it's an object, usually a rod or a staff of some kind, that holds a *very* insidious version of a fear-spell. It looks perfectly ordinary until it's been triggered, and even then it doesn't show to anything but mage-sight. It starts out just creating low-level anxiety, and works up to a full panic over the course of a day and a night. And since it isn't *precisely* attacking anyone or anything, most protective spells won't shield from it. And of course, since it wasn't active when the agent brought it into the Palace, no one knew it was there, and it didn't trip any of the protections laid around the King."

"A fear-spell?" she said softly. "But why didn't the Palace shields—oh. Never mind, it was *inside* the shields when it started to work. So of course the shields wouldn't keep anything out."

"And by the time anyone realized what was going on, it was too late to do anything about it," Amberdrake replied. "In fact, it did most of its worst work after dark—at a time when people are most subject to their fears anyway. The *mages* always slept under all kinds of personal shielding, so of course they weren't affected. Anyone with Healer training would also sleep under shields; remember, most Healers have some degree of Empathy, and this was an *emotion*—they would also have been protected against it."

"But anyone else…" She shuddered.

"And what most people did was simply to run away." Amberdrake sighed. "By morning, the Palace was deserted, and it wasn't only the nobles who ran, no matter what you might have heard to the contrary. It was *everyone*. Cinnabar said that the only ones left were the mages and Healers; there wasn't a horse, donkey, or mule fit to ride left in the stables, the servants and the Palace guards had deserted their posts, and the King was in a virtual state of collapse. She and the others called Urtho from his Tower. By the time that Urtho found the *dyrstaf*, it was too late; the worst damage had been done."

"But they didn't come back." No mistake about it: Winterhart's tone was incredibly bitter and full of self-accusation. "They could have returned, but they didn't. They were cowards, all of them."

"No." He made his voice firm, his answer unequivocal. "No, they didn't come back, not because they were cowards, but because they were *hurt*. The *dyrstaf* inflicts a wound on the heart and soul as deep as any weapon of steel can inflict on the body; an invisible wound of terror that is all the worse because it can't be seen and doesn't bleed. They weren't cowards, they were so badly wounded that most of them had gone beyond thinking of anything but their fear and their shame. Some of them, like the King, died of that wound."

"He—died?" she faltered. "I didn't know that."

Amberdrake sighed. "His heart was never that strong, and he was an old man; being found by Urtho hiding in his own wardrobe shamed him past telling. It broke his spirit, and he simply faded away over the course of the next month. Since he was childless, and everyone else in direct line had fled past recalling, Urtho thought it better just to let people think he'd gone into exile."

"What about Cinnabar?" she demanded sharply. "Why didn't *she* run? Doesn't that just prove that everyone who did really *is* a coward?"

"Cinnabar was already a trained Healer, dearheart," he said. *Not like you, little one. You might have had the Gift, but your family didn't indulge you enough to let you get it trained.* "You've worked with her; you know how powerful she is, and her Empathy is only a little weaker than her Healing powers. *She* was shielded against outside emotions, and didn't even know what was going on. Then, in the morning, she was able to tell that the fear was coming from *outside,* and she was one of the ones who got Urtho and helped him in a search for the *dyrstaf.* They all came in by way of Urtho's private Gate into the Throne Room—all but Skan; he was too big to fit. Unfortunately, by the time Urtho and the mages found it, it was too late to do any good."

"They always said her family was eccentric," Winterhart said, as if to herself. "Letting the children get training, as if they were ever going to have to actually *be* Healers and mages and all. I envied her—" A gasp told him she had realized too late that she had let that clue to her past slip.

"If your parents had allowed you to have Healer training, instead of forcing you to learn what you could on your own, you probably wouldn't be here right now," he told her quietly. "Don't you realize that if you'd been properly trained, you'd have been standing beside Cinnabar, helping her, on that day? There is nothing more vulnerable than an untrained Empath. You were perhaps the single *most* vulnerable person in the entire Palace when the *dyrstaf* started working. Didn't you ever realize that? If Ma'ar's spell of fear *wounded* others, I am truly surprised that it didn't strike you dead."

Her shoulders shook with sobs. "I wish it had!" she wept into the pillow. "Oh *gods!* I wish it *had!*"

Carefully, very carefully, he sat down on the edge of the massage table and took her shoulders in his strong hands, helping her to sit up and turn, so that she was weeping into his shoulder instead of into a comfortless pillow. For some time, he simply held her, letting her long-pent grief wear itself out, rocking her a little, and stroking her hair and the back of her neck.

She shivered, and her skin chilled. Gesten slipped in, silent as a shadow, and laid a thick, warmed robe beside him. He thanked the hertasi with his eyes, and picked it up, wrapping it around her shoulders. She relaxed as the heat seeped into her, and gradually her sobs lost their strength.

"So that was why you chose the name 'Winterhart'," he said, into the silence. "I'd wondered. It wasn't because it was Kaled'a'in at all—it was because a hart is a hunted creature, and because you hoped that the cold of winter would close around you and keep you from ever feeling anything again."

"I never even saw a Kaled'a'in until I came here," came the whisper from his shoulder.

"Ah." He massaged the back of her neck with one hand, while the other remained holding her to his chest. "So. You know, you don't have to answer me, but who are you? If you have any relatives still alive, they would probably like to know that you are living too."

"How would you know?" The reply sounded harsh, but he did not react to it, he simply answered it.

"I know—partly because one of my tasks as a kestra'chern is to pass that information on to Urtho in case any of your relations *have* been looking for others of their blood. And I know because I lost my family when they fled without me, and I have never found them again. And there is a void there, an emptiness, and a pain that comes with *not* knowing, not being able to at least write 'finished' to the question."

"Oh. I'm—sorry," she said awkwardly.

"Thank you," he replied, accepting the spirit of the apology.

He sensed that she was not finished, and waited.

Finally, she spoke again.

"Once, my name was Lady Reanna Laury…"

Winterhart spoke, and Amberdrake listened, long into the night. She was his last client—he had instinctively scheduled her as the last client of any night she had an appointment, knowing that if her barriers ever broke, he would need many candlemarks to deal with the consequences. So she had all the time she needed.

He talked to her, soothed her—and did not lay a finger on her that was not strictly platonic. He knew that she half expected him to seduce her—he also knew that given any encouragement whatsoever, *she* would seduce *him*. But the situation was too complicated to allow for one more complication, and he would have been not only unprofessional, but less than a friend, if he permitted that complication to take place.

Much as he wanted to.

She was very sweet, very pliant, in his arms. He sensed a passionate nature in her that he doubted Conn Levas even guessed at. She was quite ready to show that nature to him.

But the essence of a kestra'chern's talent was a finely honed sense of timing, and he knew that this was *not* the time.

So he sent her back to her tent exhausted, but only emotionally and mentally—comforted, but not physically. And he flung himself into his bed in a fever, to stare at the tent-roof and fantasize all the things that he wished he *had* done.

He had never really expected that he would find anyone he wanted to share his life with. He had always thought that he would be lucky to find a casual lover or two, outside of his profession.

He had certainly never expected to find anyone so well suited to him—little though she knew the extent of it. Right now, she only knew that he could comfort her, that he had answers for the things that had eaten away at her heart until it bled. He did *not* want her until she had recovered from all this—until she knew what and who she was, and wanted him as an equal, and not as a comforter and protector.

She got enough of that with Conn.

For Winterhart, whatever she *had* been, was now a strong, vital, and competent woman. She had a deep capacity for compassion that she had been denying, fearing to be hurt if she gave way to it. She had overcome her fears to find some kind of training that would make her useful to Urtho's forces, and then had *returned* to take her place there, when hundreds of others who had not been affected as profoundly as she had remained deserters. Granted, she had not come back as herself, but at this point, any attempt to reveal her name and nature would only disrupt some of what Urtho had accomplished. The House and forces of Laury answered now to Urtho and not to those who had once commanded them and their loyalty by right of birth. Why disturb an established arrangement?

He thought he had persuaded her of that—and what was more, he thought *she* had figured that out for herself, but had been afraid that saying anything of the sort would only be taken for further cowardice. It wasn't, of course. It was only good sense, which in itself was in all-too-short supply.

"It would be different," he'd told her, "if we had a situation like Lord Cory's. He was back on his estate, in retirement, and was left the only member of his line to command his levy. So he did, even though he is far too old for the task. He's a fine commander, though, so Urtho isn't going to ask him to step down—but if one of his sons or daughters ever showed up, willing to take the old man's orders, there'd be a new field-commander before you could blink."

"But the Laury people are commanded by General Micherone," Winterhart had observed, and sighed. "Bet Micherone is a better commander than I could ever be, and Urtho has the utmost confidence in her. I don't see any reason to come back to life."

"Nor do I," Amberdrake had told her. "You might ask Lady Cinnabar, since she knows the political situation better than I, but if she says not to bother, then there is no reason why you can't remain 'Winterhart' for the rest of your life." He chuckled a little, then, and added, "And if anyone asks why you have a Kaled'a'in name, tell them it's because you have been adopted into my sept and Clan. I'll even arrange it, if you like."

She'd looked up at him thoughtfully. "I would like that, please," she had replied. "Very much."

He wondered if she knew or guessed the significance of that. Kaled'a'in did not take in those from outside the Clans lightly or often—and it was usually someone who was about to marry into the Clans, someone who had sworn blood-brotherhood with a Kaled'a'in, or someone who had done the Clan a great service.

Still, he did not regret making the offer, and he would gladly see that the matter was taken care of. Because if things fell out the way he hoped...

Not now, he told himself. *Take one day at a time. First she will have to deal with Conn Levas. Only then should you make overtures. Otherwise she will be certain that she betrayed him, somehow, and she has had more than enough of thinking she was a traitor.*

All it would take was patience. Every Kaled'a'in was familiar with patience. It took patience to train a hawk or a horse—patience to perform the delicate manipulations that would bring the lines of bondbirds and warsteeds to their fulfillment. It took patience to learn everything needed to become a shaman, or a Healer, or a kestra'chern.

But oh, I have had enough of patience to last me the rest of my life! I should like some immediate return for my efforts, for a change!

He would like it, but he knew better than to expect or even hope for it. It was enough that in the midst of all this pain and death there was a little life and warmth, and that he was sharing in it.

And it was with that thought uppermost in his mind that he finally fell asleep.

CHAPTER FOURTEEN

A bird-scream woke Amberdrake out of a sound and dreamless sleep. He knew those screams; high-pitched, and sounding exactly as if a child was shrieking. He sat straight up in bed, blinking fog out of his eyes.

What—a messenger, at this hour? It was morning! What could—

But if someone had sent a messenger-bird to screech at the entrance to his tent, there was grave trouble. Anything less and there would have been time to send a hertasi rather than a bird. Before Gesten could get to the door-flap, he had rolled out of bed and flung open the flap to let the bird in. It *whirred* up from the ground and hit his shoulder, muttered in agitation for a moment, then spoke in Tamsin's voice.

"Drake, we need you on the Hill, now."

That was all there was to the message, and normally the last person that Tamsin would ask for help on the Hill was Amberdrake, despite his early training. Amberdrake knew that Tamsin was only too well aware of his limitations—how his Empathic Gift tended to get right out of control even now. He was much better suited to the profession he had chosen, and they both knew it. But if Tamsin had sent a bird for him, then the situation up on the Hill was out of hand, and the Healers were dragging in every horse-doctor and herb-collector within running distance—and every other kestra'chern who knew anything of Healing or could hold a wound for stitching or soothe pain.

He flung on some clothing and set off up to the Healers' tents at a dead run. There were plenty of other people boiling out of their tents wearing hastily donned clothing; as he had surmised, he was not the only kestra'chern on the way up there. Whatever had happened, it was bad, as bad as could possibly be.

He found out just how bad it was when he arrived at the Healers' tents, and stopped dead in his tracks, panting with effort, struck dumb by the sheer numbers of near-dead.

The victims overflowed the tents and had been laid out in rows wherever there was space. There was blood everywhere: soaking into the ground, making spreading scarlet stains on clothing and hastily wrapped bandages. The *pain* hammered at him, making him reel back for a moment with the force of it pounding against his disciplined shields.

"Amberdrake!"

He turned at the sound of his name; Vikteren grabbed his arm and steered him into a tent. "Tamsin said to watch for you; they need you here, with the nonhumans," he said, speaking so quickly that he ran everything together. "I know some farrier-work. I'm supposed to assist you if you want me—"

"Yes, I want you," Amberdrake answered quickly, squinting into the semi-darkness of the tent. After the bright sunlight outside, it took a moment for his eyes to adjust.

When they did, he could have wished they hadn't. There were half-a-dozen kyree lying nearest the entrance, and they seemed to be the worst off; next to them, lying on pallets, were some tervardi and hertasi, he couldn't tell how many—and at the back of the tent, three dyheli. There was only one division of the forces that had that many nonhumans in combat positions, and his heart sank. "Oh gods—the Second...?"

"All but gone," Vikteren confirmed. "Ma'ar came in behind them, and no one knows how."

But there was no time for discussion. He and his self-appointed assistant took over their first patient, a kyree that had been slashed from throat to tail, and then there was no time for *anything* but the work at hand.

Amberdrake worked with hands and Gift, stitching wounds and Healing them, blocking pain, setting bones, knitting up flesh—he worked until the world narrowed to his hands and the flesh beneath them. He worked until he lost all track of time or even who he was working on, trusting to training and instinct to see him through. And at last, he worked until he couldn't even see his hands, until he was so exhausted and battered by the pain and fear of others that the world went gray, and then black, then went away altogether—

And he found himself being supported by Vikteren, his head under the spout of a pump, the young mage pumping water over him frantically.

He spluttered, and waved at Vikteren to stop, pushed himself up to a kneeling position, and shook the cold water out of his eyes. He was barely able to do that; he had never in all of his life felt so weak.

"You passed out," the mage said simply. "I figured that what worked for drunks would probably work for you."

"Probably the best thing you could have done," Amberdrake

admitted, and coughed. How many more wounded were there? His job wasn't done yet. "I'd better get back…"

He started to get up, but Vikteren restrained him with a hand on his shoulder. He didn't do much but let it rest there, but that was enough to keep Amberdrake from moving.

"There's nothing left to go back to. You didn't pass out till you got the last tervardi and a couple of the humans that the others hadn't gotten to yet. The rest no one could have helped," Vikteren told him. Amberdrake blinked at that, and then blinked again. The mage was a mess—his clothing stiff with blood, his hands bloodstained. He had blood in his hair, his eyes were reddened and swollen, and his skin pale.

"We're done?" he asked, trying not to sound too hopeful.

Vikteren nodded. "Near as I can tell. They brought the last of the wounded in through the Jerlag Gate, evacuated the rearguard, and shut it down about a candlemark ago."

Evacuated? Shut the Gate down? Amberdrake blinked, and realized then that the light shining down on both of them was entirely artificial, one of the very brilliant mage-lights used by the Healers. Beyond the light, the sky was completely black, with a sprinkling of stars.

We've been working all day?

"Sunset was about the same time they shut the Gate down," Vikteren told him, answering his unspoken question. "Urtho's up at the terminus now, and—"

A ripple in the mage-energies, and an unsettled and unsettling sensation, as if the world had just dropped suddenly out from underneath them, made them both look instinctively to the north. The Jerlag Gate was in the north, beyond those mountains in the far distance.

Far, far off on the horizon, behind the mountains, there was a brilliant flash of light. It covered the entire northern horizon, so bright that Vikteren cursed and Amberdrake blinked away tears of pain and had false-lights dancing before his eyes for several moments.

It took much longer than that before either of them could speak.

Vikteren said carefully, "So much for the Jerlag Gate."

"Did he…?" Amberdrake could hardly believe it, but Vikteren was a mage, and *he* would recognize what Urtho had done better than any kestra'chern.

Vikteren nodded. "Fed it back on itself. Ma'ar may have taken Jerlag, but it's cost him a hell of a lot more than he thought it would. That's the first time Urtho's ever imploded one of his permanent Gates."

The thought hung between them, ominous and unspoken. *And it probably won't be the last.*

Amberdrake swallowed; he could not begin to imagine the forces let loose in the implosion of a fixed Gate. Vikteren could, though, and the young mage squinted off at the horizon.

"Probably a hole about as big as this camp, and as deep as the Tower there now," he said absently.

And then it was Amberdrake's turn to grab for *his* arm and steady him, as he trembled, lost his balance, and started to fall. He was heavier than Amberdrake could support in his own weakened condition; he lowered the mage down to the muddy ground in a kind of controlled fall, and leaned against him, Vikteren blinked at him with glazed eyes.

"You collapsed," Amberdrake told him gently. "You aren't in much better shape than I am."

"You can say that again, Drake." Gesten padded up into the circle of light cast by the mage-light overhead, with Aubri and two of Lady Cinnabar's hertasi with him. "The Lady told me where you were. She and Tamsin and Skan are worried sick. I'm supposed to have Dierne and Lysle help Vikteren back to his tent and get some food in *him,* while Aubri helps me get you back to yours." The hertasi patted the young mage on the shoulder. "Good work, boy. Tamsin says you two basically took care of every badly injured nonhuman that came in. *Real* good work. If I had a steak, I'd cook it up for you myself."

"Right now a couple of boiled eggs and some cheese sounds fine," Vikteren croaked, his face gone ashen. "I'd rather not look at meat just now—could look like someone I knew…"

Gesten gestured to the other two hertasi, who levered Vikteren back up to a standing position and supported him on his feet. "Get some food, get some rest. And *drink* what these two give you. It'll keep you from having dreams."

"Nightmares, you mean," Amberdrake murmured, as the hertasi helped the mage down the hill, step by wavering step. "I remember *my* first war-wounded."

"As do we all," Aubri rumbled. "Gesten, if you can get him standing— Amberdrake, you lean on my back…"

As he got to his feet, he began to black out again, and Gesten *tsked* at him as he sat abruptly back down. "I thought as much," the hertasi said. "You've drained yourself. You're going to be a right mess in the morning."

"I'm a right mess now." Amberdrake put his head down between his knees until the world stopped spinning around him. "I hope you have a solution for this. I'd hate to spend the rest of the night sleeping in the mud."

"That's why I brought Aubri. Just give us a moment." The hertasi hustled into one of the supply-tents, and came back out again with a number of restraining-straps and a two-man litter. While Aubri muttered instructions, Gesten rigged a harness over Aubri's hindquarters, and stuck one set of the litter-handles through loops in the harness. "Get yourself on that, Drake," the hertasi ordered. "I've got this inclined so Aubri takes most of your weight."

Amberdrake did manage to crawl onto the litter, but he was so dizzy that it took much longer than he thought it would, and his head pounded in time with his pulse until he wanted nothing more than to have someone knock him out. He knew what it was: he'd overextended himself, drained himself down to nothing. He was paying the price of overextending, and he wouldn't be the only Healer who'd done that today.

He closed his eyes for the journey back to his tent; when he opened his eyes again, he was being lifted into his bed. But the moment he tried to move, his head exploded with pain, so he closed his eyes again and passively let them do whatever Gesten told them to. He wound up in a half-sitting position, propped in place by pillows.

When he opened his eyes again, the tent was silent, lit only by a single, heavily shaded lantern, and Gesten was still there, although Aubri and the rest of the hertasi's recruits were long gone. Gesten turned with a cup in his foreclaw, and pushed it at him.

"Here," he said brusquely. "Drink this; you know what it is."

Indeed he did—a compound of herbs for his head and to make him sleep, so thick with honey he was surprised the spoon didn't stand in it. At this point, he was too spent to protest, and too dizzy to care. Obediently, he let the too-sweet, sticky liquid ooze down his throat.

Then he closed his eyes, waiting for the moment when the herbs would take effect. And when they did, he slid into the dark waters of sleep without a single ripple—for a while.

Winterhart had never wanted quite so much to crawl away into a hole and sleep for a hundred years. Instead, she dragged herself back to her tent and collapsed on her bedroll. She curled into a fetal position, and waited for her muscles to stop twitching with fatigue, too tired even to undress.

Urtho was losing. That was the general consensus. The only question was if their side would continue to lose ground, or if Urtho would come up with something that would hold Ma'ar off for a little longer.

We're being eroded by bits and pieces, instead of being overrun the way I thought we'd go. Even that stark certainty failed to bring her even a shiver of fear. She was just too tired.

It wasn't just tending her own charges now, it was being called up the Hill at a moment's notice whenever too many wounded came in. And it wasn't just her—it was everyone, anyone who even knew how to wrap a bandage. She'd seen Amberdrake working so long and so hard today that he'd become a casualty himself, and he wasn't the only one, either. The rest of the kestra'chern worked just as hard, and even the perchi came in to mix herbal potions and change bandages. For now, all the little feuds and personality conflicts were set aside.

Unfortunately, Shaiknam and Garber have their commands again. Although General Shaiknam no longer had nonhumans or mages under his command, he was still managing to account for far too many casualties. When he succeeded, he did so in grand style—but it was always at a high cost in terms of fighters.

I wish that Urtho would just put him in charge of siege engines and catapults. They don't die.

Well, she no longer had to parrot Garber's stupid orders, or try to make excuses for him. And the Sixth was holding its own at the moment. Perhaps they would continue to hold, and Ma'ar would give up for a while, let things stand at stalemate, and give them all time to breathe.

Footsteps outside the tent warned her in time to roll over to face the back of the tent and feign sleep. It was Conn, of course, and wanting the usual; she could not imagine where he got any energy to spare when everyone else was exhausted.

He shoved the tent-flap open roughly, and stood beside her bedroll, waiting for her to wake up. Except that she wasn't going to "wake up."

I'm tired of you, Conn. I'm tired of your so-called "temperament." I'm tired of acting like your mother as well as your lover. I'm very tired of being your lover; you have no couth and no consideration.

It occurred to her then that he had so little consideration for her that he might well try to shake her awake. Then she would have no choice but to give up the ruse.

But I'm damned if I'll perform for you, Conn. You'll get me the way I feel—too tired to move a muscle, with nothing left over for anything or anyone, not even myself.

He stood there a moment longer, and experimentally prodded her with his toe once or twice.

Very romantic, Conn.

But she had seen people fallen so deeply asleep that nothing short of an earthquake would wake them. She knew how to simulate the same thing. She remained absolutely limp, neither resisting the push from his toe, nor reacting to it. Finally he muttered something uncomplimentary and left the tent.

She stayed in the same position in a kind of wary stupor; there was no telling how Conn would react to having his wishes flaunted. He might just linger outside the tent, waiting to see if she moved or even came out. He might even come back with a bucket of cold water...

No, he won't do that. He wouldn't want to use the bedroll if it had been soaked.

But he might find some other way of waking her up and return with it.

It's a good thing he won't be able to find a messenger-bird now that it's past sunset. He'd probably bring one back here and have it shriek in my ear. The little beggars love dramatics; he wouldn't have any trouble getting one to cooperate.

But nothing happened, and when her arm fell asleep, she finally turned over, keeping her eyes cracked to mere slits.

There was a light right outside her tent, and if there had been anyone lurking out there he'd have shown up as a silhouette against the canvas. There wasn't a sign of Conn, and as her arm came back to life and she sat up, swearing softly, he didn't come bursting into the tent.

She sighed and massaged her left hand with her right, cursing as it tingled and burned. Her eyes felt dry, and gritty, as if she'd been caught in a sandstorm. She left off massaging her hand and rubbed them; it didn't stop the itching, but at least they didn't feel quite so dry anymore.

This end of camp was silent—frighteningly silent. Anyone not on duty was sleeping, wasting not a single moment in any other pursuits. As she listened, she heard the deliberate pacing of a sentry up and down the rows of tents, and the rustle of flags in the breeze, the creaking of guy-ropes and the flapping of loose canvas.

And something muttered just overhead.

She peered up, where the tent-supports met in a cross. There was a tiny creature up there, perched on the poles."

She got to her feet, somehow, and reached up to it without thinking. Only as her hand touched it and she felt feathers did it occur to her that it could have been *anything*—a rat, a bat, some nasty little mage-accident.

But it wasn't; it was only a messenger-bird. She slipped her fingers under its breast-feathers as it woke and muttered sleepily, and it transferred its hold on the pole to a perch on her hand.

She brought it down, carefully. While they were very tame, they were also known to nip when they were startled. She scratched it with one finger around its neck-ruff while it slowly woke, grumbled to itself, and then, finally, pulled away and fluffed itself up.

It tilted its head and looked up at her; obligingly, she got into the light from outside so that it could see her face and identify her. It snapped its beak meditatively once or twice, then roused all its feathers again, and spoke.

Canceling your appointment tonight, it said in Amberdrake's voice—and it was uncanny the way the tiny bird was able to imitate sheer exhaustion overlaying the words and making him slur his sentences. *Too tired. Tomorrow, if we can. 'M sorry.*

She sat back down again, obscurely disappointed. Not that she was up to so much as a walk to the mess-tent, much less halfway across camp! And *he* certainly wasn't up to giving her any kind of a massage, not after the way she'd seen him slaving today.

But we could have talked, she thought wistfully. *We could have cried on each other's shoulders... comforted each other.*

Suddenly she realized that she no longer thought of him as "the kestra'chern Amberdrake"—not even as her Healer. She *wanted* to tell him every grisly detail—the men that had died under her hands, the fighters who were never going to see, or walk, or use a weapon again. She wanted to weep on his shoulder, and then offer him that same comfort back again. She needed it, and she guessed that he did, too. His friends were as mind-sick and exhausted as he was, and would be in no position to console him.

Or else they have others they would rather turn to.

If only he hadn't canceled the appointment! If only she could go to him...

Well, why not? came the unbidden thought. *Friends don't need appointments to see each other.*

That was true enough, but...

Dear gods, it was a long walk! She held the little bird in her cupped hand, petting its back and head absently as it chuckled in content. Just the bare thought of that walk was enough to make her weep. *He* might have exhausted his *Healing* powers, but *she* had been lifting and reaching, pulling and hauling, all day. Small wonder her muscles burned with fatigue, and felt about as strong as a glass of water.

Footsteps crunched on the gravel of the path between the rows of tents, drawing nearer, but they were too light to be Conn's, so she dismissed them as she tried to muster the strength just to stand. *If I can get to my feet, maybe I can get as far as the mess-tent. If I can get as far as the mess-tent, maybe I can get to the bath-house. If I can get that far—*

The footsteps paused just outside her door-flap, and the silhouette against the canvas was not at all familiar. Until the man turned sideways, as if to go back the way he came.

"Amberdrake?" she said aloud, incredulously. The man outside paused in mid-step, and turned back to the door-flap. "Winterhart?" Amberdrake said cautiously. "I thought you were probably asleep."

"I—I'm too tired to sleep, if that makes any sense," she replied, so grateful that he was here that she couldn't think of anything else. "Oh please, come in! I was just trying to get up the energy to come visit you!"

He pushed open the tent-flap and looked down at her, sitting on her bedroll, little messenger-bird in her hands. "You got my message..." he said hesitantly.

"Since when do friends need an appointment to talk?" she retorted, and was rewarded with his slow, grateful smile. "I had the feeling we both needed someone to talk to, tonight."

"You'll never know how much," he sighed, collapsing on the bedroll beside her.

As she looked at him, sitting there in the shadows of the tent and wanting nothing more than to *talk*, a warmth started somewhere inside her and began to spread, as if a cold place within had thawed at long last, and the warmth was reaching every part of her.

"Would you like to start first, or may I?" he asked, courteous as always.

He needed her! *He* needed *her,* and not the other way around! She sensed the pain inside him, an ache that was so seldom eased that he no longer expected to find relief for it. How long had he been carrying this burden of grief? Certainly longer than just today.

"You first," she said, acting on generous impulse. "I think you must need to talk more than I do—after all, you were the one who made the long walk here."

It was too dark to see his face, but she sensed that he was startled. "Perhaps I do..." he said slowly.

She put the bird on the dressing-stand, and reached out and took one of his hands. It was cold; she cupped it in both of hers to warm it.

Sharing the warmth; sometimes that's all that's needed, I think...

* * *

Skan wheeled sideways and left an opening for Zhaneel to stoop on the pursuing makaar. The one behind him, intent upon making the Black Gryphon into shredded flesh, was a nasty, mottled deep blue, with freshly broken horns still bleeding from colliding with another of his misshapen brethren. Skandranon acted as the lure for Zhaneel's stoops, flying against the thin clouds to show up better from the ground. The gryfalcon, high above, saw through the wispy clouds easily, and it was simplicity to time when she would fall upon the pursuing makaar.

On time, a cracking sound followed by a descending scream marked Zhaneel's arrival behind him, and she shot past and under him at well over three times his speed. Skandranon's eyes blazed with approval, as they did every time Zhaneel fought beside him. He went into his follow-up while she arced upwards to retake her position of superior altitude, higher than any makaar could fly.

Beautiful! And it's working. She's unstoppable when she is in her element, and the new makaar are more fragile than the last breed. Two breeds since Kili... wonder if he's still alive? Tchah, next group...

While the battle raged behind and below them, they managed to keep most of the makaar occupied so they wouldn't harry the retreat. *Retreat! Another one! And I warned Urtho to fortify and trap the valley to at least slow Ma'ar's advance, but we ran too thin on time and resources. Now our troops are beating their way back from the latest rout, and the best the gryphons can do is keep the makaar busy dying. Granted, it's fun, but all in all I'd rather be fat and happy in a warm tent, feeding Zhaneel tidbits of rabbit.*

In broad daylight, the Black Gryphon wasn't the most effective at stealthiness, so he and Zhaneel had worked out this particular style of combat on the way. It had turned into a predictable pattern by now, and the new makaar had apparently figured out that it took Zhaneel a certain amount of time to regain her aerial advantage. It was no longer quite so easy to kill makaar, but at least the makaar at this battle were down to manageable numbers. There couldn't be more than thirty.

Another flight of makaar—four, this time, in a height-staggered diamond—closed on Skandranon sooner than the previous flights had. They were going to clash with him behind Zhaneel's upward flight path, too soon for her to strike at them, but too close for Skan to make an effective stoop of his own. The result—they could chase Skan and exhaust him, at their leisure, unless he slowed and fell to strike at them.

Either result reduces my chances of survival significantly, and I am not interested in that at all. Isn't there something better you could be doing, stupid gryphon? Maybe eating. Or dancing. Dancing—

Ah! Now that is something the makaar wouldn't expect. *They're counting on me speeding past them, or slowing—but if I pull up and stop, that might just break up their formation. Makaar without a formation are also known as scattered bodies. This may be fun again after all!*

So, that hertasi backspin-pointe that Poidon had shown him before the Harvest festival could finally come to some use, if his back could stand up to the deceleration. Amberdrake's Healing, coupled with Tamsin and Cinnabar's periodic care, should have his tendons and muscles in good enough shape to handle it. Since he was a broadwing, cupping enough air to stop should not be a problem, but the speed was going to be a critical factor.

Zhaneel was about to clear the cloud layer on her upswing, but couldn't know what was going on behind her. She'd be expecting Skandranon to be in the next quarterspan, and he wouldn't be there on time; she'd stay on station until she located him. If he slowed his flight too much right now, the makaar could guess his intention and swarm him. And even if...

You'll talk yourself out of doing anything at all, while those four uglies are debating what sauce to put on your bones! Honestly, gryphon, you should know better. Urtho's given you more than wings, you know. You have a brain to think with. That brain's learned spells, you silly side of beef, and the makaar won't be expecting that. Makaar only act on what they expect, remember? They're expecting you to be dead, dead, dead, not the proud father of little gryphlets.

Basic dazzling should do the job, but that took a moment of time and repose—*repose? Who told you that? It takes a moment of concentration, nothing more, you worrying lump. You can't do it while you're flying, but you can do it while you're falling. Falling should be in your immediate future, if you can do the backspin-pointe. You only need one calm moment.*

The makaar gained and shrieked at him, Skan recognized Kili in the lead, and that immediate future became *now*. Skandranon pointed his beak towards the clouds, and arched his body backwards. The air rushing against his throat was nearly enough to stop the blood-flow to his head, despite the cushioning effects of his feathers. Slowly and deliberately, in what seemed like years of constant effort, he changed the angle of attack of his broad wings until he kited upwards. His forward speed was decreasing rapidly, and in this deadly game, speed and endurance were all that kept a flier alive.

To the makaar, it must have appeared at first that he was surrendering. The old maxim of trading speed for altitude held true—as long as Skandranon kept his wings at a good angle of attack. He would be higher, but then eventually he'd come to a stall, and stop completely. Then, as his old enemy Kili surely knew, he would fall, and four makaar were sure to slice him open as he hurtled towards the unforgiving ground.

Zhaneel, if this doesn't work, don't tell anyone I did something this stupid, please?

The makaar screamed their glee as he slowed in midair, his arms and wings spread. Kili started to shriek a victory-cry. He straightened his body in midair with one leg pulled close, the other at pointe. The Black Gryphon hung at the apogee of his climb for a moment.

A calm moment.

Just one calm moment…

Zhaneel pumped her wings furiously, still game for the hunt but growing physically weary. The air was thin above the filmy layer of clouds that she and the Black Gryphon were using for cover, and her lungs had trouble supplying her body for long up here. Her claws hurt from hammering makaar, too.

But, she was making a *difference*. Fighting beside the Black Gryphon was everything she had dreamed it could be, and more. They worked so well together, it seemed like nothing could go wrong—but she knew better than to believe such things. Ma'ar and his commanders were cunning, and each strike the gryphon pair made could be their last. That made the elation at every success all the sweeter.

They'd been devastating on the makaar so far today, but the knowledge that it was to cover a withdrawal weighed on her mind. It was one thing to be greeted as heroes for making a glorious advance; it was quite another to dodge the enemy as you ran for home. Things looked bad enough already by the time the army came boiling out of Ma'ar's ground-Gate, rank after rank of identically uniformed humans with pole arms and bows. Urtho's mage apparently hadn't arrived in time to stop Ma'ar's mage from opening the Gate, so the two gryphons took it upon themselves to disable Ma'ar's man. Skandranon was unable to hit him until after the majority of Ma'ar's ground troops had come through, and then the makaar had clouded like gnats.

That had resulted in one of Zhaneel's proudest moments—the mighty Black Gryphon had gotten his foot caught in the camouflage net the mage had been hiding behind. He was tangled but good, anchored to the ground by the body of the mage, which was also trapped in the downed net, and the mage's men were advancing on Skandranon from the escarpment below. Zhaneel streaked in and cut the net away with her shears, then pushed the broken body of the mage, net and all, down the rocky slope to slow down the troops while Skan beat his way skyward. Just the kind of rescue she'd dreamed of!

And now, her beloved Black Gryphon was down below the clouds, waiting for her to strike again at the makaar that would inevitably be pursuing him. She lined up on where he should be, readied for her stoop, and peered through the thin clouds—and Skandranon wasn't there!

Her voice caught and she felt her throat going tight—this high up, her instinct to keen could strangle her, she realized with growing horror. The air was thinner; she couldn't let herself keen—but where *was* he? She couldn't *help* but cry out in worry!

But sure enough, there was no broadwinged black shape moving relentlessly under the haze of cloud that she could see. He *should* be right *there!* That's where his momentum would have him, and he wasn't *there!* She folded her wings and looped in a frantic search for him—

—and then there was a flash of light below her. Her eyes darted to the location of the dazzling burst, and at the center of a diamond of four stunned makaar was a falling black mass.

Skandranon!

Zhaneel fell upon the helpless makaar, as unstoppable as lightning. *No* damned makaar were going to harm *her* beloved!

Skandranon opened his eyes to find a planet spiraling closer and closer to him at high speed. Given the other things he could have been seeing at the moment—his internal organs dotting the sky, for instance, or makaar-claws in his face—seeing that he was only falling was quite a welcome sight.

There were no makaar below him or to the sides, so he followed another bit of personal philosophy—*never look behind you, there may be an arrow gaining*—and forced himself to stay stone-still so that gravity could work its magic on him. Another few seconds, and he should be moving quickly enough that his wings would do him some good. *Then* he would see what shape the makaar behind him were in, and he'd try to find Zhaneel somewhere.

She must be on station by now and looking for him, and he wouldn't be where he was supposed to be. *You've lasted this long, sky-dancer, but will you survive what she'll do to you after the worry you'll cause her?*

Before he could formulate a rebuttal to his own question, the air around him shook from a massive displacement—and a makaar wing entered his vision only a hand's-breadth from his face!

Kili's wing!

Skan desperately twisted sideways to bring his claws to bear on the enemy that was only a heartbeat away from disemboweling him. He lashed out with both foreclaws to latch onto the wing, intent upon taking the monster down with him—

—and found Zhaneel screaming past him in triumph, her shears clutched tightly in her hands. She was followed a second later by a mist of dark, cold blood, another wing, and the dying body of the now-wingless makaar flight-leader. Zhaneel arced back to come beside Skandranon and laugh along with him as he dropped the lifeless makaar wing and resumed controlled flight.

Oh, gods above, I am in love.

The other three makaar, still bedazzled by Skandranon's spell, scattered and took their remaining brethren along with them. No more makaar harried the retreat, and Ma'ar's troops had already halted to assess their own losses.

Safe again, and there she was, flying beside him, every bit as confident and beautiful as Skandranon's wildest dreams.

Yes, Zhaneel, I am definitely in love. You are worth living for, no matter what comes: You are worth anything…

CHAPTER FIFTEEN

*P*eace, at last.

Amberdrake dropped the tent-flap behind his last client for the evening; he turned with a whisper of silk to look back into the brightly lit public chamber, and sighed with relief. Gesten raised his blunt snout from the towel-chest, where he had been working, and looked straight at him and then away, as if the hertasi was going to say something, then thought better of it.

Not a comment or a complaint, or he wouldn't have hesitated, so it must be a request.

"Spit it out, Gesten," Amberdrake said patiently. "You want something. Whatever it is, you've more than earned it a dozen times over. What is it?"

"I'm tired, and I'd like to quit early and get some sleep," Gesten admitted, "but I don't want to leave you with all this mess to take care of alone, if you're tired too. I thought you felt pretty good until I heard you sigh just now."

Amberdrake shook his head, and pulled his hair back behind his neck. "That *sigh* was because it is damned nice to be doing the job I'm trained for, and not playing second-rate Healer," he told the hertasi. "It was a sigh of contentment."

Amberdrake turned aside, and went over to the portable folding table beside the couch, a table that currently held a selection of lotions and unguents, scented and not. He picked up the first, a half-empty bottle of camil-lotion, and put them in their proper order. He made very sure that the lid of each was properly tightened down before he put it away. Right now, there was no way of telling when he'd ever find replacements, and each drop was too precious to waste in evaporation or spillage. Cosmetics and lotions no longer appeared on the list of any herbalist's priorities. He knew how to make his own, of course, but when would he ever have the time or the materials?

Of course, he might not ever need to find replacements. Ma'ar might very well make the question of where or how he would find them moot at any point.

Better not to think of that. Better just to enjoy the respite and try not to think of how brief it might be.

"No, Gesten, I'm not tired. Oddly enough, I think that exhausting myself on a regular basis up on the Hill only made me learn how to make better use of my resources," he continued. "Either that, or I'm fitter now than I was before. It's just such a pleasure to get back to being nothing more than a simple kestra'chern…" A pregnant silence alerted him, and he turned to see that Gesten was grinning a toothy hertasi grin. He made a face. "And you can wipe that smug smile off your snout, my little friend. No puns, and no clever sallies. Just go get some rest. I had to clean up after myself long before *you* came along, and I think I can remember how."

If anything, Gesten's smile widened a bit more—but there was no doubt that the hertasi was as tired as he claimed. Probably more so; the past few days had not been easy ones for him, either. If anything, he had gotten less rest than Amberdrake. His scales had dulled, and he carried his tail as if the weight of it was a burden to him. That didn't stop him from exercising his tongue, however.

He bowed, and spread his foreclaws wide. "Yes, oh greatest of the kestra'chern, oh master of massage, oh summit of the sensuous, oh acme of the erogenous, oh prelate of—"

"That'll do," Amberdrake interrupted. "One of these days, Gesten, you're going to get me annoyed."

"And when that happens, the moon will turn purple and there'll be fish flying and birds under the sea," Gesten jeered. "You almost *never* get angry, Drake, not even with people who deserve it. Demonsblood! The last time I saw you get angry was with that uppity Healer, the one that came all the way down from the Hill to tell you off, and *then* you cooled off by the time you got back to the tent! You ought to get angry a lot more often; you're too polite. You've got too much control for your own good. Dams break, you know."

But Amberdrake shook his head, and continued to put the jars and bottles back into their special places, each one in order. The sandel-wood lined case had cushioned slots for each, so that no matter how roughly the case was handled, the contents would never break or spill. And, after all the times of trouble in the recent past, doing a simple task was relaxing. So was simply talking to his dear hertasi rather than trading snap opinions of how to deflect this emergency or that crisis. "It's not that I'm polite, it's that I know too much about human nature— and I know how it can be twisted and deformed until people turn into monsters. That makes it difficult to stay angry with anyone for very long, since I generally know what their feelings and motivations are. Now that I've talked with Urtho about our enemy, I even know why Ma'ar is the way he is. I *can* manage to stay angry with Ma'ar; I just wish that knowing the reasons for his behavior would make some difference in stopping him."

"But you never stay angry with anyone else," Gesten argued. "And people think you're weak because of that. They think that they can walk all over you. And they think that because you don't fight back, you must really think that *they* are in the right."

He had to raise a surprised eyebrow at that. "Do they really?" he replied. "Interesting. Well, Gesten, that's all to the good, don't you think? If they believe that I'm a weakling, they'll underestimate me. If they think I'm harboring some kind of secret guilt or shame, they'll believe that I'm handicapped in dealing with them. I'll be able to defeat their purposes or get around them with a minimum of effort, and they'll have spent their strategy-time gloating that they've already won."

Gesten snorted scornfully. "Maybe you think so—but what about all the folk like that damned Healer? The ones who look down their noses at you, think they're better'n you, and say rotten things behind your back? How're you going to stop a whispering campaign against you? How're you going to deal with people who slander you?"

Amberdrake shrugged. "I'll do what I always do: find out who they are, and what they're saying. Once I know who the dagger is likely to come from, I have options. I can duck, I can find something to use as a shield, or I can tell the right people to deal with my detractors from a position of authority without my getting personally involved."

Gesten growled, and it was clear that he was annoyed at Amberdrake's calm reasoning. "Mostly, you duck. An' they go on thinkin' you're weak. Worse, they figure you've just *proved* that they're right, because you won't come after them!"

He thought about that carefully for a moment, then lifted the now-filled chest and returned it to its proper place against the tent wall. "That's true," he said at last. "But Gesten, as long as what they say and do does me no real harm, *why should I care?* As long as I know who they are, so that I can guard against real harm in the future, there's no point in dealing with them on any level. And it makes them happy."

Gesten's mouth dropped open and his eyes widened. "I don't believe I just heard that," he said, aghast. That poison they spread—it's like stinky, sticky mud, it sticks to everything it touches and makes it filthy, contaminates everyone who hears it! Worse, it makes other people want to spread the same poison! Why would you want to make *them* happy?"

Amberdrake turned back to his little friend, and sat with a sad smile on his face. "Because they are bitter, unhappy people, and very little else makes them happy. They say what they do out of envy, for any number of reasons. It may be because I lead a more luxurious life than they, or at least they believe I do. It may be because there are many people who *do* call me friend, and those are all folk of great personal worth; a few of them are people that occupy high position and deservedly so. Perhaps it is because they cannot do what I can, and for some reason this galls them. But they have so little else that gives them pleasure, I see no reason to deprive them of the few drops of enjoyment they can extract from heaping scorn and derision on me."

Gesten shook his head. "Drake—you're crazy. But I already knew that. I'm getting some sleep; this is all too much for me. Good-night."

"Good-night, Gesten," Amberdrake said softly, rising again, and picking up scattered pieces of clothing.

I wonder if I should have told him the whole truth? he thought, as he stacked pillows neatly in the corner. *Maybe he was right, maybe I should get angry—but I don't have the energy to waste on anger anymore. There are more important things to use that energy for than to squander it on petty fools.*

If there hadn't been a war, would he still feel the same way? *No way of knowing. Maybe.* He thought for a moment about the "enemies" he had among Urtho's ranks—most of them on the Hill, Healers who felt that he was debasing *their* noble calling; some few among the officers, people he had refused to "serve" for any amount of money.

The motives of the latter were easy to guess—those who Amberdrake sent away were not likely to advertize the fact, but the rejection infuriated them. For most of them, it was one of the few times anyone had ever dared to tell them "no." But the motives of the Healers were nearly as transparent. The fact that he used much the same training and *identical* Gifts to bring something as trivial as "mere" pleasure to others sent them into a rage. The fact that he was well-paid for doing so made them even angrier.

He could see their point; they had spent many years honing their craft, and they felt that it should never be used for trivial purposes. But how was giving pleasure trivial? Why must everything in life be deadly and deathly serious? Yes, they were in the middle of a war-camp, but he had discovered this gave most folk an even greater need for a moment of pleasure, a moment of forgetfulness. Look at Skan; even in the midst of war and death, he found reasons for laughter and love.

Maybe that was why those enemies often included the Black Gryphon on the list of those to be scorned.

Oh, these are people who would never coat a bitter pill, for fear that the patient would not know that it was good for him. Never mind that honey-coating something makes it easier—and more likely—to be swallowed. And if this had been a time of peace, they would probably be agitating at Urtho's gates to have Amberdrake thrown out of the city without a rag to his name.

And they would be angry and unhappy because if this were a time of peace—I would be a very rich kestra'chern. That is not boasting, I do not think.

And in that time of peace, Urtho would listen to their poison, and nod, and send for Amberdrake. And Amberdrake would come, and the two would have a pleasant meal, and all would remain precisely as it had before—except that Amberdrake would then know exactly who was saying what.

Which is exactly what happens now. Except that it's Tamsin and Skan, Gesten and Cinnabar, who tell me these things rather than Urtho. We kestra'chern are officially serving, even as they, and it is obvious that we have a place here so far as Urtho is concerned. Besides, if they tried to rid the camp of us and of the perchi, there would be a riot among the line fighters.

But would he hate his enemies, if he had the time and the energy to do so?

I don't think so, he decided. *But I would be very hurt by what they said. I am now, though I try not to dwell on it. I may not hate people, but I do hate the things that they do. Whispering campaigns, hiding behind anonymity—those I hate. As Gesten said, they are poison, a poison that works by touch. It makes everyone it touches sick, and it takes effort and energy to become well again.*

For all of his brave words to Gesten, he felt that way now, hurt and unhappy, and it took effort to shrug the feelings off.

He immersed himself in the simpler tasks of his work, things he had not done since Gesten had come to serve him, to help push the hurt into the background. Putting towels away, draining and emptying the steam-cabinet, rearranging the furniture… these things all became a meditative exercise, expending the energy of anger and hurt into something useful. As he brought order into his tent, he could bring order into his mind.

Although Skan claims that a neat and orderly living space is the sign of a dangerously sick mind, he thought with amusement, as he folded coverings and stacked them on one end of the couch. *It's a good thing that gryphons don't have much in the way of personal possessions, because I've seen his lair.*

"Amberdrake?" It was a thin whisper behind him, female, and it was followed by what sounded like a strangled sob.

He dropped the last blanket and turned quickly, wondering if his mind was playing tricks on him. But—no, he had *not* imagined it; Winterhart stood in the doorway, tent-flap drawn aside in one hand, clearly in tears.

He quickly reached out, grasped her hand in both of his, and drew her inside. The tent-flap fell from her nerveless fingers and he took a moment to tie it shut, ensuring their privacy. "What happened?" he asked, as she took a few stumbling steps, then crumpled onto the couch, clutching a pillow to her chest with fresh tears pouring down her face. "What's the matter? Don't worry about being interrupted—my last client just left, and I have all night for you if you need it."

"I may," she said, rubbing the back of her hand fiercely across her eyes. "I'm sorry, I didn't mean to fall apart on you like this—it's just—I saw you standing there and you looked so confident, so strong—and I feel so-so—*horrible.*"

He sat down beside her, and took her into his arms, handing her a clean towel to dry her tears and blow her nose with. It might not be a handkerchief, but it was at hand.

"Tell me from the beginning," he said, as she took several deep breaths, each of which ended in a strangled sob. "What happened?"

"It—it's Conn," she said, muffled in the towel. "You knew we haven't been—for a couple of weeks now. Mostly it was because I was exhausted, but sometimes—Amberdrake, I just didn't *want* to. There's nothing there for him anymore, even if there ever was. I just wished he'd go away. So tonight, when his group came back in and he started on me—well, that's when I told him that I wanted him to leave; and not just for right then, but permanently."

"And?" Amberdrake prompted gently.

"He said—" She burst into tears again. "He started yelling at me, telling me how worthless I am. He said I was a cold, heartless bitch, that I didn't have the capacity to love anyone but myself. He said I was selfish and spoiled, and all I cared about was myself. He said I was the worst lover he'd ever had, that it was like making love to a board, and that I'd never find another man as tolerant as he was. He said I was probably a Trondi'irn because no human would have me as a Healer, and if it weren't for the fact that there's no one checking on the Trondi'irn's competence, I wouldn't even have that job. He said I was clumsy, incompetent, and if there weren't a war on, I'd be a total failure..."

She was weeping uncontrollably now, and if Amberdrake hadn't been listening carefully, he wouldn't have been able to understand more than half of what she said.

"And you're afraid that it's all true, right?" he said gently, as soon as she gave him the chance.

She nodded, quite unable to speak, her eyes swollen and bloodshot, her nose a brilliant pink. She looked horrible. He wanted to hold her in his arms and protect her from the rest of the world.

And then he wanted to take the nearest crossbow and go hunting for Conn Levas.

And I told Gesten I couldn't be angry with anyone anymore...

But none of that would solve anything. She did not need to be coddled or protected; she needed to regain confidence in herself, so that she could stand on her own feet without having to hide behind anyone else.

"You think that what he said is true, only because you are very self-critical, and there *is* just enough truth in what he said to make you believe all of it," he said firmly. "We both know what kind of a manipulator he is. He plays people the way a musician plays his instruments—and he can do that because he simply doesn't care what happens to them so long as he gets the tune he wants." He pulled away a little, and looked her straight in the eyes. "Think about him for a moment. Right now, the one thing he is afraid of is that someone will think *you* left *him* because he isn't 'man enough to keep you.' He said what he did to make you feel too afraid to leave him. Let's take the things he said one at a time. What is the first thing that you can think of?"

"Th-that I'm a c-cold bitch?" she said, in a small voice.

"By which he means that you are both uncaring and an unsatisfactory lover?" he replied. "Well, so far as *he* is concerned, that's correct. You told me yourself that you didn't care in the least for him, emotionally, when you made your arrangement with him. You used him to protect your real identity. Reanna would never have had anything to do with someone like him, which made him perfect as part of your disguise. Right?"

"Reanna would never have taken *any* lover, much less a lowborn one," she replied, her cheeks flaming. "I—I—"

He shook his head gently. "You made an unemotional bargain, and you expected it to remain that way. It didn't. In part, because he was good enough at winkling out your real feelings and using them against you. Which by definition means that you are *not* without emotion. Yes?"

She nodded, still blushing, her eyes averted.

"He also claimed that you are incompetent and clumsy, and you are professional enough to fear that he is correct in that assessment as well." He thought for a moment. "The worst that I ever heard about you—and trust me, kechara, a kestra'chern hears a great deal—was that you parroted rotten orders without questioning them, and treated your charges as if they were so many animals. No one ever questioned your competence, only your—ah—manner. And now that you treat your gryphons as the people they *are*, you have the highest marks from everyone. Cinnabar included."

"I do?" She looked at him again, shocked.

"I don't know Conn Levas very well on a personal level, nor do I wish to," Amberdrake continued. "I had him as a client once, and I managed to avoid a second session; I have seen far too many people with his attitudes, and I don't feel I need to see any more. Furthermore, every other kestra'chern that he has gone to feels the same about him as I do. The center of Conn's world is Conn; he is interested only in someone else insofar as they can do something for him. In his world, there are the users and the used; once you took yourself out of the ranks of the latter, you must have become one of the former, and thus, you went from being his *possession* to his *rival.* So that is why he flung the other insults at you, about being selfish and spoiled. To his eyes, the universe is a mirror—he sees himself reflected everywhere, both his good and bad traits. People who are good to him must be like him—and people who are bad to him must *also* be like him."

She nodded, and rubbed her eyes with the corner of the towel.

"As for the rest of his accusations..." He paused a moment, and assessed his own feelings. *Should I? What happens if I do? And what would happen if I don't?* "...would you care to have a professional assessment?"

She pulled away, eyes wide with surprise. But not with fear or revulsion, the two things he had been worried that he would see in her expression.

"You can't—I mean, do you mean...?" she stammered.

He smiled, and nodded. "The assessment would be professional," he told her, very quietly. "But the motives are purely selfish. I find you exceedingly attractive, Winterhart. I do not want to complicate our friendship, nor do I want to jeopardize it, but I wish that we were more than just friends."

She blinked for several moments, as her cheeks flushed and paled and flushed again. For a moment, he thought that she was going to refuse, and he wished that he had never said a word...

Then, to his own delight and surprise, she suddenly flung herself at him. But not like a drowning woman grasping after safety, but like an eagle coming home to her aerie after a long and weary flight, and there was no doubt left at all, of her feelings—or of his.

The afternoon respite was rare enough for Skan—and that Amberdrake had time to spare was a gift from the hand of the gods. Time for the two of them to sit in the warm sun together—and as an excuse to keep others away, Amberdrake tasked himself with repairing feadiers Skan had broken in the last engagement with the enemy.

"The word on the lines is—stalemate," said Skan, as Amberdrake imped in one of his old feathers on the shaft of a broken primary. "Again. Not a quiet stalemate though, at least not for us."

The warm sun felt so good on his back and neck... he stretched his head out and half-closed his eyes, flattening his ear-tufts and crest-feathers with pleasure.

"That seems to be the case up and down the lines," Amberdrake replied, his brows furrowed with concentration, as he carefully inserted the pin that would hold the new shaft to the old.

Skan turned his head a little, and watched him with interest, and not a little envy. He would have loved to have the hands to do things like this for himself. Even Zhaneel couldn't imp in her own feathers, for all that she had those wonderful, clever "hands." She could do plenty of other things he relied on a human for, though.

She no longer had the disadvantage of shortened foreclaws that had handicapped her in aerial combat. A human in the Sixth who had once been a trainer of fighting cocks had made her a set of removable, razor-sharp fighting "claws', that fit over the backs of her "hands." She could still manipulate objects while wearing them, for they worked best when she held her own foreclaws fisted. Now she was as formidable as the strongest of the broadwings, and wouldn't need to rely on her shears to take down makaar! These new claws were made of steel, sharp as file and stone could make them, and much longer than natural claws.

She had been so effective in claw-to-claw combat with the makaar while wearing these contraptions that the man had been pulled out of the ranks and set to making modified "claws" and "spurs" that other gryphons could wear. The makaar dropped with gratifying frequency, and gryphons wearing the new contraptions found themselves able to take out two and even three makaar more per sortie.

The trouble was, of course, that as soon as someone in the enemy ranks figured out what the gryphons' new advantage was, it would be copied for the makaar. It was only a matter of time.

As long as every makaar that gets close enough to see the new claws winds up dead, we can keep our secret weapon secret a little longer, Skan told himself. *And every makaar dead is one more that won't rise to fight us and will have to be replaced.*

"I understand that the word in the camp is much more interesting than that," Skan continued casually, looking back at his friend through slitted eyes.

Amberdrake fitted the trimmed feather onto the spike of the pin and slowly eased it into place. Skan had expected him to hem and haw, but the kestra'chern surprised him by glancing up and smiling. "If you mean what's going on between Winterhart and me, you're right," he said, with a nod. "The situation between us is not a stalemate anymore."

He looked back down and finished the work of gluing the feather to the steel pin and the place where both shafts met. "Hold still. Don't move. If you can sit there patiently until this sets, it's going to be perfect."

"Not a stalemate?" Skan asked, suppressing the urge to flip his wings, which would ruin Amberdrake's careful work. "Is that all you can say?"

Amberdrake peeled the last of the glue from his fingers, and tossed the rag he had used to clean up aside before he answered. "What else do you want me to say?" he asked. "She's the Sixth Wing East Trondi'irn, I'm theoretically the chief kestra'chern. She can't and won't abandon her duties, and neither will I. Mine take up a great deal of the evening and night, and hers take up a great deal of the daytime. Aside from that—we are managing. Conn Levas is back out in the field. He has made no moves to cause her trouble other than gossip and backbiting, which we can both ignore. He chooses to believe that she is proving what a fool she truly is by taking up with a manipulating kestra'chern, and if that makes him happy and causes him to leave her alone, then he can spread all the gossip he wants so far as we are concerned. We have an ear among the mages in the person of Vikteren, so we know everything he says."

"Huh." Skan cast Amberdrake a look of dissatisfaction, but the kestra'chern ignored it. "Tamsin and Cinnabar had a lot more to say about it than that."

"Tamsin is a romantic, and Cinnabar was raised on ballads," Amberdrake retorted, his neck and ears flushing a little. "Winterhart and I are satisfied with the arrangement we have. We are fulfilling our duties exactly as we did before. That is all anyone needs to know."

Skan raised his head, carefully, and flattened his ear-tufts. "Heyla, excuse me!" he said in surprise at Amberdrake's controlled vehemence. "Didn't mean to pry. When you're in love, you know, you like to hear that the whole world's in love too!"

Amberdrake finally looked into his eyes, and patted his shoulder. "Sorry, old bird," he said apologetically. "There've been too many people who want to make up some kind of romantic nonsense about the two of us being lifebonded, and just as many who want to turn me into the evil perchi who seduced the virtuous Winterhart away from the equally virtuous Conn Levas. I'm a little tired of both stories."

Skan nodded—but for all of Amberdrake's denials, there was very little doubt in his mind that Amberdrake and Winterhart *were* a lifebonded pair. Tamsin and Cinnabar said so, and they also said that those who were lifebonded tended to be able to recognize the state in others.

"It won't be easy for either of them," Tamsin had added pensively. "Lifebonding is hardly as romantic as the ballads make it out to be. Both of you have got to be strong in order to keep one from devouring the other alive. And you'd better hope that both of you are ready for the kind of *closeness* that lifebonding brings, especially between two people who are Empaths. You *can't* fight or argue—you feel your partner's pain as much as your own. You become, not two people precisely, but a kind of two-headed, two-personalities entity, Tamsin-and-Cinnabar, and you'd better hope that one of you doesn't suddenly come to like something that the other detests, because you wind up sharing just about everything!"

"But when it finally works," Cinnabar had added, with an affectionate caress for Tamsin, "it is a good thing, a partnership where strengths are shared and weaknesses minimized. I think that the good points all outweigh the bad, but I have reason to."

Neither of them had bothered to point out the obvious—that Tamsin was as low-born as Cinnabar was high, and if there had *not* been a war on, there would have been considerable opposition to their pairing even from Cinnabar's conspicuously liberal and broad-minded family. In fact, there had been terrible tragedies over such pairings in the past, which was why there were as many tragic ballads about lifebondings as there were romantic ones. Even Skan knew that much.

Well, if Amberdrake chose not to admit to such a tie with Winterhart, that was his business, and not Skan's. And if he preferred to make the relationship seem as casual as possible, well, that was only good sense.

"Can't help what people say, and you know that Conn is the origin of most of the spiteful talk," Skan observed. "And as for the people who are spreading it, well, you know who *they* are, too. If it wasn't Winterhart, they'd make something up about you, and that's a fact. I just want to know one thing. Are you *happy?* Both of you?"

Amberdrake nodded soberly. "I think that we are as happy as any two people can be, in this whole situation. We aren't *unhappy*, if that makes any difference." He sighed, and smoothed down the vanes of the feather, blending the old one into the new. "This is a war; she deals with the physical hurts, I try to deal with the emotional ones. Every day brings more grief; I help her through hers, and she helps me through mine. Maybe…"

He didn't finish the sentence, but Skan knew the rest of it. It was the litany of everyone in Urtho's forces, from the lowest to the highest.

"Maybe someday, when the war is over…"

The war had gone on so long that there was an entire generation of gryphons now fighting who had never known anything *but* the war. That probably went for humans, too. The war had turned the society that older folks sometimes talked about completely upside down, and even Skan could not remember most of what his elders talked about with such longing. The repercussions of that were *still* going on.

"Is it set?" Skan asked, finally, when the silence between them had lingered for some time. Amberdrake seemed to jar himself awake from some pensive dream, and checked the joint with a careful finger.

"I think so," he replied. "Give yourself a good shake. If it holds through that, it's set."

Skan did so, gratefully. There was *nothing* like being told to hold still that made a gryphon *wild* for a good shake! Amberdrake laughed, and backed out of the way, as he roused all of his feathers and then shook himself so vigorously that bits of down and dust went everywhere.

The newly imped feather held, feeling and acting entirely as strong as any of the undamaged ones. He grinned in satisfaction, and saluted Amberdrake with a jaunty wave.

"Excellent as always, my friend," he said cheerfully. "You should give up your wicked ways and become a full-time feather-artist."

"Very few gryphons are as *enthusiastic* in the performance of their duties as you are," Amberdrake countered. "I don't think I've had to imp in more than a dozen feathers in the last two years, and most of those were yours. I'd starve for lack of work."

You could always tend hawks as well as gryphons," Skan suggested.

"*You* could always pull a travel-wagon," Amberdrake replied. "Thank you, no. I enjoy my duties. I would *not* enjoy tending psychotic goshawks, neurotic peregrines, murderous hawk-eagles, and demented gyrfalcons. Have you ever heard the story about how you tell what a falconer flies?"

"No," Skan replied, with ear-tufts up. Hawks and falcons fascinated him, because they were so outwardly like and inwardly unlike a gryphon. "How do you?"

"The man who flies a falcon has puncture-wounds all over his fist from nervous talons. The man who flies a goshawk has an arm that is white to the elbow, because he never dares go without his gauntlet. And the man who flies a hawkeagle is the one with the eye-patch." Amberdrake's mouth quirked slightly, and Skan chuckled.

"I presume that must be a very old Kaled'a'in proverb," Skan told him, with the sigh that was supposed to tell Amberdrake he had quoted far too many Kaled'a'in proverbs. "But—nervous talons? What does that mean?"

"Tense birds have tense toes, and peregrines are notoriously nervous," Amberdrake said, his mouth quirking a little more, this time with a distinctly wicked glint in his eye. "Remember that, the next time your little gyrfalcon is startled when she's got some portion of you in her 'hands'."

Skan laid his ear-tufts back with dismay. "You aren't serious, surely."

Amberdrake laughed and slapped the gryphon's shoulder. "You wouldn't do anything to make Zhaneel nervous, would you?"

"Of course not," he said firmly, and wondered in the next moment if there was any chance...

Amberdrake only chuckled. "I've spent enough time with you, featherhead. There are some things I need to take care of, and I'm certain that you have plenty to do yourself. So if you don't mind, I'll get on with my cleaning, and you get back to your mate."

Skan's crest rose with pleasure at that last word. *Mate.* He had a *mate.* And that mate was Zhaneel: swift, strong, and altogether lovely...

He tugged affectionately on a mouthful of Amberdrake's hair, and then shoved the kestra'chern back in the direction of his own tent. "Back to your housekeeping, then. If you prefer it to my company. You really ought to know that a clean and neat dwelling place—"

"—is the sign of a disturbed mind; yes, I know." Amberdrake combed the hair Skan had mouthed back with his fingers, grinned, and took himself back into his tent before Skan could retort with anything else.

Such respites were doomed to be short in wartime.

The flight back to the gryphons' lairs was a short one, and normally completely uneventful. But as Skan took to the air and got above the tops of the tents, he saw evidence of a great deal of disturbance in that direction. Gryphons flew into the lairs from all over the camp, their irregular wingbeats betraying agitation. Even at a distance he saw ruffled feathers and flattened ear-tufts, crests raised in alarm and clenched foreclaws. Yet there was no other sign of agitation in the camp—so either the gryphons were privy to something the rest of Urtho's forces hadn't found out yet, or the information was pertinent only to gryphons.

It wouldn't be the first time we found out about something no one else knew, he thought with a sinking heart.

Immediately, he lengthened and strengthened his wing-strokes, to gain more speed. Whatever had occurred, it was imperative that he learn what was going on!

The lairs had been built into an artificial hill, terraced in three rings, so that each lair had clear space in front of it. There was a small field full of sunning-rocks between the lairs and the rest of the camp. That was where everyone had gathered. He landed next to a cluster of a half-dozen gryphons from the Sixth that included Aubri. All of them listened intently to what the broadwing had to say, necks stretched out and heads cocked a little to one side. Their sides heaved as they panted heavily; one of them hissed to himself; their neck-feathers stood straight out from their necks like a fighting-cock's ruff, and two of them rocked back and forth as their feet flexed. All of this was quite unconscious, and a sign of great agitation.

Aubri stopped in mid-sentence as Skan backwinged down on the top of a rock beside them, and waved Skan over with an outstretched foreclaw. "I've got bad news, Skan," he called out, as Skan leapt down off the rock and hurried over to join the group. "It's not all over camp yet, but it will be soon. General Farle's dead."

"*What?*" Skan could not have been more surprised if Aubri had told him that the Tower had just burned down. Farle? *Dead?* How did you kill a general without wiping out the entire Command? Chief officers were *never* anywhere near the front lines!

Granted, Farle had a reputation for wanting to be near the action, but the General wasn't stupid, and he was certainly the best-protected man in the Sixth! How had anyone gotten to him? Was it accident? Could it have been treachery?

"I was telling the others—we think that some kind of suicide group got through and took him out, him and most of the other chief officers of the Sixth," Aubri said. "We don't even know how or who did it—there was just an explosion in the command tent, and when the smoke and dust cleared, there wasn't much there but a smoking hole. The mages are trying to figure out just what happened, but the main thing for us is that we've lost him."

Skan swore; there was only one man of Farle's rank that was not already in a command position—Shaiknam, the General that Farle had replaced. The official story was that Shaiknam was on leave while Farle got more command experience, although the real reason Shaiknam had been taken out of the post was his incompetence.

But Urtho could not help being his optimistic self, nor could he stop giving unworthy people so many second chances that they might as well not even have gotten reprimanded. Urtho would remember all the great things that Shaiknam's father had done, probably assume that Shaiknam had learned his lesson, and would give him back the command he had taken away, rather than promoting someone else.

After all, it would look very bad for General Shaiknam if Urtho *did* promote someone of a lower rank to command the Sixth, when Shaiknam was sitting there on his thumbs, doing nothing. Until now, Urtho had been able to maintain that polite fiction that he was "seasoning" Farle, and that General Shaiknam was taking a well-earned leave of absence to rest.

He would not be able to maintain it for more than a moment after the rest of the forces learned of Farle's death. It was either shame Shaiknam, with all the attendant problems that would cause, or give the Sixth back to the man who'd never completed a task in his life.

There was no doubt in Skan's mind which it would be. Shaiknam was too well-born, too well-connected. The Sixth would go back to him.

That seemed to be the conclusion everyone else had come to as well. With Shaiknam in charge, the gryphons of the Sixth just became deployable decoys again. Right now the big question seemed to be, what, if anything, could they *do* about it?

Skan moved from group to group, just listening, saying nothing. He heard much the same from each group: *this is dreadful, and we're all going to get killed by this madman, but we can't do anything about it.* There was a great deal of anxiety—panic, in fact—but no one was emerging with any ideas, or even as a leader willing and able to represent them all.

Which leaves—me. Well, this was the moment, if ever, to act on the theories of leadership he had been researching all this time. *Can you be a leader, featherhead?* He looked around once more at the gathering of his kind; gryphons had started to pick at their feathers like hysterical messenger-birds, they were so upset.

I guess there isn't a choice. It's me, or no one.

He jumped up onto the highest sunbathing-rock, and let loose with a battle-screech that stunned everyone else to silence.

"Excuse me," he said into the quiet, as startled eyes met his, and upturned beaks gaped at him. "But this seems to be a problem that we already have the solution to. Urtho doesn't control us anymore, remember? We are just as autonomous as the mages, if we want to be. We can all fly off into the wilderness and leave the whole war behind any time we want."

A moment more of silence, and then the assembled gryphons met his words with a roar of objections. He nodded and listened without trying to stem the noise or counter their initial words; most of the objections boiled down to the simple fact of the gryphons' loyalty to their creator. No one *wanted* to abandon Urtho or his cause. They just wanted to be rid of Shaiknam.

When the last objection had been cried out onto the air, and the assemblage quieted down again, he spoke.

"I agree with you," he said, marveling that not a single gryphon in the lot had made any objection to his assumption of leadership. "We owe loyalty—everything—to Urtho. We shouldn't even *consider* abandoning him. But we do not have to tell him that. The mages all felt exactly the same way, but they were perfectly willing to use the fact that they *could* all pack up and leave as a bargaining-chit. We should do the same thing. If the situation was less dangerous for us than it is, I would never suggest this course of action, but I think we all know what life for the Sixth was like under Shaiknam, and we can't allow a fool to throw our lives away."

Heads nodded vigorously all around him—and crest-feathers slowly smoothed down, ear-tufts rising with interest. "You've got to be the one, Black Boy," Aubri called out from somewhere in the rear. "You've got to be the one to speak for us. You're the best choice for the job."

Another chorus, this time of assent, greeted Aubri's statement. Skan's nares flushed, with mingled embarrassment and pride.

"I'll tell you what, then," he told them all, wondering if what he was doing was suicidally stupid, or would be their salvation. "I was trying to come up with a plan to get the confrontation over with quickly, before Shaiknam has a chance to entrench himself. Now, we all know that where Shaiknam goes, Garber follows, and I'm pretty certain he is going to be the one to try to bring us to heel initially. This is the tactic that just might work best…"

Two messages came by bird from Garber, both of which he ignored. One of the gryphons who had a particularly good relationship with the birds smugly took the second one off for a moment when it arrived. When the gryphon was finished, the bird flew off—and shortly thereafter, messenger-birds rose in a cloud from the area around Shaiknam's tent, and scattered to the far corners of the camp.

That left Shaiknam and Garber with no choice but to use a human messenger. The gryphons of the Sixth took to their lairs to hide while the rest made themselves scarce, and Skan was the only gryphon in sight. He reclined at his ease up on the sunbathing-rock, as an aide-de-camp in the colors of the Sixth came trudging up the path to the lairs, looking for the gryphons Garber had summoned so imperiously.

The gryphons in question hid in the shadows just out of sight, although they had a clear view of Skan and the aide. They were not going to show so much as a feather until Skan gave them the word.

The young man glanced curiously around the area—which looked, for all intents and purposes, to be completely deserted. Skan wondered what was going on in his mind. The gryphons were *not* with their Trondi'irn, who obviously had not been told of this impromptu conspiracy. They were not on the practise-grounds, nor on Zhaneel's now-sanctioned obstacle-course. They were not with the Command. They could only be at their lairs, unless they had all taken leave out of the area, and leave had not been approved.

Yet the lawn in front of the lairs was completely deserted. No sign of gryphons, nor where they had gone to. There was no one in the dust-bathing pits, nor at the water-baths. No one lounged in the shady "porch" of his or her lair. No one reclined on a sunbathing-rock.

Except Skan.

The Black Gryphon watched the man's expressions as he tried to reconcile his orders with what he'd found. Skan was not precisely assigned to the Sixth, but he had been flying cover for Zhaneel. Skan would have to do.

The aide-de-camp took another look around, then squared his shoulders, and marched straight up to the Black Gryphon. Skan raised his head to watch him approach, but said and did nothing else.

"General Shaiknam has sent two messenger-birds here to rally the gryphons of the Sixth," the young man said crisply. "Why was there no answer?"

Skan simply looked at him—exactly the same way that he would have regarded a nice plump deer.

But the youngster was made of sterner stuff than most, and obviously was not going to be rattled simply by the stare of an unfriendly carnivore with a beak large and sharp enough to make short work of his torso. He continued on, bravely: "General Shaiknam orders that the gryphons of the Sixth report immediately to the landing-field for deployment."

"Why?" Skan rumbled.

The young man blinked, as if he had not expected Skan to say anything, much less demand information. He was so startled that he actually *gave* it.

"You'll be making runs against the troops below Panjir," he said. "Flying in at treetop level. Dropping rocks and—"

"And making ourselves targets for the *seven batteries* of ballistas and other sky-pointing missile-throwers," Skan replied caustically. "Scarcely-moving targets, at that. There isn't room between those cliff-walls for more than one gryphon to fly at a time, much less a decent formation. We'll look like beads on a string. If the missiles don't get us, the makaar will, coming down on us from the heights. You can tell the General that we'll be declining his little invitation. Tell him the message is from the Black Gryphon."

And with that, Skan put his head back down on his foreclaws, closed his eyes to mere slits, and pretended to go to sleep.

The aide's mouth dropped completely open for a moment, then closed quickly. But to his credit, he did not try to bluster or argue; he simply turned crisply on his heel and left, trudging back down the hill, leaving behind a trail of little puffs of dust. Skan watched him until he was well out of sight, then jumped to his feet.

"Now what?" one of the others called from the shelter of his lair.

"Now I go to Urtho before Shaiknam does," Skan replied, and leapt skywards, wings laboring to gain altitude, heading straight for the Tower.

Where would Urtho be at this hour? Probably the Strategy Room. That wasn't exactly convenient; he couldn't get to something deep inside the tower without passing a door and at least one guard. Skan was going to have to go through channels, rather than landing directly on Urtho's balcony the way he would have preferred.

He backwinged down onto the pavement in front of the Tower, paced regally up to the guard just outside the door, and bowed his head in salute.

"Skandranon to see Urtho on a matter of extreme urgency," he said, politely, and with strictest formality. "I would appreciate it if you would send him a message to that effect."

He was rather proud of the fact that, despite his own agitation, his sibilants had no hissing, and he pronounced his r's without a trill. The guard nodded, tapped on the door and whispered to someone just inside for a moment, and turned back to Skan.

"Taken care of, Skandranon," he said. "If you'd care to wait, I don't think it'll take long."

Skan nodded. "Thank you," he replied. He longed to pace; his feet itched with the need to tear something up out of sheer nerve. But he kept as still and as serene as a statue of black granite—except for his tail, which twitched and lashed, no matter how hard he concentrated on keeping it quiet.

With every moment that passed, he expected to hear a messenger from Shaiknam running up behind him—messenger-birds still probably avoided the General and his underlings, so Shaiknam would have to use a much slower method of requesting his own audience with the Mage of Silence.

As time continued to crawl past, Skan wanted to grind his beak. He felt like a very large target in the middle of all the pale stone.

Finally, after far too long a wait, a faint tap on the door behind him caused the guard to open it and listen for a moment. He flung it wide, and gestured for Skan to enter. "Urtho will see you," he said. "The mage is in the Strategy Room."

No point in the guard telling him the way, as they both knew. Skan was perfectly at home in the Tower. He simply nodded, and walked in the open door.

A second guard stationed inside gave him a brief nod of recognition as Skan passed. Urtho had planned most of his tower with creatures like his gryphons in mind: the floors were of natural, rough-textured stone, so that claws and talons did not slip on them, the doors and hallways were all made tall and wide enough for things larger than a human to pass. There wasn't a great deal to see, otherwise—just the hallway itself, plain and unadorned, with closed doors on either side of it. The room that Skan wanted was behind the third door on the right, and he hurried right to it.

The door opened for him, but by human agency, and not magical. Urtho stood behind the table-sized contour-map used for all major planning sessions. Areas held by Ma'ar had been magically tinted painted red; everything else was blue.

There was an alarming amount of red on that map.

"Urtho," Skan began, as soon as he was in the door. "I—"

"You and the Sixth Wing gryphons are staging a revolt," Urtho replied, with dangerous gentleness.

Skan's ear-tufts flattened. "How did you know?" he blurted, backing up a pace or two. Behind him, a hertasi shut the door and took himself out of the room by a side passage, leaving the two of them alone.

"I am a mage," Urtho reminded him. "While I don't squander my energies, I *do* use them on occasion to keep an eye on something. I knew you lot wouldn't care for having Shaiknam set over you, but I didn't think you'd start a revolution." He crossed his arms over his chest and gazed levelly at Skan. "That's not a particularly clever thing to do. You can't survive without me, you know."

Ah, hells. Well, might as well drop it all at once.

"Yes, we can," Skan replied, raising his head so that he looked down on Urtho, rather than dropping his eyes below the level of Urtho's as all his training screamed at him to do. "I'm sorry, Urtho, but we don't need you anymore. We know how to make ourselves fertile now. Zhaneel is the proof of that, if you doubt my unadorned word on it."

He had never in all of his life seen Urtho taken aback before. Surprised, yes. Shocked, certainly. But completely dumbfounded—never.

The expression of complete blankness on Urtho's face was so funny that Skan couldn't help himself. He started laughing.

Urtho's face flushed, and the blank expression he wore turned to one of annoyance and a little anger. "What are you laughing at, you overgrown chicken?" the mage spluttered. "What is so damned funny?"

Skan could only shake his head, still laughing. "Your face was all he was able to manage, before he ran out of breath.

Urtho reddened a little more, but then, grudgingly, he smiled. "So, you think you have the upper hand, do you?" he said, challenge in his tone.

Skan got himself back under control, and quickly, even though laughter threatened to bubble up through his chest at any moment. "Yes and no," he replied. "We can leave, now. You no longer control us by means of our future, Urtho. That doesn't mean we *will* leave, though, it just means that we won't have to put up with idiots like Shaiknam and Garber who think we're to be thrown away by the handful. Wait!" He held up a foreclaw as Urtho started to say something. "Listen to me, first. *This* is what Shaiknam planned to do with the gryphons as soon as he got the Sixth out into the field again!"

He told Urtho what the aide had told *him*, then traced out the planned maneuvers on the map. "You see?" he said, as Urtho's brow furrowed. "You see what that would do? Maybe we would provide a distraction for Ma'ar's troops, but there are better ways of supplying distraction than sacrificing half the wings!"

"I do see," Urtho replied, nodding thoughtfully. "I do see."

"We don't want to make trouble, Urtho," Skan continued earnestly, taking a cautious step nearer. "But we don't want to be blackmailed into suicidal missions. Maybe that's not how it seemed to you, but that was how it felt to us." He raised his head a little higher. "You built our urges to reproduce as strongly as our will to eat and breathe, and used that to control us. We'd rather serve you out of loyalty than coercion."

"I would rather have you out of loyalty," Urtho murmured, blinking once or twice rapidly. He coughed, hiding his face for just a moment, then looked up again. "And just how did you obtain this knowledge?" he asked. "I'm sure it was you—I can't think of another gryphon who would have tried, let alone succeeded."

Skan gaped his beak wide in an insolent grin, hoping to charm Urtho into good humor. "That, Urtho, would be telling."

CHAPTER SIXTEEN

For one brief moment when Skandranon defied him, Urtho had been in a white-hot rage. How *dared* this creature, a thing that *he* had created, presume to dictate the terms of this war? How *dared* this same creature usurp the knowledge it had no right to, and was not intelligent enough to use properly?

But that rage burned itself out as quickly as it came, for Urtho had lived too long to let his rage control his intellect. Intellect came to his rescue, with all of the answers to the questions of "how dared..." Skan dared because he was not a "creature," he was a living, thinking, rightfully independent being, as were all the rest of the gryphons. They were precisely what he had hoped and planned for, and had never thought they would become in his lifetime. They had the right to control their own destinies. Perhaps he was responsible for their form, but their spirits were their own. He was now the one who "had no right" to dictate anything to them—and he realized, in a blinding instant of insight, that he was incredibly lucky that they didn't harbor resentment against him for what he'd withheld from them. Instead, they were still loyal to him.

They would have been perfectly within their rights to fly off as they threatened, he thought, as Skan laughed at the expression on his face. *It's nothing short of a miracle that they didn't. Dear gods, we have been lucky...*

He didn't realize how lucky, until Skan told him just what Shaiknam had been planning. A quick survey of the topography of the area told him what it did not tell Skan: that Shaiknam had intended to launch an all-or-nothing glory-strike against the heavily fortified valley. Such things succeeded brilliantly when they succeeded at all, but this particular battle-plan didn't have the chances of a snowflake in a frying pan of working. It was just another one of Shaiknam's insane attempts to pull off some maneuver that would make him hailed as a military genius and a hero.

The only trouble was that military geniuses and heroes had sound reasoning behind their plans. Shaiknam, unfortunately, had only wild ideas.

Urtho cursed the man silently, as Skan pointed out all the ways that the gryphons would be cut down without being able to defend themselves. Shaiknam's father was such a brilliant strategist and commander—*how* had the man avoided learning even the simplest of strategies from him?

Well, there was no hope for it; the only way to get rid of the man now would be to strip the Sixth of all non-human troops and mages on the excuse that all the other commands were undermanned, and reassign the personnel elsewhere. Shaiknam could still *be* Commander of the Sixth, but he would only command foot-troops, all of them human. With no aerial support, and no mages, he would be forced into caution.

That should keep him out of trouble, and his little dog Garber, too.

He growled a little when Skan refused to tell him *who* his coconspirators had been, but it was a good bet that Lady Cinnabar was involved in this, right up to her aristocratic chin. And where you found Cinnabar, you found Tamsin, and probably Amberdrake. *No doubt they got in when Cinnabar asked to "look at my records on the gryphons." I thought she was looking for a cure for belly-ache!* The kestra'chern must have gotten a client to make him a set of "keys" for mage-locks; that would account for how they'd gotten into the book.

The wonder of it was that they had managed to penetrate past all the fireworks and folderol in order to find the *real* triggers for fertility.

"How many of you know the spell?" he asked, as reluctant admiration set in.

"All," Skan said, without so much as blinking an eye. "And it's not exactly a flashy spell, Urtho. It was simply good design. There was no point in holding the information back. Every gryphon outside this Tower knows the secret."

He couldn't help it; he had to shake his head with pure admiration. "And you've kept this whole thing from me all this time! Unbelievable."

"We had reason to keep it among ourselves," Skan replied. "Good reason. We didn't know how you would feel or act, and we didn't want you finding out before the time was right for me to tell you."

"So you were the sacrificial goat, hmm?" Urtho eyed Skan dubiously. "I don't know; a sacrifice is supposed to be savory, not scrawny."

Skan drew himself up in an exaggerated pose. "A sacrifice is supposed to be the best of the best. I believe I fill that description."

His eyes twinkled as he watched Urtho from beneath his heavy lids, and his beak gaped in a broad grin when Urtho laughed aloud.

"I submit to the inevitable, my friend," Urtho said, still laughing, as he slapped Skan on the shoulder. "I suppose I must consider this as your test of adulthood, as the Kaled'a'in give their youngsters. You gryphons are certainly not my children any longer—nor anyone's children."

Then he sobered. "I am glad that this has happened now, Skan. And I am glad that you are here. I need to pass along some grave news of my own, and this will probably be the best opportunity to do so."

He called in the hertasi who waited discreetly just on the other side of the door, and gave him swift instructions. "I wish you to summon General Shaiknam and take him to the Marble Office; once you have left him there, summon the commanders of the other forces to the Strategy Room."

He turned back to Skan. "I am splitting the non-human manpower of the Sixth among all the other commanders—I have reason enough, since all of them have been complaining that they are shorthanded. That will leave Shaiknam in command of nothing but humans. Is there any commander that you think the gryphons of the Sixth would prefer to serve?"

For once, he had caught the Black Gryphon by surprise; Skan's grin-gape turned into a jaw-dropped gape of surprise, and his eyes went blank for a moment. "Ah—ah—Judeth of the Fifth, I think."

Urtho nodded, pleased with his choice. "Excellent. And she has had no real gryphon wings assigned to her forces until now, only those on loan from the Sixth or the Fourth. Consider it done." Urtho regarded Skan measuringly. "Still, the gryphons should have their own collective voice, even as the mages do. There are things that you know about yourselves that no human could. There should be one gryphon assigned to speak for all gryphons, so that things will not come to the pass they have with Shaiknam before I come to hear about it." He stabbed out a finger. "You. You, Skan. I hereby assign you to be the overall commander of all the gryphon wings and to speak for them directly to me."

* * *

257

Skan's surprise turned to stupefaction. His head came up as if someone had poked him in the rear. "*Me?*" he squeaked—yes, squeaked; he sounded like a mouse. He cleared his throat and tried again. "Me? Why me? I am honored, Urtho, but—"

Urtho waved his objections aside. "You've obviously thought about becoming the leader of the gryphons, or why else would you have read all my history books about the great leaders of the past? The others clearly think that you should have that position, or why else would they have sent you here to confront me over Shaiknam?"

Is it unusually warm in here? Skan felt his nares flushing, and he hung his head. "They didn't exactly *pick me,*" he admitted. "They couldn't seem to do much besides panic and complain, so I… I took over. Nobody seemed to mind."

"All the more reason to place you in charge, if you were the only one to *take* charge," Urtho said, implacably. "How do you think *I* wound up in charge of this so-called army?"

Skan ducked his head between his shoulder-blades, his nares positively burning. "I'm not sure that's a fit comparison…"

"Now, I have a few things to tell you," Urtho continued. "I don't know if you've been aware of it, but I've been sending groups of families and non-combatants into the west ever since we first thought we'd have to abandon the Tower." He turned back to the map, and stood over it, brooding. "I didn't like having such a great concentration of folk here in the first place, and when I realized what chaos an evacuation would be, I liked it even less."

Skan nodded, with admiration. He *hadn't* realized that Urtho was moving people out in a systematic way. That in itself spoke for how cleverly the mage had arranged it all.

"I've been posting the groups at the farthest edges of the territory we still hold, near enough to the permanent Gates there that they can still keep in touch with everyone here as if nothing had changed, but far enough so that if anything happens…" Urtho did not complete the sentence.

"If anything happens, we have advance groups already in place," Skan said quickly. "An evacuation will be much easier that way. Faster, too. And if the fighters know their families are already safe, their minds will be on defense and retreat, rather than on worrying."

"I don't want another Laisfaar," Urtho said, his head bent over the table so that his face was hidden. "I don't want another Stelvi Pass."

Skan had his own reasons to second that. The lost gryphons there sometimes visited him in dreams, haunting him...

...fly again, as Urtho wills...

"Who will you pick for your second, Skan?" Urtho asked after a long silence, briskly changing the subject. "I assume it's going to be one of the experienced fighters. And——" he cast a quick glance out of the corner of his eye at Skan, who caught a sly twinkle there "——I class Zhaneel as an experienced fighter."

Skan coughed. "Well, it will be Zhaneel, of course, but because she has the respect of the others. Even gryphons who haven't trained on her course know how hard it is, and admire her for all she's accomplished. But there's something else I'd like to ask you for as well."

Urtho turned away from the table. "Oh?" he said, imbuing the single syllable with a multitude of flavorings.

Once again, Skan's stomach and crop churned with anxiety, and his nares flushed. "I——ah——did a little exploring on that level of your Tower."

"And?" Urtho's face and voice were carefully neutral.

"I found the——the models."

"How did you...?" Urtho exclaimed, flushing for a moment with anger—but he quickly calmed. "Never mind. What——"

Skan interrupted. "I met Kechara."

Urtho stared at him blankly for a moment, then grew just a little pale. "I believe," he said carefully, "that I had better sit down. You must hate me."

Skan shook his head, as Urtho lowered himself into a chair, and if he was any judge of human reactions, the mage had been profoundly shaken. "How could I hate you? The more time I spent with her, the more I realized that you had done the best you could for her. And once I had a few days to think about it, I believe I managed to puzzle out why you had her up *there*, instead of down with the rest of the gryphons. It wasn't just to protect her from being teased and getting her feelings hurt." He took a deep breath, and ventured everything on his guess. "It was because she's a very powerful Mindspeaker. Probably the most powerful you've ever seen."

Urtho's eyes widened, and he caught his breath. "Did she Mindspeak at you?" he asked.

Skan nodded, pleased that he had been clever enough to figure out the puzzle. "I realized that I had been getting a great deal more information from her than she had the words to tell me. That was when I remembered that she had hit me with a mind-blast just before she attacked me, and I figured out that she wasn't just *telling* me things with her voice, but with her mind as well."

He told Urtho the tale from beginning to end, saving only that he had gotten into the chamber in the first place with Vikteren's mage-keys. "That's why she's in the Tower, in a room with such heavy shields, and why she creates the *presence* of a dozen gryphons when there's only her. And that's why Zhaneel and I would like to have her. *We'll* protect her from teasing and ridicule, and she can act as—oh—a kind of relay for groups of gryphons that may need to speak with each other. We have Mindspeakers, of course, but nothing as powerful as she is."

"I see that you put a great deal of thought into this." Urtho mopped his forehead with a sleeve, as small beads of perspiration sprang up. "I must confess—that use for her had occurred to me. I was too softhearted to... well... misborn usually die young anyway, and I assumed that her nature would take care of the problems she represented for me. When she didn't die, though, I had to do something about her. She's as old as you are, Skan. She only seems younger because she's so childlike, and because her memory for things longer ago than a year is very poor. I knew that if anyone ever discovered her and her power, she'd be a target for our enemies. In the wrong hands, she could be a terrible weapon. I was afraid that I would have to go to war just to protect her, and I couldn't reconcile the safety and freedom of one misborn with compromising the safety of all those who depend on me. You see? That was why I hid her in the Tower and kept her existence secret. I simply could not protect her otherwise, and I would not risk a war over her."

"Urtho, I hate to point this out, but we *are* in a war, and it isn't over Kechara," Skan retorted, with a little more sarcasm than he intended. "No one is going to get into this camp to steal her, and there isn't much point in keeping her mewed up anymore."

Skandranon sat down across from Urtho. He was rather surprised to learn that Kechara was as old as he was; as Urtho said, misborn generally did not live past their teens, much less grow to be as old as he. It was something of a tribute to Urtho's care that she had lived as long as she had.

Urtho sighed. "You're right," he said, reluctantly. "She deserves a little freedom, anyway. But keep her here—if not in the Tower, then near it."

"Of course." Skan nodded. "I should like to start moving the gryphon families out to where the other non-combatants are going, if you don't mind. All pairs with nestlings and fledglings, and all fledged still in training. I don't see any reason why they can't complete their training elsewhere." He thought for a moment. "I'll tell them that you are concerned that with all of us consolidated here, we make a very tempting target for some terrible weapon. You want to get us spread out, so we aren't quite so easy to get all at once."

Urtho considered that, and studied the map. "What about here and here—" He pointed to two valleys, easily defended, at the furthest range for a permanent Gate. "I can set two of the Gates for those places, and move not only gryphons, but Kaled'a'in and all the non-humans who are not combatants there. Anyone who wants to visit them, can."

"I have an even better idea," Skan suggested. "Set up a secondary Gate and put the gryphons out further—use the excuse that we are big eaters, and need the territory. Send the Kaled'a'in to this valley in the south, and convalescents and volunteers there to the north. That gets them out from underfoot, and they can train your human youngsters while they're recovering."

Urtho snapped his fingers. "Of course—and what's more, I'll have the ambulatory and the youngsters run foraging parties! Make them as self-sufficient as possible!"

"Have them send the surplus here," Skan added, with growing enthusiasm. "It won't be much, but it will make them feel as if we need to have them out there. And a little fresh game now and then…"

His mouth tingled at the very thought. *Herd-beasts have no real flavor. A good roebuck, though…*

"With hertasi in charge, Skan, I am not certain I would be too ready to say that they 'won't send back much.' Hertasi are remarkable scavengers." Urtho's eyebrows quirked a little. "That's largely why I have them in charge of supply here. They find ways to make ten loaves feed a hundred fighters."

But Skan noticed that Urtho was much more subdued than usual. *Perhaps there is something he hadn't told me? Are things even worse than I thought?*

A light tap at the door prevented him from asking any further questions. Urtho's chief hertasi stuck his snout inside, cautiously.

"The commanders are here, Urtho," the lizard said quietly. Urtho glanced over at Skan and shrugged.

"Let them in, Seri," he said. "They might as well hear it all at once."

The commanders filed in, General Judeth last of all, impeccable and austere in her chosen colors of black and silver. They gathered around the table, and Skan saw one or two turn a little pale when they looked over the latest conquests of Ma'ar's forces.

Didn't they know? Or does this mean something I can't guess at?

"Gentlemen, ladies." Urtho nodded to the group. "I brought you here for several reasons. The first—General Farle is dead. Assassinated, so far as we can tell."

A sharp intake of breath around the table told Skan that none of the commanders had heard the bad news yet.

"I am afraid that under the circumstances, I must dismantle the Sixth as it has been known, and spread its non-human and magical resources among all of you. General Judeth—" as Urtho spoke her name, the lady sat up straighter, and lost her look of shocked dismay "—at the specific request of the new commander of all the gryphon wings, I am assigning the wings that formerly belonged to the Sixth to you. I know that you will command them well."

The General did not salute nor snap to attention, but she gave the impression that she had. "I will do my best, sir," she replied simply.

"The rest of you may decide among yourselves how to apportion up the rest of the Sixth's available manpower. General Shaiknam will command the human foot-soldiers, but all else will be available to you." Urtho nodded, and Skan saw with satisfaction that the commanders were already getting over their shock and thinking about the situation. "I am certain that you will not allow any kind of rivalry to interfere with the best possible deployment of that manpower. Now—I am certain you all know Skandranon, the Black Gryphon, either on sight or by reputation."

Nods, and some slight smiles met that, as Skan bowed his head in a brief salute to all of them, but especially to General Judeth.

"I have appointed him to be the overall commander of the gryphon wings, in the same arrangement that I made with the mages." Urtho paused, and waited for their reaction.

Skan saw only slight frowns, and one or two nods. General Judeth was the first to speak.

She cleared her throat delicately, then spoke to both Urtho and to Skan. "The arrangement is working better with the mages than we had thought it would," she admitted. "We thought it might make for problems, if not outright mutiny among the mages, but it didn't work out that way." Her mouth twitched a little, although she did not actually smile. "There are even some mages who have shown a remarkable *increase* in their abilities. Apparently having someone to evaluate their performance who *knows* what they can do has made them a little more— eager—to do their best. I trust, both because Urtho has chosen you,

Skandranon, and from *some* of your reputation, that you will act in a similar manner."

Skan's nares flushed, for there was no doubt just what the General meant by "some of your reputation," but he answered her steadily enough.

"I can promise you that no gryphon will balk at anything he is asked to do without a reason for objecting," Skan replied gravely. "We all understand there is a war, and in war, there is the risk of death. We only ask that we not be sent into a *certainty* of death. I can also promise you that if there are objections to what we are asked to do, it will be because the loss will outweigh the gain for all concerned. The gryphons will defend all the races."

The General nodded at that, and turned her attention back to the table.

"I see that you are all concerned by the amount of territory that Ma'ar has taken," Urtho continued. "You should be; I have only just updated the map, and a great deal of that gain has been within the last month. You all knew you'd lost ground, but none of you has seen the real scope of the loss until now. We are in trouble, and I will not hide that fact from you. In fact, we have lost so much, that Ma'ar himself has moved into the Palace and made it his headquarters."

They took all that without a flinch, although Skan was incensed at the idea that Ma'ar would have taken the Palace for his own. The idea of that—that beast, that tyrant, soiling the halls that great leaders had called home, soiling them with his bloody boots...

"It would be rather difficult to hide that we are in trouble, with *this* spread out before us," General Movat said dryly. "The question is, what are your plans to deal with it?"

Urtho considered the map, as heavy silence reigned. "The first thing I intend to do is to begin a quiet evacuation of the non-combatants from around the Tower," he replied. "Some preliminary work has been done in that direction, but now I want it to become a priority. I want to move them into the west. I'm going to take six of the permanent Gates here on the Tower grounds and activate them, targeting them to six points on the western border. That's mostly wilderness area, mountains and forested valleys, too steep to farm and not really suited for grazing. My very first Tower was there—" he added wistfully "—and I rather liked keeping it wilderness.'

"Yes, well, now it's a good thing it *is* wilderness," General Korad said briskly. "Ma'ar won't consider that you might have sent people into it."

"My idea precisely." Urtho tapped the map, pointing to the six places where the Gates would have their other ends. "If we have to abandon the Tower, we'll have most of the people who would be trouble already out of the way. They, in turn, will have advance camps ready for us. If we inform our people that we are doing this only to spread out our resources and make one spot less of a target, I believe we can keep them from panicking."

The Generals contemplated the plan quietly for some time, each one studying the map and making mental calculations. Urtho watched their faces; Skan watched Urtho.

He looks satisfied; well, if they have simply accepted the plan, that must mean it's strategically sound. So that's how he does it! He puts out a plan, waits to see what they think of it, and changes it with their suggestions and objections! I wondered how a mage had become such a good strategist!

General Judeth broke the silence first. "I'd like to have one strong mage with each group," she said. "Adept-class. Perhaps this would be a good place to send those who are frail, or those who have moral objections to combative magics, and those who simply do not have skill at combative magics. This way, if further Gates need to be built, there will be someone at hand, rested, and prepared to build those Gates."

Urtho nodded. "My Kaled'a'in will be *here*—" He pointed. "They will have mages enough in their ranks to cover that point. If any of you can think of particular mages who would be suitable, please let me know—especially if they are familiar with this kind of terrain."

If they can deal with primitive conditions, he means. Some of his older mages— well, they ought to go with the Kaled'a'in. The Clans can make a home anywhere, if they have to, and the horse-nomads are already set up for wandering.

There was more discussion, and they put together a tacit agreement. Skan was impressed. He hadn't known that there were humans anywhere who could agree to so much with so few wasted words.

"But this is secondary," General Korad said at last. "The real question is—how in the name of all the gods are we going to defend the Tower?"

Urtho hesitated, then said humbly, "Are you certain that we should?"

A chorus of objections met that statement, but it seemed to Skan that most of them boiled down to—"Of course we should; it's *your* Tower."

Urtho waved them to silence. "There is a great deal in the Tower that can't be moved and shouldn't be allowed to fall into Ma'ar's hands. But things can be destroyed—the knowledge that made those things possible is as portable as the minds and the books that hold it. This place may be my home, and it is true that I have invested a great deal of my life in it, but that is no reason to remain here when the situation becomes untenable. Others have lost their homes; it would be arrogant of me to think mine was any more sacred than theirs. I would be as foolish as my critics have claimed if I clung to this Tower when every wise person would have fled."

He pondered the map. "If Ma'ar breaches our defences *here* and *here*, he can spread out his troops along this line. He has manpower far exceeding ours. If he does that, he can force us to try to counter him until we are spread so thin we can't defend ourselves. From here, on the plains, he has a clear run to the Tower itself. We cannot hold a line against him, unless we can suddenly multiply our own troops by a factor of ten."

The Generals studied the map with varying expressions of gloom.

"You're right," Korad said, with no emphasis. "Damn, but I hate to admit it. If he can get that far, he's got us."

"*If* we remain at the Tower," Urtho reminded them all. "If we retreat, we can pick our place to make a stand, or make no stand at all, simply keep retreating, making *him* string out his supply lines and his forces. Eventually, even Ma'ar must become sated with conquest! We can go west, then retreat to the farthest south, in the lands that the Haighlei Emperors hold."

"The Black Kings?" said Judeth. Skan knew that referred not to their predilections, but their skin, which was supposedly as dark as a moonless, starless sky. "Would they help us?"

Urtho shrugged. "I don't know. I *do* know they would shelter us against a conqueror and despot like Ma'ar, and their magic is so different from ours that I think even Ma'ar would hesitate before he attacked them. It's not wise to attack an unknown."

Judeth bit her lip, then nodded, slowly and grudgingly. "It's our best hope, *if* Ma'ar gets that far. I am going to see that he doesn't, if it takes every drop of blood in my body to stop him." She sounded and looked grim, and Skan shivered in a sudden chill, as ice threaded down his spine as if a cold wind had just ruffled his feathers.

"How are you going to explain—everything—to Shaiknam?" Korad wanted to know, after an uncomfortable silence.

Urtho shrugged. "I'll tell him that I've seen he is best with ground maneuvers, and I'm giving him the chance to concentrate on them without the distractions and annoyances of a mixed force. Then I'll show him what I've shown you, and we'll all meet tonight to plan the overall strategy to hold Ma'ar. Right now, I want you all to go to your people and get those who are not essential ready to evacuate. I'd like to start moving people out steadily from tomorrow."

That sounded like a dismissal to Skan, and so the other commanders took it. They saluted, and filed out, with only General Judeth pausing long enough to have a brief word with the Black Gryphon.

"As soon as you've seen to your new command, come see me with the old Sixth wingleaders," she said. "And—best of luck, Skandranon. I think Urtho's chosen wisely."

She turned smartly and left, leaving Skan to gape at her back as the door closed behind her. He turned to look at Urtho.

The mage smiled wearily. "I think I've chosen wisely, too, Skan," he said. "Now—go deal with your people, while I see to mine. We both have a great deal to do, and only the Kaled'a'in Lady knows if we will be given the time to get it all done."

Skan bowed, deeply and profoundly, but he hesitated at the door. Urtho had turned back to the map, staring at it blankly.

"Urtho—" Skan said. The mage started, turned to face him, and stared at him as if he had not expected his new commander to still be in the room.

"I want you to know something. We never really considered flying off and abandoning you. We not only are loyal to you—we love you. That is *why* we are loyal to you. Love is harder to earn than loyalty, and you are more than my friend. You are my beloved Father."

He turned quickly and left, and the door swung shut behind him— but for one moment, just before it closed completely, he thought he saw Urtho's eyes glittering, as if with tears.

Packing too many people in this mess-tent made it stiflingly hot. Amberdrake stood on a table and ran one hand through his damp hair, in a nervous gesture that had become habit over the past few days. Every kestra'chern in the camp had squeezed him- or herself into the mess-tent, and they all stared at him with varying levels of anxiety. Wild tales had spread all through the camp since word came from the Sixth that General Farle had been killed and Shaiknam assigned to his old command again. Most of those tales were variations on older rumors, but some were entirely new. All the stories that Amberdrake had heard had been told with varying degrees of hysteria.

He held up a hand, and got instant silence. Lamplight glittered in dozens of eyes, all fixed on him, all wide with fear or hope. "You've heard the rumors for weeks; now the rumors are coming true," he said abruptly. "We are evacuating all non-combatants from around the Tower." A murmur started, but he shook his head, and the murmurings died away. "Urtho gave me complete control of what to tell you. I am going to tell you the whole truth, because Urtho and I are counting on you to help keep people calm. Ma'ar is in a dangerous position for us. Urtho is *telling* people that he wants the non-combatants spread out so that we don't make such a tempting target with everything clustered here. The real reason is that if he has to evacuate, he doesn't want to have civilians at the Tower; to get in the way, or have the ones left worry about them."

He let them absorb that for a moment. "We will be one of the last groups out, because we are also useful as Healers. I'm going to interview each of you tonight and tomorrow, and you will decide which of the six evacuation sites you wish to go to. I will give you an assignment chit, and when the last of the civilians are gone, you will pack up your tents and go to your chosen sites. You will *still* be able to service your clients there; the Gates will be open for two-way traffic, and Urtho expects a certain amount of coming and going."

Someone down in front waved his hand. "What if Urtho decides to evacuate completely? What about people who are visiting over here?"

"Good question. Anyone who goes from his evacuation site to the Tower must be aware that at any moment Urtho could call for a retreat. At that point, a non-combatant will have to fend for himself, and count himself lucky if he gets to *any* Gate, much less the one to his own site." Amberdrake shrugged helplessly. "You would be much better off for your clients to come to you, rather than vice versa. We are going to try to discourage traffic from the sites *to* the Tower. For instance, there is going to be a curfew in force once the civilians are theoretically gone—and meals on the Tower side will be strictly rationed to those supposed to be there; no visitors allowed."

He let them absorb that for a moment. Another hand appeared. "Is it really looking that bad?" asked a young woman with frightened eyes.

He hesitated a moment. "I can't tell you everything," he said, finally. "But Urtho is seriously worried, and he has already undertaken the enormous task of stripping the Tower of as much as possible and sending it to safer places."

Another murmur arose, but it died on its own. Finally Lily rose to her feet, and lifted her head defiantly. "There *has* to be something else we can do!" she said. "You know very well that most of our clients are going to postpone visits until the civilian evacuation is over—so there must be something practical we can do to help!"

Amberdrake relaxed, marginally, as a chorus of agreement met her brave words. "Thank you, Lily," he said softly. "I was hoping someone would bring that up. Yes. There is a *great* deal that we can do to help, both on this side of the Gates, and the other." He sat down slowly on the table-top. "The very first job is to help with the children…"

Gesten looked out beyond the campfire, counted noses, and came up with a satisfactory total. Every hertasi tribe had sent at least one representative, and most had sent several. Why *he* should have been chosen to be the leader of the whole lot, he had no notion, but Urtho said he was, and that was the end of it.

"Right," he said, and dozens of eyes blinked at him. "You know the story. Non-fighters are pulling out, and we're non-fighters. The only hertasi who are supposed to stay here after the civilians leave are the ones serving the Healers and the gryphons. Everyone else goes. Once you've gotten your own kit out, come back and start helping the families. The kestra'chern are minding the children, so you'll be doing what we do best—you'll be helping to pack up the households and get 'em moving. Once *that's* done, you go report to the Tower. If they need you, they'll tell you. If they don't, you get back over to your assigned place and *stay* there. Got it?"

"What if you're doing split duty—with a Healer and a civilian, say?" someone called from the back.

Gesten's briefing hadn't covered that, but Urtho had told him that he could and should use his own judgment when it came to things that hadn't been covered. "Depends on how close to the fighting you think you can stand to be," he said, finally. "If you're feeling brave, stay here, go full-time with the Healer. If you're not, stay on the evacuation site and help with whatever needs doing. There's going to be a *lot* that needs doing." He tilted his head to one side and narrowed his eyes as he recited the list Urtho had given him. "We'll need winter-proof housing built for everyone, and that includes the fighters, in case they have to come over. We'll need food supplies located. We'll need wells dug, sanitary and washing facilities set up. A lot of the families are going to consist of mothers with children; they'll all need that extra hand to help. We'll need facilities for the sick and injured, and overland-vehicles in case we have to retreat from there."

"Will there be mages to help us with all this?" asked an anxious voice. "And Healers? There's pregnant females with those civilians, and I don't know a *thing* about birthing babies, especially not human babies!"

"We'll have a lot of mages, all of the Apprentices, most of the Journeymen, and at least one Adept at each site," Gesten promised. "The Healers are sending some of their Apprentices, a couple of Masters, and as soon as all the civilians are over, the kestra'chern will be joining them. There's plenty of Healers with them, and they all have some Healer training."

Gesten sensed an easing of tension at that. Hertasi considered the kestra'chern the most level-headed of the humans, and the ones most likely to react properly in a crisis. "Right," he said again. "We can do this."

"We can do this," they echoed.

It was, after all, the hertasi motto.

Amberdrake rubbed his blurring, burning eyes until they cleared, then turned his attention back to the list he was compiling. *Protea to tend a crèche of tervardi little ones; that will work. Loren with the Healers, putting together packs of supplies for the evacuees. Renton, Lily, Marlina, Rilei—*

"Amberdrake? Have I come at a bad time?"

He looked up, squinting across the barrier formed by the light from his lantern, and made out the face of Lionwind, the Clan Chief of his own Kaled'a'in clan of k'Leshya. "What are you doing still awake?" he asked, out of sheer surprise to see the perpetual dawn-greeter up and active long past the hour of midnight.

Lionwind stepped further into the tent, his heavy braids swinging with each soft, silent step. "We had a Clan meeting," he said. "And we'd rather not go off with the rest of the Kaled'a'in, if it's all right with Urtho."

But Amberdrake shook his head. "You can't stay," he said flatly. "Urtho can't make any exceptions."

Lionwind half-smiled, and folded himself gracefully onto a stool on the other side of the desk. "We didn't want to stay, we just want to be where the gryphons are," he told Amberdrake. "We've supplied most of the Kaled'a'in Trondi'irn for the gryphons, we've worked with Urtho on his breeding program—and we *like* them. They'll need someone besides hertasi with them, after all. Hertasi are all very well, but they don't like to hunt, they can't lift what a human can, and they're a little short on imagination."

Amberdrake listened to this calm assessment with growing relief. He'd wondered how the gryphons were going to manage, for Urtho's plan called for a second Gate to be built from the Kaled'a'in evacuation site, and the gryphon families to be sent further out from there. The gryphons were huge eaters, and it was doubtful that they would be able to stay anywhere that there was a large concentration of any other species. All of the Kaled'a'in Clans, for instance. But if k'Leshya was basically volunteering to be sent off beyond the rest, that would solve the problem neatly.

"Are you certain you want to do this?" he asked.

Lionwind shrugged. "I'm not certain we *want* to do anything at the moment," he replied. "We don't want to run, but we don't want to stay here to be slaughtered either. We'd like it best if Urtho could suddenly produce a magic weapon that would eliminate Ma'ar and all his troops without harming anyone or anything else, but short of the Goddess working a miracle, that isn't going to happen. So this is our best choice, and if Urtho will allow it, we'll take it."

"I'm certain he'll allow it," Amberdrake said, and rubbed his eyes again as Lionwind's face blurred and went out of focus. "I'll take care of it."

Lionwind rose, and leaned over the table. Amberdrake rubbed his eyes again, but they wouldn't stop blurring.

"Is there anything else I can do?" he asked, blinking rapidly. That didn't help either.

"Only—get some rest," Lionwind answered, leaning closer. "That's your Clan Chiefs order."

"I can't, there's too much to do," he objected—as Lionwind reached across and touched his forehead. And only then did he remember, belatedly, that Lionwind was also a Mindhealer, fully capable of imposing his will on the most recalcitrant.

"'The best attack is the one no one sees coming,' kestra'chern," Lionwind quoted, and chuckled, as sleep snatched him up in surprisingly gentle talons and carried him away…

The six permanent Gates were enormous, quite large enough to accommodate the biggest of the floating land-barges. Urtho had constructed them using fused-stone arches, and tied each of them into its own node to power it. Only Urtho had ever accomplished the construction of a Gate that did not require the internal knowledge and resources of a single mage to target and power a Gate. Only Urtho had uncovered the secret of keeping such a Gate stable. Of all of his secrets, that was probably the one that Ma'ar wanted the most.

He had, for the first time in many years, left the Tower briefly to journey through one of his own creations and set up a second permanent Gate at that evacuation point. This one he targeted deep in the western wilderness, to a lovely valley he himself had once called home. The gryphon families, all those gryphons that were not fighters, and those who were injured, had all been sent there. Now the Kaled'a'in Clan k'Leshya—of all the Clans, the only one not named for a totemic animal, but called simply "the Spirit Clan"—slowly filed through the first Gate to follow them.

He could not have said truthfully that he had a "favorite" Clan, but of all of them, k'Leshya held the greatest number of his favorite Kaled'a'in. Lionwind, the Clan Chief, was one of the wisest men he knew, with a wisdom that did not fit with the smooth, youthful face and the night-black hair that hung in two thick braids on either side of his face. Lionwind's father and mother had both been shaman; perhaps that explained it. Or perhaps, as Lionwind himself had once claimed, only half in jest, he was an "old soul." The Clan Chief—not then the Chief, but nearly as wise—had been of great comfort to Amberdrake when the young kestra'chern first joined his ancestral Clan. He continued to be of comfort, on the rare occasions that Amberdrake would permit anyone to help him.

Lionwind had been first through the Gate, riding his tall, rangy warmare. He had not looked in any direction but forward, although he surely knew he would never see the Tower again, and likely would not see many of those he left behind. He had made his farewells, as had all the Kaled'a'in, and it was not the Kaled'a'in way to linger over such things.

"Long farewells give time for the enemy to aim." That was what Lionwind said to Urtho as he clasped his hand, and the words were sure to become a Kaled'a'in proverb. Although there was no enemy here, k'Leshya followed that precept now.

Urtho watched them go, hiding his pain beneath a calm smile. He did not know if he would ever see any of them again. All he could be certain of was that he had sent them into a safer place than this one. And now that the gryphons were in full control of their own destinies, he could at least be certain that no matter what Ma'ar undid of his, there would always be gryphons in the world. If Ma'ar conquered the Tower, they would scatter, using their mobility to take them beyond his reach.

So something of mine will survive, in spite of everything that Ma'ar can do.

Odd that it should be the gryphons, creatures that his contemporaries had considered eccentric toys. He had always had faith in them, though. Of everything he had created, they were his favorites. He had given them the ability to do great good; it only remained to see if they would fulfill that promise as well as they had fulfilled all the rest.

The last k'Leshya herdsman, driving the last of the Clan herds under a great cloud of dust, passed through the Gate. The Gate "sensed" that there was no one else waiting to cross it, and the view of the crowd of Kaled'a'in at the terminus faded, as the Gate shut itself down to conserve power. The space inside the arch went to black—then showed only what was on the other side of the physical arch.

Only then did Urtho realize that he was not alone.

Amberdrake stood behind and to one side of him, staring at the now-blank Gate. The kestra'chern was not wearing any of his elaborate robes or costumes, only a pair of breeches and a sleeved tunic in a soft, faded blue. His hair had been tied up into a tail at the nape of his neck, and he wore a headband of blue that matched his tunic.

Urtho regarded him with a touch of surprise. He had *thought* that it was understood that Amberdrake would go with his own Clan. The rest of the kestra'chern all had their assignments in the evacuation, and as soon as they had completed those tasks, they would head for their own evacuation sites. He was not needed as their leader anymore, and it was unlikely that anyone would have leisure in the coming days and weeks for the ministrations of a kestra'chern, however expert.

Amberdrake seemed to divine Urtho's thoughts from his expression. He raised one elegant eyebrow in a gesture so graceful it could only have been unconscious. "You're wondering why I'm still here," he said.

Urtho nodded.

"Winterhart is still here—she's the Trondi'irn of the fighting gryphon wings of the Fifth, and I am not going to leave her alone in a camp that still holds her former lover." There was a note of steel in his voice that was new to Urtho—or perhaps it had been there all along, and Amberdrake had simply hidden it better. "Skan is still here, and Zhaneel, and Gesten to serve the two of them. They are all the family I have."

Urtho allowed a bit of steel to creep into his own voice. "I said, 'no exceptions,' and you are not excused from that. You heard it clearly enough, Kestra'chern Amberdrake. You do not belong here."

"I am a Healer, Urtho. You can verify that with Lady Cinnabar

THE BLACK GRYPHON

if you wish; I volunteered for her group." Pain and fear shadowed
Amberdrake's eyes for a moment, and Urtho knew why and marveled at
his bravery. He knew all about Amberdrake's past; he knew how much it
would cost Amberdrake to work with the Healers, every waking hour—
how vulnerable he was to losing control of his Empathic abilities—how
he feared that pain, physical and mental, more than anything else.

Yet here he was, facing his worst fear, in order to remain with his odd
and tenuous "family." Urtho bowed his head a little in acknowledgement
of courage.

"I stand corrected, Healer Amberdrake. You have every right to be
here." The lines at the corners of Amberdrake's eyes softened a bit, and
Urtho decided that he would ease another of Amberdrake's worries.
"There is a single mage still working with Shaiknam and the Sixth, at his
own request. I approved his petition for field duty myself. I am told his
name is Conn Levas." He let his own eyebrow rise, just a little. "I believe
the Sixth is currently away on assignment."

Urtho turned then, not waiting for thanks. Already he had turned his
mind to the next task.

And so, probably, had Amberdrake.

Long farewells give the enemy time to aim. And they did not dare give the
enemy time for anything.

CHAPTER SEVENTEEN

Aubri's wings ached from shoulder to tip; they burned with exhaustion
on the downstroke of each wingbeat. The heavy, damp air in this
particular valley always meant difficult flying, but that was not why he
was tired. He had been flying scout for the Fifth since dawn, and it only
lacked a few hours until sunset. He had flown a double-shift already, and
by the time he finished, long after dark, it would be a triple.

At least all the innocents were far beyond the reach of any disaster
now. The last of the non-combatants, including the kestra'chern, had
passed through the Gates to their new locations several days ago. And as
Urtho had expected, there was steady traffic between the Tower and the
evacuation points, but not in the opposite direction. The word that any
non-combatant caught on the Tower side in an emergency would have
to fend for himself kept the evacuees in their new homes. Aubri missed
seeing the youngsters, missed the sound of fledglings playing—but he

would rather miss these things than have them at the Tower lairs, and at risk. One slaughtered youngster was one too many—and he had seen the pathetic corpses of considerably more than one in the time he had been fighting for Urtho.

His chest-muscles complained, growing tight and stiff from built-up fatigue poisons, and he knew that by the time he landed, he'd be one sore gryphon. At least on this second shift, he *wasn't* fighting makaar. This was all simple coordination-scouting, making sure that the Sixth and the First were where they were supposed to be, so that the mages with the Fifth didn't hit their own troops with friendly fire.

Huh. "Friendly fire, isn't." That's what the Kaled'a'in say, anyway. Ma'ar's generals hadn't pressed an attack on this point all day, holding a purely defensive line, and Shaiknam hadn't made any offensive moves, a reflection of the inertia here for the past two or three days. Both forces glared at each other from the opposite sides of a wide, shallow ravine, but the only attacking going on was from little presents the mages dropped—which were easily deflected by their opposite numbers.

The situation was a stalemate, at least here.

No—wait. He caught a hint of movement through the heavy haze. *Something's going on down there!*

Aubri circled higher, to get a better perspective on the situation. So far as *he* had been told, Shaiknam wasn't supposed to order any kind of attack unless an opportunity too ripe to ignore arose, and Aubri hadn't seen any evidence of that. Was this just false-movement? A little shuffling in place to make the enemy think that Shaiknam was about to press an attack?

He pumped harder, gaining more height, and looked down half a minute later.

At first he couldn't make out anything at all. Then the haze parted a little, giving him a clearer view of Shaiknam's troops. His wing-strokes faltered with shock, and he side-slipped a little before catching and steadying himself in the air. *Demonsblood! What does he…? Why…? He can't be that stupid! Can he?*

Shaiknam's troops had parted right down the middle, and were pulling back, leaving the easiest place to cross the ravine wide open.

This would have been a classic move, giving the enemy a place to penetrate and then closing companies in on either side of him while the troops to the rear cut his forces off from the rest. The only problem was that there *were* no other companies in place, and no time to get any in place. Shaiknam had not been positioned directly protecting one of the two vital passes, but from here Ma'ar's forces could easily *get* to one of those vital passes.

He's bluffing. Ma'ar's commanders won't believe this, and he knows it. He's just giving them something to occupy them...

He couldn't hover; the best he could do was to glide in a tight circle, panting with weariness and disbelief. Even as Aubri watched, the two groups that had pulled back moved on in a clear retreat, and Ma'ar's army marched across the ravine and into Urtho's territory with all the calm precision of a close-order drill.

What in the hell is going on here?

Now he wished he was one of those gryphons with any kind of Mindspeech; if *only* he could tell someone what was happening! By the time he lumbered through the sky to a message-relay, it would be too late to stop the advance.

Damn, it's already too late... If I can't stop it, maybe I'd better find out who ordered this. That's what Skan would do. Has Shaiknam lost what little mind he used to have? Or have his troops somehow been sent false orders?

Aubri dropped through the haze, well behind the line of advancement, and landed just outside of Shaiknam's all-but-deserted command post. He got out of sight, just in case someone from the other side was watching, under cover of a grove of trees right behind the command tent. *Predictable,* he thought savagely. *Trust Shaiknam; ignore the fact that someone can sneak up to your tent in favor of the fact that you get to sit in the shade all day. I hope there's red ants in those trees biting on his fat behind.* He'd wondered why there seemed to be so little activity going on around the command tent, but he'd figured it was simply because there was *no* activity along this section of the front lines. *Now I know, maybe. Either Shaiknam's been assassinated or replaced or—*

—or something worse has been going on.

He tried to emulate Skan, blessing Zhaneel for all those hours on the obstacle-course, as he slithered on his belly through the underbrush. The lessons were second-nature; shove the branches aside with your beak, close your eyes and let them slide over your neck, your tight-folded wings. Creep forward with fore-feet until you were as stretched-out you could get, then inch the hind-feet up until your back hunched, and start over again. Vary the intervals and your steps. Make no patterns.

And why the hell aren't there guards around the tent, after what happened to Farle? Because Shaiknam isn't there? Or because he knows he doesn't need guards? Or because he has no guards left?

He had concentrated so hard on his stealthy approach that he didn't keep track of how far he'd come. The buff canvas of the tent suddenly loomed up in a wall from out of the underbrush a few talon-lengths in front of his beak, just as he heard voices coming from inside.

Well, there's someone in there, anyway.

He closed his eyes and listened. Whoever was in there murmured, rather than speaking in normal conversational tones, as if they wanted to be certain they weren't overheard from outside.

"...going very well, my lord," whispered an unctuous voice. "And Ma'ar is keeping his side of the bargain. By the time Judeth of the Fifth realizes what has happened, Ma'ar's troops will have the pass."

"Well, good." That was Shaiknam, all right; Aubri had heard his whining tones often enough to be certain of that. "Once he has the pass, we can close behind him, and no one will know we let him through. His mages can set up Gates to pour troops down onto the plains, and I can 'surrender' with no one the wiser. My command and holdings will remain intact. And without you, Levas, I would not have been able to contact Ma'ar's commander and bring all this to pass."

Levas? Conn Levas? Wasn't that the mage Winterhart used to—

"Thank you, my lord." The unctuous voice was back. "I always make certain to be on the winning side, and I was pleased to find you are a commander as pragmatic as I."

Shaiknam laughed. "I have another task for you, if you think you're up to it. Urtho may yet be able to pull off a miracle; he has a disconcerting habit of doing so. But without Urtho..."

There was a certain archness to the mage's reply that held Aubri frozen. "I am a mercenary, my lord; you knew that when we made our bargain. There will be an additional price for additional services."

Shaiknam laughed, very softly. "Name it," he said, as arrogantly as if he had all the resources of all the world to call upon. "Whatever coin you choose."

"Twenty-four thousand silver, and the coin of bodies, my lord." The mage's voice, already cold, grew icy. "Two bodies, to be precise, and both still alive and in a condition to be amusing to me. The Trondi'irn Winterhart, and the kestra'chern Amberdrake."

"Done and done." Shaiknam replied instantly. "Neither are combatants; they should be easy to subdue. Cheap at the price. You could have sold your services more dearly, mercenary."

"Their value is peculiar to me..."

Aubri could bear it no longer.

I have to stop them! Now!

He lunged at the tent wall, slashing it open with his sharp talons, beak agape to bite the spines of one or both of them in half—

And tumbled ignominiously to the ground, unable to move even his eyes. He landed with bone-bruising impact right at the feet of General Shaiknam, skidding a little on the canvas of the tent floor.

If he could have struggled, he would have, but there wasn't a muscle of his body that would obey him. His heart continued to beat, and his lungs to breathe, but that was all the movement he was allowed.

He'd been the recipient of a spell of paralysis, of course. *Idiot! Conn Levas is a* mage! *How could you have been so incredibly stupid?*

General Shaiknam looked down at him with mild interest in his catlike eyes, then searched his pockets for a moment. Then he turned to Conn Levas, and flipped him a coin. The mage caught it deftly, and pocketed it. Shaiknam's serene, round face produced a smile that went no further than his lips. "Payment for additional services," he said, his voice ripe with satisfaction.

"Indeed, my lord," Conn Levas replied. "As I expect payment on completion of your other task."

Shaiknam shrugged, and his eyes reflected his boredom. "They have no interest for me. I will see that they are captured unharmed. It should not be terribly difficult."

"What of—*this*—my lord?" A new voice, but another one that Aubri recognized. *Garber...*

Shaiknam's second-in-command spoke from out of Aubri's line-of-sight, but there was no doubt of where he was. A toe prodded him in the ribs, waking pain in his chest muscles.

"I can dispose of him if you like," Conn Levas began, but Shaiknam held up a hand to forestall him.

"No," he said. "There is a use for him. Ma'ar is rather fond of gryphons. I believe we should send him this one, as a gift, in earnest of many more to come." He waved at the unseen Garber. "Package this up for me, would you, and deliver it to General Polden with my compliments to the Emperor."

"So the Emperor enjoys the antics of these creatures?" Conn said with interest.

"He does," Shaiknam replied. He smiled down at Aubri; the gryphon gasped, as the ice of horror and the chill of pure fear swept over him. "I hope you can learn some new tricks, beast," he said sweetly. "Other than 'playing dead.' 'Dance,' for instance, or better yet, 'beg.' Make certain to learn 'beg.' The longer you entertain the Emperor, the longer you will live. Or so I'm told."

Urtho flung a plate across the room; it shattered against the wall, but did nothing to help relieve his feelings. "*Gods!*" he cried. The cadre of hertasi and human messengers ignored him. There were no message-birds in camp anymore; Urtho had not wanted to leave these smallest and most helpless of his creatures behind even by accident. They had been the first through the Gate, to go with k'Leshya and the gryphons.

Urtho paced the side of the map-table, issuing orders as fast as hertasi and humans could take them, doing his best *not* to seize handfuls of hair and start yanking them out by the roots. What in the name of all the gods had happened? *How* had Ma'ar's men gotten past the defensive line? Why hadn't anyone noticed until they'd already taken the Pass of Korbast and had set up a Gate to bring more troops in?

Never mind, it's happened, now deal with it! This was his worst nightmare come true: the Tower still full of things he hadn't gotten out yet, the traps not yet set, and the enemy pouring down into the plains, behind his own lines. Already the Sixth and the Third had been cut off from the rest and from retreat; they would have to fend for themselves. Judeth was bringing the Fifth in, but no one knew for certain about the rest. *They have mages, they can Gate here. They can even Gate straight to their evacuation-sites. They'll be all right. I have to believe that.*

He sent the last of his messengers off on their errands, with orders to send the Healers and other support personnel to their Gates, and forced himself to stop pacing. He clutched the edge of the table and stared down at it, as if staring at it fiercely enough would make the situation reverse itself.

"Sir!" A hertasi scrambled in the door, all out of breath. "The mage Conn Levas is here from the Sixth!"

He started, and turned towards the door, just as Conn Levas pushed his way past the lizard. He looked as if he had personally fought his way through all of Ma'ar's troopers to reach the Tower; his robes were filthy, torn, and bloodstained, his hair matted down to his head with sweat.

"Go—" Urtho told the breathless hertasi. "Find me Skan and bring him here. I'll need him in a moment."

The hertasi let the door swing shut behind Conn Levas, as Urtho took three steps towards the mercenary mage. "What *happened?*" he cried, eager only to hear what had gone wrong.

Too late, he saw Conn's hand move, saw an empty bag in it, and felt the stinging of a hundred thousand tiny needles in his face and hands, in every bit of flesh left exposed by his clothing. He brushed at his face frantically, as Conn Levas laughed.

"That won't help," the mercenary said, very softly, as Urtho tried to cry out for help and realized that he couldn't do more than whisper. "*Miranda*-thorns, Urtho. Very potent. *Quite* impossible to magic away. A little invention of my new employer; I believe you might have seen their effects, once or twice. Mages never do consider that someone might attack them physically."

Urtho's knees crumpled beneath him; he managed to stagger back enough that he landed in the chair behind him before his legs gave out altogether. His entire body tingled, burned, twitched uncontrollably. His lips moved, but nothing emerged. Strange swirls of light and color invaded his vision; the furniture stretched and warped. Conn's head floated about a foot above his body as the mercenary mage approached, and the head looked down at him malevolently.

"It's a poison, of course," the head said, each word emerging from his mouth in flowing script and encapsulated inside a brightly colored bubble. "You should enjoy the effects. I knew that all the defenses of the Tower are keyed to you, of course, as well as the Node beneath it, and I knew that if I slew you outright, I would die before I had the chance to escape. I expect Shaiknam knew that, too, and was counting on not needing to fulfill his part of the bargain. But you'll live long enough for me to get clear, and he'll just have to keep his word, hmm?"

Urtho's chest nearly burst with the need to howl in anguish, but all that he could manage was a pathetic whimper. Conn Levas' head floated around the room for a moment, then suddenly produced a new body as the old one faded away. A large, furry body, of an eye-searing pink. Urtho shuddered as the fur turned into spines, like those of a hedgehog. Then Conn shook his body, and all those spines shot forward, piercing Urtho's limbs with excruciating pain. The furniture grew tentacles, and the walls opened up into pulsing star-scapes.

"I see you can't answer," the mercenary said silkily. "No matter."

He turned to go—that is, his head turned. His body remained the way it had been, and began walking backwards towards the door. With every step he took, bleeding wounds appeared in the floor, and it felt to Urtho as if the wounds were to *his* flesh. He whimpered again, and Conn's head turned back.

"Oh, one more thing," the mage said casually. "In case you might have worried about that little misborn gryphon you named so charmingly. Kechara. I offered her a nice bit of rabbit and she followed me out to the Emperor's new lines. I decided to make certain that Shaiknam would keep his word, by ensuring that the Emperor knows my name, and what he owes to me. She's my gift to Ma'ar to pave the way for my new rank and position. I expect to be a Duke at the very least."

Kechara! Oh GODS! His anguish translated into more whimpers, and streams of blood began to flow from his open hands. Conn laughed, and turned to open the door, which warped and deformed as he touched it, becoming a blood-clot lodged in an open wound. The walls throbbed in time with Conn's laughter.

But the door opened before Conn, and there was someone out there—

Skan hurried after the frantic hertasi, talons clicking on the stone of the floor. "Aubri missing, the Sixth gone silent, why did you *leave* that lying bastard alone with Urtho?" Vikteren scolded the little lizard, as they ran towards the Strategy Room.

"He told me to get you!" the hertasi wailed, caught in a dilemma between what he had been ordered to do and what Vikteren thought he should have done. "I couldn't get you and stay there at the same time!"

"Leave it, Vikteren," Skan snapped. "It's done—let's just hope that…"

The young mage sprinted for the door and shoved it open in the surprised face of Conn Levas. The mercenary mage recovered quickly from his surprise, and backed up a pace when Skan loomed up behind Vikteren.

From his greater height, Skan could see right past Conn, and spotted Urtho, clearly in terrible pain, collapsed into a chair in the corner. Conn followed his glance, paled, and began babbling.

"Urtho—" he said. "He said he wasn't feeling well. The strain…"

But Skan's hearing was better than a human's, and the word Urtho was forcing through spittle-frothed lips was "*poison*—"

Skan's vision clouded with the red of rage; he saw Conn's hands move, and didn't hesitate. The Black Gryphon lashed out with an open talon, and caught the mage across the throat, tearing it out in a spray of blood. His second blow, the backhanded return of the talon-strike, flung the mercenary's body across the room to slam against the table with the wet crack of a snapping spine.

There the body of Conn Levas lay atop the tiny space of land that was still theirs, blood pumping down onto the map, flooding the representation of the Tower and the plains around it with sticky scarlet.

Vikteren had headed straight for Urtho, as Skan stalked in through the doorway with every feather and hair erect in battle-anger. "Poison," the young mage said shortly, his face flushed and his voice tight with grief. "*Miranda*-thorns, very rare, no antidote. The bastard probably had enough in his pockets to hit us both too; that's what he was reaching for when you got him."

The hertasi gasped, and scrambled off, presumably to fetch help.

Skan only heard and heeded one thing. "*No antidote?*" he roared, so that Urtho whimpered and Vikteren winced. "What do you mean, *no antidote?*"

"Skan, I *can't change the facts,*" Vikteren shouted back. "There's no antidote! It's something Ma'ar created as an assassination-tool, and we haven't seen more than three victims since the war started! All we can do is buy him some time, and counteract some of the effects."

"Do it," Skan snapped, and spread out his bloodstained claws over the body of his creator and friend, invoking every tiny bit of magery he had. He opened himself to Urtho, found the places in his mind that the *Miranda* had muddled, bringing hallucinations and pain, and joined with Vikteren to help Urtho straighten the mental paths and banish those symptoms.

He fought with every bit of his grief and rage, every atom of energy. And still it was not enough. He saw for himself that Vikteren was right. The poison replicated itself within Urtho's body, spreading like some evil, sentient disease, and with every passing moment it destroyed a little more of Urtho's life-force, corroding it away inexorably.

At last, his mage-energies exhausted, he dropped his outstretched claws and opened the eyes he did not realize he had closed.

Vikteren supported Urtho in his chair, and the face that looked up at Skan was sane again. "The evacuation—" Urtho whispered harshly. "Get me—Healers. I have to hold on..."

Vikteren looked up into Skan's puzzled face. "I think he's keyed some kind of destructive spells into himself—if he leaves the Tower, the place is going to go unstable. And if you thought what happened with that Gate at Jerlag Pass was impressive..."

The young mage left the rest unsaid. *Leaves the Tower, or dies, he means. And there must be two dozen permanent Gates here, not to mention the Tower itself and everything still in it.* The destructive potential staggered him. Anyone still here would be obliterated by the result, pulverized to dust…

The noise of running feet from the hallway made him turn sharply, ready to attack again; but these were friends. The hertasi had returned with Tamsin and three more senior Healers, who squeezed through the door as one. *Not Cinnabar. He must have sent her through the Gate while he could…*

"We know," Tamsin said shortly, and took Vikteren's place at Urtho's side. "We'll buy him all the time we can."

Skan did not move out of the way. The Healers shoved past him, ignoring him as if he had been an inconveniently placed piece of furniture.

He started to say something, but Vikteren motioned to him to remain silent. Tears trickled down the mage's face, and his shoulders shook, but he didn't produce so much as a stifled sob to distract the Healers from their work.

Skan himself shook from beak to talons with the effort of repressing a keen of grief. He closed his eyes and clamped his beak shut, flexing his talons into the wood of the floor, feeling it splinter beneath them, and wishing he could kill Conn Levas a hundred more times.

Someone tapped him on the shoulder, startling him, making him jump. His eyes snapped open, and focused on Tamsin's face, not more than a finger away from his beak.

"We've done all anyone can," the Healer said, in a voice gone flat and dull with sorrow and exhaustion. "He needs to tell you something."

The four Healers staggered out the door, holding each other in pairs and not once looking back. Vikteren still stood beside Urtho's chair, tears falling steadily down his cheeks and dropping onto the breast of his tunic.

"Get all the gryphons you can find," one of the Healers told the hertasi who waited, trembling, beside the door. "He's going to try to get everything open that he can before the end, and he wants them to take all they can carry."

The hertasi looked up at the Healer for a moment, too grief-stricken to reply. The man spoke again. "Knowledge will always be the best weapon against tyrants," he choked out. "*Urtho* said that." And at that the hertasi ran to carry out its orders.

"Skan—there's a weapon." Urtho's voice was the merest whisper, but his words were clear enough. "Never meant to use it, but—now, Ma'ar is coming. Help me—weapons room."

Vikteren helped him to his feet, and got under one shoulder, while Skan supported him on the other side. They both knew where the weapons room was, and that it was locked, to be unsealed by Urtho's presence alone. They carried him across the Strategy Room and to the door across the hallway; Urtho had no more strength than a newborn kitten. He fell against the door to the weapons room to open it, and directed them both to a box on a stand in the far corner of the room.

"It's—like the box I gave Zhaneel. But bigger. Got one on the Tower roof. Dissolves the bonds—of spells. Take it to Ma'ar when you can, trigger it. Same thing that happened at Jerlag." Urtho did not look at Skan; the gryphon had the feeling that perhaps he couldn't bear to. "Made it for gryphons. Stick your talons—in the holes. All at once."

Skan saw then that what he had taken for decorative perforations in the side were actually holes made to fit a gryphon's talons, in a pattern of two on each side to fit the two-forward, two back-curved talons of the foreclaws.

"You have—a count of a hundred—to get away," Urtho finished. "Better have—a Gate handy. And closed fast."

The Mage of Silence tried to smile, and coughed instead. "*Go!*" he whispered fiercely, when the coughing fit was over. "Go. Get Ma'ar later. Survive now."

Skan lifted the box from its stand, and saw that it had a carry-strap meant to go around the neck. He pulled the strap over his head, awkwardly, and turned back to the mage.

Urtho's eyes were clouded with pain, and his lips formed the word, "Go."

Beak clamped down on the death-keen, Skan backed out of the room. But before he left, he saw Vikteren helping Urtho to the next door to be unlocked.

And the first of the combat-gryphons arrived, to carry away what he could.

Knowledge will always be the best weapon against tyrants. Unable to hold it back any longer, Skan fled down the hallway and into the sunset, his death-keen echoing through the Tower as he ran.

Winterhart flung books and packages through the Gate whenever there wasn't someone actually traversing it, from the pile that formed as the gryphons brought them to her, her arms and back one long pulled muscle. There would be some time after Urtho succumbed before everything went dangerously unstable. They *should* all have time to get out.

All but Urtho…

Her eyes stung with tears, but she would mourn him later, when they were all, temporarily at least, safe.

Somewhere on the other side of this Gate was another Trondi'irn, pitching packages through the Gate to k'Leshya. The further away this dangerous knowledge went, the better off they would all be. She did not bother to think about how they would continue this war, or even if they would be able to regroup. The important thing now was simply to escape, to live, and to worry about the rest later.

Other gryphons, too exhausted to be of any use, staggered up to and through the Gate while she paused in her labor. Humans and hertasi, tervardi and kyree and dyheli also presented themselves for passage, burdened with everything they could carry. There were fewer of them now than there had been; as combatants staggered in from the field, they grabbed what they could and headed for their evacuation-Gates, and by now virtually everyone who *could* make it back, had.

That left only the few faithful, like her and Amberdrake, who would stay until the bitter end to help save as much as they could from the wreckage.

She *still* did not know why Urtho was reportedly dying, although she trusted the news. It could not have been something simple like heart-failure, or the Healers would be able to save him. Had Ma'ar somehow penetrated their defenses with a mage-attack?

Another pair of exhausted gryphons and a pack of mud-stained kyree staggered up to the Gate, and she stopped long enough to let them pass. But before she could pick up another package from the pile, someone else appeared, a human this time. But he headed for her, and not the Gate, and it took her a moment to recognize Amberdrake.

His face was absolutely blank with shock, and he was as pale as snow. She leapt for him as he stumbled and started to fall, catching him and holding him upright.

"What—" she began.

"I just saw Skan," he replied dully. "I just said goodbye to him."

Something in the way he phrased that made her freeze. Goodbye? As in—permanently?

"We have to get Zhaneel out of here, now, to k'Leshya," he continued numbly. "We can't let her find out Skan is gone, or she'll try to follow him. Urtho gave him a weapon, and told him to use it to stop Ma'ar. Skan is determined that Urtho meant him to do it *now.*"

Winterhart realized that she was clutching her hand in her hair at the side of her head only when it began to hurt. She let go, slowly. "Couldn't you stop him?" she cried involuntarily.

"I tried. He wouldn't listen." Amberdrake stared at her, eyes blank and blind. "He told me that Shaiknam, Garber, and Conn Levas went over to the enemy."

A cold ring of terror constricted her throat, cutting off her gasp. "But—"

"He said he caught Conn Levas right after he'd poisoned Urtho with *Miranda*-thorns, and tore his throat out. By then it was too late; there was nothing they could do for Urtho but buy him time."

She sensed his pain, as if it was her own—if *she* wanted to mourn for Urtho, *he* would have ten times the grief to deal with—and ten times that for Skan.

"I'll—wait, there she is." Zhaneel came hurrying up with a bundle of books in her beak and another clutched to her chest, running on three legs with her wings spread to help her balance.

Winterhart grabbed the edge of her wing before she could put her burden down. "Zhaneel!" she cried. "I need someone on the k'Leshya side to make certain all this is carried as far away from the Gate as possible. We don't know how unstable these things are."

Zhaneel nodded, and darted through the Gate without waiting for further explanation. "You go after her," Winterhart ordered. "I'll follow you as soon as I get the last of this stuff across."

At least she had something to do. Something to keep her from thinking...

"Are you all right?" Amberdrake asked suddenly, a little life coming into his eyes. She knew what he meant.

Conn is dead. Conn is a traitor, and he's dead. She paused and collected herself, examined her heart.

"It's best that Skan took care of the problem," she said firmly, looking deeply into Amberdrake's eyes so that he would know she meant what she said. "If he hadn't—I'd have done so, but with less elegance. Myself."

Beneath all the pain, all the grief, she saw a moment of relief. It was enough for now. She shoved him gently towards the Gate.

"I'll see you on the other side," she said. "Take care of her." He took a last, long look at the Tower, then turned, and stumbled blindly across the threshold.

She picked up another package as soon as he was clear, and pitched it across.

* * *

Skan knew exactly who he was looking for—the Kaled'a'in Adept Snowstar, the person Urtho himself had appointed as the chief of all the mages. He knew Snowstar, knew that the man was truly second only to Urtho in knowledge and ability, and knew one other, crucial fact.

Snowstar had been working with Urtho long before the King collapsed. Snowstar was one of the mages that Urtho had with him when Cinnabar called them all to the Palace that terrible morning.

Snowstar *knew* the Palace as well as Skan did. Which meant that Snowstar, unlike many of the other mages, could build a Gate there.

And Ma'ar was at the Palace.

After three false tries, he located Snowstar at the Tower stables, turning away from the last empty stall. An odd place for a mage, perhaps, unless the mage was Kaled'a'in, and the horses here were the precious warsteeds. Skan grinned savagely to himself; Snowstar had not expected an ambush—and doubtless intended to head straight for the Kaled'a'in Gate from here, hot on the heels of his beloved equines.

There would be a brief delay.

As he turned, Skan stood in the aisle between the stalls and spread his wings to block his way. The mage looked up at him blankly. "Skandranon? What—"

"I need a favor," Skan said quietly, but with an edge to his voice. "And you don't have a choice. I need a Gate to the old Palace, and I need it now."

Snowstar's eyes went wide and he shook his head with disbelief. "Are you out of your mind?" he cried, putting out his hands to shove Skan out of the way. "There's no time for this kind of nonsense! We have to get out of here!"

"There *is* time and you *will* do this," Skan hissed. "I have a prrresssent to deliver to Ma'ar. From Urtho."

Snowstar blanched, and his eyes dropped to the box around Skan's neck as if he had only just this moment noticed that it was there. Skan was gambling on a number of things. The Black Gryphon was known as Urtho's confidant; Snowstar should assume that Urtho's request was an *order,* and that it was not meant to be implemented at some far future date, but *now.* Snowstar knew very well what kind of shape Urtho was in; he would not risk a single precious moment by going to Urtho or sending a messenger to confirm what Skan had just told him. He might even assume that Urtho had ordered Skan to *find* Snowstar, knowing that the Adept would be one of the few at full strength and capable of building a Gate that far away.

Snowstar's pupils widened and contracted, as all those thoughts—and, likely, a few more—raced through his mind.

"Right," he said then, still pale, but grimly determined. "I won't Gate you into the Palace itself, if that is agreeable to you. I have no idea who or what Ma'ar has stationed where. I could Gate you into the servants' quarters only to find out that he's got it full of soldiers or traps. But there's one place I know *very* well where you won't find much opposition, and the little you find, I suspect you can silence."

"The stables," Skan breathed, amazed at Snowstar's quick thinking.

"Exactly." Snowstar shoved at Skan again, but this time to make some room to work, and Skan gladly moved over. "I'll position the Gate to come out of the last stall in the back; it's a big loose-box, partitioned off from the rest with floor-to-ceiling walls, and with no outside windows. We never put a horse in it unless it was one that was so sick it needed dark and quiet. No grooms are likely to change that."

It sounded perfect, and Skan nodded. "Put it up, and bring it down once I'm through," he said decisively. "Then get yourself out of here."

"What about—" Snowstar began, then saw the look in Skan's eyes. The rage Skan held bottled up inside must have been blazing. Snowstar grew just a bit paler, then turned away, raised his hands, and began.

The Adept had decades of practise to refine and hone his craft; the Gate went up with scarcely a ripple in mage-energies. Skan did not even wait to thank him; clutching his precious burden with one foreclaw, he dove through to the other side.

This is poorly planned, stupid gryphon, but there isn't time. Urtho can't die without knowing Ma'ar's dead and gone. You don't do helplessness well at all. And if you can't save Urtho, you can still do something.

He landed, feet skidding a little in the straw, in the dark and empty loose-box. As Snowstar had guessed, it had not been used in so long that the straw covering the stone floor smelled musty and was full of dust. He suppressed a sneeze, and moved cautiously to the door.

He listened carefully, all senses straining against the darkness.

Odd. Lots of voices, and the sound of something struggling. What did they have penned up in here—some kind of feral stallion?

"Are you sure that's going to hold the beast?" The voice was doubtful, and very frightened. "I tell you, orders or no orders, if that thing breaks free, don't think I'm going to stand here and try to stop it!"

The *crack* of a hand on flesh, and an exclamation of pain.

"You'll do as you're told, and like it, coward!" a second voice growled. "If I tell you to stand there and let the thing take your arm off, you'll damned well *do* it!"

Not a stallion then. A bull? Some new monster Ma'ar just dreamed up?

A muttered, sullen curse; the sound of spitting. Heavy boots, walking away. More struggles; chains rattling, muffled *thuds*, more mutters, a stream of ill-wishes directed against the second voice, his family, and all his progeny to come.

The thin, high wail of a young gryphon.

"*Faaaather!*"

A voice he knew! *Kechara!*

He pushed against the stall door, and it swung wide while he stepped out and mantled. His eyes locked with those of one poor, spotty-faced groom clutching a pitchfork in one hand, a bloody rag held to his mouth with the other. The boy couldn't have been over sixteen. He took one look at Skan, went pale as milk, and fainted dead away.

Skan stepped over him, and looked into the stall he'd been guarding.

There were two canvas-covered bundles there—one thrashing, one whimpering. The whimpering bundle was the smaller, and the whimpers were definitely in Kechara's voice!

How did she—never mind. Conn Levas or Shaiknam, or both. Quickly, he squeezed into the stall, but he did not free the little one. Not yet. The larger bundle of the two also smelled of blood and *of gryphon*, and it was a scent that he thought he recognized.

"Hold still," he whispered. "It's Skan."

The bundle stilled, immediately. He took a moment to examine the situation.

Chains wrapped around the bundle, but they were not fastened to the stall itself. If he could get the gryphon inside to bend a little, he might be able to slip one loop off, and that would give him enough slack to undo the whole thing without having to unlock it.

"Can you bend this way?" he whispered harshly, pushing down on what he thought was the back of the gryphon's head. It must have been; the place bent over in response to his pressure, and he was able to work the loop of chain off as he had hoped. Once he had the slack he needed, two more loops followed, and he worked the entire chain down, with the squirming assistance of the gryphon inside.

Now he could slit the canvas bag and see if the contents were who he *thought* it was. He ripped open the canvas with a slash of his fist, and a head popped out—a head covered in an enormous version of a falcon's hood, with the beak tied firmly shut.

He pulled off the bindings, and the beak opened.

"Damn it, Skan," Aubri croaked, in a whisper no louder than his had been, "you took your own sweet time getting here!"

It took both of them to convince Kechara that she *had* to be quiet, but for once Ma'ar's men had done them all a favor. They had cut off all the primaries on both her wings and Aubri's, and in Kechara's case, that meant she wasn't tripping over her own awkward wings.

Kechara wasn't at all clear on how she had gotten there, but the picture in her mind, projected strongly, was of a blurred Conn Levas offering something that smelled lovely. Skan assured her that he had "gone away" and that Skan had made certain he wouldn't come back.

Not in this lifetime, anyway.

Aubri was a lot clearer on what had happened to him, and kept his explanation down to a terse couple of sentences. He only wanted to know one thing.

"Urtho?" he asked, with a sideways glance to see if Kechara was listening.

Skan closed his eyes, letting his grief show for just the briefest of moments, and shook his head.

Aubri's beak clamped shut, and when Skan opened his own eyes, the broadwing's eyes were blazing as red with madness as any goshawk's.

"I got Conn Levas," Skan said, around the lump of rage and grief in his own throat. "*This* will take care of Ma'ar. If we can get it to him." He tilted his head to one side. "I have to admit, I was told that I'd have a count of a hundred to get away, and then this thing will make Jerlag look like a campfire." He shook his head. "If you can think of any way you can get yourself and Kechara out of range…"

Aubri's pupils dilated, and he produced a harsh bark of a laugh. "On clipped wings? I don't think so. Besides, all I ever asked was to go down fighting. I'm sorry about the little one, but this is going to be clean, right?"

He nodded. "As clean as fire. And I can still send you both into the Light if all seems hopeless."

As you've done too many times before—Urtho, why must we feel these burdens? Why?

"Well," Aubri rumbled. "You need me. Bet we can even find a way

Kechara'll be useful. And if it gets Ma'ar…" Aubri's savage grin and the scrape of his talons on the stone told the rest. "And—ah, demonsblood, Skan, you always *were* the luckiest son of a vulture I ever saw. *Your* luck, you'll find a way out for us. I'll take my chances with you."

Skan let out the breath he had been holding in. "Well," he said lightly. "That was the hard part. Now the easy part."

"Which is?" Aubri asked, as Kechara gave a breathy squeal of glee and pounced on something. She stuffed it in her mouth and looked up innocently, the tail of a rat hanging out of one corner of her beak for a heartbeat, before she swallowed and it vanished.

Skan looked cautiously around the corner; the doors to the stable stood open wide, and the apparently deserted stable-yard stretched between them and the Palace kitchens. "Oh, it's nothing much," he replied, off-handedly. "Just getting into the Palace and the Throne Room."

The last Tower door had been opened; there were still books and devices here Urtho wished he could save, but the vital things had been carried off. He had persuaded Vikteren and the rest to leave. Now there was only the small matter of hanging on, living every possible second, for every second meant more time to ensure that all of his people who *could*, would reach safety.

The Tower echoed with the whisper of air through doors long locked, and the occasional *thud* of something falling, echoing through stone corridors suddenly more empty than imagination could bear. In all of his life, Urtho had never felt so alone.

He had never expected to die alone, much less like this. At least the mages and Healers had taken all the pain, blocked the hallucinations and the convulsions, and left him only with growing weakness.

He was so tired, so very, very tired…

No! He had to fight it, to stay conscious, awake! Every heartbeat was vital!

All we have done, and all I have learned, and I cannot slow the progress of my own death by even a candlemark.

He had never thought much about revenge, but now he burned with longing for it. *Revenge—no, I want to protect my people, my children! And when the Tower goes, I want it to be something more than the end, I want it to mean something, to* accomplish *some purpose!* He had always hoped, if it came to that, he would be able to lure Ma'ar, or at least some chief mages of Ma'ar's, into the Tower-turned-trap. He'd planned for that, all along; a desperate gambit that, if nothing else, would keep Ma'ar so busy cleaning up the damage that his children and his people would be able to get far beyond Ma'ar's reach or ability to find.

Now, when he died, the Tower would die in an expanding ring of sound and light, and it would be no more than the most impressive funeral pyre the world had ever seen—

—*wait a moment.*

Something stirred, under the morass the poison had made of his mind. An idea, and a hope. *Ma'ar cannot know that Conn Levas succeeded. What would happen if I challenged him?*

There was a permanent Gate, a small one, big enough only for one human at a time, not more than a room away. It would take no effort at all to open it. A moment of clear thought, and it could be set for the Palace, the Throne Room. Urtho had used it to step directly from his own audience-chamber into the King's—an impressive bit of nonsense that never failed to leave foreigners gaping and a little frightened. That was how he had gotten to the Palace the night that Cinnabar had summoned him; he had opened a larger Gate elsewhere for Skan. He hadn't been certain what the effect of trying to squeeze through a too-small Gate might be, and that had not been the moment to find out.

The odds are good that he'll be in the Throne Room, waiting to hear from his army. What if I opened that Gate and challenged him to come over? A fierce and feral joy flooded him, and for the first time he understood how his gryphons felt at the kill. *I open the Gate; he can't fight me through the Gate, he has to come over. I close it. He can't re-open it while I keep him busy, and by the time he gets his own Gate up, I'm dead. And so is he. If I were alive, I would never consider it—but I am dead already.*

That terrible joy gave him the strength to rise to his feet, stagger into the next room, and take his place on his own, modest version of a throne. Hardly a throne at all, really, just a large, comfortable chair, raised off the floor on a platform about half a stair-step high. He had never seen any reason to build a dazzling audience-chamber; everything in the small room was made of old, time-mellowed wood. On the few occasions that he had needed to impress someone, he'd transformed the whole place with illusions. Much cheaper, and *much* easier to clean.

He gasped with effort as he stumbled up onto the platform and lowered himself down into his throne. The exertion left him dizzy and disoriented for a moment; he closed his eyes, and when he opened them again, there was a faint haze of rainbow around everything.

The hallucinations, or what's left of them. I don't have much time. If this doesn't work—at least I tried. And Skan can make his own try, someday. That in itself comforted him, a little. Skan would get to safety, plot and plan with the sharpest minds of the Kaled'a'in, and make his own attempt. Ma'ar had not, and would not, win. Not while there was a single gryphon or Kaled'a'in left to oppose him.

He stared fixedly at the ornamental arch across the room from him, an arch built right into the wall, that seemed only to frame a shallow, purposeless nook. He wrapped his mind and his fading powers around the mage-energies woven into wood and stone beneath, and *twisted.*

Within the frame of the arch, the blank wall writhed, then turned into a swirling haze of colors, like oil on water, for just the barest instant.

Then the colors darkened, steadied—and Urtho looked across the leagues into the Throne Room of the Palace of High King Leodhan, a massive room constructed of six different kinds and colors of the rarest marbles, a place that seemed vast even when it was packed full of courtiers. Now it held only one man, but that man had presence enough to fill it.

Ma'ar stared fixedly at the Gate that had suddenly opened up in his Throne Room, a Gate he clearly had no notion ever existed. He had not been born a handsome man, but over the years he had sculpted his body into the image of a young god. His square-jawed face, with precisely chiseled cheekbones and sensuous mouth, framed with a mane of hair of dark copper, topped a body that would be the envy of any warrior in his ranks. All that remained of the old Ma'ar were the eyes: small, shrewd, and of an odd yellow-green.

"Kiyamvir Ma'ar," Urtho said genially. "It has been a very long time."

Ma'ar recovered his poise much more quickly than Urtho would have credited him for. "Urtho." He leaned back in his throne, a *real* throne, and much more impressive than the alabaster bench the King had used. This one might not be solid gold, but it certainly looked as though it was, and the single red-black ruby over Ma'ar's head, carved in the shape of the head of a snarling cat, was twice the size of the largest such stone Urtho had ever seen. "Have you called on me to offer your surrender?"

Urtho smiled gently. "Not at all," he countered. "I recall that you used to enjoy a gamble. I am offering you just that."

Ma'ar barked his laughter. "You? And what have you to offer me that I cannot take?"

Urtho waved, a gesture that made him dizzy again. "Why, this. I'm sure you realize that I've had as much carried away as I could—but I am sure you also realize that there is *far* more than could ever be carried away. I'm sure you also realize that what I did at Jerlag, I can do here."

Ma'ar's face darkened, and his lips formed a soundless snarl.

"However—" Urtho held up a finger to forestall any reply. "I'm proposing a challenge. The prize—the Tower and everything that's left. If you kill me, I obviously cannot trigger the destructive spells." *And let's hope he hasn't figured out, as Conn Levas did, that it isn't a spell that does the destruction, it's the lack of one.* "You have the Tower and everything you want. If, on the other hand, I kill you—well, I suspect that your underlings will immediately begin fighting among themselves, and leave me and mine alone. The bickering is inevitable, and I will have protected my own."

Ma'ar frowned; but he was obviously intrigued. "You underestimate what I have done here, Urtho. I took a weak land, torn apart by internal quarreling and wrecked by the greed of shortsighted idiots who thought no further than their own fat profits. I forged it into an Empire that will live long beyond me, and I intend to live a *very* long time! What makes you think I would risk all that for your stupid wager?"

Urtho leaned forward in his chair, ignoring another wave of dizziness, and spoke two words. "Knowledge. Power."

Then he settled back, and closed his eyes. "Think about it, Kiyamvir Ma'ar. You win, or I do. All the knowledge, and all the power. I can afford to wait, but feel as though I should retire. Your army is on the way, and I prefer to reset this Gate to—somewhere else, somewhere *very warm*, and leave your army with an unpleasant surprise."

He slitted open his lids just a little, and saw to his satisfaction that Ma'ar was staring at the Gate, chewing his lip in vexation.

He's going to do it!

"I always said you were the luckiest—" Aubri muttered, before Skan hushed him.

"It's not luck," he muttered back. "It's memory. Cinnabar used to play with the Princes, and she showed me all the secret passages. I took a chance that Ma'ar wouldn't have found them all, and that I could take care of the traps he put in the ones he *did* find."

He didn't like to think of how Cinnabar had shown him all the secret passages; she'd impressed them directly into his mind, and it hadn't been a pleasant experience. Nor had the circumstances been pleasant—she'd put him in charge of searching the passages for that damned *dyrstaf,* because he was the only mage there she *could* do that to.

She took the human-sized passages, and I took the ones big enough for a gryphon...

He shook off the memory; it didn't matter, anyway. What mattered was how many guards Kiyamvir Ma'ar had with him in that Throne Room.

Please, please, please, oh Lady of the Kaled'a'in, make him so arrogant that he does without guards entirely! Please... The gryphons didn't have a deity as such, and this was the first time he'd ever felt the urgent need to call on one. The gryphons had only had Urtho and themselves.

And when this is over—take Kechara somewhere safe, and warm, and bring Urtho to her—and keep Amberdrake and Zhaneel happy.

There were no peepholes in this passage, and no human would have been able to hear what was going on in the Throne Room. Anyone using the entrance here would have to do so blindly, trusting that there was no one there.

Unless that someone was a gryphon.

He closed his eyes, and concentrated, becoming nothing in his mind but a pair of broad, tufted ears, *listening...*

He's talking to someone? Demonsblood! It's now or never!

"Go!" he hissed at Aubri. The broadwing hit the release on the doorway, and rammed it with his shoulder, tumbling through as the panel gave way. Skan leapt his prone body and skidded to a halt on the slick marble, Kechara romping puppy-like behind him.

Ma'ar swung around to stare at the open panel, and now faced away from—

Urtho? Oh Star-Eyed Lady, is that a Gate?

What else could it be, when Urtho lay back in a chair framed by an archway, with a faint shimmering of energy across the portal?

Skan did not even stop to think about his incredible, unbelievable good fortune; did not stop to think about the poleaxed expression on Urtho's weary face. "Aubri!" he screeched. "Get Kechara across *now...*"

But Aubri didn't have to do anything. Kechara spotted Urtho on her own, screamed, *"Father!"* in a joyful, shrill voice, and shot across the intervening space like an arrow, squeezing through the Gate as if she'd been greased.

Aubri followed—and stuck.

Skan reached for the box, while Ma'ar stared at all of them as if he thought they were some kind of hallucination. Finally he spoke.

"All of this was to save two gryphons?"

The Black Gryphon held the weapon before him and slid his foreclaws home, and triggered the box.

"No. To save all of us."

He ducked out of the carry-strap, and slung the whole thing across the floor at Ma'ar, who dodged in purest reflex. But dodging didn't help; the box's strap caught his feet and tripped him. The fall knocked the breath out of him, and delayed any reaction he might have for a crucial moment.

Ma'ar clutched at the box, which glowed and sparked when his hands touched it. His expression changed from one of indignation to one of surprise and then—fear. Then insane anger. He stood, trembling with rage, and kicked the box aside. It clattered on the marble floor to rest by the throne.

"You think this is it?" he screamed. "This toy of Urtho's is supposed to kill me, gryphon? *Watch.*"

The Emperor drew a glittering silver knife—and with both hands, drove it into his own chest.

His face wrenched into a maniacal grin and he locked his eyes on Skandranon's. As blood streamed down his sumptuous clothing, the grin grew wider.

"You see, I know some things you don't. I have won! I will live *forever!* And I will hate you *forever*—all of Urtho's people, all your children, and their children, and I will hunt you *all* down. Do you hear?"

Skandranon Rashkae! Will you wake up? Ma'ar is playing for time! He'll keep you occupied with his little spectacle until the box goes, and takes you with it!

The gryphon snapped himself awake from Ma'ar's mesmerizing speech. Ma'ar withdrew the dagger from his chest; blood blossomed anew and dripped to the floor. Without saying anything else, the Emperor's face went ashen, and he fixed his gaze of madness on Skandranon. With both hands, he held the dagger's point to his throat, behind the chin— and in one swift movement thrust the long dagger upwards.

Skandranon was running towards the Gate before Ma'ar fell. Behind him, over the clatter of his own talons, he could hear the dagger's pommel strike chips from the stone floor, muffled only by the sound of the body. The Black Gryphon hurtled to the Gate at full speed; Aubri was still wedged there, and if this didn't work, they were both doomed.

He hit Aubri from behind with all of his weight.

With a scream of pain from two throats, they ripped through, leaving behind feathers and a little skin, and the Gate came down so quickly that it took off the end of Skan's tail.

Kechara was already cuddling in Urtho's lap, unable to understand why her father looked so sick. Skan picked himself up off the floor and limped over to the mage, who looked up with his eyes full of tears.

"I never thought I'd see you again," he whispered hoarsely. "What did you think you were doing? I meant you to *save* that weapon..."

But before Skan could reply, he shook his head, carefully, as if any movement pained him. "Never mind. You are the salvation of everyone, you brave, vain gryphon. Everyone we saved will be safe for the rest of their lives. I have never been so proud of any creature in my life, and never felt so unworthy of you."

Skan opened his beak, trying to say something wonderful, but all he could manage was a broken, "Father—I love you."

Urtho raised one trembling hand, and Skan moved his head so that the mage could place it there.

"Son," he said, very softly. "Son of all of the best things in me. I love you."

Skan's throat closed as Urtho took his hand away, and he was unable to say anything more.

Kechara looked at them both with bewildered eyes. "Father?" she said timidly to Urtho.

"Father has to go away, Kechara," Urtho said gently. "Skan will be your father for a while, do you understand? It may be for a long time, but Skan will be your father, and when the bad men who hurt you are all gone, you can come join me."

She nodded, clearly unhappy, but her one taste of the "bad men" had been enough. She gazed up at Urtho in supreme confidence that he could and would deal with the "bad men," and nibbled his fingers in a caress.

Aubri limped over to both of them. "Scuse me, Urtho?" he asked humbly. "Can that Gate go somewhere else?"

Urtho closed his eyes, then opened them with visible effort.

"I can try," he said.

Amberdrake thought that he was prepared for the inevitable, but when the great flash of light in the east turned night into full day for one long, horrible moment, he realized that he was not ready. He had accepted the loss of Skan, of Urtho, of everything he had known with his mind, but not his heart. The entire world turned inside out for a fraction of a heartbeat; as if he had crossed a Gate, the universe shook and trembled, his vision blurred—but there was no Gate, it was all in himself.

Then everything was normal again. The night sky returned, spangled with stars, but wreathed in the east with ever-expanding multi-colored rings of light, and a cool breeze brought the scents of crushed grass and dust.

Normal—except all was gone.

"*No!*" he cried out, one voice of fruitless denial among a multitude. "*Nooooooo—*"

He started to fall to his knees. A terrible moaning burst from his chest, and tears etched their way down his face in long trails of pain. *Urtho—Skan—*

Hands caught him and supported him; Winterhart. But another set of hands took his shoulders and shook them.

"Dammit, man, *no one* can fall apart yet!" Vikteren snarled at him, tears of his own leaving trails down his dusty face. "We aren't safe! Didn't you feel what happened, back there? When the Tower went up, something more happened than even Urtho thought! Gods only know what's going to happen now; we need to get under shields—"

"But—" he protested. "But—"

"Just *don't fall apart on me.* People are watching you! You can collapse after I get the shields organized, all right?" Vikteren punctuated every word with another shake of his shoulders, and Amberdrake finally nodded, weakly. Vikteren let him go, and he got a wavering grip on his emotions, turning his face into the serene mask of the kestra'chern, although deep within, pain was eating him alive.

Vikteren turned away from him, and waved his arms frantically over his head. "Listen!" he shouted, over the keens, the weeping. "Everybody! This—the trap didn't do what we thought, all right? We don't know how much is left of Ma'ar's forces, we don't know how far away is *safe*, we don't know who or how many of the rest survived. All we *do* know is that what happened was worse than we thought, and we have a couple of hours to get ready for it! It's going to be a—we'll have to call it a mage-storm, I guess. I can't tell you how bad. Just listen; I need all the mages over here with me, no matter how drained you are, and the rest of you, start getting things tied down, like for a really bad storm, the worst, you've ever seen!"

Somehow the desperation in his words penetrated; hertasi carried the bad news to the rest of the camp, to those who had been too far away to hear him. Mages pushed their way through the crowd to reach his side; the others stopped milling and started acting in a purposeful manner, glancing at the slowly expanding rings of light with a new respect and no little fear.

Winterhart went looking for her gryphons; her first duty was to them. Amberdrake let her go, then stumbled through the darkness to the small floating barge that held his own belongings.

But once there—it all left him. There was nothing left in him but the dull ache of grief. He couldn't even bring himself to care what might happen next.

He sat down on the side of the barge, and his hand fell on the feather he still had tied to his belt. Zhaneel's feather.

How would he tell her? She still didn't know...

There's nothing left, nothing left for any of us.

He didn't even hear them come up beside him, he was so lost in despair so dark that not even tears served to relieve it. One moment he was alone; the next, Zhaneel sat beside him, and Winterhart took a place next to him on the edge of the barge.

"When he did not follow, I guessed," Zhaneel said, her voice no more than a whisper, and although he had not thought that his grief could grow any greater, it threatened to swallow him now.

The tears choked his breath and stole his sight, and left him nothing.

:Nothing?: said a voice in his mind, as a hand closed over his.

"Nothing?" said Zhaneel aloud. "Are we nothing?"

And Amberdrake sensed the two of them joining, reaching into *his* heart to Heal it, reaching to bring him out of the darkness. The gryfalcon touched one talon to the feather he still held.

"Will you not redeem this now, my friend, my brother?" she asked softly. "We need each other so much..."

"And the rest of them need you," Winterhart added. "I've heard you used to ask, 'Who Heals the Healer?'—and we have at least one answer for you."

"Those who he Healed," Zhaneel said. "Giving back what he gave."

Blindly, he reached for them; they reached back, as he held tightly to feathered shoulder and human, and shook with sobs that finally brought some release.

The first flood of tears was over, for the moment at least, when he heard someone shouting his name.

"Amberdrake!" It sounded like Vikteren. "Amberdrake! *The Gate! It's opening again!*"

The what? He stumbled to his feet, and ran back to the site of the old Gate-terminus, a rough-made arch of stone. Sure enough, there was a shimmer of energy there, energy that fluxed and crackled and made him a little sick to look at it.

"What is it?" he asked, as Vikteren ran across the clearing to him.

"I don't know-can't be Ma'ar..." The energy inside the Gate surged again. "Whatever it is, whoever, it's been affected by the mage-blast." He turned hopeful eyes on Amberdrake. "You don't suppose it's Skan, do you?"

Amberdrake only shook his head numbly, heart in mouth. The energies built a third time; the mouth of the Gate turned a blinding white—

And Kechara tumbled through, squalling with fear. Winterhart and Zhaneel both cried out and ran to her to comfort her, but before they could reach her side, the Gate flared whitely a second time, and Aubri leapt across the threshold, smelling of burned fur and feathers, to land in an exhausted heap.

"Skan!" the broadwing screeched, turning his head blindly back towards the Gate. "Skan! He's still in there!"

The Gate fluxed—and collapsed in on itself, slowly, taking the stones of the arch with it. The entire structure began to fall, as if in a dream.

"*No!*" Vikteren screamed.

Amberdrake was not certain what the young mage *thought* he was doing; he was only *supposed* to be of Master rank, and Amberdrake had always been told that only Adepts could build Gates. But Vikteren reached out his hands, in a clutching, clawlike motion, and Amberdrake *felt* the energies pouring from him into the collapsing Gate, seizing it— and, somehow, holding it steady!

Amberdrake sensed Vikteren faltering, and added his own heart's strength to the young mage's—

—and felt Winterhart join him, and Zhaneel—

The Gate flared a third and final time, but this time it was so bright that Amberdrake cried out in pain, blinded.

Vikteren cried too, but in triumph.

Amberdrake's vision cleared after much blinking and eye-rubbing, and laying before them was Skandranon—shocked senseless, and no longer as he—*was*. The elegant black form they had known was thinner, and bleached to snow-white, but it was unmistakably Skandranon.

The Gate and Vikteren collapsed together.

Then there was no time to think of anything, as the eastern horizon erupted with fire—again. And for some reason Amberdrake could not understand, he could feel the death, far away, of the Mage of Silence, content that his people, including those he loved most, were safe at last.

They had just enough time—barely—to establish their shields before the double mage-storm hit. The worst effects lasted from before dawn to sunset. But their preparations held, and they all emerged from shelter to find a blood-red sun sinking over a deceptively normal landscape.

Normal—until you noticed the places where trees had been flattened; where strange little energy-fields danced over warped and twisted cairns of half-melted rocks. Normal—until night fell, and did not bring darkness, but an odd half-light, full of wisps of glowing fog and dancing balls of luminescence.

"We can't stay here," Winterhart said wearily, as she returned to Amberdrake's hastily pitched tent. It was the only one big enough to hold four gryphons—Skan and Aubri, and Zhaneel and Kechara, the former two because of their injuries, and the latter because *they* would not leave Skan's moon-white form.

"I'd assumed that. We'll have to pack up and move West, I suppose." He looked up at her, and smiled, then turned his watchful gaze back down to the slumbering Skandranon. "I don't mind, if you don't."

"Well, I wish we knew how many of the others survived," she sighed, "but the mages can't get anything through this—whatever it is. Magical noise and smoke. No scrying, no mage-messages, and we don't want to risk the poor little messenger-birds. The tervardi don't want to scout, the kyree are as scared as we are, the hertasi are traumatized, and the gryphons don't trust the winds. We'll have to go west, and assume any others are doing whatever they have to."

"So we're back to ordinary, human senses." He reached out for her, caught her hand, and drew her down beside him. "Not so bad, when you come to think about it."

"I have no complaints." She leaned her head on his shoulder, and stroked one ice-white wing-feather of the still-shocky Skandranon. Except one."

"Oh?" he replied. *She probably wishes we could stay here long enough to rest—but at least we know there won't be anyone following us—*

"This—" she pointed to Skandranon, curled around Zhaneel like a carving of the purest alabaster—"is going to make him *twice* as vain as he was!"

"Of course it will," came a sleepy rumble. A pale, sky-blue eye opened, and winked slyly. "And deservedly so."

Amberdrake smiled and held his beloved. No matter what tears were shed or what trials were faced, some things would stay the same. There would always be day and night, stars and sky, hope and rest. There would always be love, always compassion, and there would always be Skandranon. And forever, in the hearts of all the Clans, there would be Urtho—and for his memory, a moment, of silence.

THE WHITE GRYPHON

A VALDEMAR OMNIBUS

BOOK TWO
OF THE MAGE WARS

Lovingly dedicated to our parents,
Edward and Joyce Ritche & Jim and Shirley Dixon

CHAPTER ONE

*L*ight.
  From crown to talons, tailtip to wingtip, it will be a sculpture of light.

Skandranon Rashkae rested his beaked head atop his crossed foreclaws and contemplated the city across the bay. Although his city was considered dazzling at night by the most jaded of observers, even by day, White Gryphon was a city of light. It gleamed against the dense green foliage of the cliff face it had been carved from, shining in the sun with all the stark white beauty of a snow sculpture. Not that this coast had ever *seen* snow; they were too far west and south of their old home for that.

Of course, given the way that mage-storms have mucked up everything else, that could change at a moment's notice, too.

Well, even if such a bizarre change in climate should occur, the Kaled'a'in of White Gryphon were prepared for it. *We build our city to endure, as Urtho built his Tower. Let the most terrible winter storms rage, we are ready for them.*

It would take another Cataclysm, and the kind of power that destroyed the twin strongholds of two of the most powerful mages who ever lived, to flatten White Gryphon. And even *then* the ruins of its buildings would endure, for a while at least, until the vegetation that covered these seaside cliffs finally reclaimed the terraces and the remains of the buildings there…

Skan shook his head at his own musings. *Now why are you thinking such gloomy thoughts of destruction, silly gryphon!* he chided himself. *Haven't you got enough to worry about, that you have to manufacture a second Ma'ar out of your imagination! You came over here to rest, remember!*

Oh, yes. *Rest.* He hadn't been doing a lot of that; it seemed as if every moment of every day was taken up with solving someone else's problems—or at least look as if he was *trying* to solve their problems.

There was no one near him to hear his sigh of exasperation, audible over the steady thunder of the surf so far below him.

He dropped his eyes to the half-moon bay below his current perch, and to the waves that rolled serenely and inexorably in to pound the base of the rocky cliffs beneath him. On the opposite side of the bay, where the cliff base lay in shelter thanks to a beak of rock that hooked into the half-moon, echoing exactly the hook of a raptor's beak, the Kaled'a'in had built docks for the tiny fishing fleet now working the coastline. *One year of terrible travail to cross the country to get here, and nine of building. We have managed a great deal, more than I would have thought, given that we cannot rely on magic the way we used to.*

Now his sigh was not one of exasperation, but of relative content.

From here the half-finished state of most of the city was not visible to the unaided eye. Things were certainly better than they had been, even a few years ago, when many of the Kaled'a'in were still living at the top of the cliff, in tents and shelters contrived from the floating barges.

The original plan had called for a city built atop the cliff, not perched like a puffin on the cliff face itself. General Judeth was the one who had insisted on creating a new city built on terraces carved out of the cliff face. Like so many of the Kaled'a'in and adopted Kaled'a'in, she was determined to have a home that could never be taken by siege. Unlike many of them, she had a plan for such a place the moment she saw the cliffs of the western coastline.

Skan still marveled at her audacity, the stubborn will that saw her plan through, and the persuasion that had convinced them all she was right and her plan would work. Small wonder she had been a commander of one of Urtho's Companies.

The rock here was soft enough to carve, yet hard enough to support a series of terraces, even in the face of floods, winds, and waves. That was what Judeth, the daughter of a stonemason, had been the first to see. The cliffs themselves had dictated the form the city took, but once folk began to notice that there was a certain resemblance to a stylized gryphon with outstretched wings—well, some took it as an omen, and some as coincidence, but there was never any argument as to what the new city would be called.

White Gryphon—in honor of Skandranon Rashkae, who no longer dyed his feathers black, and thanks to the interval he had spent caught between two Gates, was now as pale as a white gyrfalcon. The only black left to him was a series of back markings among the white feathers, exactly like the black bars sometimes seen on the gyrfalcons of the north.

The White Gryphon regarded the city named for him with decidedly mixed feelings. Skandranon was still more than a little embarrassed about it. After all those years of playing at being the hero, it was somewhat disconcerting to have everyone, from child to ancient, revere him as one! And it was even more disconcerting to find himself the tacit leader of *all* of the nonhumans of the Kaled'a'in, and deferred to by many of the humans as well!

I thought I wanted to be a leader. Silly me.

Truth to be told, what he'd wanted to be was *not* a peacetime leader; he'd wanted to be the kind of leader who made split-second decisions and clever, daring plans, not the kind of leader who oversaw disputes between *hertasi* and *kyree*, or who approved the placement of the purifying tanks for the city sewage system...

Council meetings bored him to yawning, and *why* anyone would think that heroism conferred instant expertise in *everything* baffled him.

He wasn't very good at administration, but no one seemed to have figured that out yet.

Fortunately, I have good advisors who permit me to pirate their words and advice shamelessly. And I know when to keep my beak shut and look wise.

Somehow both the refugees and the city a-building had survived his leadership and his decisions. Most people had real homes now, homes built from the limestone that partly accounted for the city's pale gleam under the full light of the sun. All of the terraces were cut and walled in with more of that limestone, and all of the streets paved with crushed oyster shells, which further caught and reflected the light. There was room for expansion for the next five or six generations—

And by the time there is no more space left on the terraces, it will be someone else's problem, anyway.

Sculpting the terraces and putting in water and other services had been the work of a single six-month period during which magic *did* work the way it was supposed to. It had been just as easy at that point to cut all of the terraces that the cliff could hold, and to build the water and sewage system to allow for that maximum population. Water came from a spring in the cliff, and streams that had once cascaded into the sea in silver-ribbon waterfalls, carried down through holes cut into the living rock to emerge in several places in the city. It would not be impossible to cut off the water supply—Skan was not willing to say that anything was impossible anymore, given what he himself had survived—but it would be very, very difficult and would require reliably-working magic. It would also not be impossible to invade the city—but every path, either leading down from the verdant lands above, or up from the bay, had been edged, walled, or built so that a single creature with a bow could hold off an army. The lessons learned from Ma'ar's conquests might have been bitter, but they were valuable now.

Skan raised his head and tested the air coming up from below. *Saltwater, kelp, and fish. New fish, not old fish. The fleet must be coming in.* It had taken him time to learn to recognize those scents; time for his senses to get accustomed to the ever-present tang of saltwater in the air. No gryphon had ever seen the Western Sea before; his scouts hadn't even known what it was when they first encountered it.

Huh. "My" scouts. He shook his head. *I had no idea what I was getting myself in for—but I should have seen it coming. Amberdrake certainly tried to warn me, and so did Gesten and Winterhart. But did I listen! Oh, no. And now, here I am, with a city named after me and a thousand stupid little decisions to make, all my time eaten up by "solving" problems I don't care about for people who could certainly solve those problems themselves if they tried.* Now he knew what Amberdrake meant, when the kestra'chern said that "my time is not my own."

And I don't like it, damn it all. I should be practicing flying, or practicing making more gryphlets with Zhaneel...

Instead, he was going to have to return for another blasted Council session. *They could do this without me. They don't need me. There is nothing I can contribute except my presence.*

But his presence seemed to make everyone else feel better. Was that all that being a leader was about?

:Papa Skan,: said a sweet, childlike voice in his head, right on cue. *:Mama says it is time for the meeting, and will you please come!:* Even without a mage-made teleson set to amplify her thoughts, Kechara's mind-voice was as clear as if she had spoken the words to him directly. It was another of the endless ironies of the current situation that the little "misborn" gryfalcon had become one of the most valuable members of the White Gryphon community. With magic—and thus, magical devices—gone unreliable, Kechara could and did communicate over huge distances with all the clarity and strength of teleson-enhanced Mindspeech. She was the communication coordinator for all of the leaders—and, more importantly, for all the Silver Gryphons. The Silvers were a resourceful policing organization formed of the remnants of the fighters and soldiers who had made it through the two

Kaled'a'in Gates, rather than through the Gates they'd been assigned.

Kechara's ability, combined with her eternal child-mind, would have caused her nothing but trouble in the old days, which was why Urtho had hidden her away in his Tower. But now—now she was the answer to a profound need. No one ever questioned the care lavished on her, or the way her special needs were always answered, no matter what else had to be sacrificed. She, in turn, had blossomed under the affection; her sweet temper never broke, and if she didn't understand more than a tenth of what she was asked to relay, it never seemed to bother her. Everyone loved her, and she loved everyone—and with Zhaneel watching over her zealously, making sure she had playtime and naptime, her new life was hundreds of times more enjoyable than her isolation in Urtho's Tower.

:I'm coming, kitten,: he told, her with resignation. *:Tell Mama I'm on my way.:*

He stood up and stretched his wings; the wind rushing up the cliff face tugged at his primaries like an impatient gryphlet. He took a last, deep breath of the air of freedom, cupped his wings close to his body, and leaped out onto the updraft.

The cliff face rushed past him, and he snapped his wings open with a flourish—and clacked his beak on a gasp of pain as his wing muscles spasmed.

Stupid gryphon—stupid, fat, out-of-condition gryphon! What are you trying to prove? That you're the equal of young Stirka!

He joined the gulls gliding along the cliff face, watching the ones ahead of him to see how the air currents were acting, while his joints joined his muscles in complaining. Like the gulls, he scarcely moved his wings in dynamic gliding except to adjust the wingtips. Their flight only looked effortless; all the tiny adjustments needed to use the wind instead of wingbeats took less energy, but far, far, more control.

And a body in better condition than mine. I should spend less time inspecting stoneworks and more time flying!

He *could* have taken the easier way; he could have gone up instead of down, and flapped along like the old buzzard he was.

But no, I let the updraft seduce me, and now I'm stuck. I'm going to regret this in the morning.

As if that wasn't bad enough, by the time he got halfway across the bay, he'd collected an audience.

His sharp eyes spared his bruised ego none of the details. Not only were there humans and *heitasi* watching him, but someone had brought a dozen bouncing, eager young gryphlets.

A flying class, no doubt. Here to see the Great Skandranon demonstrate the fine details of dynamic gliding. I wonder how they'll like seeing the Great Skandranon demonstrate the details of falling beak-over-tail on landing!

But with the pressure of all those eyes on him, he redoubled his efforts and increased the complaints of his muscles. He couldn't help himself. He had always played to audiences.

And when he landed, it was with a clever loft up over their heads that allowed him to drop gracefully (if painfully) down onto the road rather than scrambling to get a talonhold on the wall edging the terrace. He made an elegant landing on one hind claw, holding the pose for a moment, then dropping down to all fours again.

The audience applauded; the gryphlets squealed gleefully. Skan bowed with a jaunty nonchalance that in no way betrayed the fact that his left hip felt afire with pain. Temporary pain, thank goodness—he'd been injured often enough to know the difference between the flame of a passing strain and the ache of something torn or sprained. He clamped his beak down hard, tried to look clever and casual, and waited for the pain to go away, because he wasn't going to be able to move without limping until it did.

Stupid, stupid gryphon. Never learn, do you!

The burning ache in his hip finally ebbed; he continued to gryph-grin at the youngsters, then pranced off toward the half-finished Council Hall before any of the gryphlets could ask him to demonstrate that pretty landing again.

Amberdrake took his accustomed chair at the table, looked up at the canvas that served as a roof, and wondered how many more sessions they would meet here before the *real* roof was on. Right now the Council Hall was in a curious state of half-construction because its ambitious architecture absolutely required the participation of mages for anything but the simplest of tasks to be done. The mages hadn't been able to manage more than the most rudimentary of spells for the past six months, not since the last mage-storm.

That left the Council Hall little more than the walls and stone floor, boasting neither roof nor any of the amenities it was supposed to offer eventually.

But the completion of the Council Hall was at the bottom of a long list of priorities, and Amberdrake would be the last person to challenge the order of those priorities. Just—it would be very nice to look up and see a real roof—and not wonder if the next windstorm was going to come up in the middle of a Council session and leave all of them staring up at a sky full of stormclouds.

The Kaled'a'in mage Snowstar, who had once been the mage that their Lord and Master Urtho had trusted as much as himself, took his own seat beside Amberdrake. He caught the Chief Kestra'chern's eye and glanced up at the canvas himself.

"We think the next mage-storm will return things to normal enough for us to get some stonework done," Snowstar said quietly. "This time the interval should be about nine months. That's more than enough time to finish everything that *has* to be done magically."

Including the Council Hall. Amberdrake smiled his thanks. Snowstar had been put in place by Urtho, the Mage of Silence, as the speaker to his armies for all of the human mages in his employ, and no one had seen any reason why he shouldn't continue in that capacity. General Judeth, former Commander of the Fifth, was the highest-ranking officer to have come through the two Kaled'a'in Gates before the Cataclysm—purely by accident or the will of the gods, for she was one of the Commanders who appreciated the varied talents of the nonhumans under her command and knew how to use them without abusing them. On Skandranon's suggestion, she had organized the gryphons, the other nonhumans who had served in the ranks, and the human fighters into a different kind of paramilitary organization. Judeth's Silver Gryphons had acted as protectors and scouts on the march here, and served in the additional capacities of police, watchmen, and guards now that they all had a real home.

Amberdrake liked and admired Judeth. *I would have willingly named her Clan Sister even if no one else had thought of the idea.* Members of the Kaled'a'in Clan k'Leshya comprised the bulk of the humans who had wound up together—and with no qualms on anyone's part, they had adopted the mixed bag of service-fighters, mercenaries, kestra'chern and Healers who had come through with them. The adoption ceremony had ended the "us and them" divisions before they began, forging humans and nonhumans, Kaled'a'in and out-Clan into a whole, at least in spirit. And the journey here had completed that tempering and forging...

Well, that's the idealistic outlook, anyway. Amberdrake did not sigh, but his stomach churned a little. *Most* of the people of White Gryphon were folk of good will—

But some were not. The most obvious of those had marched off on their own over the course of the arduous search for a place to build a home, and good riddance to them, but some had been more clever. That was why Judeth's people still had a task, and why they would continue to serve as the police of White Gryphon.

Because, unfortunately, the Silvers are needed.

In an ideal world, everyone here would have had meaningful work, status according to ability, and would have been so busy helping to create their new society that they had no thought for anything else.

But this was not an ideal world. There were shirkers, layabouts, troublemakers, thieves, drunks—any personality problem that had existed "back home" still existed somewhere among k'Leshya. There were even those who thought Skandranon was the villain of the Cataclysm, rather than the hero. After all, if he had never taken Urtho's "suicide device" to Ma'ar, there would never have *been* a Cataclysm. And in a way, there might have been some truth in that idea. There would only have been the single explosion of Urtho's stronghold going up— not the double impact of all of Urtho's power *and* Ma'ar's discharged in a single moment. Perhaps they would not now be suffering through the effects of mage-storms.

And perhaps we would. Even Snowstar is not certain. But there is no persuading someone whose mind is already made up, especially when that person is looking for a nonhuman scapegoat. Not even Judeth herself could reason with some of these idiots.

As if the thought had summoned her, Judeth arrived at that moment. Her carefully pressed, black and silver uniform was immaculate as always. The silver-wire gryphon badge of her new command gleamed where her medals had once held pride of place on the breast of her tunic. She wore no medals now; she saw no reason to. "If people don't know my accomplishments by now," she often said, "no amount of medals is likely to teach them, or persuade them to trust my judgment."

She smiled at Amberdrake who smiled back. "Well, this is three— Silvers, Mages, Services—and I know that Cinnabar can't be spared right now for Healers, so where is our fourth?"

"On the way," Snowstar said promptly. "Zhaneel had Kechara call him."

"Ah." Judeth's smile softened; every one of the Silvers liked Kechara, but Amberdrake knew she had a special place in her heart for the little misborn gryfalcon. Perhaps she alone had any notion how hard Kechara worked to coordinate the Silvers, and she never once took that hard work for granted. "In that case—Amberdrake, is there anything you want to tell us before Skan gets here?"

"Only that I am acting mainly as Chief Kestra'chern in this, rather than as Chief of Services." With no one else to coordinate such common concerns as sanitation, recreation, medical needs, and general city administration, much of the burden of those tasks had fallen on Amberdrake's shoulders. After all, the kestra'chern, whose unique talents made them as much Healers as pleasure-companions, and as much administrators as entertainers, tended to be generalists rather than specialists. Amberdrake had already been the tacit Chief of Urtho's kestra'chern, and he was already Skandranon's closest friend. It seemed obvious to everyone that *he* should be in charge of those tasks which were not clearly in the purview of Judeth, Snowstar, or Lady Cinnabar.

Judeth raised an eyebrow at that. "Is this an actionable problem?" she asked carefully.

"I think so." He hesitated.

"I think you should wait long enough for me to sit down, Drake," Skandranon said from the doorway. "Either that, or hold this meeting without me. I could always find something pointless to do."

The gryphon grinned as he said that, though, taking any sting out of his words. He strolled across the expanse of unfinished stone floor to the incongruously formal Council table, the work of a solid year by one of the most talented—and unfortunately, disabled—woodworkers in White Gryphon. Since an injury that left him unable to walk or lift, he had been doing what so many other survivors at White Gryphon had done—used what they had left. He'd built the table in small sections, each one used as an example to teach others his woodworking skills, and then had his students assemble the pieces in place here. Like so much else in the settlement, it was complex and ingeniously designed, beneath an outer appearance of deceptive simplicity.

"So, what is it that was so urgent you had to call a Council meeting about it?" Skan said, arranging himself on the special couch that the same woodworker's students had created to fit the shape of a gryphon. "I know you better than to think it's something trivial—unless, of course, you're growing senile."

Amberdrake grimaced. "Hardly senile, though with an active two-year-old underfoot, I often wonder if I'm in danger of going mad."

Skan nodded knowingly, but Amberdrake was not about to be distracted into discussions of parenthood and the trials thereof. "I'm afraid that as Chief Kestra'chern, I am going to have to bring charges against someone to the Council. That's why I needed three of you here—I'm going to have to sit out on the decision since I'm the one bringing the charges. That means I need a quorum of three."

Snowstar folded his hands together on the table; Judeth narrowed her eyes. "What are the charges?" Snowstar asked quietly.

"First, and most minor—impersonation of a trained kestra'chern." Amberdrake shrugged. "I do not personally *remember* this man being in Urtho's service, as a kestra'chern or otherwise. I can't find anyone who will vouch for his training, either. I *do* know that his credentials are forged because one of the names on them is mine."

"That's fairly minor, and hardly a Council matter," Snowstar said cautiously.

"I know that, and if it were all, I wouldn't have called you here. I'd simply have examined the man and determined his fitness to practice then put him through formal training if he was anything other than a crude *perchi* with ambitions." Amberdrake bit his lip. "No, the reason I bring him up to you three, and in secret session, is because of what he has done. He has violated his trust—and if he had been less clever he would already be in Judeth's custody on assault charges."

Judeth's expression never varied. "That bad?" she said.

He nodded. "That bad. We kestra'chern are often presented with—some odd requests. He has used the opportunities he was presented with to inflict pain and damage, both emotional and physical, purely for his own entertainment."

"Why haven't we heard of this before?" Skan demanded, his eyes dangerously alight.

"Because he is," Amberdrake groped for words, "he is *diabolical*, Skan, that is all I can say. He's clever, he's crafty, but above all, he is supremely adept at charming or—manipulating people. He has succeeded in manipulating the people who came to him as clients so thoroughly that it has been over a year from the time he began before one was courageous enough to report him to me. Even the other kestra'chern were fooled by him. They couldn't tell what he was doing behind his doors. But I know—I have felt what his client felt."

Skan's beak dropped open a little. "What *is* this man?" the gryphon asked, astonished. "Some sort of—of—evil Empath?"

"He might be, Skan, I don't know," Amberdrake replied honestly. "All I know is that the person who came to me needed considerable help in recovering from the damage that had been done, and that there are more people who are more damaged yet who have not complained." Amberdrake had been very careful not even to specify the client's sex; while the victim had not asked for anonymity, Amberdrake felt it was only fair and decent to grant it. He spent several long and uncomfortable moments detailing exactly what had been done to that victim, while the others listened in silence. When he had finished— as he had expected—all three of them were unanimous in their condemnation of the ersatz kestra'chern.

"Who is he?" Judeth asked, her voice a low growl as she reached for pen and paper to make out the arrest warrant.

Amberdrake sighed and closed his eyes. He had hoped in a way that once the charges had been laid and the Council decision arrived at, he would feel better. But he didn't; he only felt as if he had uncovered the top of something noisome and unpleasant, and that there was going to be more to face before the mess was cleaned up.

"Hadanelith," he said softly, as Judeth waited, hand poised over the paper.

She wrote down the name.

"Hadanelith," she repeated as she sealed the order with her signet ring. "Can I deal with him now, or is there something else you want to do with him first?"

"Now," Amberdrake said quickly, with a shudder. "Arrest him now. He's done enough damage. I don't want him to have a chance to do any more."

"Right." Judeth stood up. "Skan, would you have Kechara call Aubri, Tylar, Retham, and Vetch, and have them double-time it over here to meet Amberdrake and me?" She handed the arrest warrant to Amberdrake, who took it, trying not to show his reluctance. "I'll be going with you to take this Hadanelith down. This could look bad—I am considered to be the military leader here. A military leader arresting a putative kestra'chern under any circumstances will cause some discontent. Still, I don't want to be seen as being above getting my hands dirty or unfit for service with the other Silvers. And I definitely do *not* want someone like that loose to deal with later. Hate to saddle you with this, Drake, but—"

"But I'm the one bringing the charges, so I had better be there. It's my job, Judeth," he replied as he wrung the warrant loosely in his hands. "Though it's times like these when I wish I was just a simple kestra'chern."

Judeth snorted and gave him a sideways look. "Drake," she said only, "you were never a *simple* kestra'chern."

"I suppose I wasn't," he murmured as she, Snowstar, and Skan left the table and the Council Hall.

Hadanelith whittled another few strokes at the wooden bit before setting it down. After some more cutting and rounding—not too much rounding, though, it needed to remain a challenge for the client, right?—he'd add the pilot holes for the wooden pegs and straps later. Carving wood was so much like what he did for a living with his clients, it was natural that he would be excellent at it. He could grasp the roughness, grip it firmly, and then cut away at every part that didn't look like the shape he had in mind.

Telica, here, was one of his works. A slice here, a chunk taken off there, and before long she'd be another near perfect item. Her mind was his latest work. She was nude, kneeling on the floor, held in place by several lengths of thread binding her neck to her wrists, her wrists to her ankles. The thread was completely normal in composition, which was what made it so amusing to him.

Virtually any effort at all would have snapped them, without leaving so much as a welt; no, the real bindings here were those of his will over hers. The regular training that made her one more of his items held her as firmly in place as any set of iron shackles or knotted scarves. She was one of his carvings, inside, though she didn't presently show so much as a scratch on her alabaster-smooth skin.

Every time Telica came to him for one of her appointments she knew she would be trained and tested in a dozen ways. All of his girls knew this. They could be trapped or tricked, hurt or caressed, abused or set up for humiliation, and after a while, they came to love him for it—or at least obey him. Obedience was close enough for him, he'd take that over love any day.

So it was with no worry at all that he took three steps to stand before her steadily breathing, still form, and put a hand to her jaw. "Open," he said in his rich voice, and her lips parted in instant compliance to receive the wooden bit he'd been trimming. As he pressed it deeper into her mouth, he noted that it scraped the gums, and probably pressed the palate about *there.* Good, good. It would serve as another test of her training in itself, then, and the soreness that lingered after Telica's visit would simply be another reminder of his attentions, and who she served now.

Who *she* served? That was another delicious irony. Hadanelith was, as far as anyone else knew, serving *her*, but behind these doors, she was *his* as surely as any other of his whittled treasures. His treasures were six now; Dianelle, Suriya, Gaerazena, Bethtia, and Yonisse, and Telica here, each one a good but still slightly flawed carving.

There was always something wrong with them by the time he'd made them his artworks. Why was that? Why was the wood always unseasoned, or knotty, or split down the middle, when he'd finally carved away enough of the bark to make something beautiful? It was as if the wood that looked so promising on the outside failed to live up to the promise; that by the time he'd gotten enough of the useless wood shaved away to refine the details, the flaws in the material showed themselves.

Telica here, for instance, was too quiet. It was nearly impossible to get as much as a whimper out of her. He was no more lusty than any other man, he felt, and there were times, just as when one craved a certain dish or fruit, when he simply had to hear a muffled cry of anguish or a sob. Telica was mute as a stick unless he lacerated her with a blade or pierced her flesh with a needle. She was just as flawed in her silence as Gaerazena was in her garrulous, hysterical chattering and Yonisse was in her shuddering anxieties.

It couldn't be his skill; it had to be the material itself. If only he could get his hands on a woman of real substance, breeding, true quality. A woman like Winterhart…

That one he had yet to touch, although he had watched her hungrily for ten years. Now there was a creature fit for an artist! Not wood at all, she was the finest marble, a real challenge to carve and mold. But he could do it. He was more than a match for her, just as he was more than a match for any of them. What sculptor was ever afraid of his stone? What genius was ever afraid of his toys? The challenge would be to unmake and then remake her, but to do it so cleverly that she *asked* for every change he made to her.

What a dream…

But a dream was all it ever would be. She would never come to him, not while she was mated to the oh-so-perfect Amberdrake. And not when the whole city knew how disgustingly contented she was with her mate. It was all too honey-sweet for words, just as sickeningly, cloyingly sweet as that sugar-white gryphon, Skandranon, and *his* mate.

It was just a good thing for him that not everyone in this little Utopia was as contented with life as those four were.

He would certainly enjoy giving all of them a bitter taste of reality when the time was right. Especially Winterhart. Get under that cool surface and see what seethed beneath it. Find out what she feared.

Not the ordinary fears of his six creations, he was certain of that. No, Winterhart must surely fear something fascinating, something he would have to work hard to discover. What could he cut free from inside her? Now there was an interesting image, a hollow woman, emptied out slice by slice, with only a walking shell left for everyone else to see. How could it be done? And how thin could he carve those walls before the sculpture collapsed in on itself? Well. If the wood was good enough, he could scoop out quite enough to satisfy his needs.

These thoughts were on his mind as he lowered his knife down between Telica's thighs. That, and his craving for her to make some noise for him.

The blade touched the birch-white skin of one thigh.

At that moment, a shadow moved across Telica's still skin. The lighting in the room shifted as someone—no, several someones—came into the room uninvited. Now *this* was an outrage! Hadanelith whirled, knife in hand, to confront these presumptuous invaders. Before he could utter more than a snarl, a boot to his face made things quite different than a minute before, when *he* was the one in control.

Amberdrake's trepidation had hardened into a dull, tight pain in his gut. It certainly wasn't because he hadn't seen horror in his life, or felt himself grow ill from feeling others' suffering. It wasn't precisely because he feared a violent confrontation, or the cleaning up that was always needed after such a thing happened. The sensation he had, as the group arrived at Hadanelith's home—or perhaps it should be called a lair— was dread for its own sake. Amberdrake had the feeling that nothing good was going to come of this arrest. Morally it was the right thing to do, by Law it was the right thing to do, yet still there was that gnawing in his gut that told him they were doing more harm than good.

Aubri, the Eternally Battered, apparently felt it also, although it might have just been a bad breakfast that caused his disgruntled expression. He was a gryphon who never had any good luck, if you believed what he said.

"It's too quiet in there, Drake," he wheezed, as they held themselves poised just outside Hadanelith's door. "We know he's got someone in there, so why isn't there any sound?"

316

"I don't know," Amberdrake replied, in an anxious whisper. "I don't like it, either, Judeth?"

"I've got a bad feeling about this," she said shortly. "Let's get in there—now."

With a wave of her hand, she led her group of ex-fighters through the door in a rush. Amberdrake trailed behind, warrant still held in his clenched hand, dreading what they would find.

So he didn't actually *see* Judeth kick Hadanelith in the jaw and send him sprawling to the floor, but once he saw what had prompted that action, he also saw no need to protest what might be considered an act of brutality.

The young woman was bound only by thread, in one of the most excruciatingly uncomfortable positions Amberdrake had ever seen. Her skin was sheened with sweat, and her muscles trembled with the effort of holding herself in place. There were faint scars in many places on her pale skin. With Hadanelith's carving knife lying on the floor where Judeth had just kicked it, there wasn't much doubt in Amberdrake's mind where those scars had come from.

But most horrible of all—she acted as if she were completely unaware of their presence.

No. She's not acting. She is *unaware of our presence. She will not acknowledge that we are here because he has not told her to.*

That was what held him frozen, and what made Judeth's eyes blaze with black rage; that one presumably human person had done *this* to another.

The scars are only the least of what he has done to her. This will take months to undo. This is a case for the Healers; my people can't possibly make this right.

With trembling hands, Amberdrake unrolled the arrest warrant and read it out loud. Hadanelith did not move from the place where he lay sprawled across his own floor, not even to finger the growing bruise on his jaw. He only glared up at Amberdrake in impotent fury as the kestra'chern read out the charges and the sentence.

"You've heard the charges. We've seen the evidence before our eyes. You've been caught, Hadanelith," Judeth said fiercely, biting off each word as if she bitterly regretted having to say anything to him at all. "Have you got anything to say in your defense?"

In answer, Hadanelith spat at her. Since he was lying on the ground and she was standing over him, it didn't get very far. The glob of spittle hit the top of her boot and ran down the side. One of the human Silvers snarled and pulled back a fist; Judeth caught his arm.

"No point in soiling your hands, Tylar," she said coldly. She looked around, picked up a piece of expensive silk that Hadanelith was using for a couch drape, and deliberately wiped her boot with it, dropping it at her feet in a crumpled heap. Only then did she turn to look at her prisoner.

"There are a lot of things I would *like* to do to you, scum," she said, her voice flat and devoid of all emotion. "However, we've got one Law to deal with people like you. Hadanelith, by reason of being caught in the acts described, you will be taken as you are to the plateau above White Gryphon in chains. You will be taken to the edge of the lands we have claimed and cultivated. There you will be freed of your chains, and you will be given from now until darkness falls to take yourself outside our border marker. If, by tomorrow at dawn, you are still inside them whoever finds you is permitted to take any steps he deems necessary to get rid of you."

Hadanelith's rage showed clearly in his eyes, but his voice was as cold as Judeth's. "As I am? What, no weapons, no food, no—"

"You are a mad dog, scum. We don't supply a mad dog with food and weapons." Her lips thinned, and her eyes glinted as she looked down at him. "You think that you're so clever—I suggest you start using that cleverness to figure out how to survive in the forest with only what you're wearing." She jerked her head at the rest of the Silvers. "Chain him up, and get him out of here before he makes me sicker than I already am."

The Silvers didn't need any urging; within moments they had their prisoner on his feet, collared and manacled.

Amberdrake had expected Hadanelith to fight, to heap verbal abuse on them—to do or say *something*, at any rate. This continued silence was as unnerving as his continued certainty that no good was going to come of this.

He is a mad dog. The forest is going to kill him, but painfully, and perhaps slowly. Shouldn't we have at least had the compassionate responsibility to do it ourselves?

But his crimes had not warranted execution, only banishment. He could not be cured, that much was obvious, so the rulers of White Gryphon had an obligation to remove him from among those he was preying upon. That meant imprisonment or banishment, and White Gryphon did not yet have a prison.

Hadanelith glared at Amberdrake all the time he was being bound, and continued to glare at him all the time he was being hauled out of the room, as if he held Amberdrake personally responsible for what was happening to him. That just added another level of unease to all of the rest.

If they had found Hadanelith alone, Amberdrake might have turned and bolted at that moment—but they hadn't, and through all of this, the young woman had not moved so much as an eyelash. Amberdrake's personal unease gave way to a flood of nausea as he knelt down beside her.

He eased down his own shields, just a trifle, and touched her arm with a feather-brush of a finger to assess the situation.

He slammed his shields back up in the next instant, and knew he had gone as white as Skan's feathers by the chill of his skin.

He looked up at Judeth, who hovered uncertainly beside him.

"It's not good, Judeth, but I can take it from here." He took a deep, steadying breath and reminded himself that this was no worse than many, many of the traumas he had helped to heal in his career as the Chief Kestra'chern of Urtho's armies. He looked up again and manufactured a smile for her. "You go on along. I can manage. She'll have to go to Lady Cinnabar, of course, but I can snap her out of this enough to get her there."

One of Judeth's chief virtues was that she never questioned a person's own assessment of his competence; if Amberdrake said he could do something, she took it for granted that he could.

"Right," she replied. "In that case—I'll go along with the others. I want to make personally sure that chunk of *sketi* gets past the border markers by sundown."

She turned on her heel and stalked out the door, leaving Amberdrake alone with the girl, a young woman whose name he didn't even know.

And that's the next thing; go through Hadanelith's records and find his client list. Where there is one like this, there will be more.

You knew it could be this bad, Drake. Just think how much worse it would be for her if you weren't here.

Hadanelith would not run, no matter how grim and threatening his captors looked. He walked away from them at a leisurely pace, as if he was out for an afternoon stroll, keeping his posture jaunty and his muscles relaxed.

It wasn't easy. The back of his neck crawled, and despite that officious bitch Judeth's assertions that they were not going to physically harm him—*themselves*—he half expected an arrow in the back at any moment.

But no arrows came, and he completed his stroll down the furrow of planted ground without incident, carefully stepping on each tiny seedling before him as he walked, and grinding it into powder beneath his feet. A petty bit of revenge, but it was all that he was likely to get for some time.

At the end of the furrow was the land that had not been claimed from the forest—forest that held so many dangers that sending him out here might just as well have been a death sentence. Even the field workers came out under guards of beaters to drive the beasts away, and Kaled'a'in whose specialty was in handling the minds of wild beasts in case the beaters couldn't frighten predators off.

And archers in case both fail. Thank you so much for your compassion, you hypocrites.

He did not pause as he reached the trees and the tangle of growth beneath them. He pushed right on in and continued to shove his way grimly through the bushes and entwined vines, ignoring scratches and biting insects until he finally struck a game path.

Then he stopped, a little out of breath, to take inventory of his hurts. He wanted to know every scratch, every bruise, for he would eventually extract payment for all of them.

There was the kick to his jaw, the other to his hand; the one had practically broken the jawbone, the other had left his hand numb. His guards hadn't been any too gentle on the trip up here, either; they'd just about dislocated his arms, wrenching him around, and they'd gotten in a few surreptitious kicks and punches that left more bruises and aching spots under his clothing.

Nevertheless, Hadanelith smiled. They'd been so smug, so certain of themselves—they'd said he was to be sent into this exile *as he was,* and then were bound by that word from searching him!

Fools. They assumed that a kestra'chern at work would be completely unarmed—but Hadanelith was not exactly a kestra'chern.

And Hadanelith was never unarmed.

He began to divest himself of all his hidden secrets, starting with the stiletto blades in the seams of his boots.

Shortly, he would resume his journey to the boundary markers, and he would be very careful to remain outside them for the few days it took to convince these idiots that some beast or other had disposed of him.

Then he would return.

And then the repayments would begin.

CHAPTER TWO

Skan cupped his wings and settled onto the ledge of the lair he and Zhaneel had chosen when White Gryphon was first laid out, this time only stubbing two talons upon landing. That wasn't unusual; he was often less careful when he thought no one was watching him, and the pain was negligible. This was his home. He could blunt his talons on the stone if he felt like it.

Together with a small army of hertasi, they had carved it from the rock of the cliff, used the resulting loose stone for mortared walls and furniture, then filled it with such gryphonic luxuries as they had brought with them. It had a glorious view of the surf on the rocks below, but was sheltered from even the worst winter storms by an outcropping of hard, black stone covered with moss and tiny ferns. It was easily the best lair in the city; mage-fires kept it cozy in the winter, breezes off the sea kept it cool in the summer, and there were plenty of soft cushions and carved benches to recline upon. Occasionally rank *did* have its privileges.

One of those privileges was absenting himself from the likely unpleasant confrontation with this Hadanelith character. He felt rather sorry for poor Amberdrake but, on the whole, rather relieved for himself. Perhaps he could soothe his guilt later by visiting Amberdrake with a special snack or treat.

At least that Hadanelith mess was one decision I didn't have to make. All I had to do was agree with Drake. What's happened to me, when not deciding someone else's fate is an event.

His wing muscles still ached, distantly, from his landing, and he felt a lot more tired than he should have been after two relatively short flights. *I'm going to have to increase the time I spend sky dancing,* he decided. *No matter how I have to juggle my schedule. I shouldn't be tiring this quickly. After ten years you'd think I'd get most of my endurance back!*

He folded his wings, and glanced back down at the surf before pushing open the door to the lair. Cinnabar kept warning him, even after all these years, that the time he spent between Gates followed too quickly by the perils of their cross-country trek had burned away every bit of his reserves. He was stripped to the bone by the strain, so many years ago—but he should have gotten all of it back by *now!* Amberdrake, Gesten, and Lady Cinnabar had done their best for him, too. *This is all the fault of a sedentary life! I spend more time strolling around the streets than I do in exercises, and no one says anything because I'm Skandranon—but if I were any other gryphon, there'd be jokes about my sagging belly!*

He closed the door neatly behind him and stepped over the wall across the entrance—a necessary precaution to keep unfledged, crawling, leaping gryphlets from becoming hurtling projectiles off the balcony. The gryphons had never had to face that particular problem when their lairs had been on the ground, but a small inconvenience seemed a trivial price for the added safety of their youngsters.

Small mage-lights illuminated the interior of the lair—unusual in the city at the moment, as were the mage-fires that heated the lair by winter. Mage-lights and mage-fires were far down on the list of things the mages needed to create during the brief times that magic worked properly. Skan had made most of these, and Vikteren had done the rest.

There we are again. Another reason why I am such a feathered lump. Lying in place for days on end to make mage-lights. Staring at a stone to enchant it to glow like a lovesick firefly while hertasi and humans bring me enough food to sink a horse. What would Urtho think of me now!

The humans and hertasi had to make do with candles and lanterns; while mage-lights and mage-fires were in limited supply, they went first to the Healers, then the gryphons and *tervardi*, then the *kyree*. Only after all the nonhumans had sufficient lights and heating sources would humans receive them for their homes. This had been a decision on Skan's part that although it seemed slightly selfish, had a sound reason behind it. The Healers obviously needed mage-lights and heat sources more than anyone else—and as for the gryphons, tervardi, and kyree, well, the former had feathers, which were dangerous around open flames, and the wolflike latter didn't have hands to light flames with.

Freshly crisped gryphon and roasted tervardi, mm-mm! Served fresh in their own homes, in front of their children—Ma'ar's secret recipe! That was the very phrase he'd used to persuade the rest of the Council to agree to the edict, and as he'd figured, the invocation of Ma'ar's name did the trick, more than logic had.

He hadn't enjoyed manipulating them, though. Tricks like that left a rather bad taste in his mouth. He really didn't like manipulating anyone, if it came right down to it. Neither had Urtho.

There were many things Urtho didn't like, gods bless his memory. I always secretly pitied him for the position he was put in by others' need for him. He never liked being the leader of all those who craved freedom from Ma'ar, but it was something he had to do. I remember him looking at me once, with a look of quiet desperation, when I asked him why he did it.

Skandranon paused, eyes unfocused, as his memory brought the moment back in sharp detail. *He said, simply, "If not me, then who!"*

Now I know how he felt then. It wears a soul down, even though the sense of fulfilling a duty is supposed to make a soul enriched. A noble heart, the stories say, is supposed to live and find joy in the responsibility. But I am satisfied less and less, doing a great deal I don't like—including getting fat!

"Zhaneel?" he called softly, when a glance around the "public" room showed no signs of life, not even a gryphon dozing in the pile of pillows in the corner. "I'm—"

He'd called softly, hoping that if the little ones were sleeping, he wouldn't wake them. Stupid gryphon. Vain hope.

A pair of high-pitched squeals from the nursery chamber greeted the first sound of his voice, and a moment later twin balls of feathers and energy came hurtling out of the chamber door. They each targeted a foreleg; Tadrith the right and Keenath the left.

They weren't big enough to even shake him as they hit and clung, but they made it very difficult to move then they locked on and gnawed. And Amberdrake and Winterhart thought *they* had problems with their two-legged toddler! Young gryphons went straight from the crawling stage into the full-tilt running stage, much like kittens, and like kittens they had three modes of operation—"play," "starving," and "sleep." They moved from one mode to another without warning, and devoted every bit of concentration to the mode they were in at the time. No point in trying to get them interested in a nap if they were in "play" mode—and no point in trying to distract them with a toy if they were squalling for food.

Zhaneel followed her two offspring at a more sedate pace. She was more beautiful than ever, more falconlike. Her dark malar-markings were more prominent; now that she wasn't trying to look like the gryphons whose bodies were based on hawks, and now that she had learned to be self-confident, she carried herself like the gryfalcon queen she was. "Don't worry, I wasn't trying to settle them for a nap," she said calmly over their wordless squeals of glee, as Skan tried vainly to detach them. "We were just playing chase-mama's-tail."

"And now we're playing burr-on-papa's-leg, I see," he replied. Zhaneel took one bemused look at what her children were doing and began chortling. At the moment, still in their juvenile plumage, the gryphlets looked like nothing but balls of puffy, tan-and-brown feathers, particularly absurd when attached to Skan's legs. "The Council session broke up early,"

Skandranon continued, "and I decided that I'd had enough and escaped before anyone could find some other idiot's crisis for me to solve."

It came out a lot more acidic than he'd intended, and Zhaneel cocked her head to one side. "Headache?" she inquired delicately.

He succeeded in removing Tadrith from his right leg, but Keenath, being the older of the two tiercels, was more stubborn. "No," he replied, again with more weariness than he had intended. "I am just very, very tired today of being the Great White Gryphon, the Wise Old Gryphon of the Hills, the Solver of Problems, and Soother of Quarrels. No one remembers when I was the Avenger in the Skies or Despoiler of Virgins or Hobby Of Healers. Now they want someone to do the work for them, and I am the fool that fell into it. I am tired of being responsible."

He slowly peeled Keenath from his foreleg, as the young gryphlet cackled with high-pitched glee and his brother pounced on Skan's twitching tail.

"You want to be irresponsible?" Zhaneel asked, with a half-smile he didn't understand, and a rouse of her feathers.

"Well," he replied, after a moment of thought, "Yes! The more people pile responsibilities on me, the less time I have for anything else! All of my time is taken up with solving other peoples' problems, until I don't have any time for my own! And *look* at me!" He shook himself indignantly. "I'm *fat*, Zhaneel! I'm overweight and out of condition! I can't think of the last time I sat around chatting with Amberdrake and Gesten just because I enjoy their company, when I spirited you off for a wild storm ride, or just flew off somewhere to lie senseless in the sun for a while! Or for that matter, to lie on *you* a while. And the longer this goes on, it seems, the less time I get to even think!"

Zhaneel reached out a foreclaw and corralled her younger son before he reattached himself to his father's leg, nodding thoughtfully. "But the city is almost finished, except for the things that people must do for their own homes, which you cannot be responsible for," she pointed out. "So—surely they must not need you as much?"

He sighed and shook his head. "Except that the more things get done, the more they find for me to do. As the months go by, the things are always less vital, but they're frozen without my word of approval or decree. It's as if they've all decided that I am the only creature capable of making decisions—never mind that I'm only one member of a five-person Council!"

As she fixed her eyes on his, he struggled to articulate feelings that were not at all well defined. "I don't know if this is some twisted joke that fate has played on me, Zhaneel, but I'm beginning to feel as if I'm not me anymore. It's as if the old Skandranon is being squeezed out and this—this faded, stodgy, dull old White Gryphon is taking his place! And it is happening in my body, and I can only watch it happen."

As Tadrith raced around to attack Skan's other side, Zhaneel cornered him as well, tumbling both gryphlets together into a heap of cushions, where they attacked each other with exuberant energy, their father utterly forgotten. She sat down beside him and nibbled his ear-tuft, with an affectionate caress along his milky-white cheek. "The wars are over, my love," she pointed out with inarguable logic. "There are no more secret missions to fly, no more need to dye your feathers black so that you do not show against the night sky—no more real need for the *Black* Gryphon. We all have changed, not just you."

"I know that," he sighed and leaned into her caress. "But—that was more than a part of me, it was who I was and I miss it. Sometimes I feel as if the Black Gryphon died—with—with Urtho—and now all I have left is a shell. I don't know who or what I am anymore. I only know that I don't like what's happened to me."

Zhaneel clicked her beak in irritation. "Perhaps you do not care for what you are, but there are many of us who were very pleased to see a Skandranon who had learned a bit of responsibility!" she said crisply. "And we would be very annoyed to see that particular lesson forgotten!"

She glared at him just as she would have glared at a foolish young brancher for acting like one of the fledglings.

He shook his head, trying to bite back a hasty retort and instead make her see what he was talking about. "No, it isn't that," he replied, groping for words. "I—it's just that it seems as if I've gone to the opposite extreme, as if there just isn't any time for me to be myself anymore. I'm tired all the time, I never have a moment to think. I feel—I don't know—thinned out, as if I've stretched myself to cover so much that now I have no substance. My duty has consumed me!"

The slightly frantic tone of his voice was enough to make both the youngsters look up in alarm, and Zhaneel patted his shoulder hastily. "You'll be all right," she told him, clearly trying to placate him. "Don't worry so much. You gave a lot of yourself in the journey here. You lost almost all of your strength when you were trapped in the Gates. You just need more rest."

That's always the answer, any time I complain that I don't feel like myself.

"And that's just what I'm not getting," he grumbled but gave up trying to explain himself to her. She didn't understand; how could he expect her to, when he didn't really understand what was wrong himself?

The gryphlets came galloping over to him again, and he settled down on the floor and let them climb all over him. What *was* wrong with him, anyway? He had everything he had ever wanted—a lovely mate, a secure home, peace—and he was the leader he had always dreamed of being. Shouldn't he be content, happy?

Well—except that he *wasn't* the leader he had dreamed of being, back when he fought against the sky, *makaar*, and all the death-bolts an army could hurl at him. The stories he was raised on, of heroes and hopes, said nothing about the consumption of the leader by his duties. He had dreamed of dramatically-lit skies against which his glorious form would glide across the land he protected, and below him the people would cheer to behold him and flock to his presence.

Maybe the problem was simply that he was, at best, a reluctant leader when it came to peacetime solutions, and his discontent with that situation spilled over onto everything else.

Zhaneel nibbled his ear-tuft again, then disappeared into the depths of the lair, presumably with some chore or other to take care of now that he was keeping the youngsters out of her feathers for a while. Skandranon might be caught in chasms of distress, but he would always have affection for his little ones. He loved them day to day as much as he had enjoyed conceiving them. He fisted his claws and bowled the little ones over with careful swats, sending them back into the pile of cushions. They squealed and chirped, rolling around and batting at him in boundless exuberance—for the moment—and he wished that he could be as carefree and happy as they were.

Was everyone as unhappy as he was? He didn't think so. In fact, he wasn't quite certain when his current discontent had begun. It was simply that today, he was devoting concentration to realizing it was *there*, and just how deep it festered.

As arduous as the journey here had been and as fraught with danger and uncertainty, *his* job had actually been easier then than it was now. He'd only needed to offer encouragement, to keep peoples' spirits up. He could step up and make a rousing speech, inspire hope, and tell well-timed stories. He was the cloud-white cock of the walk at critical times. Judeth had been in charge of protecting the army of refugees, Gesten and Amberdrake in charge of keeping everyone fed and sheltered. Lady

Cinnabar had taken over anything remotely concerned with the health of the group. All *he* had been asked to do was to provide a figurehead, a reminder of the old days, and what the best of those days had meant.

Skandranon snorted to himself. *In other words, vain gryphon, your job was to be their living legend.*

Now he had to make decisions—usually difficult, uncomfortable decisions. Worst of all, he was the only "authority" anyone could agree on to arbitrate in disputes between non-humans and humans—and even though the disputants might agree on him as arbitrator, they were seldom entirely satisfied with him. Humans, he suspected, always were sure he was favoring nonhumans, and the nonhumans were always convinced he would favor humans because of his special relationship with Amberdrake. Annoying, but there it was. And that just led to another source of discontent for him; if people were going to insist he solve their conflicts, the least they could do would be to pretend that they liked the solution! But no matter what he did or did not do, *someone* would grumble about it!

It almost seemed as if the easier life became, the more *trouble* people caused! In the beginning, when White Gryphon was nothing more than a collection of tents perched on the terraces, people just never seemed to have the energy or time to quarrel with one another.

Maybe that's it. Maybe the problems are coming because people have too much spare time!

Surely that was too easy an answer...

And it wasn't true for everyone, either.

Maybe it was just the curse of civilization. *I know that Urtho's army had all the troubles that plague any big gathering of people. It stands to reason that once people aren't completely absorbed in the business of trying to get the basic necessities, they'll go back to their old ways. Look at that Hadanelith creature, for instance! I'll bet ten years ago he was playing those same games down among the* perchi; *I'll bet the only reason he didn't get caught then was because his clients just didn't come back to him for more, rather than complaining about him. Or else—his clients just didn't come back from the battlefield.*

Or maybe Hadanelith hadn't been old enough, ten years ago, to ply any kind of trade; Amberdrake hadn't mentioned his age. That could be why he had been able to fake being trained—if he had lied about his training he could just as easily have lied about his age and experience. Most of the kestra'chern attached to Urtho's armies had *not* wound up with the Kaled'a'in Clan k'Leshya, instead they had gone through the

Gate that had taken the noncombatants from the purely human forces. That only made sense, of course; why should they have gone where the skills they had trained for would not be needed? The Kaled'a'in Clan k'Leshya had chosen to go with the gryphons and the other nonhumans because of their own special relationship with Urtho's magically-created creatures—but the other Kaled'a'in Clans had not gone to the same refuge for purely pragmatic reasons. It was best not to put all the refugees in one place. If the Kaled'a'in were to survive as a people or even as a vestige of a people, it was best that the Clans split up, to distribute them over too large an area to wipe out. That Amberdrake was here was partly the result of his own friendship with Skan, and partly the fact that he had joined k'Leshya himself; besides him, there were only the k'Leshya kestra'chern and perhaps a handful of others.

So when there was leisure again, and people began to look for some of the amenities of the old days, there were some things—like trained kestra'chern, for instance—that were in short supply.

Which means that the more subtle unethical people will have the opportunity to revert to type, an opportunity that hasn't been there until now. That makes sense. Probably too much sense, actually. Urtho might have been the most principled creature in the known lands, but there were not too many like him, in his army or out of it. I suppose, given how many people were pouring through whatever Gate was nearest there at the end, that we shouldn't have expected that everyone with us was of an angelic nature. We shouldn't have expected anything. We were just glad to be alive at the time. And later—everyone was too busy to get into trouble, even the potential workers of trouble.

That only depressed him more. Perhaps he was overly idealistic, but he had really hoped that they had left things and people like Hadanelith behind them. *I suppose there is going to be crime now, theft and assault, fraud and chicanery, who knows what else.* He sighed. *More work for the Silvers; I'd thought Judeth was just creating makework for them, but maybe she had more vision than me.*

Or maybe she had just had less blind optimism.

Or maybe she is just smarter than the White Fool.

Well, whatever the reason, General Judeth had done her work well. The Silver Gryphons, with their silver badges and ornamented bracers to show their station to even the most drunken of viewers, were as well-trained as they were well-equipped. Fortunately for Skan's peace of mind, the. stylized silver-wire badges they wore, created by a displaced silversmith who was tired of never being able to make jewelry anymore, bore no resemblance to Skandranon, White or Black. After all, there was only so much adoration a sane mind could accept. The former soldiers had applied their military training to other matters under Judeth's supervision, and at the time Skan had only felt relief that she was giving them something to make them feel useful.

I thought that gradually we'd be able to phase all those old warhorses out, that once we knew we weren't going to need protection against whatever is out there in the wilderness, they'd become mostly decorative, rescuing children from trees and the like. Silly me. So now we have police; and it looks as if we are going to need them.

No wonder that Judeth had insisted that the Silvers always travel in pairs, with one of the pair being a Mindspeaker—and no wonder she had politely requisitioned Kechara's talents and service. Skan hadn't thought much about that, either, except to be glad that Judeth was giving poor little Kechara something to do to make *her* feel useful. He'd been too grateful to care, since that got her out from under Zhaneel's feet most of the day. The eternal child, she'd been fine until Zhaneel gave birth to the little ones—and the sheer work caused by the presence of three children in the lair, one of them half the size of an adult, was just a bit much for Zhaneel.

Even the addition to the household of another hertasi, a young lizard named Cafri, who was Kechara's best friend, playmate, and caretaker all rolled into one, had not helped until Judeth had come to Skan with her carefully-phrased request. Now Kechara went up to a special room in the Silvers' headquarters in early morning and did not return until after dark—not that Judeth was abusing her or overworking her. The "special room" was very special; it had a huge open high-silled window, a fabulous balcony, was cooled by the breezes in summer and warmed carefully in winter. It was also crammed full of all the toys the grandmothers could make. There were playmates, too. The mated gryphons among the Silvers brought their own offspring to play there as well. It was just that Kechara of all the "children" would be asked from time to time to Mindspeak a message to someone. She would stop whatever she was doing, happily oblige, then get back to her latest game.

Mindspeech seemed to take no effort whatsoever on her part which, in itself, was rather remarkable. She often forget to say things with words, in fact, projecting her thought or feeling directly into the mind of whoever she was "talking" to, particularly when she was impatient. Acting as message-relay for the Silvers did not bother her in the least—in fact, she was rather proud of herself, insofar as Skan could tell, because *she* had a job, and none of her playmates did.

:Papa Skan!: said that cheerful little voice in his head, suddenly, and he wondered with startlement if she had somehow picked up his thoughts about her and assumed he was trying to talk to her. *:Papa Skan, Unca Aubri says you need to know something.:*

He sighed with mingled relief and resignation. Relief, because he didn't want to have to explain what he had been thinking to Kechara, and resignation because Aubri had been assigned to the unpleasant task of ejecting Hadanelith from White Gryphon. Something must have gone wrong…

:What does Uncle Aubri want, sweetling!: he asked carefully, keeping his own feelings out of what he sent. She was quicker to pick up on emotion than thoughts.

Her reply was prompt and clear. *:Unca Aubri says to tell you he's up on the cliff and that there's a ship that isn't ours, and it's coming in to the docks and he wants you to come where he is right away please.:*

His head snapped up. A ship? A strange ship? Friend or foe? *:Tell him I'm coming, sweet,:* he replied quickly. *:Can you please tell Uncle Snowstar and Uncle Tamsin what you just told me! And ask Cafri to run and tell Judeth the same thing!:*

:Yes, Papa Skan,: she said with a giggle, largely because she really liked to Mindspeak with "Uncle" Tamsin. She told Skan it was because "he has a furry mind, and it tickles," whatever that meant. *:There, Cafii is gone, I'll talk to Unca Snowstar now.:*

Her "presence," as strong as if she had been in the same room with him, vanished from his mind. He leaped to his feet and called to Zhaneel, who came quickly out of the rear of the lair.

"Aubri's seen a strange ship coming in to the docks," he told her hastily, and her golden eyes widened as the hackles on the back of her neck stood up a little.

"Who?" she asked.

He shook his head. "We don't know. I've had the Council summoned; we'll have to go down and meet it, whoever it is. I don't know how long I'll be."

She nodded, and shooed the twin gryphlets into the nursery—which just happened to be the most defensible room in the lair. *She* knew; she was a child of the Mage Wars, after all. They dared not assume this was a friend, or even a neutral party. They *must* assume the worst.

"Stay safe," was all she said, over her shoulder, her eyes wide with worry that she would not voice. "I love you, Skandranon Rashkae."

"I love you, Brighteyes," was all he *could* say—then he was off, out the door of the lair and onto the landing porch, using the low wall to leap from. A wingbeat later, and the White Gryphon was clawing his way against the wind to the top of the cliff, where Aubri was waiting.

Amberdrake shaded his eyes and stared at the bobbing sail just beyond the mouth of the bay, even though he knew he would not be able to see anything. Even if he had not been half-blinded by the sunlight on the water, the ship was too far away to make out any kind of detail.

That, however, was not true of the gryphons, whose eyes were infinitely better than the humans'. Aubri roused all his brown feathers, then widened his eyes rather than narrowing them as a human would; his pupils flared open, then constricted to mere pinpoints, then flared again with surprise.

"They're black," Aubri announced, his voice startled and his beak gaping open, as he peered across the waves at the oncoming ship. "The humans in that ship, Skan, Drake, they're *black.*"

"They're what?" Skan craned his neck as far as it would go and widened his eyes as well. His pupils flared to fill his eyes. "By—Drake, Aubri's right. These humans have *black* skin! Not brown, not painted, not sunburned—they're really, really black!"

Black? But—Amberdrake blinked because he, and perhaps he alone of all of the Council, knew what that meant, and recognized who these people must be.

"They must be—but we aren't that far south—" He was babbling, he knew; speaking aloud what was running through his head, without thinking. He scolded himself. That would be a horrible habit for a kestra'chern to get into!

"They must be *what,* Amberdrake?" The Kaled'a'in Adept, Snowstar, stared at him out of silver-blue eyes in a gold-complected face, his expression one of impatience. He tossed his braided silver hair over his shoulder and stared hard at his fellow Kaled'a'in. "What are you babbling about?"

"They must be Haighlei," he replied vaguely, now concentrating on his effort to try to make out some details of the ship, at least, something that might confirm or negate his guess.

"They must be highly *what?*" Snowstar asked sharply, perplexed and still annoyed.

"Not *highly,*" Amberdrake repeated, rather stupidly, shading his eyes against the glare of the westering sun on the water. "*Haighlei.* From the

Haighlei Emperors. You know, the Black Kings. They're called that because they *are* black. They're the only black-skinned people that I know of, but how on earth they came here, I haven't a clue."

Out of the corner of his eye, he saw Snowstar's mouth form into a silent "o," and the Adept also turned his attention to the boat that was tacking into the bay.

"Aren't we more than a bit north and west for them?" General Judeth asked, her voice troubled. She was right to be troubled; the Haighlei Empire was vast and powerful, even by the standards Ma'ar had set, and they were as mysterious as they were powerful. She shaded her sharp, dark-gray eyes with one hand, her strong chin firming as she clenched her jaw.

Amberdrake gave up trying to make out any details for the moment, and shrugged. "I don't know," he admitted. "I don't know of anyone from our lands who had even the vaguest idea how large their Six Nations are. For all I know, they could run from this Sea to the Salten Sea in the East!"

The only person he had ever met who knew anything about the Haighlei Emperors was his old teacher, the incomparable kestra'chern Silver Veil. At the start of the war with Ma'ar—had that really been twenty years ago?—she had been heading south, toward a promised position in the court of one of the Kings. She would be perhaps fifty now; no great age for a kestra'chern of her lineage and training—and she was one of those women who would never look anything other than agelessly elegant. Had she gotten that position? Was she prospering? He hadn't found out; the wars had eaten up all his time and energy, leaving none to spare for trying to trace his mentor's whereabouts.

He turned his attention back to the ship. The ship had entered the bay, now, and it was finally possible to make out the details of its fittings and crew. The White Gryphon "fishing fleet" was made up of fairly crude vessels fitted with oars and a single, basic sail—large enough for four men at the most. This was a real *ship*, clearly able to carry several dozen people, and Amberdrake didn't know enough about ships to know if it was of a type any of their few folk familiar with such things should recognize or not. It was quite elaborate, that much he knew on sight; it had three masts and several sails striped in red and white, and there were people swarming all over it. The hull was painted in blue and red, with a pair of eyes on the front; the sails were augmented by a network of lines and rope-ladders. There was a raised, houselike section in the middle of the boat that had a door and several windows in it. The men actually doing all the work were dressed simply, in white breeches, many with colored cloths wrapped around their heads and colored sashes around their waists, but there were three people in much more elaborate clothing standing in front of the door in that houselike section, peering at the people waiting on the dock. Rich hues of red, orange, and the gold of ripe grain, ornamented with winking glints of metal and the sharper gleams of gems marked the costumes of these three notables. The cut of their clothing was entirely unfamiliar to Amberdrake.

It did not comfort Amberdrake in the least to see, as the boat drew nearer, that every man in the crew had enormous knives stuck through their sashes, and that there were racks of spears visible behind the elaborately-garbed men watching them.

They're tall. They are very *tall.* The ship was finally close enough for Amberdrake to make some kind of guess as to the general appearance of these people. The thing that struck him first was their height. The shortest of them would probably top the tallest Kaled'a'in by at least a head. Their features were handsome enough, finely sculptured, although they were not as hawklike as the Kaled'a'in. Amberdrake was amazed by the garments the three—officials?—were wearing; although the material was very light by the way it fluttered, it was woven with incredibly detailed geometric patterns in bright yellows, reds, and oranges. The robes fastened high up on the side of the neck, with the openings running down the left of the front rather than the middle. The robes boasted high, stiff collars that matched the cylindrical hats each of them wore. Heavy, jeweled neckpieces lay on their breasts and shoulders, and heavy, matching brooches centered their odd hats.

Although their hair was as tightly-curled as a sheep's fleece, it was so black that it swallowed up all the light. The sailors wore theirs at every length, although perhaps "length" was the wrong term to use for hair that stood out rather than draping down the owner's back. Some of them had cropped their hair so close to the skull that there was nothing there but a short frizz, others had clearly not cut their hair for months, even years. It stood out away from their heads as if lightning had just struck them. But the three men waiting with folded hands wore their hair as short as they could and still be said to *have* hair. The hats fit too closely to allow for any amount of hair.

They were all, without a doubt, beautiful to behold. Unfortunately they did not look pleased, if Amberdrake was any judge of expressions.

They did not bring the boat to the dock; instead, they anchored out in the bay, with a sophisticated set of tensioned fore- and aft-anchors that held them steady against the waves.

And there they waited. The sailors formed up in loose ranks on the deck of the ship and remained there, unmoving.

No one spoke a word; the ship hung at anchor, with the only sound being the steady pounding of the surf on the rocks.

"It appears that they expect us to come to them," Judeth observed, in her usual dry manner.

Of course they do. We're the interlopers, the barbarians. Amberdrake would have called for a boat to take him and the rest of the Council to the strangers if there had been any—but there weren't. Every vessel they owned was out fishing or dropping nets.

"They aren't stupid," Skan rumbled. "They can see we don't have the means to come to them. Besides, if they came this far, they can go a few more feet."

And be damned annoyed when they do, Amberdrake thought silently, but he held his peace. There wasn't any way they *could* go out to the waiting vessel, except by flying, and he was not about to suggest that Skan go out there by himself. There was no point in wrapping a potential hostage up like a gift and presenting him to a possible enemy.

The tense moments passed, marked by the waves breaking against the rocks, as the Haighlei stared and the Kaled'a'in stared back, each of them waiting for the other to make the next move. But as it became clear that there were no other vessels available, not even a tiny coracle, the Haighlei leaders turned to the sailors, gesturing as they ordered their men to bring up the anchors and move in to the docks.

To make up for the loss of face, the Haighlei brought their ship in with a smooth expertise that Amberdrake watched with envy. There were no wasted motions, and nothing tentative about the way the captain and pilot maneuvered the ship. Even though the dock was completely unfamiliar to them, they had their vessel moored and comfortably snugged in to the wooden piers in a fraction of the time it took their own people to do the same with a much smaller boat.

"They're good," Judeth muttered, with grudging admiration. "They're damned good. I'll have to remember to dredge some sandbars to hang them up on if they turn hostile and bring friends. It would cut back the effectiveness of the drag-fishing nets, but we could work around that. If there are hostilities, the gryphons and kyree wouldn't be free to pull nets in, anyway."

Amberdrake nodded, impressed all the more by the fact that Judeth's mind never seemed to stop examining resource management and strategy, even while watching the ship draw in.

Within a few moments, the Haighlei sailors had run a gangplank down to the dock, and were unrolling a strip of heavy woven material patterned in bright reds and browns to cover it. Then they scrambled back aboard their ship, and formed a line of alert bodies along the railing—all this without another issued order.

Only then did the three envoys—if that was what they really were— deign to descend to the dock. And there, standing on the strip of material, they waited, hands tucked into the sleeves of their elaborate, fluttering robes.

Amberdrake started to step forward, hesitated, and caught both Judeth and Skandranon's eyes. Judeth nodded, slightly, and Skan made an abrupt motion with his beak. Amberdrake assumed the leadership position of the group, and the others followed.

He was the only one of the lot properly garbed to meet these people; Snowstar was wearing simple Kaled'a'in breeches and a wrapped coat, both old and worn. Judeth, though her pepper-and-salt hair might have given her the authority of age, wore one of her old black uniforms with the insignia removed and only the silver gryphon badge on the breast. Bearlike, red-haired Tamsin, who shared the Healers' Council seat with his love, Lady Cinnabar, was as shabbily dressed as Snowstar. Only Amberdrake kept up some pretense of elegance these days; somehow it didn't feel right for a Council member to show up in public dressed as if he had just been weeding his garden (as Snowstar had been) or scrubbing medical equipment (which was where Tamsin had been). As the best-dressed Council member, perhaps it was wisest for him to pretend to the position of leader.

He stopped, within easy conversational distance, but no closer. The stern, forbidding expressions on the faces of the envoys did not encourage hearty greetings.

"Welcome to White Gryphon," he said, slowly and carefully—and hoping frantically that these people *might* be able to speak his tongue! "We are the Ruling Council of the city. I am Amberdrake." He introduced the rest of his colleagues as the Haighlei stood there impassively, giving no indication of whether they understood him or not. "May we ask what brings you to our settlement?" he finished, a little desperately.

The man in the middle removed his hands from his sleeves, and cleared his throat. "You trespass upon the lands of King Shalaman, and violate the sanctity of Haighlei territory," he said, coldly, clearly, and in a precise but dated form of their own tongue. "You will leave, or you will be removed."

Amberdrake stood there, stunned. A hundred things ran through his mind. *Should I apologize? Should I beg for mercy? Should I explain how we came here? What should I say?*

Judeth stepped forward and folded her arms over her chest, matching the envoys stare for stare. "We will stay," she stated, baldly, her eyes meeting theirs without blinking. "There were no territory markers here when we arrived, and there are no signs of habitation for two days' *flight* in any direction. We can withstand any force your King may bring against us. We have been settled here almost ten years, and we are staying."

Amberdrake nearly bit his tongue off, suppressing a yelp of dismay. *What is she doing? Who does she think these people are? What—*

"Drake," Skan said—as softly as a gryphon could—in Kaled'a'in, "Judeth's calling their bluff. They can't force us out, not now, not without bringing a lot of troops up here, way off from their own nearest city, and not without a big expense. They weren't using this land for anything. And Judeth knows we have to look as if we're operating from a position of strength or they won't take us seriously."

Judeth, who understood Kaled'a'in quite as well as any gryphon, nodded ever so slightly.

The impassive masks of the envoys cracked the tiniest fraction with shock, as if they had no idea that someone might actually *challenge* them. "You will leave," the middle envoy began again, as if by repetition he could make his point.

"I said, we will *not*," Judeth replied, this time with more force. She smiled, slightly, as the wind stirred her short curls. "We *are*, however, willing to make alliance with King Shalaman in return for the use of this land."

The envoys did not actually faint with indignation at Judeth's bold statement, but they were certainly shocked. They were shocked enough to turn away and confer together in buzzing whispers, all the while casting dubious glances over their shoulder at the Council members.

"I hope you know what you're doing, Judeth," Amberdrake muttered, watching the three envoys—though what he would do if they announced that they were leaving then and there, he had no idea.

"I had my hand in some of Urtho's diplomatic doings," Judeth said with equanimity. "Not a lot—but I know a bluff when I see one. Skandranon is right. These people can't possibly have any way of dislodging us without a lot of trouble. If we take a strong stand now, they're more likely to give us some respect. It'll suit them better and save face all around if they decide to make an alliance with us and pretend it was all their own idea."

Before Amberdrake could reply, the middle envoy turned abruptly and centered his gaze on Judeth. "Flight, you said," he said to her, frowning. "Two days' flight."

Although it was not phrased as a question, it clearly was one. Skan read it that way, too, and stepped forward himself. The envoy had ignored his presence and that of Aubri up until this moment—a rather difficult proposition, considering that he was the size of a small horse.

"Indeed," Skandranon told the man in his deepest and most impressive voice, fanning his wings for emphasis. "We gryphons, who are also citizens of this settlement, made flights in all directions before we settled here." He tilted his head toward the man, whose mouth had actually dropped open in shock on hearing the "beast" speak. Skandranon looked up, with his head lowered at just the right angle to make his brows and eyes appear even more raptorial than usual. "You might be amazed at the things we do."

The envoy closed his mouth quickly, as if he had just swallowed a bug; the other two were looking a bit ill, with a grayish tone to their skin beneath the natural deep black color. The middle man looked at his two colleagues, who simply blinked at him uneasily. He turned back toward Amberdrake.

"We will confer," he said shortly, and without another word, he marched back up the gangplank, followed by his fellows.

Two sailors sprang down onto the docks and quickly rolled up the strip of carpet, taking it back aboard the ship. They did not retract the gangplank, however, which might be a sign that the envoys were not done with White Gryphon yet.

Amberdrake could only hope.

"Now what?" he asked Skan and Judeth. Judeth shrugged.

Skan actually chuckled. "I think that is obvious," he replied. "Now we wait. And of course—we eat. Is anyone besides me hungry? I think that if Aubri and I bite through a few leg-sized bones while we're in eyesight of these diplomats, they might just reconsider any conflicts and be friendly."

* * *

Judeth, at least, made one concession, a concession that really didn't do much to mitigate Amberdrake's anxiety; she suggested that the rest of the Council members drift off one at a time and return wearing clothing a little more appropriate to the situation. "Except Drake, of course," she added, with an enigmatic half-smile. "He is never underdressed."

Amberdrake wasn't certain whether to take that as a compliment or the opposite.

She also suggested that Tamsin send Lady Cinnabar in his stead, a suggestion that everyone else seconded.

Tamsin was hardly offended. "I was going to suggest that myself," he said, with obvious relief. "Cinnabar has a lot more experience at this sort of situation than I do!" He thought for a moment, then added, "I'll Mindspeak Kechara while I'm on my way up; I've got some ideas that may speed things up a bit."

He sprinted for the path to the top of the cliff; Amberdrake did not envy him the climb that was ahead of him. But when Lady Cinnabar appeared, long before even their most athletic youngster could have made it up the winding path, it was obvious that at least one of Tamsin's ideas had been to have Kechara send her down directly.

She was wearing one of her seldom-used court gowns, a lush creation of silver brocade and emerald silk that went well with her pale blonde hair, making her a fit match for Amberdrake's beaded and embroidered, bronze-and-brown finery. And with her were two *hertasi* laden with "proper" clothing for Judeth and Snowstar, at least by Amberdrake's standards of the clothing appropriate to diplomatic receptions. Judeth sighed when she saw the particular uniform that her *hertasi* had brought, but she made no other complaint. Both of them headed for one of the nearby boathouses to change, while the two gryphons, Amberdrake, and Lady Cinnabar waited, keeping their vigil.

It would not be too much longer before the fishing "fleet" came in, and what they were going to make of this imposing vessel, Amberdrake had no notion. He had confidence in the basic good sense of everyone out on the water, though; the sea was a harsh teacher, and those who were not possessed of good sense had not survived the first two years of experimenting with boats and fishing.

"I met Tamsin on the way down, and he told me everything you know so far," Cinnabar said, as she examined the Haighlei ship without appearing to pay any attention to it at all. "I don't entirely agree with

Judeth's approach, Amberdrake. I'm not sure it was necessary to be quite so blunt with these people."

Amberdrake shrugged. "I feel the same way," he agreed. "But she'd already gotten the bit between her teeth and was galloping away before I could stop her. The little that I know about the Haighlei is that they are extremely formal, that their culture is very complicated. I'm afraid we shocked them, and I only hope we didn't utterly revolt them."

Cinnabar pursed her thin lips, but made no other change in her expression. "That could work to our advantage," she told him. "If we follow up on the shock in the right way, that is. Now that we have shocked them with our barbaric directness—which could be a sign of power, and they can't know one way or another yet—we need to prove we can play the diplomatic game as well. We can't simply let them dismiss us as beneath them; we have to complicate the issue for them."

Amberdrake nodded, relieved to have someone on his side in this. "We also can't afford to have them out there, waiting, watching for us to make a fatal mistake," he agreed, "And if we shock and frighten them too much, that's exactly how they may decide to treat us." Then he smiled weakly. "Although on the surface of things, it does look as if it would be very difficult for them to insert a spy among us without a boatload of makeup."

Judeth emerged from the boathouse at that moment, looking as if she had just come from a dress parade. Somehow, despite the fact that the stiff, severely tailored black-and-silver uniform she wore was over ten years old—this time *with* all her medals and rank-decorations on it—her *hertasi* had made it look as if it had just been fitted for her yesterday. With it she wore her favorite thigh-high, black leather boots, marking her former position as a cavalry commander.

"I'm glad to see you here so quickly, Cinnabar," Judeth said with a smile. "This is not my strong suit. Telling them they have no choice but to live with us—now that is my strong suit! But from now on—" she made a helpless little gesture with one hand. "—I'm in the woods. You and Amberdrake play this the way you see fit."

Amberdrake relaxed a trifle; it would have been very difficult to get anything done if half of the Council members were at odds with the other half...

"I agree," Skan put in, "with one proviso. I do not believe that these people are familiar with gryphons or kyree—creatures that they *think* are mere animals—being intelligent. Look at the way they reacted when

I spoke! If you wish, you may put me forward as the titular ruler here, and that will throw them further off balance, a state which we can use to our advantage."

"Now that is a good idea," Cinnabar said thoughtfully. "It might be the factor that turns us from mere barbarians into something so very exotic that we take ourselves out of the realm of anything they can calculate. We might be able to get away with a great deal more than we would as barbarians. They will certainly assume we are the most alien things they have ever seen, and make allowances. I like it."

"So do I," Amberdrake replied, as Snowstar emerged from the boathouse, garbed in one of his sweeping, midnight-blue silk robes, with dagged sleeves faced with white satin and a white leather belt. He had braided ornaments of white feathers and crystals into his hair as well, and now was more splendid than Amberdrake.

"Well, look who's putting us in the shade," Judeth chuckled, as Snowstar rejoined them. "Where were you keeping *that* rig all this time?"

"In a chest, where it belonged," Snowstar replied serenely. "It's not exactly the sort of thing one wears for building walls, weeding gardens, or trekking across the wilderness." He half-bowed to Lady Cinnabar, who smiled back at him. "One wonders what our visitors will make of our transformation."

They did not have to wait much longer to find out. As the first of the fishing vessels came up to the dock and tied up—be it noted, carefully and cautiously—the three envoys emerged from the cabin of their ship, waited for the sailors to unroll the carpet again, and trooped down the gangplank to face the Kaled'a'in delegation.

The Haighlei did not miss the change in wardrobe; each of the envoys gave them a penetrating glance, although they said nothing. Skan did not pause to give them a chance to speak first.

"You surprised us with your coming," he said graciously, rumbling deeply despite the clear volume—offering an apology that was not an apology. "We of the White Gryphon Council are as much responsible for the work of our settlement as any of our citizens. We were dressed for labor when you arrived, as is our duty. Nevertheless, we deemed it important to be here at your arrival—and felt it was irresponsible to keep you waiting as clothes were changed. Healer Tamsin was required urgently above; in his place is the Honorable Lady Cinnabar, also a Healer and a member of our Council."

Cinnabar inclined her head toward them in an acknowledgment of equal status, and her formal, perfectly fitted gown left no doubt as to her rank. The meaning of the salute was not lost on them.

Amberdrake felt the appraising eyes of the two silent envoys assessing every detail of the new costumes, reckoning value, perhaps even assigning a tentative rank to each of them as the Haighlei judged such things. He thought he sensed a marginal relaxation, now that they were no longer forced to deal with what looked like a band of scruffy workmen.

The leader nodded graciously. "We see now that you are not the piratic interlopers we first took you for," he said, offering his own not-quite-apology for their first demand. "Our agents reported that they had seen something like a river's base being constructed; we see that you have built a formidable settlement here, made for the ages rather than the moment, and worthy of the name of 'city.'"

I think he's saying that they've had a good look, and Judeth's right; they can't dislodge us without a nasty fight.

The envoy's next statement confirmed Amberdrake's guess. "We see that you would also make valuable allies and we have been advised to offer you the opportunity to come to King Shalaman's Court, to negotiate."

"We see that you are civilized and responsible," said the man to the envoy's right, a gentleman who had been silent until now. "We noted the careful planning of White Gryphon, and it appears that you have endeavored to despoil the land as little as possible. We had expected brigands, and we find builders, architects." He smiled, revealing startlingly white teeth in his black face. "Such people would be valuable guards upon our northernmost border."

Amberdrake smiled back, and Skan bowed slightly. "I am of the same opinion," the gryphon said, with complete equanimity. "When would your monarch care to open negotiations?"

"Immediately, if possible," the envoy replied without a moment of hesitation. "We would be pleased to host a delegation of two with families and retainers, one human and one—other, such as yourself. There is room in our vessel to convey your initial delegation; others may follow you, if you so desire. We are authorized to wait here until you are ready to leave."

That made Amberdrake's eyebrows rise. Either these envoys had extraordinary power in making a decision here, or they had some way to communicate directly with their superiors.

Very possibly the latter. If their magic was working more reliably than magic used by the Kaled'a'in refugees, such communication would be simple enough.

Skandranon was equal to the challenge. "We would be pleased to host you in our city above for the night and show you a pale reflection of the hospitality we will be able to offer when our city is complete. In the morning Amberdrake and I and our families will be ready to leave with you. We are as anxious to conclude a treaty as you are."

"Excellent," the envoy said, as if he meant it. And for the first time, the three envoys stepped off their little strip of carpet and onto the dock.

Leaving their territory for ours? Whatever the gesture meant, it seemed they were perfectly prepared to make the trip up the cliff.

Well, none of them are very old, nor do they look out-of-shape… and how better to show them that we're fortified for defense! Each of the envoys fell in beside one of the Councilors as they all began the walk to the path leading upward; the chief speaker beside Skan, the second man who spoke beside Amberdrake, and the one who had been silent the whole time beside Judeth.

The second man was thinner and a little taller than the other two, putting him at least a head taller than Amberdrake, who was not undersized by Kaled'a'in standards. His garments of red, black, and orange, while trimmed with heavy embroidery in gold threads, were made of very light material, perhaps silk. His walk and posture were relaxed now, and he strode beside Amberdrake with an easy gait that made the kestra'chern think that he was used to walking long distances. Perhaps they had no beasts of burden in his land.

"If you don't mind my asking," Amberdrake said hesitantly, "How is it that you speak our language so fluently? Our people have heard of the Haighlei Emperors, and how powerful they are, but nothing of any detail and certainly not your tongue."

"Oh," the man said, with a flashing smile and a wave of his hand, "That is simple. We have had many northern kestra'chern in the Courts of the Kings over the years—there is one with King Shalaman now."

"There is?" Amberdrake wondered—

"Oh, yes. A most remarkable and talented woman, and a great confidant of King Shalaman. Since he has no wife, she serves as Royal Companion. He even made her his Advisor for her wisdom. They call her *Ke.Azigat Osorna*—that is, in your tongue and hers, The Silver Veil."

Somehow, Amberdrake managed not to choke.

CHAPTER THREE

W interhart closed the pale-blue gauze curtains over the doorway to the balcony of the palace bedroom she shared with Amberdrake, and sighed contentedly. She left the doors open to the light breeze, a breeze that was already turning oppressively hot, and turned with all the grace of a courtier born, poised and elegant in the gown Lady Cinnabar had lent her. It was of a light cream silk, which complemented her skin. Her long hair, laced with cords of matching cream silk ornamented by bronze beads and cream-colored feathers, brushed her face as she smiled slowly at Amberdrake, and flicked her braids over her shoulder.

Then with all the abandon of a child, she flung herself between the pale-blue gauze bedcurtains into the heap of pale-blue silk pillows topping the bed. She grabbed one and hugged it to her chest, looking up at Amberdrake with a face full of mischief.

"A maid for the bath, another for the rooms—*two* nursemaids for Windsong—eating incredible delicacies at the royal table—and a suite of five rooms all to ourselves! And all Gesten has to do is oversee the Haighlei servants! I could get used to this very quickly," she said contentedly. "It certainly is a cut above spending my mornings weeding the vegetable garden, my afternoons tending to minor gryphonic ailments, and the rest of the time chasing a two-year-old with endless energy and a positive fascination for heights!"

Amberdrake smiled, and sat down on the bed beside her, reaching out to touch her cheek. "As far as I am concerned, the main benefit is the nursemaids, who give us the chance to be alone together! How is it that Windsong always, knows the *moment* you and I—"

"Empathy, I suspect," Winterhart said impishly. "She certainly takes after you in every other respect, so I can't see any reason why she shouldn't have your gifts as well. And you know how little ones are, they want to be the center of attention, so when Mum and Da begin to shift that attention to each other…"

Amberdrake sighed. "It is a perfectly rational explanation," he said ruefully. "But it doesn't suggest a solution to keep her from interrupting."

"But the nursemaids *will,*" Winterhart said gleefully and waved her legs in the air, looking for all the world like a giddy adolescent. "Which means that we can spend as much time together as you can spare from being a diplomat."

"You are as much the diplomat as I, no matter how much you bounce on the beds," he reminded her with a slight grin. *Small wonder—she never had a chance to be giddy when she was an adolescent.* He ruffled her hair affectionately. *She is good at this business; she looked every bit as regal as the highest of the Haighlei at the court reception this afternoon.*

It had taken two weeks to sail down the coast to King Shalaman's capital city of Khimbata; a second vessel with more room for passengers would be arriving at White Gryphon shortly, to bring the rest of the delegation. The initial party consisted of Amberdrake and Winterhart, Skan and Zhaneel, the twin gryphlets and Windsong, and three hertasi, Gesten, Jewel, and a little female named Corvi. Jewel and Corvi were with Skan; Gesten mostly served (and lectured) Amberdrake these days, but he often stuck his bossy little snout into Skandranon's quarters to make certain that Jewel and Corvi were "doing things right by the old bird."

The first few days had been occupied with settling into their new quarters, a pair of side-by-side suites in the Royal Palace itself. The architecture of Khimbata was strange and fascinating, even to those who were used to the weirdly lovely buildings Urtho, the Mage of Silence, had raised over his lands. It had an oddly organic feeling, to it, with pronounced woodgrains, and no exterior surface was ever left unornamented. The swirling curves were covered with mosaics and sculptured reliefs of plants, birds, and animals. There was seldom anything as simple as a straight line, either, even in the interiors of buildings. The corners and the joining of walls and ceilings were always gently rounded, forming arches; ceilings sloped slightly upward to the center of a room, where there was always a flower-shaped or globe-shaped lamp. There wasn't a right angle to be seen here, unlike the carved stone austerity of the buildings of long-lost Ka'venusho.

The private rooms all seemed to be decorated in pastels, and featured a number of ingenious ways to at least simulate coolness. There were gauze curtains to reflect away the worst of the sunlight, and huge windows and balcony doors to catch the least breeze. Fabrics were light and airy, smooth and soft to the touch. That was just as well because Khimb'ata lay in the heart of a jungle, and it was the most northerly of all the Haighlei Kingdoms. Amberdrake did not want to think about spending summer in one of the more southerly regions. One, at least, was a desert, with temperatures literally high enough to kill a man standing under the open sky for more than a few moments. So he had been told, at any rate, and he saw no reason to dispute the claim.

In the public chambers, however, the Haighlei love of color ran riot.

The Haighlei felt as much at home in the jungle as within a building, and brought the jungle into their buildings as a pleasant reminder of the wealth of life lying outside the city. Huge, lush plants prospered inside, placed where sunlight would reach them and accompanied by cheerful fountains or pools with lazy fish of gold, white, and black. Tiny, huge-eyed furry creatures scampered tamely up the plants' trunks, and out onto their limbs, and loud, rainbow-bright birds sang, whistled, or spoke mockingly down at the humans passing beneath.

The birds made Amberdrake feel comfortable amid all the alien architecture. They were like the tiny, rainbow-hued messenger-birds that the Kaled'a'in had brought with them, cherished, carefully nurtured, all the way from Urtho's Tower. These birds were larger, but like the messengers, spoke in human voices, with sense to their speech. He had already made friends with two, a salmon-pink one with a backward-curving crest of deep red, and one seemingly painted in blue, gold, and green.

The walls were covered with mosaics that were just as colorful as the birds, and cool, dim, deep-green passages between the vast public rooms brought to mind the cool, dim trails between huge forest giants.

The Haighlei themselves were as harlequin-bright in costume as their architecture; the clothing the three envoys had worn was fairly typical. Silk, raime, the finest linen imaginable, and a gauzy stuff made from fluffy plant fiber were dyed and fashioned into elaborate, fluttering robes, billowing trousers, and draped gowns, none of which incorporated less than three colors.

Amberdrake had pulled out all his most elaborately beaded and embroidered robes in anticipation of this; Winterhart would have been in some sartorial difficulty if it hadn't been for Lady Cinnabar. The Lady, it seemed, had used all of her old court gowns as padding on the floor of her floating-barge when planning for the evacuation of Urtho's Tower. That was clever of her, and reasonable given that fabric for padding was not a high priority and that her gowns were not made of stuffs that could be used as bandages or other useful articles. The clever aspect was that she had packed her gowns in a way that allowed her to retrieve the robes and dresses unharmed. "All" of her court gowns comprised a formidable number, and most of them were utterly unsuitable for the life of a Healer in a half-finished city.

Not all of the gowns were still pristine, and the lighter the fabric, the more it had suffered from wear and the intervening decade. Winterhart, however, was smaller than the aristocratic Cinnabar, and even those articles showing signs of wear or weakness at the seams could be cut down for her and look new. Jewel and Corvi had spent most of the sea voyage frantically—but delightedly—retailoring those gowns to suit their new owner. There was nothing a hertasi enjoyed more than costume-making, and there had been little enough of that during the war with Ma'ar or the search for a new home. Even Gesten had gotten into the act, much to the amusement of Skandranon.

So now Winterhart could put on as fine a display as Amberdrake, wearing her elaborate gowns with all the aplomb of the lady of nobility she had once been. The difference was, now she was not suffering under the expectations of her high-ranking family; now it was Amberdrake who was under the careful scrutiny of countless critical eyes, and she who needed only smile and whisper a bit of advice unless she chose otherwise.

She was enjoying it; Amberdrake was quite sure of that. He thought about Winterhart with a wry smile as he looped string on his fingers, preparatory to making a cat's cradle. She was enjoying the luxury and pampering she had not had in decades. For the past ten years she had done all of her own chores, her own cleaning, her own cooking—or rather, she had done those things with the help of Gesten and Amberdrake. For years before that, she had lived the rough life of a trondi'irn in Urtho's army, a healer and tender of Urtho's gryphons, a post where there were few luxuries and no pampering. Even Urtho himself had lived a life positively austere by the standards of the Haighlei Courts.

"Is Silver Veil able to visit us this afternoon?" Winterhart asked suddenly. Amberdrake covertly searched her face for any hint of jealousy, but to his relief, there didn't seem to be any signs of it. He would not have been at all surprised to discover that Winterhart was jealous of The Silver Veil. His mentor was one of those fine-boned, ageless women who, once they achieve maturity, seem to hover at an indefinable perfection until they are very old indeed. Her hair had turned silver in her teens, and she had capitalized on what might have been a handicap for someone in her profession by growing and cultivating it until it reached the floor, making it the trademark that had become her name. She was as strikingly graceful and beautiful now as she had been when he knew her, and it would not have been unexpected for Winterhart to react with jealousy at the inevitable bond between astonishingly beautiful mentor and student.

"What do you think of her?" he asked cautiously, looping another strand. "Your own opinion, not what you think I want to hear."

"I like her," Winterhart said thoughtfully, her gaze turned inward for a moment. "If you can say you 'like' someone as self-contained as she is, that is. I want her to like me, and not just be polite to me, and that's not just because she is your old teacher and your friend. I like to listen to her talking; I think she is fascinating. I hope that I may age as gracefully."

Amberdrake nodded; it was a good observation. "To answer your question, she said she wanted to come to our suite this afternoon, if that is all right with you."

"When everyone else is taking a nap, which is a good time for northerners like us to get together and pretend we are accomplishing something even though we aren't," Winterhart chuckled. "I thought that was so absurd when we first arrived here, for everything to stop at the height of the day—but now, I can't imagine even trying to get anything done when it's so horribly hot. Even Windsong takes her nap without arguing now, and I thought that was nothing short of miraculous."

"But it's the perfect time of day to socialize," Amberdrake pointed out, verbally, since his fingers were weaving and unweaving intricate knots. "Especially if little 'why-mama' is chasing dream-butterflies. And if we northerners can't bear to sleep during the day when we should be getting work done, at least we can keep each other company."

Gesten appeared in the doorway, as if on cue. "Windsong is asleep, and Silver Veil is here, Drake," he said. "Would you prefer the sitting room or the garden?"

Amberdrake raised an eyebrow at Winterhart, signifying that it was her choice. After all, his hands were tied at the moment. "The garden, I think," she replied after a moment. "I hope the fountains in the pool will make it cooler than the sitting room."

By now, as always, even the cool stone of the floors was not helping cool the air much. It was always like this; shortly after noon, the heat began to collect, and it weighed down the very air until the sun neared the western horizon.

Gesten shrugged. "They're supposed to, so they tell me," the little hertasi said philosophically. "I'll have Jewel tell someone to send up the usual refreshments."

"I'd appreciate it if you'd serve us yourself, Gesten," Amberdrake said before Gesten could leave. "I don't think we're likely to say anything dubious, but it's hard to tell how the Haighlei would translate some of our conversations or mannerisms."

Gesten nodded and went off to attend to all of it; no need to elaborate with him. They all knew that the so-attentive servants were reporting whatever they saw and overheard to their superiors, and possibly to masters besides their superiors. That might have been the reason for Winterhart's choice of the garden as well; the sound of the fountains would cover any conversation from more than a few feet away.

Discretion, discretion. Still, this is better than facing the Haighlei warships. They were on sufferance here; how much, perhaps Silver Veil could tell them. That was what she had implied when she asked for this meeting; that she could tell him more about their position here, now that the delegation had settled in.

Winterhart smiled as Amberdrake showed off the finished cat's cradle, then she slipped off the side of the bed and smoothed down her skirt. Amberdrake unraveled the elaborate finger and string sculpture, rose to his feet and straightened wrinkles out of his robes. Together they made their way to the tiny garden in the center of every suite of rooms. The Palace sprawled out across the Royal Compound, rather than being built in the vertical as Urtho's Tower had been. It was a vast complex of suites connected by corridors, with tiny gardens everywhere, as if they had been scattered like seeds and the Palace had been built around them. Every garden had one huge tree growing in the middle, shading everything, and most had more of the same ubiquitous fountains and pools that their own garden had. The theory was that this allowed more air to flow through the rooms, and the falling water cooled the breeze further. Since there was no need to worry about *heating* this vast pile, there was no need to build so as to conserve heat.

Their garden was mostly water, a complex of fountains and connected pools with a fabulous collection of water-lilies, water-irises, and flowering reeds to set off the fat fish in their armor of red and black, gold and white. Their tree was a huge giant, towering far above the roof three stories above, and shading the entire courtyard perfectly. Gesten had set a low wooden table and three upholstered lounges out in the flagstoned midst of the pools, and Silver Veil was already there, wearing a thin gown of finger-pleated linen with gold ornaments on her arms and bare ankles, trailing her fingers gracefully in the water. Feeding the fish, perhaps? They were always greedy for crumbs. She rose as they approached. Her thin, delicate face was suffused with pleasure.

She kissed both of them on the cheek, impartially, and they all took their seats as Gesten arrived with cool beverages and slices of fruit arranged artfully on a plate. At the moment, the earlier breeze had

died away to nothing, leaving only the heat and the babble of water;
Winterhart picked up a fan made of woven palm leaves and created a
breeze of her own. The palm-leaf fans woven into fanciful shapes were
another Palace fixture; servants left stacks of them everywhere.

"Does it ever get cold here?" she asked, a little desperately, as Silver
Veil followed her example with a fan shaped like a spade blade.

Silver Veil shook her head, and her silver hair followed the motion.
"Never; in the deep of winter it is sometimes very cool during the night,
but only so that one wants a brazier of coals in one's bedroom, and
perhaps a light blanket. I never thought that I would long for snow
before I came here."

"Well, we of White Gryphon have snow enough in winter for you,"
Amberdrake replied, "if you can get leave to come visit. You would be
very welcome."

But Silver Veil only sighed. "I fear not," she said reluctantly. "I am
one of Shalaman's Chief Advisors, you know; there is only Truthsayer
Leyuet and Palisar, the Speaker to the Gods, besides me." She coughed
delicately. "I fear that their advice is rather biased in some areas. I would
rather be here to counter them, so to speak. In fact, that was why I
wished to speak with you both, now that you have had time to settle in
and view the situation."

"Oh? I am flattered that you would hold our welfare in such esteem,
Lady," Winterhart said carefully.

Silver Veil laughed; it sounded like one of the fountains. "So discreet,
Winterhart!" she exclaimed, with no hint of mockery. "From what
northern court did *you* spring? It took me years to learn such discretion."

"Some are born with such grace," Amberdrake replied quickly, to
save Winterhart from the question. Nevertheless he was enjoying the
exchange, for this was like some of the conversations he had shared with
her in the past, during the few moments of tranquility during their flight
from Kiamvir Ma'ar's forces. Now, however, the conversation was better,
because it was between equals, not world-wise mentor and overstressed
pupil. *I would not want to repeat that time for any amount of money, but I am glad
to have experienced it, in a peculiar way. Certainly I am grateful for the privilege of
learning from her.* When all was lost to him, she had taken him in. When
he was adrift, she found him the avocation best suited to his talents. Who
else would have done such a thing?

Silver Veil bowed her head in ironic acknowledgment of the truth
of his answer. "Well, here and now comes the time to leave a certain

amount of discretion outside the garden, and speak frankly, northerner to northerner, friend to friend." She leaned forward, her violet-gray eyes darkened momentarily. "I need to give you some small idea of the world you have blundered into."

"It baffles me," Amberdrake confessed. "I am not certain how to act, and I find myself doing nothing rather than chance an incident." He looked to Winterhart for confirmation, and she nodded.

Silver Veil fanned herself quietly. "Your instincts must be guiding you correctly," she told them both, "For that is the safest thing to do here; *nothing.* Had you noticed anything odd about the Court itself? Physical things, I mean, things that seem familiar, but antique."

Amberdrake frowned, for he had, although he could not name precisely what had set off those strange feelings of familiarity at one remove. But Winterhart was quite certain.

"There are strange echoes of our past here," she said. "I see it in the clothing, some of the customs, even some of the food. But none of it is like the North we left."

"Precisely," Silver Veil said, with a nod. "It is like the North of years, decades, even centuries ago. That was what gave me the key to understanding these people. *They both abhor, and adore, change.*"

Amberdrake shook his head. "I'm not sure I understand," he began.

Silver Veil interrupted him with a gesture of her fan. "The Haighlei are a people who avoid change at all cost. Their own customs go back in an unbroken line for hundreds of years. To them, our way of life with its constant changes and readjustments is one short step below blasphemy, for if the gods wanted men to change, would the gods not decree it?" She shrugged. "The point is, they not only hate change, it is mandated against by their holy writings. Change comes as the gods decree, when the gods decree."

Winterhart frowned. "But if that's the case, how is it that customs of ours have ended up in practice here?"

"A good point." Silver Veil looked pleased. "That is one reason why change, with all the attraction of the forbidden, is very appealing to many of them. And the answer to how change comes to them is this; someone, at some point, understood that without some changes taking place, this society would rot from within. So at some point in the past, the holy writings were modified. There is a celebration connected to an eclipse that takes place once every twenty years. The more of the sun that vanishes, the more change can be integrated into the society. Thereafter, however, it does not change, except for deep exploration of the details. That is why you see things here that have only been written about in our lands. And that is why the office and position of kestra'chern were established here in the first place."

"But it is the kestra'chern of a hundred years ago that they imitate?" Amberdrake hazarded.

"More like two hundred or more, the kestra'chern who were the pampered and cultured members of the households of the very elite, and never seen by the common folk at all." She pointed her fan at the two of them. "You are on sufferance here; you embody change. Only if Shalaman accepts you and adds you and your presence here to the Eclipse Ceremony will you be actually accepted by the Haighlei as a whole." She flicked her fan idly at a blue fly blundering past. "You don't have many friends here. The Speaker to the Gods is firmly against your presence. Others are curious, but fearful of all the changes you represent."

He nodded, slowly. "I understand. So the question becomes, how do we persuade others over to our side?"

She shook her head, and her jewelry sang softly. "Gentle persistence. It helps that you have Skandranon with you; he is such a novelty that he is keeping peoples' minds off what you folk truly represent. I was accepted because what I *am* fell within the bounds of what they had already accepted. You must tread a careful path, Amberdrake. You dare not give offense, or give reason for the Haighlei to dismiss you as mere barbarians."

"What else do we need to know?" Winterhart asked urgently.

"Mostly that the Heighlei are very literal people; they will tell you *exactly* what they mean to do, not a bit more, and not a bit less." She creased her brow in thought. "Of course, that is subject to modification, depending on how the person feels about you. If you asked one who felt indifferent toward you to guard your pet, he would guard your pet and ignore the thief taking your purse."

Amberdrake nodded, trying to absorb it all.

"What can you tell us about this Eclipse Ceremony?" he asked.

Silver Veil smiled.

"Well," she said, with another wave of her fan, "Obviously, it begins, ends, and centers around the Eclipse…"

Zhaneel found the hot afternoons as soporific as any of the Haighlei, and usually followed their example in taking a long nap. Even the youngsters were inclined to sleep in the heat—her Tadrith and Keenath and Winterhart's energetic girl Windsong. Well, since the twins had been born, *she* had been short on sleep, so now she might have a chance to make it up at last. Let Skandranon poke his beak in and around the corners of this fascinating Palace; while it was this hot, *she* would luxuriate in a nest of silken cushions, or stretch her entire length along a slab of cool marble in the garden.

She was doing just that, when one of the servants entered, apparently unaware of her presence. The twins were asleep in the shade, curled up like a pair of fuzzy kittens beside one of the pools, for they liked to use the waterfall as a kind of lullaby. The servant spotted them and approached them curiously, then reached out a cautious hand to touch.

Not a good idea, since the little ones sometimes woke when startled in an instinctive defensive reaction. An unwary human could end up with a hand full of talons, which would be very painful, since each of the twins sported claws as formidable as an eagle's. She raised her head and cleared her throat discreetly.

The servant started, jerking upright, and stared at her for a single, shocked second, with the whites of his eyes showing all around the dark irises. Then he began to back up slowly, stammering something in his own language. She couldn't understand him, of course, but she had a good idea of the gist of it, since this wasn't the first time she'd startled a servant.

Nice kitty. Good kitty. Don't eat me, kitty—

She uttered one of the few phrases in his language she knew, the equivalent of "Don't be afraid, I didn't know you were coming in; please don't wake the babies."

He stared at her in shock, and she added another of the phrases she'd learned. "I prefer not to eat anything that can speak back to me."

He uttered something very like a squeak, and bolted.

She sighed and put her head down on her foreclaws again. *Poor silly man. Doesn't anyone* tell *these people about us!* It wasn't that the Haighlei were prejudiced, exactly, it was just that they *were* used to seeing large, fierce, carnivorous creatures, but were *not* used to them being intelligent. Sooner or later she and Skan would convince them all that the gryphons were neither dangerous, nor unpredictable, but until they did, there would probably be a great many frightened servants setting new records for speed in exiting a room.

Those who accept us as intelligent are still having difficulty accepting us as full citizens, co-equal with the humans of White Gryphon, she reflected, wondering how they were going to overcome that much stickier problem. *At least I don't have to worry about that. Skan does, but I don't. All I have to do is be charming and attractive. And the old rogue says I have no trouble doing that! Still, he has to do that himself, plus he has to play. "Skandranon, King of White Gryphon."*

The sound of someone *else* discreetly clearing her throat made Zhaneel raise her head again, wondering if she was ever going to get that nap.

But when she saw who it was, she was willing to do without the nap. "Makke!" she exclaimed, as the old, stooped human made her way carefully into the garden. "Can it be you actually have nothing to do? Can I tempt you to come sit in the garden?"

Makke was very old, and Zhaneel wondered why she still worked; her closely-cropped hair resembled a sheep's pelt, it was so white, and her back was bent with the weight of years and all the physical labor she had done in those years. Her black face was seamed with wrinkles and her hands bony with age, but she was still strong and incredibly alert. Zhaneel had first learned that Makke knew their language when the old woman asked her, in the politest of accented tones, if the young gryphlets would require any special toilet facilities or linens. Since then, although her assigned function was only to clean their rooms and do their laundry, Makke had been Gesten's invaluable resource. She adored the gryphlets, who adored her in return; she was often the only one who could make them sit still and listen for any length of time. Both Zhaneel and Gesten were of one accord that in Makke they had made a good friend in a strange place.

"I really should not," the old woman began reluctantly, although it was clear she could use a rest. "There is much work yet to be done. I came only to ask of you a question."

"But you should, Makke," Zhaneel coaxed. "I have more need of company than I have of having the floors swept for the third time this afternoon. I want to know more about the situation here, and how we can avoid trouble."

Makke made a little gesture of protest. "But the young ones," she said. "The feather-sheath fragments, everywhere—"

"And they will shed more as soon as you sweep up," Zhaneel told her firmly. "A little white dust can wait for now. Come sit, and be cool. It is too hot to work. Everyone else in the Palace is having a nap or a rest."

Makke allowed herself to be persuaded and joined Zhaneel, sitting on the cool marble rim of the pond. She sighed as she picked up a fan and used it to waft air toward her face. "I came to tell you, Gryphon Lady, that you have frightened another gardener. He swears that you leaped up at him out of the bushes, snarling fiercely. He ran off, and he says that he will not serve you unless you remain out of the garden while he works there."

"He is the one who entered while I was already here." Zhaneel snorted. *"You* were in the next room, Makke," she continued in a sharp retort. "Did you hear any snarling? Any leaping? Anything other than a fool fearing his shadow and running away?"

Makke laughed softly, her eyes disappearing into the wrinkles as she chuckled. "No, Gryphon Lady. I had thought there was something wrong with this tale. I shall say so when the Overseer asks."

Zhaneel and Makke sat quietly in easy silence, listening to the water trickle down the tiny waterfall. "You ought to be the Overseer," Zhaneel said, finally. "You know our language, and you know more about the other servants than the Overseer does. You know how to show people that we are not maneating monsters. You are better at the Overseer's job than he is."

But Makke only shook her head at the very idea, and used her free hand to smooth down the saffron tunic and orange trews that were the uniform for all Palace servants, her expression one of resignation. "That is not possible, Gryphon Lady," she replied. "The Overseer was born to his place, and I to mine, as it was decreed at our births. So it is, and so it must remain. You must not say such things to others. It will make them suspect you of impiety. I know better because I have served the Northern Kestra'chern Silver Veil, but others are not so broad of thought."

Zhaneel looked at her with her head tilted to one side in puzzlement. This was new. "Why?" she asked. "And why would I be impious for saying such a thing?"

Makke fanned herself for a moment as she thought over her answer. She liked to take her time before answering, to give the question all the attention she felt it deserved. Zhaneel did not urge her to speak, for she knew old Makke by now and knew better than to try to force her to say anything before she was ready.

"All is decreed," she said finally, tapping the edge of her fan on her chin. "The Emperors, those you call the Black Kings, are above all mortals, and the gods are above them. The gods have their places, their duties, and their rankings, and as above, so it must be below. Mortals have their places, duties, and castes, with the Emperors at the highest and the collectors of offal and the like at the lowest. As the gods do not change in their rankings, so mortals must not. Only the soul may change castes, for each of the gods was once a mortal who rose to godhood by good works and piety. One is born into a caste and a position, one works in it, and one dies in it. One can make every effort to learn—become something of a scholar even, but one will never be permitted to *become* a Titled Scholar. Perhaps, if one is very diligent, one may rise from being the Palace cleaning woman for a minor noble to that of a cleaning woman to a Chief Advisor or to foreign dignitaries, but one will always be a cleaning woman."

"There is no change?" Zhaneel asked, her beak gaping open in surprise. This was entirely new to her, but it explained a great deal that had been inexplicable. "Never?"

Makke shook her round head. "Only if the Emperor declares it, and with him the Truthsayer and the Speaker to the Gods. You see, such change must be sanctioned by the gods before mortals may embrace it. When some skill or position, some craft or learning, is accepted from outside the Empire, it is brought in as a new caste and ranking, and remains as it was when it was adopted. Take—the kestra'chern. I am told that Amberdrake is a kestra'chern among your people?"

Zhaneel nodded proudly. "He is good! Very good. Perhaps as good or better than Silver Veil. He was friend to Urtho, the Mage of Silence." To her mind, there could be no higher praise.

"And yet he has no rank, he offers his services to whom he chooses, *and* he is one of your envoys." Makke shook her head. "Such a thing would not be possible here. Kestra'chern are strictly ranked and classed according to talent, knowledge, and ability. Each rank may only perform certain services, and may only serve the *nobles* and noble households of a particular rank. No kestra'chern may offer his services to anyone above or below that rank for which he is authorized. This, so Silver Veil told me once, is precisely as the kestra'chern first served in the north, five hundred years ago, when the Murasa Emperor Shelass declared that they were to be taken into our land. I believe her, for she is wise and learned."

Zhaneel blinked. Such a thing would never have occurred to her, and she stored all of this away in her capacious memory to tell Skan later. *No one can rise or fall! So where is the incentive to do a good job!*

"We are ruled by our scribes in many ways," Makke continued, a little ruefully. "All must be documented, and each of us, even the lowest of farmers and street sweepers, is followed through his life by a sheaf of paper in some Imperial Scribe's possession. The higher one's rank, the more paper is created. The Emperor has an entire archive devoted only to him. But he was born to be Emperor, and he cannot abdicate. He was trained from birth, and he will die in the Imperial robes. As I will be a cleaning woman for all this life, even though I have studied as much as many of higher birth to satisfy my curiosity, so he will be Emperor."

"But what about the accumulation of wealth?" Zhaneel asked. "If you cannot rise in rank, surely you can earn enough to make life more luxurious?" *That would be the only incentive that I can imagine for doing well in such a system.*

But Makke shook her head again. "One may acquire wealth to a certain point, depending upon one's rank, but after that, it is useless to accumulate more. What one *is* decrees what one may *own;* beyond a certain point, money is useless when one has all one is permitted by law to have. Once one has the home, the clothing, the possessions that one may own under law, what else is left? Luxurious food? The company of a skilled *mekasathay?* The hire of entertainers? Learning purely for the sake of learning? It is better to give the money to the temple, for this shows generosity, and the gods will permit one to be reborn into a higher rank if one shows virtues like generosity. I have given the temple many gifts of money, for besides dispensing books and teachers, the temple priests speak to the gods about one's virtue—all my gifts are recorded carefully, of course—and I will probably give the temple as many more gifts as I can while I am in this life."

Zhaneel could hardly keep her beak from gaping open. "This is astonishing to me," Zhaneel managed. "I can't imagine anyone I know living within such restrictions!"

Makke fanned herself and smiled slowly. "Perhaps they do not seem restrictive to us," she suggested.

"Makke?" Zhaneel added, suddenly concerned. "These things you tell me—is this forbidden, too?"

Makke sighed, but more with impatience than with weariness. "Technically, I could be punished for telling you these things in the *way* that I have told you, and some of the other things I have imparted to you are pieces of information that people here do not *talk* about, but I am old, and no one would punish an old woman for being blunt and speaking the truth." She laughed. "After all, that is one of the few advantages of age, is it not? Being able to speak one's mind? Likely, if anyone knowing your tongue overheard me, the observation would be that I am aged, infirm, and none too sound in my mind. And if I were taken to task for my words, that is precisely what I would say." Makke's smile was wry. "There are those who believe my interest in books and scholarly chat betokens an unsound mind anyway."

"But this is outside of my understanding and experience. It will take me a while to think in this way. In the meantime, what must we do to keep from making any dreadful mistakes?" Zhaneel asked, bewildered by the complexity of bureaucracy that all this implied.

"Trust Silver Veil," Makke replied, leaning forward to emphasize her advice and gesturing emphatically with her fan. "She knew something of the Courts before she arrived here, and she has been here long enough to know where all the pit traps and deadfalls are. She can keep you from disaster, but what is better, she can keep you from embarrassment. I cannot do that. I do not know enough of the higher stations."

"Because we can probably avoid disaster, but we might miss a potential for embarrassment?" Zhaneel hazarded, and Makke nodded.

And in a society like this one, surely embarrassment could be as deadly to our cause as a real incident. Oh, these people are so strange!

"There is something else that I believe you must know," Makke continued. "And since we are alone, this is a good time to give you my warning. Something of what Gesten said makes me think that the Gryphon Lord is also a worker of magic?"

Zhaneel nodded; something in Makke's expression warned her not to do so too proudly. She looked troubled and now, for the first time, just a little fearful.

"Tell him—tell him he *must not* work any magics, without the explicit sanction of King Shalaman or Palisar, the Speaker to the Gods," Makke said urgently but in a very soft voice, as she glanced around as if to be certain that they were alone in the garden. "Magic is—is strictly controlled by the Speakers, the priests, that is. The ability to work magic is from the hands of the gods, the knowledge of how to use it is from the teachers, and the knowledge of *when* to use it must be decreed by priest or Emperor."

Zhaneel clicked her beak. "How can that be?" she objected. "Mages are the most willful people I know!"

Makke only raised her eyebrows. "Easily. When a child is born with that ability, he is taken from his parents by the priests before he reaches the age of seven, and they are given a dower-portion to compensate them for the loss of a child. The priests raise him and train him, then, from the age of seven to eighteen, when they return to their families, honored priests and Scholars. I say 'he,' though they take female children as well, though females are released at sixteen, for they tend to apply themselves to study better than boys in the early years, and so come to the end of training sooner."

"That still doesn't explain how the priests can keep them under such control," Zhaneel retorted.

"Training," Makke said succinctly. "They are trained in the idea of obedience, so deeply in the first year that they never depart from it. This, I know, for my only daughter is a priest, and all was explained to me. That, in part, is why I was given leave to study and learn, so that I might understand her better when she returned to me. The children are watched carefully, more carefully than they guess. If one is found flawed in character, if he habitually lies, is a thief, or uses his powers without leave and to the harm of others, he is—" she hesitated, then clearly chose her words with care. "He is removed from the school and from magic. Completely."

A horrible thought flashed through Zhaneel's mind at the ominous sound of that. "Makke!" she exclaimed, giving voice to her suspicions, "You don't mean that they—they *kill* him, do you?"

"In the old days, they did," Makke replied solemnly. "Magic is a terrible power, and not for hands that are unclean. How could anyone, much less a priest, allow someone who was insane in that way to continue to move in society? But that was in the old days—now, the priests remove the ability to touch magic, then send the child back to his family." She shrugged. "It would be better for him, in some ways, if they *did* kill him."

"Why?" Zhaneel blurted, uncomprehendingly.

"Why, think, Gryphon Lady. He can no longer touch magic. He returns to his family in disgrace. Everyone knows that he is fatally flawed, so no one will trust him with anything of any consequence. No woman would wed him, with such a disgrace upon him. He will, when grown, be granted no position of authority within his rank. If his rank and caste are low, he will be permitted only the most menial of tasks within that caste, and only under strict supervision. If he comes from high estate, he will be an idle ornament, also watched closely." Makke shook her head dolefully. "I have seen one of that sort, and he was a miserable creature. It was a terrible disgrace to his family, and worse for him, for although he is a man grown, he is given no more responsibility than a babe in napkins. He is seldom seen, but the lowest servant is happier than he. He is of very high caste, too, so let me assure you that no child is immune from this if a flaw is discovered in him."

Zhaneel shook her head. "Isn't there anything that someone like that can do?"

Makke shrugged. "The best he could do would be to try to accumulate wealth to grant to the temple so that the gods will give him an incarnation with no such flaws in the next lifetime. It would be better to die, I think, for what is a man or a woman but their work, and how can one *be* a person without work?"

Zhaneel was not convinced, but she said nothing. At least the Black Kings certainly seemed to have a system designed to prevent any more monsters like Kiamvir Ma'ar! There was something to be said for that.

Almost anything that prevented such a madman from getting the kind of power Ma'ar had would be worth bearing with, I think. Almost. And assuming that the system is not fatally flawed.

"Have the priests ever—made a mistake?" she asked, suddenly.

"Have they ever singled out a child who was *not* flawed for this punishment, you mean?" Makke asked. Then she shook her head. "Not to my knowledge, and I have seen many children go to the temples over the years. Truly, I have never seen one rejected that was not well-rejected. This is not done lightly or often, you know. The one I spoke of? He has no compassion; he uses whomever he meets, with no care for their good or ill. Whilst his mother lived, he used even her for his own gain, manipulating her against her worthier offspring. There are many of lesser caste who have learned of his flawed nature to their sorrow or loss."

Zhaneel chewed a talon thoughtfully.

"There is one other thing," Makke said, this time in a softer and much more reluctant voice. "I had not intended to speak of this, but I believe now perhaps I must, for I see by your face that you find much of what I have said disturbing."

"And that is—?" Zhaneel asked.

Makke lowered her voice still further. "That there is a magic which is more forbidden than any other. I would say nothing of it, except that I fear your people may treat it with great casualness, and if you revealed that, there would be no treaty, not now, and not in the future. Have your people the magic that—that looks into—into minds—and hears the thoughts of others?"

"It might be," Zhaneel said with delicate caution, suddenly now as alert as ever she had been on a scouting mission. All of her hackles prickled as they threatened to rise. There was something odd about that question. "I am not altogether certain what you mean, for I believe our definitions of magic and yours are not quite the same. Why do you ask?"

"Because *that* is the magic that is absolutely forbidden to all except the priests, and only then, the priests who are called to special duties by the gods," Makke said firmly. "I do not exaggerate. This is most important."

"Like Leyuet?" Zhaneel asked in surprise. She had riot guessed that Truthsayer Leyuet was a priest of any kind. He did not have the look of one, nor did he wear the same kind of clothing as Palisar.

"Yes." Makke turned to look into her eyes and hold her gaze there for a long moment, with the same expression that a human mother would have in admonishing a child she suspects might try something stupid. "This magic is a horror. It is unclean," she said, with absolute conviction. "It allows mortals to look into a place where only the gods should look. Even a Truthsayer looks no farther than to determine the veracity of what is said—only into the soul, which has no words, and not the mind. If your people have it, say nothing. And do *not* use it here."

We had better not mention Kechara, ever, to one of these people! And Amberdrake had better be discreet about his own powers!

That was all she could think at just that moment. While Zhaneel tried to digest everything she'd been told, Makke stood, and carefully put the palm fan on the small pile left for the use of visitors. "I must go," she said apologetically. "A certain amount of rest is permitted to one my age, but the work remains to be done, and I would not trust it to the hands of those like that foolish gardener, who would probably think that Jewel and Corvi wish to rend him with their fearsome claws."

Since neither Jewel nor Corvi had anything more than a set of stubby, carefully filed down nails, Zhaneel laughed. Makke smiled and shuffled her way back into their suite.

The gryphlets looked ready to sleep for the rest of the afternoon; not even all that talking disturbed them in the least. Zhaneel settled herself on a new, cooler spot, and lay down again, letting the stone pull some of the dreadful heat out of her body.

She closed her eyes, but sleep had deserted her for the moment. *So Makke is an unTitled Scholar! No wonder she looks as if she were hiding secrets.* Now, more than ever, Zhaneel was glad that she and Gesten had made friends with the old woman. Next to the Silver Veil, it seemed they could not have picked a better informant. *That explains why she bothered to learn our language, anyway. She must have been very curious about Silver Veil and the north, and the best way to find out would have been to ask Silver Veil. It must have taken a lot of courage to dare that, though.*

But Makke was observant; perhaps she had noticed how kind Silver Veil was to her servants, and had decided that the kestra'chern would not take a few questions amiss.

An amateur scholar would also have been fascinated by the gryphons and the *hertasi*. Perhaps that was why Makke had responded to the overtures of friendship Zhaneel and Gesten had made toward her.

And when it became painfully evident how naive we were about the Haighlei— Zhaneel smiled to herself. There was a great deal of the maternal in Makke's demeanor toward Zhaneel, and there was no doubt that she thought the twins were utterly adorable, even if they looked nothing like a pair of human babies. Perhaps Makke had decided to adopt them, as a kind of honorary grandmother.

She said, only daughter. *She could have meant only child as well. And if her child is now a priest—do the Haighlei allow their priests to marry and have children! I don't think so.* Zhaneel sighed. *I wonder if her daughter is ashamed of Makke; she is only a cleaning woman, after all. For all that most priests preach humility, I never have seen one who particularly enjoyed being humble.* If that were the case, Makke could be looking on Zhaneel as a kind of quasi-daughter, too.

I shall have to make certain to ask her advice on the twins. I don't have to take *it, after all! And that will make her feel wanted and needed.* Zhaneel sighed, and turned so that her left flank was on the cool marble. *But the warning about magic—that is very disturbing. Except, of course, that we can't do much magic until the effect of the Cataclysm settles. That might not even be within our lifetimes.*

She would warn Skandranon, of course. And he would warn Amberdrake. Zhaneel was not certain how much of what Amberdrake did was magic of the mind, and how much was training and observation, but it would be a good thing for Drake to be very careful at this point. Winterhart, too, although her abilities could not possibly be as strong as Drake's…

Healing. I shall have to ask Makke about Healing. Surely the Haighlei do not forbid that!

But the one thing they must not mention was the existence of Kechara. If the Haighlei were against the simpler versions of thought-reading, surely they would be horrified by poor little Kechara!

The fact that she is as simple-minded as she is would probably only revolt them further. And she is *misborn; there is no getting around that. It's nothing short of a miracle that she has had as long and as healthy a life as she has. But she is not "normal" and we can't deny that.*

So it was better not to say anything about her. It wasn't likely that anyone would *ask*, after all.

Let me think, though—they may ask how we are communicating so quickly with White Gryphon. So—this evening, Skan should ask permission from King Shalaman and Palisar to "communicate magically" with the rest of the Council back home. Since they do *that, they shouldn't give Skan any problems about doing the same. He's clever; if they ask him how he can communicate when things are so magically unsettled, he can tell them about the messages we send with birds, or tell them something else that they'll believe, and not be lying. Then, when we get instant answers from home, they won't be surprised or upset because we didn't ask permission first.*

So that much was settled. If the Haighlei sent resident envoys to White Gryphon, there was no reason to tell them what Kechara was—

And since she is there among all the other children of the Silvers, her room just looks like a big nursery. Would they want to talk to her, though?

Would an envoy have any reason to talk to *any* child, except to pat it on the head because its parents were important? Probably not. And Cafri could keep her from bounding over and babbling everything to the envoys; he'd kept her from stepping on her own wings before this. With all of that sorted out to Zhaneel's satisfaction, she finally felt sleep overcoming her. She made a little mental "tag" to remind her to tell Skan all about this conversation and the things she'd reasoned out, though. Gryphonic memory was excellent, but she wanted to make certain that nothing drove *this* out of her mind, even on a temporary basis.

Then, with her body finally cooled enough by the stone to relax, she stretched out just a little farther and drifted off into flower-scented dreams.

CHAPTER FOUR

Winterhart moved easily among the Haighlei in their brilliant costumes of scarlet, vermilion, bittersweet and sunset-orange, wheat and burnt umber and the true gold of the metal; she seemed one of them despite her dress and light skin. She was distinctive, a single, long-stemmed lily among a riot of dahlias. Lady Cinnabar's refitted gown of white silk gauze and emerald silk damask was as startling in this crowd as one of the common robes of the Haighlei would be in a Northern Court.

A Northern Court...

Assuming there *was* such a thing as a Northern Court anymore. The few bits of information trickling in seemed to indicate that the Cataclysm had a far more widespread effect than any of the Kaled'a'in had dreamed.

We were so concerned with our own survival, we never thought about what would become of the lands we left behind, she reflected, as she exchanged a polite greeting with a highborn maiden and her bored brother. *Oh, we knew that Urtho's Tower was gone, and the Palace with it, but we never thought about other lands.*

Without Ma'ar at the helm, the kingdoms he had conquered—the few that survived the Cataclysm—fell into chaos and intertribal warfare, the same kind of warfare that had devastated them before he came to rule.

And Winterhart could not help but feel a certain bitter satisfaction at that. If they had not been so eager to listen to his mad dreams of conquest, he would never have gotten as far as he had. Now, from being the acme of civilization, they were reduced to the copper knives and half-wild sheep herds of their ancestors, with the hand of every clan against members of any other clan. Their cities were in ruins, their veneer of civilization lost, all because they had followed a madman.

But beyond Ma'ar's lands, the Cataclysm utterly devastated other nations who relied heavily on magic. A few refugees had reached the Wtasi Empire to the east, on the Salten Sea, after all this time, and the word they brought of far-reaching consequences of the double explosion was terrible. Many lands had once relied on Gates to move supplies and food, especially into the cities. It wasn't possible to erect Gates anymore; there was no certainty that they would work. With no Gates, these cities starved; once people were starving and desperate, order collapsed. And worse was to come, for no sooner had the authorities—or what passed for them—sorted out some of the chaos, in poured hordes of leaderless troops who took what they needed by force of arms. Winterhart could only hope that those were Ma'ar's leaderless troops who were acting that way—but in her heart she knew better. It was likely that their own people, when faced with privation, would act just the same as their former enemies.

It is easy to assign the persona of a monster to the faceless enemy, but the fact is that most of them were just soldiers, following orders, no worse than our own soldiers. It had taken her a long time to work her way around to that conclusion, and it still wasn't a comfortable thought. But that was one unexpected result of living with Amberdrake: learning to seek or reason out truth, and accept it unflinchingly, no matter how uncomfortable it was.

The result of the Cataclysm was that there were no central governments worthy of the name up there now. For the most part, the largest body of organization was the small town, or the occasional place that those aforementioned soldiers had taken over and fortified. Old skills that did not require magic had to be relearned or rediscovered, and that took time. Civilization in the north was gone, as far as the Haighlei were concerned.

And where the Clan k'Leshya was concerned, as well, and all the adopted Kaled'a'in with them, Winterhart among them. There had been no communication from any of the other Kaled'a'in Clans, and no one really expected there to be any. K'Leshya had traveled far beyond the others, the distance of the maximum that two Gates could reach, rather than just one. That was too far for anyone except Kechara to reach with Mindspeech, and too far for the messenger-birds to go, assuming anyone was willing to risk them.

We are on our own, and we can only hope that the other Clans survived as well as we did. Our future is here, and we had better build a firm foundation for it.

So she walked among these strange people in their strange garb and accustomed herself to them, until they no longer seemed strange, until it was *her* dress and *her* pale skin that seemed odd. She moved through the gathering like one of the graceful slim silver fish that lived in the ponds with the fat, colorful ones. Unconsciously she imitated the slow, deliberate pace of their steps and the dancelike eddies and flows of the Court itself. She took all that into herself and made it a part of her.

That was, after all, precisely what she had been trained to do, so long ago. This was what she had been before she became the Trondi'im Winterhart, serving the Sixth Wing gryphons in the army of Urtho, the Mage of Silence. Before, when she had borne another name, and a title, and the burden of rank, she had moved to the dancelike pattern of another Court.

Now rank was no longer a burden, but a cloak that trailed invisibly from the shoulders. The name she wore was hers, with no invisible baggage of long and distinguished lineage. The title? Hers as well, truly earned, like the name.

But the rest was familiar, as familiar as the feel of silk sliding along her body, as real as the exchange of banal courtesies and pleasantries. And since this was a Court like any other—with the folk of White Gryphon a strange and possibly hostile presence—there was caution and even malignity beneath the courtesies, and fear beneath the pleasantries. It was her task to discover where, who, and what hid under the posture and counterposture.

She often felt at a time like this as if she were a sword sliding into an old, well-worn sheath, or a white-hot blade sinking into a block of ice. She was Winterhart, the trondi'im—but she was also much more than the Winterhart her fellow refugees knew. She had not used these old skills in a very, very long time, but they were a significant part of her, long disregarded. She stretched muscles long unused, and she relished the sensation.

Amberdrake, to her bemusement, simply smiled and bid her follow her instincts and her inclinations. "I have been *among* the well-born," he'd said this very evening, before they made their entrance. "I know how to act with them and comfort them. But I never was one of them. You were, and all that early training makes you something I cannot be, and can only imitate. It gives you an assurance that is part of you rather than assumed. Believe me, my love, it shows. So go and be your own gracious self, and show me how it is done. After all," he said with a grin and a wink, "I enjoy gazing at you anyway."

Like a hawk with the jesses cut, he sent her off, trusting she would return to his glove. And she would, of course, for like a *true* falconer and his bird, they were partners.

Or *perhaps we are more like those Kaled'a'in scouts with their specially-bred birds, the bondbirds, who Mindspeak with the ones they are bonded to.* She wondered what the Haighlei would make of those! They had relatively few domesticated animals, and most of them were herdbeasts. No horses, though—

They have sheep, goats, and cattle. They have those misshapen, hairy things that need so little water for riding and bearing burdens in the deserts, and donkeys for pulling carts. Dogs the size of small ponies! A few, a very few, of the Great Cats that have been partly domesticated. No house cats, no horses, no birds of prey. She smiled and nodded and exchanged small-talk with the envoy from the Kmbata Empire, and let part of her mind consider the possible impact that the introduction of each of these domesticated creatures could have on the Haighlei. The cats alone would cause a stir—those huge dogs had been bred to hunt equally large cats, and she could well imagine the delight that the elegant Haighlei would take in the graceful "little tigers" that the adopted Kaled'a'in had brought with them from their homes.

Trade and the possibilities of trade... it would be much easier on the citizens of White Gryphon if they could get their hands on *proper* plows, and not the trial-and-error instruments they had now, made by a weaponsmith who thought he recalled the one lesson he'd had in forging such things, twenty years ago. Proper boats, made for fishing, would save lives if the fishing fleet was ever caught by a big storm. Seeds bred to grow here—and the odd plants that the Haighlei themselves grew to eat—that would not fail in the heat, or sprout too late or too soon.

And in return—horses and cats, for a beginning. Lionwind, the k'Leshya Clan Chief, would be happy to learn of a "proper" market for his riding horses, which just at the moment were, to his injured pride, often trained to harness for pulling carts and plows. After that, there were surely skills they could exchange. Haighlei jewelry, for instance, was lovely and costly, but massive. Not crudely made, but with none of the detail that—for instance—the silversmith who made the Silver Gryphon badges could produce. Would the Haighlei like that sort of thing? They'd certainly admired the delicacy of Winterhart's ornaments, so they might—particularly if the northern jewelry became a fad item.

Odd. I feel so at home here, as if I were born for this place and this court, so rigidly structured, so refined in its subtleties... The longer they were here, the more comfortable she felt.

The Haighlei ruled a territory more vast than anyone up north had ever dreamed; two Kingdoms—or Empires, for they had aspects of both—here, sharing the land between the Salten Sea and the Eastern Sea. Four more farther south, dividing yet another continent among them, a continent joined to this one by a relatively narrow bridge of land. The Haighlei called their rulers both "King" and "Emperor" indiscriminately, something that sounded strange to Winterhart's northern ears.

Another member of the Court greeted her, and Winterhart smiled warmly into Silver Veil's eyes, oddly relieved to see that she was no longer the only pale face with a northern gown here this evening. Silver Veil wore her hair loose, as always, and a pale gray silk gown that echoed the silver of her hair. "You are doing well, little sister," Silver Veil said softly. "I have been listening, watching. Amberdrake is respected for his office and his training, but *you* are acknowledged to be a Power."

She flushed, with embarrassment as well as pride. "Well, Skandranon has us all bested. He is doing more to impress the Haighlei simply by being himself than I could with all the clever words in the world."

But Silver Veil shook her head. "You underestimate yourself, my dear. That is your one fault, I think. But be aware that my people do not underestimate *you*. You are a Power among them, and they will all, from highest to lowest, accord you that respect."

Then she drifted away on another eddy of the crowd, as the dance of the Court carried them both off to other partners. Winterhart smiled and murmured greetings, and wondered about Silver Veil's words. *She* certainly didn't think of herself as particularly important beyond the fact that she was an envoy... but the kestra'chern was right, people were treating her with that sort of deference.

Not as if she were nobly born, but as if she were royal.

As royal as King Shalaman.

The King himself was here, sitting like a stiff statue on a platform about three steps above the rest of the room. He didn't have a throne, precisely; he sat on a gilded bench, shaped like a Hon, with the head at his right and the tail at his left. He wore the pelt of the Hon over one shoulder, but the rest of his costume consisted of a robe of a brilliant saffron color, belted with a sash made of thousands of links of pure gold, so finely made that at a distance it appeared woven. His pectoral collar was made to match, with the stylized mask of a lion on the front. He looked neither to left nor to right, and Winterhart found herself admiring him for the fine figure that he presented. It was difficult to believe that he was over sixty; if she had not been assured of that figure, she would have assumed he was a vigorous warrior in his early thirties at most, and that his white hair was due to premature graying—or to the fact that he was also an Adept-class mage, and working with node-magic had turned his hair white.

Evidently he was only supposed to grace these gatherings with his presence, he wasn't actually expected to mingle with his courtiers. She had the definite feeling, though, that he missed very little, and that what he himself did not notice, one of his advisors would tell him later.

Well, let them tell him that the Lady Winterhart is charming, well-spoken, and utterly opaque.

She smiled at that, and turned the smile on yet another Haighlei courtier. Even a smile could not be wasted. Not here, and not now.

Palisar watched the dance of the courtiers with only one eye, for the other was on his Emperor. The Emperor was watching one particular section of the dance, and Palisar did not care for the fact that the pale-skinned foreigner in her bizarre gown was at the center of that section.

"The Outland woman—" Shalaman murmured to the Speaker to the Gods. "She seems well at ease among us."

"She does, Serene One," Palisar replied, cautiously. *He* did hot care for any of these new Outlanders, but it would not be a good idea to allow Shalaman to learn of this. Not while The Silver Veil, who favored them, was so great a favorite of the King, at any rate.

He was prepared to make many exceptions for The Silver Veil, who was a kestra'chern, and who had served Shalaman well and loyally for many years. That she so favored these Outlanders was understandable, since one of them was her own pupil. And their own audacity was forgivable, given that they *had* made their home in territory so far north that it was virtually uninhabitable. Still.

It does not make them our equals. Let them be made our clients, a liege-alliance, and then let them go home again. That was what Palisar devoutly wished. But Shalaman's next words to his Advisor nearly shocked Palisar into revealing his true feelings in the matter. "I would like you to bring her the Lion Lilies, impart to her my pleasure that she has blended so well into my court, and invite her to walk in the Royal Gardens tomorrow, if she so desires."

The Royal Countenance remained inscrutable, the Royal Voice was even and thoughtful. He might have been suggesting that Palisar order a new lionskin for him, rather than asking Palisar to upset every well-born princess in the court, and shock half of his courtiers numb and insensible. Granted, Shalaman was the son of the gods, but this—

—even the son of the gods could not reign for long by violating all the laws!

Only many years of serving Shalaman enabled Palisar to keep an outward seeming of composure. But he could not help but interject a note of caution—

Better a note of caution than to shout to the King that this could mean utter disaster!

"Is that entirely wise, Serenity?" he murmured, as if only faintly troubled. "So soon after they have arrived? This could betoken favoritism. You have other allies you have not invited to walk in the garden—and there are many other ladies, far more appropriate, to whom you have not sent the Lion Lilies."

All the while, he was choking on the words he wanted to say. *This is insanity! How can you even think of courting this barbarian Outlander when you have two, nay three dozen princesses from Haighlei Kingdoms here in your own court, waiting for such a gesture! You will offend your fellow Kings! You will offend the women themselves! And what has this woman done to deserve such attention, that The Silver Veil cannot do with more grace!*

But he knew the answer—for this woman was *like* Silver Veil, but differed from the kestra'chern in three important ways. She was not familiar. She was younger. And she was theoretically a good candidate to cement an alliance.

"My other allies do not need to be examined, for I know what they can and cannot do," Shalaman said, reasonably. "They are firmly my allies, and I need not strengthen those alliances any further than to see that the daughters are disposed of to high officials of my court. That *is* what they are here for, after all. And the 'appropriate' ladies do not interest me enough that I should send them the Lion Lilies. Impart to Lady Winterhart my words, give to her the Lilies, and bring me back word of what she said."

This was a direct order, which Palisar was helpless to disobey. With a sinking heart, he gathered up the Lilies from their brass vase, on an ebony stand beside the Lion Throne, while a stir of interest rippled through the court at his gesture. The Lilies, huge, tawny-gold, many-petaled bells on long, slender stems, spread their heavy fragrance as he moved them. There were three Lilies in the vase, as always, since Shalaman had not begun to court a consort in earnest. Three—for interest. Four betokened more than interest.

A dozen, along with the betrothal-necklace of ancient amber, gold, and bronze, became a proposition.

He bore the Lilies with a sinking heart, as the ladies he had to walk past looked hopeful, then excited, then downcast as he passed them by. He bore them toward Winterhart, that pallid, sickly-looking creature, like one of the Lilies herself, but a blighted one, colorless, stiff, and thin. All eyes followed his course across the highly polished floor of inlaid woods, and she, of course, must turn to see what everyone else was watching. When he stopped before her, he saw puzzlement in her eyes, quickly covered, as she bowed gracefully to him.

At least she can do that much. Pray to the gods she is feeble-minded, with no interests of her own. One conversation, and Shalaman will tire of her.

"Lady Winterhart," Palisar said, allowing no hint of his innermost thoughts to show in his voice. "The Emperor sends you the Lion Lilies, and has instructed me to convey his pleasure in the fact that you have fit yourself into our Court so gracefully and easily. He invites you to walk in the Royal Gardens in the afternoon."

He handed her the Lilies, praying that she might drop them, which would be a dreadful omen and would surely erode Shalaman's interest in her. But she smiled and took them from him without mishap. Clearly, she had no idea what an honor had just been bestowed upon her, nor what it might lead to. He was not inclined to tell her.

If she does not know, she may yet say or do something that Shalaman will not approve of.

"Please tell the Emperor that I am unworthy of his notice or his compliments, but that I am grateful that he deigns to allow his sun to shine upon this poor northern lily. I will accept his invitation for the morrow with great pleasure, though I by no means deserve such a privilege."

Palisar smiled, although he felt more like gritting his teeth. How had she learned precisely what the best sort of reply would be? It was exactly the right mixture of humility and graciousness. And that—that *dung* about "allowing his sun to shine upon this poor northern lily"— making a delicate play upon the Lion Lilies themselves, and making the comparison to herself that *he* had even noted—

Clever—no, not merely clever. Brilliant.

He bowed, and made his way back to the Emperor. Already a headache throbbed in his left temple. By the time court was over, it would be a torment. He always got these headaches when something went wrong, and he had the feeling that this was only the first of many such torturous headaches.

Shalaman waited for several long moments after Palisar took his place again before speaking to his Advisor. He watched Winterhart cradle the flowers carefully, watched her ignore the envious or avid glances from those other ladies who were too unschooled in the ways of the court to conceal their feelings beneath an urbane mask. Then, when at last the Emperor spoke, he spoke in that low voice that only Palisar was meant to hear, but casually. In fact, from the tone of his voice, he might have been asking what the weather in the gardens was like, and nothing of more import. But Palisar was not deceived by the casual tone. Shalaman knew the ways of dissembling better than anyone in his entire court.

"Well?" the Emperor said. "And what did she say?"

Palisar told him.

There was silence for a few more moments, then a sound which, again, only Palisar heard, but which was enough to make his headache worsen tenfold.

For quietly, deep within his chest, Shalaman was chuckling.

* * *

How do they light this garden so well! They are not using mage-lights, but the place is brighter than a night with a full moon! We need to learn how to do this, ourselves. White Gryphon would be made even brighter with such knowledge. Skandranon looked out into the Great Garden—which was more than a simple garden although it was shaded with more of the enormous trees that grew everywhere in the Palace. It was also a natural bowl-shaped amphitheater floored with grass, with carefully placed trees and beds of flowers beside carved benches on little terraces going up the sides for seating an audience. The only break in the bowl was the door from the Palace where he now stood. He gave his feathers a great shake to settle them, before stepping carefully into the bottom of the bowl.

As always, Evening Court was followed by some other kind of gathering, one which the King was not obligated to attend, although he often did. Perhaps the afternoon nap made people too restless to sleep until well after midnight, although Skan could think of things a lot more exciting to do than caper about at an official function, particularly with all those charming private and semiprivate gardens available.

And think, to one day have these in the White Gryphon settlement—grottoes and gardens for dalliances and courtship. Hertasi, tervardi, kyree, humans, and gryphons amid such beautiful landscaping. And perhaps even some Haighlei!

Tonight there was to be an enormous formal Dance, ostensibly in honor of the envoys from White Gryphon. This wasn't a dance as Skan was accustomed to thinking of a dance; more of a performance, really, rather than a gathering with music where everyone danced.

They didn't seem to have such things here. Instead, a Dance meant that most of the courtiers would be watching the trained dancers go through a long set-piece. All of the Royal Dancers and some of the courtiers would be participating, the courtiers as a kind of untrained, minimally-moving background to the Dancers, all two hundred of them, who were schooled from the time they were five and performed until they were deemed too old to be decorative.

That was interesting; there were a few people Skan had known— most of them kestra'chern or the odd perchi—who had gotten formal dance training. Virtually everyone else was self-taught.

But Drake said that before the wars there were dance troupes, so there must have been performances and people gathering to watch rather than participate.

These Dancers were different from that, though. They "belonged," in a sense, to the King—as the mages belonged to the Priests. They performed only for the King and his court. When they were too old to dance, they were turned into teachers for the next generation, if they had not already married. It was considered a great honor to be permitted to wed a Royal Dancer, and the marriage could not be consummated until the Dancer had a replacement.

The four envoys would be sitting on top of a little pyramid-shaped affair in the center of the performance area, a wooden structure erected for this purpose, surrounded by the dancers and the pivot point of the dance. Skan was rather disappointed that he wouldn't be able to perform this time; he had a notion that he could give these folk an eyeful!

Next time, he consoled himself. *Next time. The Dance-master has promised I may participate, and is planning aerial maneuvers to compliment the dancing on the ground.*

In fact, the Dancemaster already had a title for the next performance; *Phoenix Dancing with Dragon,* an old legend among these people. Skandranon would be the Phoenix, Air-Spirit and Fire-Spirit in one; the dancers would join together to form the earthbound serpentine Dragon, who embodied Water and Earth together.

The very notion had him chuckling with glee. He could hardly wait!

This performance would give him a good notion of how these people danced, and how to adapt his own skydancing techniques to their style.

Without that, I would look more alien to them than I really want to. Perhaps it's just as well that I'm not dancing tonight.

The others, including Zhaneel, had already preceded him, according to some sort of strict protocol that mandated that he, supposedly the highest in rank, be the last one seated. Now four of the Royal Dancers paced gravely up to him in their flowing robes of blue and green with short, cylindrical hats strapped to their heads; four young girls who could not be older than eleven, who looked up at him with solemn eyes and bowed to him until their foreheads touched the grass.

He bowed in return, just as low, and just as gracefully, bending over one extended foreleg until every muscle complained.

They took their places around him, forming a square with himself in the middle, and they all marched out into the garden together.

Murmurs of conversation rose on all sides, and he sensed the curious eyes of those ranked on the benches above him. What did he look like, the white gryphon parading on the green grass? Dangerous—or handsome?

Both? Oh, I hope so. I know I'm handsome, but I haven't felt dangerous all day.

The four girls split off as they all reached the pyramid, a smallish construction with a flat platform on top. He went on alone, climbing the wooden steps with ease, and discovered as he took his place beside Zhaneel why this was such a place of honor. From here, elevated above the dancers, you saw not only the dancers themselves, but the patterns they formed, abstract constructions created by the special colors of the costumes they wore.

Well, this should be fascinating. I can study their dance steps very well from here; the patterns ought to be incorporated into what I will do as well. As he settled in, a touch of a color he hadn't expected caught the corner of his eye— Zhaneel was buff and gray, Winterhart had worn green and white, and Amberdrake was all in green. So why the vivid, warm golden-yellow? He turned out of curiosity, and saw that Winterhart was cradling a bouquet of three large, tawny-gold lilies in her arms.

That's interesting. She didn't have those when we came down to Court, so she must have gotten them at Court itself. I wish I hadn't been so busy talking to Leyuet; I must have missed something. Wonder who gave them to her?

Chances were it was Amberdrake, that incurable romantic. But where had he found them? Skan had never seen anything like them before, and he *knew* there wasn't anything like them growing in the gardens. Gesten would have noticed; Gesten was always on the lookout for plants to take home to White Gryphon, and he would love these.

But before he could say anything to Winterhart, the musician struck up; Haighlei music wasn't anything like the Kaled'a'in stuff Skan remembered, nor like the music of the minstrels and Bards of the old northern courts. Like the Royal Dancers, these Royal Musicians were all trained to play together as a group, and their music lessons began in earliest childhood. They even wore a uniform that was unique among the Haighlei garments, in that there were no trailing sleeves or other encumbrances to interfere with the playing of instruments.

There were at least a dozen different kinds of drums alone in that group, plus gongs, bells, cymbals, zills—at least half of the musicians played percussion of one sort or another. The rest were equally divided between instruments with plucked or bowed strings, and various flutes.

As might be expected with that kind of balance, the music was heavily percussive in nature, and Skan was glad he wasn't sitting too near the ensemble.

You could go deaf quickly with that much pounding in your ears—and I pity the poor creature with a headache! But when it all blends together, it is deep and driving. I like this a lot. It reminds me of—

Skandranon realized what it reminded him of. It was visceral. It reached deep into him; the vibrations carried through his chest, through his wings, through his bones. It felt like sex; it felt like skydancing and mating, when the blood thrummed in his ears and all the world shook.

Oh, I remember those times, when I weighed less. I was strong and virile. And fast. And sleek and glossy black.

Skandranon suppressed a delighted laugh. Those were the days!

Then the dancers struck their initial poses, right arms with their trailing sleeves raised high, left arm bent toward the earth, and bodies curved backward until it made *his* back ache to look at them. He forgot everything else from that moment on in his absorption in the dance, studying the details.

"Enjoy yourself?" Zhaneel asked with a saucy gape-grin on her delicate gryfalcon face, as they looked in on the twins before taking to their own bed. Skan was yawning; the performance had gone on for a very long time, and it was well after midnight when all the congratulations had been made to the Dancers, the Musicians, and the Dancemaster, and they could return to their rooms again.

Not that he hadn't savored every minute of it!

The little ones were curled up in their nests of cushions, making a ball with two heads, four wings, and an indeterminate number of limbs—in other words, the usual nighttime position. In the heat of the day, they sprawled, belly-down on cool stone, looking rather squashed. But for now, they were puffballs.

"I liked it a great deal," he told her, as they left the twins to their dreams of mischief among the fishponds, and walked into their own room. The servants had already been and gone, leaving the suite prepared. The door to the balcony was wide open, the curtains pulled aside to allow entry to the cool breeze that always came up around midnight. The air that drifted in was scented with the heavy perfume of a flower that bloomed only at night, a tiny white blossom like a trumpet.

She is just as sweet. I wonder if she is in the mood!

Skan stretched luxuriously. "These Royal Dancers are quite amazing. I don't remember ever seeing anything like that be—"

Someone pounded on their door. Skan and Zhaneel exchanged startled glances as one of the Haighlei servants ran out of the servants' rooms to answer it.

Who can that be at this hour! Surely nothing can be so important that they *need to summon us now! Unless—*Skan suddenly felt a rush of chill. *Unless something's happened to Drake or Winterhart—*

The servant exchanged some half-dozen words with whoever was there, then quickly stood aside and flung the door open wide. Leyuet, the Truthsayer and Advisor to King Shalaman stood firmly in the doorway, looking both solemn and very upset, and with him were ten of Shalaman's guards, all armed to the teeth.

I don't like the look of this!

"You will please come with me," Leyuet said, trembling, his voice shaking a little as he looked into Skandranon's eyes, past the formidable beak. "Now."

Skan pulled himself up to his full height, and glared down at the thin Truthsayer standing in the doorway. *Better act important and upset. If this is some kind of a trap, I might be able to bluff my way out of it.* "Why?" he demanded. "It is midnight. It is time for sleep. And I am the envoy of my people and a ruler in my own right. What possible cause can you have to come bursting in here with armed guards at your back? What possible need can anyone have of my presence? What is so urgent that it cannot wait until morning?"

Is this some way to try and separate us! Have we come all this way only to find we've willingly become hostages! Was Drake wrong in trusting that Silver Veil would protect us!

But Leyuet only looked tired, and very, very frightened, but not by Skandranon. "You must come with me," he insisted as he clasped his hands together tightly in front of his chest. "Please. You must not make me compel you. I tell you this for your benefit."

"Why?" Skan demanded again. *"Why!"*

"Because," Leyuet said at last, his face gray under the dark color of his complexion, "there has been a murder. And it was done by a creature with wings, with magic, or with both."

Zhaneel was not wanted along, so she stayed behind under guard. Skan was just as happy to have her elsewhere, although he doubted that she would get any rest until he returned. It looked as though it was going to be a long night for both of them.

And we were just getting our *stamina back, too!*

He was not under arrest. *Fortunately,* he and the others had been sitting in the middle of that Dance, under the scrutiny of the entire court, all the Dancers, and however many servants had managed to steal a moment and a place to watch from. Or rather, his "arrest" was a token only, and meant to last only so long as it took for half a dozen witnesses to be hauled from their beds and swear before the King that Skan had not once left his seat from the moment the Dance began. As he was counted as the highest authority among the newcomers, protocol dictated that he would be questioned first; presumably this was so that he would have the option of naming any of his underlings guilty of the crime, and thus save face.

Shalaman waited on his bench-throne, face stern and impassive, as six sleepy Haighlei—a Dancer, a servant, three courtiers, and an envoy from one of the other Kingdoms—all vouched for him at different times during the Dance. Evidently, they were leaving nothing to chance.

When the last of them left, Leyuet listened for a moment while the King spoke, then turned back to Skan. "The King would like your opinion on what transpired, and he requests that you accompany us to investigate the scene. As you pointed out, you have wings, and you know magic. The King believes that you will have insights into this tragedy that we may not."

As if I have any choice. If I refuse, it will look bad, perhaps suspicious, and these people are suspicious enough of me already.

Best to put a good face on it, then. He bowed as he had to the dancers. "Tell the King that I will be pleased to add whatever I can to help determine who is the author of this murder." He tried to look calm, dignified, and just as impassive as Shalaman himself.

His innocence ascertained, the King waited for Palisar, Silver Veil, and a gaggle of priests and official-looking fellows with spears that were both functional and decorative to arrive. Then all of them, Skan included, trooped off together to a far corner of the Palace, to one of the towers that housed some of the higher-ranking nobles.

The corridors were deserted, but not because people were sleeping. Skan sensed eyes behind the cracks of barely-opened doors behind them, and sensed fear rising like a fog all along their path. People knew that something terrible had happened although they didn't know what it was. Rumors were probably spreading already.

I only hope I look like an investigator and not a prisoner or a suspect in custody!

Up the wooden stairs of the tower they went, four stories' worth of climbing, with a landing and a closed door giving onto the staircase at each floor, until they came out onto the landing of the suite belonging to the victim. This was the uppermost floor of the flat-roofed tower, with only the staircase as an access route. Leyuet took pains to point that out, as they opened that final door into the victim's suite.

They didn't exactly have to search to find the body—or rather, most of the body. It was all still in the first room of the suite.

Skan didn't know the victim. When Leyuet had mentioned the name, it hadn't triggered a feeling of familiarity; there were a lot of high-ranking nobles, and he'd hardly had time to learn all of them by name. He might have recognized the face—if there had been anything left of the face to recognize.

The problem was that there wasn't anything left to recognize. The body had been shredded, flesh sprayed all over the walls and furniture with such abandon that the hardened guards looked sick, and the more susceptible Palisar and Leyuet had to excuse themselves. The King, who presumably had seen quite a bit of carnage over his lifetime, if only on one of his fabled lion hunts, was visibly shaken. Silver Veil's face was as white as her dressing gown, but her features remained composed. Skan wondered how she managed it.

Then again, she took her wagon and her apprentices through Ma'az's battle-lines, and before that, through the areas he'd "pacified." Perhaps this isn't anything worse than she saw back then.

Well, that was a horrid thought. And, unfortunately, probably true.

Skan paced slowly around the room, avoiding the blood and bits of flesh, noting how and where the blows had fallen. There wasn't a great deal of furniture in this room, which made his task easier. "I hope your Serenity will excuse what might seem callousness on my part," he said absently, crouching to examine the path of a particular blood spurt. "But I am a warrior. I have seen worse than this visited upon my own people in my very presence. Silver Veil will have told you of Ma'ar, of the wars. I assume that I am here in part because of that experience, as well as the fact that I am a mage and I am capable of flying."

Silver Veil translated, and Shalaman nodded. He said something, and Silver Veil turned toward Skan.

"His Serenity says that the woman who died was seen in Court this evening, and left just as you entered the garden for the Dance in your honor. She was known to oppose the alliance, and chose to make her opposition public with her withdrawal."

Charming. My enemy, which makes me suspect all over again. "I was not aware that this particular woman felt that strongly," Skan said mildly. "I do not feel it is my place or my duty to interfere in the opinions of the Haighlei.

Firstly, they are your people, not mine, and your Serenity will deal with them and their opinions as he sees fit. Secondly, actions tell more than words; I behave with honor and candor, and that will do more to reverse a poor opinion of me than all the arguing and attempts at persuasion of all the learned diplomats in the world."

Shalaman smiled faintly as Silver Veil translated this, and Skan went back to his examination. Since he had tacit permission to do so, he invoked mage-sight, although he frankly wasn't expecting it to work correctly. Sometimes it did, these days, and sometimes all it showed him was a wash of magical energy over everything like a fog, impossible to see through. Once in a while, very rarely, it showed him nothing. That might mean that it wasn't working—or it might mean there was nothing to see.

This time, he got that foggy wash of energy over everything, which was hardly useful.

He examined the windows, which were unlocked and open, and found nothing there, either. No bloodstains showing that the murderer had escaped that way, and no signs of clawmarks as there would be if the murderer had landed on the window ledge and grasped it as a gryphon would.

He reported both those nonfindings dutifully.

"Could a mage have done this?" Leyuet prompted.

"Certainly," Skan replied. "*If* any mage could gather enough power to overcome all the present difficulties in working magic—difficulties I am certain that Your Serenity's priests have already advised you of—this could be done at a distance, without the mage needing even to be near this room. It could also have been done physically. My opinion is that most of the damage was done while the victim was already unconscious or dead, probably the latter."

He pointed out with clinical precision why he had come to that conclusion—the lack of force in the blood sprays, the apparent lack of movement on the part of the victim. Leyuet looked sick but continued to translate.

I had better learn this language quickly if I am going to find myself fending off accusations of murder!

"I cannot tell if this was done by magic means or physical," he concluded. "There was time enough for someone to have done this by physical means before the body was discovered, since the victim dismissed her servants to brood alone during the Dance. I cannot tell if someone flew here or climbed up from below. The latter would be easy enough, for the north side of this tower is all in shadow, and does not overlook a guard post or a garden where someone might have been walking. If the murderer was very, very good, he could even have come up by the stairs and left the same way without anyone seeing him." He shrugged. "I am sorry to be of so little use."

Leyuet nodded, as Silver Veil translated, and then said something to Shalaman himself. The King spoke, and both of them listened gravely.

It was Silver Veil who translated the reply. "Skandranon," she said hesitantly, "I do not care to be the one who tells you this, but His Serenity decrees that while he is convinced for the moment that you had nothing to do with this, there are others who will not be convinced. You must therefore submit to his supervision."

Skan ground his beak, and Leyuet winced at the sound. "And what sort of supervision will that be?" he asked harshly. He could already tell from Silver Veil's expression that he wasn't going to like it, whatever it was.

"You must have one of the Spears of the Law with you at all times, or submit to being closed inside a locked and windowless room if you must have privacy," she told him apologetically. "That is the only way we can be certain of your whereabouts at all times. It is as much for your sake as ours, you know."

Oh, lovely. Either have one of these ebony spearcarriers watching my every move, or get closed up into a closet. Charming. This is not going to do a great deal for my love life! Somehow I doubt that Zhaneel will welcome a third party to our little trysts...

And the idea of any kind of exertion in a locked and windowless room, especially in this climate, was not a pleasant one.

I shall certainly lose weight. It will be steamed off!

But what other choice did he have?

None, and that's the problem, isn't it!

"Very well," he growled, making no secret of his displeasure. "Tell everyone that I will suffer that they may feel more comfortable. Tell them I will voluntarily be their hostage in a closet. I can't see any other solution."

"Neither can I," Silver Veil replied with a sigh.

It was matched by Skan's. And there was one more problem to be faced.

I have to explain this one to Zhaneel!

There was a windowless room in their suite, as it turned out; normally used as a storage room, and hastily turned into a sleeping chamber. Fortunately for him, it might have been windowless, but it wasn't *airless;*

he had forgotten the humidity that went along with the heat in this land. You didn't dare close things into an airless chamber, not and expect to extract them again in the same shape they went in. Mildew and mold were the twin enemies that housekeepers fought here, and mildew and mold would thrive in a completely closed chamber.

So there were air-slits cut just below the ceiling, no broader than the width of a woman's palm, but cut on all four walls, and providing a steady stream of fresh air into the room.

"At least it will be dark when we wish to sleep," Zhaneel said philosophically as she set a tiny lamp up on the wall, trying to make the best of the situation. It was a good thing that she *had* handlike foreclaws, and not Skan's fighting claws—with no mage-lights available, it was either a lamp or nothing, and *he* couldn't light a lamp. Except with magic, which he'd been warned not to use. "These slits cannot let in much light. And if the little ones wake at dawn and begin to play, the walls will muffle the noise."

Skan tried not to growl. It was not exactly compensation for being shut into a closet at night.

"I won't say I like this," he said, throwing himself down on their bed, and resisting the urge to claw it to bits in frustration. "I wish I had a better solution. *Sketi*, I wish I'd never come here in the first place! If I wasn't here, there'd be no one from White Gryphon to suspect!"

"I would not count on that," Zhaneel countered thoughtfully, stretching herself down beside him, and beginning to preen his ear-tufts to soothe his temper. "Consider; what if this were devised *precisely* to implicate you? Or rather, to implicate one of the White Gryphon envoys. If Judeth had been here in your stead, the murder might seem to have been performed by a fighter; if Lady Cinnabar, the victim might have been dissected with surgical precision. Or a weapon from the north might have been found in the room."

"Hmm." Skan pondered that; it had the right sound and feel to it. "But what does that mean for us at the moment?"

Zhaneel delicately spat out a tuft of down and answered him. "Whoever did this in the first place must not realize that you were under the eyes of hundreds of witnesses at the time of the murder. The best that we can do is be graceful and gracious beneath this burden, and wait for some other evidence to surface. What is needed is motive. Perhaps this courtier had some great enemy, or perhaps she owned something that will prove to be missing." She shrugged and went after the other ear-tuft. "In any case, it hardly matters at the moment. I think that there is magic involved."

"How, when mages are so watched and bound by laws and priests?" Skan asked skeptically.

She had no answer for that, but there was no reason why he couldn't pursue that particular quarry for a moment. "I suppose that accidents could happen," he mused aloud. "This is a large country. A child could be overlooked, or even run away from the school. Once he knew what he was, if he didn't turn himself in—"

"Then obviously he would already be a criminal," Zhaneel stated.

"A good point. Which would mean he would drift into the company of other criminals." He nodded, and leaned a little more into her preening; she knew where all the really itchy spots were.

"Which would mean that he would become a weapon in the hands of other criminals," she replied. "I think the most likely is that this woman had a great enemy, and that the enemy decided to rid himself of the woman during a time when he was unlikely to be caught."

"During the Dance, you mean? But everyone knew we were going to be there, didn't they? After all, it was supposed to be in our honor."

"That would be known to those in the Court itself. The fact that the murder looked as if a gryphon did it might actually only be a coincidence, if this was a crime of terrible and profound anger," she pointed out. "And the murderer could simply be incredibly lucky, to have gotten into his victim's suite, killed her, and gotten out without being seen. People *do* have that kind of luck, you know." She glanced at him slyly. "Certainly, you did."

"Huhrrr." He thought that over. It was possible. Not likely, but barely possible. "He'd have to be lucky *and* good. And if that's the case, we'll never catch him."

"But when nothing more happens, this will all evaporate in a few days," Zhaneel pointed out. "After all, *you* could not have done the deed, even Palisar admits that. As unreliable as magic is, even if you had done this by magic, you would still have needed privacy and a great deal of time, and there would be traces. So, when nothing more is discovered, all the attention upon us will fade in importance in no more than a week, and they will remove their guards and precautions." She glanced at him, with a sideways tilt of her head. "They may never find the murderer, but this will soon become only the interest of what passes for a policing force here."

Skan sighed, and nuzzled her tiny ear-tufts. "You're right, of course," he said as she craned her head upward to blow out the lamp. "In a few days their suspicion of us will be forgotten."

There. I have said what will comfort her. Why don't I believe it myself!

CHAPTER FIVE

T here was a familiar knock at the door, a little after dinnertime and just before Court. The servant spoke a sentence or two in hushed tones.

"Don't tell me," Skandranon groaned, as the servant—once again—ushered in Leyuet and the Spears of the Law. This was the third time in six days. "Another murder."

Leyuet nodded grimly. His dark face was drawn and new worry-lines etched the corners of his mouth. And was there more gray in his hair? It seemed so. "Another murder. Another professed opponent of the treaty. This time, in a room locked and barred from within. It *must* be by magic. You were, of course, watched all afternoon during your sleep period?"

Skan gestured broadly to indicate the pair of heavily-muscled spear-bearers, standing stoically in what passed for the corners of the room. "They never left my side, and they never slept." After the second murder, a single watcher had not been deemed enough to insure Skandranon's innocence by some parties, so a second Spear of the Law had been added to make certain that the first was not duped or slumbering. "I've either been here or in the garden. Just ask them."

Leyuet sighed, a look of defeat creeping over him. "I do not need to, for I know that they will confirm your words. But I also know that no magician of the Haighlei could have done this. As you rightly pointed out, to overcome all the disturbances in the use of magic would require more power than any of our priests or mages has available to him. Thus the mage must be foreign, with foreign ways of working magic." He rubbed his eyes, a gesture that had become habitual over the past several days, as Leyuet clearly got less and less sleep. "No Haighlei would ever have committed murder so—so crudely, so impolitely, either."

Skan coughed to keep from choking with astonishment. Every time he thought he understood the Haighlei ways, someone said something that surprised him all over again. "You mean to tell me that there is a polite way to commit *murder!*" he blurted.

Leyuet did not rise to the bait; he just shook his head. "It is just the

Haighlei way. Even murder has a certain protocol, a set ritualistic aspect to it. For one thing, a murderer must accomplish certain tasks to be certain that the spirit of his victim has been purged from the earth. How else could the perpetrator feel satisfaction? But this conforms to nothing Haighlei. It is not random, but there is no pattern to it, either."

Zhaneel coughed politely, drawing Leyuet's gaze toward her. "All the victims were women as well as being opposed to the alliance," Zhaneel suggested delicately. "Could it be a case of a jilted lover? Someone who approached all three of the women about an assignation and was rebuffed—or someone who once had affairs with them and was cast off for another?"

But Leyuet only shook his head again. "There would be even more of ritual in that case. No, this has no pattern, it was done by magic, and it is like nothing we have ever seen in the Empire."

As if some madman among the Haighlei could not act in a patternless fashion. "It is new, in other words," Skan said flatly. "And since it is new, and we are new, therefore—"

"Therefore I must summon you before the Emperor Shalaman once again," Leyuet finished for him, spreading his hands wide. "It is the pattern."

Skan simply bowed to the inevitable. *I have no choice, after all. I cannot even try to go back to White Gryphon now; they might decide that retreat was an admission of guilt and send an army.* "Lead on," he replied, gesturing with his foreclaw. "I am at your disposal."

And I only hope that isn't a prophetic phrase! I would very much prefer not to be "disposed of!"

Kanshin worked the little wooden ball up and around his fingers, from the index to the littlest finger and back again, in an exercise often used by street-entertainers who practiced sleight-of-hand and called it magic. He was no street entertainer, however. He was a thief, and a master thief at that. More than any street-entertainer, he needed to keep his hands supple.

His father would be horrified, if he still lived, to know what "trade" Kanshin now plied. *Better to be a master thief than a master-ditchdigger.* That was what Kanshin's father had been, and his grandfather, and so on back for ten generations. That, so the priests and the gods decreed, was what Kanshin should have been.

Kanshin sneered at them all, at his father for being a fool, at the priests for the "decrees" that duped so many. *A pox upon priests and gods together. Assuming there even are any gods, which I doubt.*

He worked the ball around his left hand, across the palm, and up to the index finger again. *My father believed in the gods and the priests, and we starved. I like my way better.*

Kanshin had more intelligence than to believe the pious rhetoric spewed out in regular, measured doses by the priests—especially when the only way to "be certain" of a better position in one's next life was to bestow all of one's wealth on the priests in this one. Not that a ditchdigger was going to acquire much *wealth* over the course of a lifetime, but Kanshin's father had devoted every spare coin to the purchase of that new life, to the detriment and hardship of his own children.

Perhaps that was why Kanshin had seen through the scheme by the time he was five. Hunger undermined manners. Polite people didn't question.

He glanced at the door to the guest room, thinking he had heard a sound, but it was nothing.

Even our guest would certainly agree with me and not with my father. He might be insane, but he certainly isn't stupid.

He had hoped for a while that he might escape the endless cycle of backbreaking labor and poverty by being taken by the priests as a mage—but that never happened. *No mage-craft and easy life for me. What a joke! If the gods really existed, they'd have arranged for me to have the powers of magic, wouldn't they! If they had, I'd be one of their fat priests or fatter mages right now, and there would be many people still in the incarnations I cut short.* But there were no gods, of course, and no priest had come to spirit Kanshin away to a better life. So, one day, when his father and mother and bawling, brawling siblings were all sleeping the sleep of the stupefied, he ran away. Away to the city, to the wicked, worldly city of Khimbata, and a chance for something better than blisters on his hands, a permanently bent back, and an early grave.

Kanshin smiled with satisfaction at his own cleverness. So much for the gods, who sought to keep him in his place. For although he could not go higher in caste to win himself the fortune and luxury he craved—he *could* go lower.

He transferred the ball to his right hand, and began the exercise all over again.

He had started out as a beggar, self-apprenticed to one of the old hands of the trade, aged Jacony. Jacony had taught him everything; how to wrap his body tightly with bandages to look thinner, how to make his face pale and wan or even leprous, how to create sores from flour, water, and henna, how to bind his leg or arm to make it look as if he were an amputee. That was all right for a while, as long as he was young and could look convincingly starved and pathetic—and as long as the sores and deformations his master put on him were strictly cosmetic. But when the old man let drop the fact that he was considering actually *removing* a hand or a foot to make Kanshin into a "wounded lion hunter," Kanshin decided that he'd better find another trade and another master.

I can't believe the old man thought I'd stand for that. I wasn't that desperate! But—maybe he was. And missing a hand or a foot, I'd be a lot more conspicuous if I tried to run off—a lot more dependent on him, too, I suppose.

It didn't take him long to find a new master, now that he knew his way around the city. By that time, he was quite conversant with the covert underground of beggars, whores, and thieves that swarmed the soft underbelly of the lazy metropolis, like fleas living in the belly-fur of a fat, pampered lapdog. And he knew what he wanted, too.

There were other masters ready to take me at that point. Lakshe, for instance. He hadn't ever given Lakshe's offer serious thought because he didn't intend to become a boy-whore, although the trade paid well enough. He would have only one chance in ten of earning enough before he became too old to be called a "boy" anymore, and there wasn't a lot of call for aging catamites.

And the odds of becoming a procurer like Lakshe are even lower than earning enough to keep you for the rest of your life.

He'd tried being a beggar, and he just looked too healthy, too strong; not all the paste-and-henna sores in the world would convince people he was really suffering, not unless he *did* undergo a self-amputation. *I didn't like begging, anyway. No chance for a fortune. And scraping out a living that way was hardly better than digging ditches.*

So—that left thief, an avocation he was already attracted to. He smiled as he worked the ball across his fingers. *I'd even picked a pocket or two by then, so I was ready, ready to learn more.*

He was still young enough—just—to get a master. He chose one of the oldest thieves in the city, an alcoholic sot who lived on cadged drinks and a reputation many doubted. *No one knew that Poldarn was more than a drunk and a liar.* Kanshin had not doubted him after several of the stories had, on investigation, proven to be true. Nor had he doubted the man's ability to teach him, if only Kanshin could keep him sober and alive long enough to do so.

He had managed both, and now, if he was not *the* master-thief in the city, he was certainly among the masters. *Poldarn did know every trick of the trade, from picking locks to climbing up walls with no more gear than ten strong fingers and toes. He was good, I'll grant him that. Too bad drink addled his wits.*

And his master? Dead, now; collapsed back into the gutter as soon as Kanshin left him on his own. *He couldn't stay sober a day without me. He was drunk the day I set up on my own, and I never saw him sober after that. I don't think he lived more than a fortnight after I left.*

Hardly a surprise; the man's liver must have been the size of a goose. *Either that—or he went back to drinking the same quantities of strong liquor that he had of weak, and the drink itself killed him. Small loss, to the world or to me. Where were the gods for him, when he was drinking himself into a stupor.*

The young thief had been good—and careful. He neither over- nor under-estimated his own abilities, and he always brought back the goods he'd been paid to take. Now Kanshin had all the things he had dreamed of; a house, slaves, fine foods to eat and wines to drink. The food was as good as that from the King's table, and the wines were often better.

The house was a grand affair, like the dream of a palace on the inside—granted, the house was in the heart of the Dakola District, but no one was stupid enough to try to rob Kanshin. The last fool who'd tried was still serving out his punishment, chained to a wall in Kanshin's basement, digging a new cesspit. That was a *far* more effective deterrent than simply killing or maiming interlopers. After all, most of them, like Kanshin himself, had become thieves to *avoid* hard labor. When they found themselves little better than slaves, forced to wield shovels and scrub dirty dishes, they never tried to rob him a second time.

He listened very carefully, and smiled when he heard the faint scrape of a shovel on dirt. Now *there* was one unhappy thief who would not be making a second visit to Kanshin.

The house itself looked like every other filthy, rundown heap in the district—outside. Inside, it was crammed with every luxury that Kanshin could buy or steal. Perhaps service was a little slower than in the homes of the nobles—the slaves were hobbled with chains to hinder their escape—but Kanshin didn't mind. In fact, he rather enjoyed seeing people who could probably boast higher birth than he, weighted down with iron and forced to obey his every whim. Slavery was not legal in this kingdom, but none of these people would dare to complain of their lot.

Not all of this was due entirely to his own work, but it *was* due to his own cleverness.

He set the ball aside, and began to run the same exercises using a coin. *It was clever to find this perfect partner. It was clever to see* his *cleverness.* Some eight or nine years ago, right after that strange winter when the priests all seemed to vanish for a time and there were rumors all over the city of magic gone horribly wrong, a young and comely stranger began walking the streets of the Dakola District. He claimed to be a mage, which all men knew to be impossible, since no mage—by definition a Law-Keeper—would ever frequent the haunts of the Law-Slayers. So all men laughed him to scorn when he told them this, and that he was looking for a thief to partner him in certain enterprises.

No one believed him. They should have known that a story so preposterous had to be true.

All men laughed at him but one—Kanshin, who bethought him that if a ditchdigger could slip through the Law to become a master-thief, could not a renegade mage slip through the Law as well to retain his magic? So he sought out this man, and discovered that what no one else would believe was nothing more nor less than the barest, leanest truth.

He—the man called himself "Noyoki," which meant "No one"—*was* a mage. And he had, by sheerest accident, slipped through the hands of the priests. At seventeen he had been discovered in some unsavory doing by the priests, his teachers—what, Kanshin never bothered to find out for true, although Noyoki said it had been because he used his powers to cheat at games of chance.

That seems unlikely... but then again, these priests find cheating to be a sin only second to murder. I suppose it never occurs to them that they *are the real cheats.* They had, of course, decreed that he should have his powers removed, as always. No child caught misusing his powers could be allowed to retain them. For that matter, it was rumored that adult mages had been stripped of their powers for misuse.

A useful tumor to circulate I suppose, if you are intent on preserving the illusion of the integrity of your adult mages.

It was the mad magic that had saved Noyoki, that first wave of mad magic ten years ago that had lit up the night skies, created abortive and mismade creatures, muddled everything and turned the world of the mages upside-down. The priest that should have burned the magic out of his head had been struck down unconscious and died the following week without ever waking again, but Noyoki had the wit to feign the sickness that came when such a deed had been done. And with magic gone quite unpredictable, no one of the priests could tell that it had *not* been done.

So he was sent back to his family in disgrace—powers intact, and lacking only a few months of training to be a full mage.

They were told he should never be trusted, never given power, a high office, or any responsibility. Kanshin smiled at that. Another challenge to the nonexistent gods; if they had never given this boy magic, he would never have turned against the world and cultivated Kanshin. If he had never met Kanshin, there were things stolen and deaths recorded that would never have happened.

So much for the gods.

It was a lofty house, for Noyoki had quarters of his own within the Palace itself. Noyoki had waited until they ceased to put eyes on him wherever he went, and left him in scorn to seek whatever excesses might soonest bring his cycle to the earliest end. That was what he was supposed to do. No one dreamed he had any ambitions at all; they should have been burned out with his magic.

Then, once no one bothered to watch him anymore, he went down into the quarter of the thieves, to seek a thief as a partner.

Kanshin and Noyoki were successful beyond Kanshin's original dreams of avarice—though Noyoki never seemed to want the gems and artifacts, the drugs and the rare essences that Kanshin stole with his help. No, Noyoki was most interested in paper, documents—

Well, that was fine with Kanshin. Let Noyoki have the documents; Kanshin knew better than to try to take them to use himself. That required subtlety which Kanshin had, but it also required knowledge of their owners and the enemies of their owners which he did not have. He was smart enough to know that he could and would never learn these things in time to make proper use of the stolen papers.

Noyoki also had another power—rarely used and hard on him— that allowed him to place Kanshin within a locked and barred room and extract him again. At first he had not been able to do this more than once a year or so, but lately, he had been able to accomplish it much oftener. For a thief, such a talent was beyond price, and Kanshin treasured his partnership, suffering insults and slights from Noyoki he would never have suffered from another living being.

Things have been going well. Kanshin frowned. *So why has Noyoki suddenly gotten greater ambitions!*

Everything had gone according to the plan Kanshin had worked out for his life—when the unexpected happened. Kanshin had wealth, power, a certain amount of fame, and needed only to work when he chose. But one day not long ago, Noyoki had brought the madman now in Kanshin's guest chamber to Kanshin's home and bade him care for the pale-skinned creature.

Hadanelith was the madman's name, a man with the white skin of a leper, the pale-blue eyes of a lemur, and hair like bleached straw. Kanshin would have thought that this "Hadanelith" was some kind of misbegotten sport, created from a normal man by the mad magic, if he had not once seen the Emperor's kestra'chern, The Silver Veil, with his own eyes. She had skin as pale, eyes as washed-out, and hair of an even stranger silver color. So the madman was not a misbegotten thing, but only a man from another land.

I do not understand this creature. Hadanelith found humor in things not even Kanshin found amusing; he made slaves of the slaves, manipulating their minds in such a way that Kanshin could remove their chains at any time and never fear their escaping. Of course, once Hadanelith had done with them, they were useless to anyone but him. Kanshin was just glad he had not given the man access to more than three, of which only two were female. Hadanelith had no use for males. Kanshin refused to allow himself to be intimidated by the man, but his strange behavior unnerved him.

On the other hand, he is frighteningly intelligent. He had learned their language so quickly that Kanshin wondered now and again if the man had plucked it from their minds. But no—he had only learned by listening, and when he finally spoke, it was with no real accent. He might giggle like an hysterical girl with pleasure in the work he had done for them, but it was competent work, and within the limits he and Noyoki set, Hadanelith worked well.

One of the slaves—one that Hadanelith had not spoiled—came to the door of Kanshin's work room, a chamber filled with the tools of his trade and the instruments he used to keep his body as supple as that of the *young* thief he had once been. "Master," said the man, his head lowered submissively, "Noyoki awaits your pleasure in the reception chamber."

"Good." Kanshin placed the coin back in the holder beside the ball, and rose from his chair. "Tell him I will be with him shortly."

With a faint clinking of chain, the slave bowed and shuffled out. Kanshin smiled at his back.

Then he surveyed himself in the full-length mirror to be certain there was nothing lacking in his appearance. He suspected Noyoki to be of extraordinarily high birth, and he had tried, since the beginning, to look as outwardly respectable as someone of high caste could. Noyoki himself cultivated a rapscallion appearance, wearing untidy robes of odd cut, his hair woven into braids like a working man, but that did not mean he was not influenced without his realizing it by the appearance of respectability. Every trick that came to hand was necessary when dealing with Noyoki.

There was nothing to mark Kanshin as a person of anything less than the caste of bankers and professionals. He smoothed his robes with a proprietary hand and went in search of his partner.

Noyoki sprawled casually on one of the couches in the reception chamber, his hair beaded as well as braided, his bright cotton robe made of patchwork material, like that of a mountebank or street-entertainer. He was examining a piece of carving that Hadanelith had left on one of the tables, looking it over with intense scrutiny, a frown of concentration on his handsome, chiseled features.

"What do you make of this?" he asked as Kanshin entered, followed by the slave with a tray of fruit ices for their refreshment. He held it up; there was no mistaking what it was meant for, but the shape was odd. It was carved to resemble a rabbit, with long ears pressed tightly together, and a misshapen, bulbous body. The expression on the rabbit's stupid face was that of sheer terror. Not the sort of expression one would expect to find on a toy of that nature. It was not unheard of for these toys to be shaped like animals, but the animals always looked as if they were cheerfully enjoying themselves.

"It is one of your friend's toys," Kanshin replied easily. "And I suspect it would give us a great deal of insight into his way of thinking if we knew why he had carved it that way. He presented me with it this afternoon. There was blood on it."

"Charming." Noyoki did not put it down immediately, as Kanshin had thought he might. Then again, given that he had turned to blood-magic, perhaps the thing held some arcane significance for him. "He performed well this afternoon."

"You would be the one to know, not I, by the results of your working." Kanshin raised his eyebrows in inquiry; Noyoki only smiled, and ran his fingers along the smooth wood of the carving, caressing the toy with his touch.

"If that is a question, yes, the blood-power came through strong and clear. It more than tripled the reserves I expended to put him in place and take him out again." Noyoki had told Kanshin that only the power that came through pain and spilled blood was strong enough to allow him to work magics in the old way, before magery had run wild. *What* he was doing, Kanshin did not ask. He really did not want to know. *The less I know of his doings, the safer I am.* He knew very well that Noyoki would not hesitate to be rid of him if the mage thought he knew too much.

Whatever magics the man worked now, it was something to put Noyoki back in a position of power, though whether overt or covert, Kanshin would not even guess. He knew that the victims Noyoki had chosen for his "pet" to slay were all rivals or former rivals; perhaps he was ridding himself of his male rivals by using the deaths of their females to undermine them.

"It is a pity that we cannot persuade the man to broaden his—ah—interests," he said carefully.

Noyoki frowned. "If I could find a way to coerce him to take men—well, perhaps coercion would be a bad idea. He *is* an artist in his way, and when one coerces an artist, the work is always flawed."

Kanshin nodded, although the turn of Noyoki's phrase surprised him. Had the mage spoken from past experience?

Their dual role in this was to use Hadanelith to simulate murder by magic. Kanshin would find a way to insert Hadanelith into the victim's chambers and get him out again; if there was no other way in, Noyoki would spirit him in and out by that odd talent of his when he was done, using the excess of the power released from the victim's suffering and death. In between, Hadanelith had free rein to work whatever atrocities on the victim that he chose, up until the moment he received the signal to kill.

A clever plan, which required a minimum of magic to carry out. At the moment, Kanshin's payment was coming through Noyoki, and both maintained the polite fiction that Noyoki was working for someone else, some great noble who wanted obstacles removed from his path, but in such a way that these dangerous new pale-skinned allies were also placed under suspicion.

It is easier to discredit foreigners anyway. It is just a good thing that their arrival coincided with the beginning of our plan. Kanshin had not told Hadanelith any more than was strictly necessary to carry out the work, but he wondered if the man had guessed who was taking the blame for the murders. If so, he did not seem at all displeased by the idea of what might be his own countrymen being falsely accused.

Perhaps he simply doesn't care. Or perhaps these people drove him out of their ranks… That was an interesting thought. If Hadanelith had tortured and killed before, it would account for his peculiar competence in that area.

He was a good, if flawed, tool. He followed his instructions to the letter, as long as he knew why he was supposed to be doing something. When the signal to kill came, he never balked.

The trouble is, we cannot be certain how much longer he will remain tractable.

As Kanshin understood it, for Noyoki's blood-magic to work, the power he received had to be incredibly strong, which meant the murders must be committed with a diabolical, rabid brutality. Despite the fact that the Emperor was trying to keep the news suppressed, rumors of the murders were already in the lower districts of Khimbata, and hardened criminals spoke of the scenes and the victims with troubled awe, as if even they could not imagine doing such things.

"How much longer do you think we can keep a leash on our dog?" Noyoki asked, as if he was aware of Kanshin's doubts.

Kanshin shrugged. "How much longer do you need him? He seems stable enough for now. I think as long as he knows that we are the only route to what *he* wants, he will obey. But he is not sane, Noyoki. He could suddenly change, and we would have no warning of it."

Noyoki nodded, face solemn, the beads on the ends of his braids clicking with the movement of his head. "His carving might give us a clue."

"True." Hadanelith had a mania for carving; he always had a knife in his hands and a piece of wood, and there were more of his twisted little sculptures all over the house. Kanshin didn't mind the mess and the shavings at all; while Hadanelith carved, he was not getting into other mischief.

"I think he knows about the visitors taking the blame for the murders," Noyoki said, suddenly switching topics. "I think it pleases him. Perhaps these people were his enemies."

"Perhaps they were his jailers!" Kanshin retorted sharply. "Never forget what this man does, Noyoki! Never forget that Hadanelith is mad, and he could decide he wants to do it to you! We may turn the tiger upon the tracks of our foes, but the tiger can decide to turn back again and seek us instead!"

"Yes," Noyoki replied with an odd and disquieting smile. "And that is what makes the game all the more interesting, is it not?"

Madness must be contagious, for he surely is mad! Kanshin thought with astonishment.

"I am not mad, Kanshin," Noyoki said, in another uncanny answer to words left unspoken. "I am simply interested in a challenge, and

Hadanelith presents such a challenge. If it is possible, I should like to tame him to my hand as I have tamed the lion and the pard."

Kanshin shrugged. "On your head be it," he replied. "I am interested only in getting rid of him once our tasks for him have been completed. If you choose to take him into your own household, I simply ask that you take him as far away from me as possible."

"Perhaps I will," Noyoki observed, stretching like a well-fed and very lazy cat. "And with that, I shall take my leave of you; I will bring you the information on the next of Hadanelith's playfellows tomorrow."

Kanshin bowed him out to the street and stood in the doorframe, watching his back as he disappeared into the swirling crowds. *He is not a fool, but he is foolhardy,* the thief thought as he closed the door and retreated into the perfumed safety of his own home and away from the noisome babble and stenches of the streets. *Too foolhardy for me. Once this set of jobs is over, I am retiring, far away from here.* He had just the place in mind too; a lake big enough to be considered an inland sea. *Such recklessness is like teasing a lion; you never get a second chance to learn how much is too much.*

He retreated deeply into the depths of his home, past rooms that only opened when he had picked a complicated lock, and which relocked themselves when the door closed. He took himself to the farthest of those rooms, a place where Hadanelith did not go and where, hopefully, he could not go.

The trouble was, the madman learned at a terrible speed. There was no reason why he could *not* learn to master all those locks, as he had already mastered the language and the thief's tricks that Kanshin had taught him.

Kanshin flung himself down on a couch, and laid his right arm across his eyes. How long would the madman remain "safe?" That was a good question.

He only wished he had an answer.

Skandranon was making some decisions as he marched toward the Audience Chamber under armed guard for the third time in a week. For one thing, he was getting *damned* tired of taking the blame for someone else's murders! Especially when the law-keepers didn't seem to him to be making much of an effort to find the real culprit!

His control over his temper had improved over the past several years, but he was just about to lose all that hard-won control. He felt the hackles on the back of his neck rising, despite a conscious effort to make them lie flat.

How can they even pretend that I'm still a suspect? he growled to himself. *I've been under guard for two of the three killings! After the second, they should have removed my guard, not doubled it!*

The situation was uncomfortable enough for him personally, but by now it was obvious that someone, probably someone in Shalaman's own court, was trying to discredit the Kaled'a'in. *We should be uniting to find the culprit,* he seethed. *They should have asked me to bring in the other mages from White Gryphon, mages who might know other techniques to get at the truth! Instead—here I am, being hauled up in front of the King again!*

These murders were jeopardizing everything he had worked for since Urtho's death, threatening to put the Kaled'a'in in the position of having to make an untenable choice—abandon the city and rebuild elsewhere, where the arm of the Haighlei did not reach, or stand and fight for what they had built so far, against a vastly superior force.

By the time they reached the Audience Chamber, Skan was so angry he was just about ready to disembowel something.

So instead of parading meekly into the chamber as he had the past two times, *this* time he shouldered his guards aside and pushed his way up to King Shalaman. The courtiers quickly leaped aside when they saw the look on his face, the parted beak, the raised hackles, the anger in his eyes. The King's bodyguards instinctively stepped forward when the last of the courtiers jumped out of his way, leaving nothing between him and Shalaman but those two guards. But Skan waited for Leyuet and the escort to catch up—which didn't take long—and then he opened his beak and let the words pour out.

Leyuet was babbling, trying to keep up with his own flowing torrents of words. Skan ignored him, in part because he had a suspicion that Shalaman didn't need an interpreter.

"...and what I don't understand is why no one has even *begun* to look for a suspect besides me!" he ranted, his voice coming close to a shriek on the last few words. People winced and tried to cover their ears: "What is wrong with you people? I mean, I know that magic's gone bad, but surely with enough power behind a simple spell your mages could make it work! If your mages don't know anything about using magic to find criminals, then *mine* do, and I'll bring them here from White Gryphon if that's what it takes!" He was in fine style now, pacing and lashing his tail, radiating enough anger to have sunburned anyone near him. "Are you deliberately obstructing the investigations? Have you even started them? I saw no signs of it!"

There was horrified scandal in the murmurs he heard, the faces he watched as he paced and ranted.

He was actually beginning to enjoy himself. Evidently this was something that was just Not Done in Haighlei society.

Well, murder is Not Done, and accusing someone falsely of murder is Not Done—and it's about time someone woke them up to that fact.

Since the polite approach had produced no obvious cooperation on their part, perhaps violating all their social rules would!

Leyuet watched in horror as the huge white gryphon broke away from his escort and began to force his way through the courtiers—although it didn't take long for the courtiers to notice what Skandranon was doing, and leap hastily out of the way. What did the creature think he was doing? Surely he wasn't going to—

But Skandranon stopped short of the throne and began to pace back and forth, his voice raised to a shout, accusing the Haighlei of trying to blame him for the murders for the sake of convenience. Accusing the *King* of originating the plan!

The gryphon was angry, showing more anger than Leyuet had ever seen demonstrated in his life. His rage was a palpable thing, radiating from him in waves of passion as he paced and turned, never once ceasing in his accusations.

He is innocent. Leyuet was sure of that on all counts; such rage could not be the product of guilt, and that was nothing more than simple fact. Leyuet himself had ascertained the gryphon's innocence a dozen times over, with far more than the simple facts to guide him.

So now what do we do! For the very first time since the strangers had arrived here, Skandranon was acting like a King, like the equal of any of the Haighlei Emperors, addressing Shalaman as an equal, demanding his rights, demanding action. This, along with their basic understanding of the gryphon's position as the Kaled'a'in leader, only confirmed his real position in Leyuet's eyes—and presumably in the eyes of every other Haighlei present.

And that only complicated the situation.

I will have to remove the guards, of course. A King simply could *not* be imprisoned or under guard—or held for ransom—or even *questioned* publicly!

"I swear to you, to you all, if *you* don't do something, I will!" Skandranon shouted, his feathers standing on end with rage, his beak snapping off the words as if he would like very much to be closing it on someone's arm. "I will find the murderer! I will bring him to justice!"

Leyuet's dismay deepened, as he surreptitiously gestured to Skandranon's guards to take themselves elsewhere. *Now* what were they going to do? Kings didn't run about trying to solve a murder! They left that up to the Truthsayers and the Spears Of the Law!

Except that the Truthsayers and the Spears hadn't been doing very well. The gryphon was right enough about that.

Whatever were they going to do?

The Emperor caught Leyuet's eye and gave a slight nod in Skandranon's direction. Leyuet cast his own eyes upward for a moment, then nodded back. Some called it magic, some felt that it bordered on the blasphemous powers of seeing into another's mind, but the Truthsayers were trained by the priests to know, infallibly, whether or not someone was speaking the truth. And Leyuet had just told Shalaman without words that the white gryphon was doing just that. It was only a surface touch of the soul; Leyuet dared not go deeper, as he would with a human. He had no notion how his own soul would react to such an intimacy. But at the moment the surface touch was all that was needed.

The skin around Shalaman's eyes twitched. That was all, but it was an unusual display of emotion from the Emperor.

We are in a tangle, and I see no way out of it. But I am not the King. Perhaps Shalaman—

The gryphon finally ran out of words—or his rage overcame his ability to speak—and he stood quietly, sides heaving with angry pants, glaring at Shalaman. The silence that fell over the court was so profound that the calls of birds and monkeys penetrated into the Audience Chamber from outside.

"I understand your anger," Shalaman said quietly in the foreigners' own tongue—shocking Leyuet. The Emperor *never* demeaned himself by speaking the language of another!

Unless, of course, the other was a King in his own right. In one stroke, Shalaman had just confirmed the gryphon's status and changed the rules of the game.

"I understand it and sympathize with it," he continued. "Look about you—you are no longer under any sort of guard."

Skandranon nodded shortly without looking around. *Good. He is willing to take Shalaman's word for it.* Leyuet let out a tiny sigh of relief, for that was one small obstacle dealt with.

"I know that you have not seen any of our investigations; be assured that they are going on, even at this moment," Shalaman continued. "It is only that all such things must take place *within the grounds of the temples.* That is our way. That is probably also why you have noticed nothing of a magic nature taking place in the vicinity of the palace."

"Ah," the gryphon replied, a little more satisfied. "Now I understand. I had taken the lack of spell-energy for lack of effort."

"It is an effort," Shalaman admitted. "As you yourself are aware, that event you call the Cataclysm has changed everything for both our peoples. The mages and priests have, thus far, come up with no suspects—but they *have* eliminated you, which gives you yet one more voucher of innocence."

The gryphon muttered something under his breath. Both Leyuet and the Emperor pretended not to notice.

"Please, I earnestly ask you, do not bring your foreign mages here," Shalaman continued. "Such an act will only serve to drive a wedge between yourselves and our priests. That would be a bad thing for all concerned."

"Then what *can* I do?" Skandranon demanded.

"Be patient," Shalaman told him. "Please. You are once again free to come and go as you will in this Court and Palace. You will not be guarded nor watched."

Leyuet wondered if the gryphon realized that Shalaman was giving him tacit permission to go fly off and perform his own investigations.

Probably, he decided. *The gryphon is not stupid. If he can master the court dances the way he has, he will be able to read what is not said as well as what is said.*

But that would only give him one more personal headache; how to keep the gryphon safe while Skandranon was winging his way everywhere.

The gryphon's feathers slowly collapsed, bringing him down to a more normal appearance. He and Shalaman exchanged several more words, now in calmer tones, and with less vehemence behind them. That was when the gryphon surprised Leyuet yet again by replying to one of Shalaman's questions in the Haighlei tongue, neatly turning the diplomatic tables on the Emperor.

Although all of this was very good, a headache still throbbed in Leyuet's temple when it was all over and the gryphon had gone away, bowing gracefully.

Leyuet did not follow; the Emperor's eyes held him where he stood. For a moment, he feared that Shalaman would summon him to the side of the throne, but once the gryphon was well away, the Emperor only nodded, releasing Leyuet from any further need to dance attendance on him.

Shalaman's nod was accompanied by the faintest of sympathetic smiles, telling Leyuet that the Emperor had noticed the lines of pain about his eyes and mouth. Shalaman was good at noticing things, and was only unkind to his subordinates when need drove him to unkindness.

Leyuet took himself out, quickly.

Silver Veil had not been in *her* Advisor's position at the throne, and neither had Palisar. The latter was probably in the temple complex located on the Palace grounds, overseeing the magical investigations into the murders. The former must be in her quarters.

This was, for Leyuet's sake, a very good thing, the first good thing that had happened today.

A Truthsayer must always find the truth. A Truthsayer could not be bought for any coin. This was a weighty responsibility; and all those bearing weighty responsibilities went to Silver Veil for solace. That solace was generally *not* the kind of physical comfort that the lower classes assumed. Leyuet could have that at any time, from any number of skilled ladies. No, the solace that Silver Veil provided was of another order altogether.

His feet took him to Silver Veil's suite without a conscious decision on his part, purely in the hope that she might not be giving another the privilege of her skills. He had not gone to her in many days, respecting her need for privacy in the wake of the horrifying murders—but now, his own pain and need were too great. The physical pain of the headache warned him of worse to come if he did not have it tended to, *now*.

Silver Veil's servants answered his knock and ushered him into a room he knew well, a room where the harsh light of the sun was softened by gauze curtains drawn across many windows, where the scents of flowers blended gracefully with those of soothing herbs, where the only furnishings were low couches covered in soft, absorbent fabrics, couches that could also be used for massages.

The colors here were all cool; deep greens and blues, strong, clear colors that accentuated Silver Veil's pale beauty. She entered once the servants had settled him on one of the couches, and had clothed him in a light robe suitable for a massage.

She slipped among the gauze hangings like a slim silver fish through water-weeds, a silver-chased basket in her hands. She put it down beside him, and experimentally touched his shoulders with her fingers.

"My goodness," she said with an upraised eyebrow. "You should have come to me several days ago! Palisar certainly didn't hesitate."

"I am not Palisar," he reminded her.

"No, you aren't. You are Leyuet, who sacrifices his own comfort far too often. Here——" She flipped open the lid of the casket, revealing the contents.

It contained neither massage oils nor treasure, but Leyuet's own secret passion and guilty pleasure: sugar-powdered pastries and cookies.

"Oh——" he said ruefully, in mingled appreciation and concern. "Oh, my dear child, I shall eat these and put on so much weight that my robes will strain across my stomach!"

"You will eat those because a little bird told me you have eaten next to nothing these past three days," she said firmly. "You will eat these because you need them, for the soothing of your spirit, because you deserve them. Besides, they are good for you. I used special recipes. I do not ascribe to the belief that what is good for you must taste like so much old, dried-up hay."

Leyuet finally broke into a smile, selecting a plump pastry. He held it and devoured it first with his eyes, anticipating the sweet savor, the way that the first bite would melt away to nothing on his tongue, releasing the mingled flavors of almond, vanilla, and honey. He closed his eyes, brought the pastry to his mouth, and bit into the flaky crust, as sugar-glaze broke and scattered over his hand.

It tasted every bit as good as he had imagined, and before he realized it, he was licking the last crumbs from his fingers.

Leyuet opened his eyes to see that Silver Veil was watching him with a pleased smile on her lips, her hands folded in her lap. He laughed.

"Silver Veil," he asked, feeling a warm contentment begin to loosen those knotted muscles in his shoulders before she could even place a finger upon them, "how is it that you always know what someone needs before he himself knows? How is it that you can do the things that are *kind* as well as the things that are duties, in the face of all obstacles?"

She continued to smile serenely. "I could say it is a professional secret, dear heart—but the truth is that I simply think of another's hopes before my own, and the kindnesses follow, as naturally as flowers follow buds. It is really no more mysterious than that."

Leyuet shook his head. "If these strangers, these folk of the Gryphon King, could possibly be anything like you——"

"At least one is, for I taught him, and I think that I know him as well as any person can be said to know another," she interrupted, directing him to turn his back to her so that she could begin to work on the muscles of his neck and shoulders. He was tempted by the still-open casket beside him, but resisted the temptation.

"Amberdrake, you mean." He sighed. "He is so foreign—and their King, more alien still. I do not understand them, and I wonder how they could ever understand us. They *seem* to, but how could they, really? How could anyone who has a King like theirs ever hope to understand us?"

"Would that not make it easier?" she countered. "If someone can understand the ways of a creature like a gryphon, should it not be easier for them to understand the ways of fellow humans?"

He let out his breath in a hiss of pain as she struck a nerve, then shook his head again. "You and they are of a piece, my dear. Their lands gave birth to you and nurtured you. Yet somehow *you* fit in here as well as with them, and I find that even more mysterious than anything else about you. How can you move so well in two different worlds?"

Silver Veil worked on his muscles for a little longer before she answered.

"Perhaps—" she hesitated. "Perhaps because I have lived long enough that I no longer pay a great deal of attention to what is different, only to what is the same," she answered slowly. Then her tone grew lighter. "And one of the things that is universal is that no one can truly have his back worked on while he is sitting up like an old nursemaid displaying perfect posture!" She rapped him reprovingly on the shoulder. "Down, Truthsayer! Give me the space to work my will upon you!"

Chuckling, he obliged her, and for the space of an hour at least, he forgot the troubles that had brought him there.

CHAPTER SIX

Hadanelith carved another delicate sliver of dark wood from his current sculpture, and surveyed the result critically, lips pursed, humming a bit to himself.

Not quite perfect. Not yet. Soon, though. A little more here, and here...

He had every reason to feel pleased. The last game he'd run for his "hosts" had been very satisfactory, particularly since they had consulted him before they told him what they wanted done. In fact, they had *asked* him for descriptions of some of the more interesting spells that dear old Ma'ar had used on his foes.

It's a pity I was never a mage. I'd know more about spells of destruction. Still,

Hadanelith had a very good memory, and as a youngster he had always been very attentive when bodies were brought in from the front lines. No one ever paid any attention to him then; he'd been quite an unremarkable child, and since the concern of the Healers was for the living, he'd often been able to examine the dead quite closely. He remembered quite precisely what some of the most amusing effects Ma'ar had produced looked like. Well enough to counterfeit them, in fact, and that was what he had assured Noyoki and Kanshin.

His hosts had particularly liked the description of the flaying-spell, the one Ma'ar had preferred to use on gryphons.

"Copy that," they'd told him, leaving the ways and means up to him. That rather, clever thief, Kanshin, had smuggled him into his target's rooms by way of a ventilation shaft, and had taken pains to assure him of a relatively satisfactory length of time alone with her.

Skandranon certainly recognized the result, although I doubt he guessed the method. What Ma'ar had accomplished with profligate use of magic and an exquisitely trained and honed talent, Hadanelith had duplicated with nothing more than determination and precise surgical skill. He'd taken care to leave nothing behind to betray that fact. *Poor Skandranon. By now he must be sure there's another Ma'ar around.*

Hadanelith giggled at the thought; he had thought that the role of a kestra'chern would give him ample scope for his fantasies, but what he had accomplished then was a pale shadow of the pleasures he had now. This situation had so much to recommend it! A free hand with his targets—even if they weren't of his choosing—was worth any amount of interference from his hosts, and, in fact, they actually gave him very little interference. The delicious moment when his targets realized that they were completely in his power and there was no help coming—that was better than all the tame slaves in the world!

Add to that the chance to terrify the so-powerful Skandranon and a way to undo everything that those presumptuous prigs from White Gryphon were trying to accomplish, and he had pleasure and revenge all in one tidy little packet.

All of these were equally delightful reasons to pursue his current course. But beyond those was the most delightful of all.

Personal revenge. Revenge on Amberdrake, who had dared to sit in judgment on *him.* Revenge on Skandranon, who had given Amberdrake the authority to throw Hadanelith to the wolves. Revenge on *all* of those fools of White Gryphon, who agreed with Amberdrake and Skandranon and who tamely went along with anything those two wanted.

Hadanelith would prove that he was cleverer, craftier, superior to all of them. Wasn't he proving it now? His hosts thought that they were the ones in control of the situation, that they held Hadanelith's leash. They didn't know he was the one using them.

Once the news of the Kaled'a'in settlement reached the Haighlei, Noyoki had scryed the area around White Gryphon during one of the few times that his magic worked properly. He was nobly educated; he knew several northern languages, and he had probably done his scrying in the vague hope of discovering a malcontent among the Kaled'a'in that he could make use of. He found Hadanelith, skulking around the guarded periphery, stealing from the gardens—and he'd scryed out people who knew something of Hadanelith's so-called "crimes."

He'd sent swift hunters and a small, fast vessel of his own to find Hadanelith and bring him back. That much, Noyoki had conveyed to him in his own language, obviously hoping to get some sort of gratitude in return.

Hadanelith kept his own counsel and simply looked agreeable. After he'd used his own rudimentary powers of mind-magic to pluck their own language out of their heads, he had made one small error out of sheer pique. He'd been so annoyed with Noyoki's callous remarks about how he planned to exploit Hadanelith's "madness" that he'd revealed his own knowledge of their tongue before he'd taken thought to what that slip might cost him.

Still, that sudden expertise in their tongue had impressed them no end. And he'd discovered with that slight mistake just how horrifying they found the bare concept of mind-magic. Forewarned, he'd managed to pass his sudden proficiency off as simple intelligence, and perhaps a side-effect of his "madness," rather than the use of anything forbidden.

So now he had a double advantage over them; he knew their language much better than they had any notion that he did, and he could occasionally read their thoughts, knew that while they were aware he was of the same general race as Amberdrake, they did not know that he actually *knew* Amberdrake. They had no idea that he had his own little vendetta to pursue, and that they were helping him to do so.

So much the better. The less they realized that he *wanted* to do what he was doing for more reasons than just the obvious, the more power over them he held.

He shaved another sliver of wood from a curve of the sculpture and ran his finger over it to assure himself that there were no splinters or rough spots there. That would not do at all.

It was interesting that his "partners" were not at all horrified by the various acts he perpetrated on their chosen targets. In fact, so far as Noyoki was concerned, the more—artistic—the better. Noyoki apparently had more reasons than one himself for choosing these women; Hadanelith had sensed a deep and abiding resentment, even hatred, for each of them. That was interesting, too. Hadanelith intended to continue watching Noyoki's thoughts for more such information. Information was power, and one could never have too much power.

As for Kanshin, he was indifferent to the fate or plight of anyone except himself. Hadanelith found that attitude laudable as well as practical—and the exact opposite of those idiots from White Gryphon, who concerned themselves over the fate of every little social butterfly, slave, and useless leech.

Together the two of them fit very neatly into his plan. Noyoki obviously wanted the envoys from White Gryphon discredited and disgraced at the very least, and possibly destroyed at the most. Kanshin wouldn't care what Hadanelith did as long as *he* continued to get paid.

So now that some shadows had been cast over the reputations of the newcomers, Hadanelith would pour a little more fuel over the fire.

Before Amberdrake died—and he *would* die, in disgrace and despair—Hadanelith would see that he suffered all the agonies that only so sensitive a person was capable of suffering.

He had arranged via Kanshin to have some of Amberdrake's distinctive finery filched from the Palace laundry. Not enough of it to be missed, at least not immediately, but just enough to leave a few incriminating clues at the site of the next little exercise. Amberdrake's combination of Kaled'a'in styles and kestra'chern construction and luxury, with the specially woven fabrics and elaborate bead-fringes, were absolutely unique to him and him alone.

Hadanelith took up a fine wood rasp and began smoothing the surface of the carving, smiling with anticipation. This would be so sweet, so very sweet! The next victim would be left bound and gagged as well as whatever else Noyoki wanted him to simulate, and the Haighlei would find the tantalizing little bits of evidence nearby, as if torn from the murderer's clothing. There was no way that they could mistake these things for something Haighlei—oh, no. They would be identifiable immediately as distinctly foreign, and then as distinctly in the style of no one else but Amberdrake.

Suspicion would move from Skandranon—for the moment—to Amberdrake. Unlike Skandranon, however, it was not likely that Amberdrake would have any watchers to provide him with an alibi.

There *was* one small flaw in this plan. It was just barely possible that Amberdrake would recall Hadanelith and his predilection for bindings and gaggings… and might remember that Hadanelith knew more about him than anyone else outside the White Gryphon delegation. It might occur to him to wonder if somehow Hadanelith had found his way *here*, to Khimbata, Shalaman's capital.

But even if he did, there was still the large matter of convincing the Haighlei that Hadanelith could be the guilty party. His story of a mad kestra'chern banished into the wilderness, who had mysteriously transported himself to the capital to begin murdering high-ranked Haighlei, would be so ridiculous that no one would be foolish enough to give it credence. It would sound like something made up out of pure desperation—and not concocted very well, either.

In fact, if I told myself my own story, I wouldn't believe it. Hadanelith giggled and continued to smooth the dense, dark wood with his rasp. *No matter how logically he presents it, no one would* ever *believe a wild tale like that. He could bring all the witnesses he liked, and it would make no difference. No one here has seen me but my two partners, and my little playmates. My partners aren't likely to talk, and as for my playmates—unless someone here has the ability to speak with the spirits, they are otherwise occupied.*

He giggled hysterically at his own wit while he continued to work on his latest sculpture. Perhaps, when he didn't need it anymore, he would present this one to Noyoki.

I may never come to truly understand these people, Amberdrake thought with resignation. Winterhart told him that he didn't need to understand them as long as he could follow the logic of their customs, but he had been a kestra'chern for too long to ever be content with anything that superficial. Life at Court had gotten back to a semblance of normalcy— as normal as it could be, with three murders being gossiped about, and foreigners under suspicion. Nevertheless, the Haighlei being what they were, custom, even in the face of murder, must be observed.

Which meant that every night must contain Evening Court, and every Evening Court must be followed by an Entertainment. Tonight the Entertainment was a play, a very stylized play, accompanied by equally stylized music. Amberdrake had to admit that this one baffled him, even with his experience in all manner of entertainments. The actors wore heavy masks and their dialogue was chanted to the sounds of a drum and two particularly nasal-sounding instruments, one a stringed thing and one a reed flute. Their multicolored, multilayered costumes were so complicated that the actors had to move slowly when they could move at all. The scenery was sketchy at best—a plant in a pot represented the jungle, a screen invoked a bedroom, a spindly desk someone's office or study. The tiniest gesture of a finger was supposed to convey entire volumes of information, but the gestures were so arcane that only an aficionado could ever decipher them. The result was that Amberdrake had given up even pretending to watch the play, and had moved away so that the music didn't give him a headache.

He wasn't the only one ignoring the piece, however; it seemed that most of the Haighlei were doing the same. One wasn't required to sit and be a "proper" audience for this piece the way one was for a performance of the Royal Dancers, and little knots of conversation had formed all over the room. Only a few folk still sat on the cushions provided in front of the tiny stage. Either the rest of them already knew this thing by heart, or it was as annoying to the natives as it was to a foreigner.

Very possibly the latter! he thought with amusement. It must be rather disheartening for the performers, however. Perhaps they were used to it. Perhaps they didn't care as long as they were paid. Or perhaps they were content to display their complicated art for the benefit of the few faithful. He managed to have a rather lively discussion with another envoy regarding the merits of several different massage-lotions for the treatment of aged joints, and he was looking for Winterhart when the musicians suddenly stopped in the middle of a phrase with a decidedly unmusical squawk, and the performance end of the room, where both Emperor Shalamari and "King" Skandranon were ensconced erupted into frenzied activity.

Naturally, Amberdrake and everyone else at his end of the room hurried over to find out what the fuss was about, expecting it to be something minor—someone who'd been slighted or insulted by another courtier, perhaps, or even word of a dangerous lion attacking a village. King Shalaman was famous for his lion hunts, but he never hunted anything but man-killers, and there hadn't been one of those in several years. Amberdrake found himself shuffled right up to the front of the crowd with absolutely no expectation of trouble in his mind—just as a grim-faced Leyuet and his brace of Spears of the Law laid bloody evidence of yet another murder down in front of Shalaman and Skan.

Amberdrake froze, as did everyone else within sight of the relics. There were bloodstained ropes and a ball-gag, torn clothing—

And then Amberdrake's heart stopped beating completely, for among the evidence was a bit of beaded fringe that could only have come from one of his own costumes.

No—no, it can't—

His face froze into an expression of absolute blankness, and his mind went numb, as he recognized more of the bits of torn clothing as his own.

This isn't possible!

Fear clutched a chilling hand around his throat, choking off his breath, and he went cold as all eyes turned toward him. He was not the only one to have recognized those telltale bits of finery.

*How did that—where—how—*His thoughts ran around like mice trapped in a barrel.

Skandranon rose from his seat, his hackles raised and his eyes dilated with rage, as a murmur passed through the crowd. At that point the courtiers began to back away from Amberdrake, leaving him the center of a very empty space, the evidence of terrible murder lying practically at his feet.

"These things—" Leyuet poked at the bead fringe, the torn cloth, with the end of his staff, "These things, clearly the property of the foreigner Amberdrake, were found with the body, oh King," he said stiffly, clearly continuing a statement he had begun before Amberdrake got there. "The bit of fringe was found in her hand. The death occurred at the afternoon recess, when Amberdrake dismissed his servants and there are thusly no witnesses to Amberdrake's whereabouts save only his own people—"

Skandranon let out his breath in a long, startlingly loud hiss, interrupting Leyuet in mid-sentence. "I can vouch for Amberdrake's whereabouts," he said fiercely, yet with surprising control. "But I will do more than vouch for it." He faced Shalaman, who sat his throne as impassively as a carving. "If you suspect Amberdrake of murder despite that, then I must stand prisoner alongside him. Pray recall, Serenity, that you suspected *me* of these murders less than a week ago!"

There was another murmur running through the crowd, these time of surprise mingled with shock, as Skandranon held up his head and challenged both the Emperor and Leyuet with his gaze. "I am as good as any of my fellows and companions from White Gryphon, and they are as trustworthy and law abiding as I. If their integrity is to be under question, then so must mine. I will offer my freedom in trust for their innocence."

Skan's voice carried to the farthest reaches of the room, and Amberdrake managed to shake himself out of shock enough to look around to see the effect of those words. *Oh, sun above, has Skandzanon lost the last of his sanity. What is he doing...* The dumbfoundedness he saw on every face told him without any explanations how unheard of this kind of declaration was. Obviously, no Haighlei ruler would ever have stood personal surety for the honor of a subject; this went quite out of their understanding.

But Urtho would have done the same—

Skan raised himself to his full height, and Amberdrake realized that he was slimmer and more muscular than he had been a few weeks ago. He was changing somehow. Had the gryphon been exercising in secret? "Let it be known that the honor of those I trust is *my* honor!" he said, in the Haighlei tongue, clearly as the call of a trumpet. "This so-called evidence was concocted to cast suspicion upon one who is innocent, just as the other murders were accomplished in such a way as to cast suspicion on me! Amberdrake is innocent of any wrongdoing—and just as I urged the Spears of the Law to seek for the true perpetrator in the last murders, I urge them to do the same now! If you imprison him, you must imprison me as well, for I am as guilty or as innocent as he. I *demand* it! I stand by my companions, in honor and in suspicion!"

Amberdrake nearly choked. Did Skan realize what he was saying? By these peoples' customs, he was linking his *own* fate with that of Amberdrake!

Not that Urtho would not have done the same as well, but—but that was Urtho, Mage of Silence and Adept of more powers than Amberdrake could number!

"And if it is proved that Amberdrake *did* murder, will you die beside him?" That was Palisar, as cagy and crafty as ever, making certain that Skandranon knew what he was doing with his assertions, so that he could not claim later that he was not aware of all of the implications.

Skan snorted contemptuously. "No, of course not," the gryphon replied immediately. "That would be ridiculous. My friends and I are honorable, but we are not stupid. But if you could *prove*, beyond a shadow of a doubt and to my personal satisfaction, that he had done such a thing, I would deliver the death sentence upon him myself, and I would carry it out myself."

The murmuring swelled to a low rumble, as Leyuet and Palisar stared at both Skan and Amberdrake, and the King blinked thoughtfully. Skandranon had now made it impossible to imprison Amberdrake and perhaps "question" him under torture to extract a spurious confession, yes, but—

But has he lost his mind! Amberdrake was practically ready to gibber and foam at the mouth, although the shrieking voice was only in his own thoughts. *Oh, he's been clever, all right—he's thinking on his feet—*

—and he moved like the old Skandranon, alive with a fire and an enthusiasm that could not be denied. But had he lost his reasoning to recklessness? *And what about me!* his thoughts wailed, as his knees turned weak with fear. *They think I've committed murder, and there's no way to prove them wrong! We can't use magic, we haven't any way to hunt a criminal out, we're strangers here, and the natives aren't likely to look for one of their own when they have a convenient suspect! What am I going to do!*

Never mind that Skan had already been a suspect—*he* at least had solid alibis. Amberdrake had nothing. And whoever was behind these deaths was smart enough to see to it that things remained that way. Except for the first murder, when Amberdrake had been watching the Dance with the others, *he* had no alibi at all for the times those other deaths had taken place. He could be charged, not only with this murder, but with all the rest as well!

What am I going to do? He wanted to run, but he knew he didn't dare even move. He felt horribly like a mouse looking up at the talons of an owl. Anything he did could look suspicious at this point!

As he stood there, frozen with fright and indecision, terror and shock, Skandranon continued to speak, taking the attention of everyone—even Leyuet—off of him. The removal of their multiplied regard freed him somewhat, and he felt the paralysis that had held his limbs weaken its hold over him, but he still didn't know what his very next action should be. How was he going to disprove all this? He was a kestra'chern, his skills didn't lie in investigation! And where was Winterhart? Had they already taken her into custody as an accomplice?

Oh, Star-Eyed, if they've taken her and they're torturing her right now— Paralysis was replaced by panic.

A gentle touch on his arm at that precise moment made him jump, and he began to shake as he turned. *Now* it came—despite anything Skan had said. Leyuet had sent Spears around to take him, arrest him, and carry him off under the cover of the crowd. They'd have a confession out of him in no time and—

But it was *not* a frowning, brawny man who had touched him to get his attention. He turned to gaze into the face of, not a dark and forbidding stranger, but an oh-so-welcome, calm visage he knew just as well as the face in his mirror.

"Silver Veil—what—is happening to—" he began, then forcibly shut his lips on what threatened to turn into hysterical babble as she laid a finger on her own lips.

"Come with me," she said, tucking her hand into the crook of his elbow and leading him to a side entrance of the Audience Chamber. "You and I must talk—and quickly."

Zhaneel did not want to attend Court or the Entertainment, and she had a perfect excuse not to: the gryphlets. Makke was better company than all the courtiers rolled into a bundle.

What was more, Makke was willing to help with them and more willing to learn about them than either of the "nursemaids."

"So, you see?" Zhaneel said, as Makke wiped down the feathers of both gryphlets with a very lightly oiled cloth. "First the bath, then the drying, then the oil. When they are older, they will oil themselves like any bird, but for now we must do so for them. Otherwise, if their feathers get too wet, if they decided to go fishing in the fountain after dark, for instance, they could take a chill."

Makke nodded and sent both of the little ones tumbling away with pats to their hindquarters. In the past few weeks, she had been spending more and more time in the gryphons' suite, time that had nothing to do with any cleaning that was needed. All Makke's children were gone, and the twins had obviously aroused in her all the old maternal urges. Zhaneel had been more confident with Makke in charge of the nursery than she had been in entrusting the safety of the little ones to the young and obviously childless "nursemaids" supplied by the chief of the serving staff.

Makke was clearly surprised, despite all her earlier talks with Zhaneel, that anyone of Zhaneel's rank would grant her such a privilege. She had even protested, once or twice, that this was not the sort of thing that she should be allowed to do.

"But you have been a mother, have you not?" Zhaneel had said, with patient logic.

Makke had nodded slowly.

"And you know and love children, you see my two imps as *children* and not as some sort of odd pet." That was the problem with the "nursemaids," who had probably been brought in from the ranks of those normally in attendance on the many animals that courtiers brought with them. The girls treated the gryphlets as beloved pet animals, not as children—expecting a degree of self-sufficiency from them that the youngsters simply didn't have yet. They might be as large as any of the biggest lion-hunting mastiffs, but you simply *couldn't* leave them alone for any length of time without them getting themselves into some kind of trouble. Tadrith, in particular, had a genius for getting himself into situations he couldn't get out of.

"That is so, great lady," Makke had admitted.

"Then you are the correct person to help me with them," Zhaneel had said firmly. "We of White Gryphon count what is in one's heart far more important than what caste one is born into. For those of us who shared the same trials, bore the same burdens, rank has come to mean very little."

Normally Makke came to the nursery with smiles wreathing her wrinkled old face, but tonight she had been unaccountably gloomy. Now she watched the two youngsters play with such a tragic hunger in her eyes that it might as well be the *last* time she ever expected to do so. Even as Zhaneel watched, the old woman blinked rapidly, as if she were attempting to hold back tears with an effort."

"Makke!" Zhaneel exclaimed, reaching out to her. "What is wrong?"

"Nothing, nothing, great lady—" Makke began, but then her resolve and her courage both crumpled, and she shook her head, tears spilling out of her soft dark eyes and pouring over her withered cheeks. "Oh, lady—" she whispered tightly, blotting at her eyes with her sash. "Oh, lady—I am old, my children are gone, I have nowhere to go—and I must leave the Court—I have disgraced myself and I will be dismissed, and once I have been dismissed, I will die. There is nowhere that will shelter me—"

"Dismissed?" Zhaneel interrupted sharply. "Why? What could you possible have done that they would dismiss you for? I *need* you, Makke, isn't that—"

"But you cannot trust me, lady!" Makke wailed softly, her face twisted with despair, the tears coming faster. "You must not trust me! I have failed in my duty and my trust, and you cannot ever dare to trust me with so precious a thing as your children, can you not see that? And I will be dismissed because I have failed in my trust! I *must* be dismissed! It is better that a worthless old rag as I should go after so failing in my duty!"

"But what have you *done*?" Zhaneel persisted, now seriously alarmed. "What on earth have you done?" A hundred dire possibilities ran through her mind. Makke was old, and sometimes the old made mistakes—oh, horrible thought! Could she have accidentally hurt or poisoned someone? Could she have let the fact that she suspected the Kaled'a'in of having mind-magic slip to one of the Priests? Could she have allowed someone of dubious reputation into the Palace?

Could she even, somehow, have been indirectly involved in the murders Skan had been accused of?

"Tell *me*!" Zhaneel demanded, insistently. "Tell me what you have done!"

"I—" Makke's face crumpled even further, and her voice shrank to a hoarse whisper, as she yielded to the long habit of instantly obeying those in a caste above hers. "I—oh, great lady! It is dreadful—dreadful! I have cast disgrace over myself for all time! I lost someone's—" Her voice fell to a tremulous whisper, *"laundry."*

*She—no—*Zhaneel felt her beak gaping open. "You—what?" She shook her head violently. "You lost—laundry? And for *this* you would be dismissed and disgraced?" She shook her head again, and the words made no more sense than they had before. She blurted out the first thing that came into her mind. "Are you people *insane!*"

She did not doubt Makke, nor that events would follow precisely as Makke described. But—dismissal? For *that!*

"Great lady—" Makke dabbed at her eyes and straightened a little, trying to meet Zhaneel's gaze without breaking down again. "Great lady, it is a matter of honor, you see. If it were my own laundry, or that of the Chief of Servants—or even that of a ranking lady, it would be of—of less concern. But it is the *envoy's* laundry that I have lost. I *must* be dismissed, for there is no greater punishment for such carelessness, and it is our way that the punishment must equal the rank of the victim. This is—in our law, it is the same as if I had stolen his property. I am a thief, and I deserve no better, surely you must see this."

"I see nothing of the kind," Zhaneel said stoutly. "I see only that this is all nonsense, quickly put right with a word to Amberdrake. Unless—" She clenched her claws in vexation; if Makke had already told the Chief of the servants what had happened, there was no way that Zhaneel could save the situation. "You haven't told anyone but me yet, have you?"

Makke shook her head miserably. "I have not yet confessed my crime, great lady," she said, tears pouring down her cheeks afresh. "But

I wanted to say farewell to you and to the little ones before my dismissal. Please forgive—"

"There is nothing to forgive, Makke, and I do *not* want you to report this until you and I have had a chance to speak with Skandranon and Amberdrake—" Zhaneel began, reaching out her left talon to surreptitiously hook the hem of Makke's robe so that the old woman could not run off without tearing herself free of Zhaneel's grip. "I—"

The door to the suite opened, thudding into the wall.

Makke and Zhaneel turned as one, as surprised by the fact that no one had knocked as the fact that the door had hit the wall.

Winterhart stood in the doorway, one hand clutching a wreath of tawny-gold lilies, the other at her throat, convulsed around an elaborate necklace of carved amber lilies and solid gold and bronze sun-disks. Her face was as pale as a cloud, and her expression that of a stunned deer.

She stumbled into the room as Makke and Zhaneel stared, and fumbled the door shut behind her.

"Winterhart?" Zhaneel said, into the leaden silence. "What is wrong?"

Winterhart looked at Zhaneel as if she had spoken in some strange tongue; she licked her lips, blinked several times, and made two or three efforts to reply before she finally got any words out.

"The—King," she said hoarsely, her eyes blank with disbelief. "Shalaman—"

"What *about* him?" Zhaneel persisted, when she fell silent.

But when Winterhart spoke again, it was Zhaneel's turn to stare with disbelief.

"He—" Winterhart's hands crushed the lilies, and her knuckles whitened under the strain. "He has asked me to marry him."

"You must confine us both to our suites," Skandranon was insisting, to an increasingly alarmed Leyuet. "You must place us under guard, if you will not imprison us."

Frantically, Leyuet looked around for a higher authority, but the King and Palisar were both gone, Silver Veil had vanished earlier with Amberdrake, and only he and Skandranon were together in this little side-chamber. This, of course, was precisely the way Skan wanted things.

He's one of Shalaman's protocol administrators. These demands are going to send him into a spinning frenzy. He can't grant them, of course. I already made the bold, dramatic gesture, which forced the King to counter it with a bold, dramatic sign of trust.

"The Emperor has decreed that nothing of the kind is to occur," Leyuet said at last, forced to rely on his own judgment. "You must *not* be placed under arrest. Such a thing would be dishonorable. It is impossible to agree to this demand of yours."

I know, Skan thought smugly. *That's why I made it.*

"Are you saying that I am free to move about this Court as I will? That this is what the Emperor wants?" Skan retorted, allowing skepticism to creep into his voice. "That can't be right."

"I tell you, it is!" Leyuet insisted, his face now so contorted with concern that it resembled a withered fruit. "You must move freely about the Court—nay, the Court, the Palace, the entire city! This is the King's decree! This is how he shows his trust in you!"

There is a certain glint in his eyes... I think he has finally figured out that this might be a better move on their part than trying to keep us locked up. After all, that didn't work before. If we actually were guilty, this kind of freedom might make us careless, and give them a chance to trap us, and I'm sure those are precisely the thoughts that are going through Leyuet's mind at this very moment.

So, there would probably be watchers, covert and overt, keeping an eye on Skan and Amberdrake at all times. That was just fine with Skandranon. He *wanted* to be watched.

He continued to express doubt, though, and Leyuet continued to express the King's wishes, and all the while he was making plans, grateful that it was very difficult to read a gryphon's facial expressions.

I will wait until Kechara contacts me tonight, and I will tell Judeth to send only the Silvers and keep the rest of the delegation at home. I'll tell her to fortify White Gryphon. We might yet need to defend the settlement before this is over.

And he had one more request of Judeth; one he knew that she would understand. He had a list of things he wished her to take out of the storage chests in his lair—and he would ask her to prepare and send a cask of ebony feather-dye.

And last, but by no means least, he would bid her to tell the settlement of White Gryphon that the Black Gryphon was back.

The Black Gryphon is back.

Shalaman had long been in the habit of listening to his court secretaries with half of his mind, while the other half mused on subjects that had nothing to do with the minor issues at hand. Whatever he left to the secretaries to read to him *was* minor, after all; that was why he had them read these letters to him after Evening Court and the Entertainment, and just before he retired. He had a mind that was, perhaps, a trifle too active; he needed to tire it or he would never be able to sleep.

So the secretaries read the innumerable petitions, and he grunted a "yes," "no," or "later—delay him," and he let his thoughts circle around other quarry.

Tonight, they circled Winterhart, that strange, pale beauty from the North. Engaging—nay, fascinating! She had many of the attributes of the incomparable Silver Veil, but unlike a kestra'chern, Winterhart was attainable…

Silver Veil could never give heart and soul to any single person. No kestra'chern can. That is why they are kestra'chern; their hearts are too wide for a single person to compass. But Winterhart—ah, Winterhart—

Like Silver Veil in elegance, in grace… not precisely a shadow of the kestra'chern, but reachable. Shalaman had learned, if he had learned anything at all, that there was no point in yearning for the unattainable. Better to have the moonflower that one could touch than to lose one's heart to the moon.

Logic gave him plenty of arrows to spend against the target of Palisar's inevitable objections. *This would be a valuable gesture; even in the light of the murders. Should Amberdrake prove to be the murderer, he will be repudiated, and wedding her would mollify the northerners. Marrying her would create the kind of alliance that would bring them into my Kingdom as vassals rather than allies. The gryphons alone are worth wedding her for!*

So he would tell Palisar and Leyuet—though he did not think that the Truthsayer would object, only the Speaker.

He would not tell them his other reasons.

This is the kind of woman, like Silver Veil, who could make me happy when I am not in the Court's gaze. Silver Veil was not always there when he needed—company, companionship, pure and simple. She had other duties, others who needed her skills as much as he. Winterhart could be only for him.

She said little enough about herself, but he sensed that she hid depths that she had not disclosed. She carried herself well, unconsciously projecting a nobility of spirit that spoke of noble birth, just like Silver Veil. But unlike Silver Veil, her surface was not entirely flawless; there were hints of vulnerability. One could reach her if one tried.

He had ten Year-Sons and two Year-Daughters, born of the Year-Brides of his first decade of rule. He need not wed her for heirs, for he needed none. He could wed her for himself alone.

The first secretary coughed and reached for water, his throat raw.

Shalaman waved to the second to begin where the first had left off, as his thoughts drifted northward—not to Winterhart, but to the place where she had come from.

White Gryphon; no parrot in the world can crack that palm-fruit. His spies had drifted through the city in the guise of sailors and other harmless sorts, and the word that they sent back was of caution. The city was built for defense, and with very little work could be made impregnable. Technically, it was within his borders—but only technically. If he had to make war upon them, his allies would rightly say that a settlement perched so precariously on the edge of his lands was not worth disputing over. His allies would be correct. There were troubles enough in his Empire without taking on a nasty little border war. The sudden failure of magic and the strange creatures emerging from the deserts and jungles in the wake of magical catastrophe were quite enough to occupy the rest of his tenure on the Lion Throne.

As for the newcomers themselves, unlike Palisar, he saw no harm in them. They were a fact; they were not going to leave, and their very existence meant a change in Haighlei ways, whether or not anyone admitted it. Precedent was important, too, since there might yet be more Northerners to come. If they came, they would mean change, too.

We desire change even as we fear it. Like children looking for demons in the dark, but hoping the demons will bring us three wishes, or wealth, or magic carpets to ride...

And whether or not Palisar liked the presence of the newcomers and the changes they would bring, their discovery on the eve of the twenty-year Eclipse Ceremony was too serendipitous to be coincidental. *If I were a religious man, I would call it an omen.*

Even Palisar would accept and embrace a change that was mandated at the height of the Eclipse. *When the sun vanishes at midday, then change comes to the Haighlei.* That was the word in the holy books themselves, many of which had been written following changes that came with the Ceremonies of the past. *It was wise of our gods to give us this. We love things to remain the same, but if they remain the same forever, we will rot as a people. Pah, if they had remained the same forever, we would still be a collection of little villages of thatched huts, hunting with copper-headed spears, growing only yams, lying in fear of the lions in the dark! Or else—a nation more flexible would have discovered us and carried us away to be slaves in their fields.*

"Tell him it is impossible until after the Eclipse," he said, in answer to one of the petitions. "If it is still an issue then, I will reconsider."

Many of the current petitions could be put off until after the

Eclipse. Many of them were not problems at all, only the perception of a problem, and simply delaying a decision would make it less of a perceived problem with every passing day. Others—well, they tied in with the decisions *he* would have to make about these people from White Gryphon, and none of them could be resolved until he decided what he was going to do about them *and* made his decrees…

…or did not.

At that point, it would become the problem of his successor, for he did not foresee himself living to see another Eclipse Ceremony. Nothing whatsoever could be done about the outlanders until the next Ceremony.

And there are a fair number of Emperors who resolved such tricky problems by just such a postponement, he thought wryly.

But again, Winterhart came into his thoughts. She could be the perfect, symbolic embodiment of that change; the focus for it, the way to present it to Shalaman's more doubting or hidebound subjects in an acceptable form.

If only Silver Veil—

But Silver Veil was a kestra'chern, and she, too, was bound by the edicts of the ages. She was not for any one man. Her office was too important, and not even the Emperor could take her for himself.

He had already proposed marriage to Winterhart anyway, this evening, before that dreadful interruption of the Entertainment.

She had been overwhelmed, of course, as any woman would. She had stammered something about being bound to Amberdrake, though, and there *was* a child, now that he came to think about it—

Shalaman was too well-schooled to frown, but his thoughts darkened for a moment.

Still, that may not be a problem for long, after this evening. In a way, the fourth murder had come as something of a blessing. It was rather difficult for even the most sensitive to be dreadfully upset about the death of that harridan, Lady Fanshane. She had moved into the life of Lady Sherisse years ago, turning the poor thing into a man-hating recluse, and she was cordially detested by most of the wiser folk in Shalaman's Court. And once Lady Sherisse had drunk herself into an early grave, Lady Fanshane had been circling the court like a vulture, looking for another victim to fatten on.

Still, she *had* been murdered, and murder was a crime most foul (and never mind that in the laws of return, Lady Fanshane could be considered guilty of the murder of her former paramour), and evidence was mounting that it was Amberdrake who was guilty of that crime, and perhaps the previous three murders as well. Once there was enough evidence, Amberdrake would be out of the way, and Winterhart would be free to accept the honor that the Emperor had offered her.

He might be innocent, muttered a third part of his mind, a part he seldom heard from. *This might be some strange conspiracy, and Amberdrake the victim of it as much as those who were slain.*

No. That was utter nonsense. If—if—Amberdrake were truly innocent, why had he not asked for the services of the Truthsayer immediately? If his conscience was clear, the Truthsayer would know; as the King's guest, he was entitled to the offices of the highest Truthsayer in the land, Leyuet, who was also the leader of the Spears of the Law. If Leyuet declared him innocent, not even Palisar would challenge that declaration.

So, obviously, he had something to fear from a Truthsayer's examination.

But what if these people know nothing of Truthsayers? niggled that annoying little voice. *What if he does not know he* has *the right to such an examination! It is magic, after all, and all the outlanders have been cautioned against the use of magic. Why, what if they do not even have such a thing as Truthsayers among them? How can he ask for something he is not aware exists!*

Oh, that was nonsense! Of course these people must have Truthsayers! How could any society exist without the means to tell truth from falsehood? That was insane! Besides, wouldn't Silver Veil have said something if there were no such things as Truthsayers among the cultures of the north?

No, Amberdrake, if not directly guilty, knew something of the murders, enough to make him fear the touch of Leyuet's mind on his. That would make him guilty of conspiracy to murder, which was just as great a crime as murder itself.

It would be only a matter of time now. Either the evidence would become irrefutable, Amberdrake would slip up and be caught, or he would finally break down and confess.

And then Winterhart would be free—and once she was free, she would be his. Then he would be lonely no more.

Hadanelith flung open the windows of the darkened chamber, and the night breeze blew the gauzy curtains about, giving them the uncanny semblance of grasping, ectoplasmic hands.

This would be the first time he had dispatched two victims within a day of each other—but the Haighlei were expecting the same pattern as the last time, and they had all let their guards down in the wake of the last murder.

Fools, they patterned their lives like pieces on a gameboard, and expected everyone else to do the same!

Even this rather ineffectual old biddy; she had followed the same pattern every night for as long as he and Kanshin had watched her. It had been child's play to insinuate himself up the wall and into her chamber after she dismissed all of her servants for the night. She hated the sounds of other people breathing in their sleep (or worse, snoring), or so Kanshin said, and she would not abide another human being or animal in her chambers after she retired for the night. She would ring a bell to summon her servants once she awoke, but from the moment she took to her bed to the moment she left it, she was alone. And not even a murderer on the loose would induce her to change that pattern.

Fool.

Hadanelith had pinned Lady Linnay to her bed, stuffed the end of his latest special carving down her throat to prevent even the slightest sound out of her—

That was a bit unsatisfactory. I would have liked to have heard her beg.

Then he had dragged her over to the window, his skin pressed against her bedclothes, at precisely the spot she *might* have stood if she'd heard something large—say, the size of a gryphon—land on her balcony. Then he pretended to let her go.

Predictably—*Pah, these fools are so tediously predictable!*—she had turned to run, and he had struck her down from behind with his new sculpture, a club carved into the exact likeness of a gryphon's foreleg.

He opened the window now, so that the overwhelming body of evidence would be that it was open before she died. Then he stood over her unconscious body, and raised his club again.

As he brought it down in a punishing blow, regretting the necessity of doing this in the dark, he felt just a little bored. These Haighlei as a whole were just not interesting prey—the Kaled'a'in may have been sanctimonious, sickeningly sweet prigs, but at least they *did* something once in a while. The Haighlei just lined up like good little sheep for his knife. They didn't even alter their habits when it was obvious who and what kinds of folk his targets were!

Well, they aren't really important, he consoled himself with a grim smile, bringing the club down on the body with all of his strength. *They aren't my real prey, anyway. They're only tools. Their deaths are not the end, only the means. They're only the stepping stones to my real goal, the ladder to reach my revenge.*

Although—actually, this was turning out to be a little more interesting than he had thought it would. *I've never actually beaten anyone to death before. Hmm. Fascinating. I didn't realize how much punishment a body could take and still breathe!* He knew it could be done, of course; provided nothing like the spleen or the skull was injured, a great deal of injury could be inflicted in theory before the body was so broken that it literally bled to death from bruising. But he'd never actually witnessed such a thing.

In fact, he thought, beginning to feel some of that manic strength coming into his arm that only the best kills brought out in him, *this is rather fun!*

He wanted to giggle, but he kept his mirth well-contained as energy poured into him and the club felt as if it weighed no more than a straw. It rose and fell of its own accord, and he brought it down, over and over, harder and harder, the thudding of wood into flesh pounding in his ears like the thumping of his own heartbeat pounding with excitement and—

The club splintered. He heard the *crack* of the wood over the dull sound of the blow.

He stopped in mid-swing, immediately. *He* was too well-trained, and much too clever, to risk a final strike and leave behind even a single shred of evidence that it had *not* been the claw of a gryphon that had done the deed. Instead, he stood over the now-motionless body, breathing heavily, while he surveyed his handiwork as best he could by moonlight.

Quite impressive. He'd left the head intact except for the initial blow that had rendered her unconscious. For the rest—there was nothing to show that she had *not* been bludgeoned to death by the fisted claw of a gryphon. There were the cuts and tears in the skin that even a claw closed tightly could and *would* leave, and the telltale signs of the essentially bony nature of the "hand" that had beaten her. Virtually every bone in her torso had been smashed, however, and the stiff and structured Haighlei would assume that no human could do that.

Which will leave the obvious, of course. Skandranon.

Lady Linnay had been one of Lady Fanshane's few friends, and had been one of the loudest in her insistence that Amberdrake was guilty and must be made to pay then and there. And as such, she became an obvious target for Kaled'a'in elimination.

Hadanelith grinned as he moved carefully away from the body. Somewhere nearby, Noyoki was capturing all of the potent energy released by this death, and channeling it into whatever project *he* had in mind. Kanshin waited above, with a rope-ladder, ready to spirit him off the balcony and across two rooftops. Noyoki would meet them both there, and use a bit more of that channeled energy to lift them down to the ground, noiselessly, and efficiently, putting them all in a garden cul-de-sac where Kanshin had concealed the servants' livery they had worn earlier to move through the Palace grounds.

Of course, no one who was not a Palace servant would ever even *think* of wearing Palace livery—nor would the Spears of the Law consider that possibility. It was simply Not Done. Here, all crimes worked by ritual and custom!

Hadanelith backed up onto the balcony, glad for the first time of his pale skin, which blended into the stonework very nicely. Of course, Kanshin would have contrived to look like a shadow, but still—

Still, even he hasn't got the audacity to do work like this in the nude. Even if this murder was discovered before they got off the Palace grounds, watchers would search in vain for bloodstained clothing. There wouldn't be any. And one quick wash with the bucket of water that Kanshin had up there with the ladder would remove any trace of evidence from Hadanelith's person.

I will never forget their faces when I told them how I planned to avoid getting blood on my clothing. And of course, for all but one of these old hags, the sight of a naked man in their rooms was shocking enough to stun them all by itself. They didn't even think to scream until I'd made screaming impossible.

The only time he had worn *anything* had been this very afternoon, when he'd worn just a bit of Amberdrake's stolen finery. He'd let his target struggle just enough to tear the clothing from his back in an artistic fashion.

That time he'd brought his change of livery with him, of course. And he'd cleaned himself up in the pool in the prey's own little garden. Had anyone noticed a sign of blood there?

Probably not. But if they did, they'd assume it was Amberdrake cleaning up after himself.

That was the essence of making all of this work; attending to detail. With no bloody clothing to dispose of, that left one detail already taken care of. With no *blood* about, there was nothing for a mage to trace.

He would have to remind Noyoki to cleanse this club very thoroughly, though.

The rope-ladder dropped down from above, and Hadanelith grabbed it, clenching the end of the club between his teeth so that he could use both hands in climbing.

The night breeze felt very good, slipping along his skin like a caress. Was this how a gryphon felt when it flew? Was this how a gryphon felt when it made a good kill, and launched itself up into the vast dark vault of the night sky?

I should have been born a gryphon! he thought, laughing to himself, as he let his energy carry him up the ladder effortlessly. *But no, not a gryphon. Tonight—I was better than a gryphon! Tonight—I was the ultimate predator, the killer of gryphons! Yes. Oh, yes. Tonight, I was* makaar!

CHAPTER SEVEN

Leyuet was a sorely puzzled man, and his worries dogged his footsteps as he passed through the cool, dimly-lit hallways of the Palace. The rest of the Entertainment had been canceled, of course. That left most of the courtiers at loose ends, with nothing to do but gossip until their normal time to retire. And gossip they certainly would—but Leyuet felt certain that most of them would not come within a bowshot of the truth of tonight's drama.

Even though all the evidence pointed to the foreigner Amberdrake as the author of the latest murder, he himself would never have believed it to be so, *after* he witnessed the foreigner's reaction. Amberdrake had been as shocked as anyone in the room at the revelation of a fourth murder, and his reaction on being accused was to freeze, like a terrified bird. He had not been plotting means to escape the room, he had not come forth immediately with plausible alibis—he had frozen, struck dumb, as any innocent man would.

And seeing his bewilderment and terror, Leyuet would bet his professional reputation that, if he had been asked to perform a Truthsaying on the man, the results would mirror his intuition.

Furthermore, it occurred to him on reflection that the person who spirited himself into four rooms without detection, committed butchery without detection, and spirited himself out again without detection, would not have been stupid enough to leave so many clues behind as to his identity.

Still, though, the first three murders had been made without leaving a signature, as was customary among professional assassins. The foreigners' ways were not those of the Haighlei, though, so perhaps the murderer did not know what should be done. Even in assassinations, customs were to be observed—but only if the assassin knew the customs.

The foreigners don't know the customs of assassination any better than they know how to address a social convention in Court, if that is the case. That is circumstantial evidence, but evidence nonetheless, that a foreigner committed the murders.

He would have said as much to the Emperor in private, if the Gryphon King had not interrupted with his theatrical posturings and outrageous statements. By the time Skandranon was finished and Shalaman had been forced to order both of them free on their own recognizance, there was no point in saying anything, at least not until things calmed down a trifle.

Leyuet had intended to speak to the Emperor in private even before the murder was discovered, but he never got the chance. The Gryphon King had been spending a great deal of time today in the air, although Leyuet had not seen Skandranon anywhere near where the fourth murder had taken place—and anyway, there had been no way to get into the murder room from outside the building. But *why* was he flying about, spying? There was no reason for him to do so. This observation was of a piece with everything else about this series of murders—strange things were occurring all over the Palace, yet none of them fit with the murders or even with each other.

Strange things—such as the Emperor absenting himself from the Entertainment, and only reappearing after the Ho Play was well underway. I could not find him. Silver Veil and Palisar could not find him. Where was he? What was he doing! This play was about his own grandfather, what could have kept him from watching it.

There were others absent this evening, but the Emperor was conspicuous in his absence. He only appeared after several people had been asking for him.

But there were other questions, more troubling than that, which plagued Leyuet this night—and they *were* about the murders.

I am the Chief Truthsayer of this Kingdom, and at the moment I would be willing to swear that Amberdrake is as innocent of murder as I. What is more, I would be willing to swear that Shalaman thinks so, too. So why *did he not call upon me to exercise my office and settle the accusation immediately.*

When it first appeared that the Gryphon King was a suspect, Leyuet had shrunk from the notion of touching such a strange creature's soul for a full and formal Truthsaying, and Shalaman had not asked it of him. There really had been no need, since the first murder had occurred when Skandranon—and his mate, which accounted for the only two gryphons besides their flightless children—was under the eyes of hundreds of spectators, and the next two when he was under guard. The suspicion was really only in the minds of those who hated and feared the foreigners in the first place, and was eventually dismissed without Leyuet's intervention, as the Truthsayer had hoped.

I could understand and appreciate the Emperor's reluctance to ask me to examine the mind of the Gryphon King—after all, I was reluctant myself and he surely saw that. Skandranon is not human, and I might not be able to read his soul, or trying to do so might cause me damage or distress. But Amberdrake is as human as I, and there should be no question of my being able to read him. Even if the foreigners are unaware that calling a Truthsayer is their right, the Emperor *certainly knows! So why did he not call upon me! I was waiting!*

Shalaman seldom forgot anything; with Leyuet standing there and Amberdrake accused of a terrible crime, surely he could not have "forgotten" to ask Leyuet to exercise his chief office! So *why* had Shalaman done nothing? Innocence *or* guilt could have been settled in a single evening!

And while under Shalaman's gaze—and command—it would have been improper of me to volunteer. Protocol must be observed.

Leyuet turned a corner and realized that he had quite missed the corridor he wanted; his feet had taken him in the direction of the Guest Quarters—and Silver Veil's suite—without him intending anything of the sort. He knew that Silver Veil was with Amberdrake now, possibly advising him, so there was no point in going on.

My heart knows what I need—but he has need of advice more than I. Surely I can unravel this by myself, if I can only see all the clues.

He turned, and was about to retrace his steps, when he saw that he was no longer alone in the corridor.

Stumbling blindly toward him, a look of stunned bewilderment on her face, was the foreign woman Winterhart. Leyuet would have attributed her expression to the terrible accusation laid against her mate, if not for two things. One, was that he knew that *she* had not been in the room when the accusation was laid.

And where was she if she was not there?

And two, an observation that left *him* stunned—she wore the Royal Betrothal Necklace of amber lilies and golden lion heads about her neck, and she carried in one hand the wreath of ten Lion Lilies, signifying the King's intention to wed her.

Her eyes saw nothing, and he pressed himself back up against the smooth wooden paneling of the wall, hoping the dim light would disguise his identity. With luck, she would take him for a servant.

She walked numbly past him, clearly lost in her own thoughts and paying no attention whatsoever to him, as he stared at her with his mouth slightly agape. His own thoughts swirled with confusion for a moment.

And suddenly, the reason for the King's inaction became blindingly, painfully clear.

Shalaman wanted Winterhart.

But Winterhart was bound to Amberdrake, by whatever simplistic rites these barbarians used as marriage. There was a child, in fact, a girl-child called Windsong, or so Silver Veil had told him.

Now, if Winterhart *chose* not to be bound by such things, then she would not be considered wedded, not by the laws of this land. Even among the Haighlei, most women would be so overwhelmed by the King's offer that even a legal marriage would be—dealt with.

Such things had happened before. If the woman were already wedded, she and her family, and possibly even her *husband* and his family, would do all that they could to hurry through a divorce so that she could be free to wed the King. Most marriages were arranged by parents, anyway, and a woman had only to declare her soul at complete opposite to that of her husband for a priest to make a marriage null and void. There was no particular disgrace in that, provided the husband also agreed. And in the case of the King's indicating his interest—well, there could be considerable status and profit in being the amiable and agreeable ex-husband of the new Royal Consort.

Fortunes had been made, and noble rank achieved, by men who had been willing to honor the King's interests before their own.

But that was only true where there were no bonds of the heart and soul. Now, admittedly, Winterhart was so poised and self-controlled that Shalaman might not be aware of any real attachment to Amberdrake— but it was Leyuet's experience in many long years as a Truthsayer that no woman packed up herself *and* a young and restless child to follow her mate into a strange land if she did not love him dearly, and could not bear to be parted from him.

Which meant that the King's interests would never be fulfilled.

Ordinarily.

He did not think that Winterhart was so dense as to be unaware of how singular an honor this was—but he also did not think that questions of status and opportunity would ever enter into Winterhart's considerations on this subject, either. In fact, he guessed that no threat or bribe would ever force her to break the bonds of the heart that she shared with Amberdrake.

But the death of Amberdrake, as a punishment for murder... *that* would break at least the earthly bonds of marriage, leaving the way clear for Shalaman. Even his imprisonment on suspicion alone might do that, if the imprisonment were made for life.

Or if something unfortunate happened to him in prison. Disease, a vengeful relative taking matters into his own hands—these things have happened before, too.

Leyuet stood frozen, his back still pressed up against the paneling of the corridor. It all made sense—horrible, dishonorable sense, but sense still.

He tried to find some other plausible reason for Shalaman's inaction. *The King might not know that they are unaware of the real meaning of my office. I only knew, because Silver Veil asked me about it when she first arrived, and she was astonished to hear that we had such a thing. He might not know that they do not know they can demand my services if he does not offer.*

He might not—but Leyuet had the horrible feeling that Shalaman would not raise even a whisper to find out. Not with Winterhart at stake.

Leyuet clenched his hands into fists at his sides, every muscle tight with anxiety. Oh, how was he to deal with this? What was he to do? It was a *dreadful* dilemma!

My duty as Chief Truthsayer is clear. If I even suspect there has been an attempt to circumvent my office, I must arrange for the barbarians to be informed of my function and my duties, and offer myself to them immediately. I must! That is fundamental to all of the oaths I swore! "Let no man be denied the Truth"—no man, be he Haighlei or foreign, and not even the King can deny that!

But his other oaths—the ones he swore when he took office as the King's Advisor, were now in direct conflict with his oaths as a Truthsayer.

I have a duty to honor the wishes of the King. All of this is supposition and suspicion on my part—except for the fact of the Lilies and the Necklace, which make the King's wishes clear to me.

His hands rose of their own accord to hold his temples. This was giving him a headache that surely rivaled any of Palisar's.

I shall never again be tempted to think lightly of his pain!

Which of his duties was the deeper? Shalaman *needed* a Consort; indeed, he and Palisar had been urging him for many, many years to select one. How could he continue in the next twenty-year cycle if there was no female principle beside him to balance his male? And he needed a Consort for his own sake as well; the Royal Consort was the equivalent of a personal kestra'chern in many ways, a kestra'chern Shalaman would never have to share with anyone.

Winterhart looked, to Leyuet's eyes at least, to be fully capable of serving that position admirably. In addition, wedding her would bring the foreigners neatly into the fold without having to concede anything. There would be no need for elaborate arrangements, or for special inclusion in the Eclipse Ceremony—they would become allies by virtue of marriage, the simplest way of all.

But my duty as a Truthsayer—

There had been nothing whatsoever in his training, arduous as it was, that dealt with a situation like *this!*

What do I do when the King, who is the embodiment of the honor of the Haighlei, is—is possibly—*acting with less than honor!*

Should he confront Shalaman? What good would that do? It was not his place or his right to confront Shalaman over anything—and anything less than an accusatory confrontation would serve no purpose. If Shalaman were innocent of these suspicions, he still would be shamed and lose face before Leyuet.

That would be unthinkable—and for suspecting such a thing, I should offer to take my own life.

If he were guilty—he would deny his guilt and probably still contrive to keep Amberdrake from exercising his rights.

And he might demand that I take my own life. How would I know without Truthsaying if he were innocent or guilty! I cannot Truthsay the Emperor without his leave!

There was really only one solution, and that was for Leyuet to redeem Shalaman's honor himself. *The only way to save this situation is to remove the temptation for Shalaman to act wrongfully. If I circumvent the need to confront him, then events will fall as they would have if he had not neglected to call me forward in the first place.*

That meant that Leyuet, who abhorred taking direct action, would have to do just that.

You must make it impossible for Shalaman to make his "convenient" oversight, *Truthsayer,* said a stern, internal voice, his own voice. *That is the deeper duty, both to your office and to your King. If he is acting without honor, he will be forced to confront that for himself without having an outside force confront him. If he was simply forgetful, he will be saved from the results of that neglect, as is your duty to him as an Advisor. You, yourself, must go to the barbarians and make it clear to them what their options are.*

It might possibly be, still, that Shalaman knew something that Leyuet did not. He might be aware of some reason why the barbarians would not want Leyuet inside their hearts and souls. But Leyuet would not *know* that unless he went to the barbarians himself. Only then would his own conscience and honor together be clean.

And I cannot sleep this night until I make them clean.

With a weary sigh, Leyuet turned again, and walked slowly in the footsteps of Winterhart, making his way to her suite in the Guest Quarters. He would tell her what he must. The next steps would be up to her—

And to Amberdrake—for Amberdrake, after all, was the one person around whom this tragedy was revolving, and the one person who had the power to resolve at least part of it.

And all of this so close to the Eclipse. Why do the gods torment and taunt us this way!

Amberdrake's head and heart were already full of confusion when he walked in through the door of his rooms, although he had been relieved of a considerable burden of fear and tension by his graceful mentor.

Now the problems are not threatening my life—at least not immediately—but oh, the problems we've uncovered!

Thanks to Silver Veil, at least *now* he had the means to prove his innocence; the services of someone called a "Truthsayer" would put an end to any accusations. Unfortunately, now there were greater questions to be answered, for it was painfully obvious that someone in this land wanted the Kaled'a'in dead, discredited, or both. And it was absolutely imperative he find out who and why, and soon.

And all this must be done before their Eclipse Ceremony, or we can bid farewell to any kind of arrangements with the Haighlei for another generation or more!

He was hoping to find Winterhart, sanity, and a tiny space of peace in which to muster his thoughts and come up with some plan of action.

Instead, he walked into chaos as soon as he opened the heavy wooden door.

The servant Makke was sitting on the floor and wailing, her face buried in her hands as she rocked back and forth. Zhaneel—and what was *she* doing there?—stood over her with wings mantled and hackles up, as if Makke were one of her gryphlets and under attack. Winterhart sat in the chair by the door that the servants used, staring blankly into space, her face white with shock and a crumpled wreath of flowers at her feet.

And the moment he entered, all three of them started, stared at him as if he was one of Ma'ar's worst creations, then began babbling like a trio of lunatics.

"Forgive me, great lord—I have betrayed you, I have stolen from you—"

"She didn't do anything, neither of them did anything, it is not their fault—"

"Oh, gods—I didn't mean to encourage him—please believe me— Drake, please, you must believe me—"

He clapped his hands over his aching temples and shook his head violently. What on *earth* were they all babbling about?

"Please—" he said faintly, over the din, "Please, one of you at a time—"

As if his plea, faint as it was, had been a thunderous roar, they all fell silent at once, staring at him. He knew he felt as if he had walked through the seven hells in his bare feet, but he didn't think he *looked* that way!

Unfortunately, the silence was just as uninformative as their babbling had been.

I must look worse than I thought. I must look like I've been dragged behind a horse through all the hells of all the religions of the world. They must not have heard... they expected me to be Amberdrake the Imperturbable, and I look as shaken as they are, and they don't know why.

This was clearly no time to fall apart and hope for them to pick *him* back up and put him together. It was also clear that what had happened to Winterhart, Zhaneel, and Makke was as serious as a murder accusation, at least in their own eyes.

My immediate problem is settled. Come on, Drake, get a hold on yourself, they need you! He took a deep breath, and pulled himself together. *I am a kestra'chern, dammit! I was a pillar of strength for others as a profession! If I cannot be a rock of sanity at this moment, I can at least* pretend *to be sane and calm!*

"Easy," he said, in a calm and soothing voice. "Let's sit down and get all this sorted out, shall we?" He smiled at Makke. "Now, what's all this about betrayal?"

In a few minutes, and at the expense of his own nerves, he had a sketchy idea of what had happened while *he* had been dealing with accusations of murder. He told them, with equal brevity, what had happened at the Entertainment. And there was a feeling of sickness in the pit of his stomach about the betrothal offer in light of what he had learned from Silver Veil, a nauseous unease that warned him that there was danger there he had not ever expected. There was also a rising sense of anger. King Shalaman wanted his *mate*. He had been struggling to be at peace with the King, and all the while, Shalaman had been coveting Winterhart! Had they all been fools, assuming that because the Haighlei were formal and civilized, they could not possibly be lustful or treacherous? What were Shalaman and his advisors orchestrating?

But he hadn't even begun to sort it all out, much less get the details from any of the three, when there was a knock at the door. Reflexively, because a kestra'chern was trained to *always* answer a knock, because it might be someone in grave need, he answered it.

He thought, when he opened the door, that he was either hallucinating or caught in a nightmare. It was Leyuet, the leader of those who administered Shalaman's justice—the very man who had just accused him of killing a woman in cold blood.

He's come to imprison me!

That was the first, panicked, thought. But there were no Spears of the Law with the Advisor, which meant he could not have come here for that, at least. But why? And in the name of the gods, why now?

"Ah, Leyuet—" he stammered, trying to think of what the Haighlei protocol would dictate in this situation, "I appreciate that you have come to my quarters, I presume to ask me some questions, but it is very late and this is not a good time—"

"I must speak with you, Lord Amberdrake," the rabbity little man said urgently, actually stepping forward so that Amberdrake had to move back, and thus managing to get himself inside the door. "I must. My honor, the King's, and your life may all depend upon this."

As Leyuet entered, he shut the door behind him, thus preventing Amberdrake from coaxing him out with similar trickery. And at the moment, he did not really look rabbity at all. Haggard, yes—but rather more like a determined and stubborn goat than a rabbit.

Determined, stubborn, and in extreme discomfort. The man was so ill at ease that he radiated it; even Winterhart stared at him with narrowed eyes as if she sensed it, and she was not as Gifted with Empathy as Amberdrake.

"You must listen to me—it is exceedingly important that you understand what I am and what my duties are," Leyuet blurted out, and then launched into a detailed explanation of what a Truthsayer was and did—and that his position as Advisor and Chief of the Spears of the

Law was strictly secondary to his vocation as a Truthsayer.

"You are *entitled* to a Truthsayer to establish your innocence, Lord Amberdrake," Leyuet finished, his insides clearly knotted with anxiety, if the state of Amberdrake's own stomach was any indication. "Furthermore, as an envoy, you are entitled to the services of any Truthsayer you may wish to summon. It is serving no purpose to conceal from you that I am one of the best of my kind. If I declare you innocent, there can be no doubt of it."

Since Silver Veil had already gone through an even more detailed explanation of a Truthsayer's abilities and duties, Amberdrake saw no reason to doubt him. She had not recommended Leyuet by name—

But the hints she dropped were certainly specific enough that I should have made the connection already. Amberdrake nodded, aware that there was a lot more going on in Leyuet's mind and conscience than the Advisor wanted to admit—or be questioned about. The important thing was that he had offered his services, of his own accord. Silver Veil was of the opinion that the effectiveness of a Truthsayer was affected by whether or not he was bringing his gifts into play reluctantly, and she had warned him that he must find a Truthsayer who brought himself to his task with a whole heart. Leyuet, obviously, had made up his mind that he was not going to be reluctant.

Best not to question further. I do not want to know what he does not want to reveal.

"Leyuet—my Lord Leyuet—*thank* you for bringing this information to me, and so generously offering yourself as my Truthsayer," Amberdrake said, making sure that he projected sincerity and profound gratitude into every word. "Rest assured, your services will be called for shortly, perhaps even tonight—as it happens, the kestra'chern Silver Veil gave me identical advice, although she did not suggest you, specifically, and if anyone questions me I must in all honesty say that I ask for a Truthsayer on her word."

He had said precisely the right thing. Rather than taking offense, Leyuet visibly relaxed when Amberdrake said he would be giving Silver Veil the "credit" for advising him.

He doesn't want anyone to know he came to tell me the same things as Silver Veil. I think perhaps I'll ask her why later.

"I cannot begin to tell you how pleased I am that you have a true friend like The Silver Veil in this Court," Leyuet said, fervently, "And I will remain awake for a while yet, if you think you may wish to call upon me tonight—it is not that late—we would all still be watching the

Entertainment under other circumstances—"

He broke off, embarrassed, as if he realized he was babbling.

There is a great deal of babbling going on tonight.

"I believe that will be the case," Amberdrake told him, gravely. "And I thank you in advance for going to such, lengths for me."

"It is nothing more nor less than you deserve," Leyuet protested, opening the door and letting himself out quickly, as if he feared Amberdrake might want to question him further. "It is only my duty; it is only what is right. I bid you good night—for now."

And with that, he gratefully took himself out. Amberdrake had the feeling that if it had been within the bounds of propriety to *run* away, he would have.

There is something that he doesn't want me to ask about, and I would bet that it has to do with the King's proposal to Winterhart.

He turned back to the three anxious faces that were, at least, a little less anxious for hearing Leyuet's speech.

"Now," he told them, "let's get comfortable. The garden, I think—we're less likely to be overheard there. Makke, would you go fetch Gesten and have him bring us something to drink that will help keep our nerves steady? We have a great deal to sort out, and we must find a way to do it in a way that will keep anyone from being hurt."

When Makke rejoined them in the garden, with Gesten and a tray of strong tea and another of sugar-cakes, he ordered her to remain. "You have a part in this, little mother," he told her, patting a seat beside him and smiling at her as she took it, timidly. Gesten went around the garden lighting the insect-repelling lamps and candles. "Let us begin with the lost clothing, for that is what brought *me* to such a terrible accusation. I think you do not realize that you have been betrayed as badly as you believe you betrayed me."

She bowed her head to hide her face, her shoulders trembling. *Odd. I feel steadier now than I have all evening. I wonder why!* Was it because he was pretending to be the ever-serene kestra'chern? Or was it because they needed him to *be* the calm one?

Well, as a servant, she cannot demand the services of the Truthsayer, I suspect. But because the loss of my property is what led to my being accused of murder, I can demand she be examined myself. I think Leyuet will find she did not lose anything— that the missing clothing was stolen, and she cannot possibly be blamed for having clothing stolen by the crafty fiends who have successfully completed four murders!

He sensed Winterhart's anguish even as his mind raced through plans dealing with his quandary and Makke's, and he reached out for her hand even as he spoke soothing words to Makke. When the old woman finally raised her eyes to his, he smiled encouragingly at her and turned his attention to his own beloved.

"Amberdrake, I—" she began.

He managed a weak chuckle. "You are as blameless as poor Makke, if you think you somehow encouraged Shalaman to think you were interested in him," he said, taking a cup of tea from Gesten and pressing it into her trembling hand. "All you did was to be yourself. Dear gods— that was certainly enough to ensnare *me*, wasn't it?"

Her manners are flawless, in a Court which values manners and those things that have no flaws. Her mannerisms are all charming. She fits here as well as Silver Veil, and it is obvious even to a fool that she would never do anything that would disgrace her, in the purest sense of the word! Winterhart is surely as exotic as Silver Veil—though why Shalaman hasn't made this offer to her—well, it might be some stupid caste issue, I suppose. It irritated him to think that Silver Veil might somehow be considered unworthy of the King's matrimonial attentions, when he was obviously taking advantage of every one of that redoubtable lady's many talents.

Silver Veil would make such a Queen—and she loves him. Why can't he see that! Oh, damn. Let me get this settled first. A little matter of a murder accusation—I'll deal with hearts and minds later.

"All you did was to be yourself," he repeated. "And that was just a temptation that was too much for the Emperor to resist. I understand his desire, and I can hardly blame you if I can't blame him!"

She sensed his sincerity, even if she could not share his thoughts, and she managed a tremulous smile.

"The problem is—" he hesitated a moment, then said it out loud. "The problem is, it does appear that Shalaman was perfectly willing for me to stand accused of murder so that his way was clear to take you as his wife."

Makke's face turned gray, but both Zhaneel and Winterhart nodded. Zhaneel's hackles were up, and Winterhart's jaw clenched.

"The obvious answer is to demand Leyuet's services in Court," he continued, but Winterhart interrupted. And not, as he might have supposed, with angry words about the Emperor.

"You have to be careful not to imply in any way that Shalaman was using the accusation as a way to obtain me," she pointed out. "You can't even let other people make that implication. If *anyone* besides Leyuet suspects him of dishonorable intentions, he'll never forgive us."

Oh, that is the lady I love—thinking ahead, seeing all the implications, even while her own heart is in turmoil! He felt better with every passing moment, more alive than he had in years—the way he had right after the Catastrophe, when every day brought a new crisis, but she was there to help him solve it.

"Even if it all simply slipped his mind in the excitement, people could still suspect that if I act in public," he replied, thinking out loud. "If he *was* operating with those intentions—he'll become our enemy for exposing him. And if he wasn't, well, when people put facts together and come up with their own suspicions, however erroneous, wouldn't he lose face with his own Court?"

Winterhart nodded as Zhaneel looked from one to the other of them. She toyed with the necklace as she spoke. "It is almost as bad for the Haighlei to lose face as to *be* dishonorable, and while he might not become our enemy over his own mistake, he isn't going to be our friend, either." Winterhart frowned: "But we can't simply leave things the way they are!"

"If he is disgraced before his own people, might he not even declare war upon us in an attempt to show that he did not want Winterhart after all?" Zhaneel hazarded, her eyes narrowed with worry. "Oh, I wish that Skandranon were here!"

I'm just as glad he's not. He's more than a bit too direct for a situation like this one.

"In any event, if we do this in public, and everything came out *well*, we still must have Makke's part of the story—and that makes her a conspicuous target for anger," Amberdrake said, as Makke nodded and turned even grayer. "I can't have that. And we have to remember something else—there is *someone* out there who wants all of us dead or gotten rid of, and if we take care of this in public, he'll only try again to do just that. The next time he might be still more clever about it. As long as we don't know who our enemy is, we can't guard against him without just going home."

Winterhart clasped her hands together in her lap, around the cup of tea, and Amberdrake pretended not to notice that her knuckles were white.

"You are saying that we can't do anything, then?" she asked tightly. "But—"

"No, what I'm saying is that this can't be public. I spoke at length with Silver Veil, and she gave me another piece of advice—'That which is unthinkable in public is often conducted in private.' Is there a way, do you think, that we could get Shalaman alone, without any witnesses to what we say to him?"

"I don't see how," Winterhart began. "He always has bodyguards with him, even when he gave me the Necklace and the Lilies—"

Makke cleared her throat, interrupting Winterhart, and all eyes turned toward her.

"A bride-to-be accepts her betrothed's proposal in her own house," she said carefully. "She does so in private. This is an old custom, and one that dates back to the days when the Haighlei were barbarians, and occasionally kidnapped women they wished to wed. By making the groom come to her, alone, she prevents being coerced into acceptance."

"So—if I sent a message to Shalaman saying I wished to see him here, alone—" Winterhart began.

Makke nodded. "He would assume that you were going to accept the Necklace, and he would send away his guards, arriving at your door unaccompanied. He would, of course, expect that you would be alone as well." She coughed delicately. "It is often said that there are many children whose births come at intervals that are easily calculated back nine months to the date of the bride's acceptance…"

"Would now be too soon?" Winterhart said, blushing furiously. "I—I wouldn't want to seem too forward."

"I suspect," Makke replied, with a hint of her old spirit, "that our King is pacing the floor, hoping that *you* will find it impossible to sleep until you have answered him."

Winterhart smiled, but it was a tight, thin smile. "So I shall," she said. "So I shall."

Skandranon, predictably, arrived just at the moment when they were about to send that carefully worded message to the King.

"I was on the roof," he said, looking at all of their tense faces with puzzlement. "I was waiting for Kechara to contact me. I was concerned that there might be an off chance that there was someone capable of sensing mind-magic at work within the Palace."

"Why go on the roof?" Amberdrake asked.

He shrugged. "If that was the case, I didn't want anyone to associate the messages passing between myself and our little gryphon with *me*. It wasn't our roof, you see."

They had to explain it all over again to him, which took a bit more time. Amberdrake was a little worried that Skan might come up with another one of his wild plans instead of falling in with theirs. To his relief, Skan was in complete agreement with all of them.

"I must admit I didn't expect you to go along with this without an argument," Amberdrake finally said, as Skan settled himself into a corner with Zhaneel tucked under a wing.

The gryphon looked up at him thoughtfully. "Not an argument, exactly," he replied. "More of an addition. It's unethical, of course—but you've had a game played on you that was worse than unethical, and I think this would just even the scales between you and Shalaman."

Amberdrake winced; whenever the gryphon suggested something "unethical," or something to "even the scales," there was no predicting what he was going to say. Gryphons were carnivores, and they showed it in their ideas of justice and fair play. "Well—what was your suggestion?"

"Two things, really," Skan said, preening a talon. "The first is the unethical one. You've got a rather formidable Gift in that Empathy of yours. Use it. You know very well you can make people feel things as well as feeling them yourself—so use that. Make Shalaman feel *very* guilty and in your debt for not exposing him. Shove your sincerity and good-will down his throat until he chokes on them. Make him eat kindness until he has to do us major favors or burst."

Amberdrake gritted his teeth over that one, but he had to admit that Skan had a good idea. He *hated* using his powers that way, but—

But if I'm going to ensure the success of this, I have to use every weapon I have. He's right.

"And the other?" he asked.

"Tell him you're lifebonded." Skan finished preening the talon, and regarded him with that direct gryphonic gaze. "From what I've learned, it's unusual here and it's important to these people. Leyuet can probably confirm that to him. I think telling him might just tip the scales in our favor."

Amberdrake considered that for a moment. "Well, I can't see why it should, but I also can't see how it can hurt. All right, Gesten—are you ready to play messenger?"

The hertasi nodded tightly. "This is going to need a lot of fancy footwork, Drake, I hope you know that."

"Believe me," Amberdrake replied grimly. "No one knows it better than I do." He handed the hertasi the carefully worded messages, one to the Emperor and one to Leyuet. "We'll be waiting."

Gesten slipped off, and the five of them arranged themselves very carefully. Makke was off to one side, out of the way. Zhaneel and Skan placed themselves on either side of the door, ready to interpose their bodies if the King should decide to storm out. He would not get past them; they could simply block the door with their bodies, or an extended wing, using no force and no violence. Amberdrake stood beside Winterhart, who was seated on the floor, with the Necklace gleaming on a pillow, arranged in a pattern that Makke said signified "polite refusal." It seemed there were customs for the arrangement of the necklace, which included "angered refusal," "fearful refusal," "wistful refusal," "unexplainable refusal," and so on. There was a ritual for everything.

"What did Judeth have to say?" Amberdrake asked Skan, to fill in the time. "How much did you tell her?"

"Oh, as relayed through the little one, she was apoplectic about the murder accusations, of course," Skan said casually. "She wanted us to come home. I pointed out how stupid that would be, and how it might only get us in deeper trouble. Then she was going to cancel the next lot of diplomats; which wasn't a bad idea, but I had a better one. I told her to send us some of the human Silvers instead, ones that can at least go through diplomatic motions and leave the real work to us. She thought that was a pretty good notion, giving us our own little private guards. She wanted to send mages, but I told her that would be a very bad idea and why. She agreed, and started working out the details so things can move quickly and the Silvers can sail with the tide. That's pretty much where things stand."

Amberdrake had a shrewd notion that wasn't *all* Skan had told Judeth to do, but it hardly mattered. At the moment, more strategy was required than diplomacy—the kind of leadership of a field commander rather than that of an administrator. Those were, and had always been, Skan's strengths. He was never better or more skillful than when he was alone, making decisions that only a single person could implement.

He hates being a leader. Now he's in his element. As dreadful as this situation is, it's good for him. And—is he losing weight!

At least this meant that there would be some skilled fighters showing up shortly, and if worse came to worst, as Skan said, they would have their own little guard contingent. If everything went wrong and they really did have to flee to save their lives—provided they could all escape the city—with the help of several skilled fighters, they *could* probably make their way across the jungle and back to White Gryphon.

It occurred to him that they ought to start making emergency escape plans, just in case. But before he could say anything, the sound of footsteps out in the hallway, coming through the slightly-open door, put all of them on alert.

Shalaman pushed the door open and took three eager steps into the room before he saw that there was a group waiting for him rather than Winterhart alone. His expression was so eager, and so *happy*, that Amberdrake's heart went out to him—despite the fact that Shalaman wanted him out of the way. Perhaps that was only a sign of how much a kestra'chern he was, that he could always see someone else's side.

Oh, gods, if only everyone could have everything they wanted out of this situation—But he knew very well that there were never such things as unadulterated happy endings, and that the very best that anyone could hope for here was that hearts would not be broken too badly…

Shalaman was clearly taken aback when he saw Amberdrake; he stopped dead, and his face lost all expression. In the next heartbeat, his eyes dropped to Winterhart, then to the necklace on the pillow in front of her.

His eyes went back to Amberdrake, and turned cold. His face assumed an expression of anger. But his words surprised the kestra'chern. "Lady," he said softly, "if this man has threatened you—if—"

Winterhart raised her eyes to his, as Skan and Zhaneel closed the door very softly and put themselves between Shalaman and the exit. He did not appear to notice anything except Winterhart and Amberdrake.

"This is *my* answer, Serenity," she said steadily. No one who knew anything about her would ever have doubted the firm resolution in her voice. "If you think that anyone could threaten me to perform any action against my will, you are very much mistaken. Amberdrake is here because I wish him here, I asked him here, and because I wish to show you that we are of one heart in this and in all else."

Shalaman's face fell—but before he could react any further, Amberdrake spoke.

"You desired my lady," he said very gently, without even a hint of threat. "And you did not advise me that I had a right to a Truthsayer when accused of murder. I cannot think but that the two are connected."

He tried to keep the words neutral, tried to make his statement very casual, but the accusation was still there, and there was no real way to soften it.

Shalaman went absolutely rigid, as if struck with a sudden paralysis. His face froze except for a tic beside his right eye, he opened his mouth slightly, as if to speak, but nothing emerged.

Amberdrake sensed a turmoil of emotions—chief of which was panic. And overlaying that, real guilt. And beneath it all a terrible shame. All of his own doubts were resolved; consciously or not, Shalaman had tried to rid himself of his rival by underhanded means and had just been forced to acknowledge that.

Caught you. Now to soothe you.

"Serenity," he said swiftly, using his Gift just as Skan had advised, to emphasize his words and gently prod the Emperor's emotions in the direction *he* chose. "Winterhart is a beautiful woman, full of wit and wisdom and grace. She is a fit consort for any King, and I cannot fault you for desiring her.

We are private in our emotions, and you could not know that this was not a marriage of convenience between us."

"You are generous," Shalaman growled.

Amberdrake noted the dangerous anger behind that simple statement. *Time to turn that anger in the proper direction.*

"I also cannot fault you for falling into a trap that was laid for all of us," he continued with a little anger of his own. "A trap contrived by someone—or a conspiracy of someones—who must be the most clever and fiendish I have ever had the misfortune to encounter. The party behind it—whoever he or she is—saw your interest and did not scruple to use it against all of us."

Shalaman knitted his brows slightly in puzzlement. "I do not understand," he told the kestra'chern. "What are you trying to say? That these murders are serving another purpose?"

Amberdrake nodded. "There is *someone* in this land who wishes to be rid of the folk of White Gryphon. I dare say he or she would not be averse to seeing *you* come to grief as well, and this person contrived to put you in a situation where you might not see the threat to your honor." *There. No accusation, only point out the existence of the threat.* "That is why—or so we believe—these dreadful murders have occurred, all of them of people who objected to our presence but were completely loyal to you. That is why—so we conjecture—this person arranged a situation that *you* would also be entrapped by."

"So—I have a traitor in my own ranks?" the King asked, his expression darkening to anger, seizing gratefully on the suggestion that his actions had been manipulated by someone else—just as Amberdrake had known he would. It was an easier answer, one that was more palatable.

Better that, than be thought dishonorable, even by barbarians. Interesting. Amberdrake had the feeling that he was finally beginning to understand these people.

"We believe so. The problem is that we will never find this person unless we lull him into carelessness," Amberdrake told him earnestly as Skan and Zhaneel moved quietly away from the door. "So, before we go any further, that I may clear my name and honor before you, at least, I should like the services of Truthsayer Leyuet—but only in private."

Again, the King was taken aback. "Why in private? Do you not wish your name to be made clean?"

Amberdrake shrugged. "We are gambling with more than just my personal honor here," he said philosophically. "To ask for the Truthsayer before the Court would reveal that we are aware of some of what is going on, and I am willing for others to continue to suspect me if it will help us to catch the true villain. *That* is more important, and I can abide suspicious glares and the anger of your courtiers to achieve justice for the murders."

Sincerity, honesty, graciousness... do believe me, Shalaman. It all happens to be true.

Shalaman nodded cautiously; too much the diplomat himself to take even this at face value.

"I also request Leyuet's services on behalf of the servant Makke," he continued persuasively. "The reason will become clear when you hear what she has to say."

Shalaman frowned but nodded again. Gesten—who had left his message with Shalaman only to go fetch Leyuet—knocked in his familiar pattern at that precise moment, and Skan moved to open the door to let the hertasi and the Truthsayer in.

They almost lost their advantage at that moment as Shalaman realized how *they* had manipulated him. But his own good sense overcame his temper, and he managed to do no more than frown at his Advisor as Leyuet came in.

Leyuet made a formal obeisance to his leader which appeared to mollify the King somewhat. Shalaman gestured to the rest of them to take seats, then appropriated the best chair in the room and sat down in it with ill grace.

"I see you have all this planned," he growled, waving his hand at Leyuet. "Continue, then, before I lose my patience. Truthsayer, examine the man Amberdrake."

Good. He's angry. Now to turn that anger away from us and toward whoever is conspiring against us.

"There is only one thing more that I need to tell you, Serenity," he said, very carefully. "But I needed the Truthsayer here to confirm it so that you will believe it. If you would, please, Leyuet?"

The Truthsayer nodded and then knelt upon the floor at Amberdrake's feet, closing his eyes and assuming an expression of intense concentration. As Silver Veil had explained it, Leyuet would *not* actually read Amberdrake's thoughts as a Mindspeaker might, nor his emotions as an Empath would. She could only describe it as "soul-touching, perhaps, or heart-reading"—that Leyuet would take in what Amberdrake *was*, with no emotions or surface thoughts intruding, and relate that to the truth or falsehood of what he was saying. As she described it, the act would be far more intimate on Leyuet's part (for Amberdrake would sense nothing) than any Empathic sensing of emotion. It was impossible to lie to a Truthsayer, she claimed. If that was the case, Amberdrake did not envy Leyuet his Gift—

There are more than a few slimy souls I would never have wanted to touch in that way. Ma'ar, for instance, or Shaiknam. The very idea makes me shudder.

"I wish to prove to you why my lady and I are more than we appear. Winterhart and I have a very unusual bond," he said, choosing his words with care. "In our tongue, it is called 'lifebonding.' I have not been able to find the equivalent in yours, but it is a binding of soul to soul—a partnership that completes both of us. What one feels, the other feels as well—" He continued, trying to describe their relationship in terms that Shalaman might understand, groping through the unfamiliar Haighlei words, until suddenly Leyuet's eyes flew open and the Truthsayer exclaimed with dismay—

"Serenity! These two are *loriganalea!* Oh, dearest gods—what did you think you were doing?"

The look of horror on Leyuet's face was mirrored in Shalaman's.

What on earth! Why—

Amberdrake had no time for any other thoughts, for suddenly, the Emperor himself, the great Shalaman, was on *his* knees, clutching the hems of Amberdrake's garment and Winterhart's in turn, begging their forgiveness. Amberdrake had not seen anyone so terrified in ten years. What had Leyuet said?

Amberdrake was taken so aback he didn't know what to say or do next. Leyuet seemed to be completely paralyzed.

Finally it was Skan who broke the impasse.

"Well," he said, in a completely casual tone, as if he saw all-powerful Emperors groveling in front of his friends every day, "I always said you and Winterhart were something special."

Things were very confusing for several long moments. When a greatly-shaken Shalaman—who had by this time lost every aspect of Emperor and seemed to have decided that he would be, for now, only Shalaman the man—was calmed down and assured of both their forgiveness, they finally learned from him and from Leyuet why their reaction had been so violent. In fact, Leyuet was still looking a bit gray about the lips.

"This is a sacred bond," Leyuet said, carefully, so that there could be no mistake. "This is a marriage, made not for lust or for power or the sake of convenience, but made *by the gods.* The holy books are very plain; interfering in such a bond will bring the curses of the ages upon anyone who tries to break it, anyone who *helps* to break it and anyone who does not aid the bonded ones. If he who tried to interfere in the bonding is a ruler, the curses would fall even upon the people as a whole. You have done a good thing, Amberdrake, by recognizing this bond and telling us of it. You have not only saved the Emperor's honor, you have prevented the curses of all of our gods and yours as well from falling upon this land."

"You were well within your rights to withhold this knowledge from me," Shalaman said miserably, shaken to his bones. "If I had not the opportunity to obtain your forgiveness, it is possible that the curses would *still* have come, and you would have had your revenge upon me threefold. It would only have been justice—your withholding of information in exchange for my omission."

The Emperor shuddered, his lips pale with strain. "There is nothing I can give you in my entire Empire that can compensate you—"

This was too much. Amberdrake cast a glance of entreaty at the Truthsayer for help, since nothing he had said seemed to penetrate the Emperor's reaction. Leyuet placed a hand upon Shalaman's, keeping him from saying anything more. "It is enough. It did not happen. Amberdrake and Winterhart understand and forgive. They both know—well, enough."

"That is the truth," Amberdrake said hastily. "Remember, we were *all* caught in a web of deception. The blame should rightly fall on the spider who spun it; let the curses fall upon him."

That was evidently exactly the right thing to say; the Emperor closed his eyes and nodded, relaxing a little.

But Leyuet was not finished. "And *you* know, my Emperor, that even if Amberdrake were to perish in the next instant, Winterhart would *still* not be for you, nor for any other man. You may wish to consult Palisar on the matter, but I would say this proves that the gods regard those of White Gryphon as they would the Haighlei, in matters of the soul and love."

That last was said with a certain stern relish that made Amberdrake wonder if the pointed little reminder were not Leyuet's tiny act of revenge for his own mental and emotional strain over this situation. Poor *Leyuet. He walked a thread above a chasm, and he survived. I should not be surprised if he garnered more white hairs from this.*

Shalaman nodded weakly. "I know. And I swear that I will think of her from this moment as I would my own sister, my own mother, my own daughter—and with no other thoughts in my heart." He shook himself a little, then looked up at Amberdrake. "Now, you will assert your innocence in this matter, and Leyuet will verify it, and I will make this public if there is no other way to prove that you are blameless. Will that suit your plan to trap this plot-spinning spider?"

"It does. But do not reveal my innocence unless there is no other way to save my life," Amberdrake reminded him. "We must make our enemy think that he has us trapped, all of us. He will never make any mistakes unless he becomes overconfident."

We *have to think of other things that will make it look as if I am still the chief suspect...*

Leyuet assumed his Truthsaying "trance" again, and Amberdrake carefully stated his innocence in *all* the murders. There was no point in doing this if Shalaman would still be wondering if Amberdrake had anything to do with the other three deaths. "Nor would I harm any other member of your court," he added, "except to bring this killer to justice."

There. I think that covers everything.

Shalaman hardly looked at Leyuet, who confirmed everything Amberdrake said in a dreamy, detached voice. *Odd; he looked so strained before, but now he actually seems to be experiencing something pleasant! I wonder why!*

"Now, for Makke—" Amberdrake brought the trembling woman to sit in front of Leyuet. She seemed to be on the verge of tears, but bravely held them back, looking only at Amberdrake. She seemed to take comfort and heart from his presence, and he put a steadying hand on hers as he knelt beside her chair, out of Leyuet's way.

"Makke, you are the servant and cleaning woman for myself,

Winterhart, Zhaneel, and Skandranon, are you not?" he asked in a gentle voice.

She nodded mutely, and Leyuet echoed the gesture.

"One of your tasks is to see that our clothing is taken to the laundresses and returned, is that not so?" he continued; she nodded, and Leyuet confirmed the truth of the statement.

"Now—today, this morning, when you fetched the clean clothing, some of it was missing, correct? Whose was it?"

Makke's voice trembled with suppressed tears. "Yours, great lord."

"And that was before the afternoon recess, when all the Court takes a rest, was it not?"

"Yes, great lord," she replied, a single tear seeping out of the corner of her eye and escaping into the wrinkles of her cheeks.

"When you took it away yesterday, did it *ever* leave your hands from the moment you received it to the moment you delivered it to the laundresses?" he asked. She shook her head mutely.

"And when did you discover that there was a piece missing?" he asked her.

"When I opened the bundle as it came from the laundresses, in these rooms, great lord," she said and sobbed as she lost her tenuous control of herself. "I am—"

"No," he said quickly, putting a hand on her shoulder to stop her from saying anything more. "Describe the missing piece, if you can."

As he had hoped, she remembered it in minute detail, and it was obvious to anyone who had seen the bloody fragments that the robe she described and the pieces found with the last victim were the same.

"Good," he said. "Now, simply answer this. Did you leave the bundle anywhere, after you received it from their hands? Did you even leave it alone in our rooms?"

She shook her head.

"So during the entire time when the clothing was in *your* control, you did not leave it anywhere but in the hands of those who were to clean it?" It was a rhetorical question, but she nodded.

"The woman speaks the truth," Leyuet said tonelessly.

"So—*first*, the clothing that turned up with the last murder victim was missing from my possession this morning, so I could not have been wearing it," Amberdrake said triumphantly. "And *second*, it cannot possibly have been Makke's fault that it came into the possession of someone else. She was not careless, she didn't lose anything—it was stolen, and she can hardly be held responsible for the acts of someone who is a murderer, a traitor, and a thief."

Shalaman sighed wearily, and Makke suddenly looked up, her expression changing in an instant from one of despair to one of joy.

"That is so, Emperor," Leyuet said slowly as he shook himself out of his trance. "Though I fail to see why it was so important—"

He stopped himself, flushing with shame. "Forgive me, woman," he said to Makke, with stiff humility. "It was important to you, of course. Not all troubles involve the curses of gods and the fate of empires—but sometimes the fate of empires can devolve upon the small troubles."

Makke obviously didn't understand what Leyuet was trying to say, but she nodded timidly, shrinking back into the chair.

"The question is," Leyuet said, "what do we do with her? I do not know that she should continue as your cleaning woman. Perhaps a retirement?"

Makke shrank back further still.

"If I may make a request?" Zhaneel put in. "Makke is the only one who knows that the clothing was missing. This puts her in danger, if the murderer thinks of it. Could she not be protected if she were here, in our personal train? If she were to be made—oh—" Zhaneel's expression became crafty "—the nurse of my little ones? She would then be in our suite all the time, and under our guarding eyes and talons!"

Leyuet looked dubious. "Is this permitted?" he asked Shalaman. "She is of the caste of the Lower Servants, is not a nursemaid of the caste of Upper Servants?" He seemed far more concerned over the possible breach in caste than by the threat to Makke's life. Shalaman's brow creased with a similar concern.

Hang these people and their ranks and castes!

Skandranon snorted with derision before anyone else could say anything. "At the moment, the servants watching the little ones are from whatever caste takes care of pet dogs and parrots!" he said with thinly-veiled contempt. "This is, I believe, on the judgment of whoever it is that decides who should serve where. I hardly think that they can be of any higher caste than Makke. They are *certainly* of less intelligence!"

Leyuet looked a little happier. "It is true, Emperor, that there is no description or caste for one who would be a nursemaid to—to—" He groped for a tactful description, and Skan supplied him with an untactful one.

"Nursemaid to the offspring of intelligent animals," he said shortly. "And I don't see any reason why Shalaman can't declare it to be in Makke's caste and give her the job here and now."

"Nor do I," Shalaman said hastily, obviously wanting to get what seemed to him to be nonsense over with. "I declare it. Leyuet, have a secretary issue the orders."

Leyuet emerged from his trance feeling more like himself than he had since the foreigners arrived. His stomach was settled, his headache gone, his energy completely restored.

And it was—it was a pleasure to touch the soul of Amberdrake, he realized with wonder. As *noble a soul as Silver Veil—and how ever could I have doubted that? Was he not her pupil! Is he not still her friend! Why should I have forgotten these things!*

He did not even express impatience with the amount of time spent on the servant woman, where a few days ago he would have been offended at this waste of his gifts, and insisted that a lesser Truthsayer attend to her.

It would, of course, have been a great pity if anything happened to her, so the female gryphon's suggestion about how to keep her safe was a good one. But it was an insignificant detail in the greater work of this evening. He and Amberdrake between them had managed to engineer all of it without ever having Shalaman's honor publicly called into question.

And Amberdrake saved us all from the curses of the gods—and on the eve of the Eclipse, too! His relief at *that* was enough to make him weak in the knees. *The disaster that would be—the* curses *could have persisted for the next twenty years, or worse!*

But of course Amberdrake's forgiveness came quickly and readily; that was the kind of soul that Leyuet had touched.

He simply rested from his labor as Skandranon, Shalaman, and the rest worked out what the next moves would be.

"I think perhaps that we should do more than continue to foster the illusion that I am the chief suspect," Amberdrake said gravely. "In fact—Winterhart, if you have no objections, perhaps we should also foster the illusion that you and I have quarreled over this, and that you have accepted the King's proposal."

Leyuet woke up at *that*. It was a bold move—and a frightening one. He would have been more concerned, except that he had violated custom and Read the King, and he knew that Shalaman had been truly frightened by his narrow escape, and that he would, indeed, regard Winterhart as purely and without lust as if she was his daughter from this moment on.

In the face of so great a threat, the violation of custom is a small matter. Shalaman could not have been permitted Winterhart's company if his heart had not changed.

"I don't object—as long as I can still—" Winterhart bit her lip and blushed redly, and Shalaman laughed for the first time that evening. These pale people showed their embarrassment in such an amusing fashion!

How far down does the red go, one wonders? It certainly crept down her neck and past her collar.

"I shall have Leyuet give you the key to the next suite," Shalaman said indulgently. "Just as the gryphons' suite connects to yours, there is one that connects to theirs. I shall put you there—it is a suitable arrangement for a Consort-To-Be, since the bride must remain with her relatives, and they are the closest you have to relatives here—and it will look as if I am placing the gryphons between you and Amberdrake as a kind of guard upon your honor and safety."

"Meanwhile, we are anything but. I like it," Skandranon said. "Just don't keep us awake at night, scampering through our quarters, all right, Amberdrake?"

Shalaman chuckled at this, as did Amberdrake. So did Leyuet. If the King had been having second thoughts, he would have put Winterhart in the Royal Apartments. All was well.

He relaxed back onto his cushion; his opinion was not needed in this, but he did need to know what they were planning, for Palisar and Silver Veil would have to be informed.

I shouldn't be relaxed, he tried to tell himself. *This is a perilous and horrible situation. There is a killer among us, a killer who is likely also a traitor, who kills in terrifying and obscene ways. It could be anyone! Well, almost anyone. Four ladies of the Court are dead—I did not know them, but still, I should not be sitting here thinking about being able to enjoy a meal for the first time in days…*

On the other hand, there was nothing more that he could do, and his Emperor was acting again like the Shalaman he knew, the warrior, the leader.

And he was seeing a side to the foreigners, especially Amberdrake, that he had never, ever guessed. They had seemed so different from the Haighlei before this moment—alien, tricky, crafty, possibly deceitful.

Amberdrake, in particular, had seemed too opaque to be trustworthy. How could he not have noticed that this very opacity was like Silver Veil's mannered detachment?

I thought that Silver Veil was unique. Is this how all northern kestza'chern are! Oh, perhaps not. Anyone can call himself a kestra'chern, after all. We have kestra'chern who are hardly worthy of the name. And there have been very few even of the good ones who have risen to the rank of Advisor.

But here were two who were worthy of the name and the highest of ranks—Silver Veil and Amberdrake—and an equally brilliant soul, if of a different order, in Winterhart. The strangers had turned out to be not so strange after all, despite their odd ways and their even odder friends, the gryphons.

Perhaps—one day I shall venture to read the gryphons. If they can be the friends of Amberdrake, then I think I should be in no danger of harm...

With a start, he realized that the conference was coming to an end, at least as far as he was concerned.

"You may go, Leyuet," Shalaman said, dismissing him with a wave of his hand. "We have taken up enough of your rest as it is. In the morning, see that Palisar and Silver Veil learn of what we have discussed, but keep it all among yourselves."

Unspoken, but obvious to Leyuet—he should keep to *himself* the King's near-debacle in the matter of honor.

It was not the first time that he had kept such things to himself. That was something of the nature of a Truthsayer; he examined and watched the King more often than the King himself knew.

He rose, smiled his farewells, and bowed himself out.

But not to go to his rooms.

Silver Veil would probably learn of all of this from Amberdrake, he could make sure of that in the morning. But the rest of this was critical enough that Palisar should hear of it now.

Let Shalaman preserve his illusion that his Advisors wasted time on sleep when there was a delicate situation to be handled. Leyuet knew his duty, and so did Palisar. It would be a long night, but one well-spent.

Besides, he thought, humming a little to himself, *suddenly I seem to have much more energy than I did earlier.*

I wonder why that is?

CHAPTER EIGHT

Skandranon woke early and went scouting on the wing, just after dawn, despite the late hours they had all kept the night before. He was restless and found it hard to sleep with so many problems burning away at him.

First and foremost, of course, was *who* the murderer was, and how he was accomplishing his crimes.

Skan was so angry that his muscles were all tight, but it was not the kind of hot, impulsive anger that had driven him in the past. This was a slow, smoldering rage, one that would send him wherever he had to go, to do whatever he had to do to catch the culprit. And when he caught the blackguard—well, he would probably wish that Leyuet and his Spears of the Law had gotten there first. *Whoever this smelly chunk of sketi is, he has to be getting into those rooms somehow. Maybe he left some sign on the roofs. Maybe I can find it. I doubt that Leyuet's people were really looking for it, not after they'd made up their minds that Drake or I had killed those people.*

He flung himself off the railing of his balcony and up into the air with a great lunge of his hind legs—a lunge no longer accompanied by the plaint of his muscles, although there was a tiny creak of his joints that was probably unavoidable. At least his campaign of reconditioning himself had worked. The creaking was because of the damp, and there wasn't much to be done about that. This place was always damp; cool and damp by night, hot and damp by day. The climate made for some spectacular foliage, thick with lushly beautiful flowers that were even now sending their fragrances up on warm thermals, but it was also rather bad for middle-aged joints.

It belatedly occurred to him as he took to the air and began a series of slow, lazy circles in the damp morning air that he made a dreadfully conspicuous target. *It isn't as if their are a lot of creatures the size of a horse or larger, pure white, flying about in the sky around here. If someone who happened to like one of those women happened to decide to take the law into his own hands, I could be in deep—*

Something sent a warning shrilling along his nerves.

Only years of dodging the inventive weaponry used by Ma'ar's soldiers—and the fact that his fighting instincts were coming back with a vengeance—saved him at that moment.

He thought later that he must have caught a hint of swift movement coining up from below, movement so subtle it didn't register consciously. His nerves just screamed a sudden alarm at him, and he sideslipped in the air, violently and unpredictably altering his path.

What in—oh, sketi!

And an arrow passed through the part of the sky where his chest had been a moment before, actually whiffling through his outermost three primaries on his left wing without touching the wing itself.

It was close enough that he reached out, still without thinking, to snatch it out of the sky.

A foolish move, of course—although it did give him the satisfaction that his reactions were quite good enough now that he caught it. He spiraled violently away before a second arrow could follow it, scanning the ground below him for signs of the archer.

There was nothing, of course. Whoever had sent off the shot wasn't willing to risk a second. And he wasn't about to show himself with a bow in his hand, either.

The arrow was plain, quite ordinary, without owners' marks or fancy fletching. It was probably nothing more than a plain target arrow, one of a hundred thousand like it in this city alone. It might not even have been shot at him; someone might have been stupid, overly exuberant, or a very bad hand with a bow.

Oh, yes. Surely. And pigs are flying in parade formation around the sun at this moment.

There was no point in pretending that this arrow had come zinging at him with any innocence involved in its flight. Someone down there on the ground did not like him. Someone in the Palace wanted him perforated. Suddenly he could hardly wait for a particular barrel to arrive with the augmented "diplomatic" corps. For some reason, even by day, it was harder to hit a black target in the air than a white one. Human perception, perhaps.

But this arrow carried far more implications than that. For someone among the Haighlei to bypass law, custom, and protocol and go shooting at Skandranon personally meant that the situation had eroded to a very dangerous point indeed. These people simply did not *do* that. They were so law-abiding that it was ridiculous.

And neither he, nor anyone else, had taken that possibility into their considerations last night. It might be a lot more dangerous to be the chief suspect of all these killings now than they had thought. That put Amberdrake in a very precarious position.

I think I'd better talk to Drake. Quickly. Besides, the sky is not a healthy place to be at the moment.

Mere heartbeats later, he was backwinging to a landing on Amberdrake's balcony—and Amberdrake, much to *his* surprise, was pushing his way through the curtains to meet his early-morning visitor.

The kestra'chern looked as if he hadn't gotten a lot of sleep, either. His eyes were red and a little swollen with a hint of dark circles beneath them, his long hair was tangled, and the loose robe of rich, multicolored silk was something he had clearly just pulled on when he heard Skan's wings outside his bedroom.

It's a good thing that Winterhart sleeps as deeply as she does, or I'd be in trouble. She hates being wakened too early. At least Drake will put up with it.

He made one of the better landings of the last several months, at least, touching down gracefully and sending Amberdrake's hair whipping around his face with the wind from his wings.

"Drake, we have more trouble," he said shortly, as Amberdrake looked up at him, with one hand absently rubbing his temple, a sure sign the kestra'chern had a headache. Well, there were a lot of headaches in the Palace this morning. "Look." He held out the arrow, and Amberdrake took it. "Someone thinks foreigners make great targets, especially flying foreigners. That could change, though. Walking targets in silk robes might be next on the target range."

Amberdrake chewed his lip thoughtfully, his brows knitted with worry. "Meant to warn, or to strike?" he asked, coming straight to the point.

"To strike, unless they were counting on my being able to dodge it," Skan told him bluntly. "The thing is, you don't get out of the way as well as I do, especially if you're on a balcony or in a corridor. We might want to rethink this plan of ours; Winterhart isn't going to be very happy with me if you end up full of holes."

You're not a warrior-hero, Drake, he thought silently, willing the kestra'chern to be sensible. *You were never meant to be on the front lines. You don't have to do this if you don't want to. Don't pretend to be something you aren't.*

"If I become the chief suspect, I can keep to my rooms," Amberdrake pointed out reasonably. "In fact, if I become the chief suspect, I'll have a good reason to keep to my rooms. The others will be here in a few days, I'll have guards enough then to keep me safe, don't you think?"

"You can never have enough guards," Skan muttered, but he nodded reluctantly. "I want to go on the record as thinking this is a very bad idea, though," he continued. "You aren't and never were a fighter, no matter what most of the Kaled'a'in are. You never got any closer to the front lines than the Healers' tents. You haven't got a fighter's instincts. I—"

"Skan, you forget what I was before I was a kestra'chern," Amberdrake interrupted softly. "I haven't been sheltered from violence my entire life. I weathered the flight from Ma'ar's troops as a boy, I weathered the war with his army, and I managed to do all right on the journey into the West. And I may not be a fighter, but I've kept myself in shape the whole time."

If that remark was supposed to annoy the gryphon, it fell wide of the mark. "I've gotten myself back in shape, too, Drake," Skan said, just as pointedly. "I make a better target than you. I'm not human, and I *am* a fighter, with plenty of practice at dodging whatever is thrown or shot at me."

"You make a much more conspicuous target than I do, and I'd say that disqualifies you," Amberdrake snapped, then looked contrite. "I'm sorry; I'm short on sleep and on tolerance, and this hasn't helped. I promise, I will be *very* careful, but this thing is too important not to take some risks in order to get it solved. Is that enough?"

Skan closed his eyes for a moment, trying to quell the sick feeling he had in the pit of his stomach when he thought of pulling that same arrow in his talon out of Amberdrake. *Odd. I was always the one who went charging off into danger, and it never bothered me like this. But put Drake on the line of fire—*The sick feeling rose to his crop, and he fought the nausea down. *Is this how my friends felt about me! I can't stand the idea of him being in danger! I not only want to protect him, I want to keep him out of it!*

Yet wasn't it Amberdrake's right to decide what he did, what he volunteered for? *I certainly didn't need anyone telling me what to do with my life, and I'd have resented anything Drake did to "protect" me. And he is right, damn him. These murders are going to wreck everything with the Haighlei and may send us into a war neither side can win if we can't solve them.*

"If you *aren't* careful," Skan said savagely, through a clenched beak, "what this enemy of ours does to you will be *nothing* compared to what *I'll* do to you if you get hurt!"

"Fair enough." Amberdrake ran a hand through his long, tangled hair, and smiled wanly up at Skan, who glowered down at him. "As long as I'm awake, why don't you tell me everything you said to the people back home, and what they said to you. The less Winterhart knows, the better, and I don't want to worry Zhaneel, but I need to know what you've ordered. If I'm going make a target out of myself, the least you can do is keep me completely informed."

Of all the nerve! Skan folded his wings tightly, and gave Amberdrake a nasty look. "That's not fair, Drake," he growled. "That's blackmail."

"So it is." Amberdrake nodded agreeably, then pulled his robe more tightly around himself, folded his arms, and leaned against the wall. It constantly amazed Skan how the man could look so attractive even when he was disheveled. "You might as well talk because I'll continue to make you feel guilty until you tell me what I want to know. I'm very good at it—as you very well know."

Damn him. He is good at it. All he has to do is put on a certain expression—or drop the right word or two. He could have been my mother.

Skan growled wordlessly and gave in. "Mostly, I told *them* what was going to happen. If they're going to insist that I'm their leader, then in a situation like this one, damn if I'm not going to get arbitrary."

Amberdrake nodded as if he had expected something of the sort. "And who were 'they'? You mentioned Judeth; who else was in on the conversation?"

"Judeth, Snowstar, Vikteren, Aubri. That was the most Kechara could handle over the distance, and she simply repeated to me what Judeth and Vikteren were saying rather than relaying their mind-voices." He tilted his head to one side. "I put Snowstar in charge of White Gryphon, taking my place indefinitely. He didn't like it, but he agreed. Vikteren is staying, too. Judeth and Aubri are coming here themselves."

I think Snowstar guesses I plan to put him in charge permanently. I'm no leader—and I think once people get used to deferring to Snowstar in this emergency, they won't have any more trouble deferring to him ever again. I suspect he'd have been made the Kaled'a'in k'Leshya Clan Leader if Lionwind hadn't been so charismatic and capable.

"Your idea or theirs?" Amberdrake asked, raising an eyebrow in inquiry.

"Theirs mostly, but—hell, Drake, we've worked together before, and I'd rather have them than some green gryphlet who thinks I'm only a legend." He turned away from Amberdrake for a moment and gazed back north, in the direction of the settlement. All that was visible past the buildings of the city and Palace were trees, but his heart knew where home was, and he wished he could be back there now.

And yet—no, he wouldn't have missed this for the world. He felt his blood stirring again, felt *effective* for the first time in years. "I told them to bring black feather-dye with them. I'm going to be the Black Gryphon again."

He expected Amberdrake to protest, but there was only silence from the kestra'chern. He turned back to see his friend nodding.

"Oddly enough, this is not a surprise," Amberdrake said, startling him a little. The kestra'chern smiled at Skan's reaction. "You are remembering who you are, after being made into someone else by the needs of others. Others may not see it, but a close friend or a kestra'chern can. I *am* a kestra'chern. Accurate perception is part of the job."

"So it is." Skan bowed slightly in his direction. "Well, I told them what the situation was here—that we had an enemy who was more interested in taking us out than confronting us. I told them that there was no point in arguing about whether or not we were going to do something about him, because we couldn't afford not to."

"True enough. We discussed that to death last night." Amberdrake sighed, and leaned his head back against the stone of the wall. "Who's coming, then?"

"No mages," Skan said quickly. "Judeth wanted Vikteren there; he didn't want to go because we're still getting magestorms and you never know what they're going to kick up. I thought about it, and agreed with him—more because these people don't want mages around than because I think he's right about being indispensable."

"There *is* Snowstar, after all," Amberdrake pointed out with a smile. "Vikteren would be very useful, if we could just keep the fact that he's a mage a secret."

"Oh, yes, we all know Snowstar is more powerful than he is, and there are half a dozen others as good as he is. Still." Skan clicked his beak a little. "On more reflection, I would still want him in place in White Gryphon. He *does* have a knack for handling situations no one else has ever seen or heard of before. So he stays. The main thing I told them, though, was that I had to get to the heart of this mess, or I might not have a settlement to come back to—" he snapped his beak, "—or else, the Black Gryphon Skandrarion might come back to a blackened city. That would be bad. So all I wanted on this job were experienced Silvers with good sense and good judgment—which ought to let out Aubri, but I'm sentimental," he added with a gape-grin.

"I hope you haven't emptied White Gryphon of every competent Silver there," Amberdrake protested. "We can't bring an army in here, either!"

Skan shook his head. "Only asked for a couple of them who are as long in talon or tooth as we are—even if I haven't *got* any teeth—and a couple of youngsters who never saw fighting against Ma'ar but proved themselves since. Judeth's entire contingent won't number more than ten. Enough to be useful, not so many as to be a burden or get in the way. If we *have* to cut our way out and run, we'd better not have too many people to keep track of."

Amberdrake nodded agreement. "I suppose that's all I needed to hear, then, if that's *all* you said and did." He squinted tiredly against the sunlight.

Skan chuckled. No point in telling Amberdrake about the "no questioning allowed, this is orders," attitude he'd taken with the folks back home. What would the point be, after all? Amberdrake would only worry about his "image," and he frankly didn't care about his "image" at the moment.

And no point in telling him about Kechaia, either, he thought with a pang.

The little misborn had been unhappy that her "Papa Skan" had been away so long, and even more unhappy when she sensed the worry in the others as Skan issued his orders. He had spent quite a bit of time Mindspeaking only to her before he went to sleep.

I tried to tell her that everything was fine. I tried to reassure her. He thought he'd been very convincing, but then again, it wasn't too hard to convince Kechara of much of anything. She believed him because she was Kechara, and she believed in everyone and everything.

He'd told her how proud he was of her, praised her for her hard work in watching all of them from such a great distance. Judeth had told him about that—how Kechara had decided all on her own to keep a watchful eye on all of them, touching their surface thoughts several times a day without them ever being aware of it. He was only grateful that purest chance had caused her to pick times when none of them had been worried about their situation.

Then she had to ask me when Father Urtho was coming back, and if he was with me here. That had given him a serious wrench, although he'd managed to cover it without her noticing.

So far as Kechara knew, her "Father" was still alive, somewhere, doing something vague but important. No one had ever tried to tell her anything to the contrary. The deception made her happy, after all—and in a sense, that was probably just what Urtho, or Urtho's spirit, *was* doing.

Besides, no one was entirely sure she understood what death meant—and if she didn't know, no one wanted to be the one to tell her.

I had to tell her he wasn't with me, and that I didn't know when he'd be back. Sketi, I'm not altogether certain that I'm going to be back. How could I tell her that!

He had tried to prepare her—if anyone could prepare simple little Kechara for such a terrible revelation—that sometimes people went away and didn't come back again. He'd meant Urtho, but—well—he could only hope and pray that it *wasn't* going to apply to him…

Damn it, it's not going to apply to any of us!

Amberdrake yawned hugely, then apologized, covering his mouth with his hand. "Skan, I'm tired, and I'm going back inside; frankly, the less I show of myself, the more people are going to talk, and that's good for us right now. So I'm going to get some sleep. The Morning Court can proceed without me. I wouldn't be popular there today anyway. But tell Leyuet about this as soon as you can."

Skan ruefully regarded the arrow in his talons. "Given that the skies seem to be more than a bit dangerous today, I probably ought to do the same, at least as far as going back inside and not doing any more flying today goes," he admitted. "I wish I could have spotted the archer. I think I'm strong enough now to lift a struggling body—or a dead one. Just— watch your back for me. Tell Gesten about this."

"Gesten already knows," said a rasping, humorless voice from inside the room, in tones of disgust. "You didn't think you'd get away with me not finding out, did you?"

"Hardly," Skan snorted. "You are the Emperor of all busy-bodies, the King of eavesdroppers. I would never even dream of having a conversation you didn't manage to overhear. I hold all my conversations assuming you will be lurking behind a curtain or beneath a piece of furniture." Then, since he seldom got the last word in any such exchange with the hertasi, he took advantage of the situation and vaulted lightly over to the next balcony, his own, before Gesten could manage to form a reply.

Behind him, he heard Gesten giving Amberdrake a healthy piece of his mind, and chuckled with relief. *Now there is one danger I am glad to avoid! Gesten's tongue is worse than all the arrows in the Haighlei arsenal!*

Amberdrake woke for the second time that morning, this time when Winterhart came back in from attending Morning Court in her new role as Consort-To-Be. He stretched with care, and sat up, feeling much the better for the few extra hours of sleep.

She had dressed very carefully for Morning Court, and the transformation she had undergone while he was asleep was amazing. She looked spectacular.

The amber silk gown she wore had been altered slightly, enough to make it into something of a compromise between a northern costume and Haighlei robes. Bands of geometric applique in white and gold had been applied to the wide sleeves and the hem, although there was no matching band at the collar the way a Haighlei costume would have been adorned. Instead, the gold and amber Betrothal Necklace took the place of such a decoration. Her hair had been put up in an intricate arrangement of braids with one of the Lion Lilies nestled in the front, and she wore bracelets matching the Betrothal Necklace around her wrists and a belt of amber plaques carved in lions' heads at her waist. She looked like a statue of marble and golden amber, and not human at all.

Some of the strain she was under showed in the serene expression she wore; the worse she felt, the more like a statue she looked.

"So it's official?" he asked, as she sat down on the side of the bed beside him. "Is that where the bracelets and belt came from?"

She nodded and sighed, fingering the heavy gold of the bracelets. "The rumor is that I have abandoned you for your terrible crimes, even though nothing has been proved against you yet. I, of course, have said nothing. We've already taken enough of my belongings over to the other suite that it will look credible—and I took Windsong with me, too. Or, to be precise, I moved her into the nursery with Tadrith and Keenath." She eyed him apprehensively as if she expected him to object. "She'll be safer there, in case this person gets the bright idea to go after the children."

His stomach turned over at the merest suggestion that harm could come to their daughter. *Gods. That was a possibility I didn't want to think of. I'd better warn Skan.*

He smiled wanly, though, and tried to make light of the situation. "Well, at least I'll be able to sleep late in the morning, now, and she'll have her two playmates from the moment she opens her eyes. Frankly, I pity anyone trying to get in at her—especially if they're trying to get past Makke."

He meant it as a joke, but she only raised an eyebrow, and said quite seriously, "So do I. There's more to Makke than you think."

He raised his own eyebrow. *One mother recognizes and trusts another, I suspect. I must remember never to underestimate maternal protectiveness. Or Makke, for that matter.* "So, from now on, officially you are no longer associating with me." He couldn't help the feeling of depression and abandonment that gave him, though he tried not to show it. That was the one part he really hated about all this. He'd been alone for so very long, and then found Winterhart—he'd never thought he'd have to face an empty bed again.

Now she dropped her mask of serenity. From the bereft expression in her face, she felt the same as he did about any kind of separation—

That gave him a perverse kind of comfort. It made him feel better, knowing that she would be as lonely as he, it made him feel needed and valuable. Did she know that? She might.

It was a good thing, though, that she was a consummate actress. He knew her, and knew without a shadow of a doubt that she would never betray how she felt in public. She had managed a much more difficult task in her past—of completely hiding who and what she was from people who might have recognized her.

And it is just as well that I am as certain of her as she is of me, or when we met in public I would have terrible doubts. He laid his hand on hers as her eyes darkened with unspoken unhappiness. He sensed her heart growing as heavy as his own.

She squared her shoulders and tried to shake her mood off with brave words, as he had known she would. "It won't be forever. And at least if I have to avoid you in public, things can be the same in private." She bit her lip, and he tightened his hand on hers. "In case you are curious, Shalaman has been very sweet, attentive, and entirely brotherly. I doubt anyone else has noticed the difference, but he treats me as if I were a sacred object, and not for such profane hands as his."

"And you are conducting yourself as if you were not only his affianced, but had lost all faith in me." He smiled as she nodded, comforted no end, as much by the fact that she knew to give him that comfort as by the words themselves. "That has to be feeding right into our nonfriend's plans. The more he can sow dissension in our own ranks and make us avoid each other, the more chance he has of implicating all of us in one or another of these murders."

Well, the worst was over, the actual acknowledgment of the separation, the physical fact of it. He found his mind was working again, thinking of possible parameters, now that the emotion was out of the way. In a curious way, he realized that he was enjoying this, despite all the danger, implicit and real, despite the artificial rift between him and his beloved. Skan might be the strategist, but *he* was turning out to be a more than adequate coordinator.

And speaking of that—he should change the subject. Thinking of strategy and tactics would keep both of them from becoming too depressed by their personal thoughts. "Skan Mindspoke with Judeth and some of the others last night. Judeth is coming, along with nine of the Silvers, instead of the diplomatic experts that were originally supposed to join us."

She pondered that for a moment, tracing a pattern on the bed with her fingers. "That's not a bad idea, but I wish we dared have some mages among them. Well, it's not possible, since we don't dare offend Palisar; he's just marginally on our side at the moment, and if we had a mage—"

"He'd probably make up his mind that we'd had somehow had the mage working the killings, and never mind what the Truthsayer said." At her nod, he felt a great deal of satisfaction in his reading of the third Advisor. "How does he feel about the Consort-To-Be?"

She laughed, but without real humor. "He'll put up with me, but only because this isn't real. He really doesn't like us very much. I think we disturb him."

"And I think I need a bath." Amberdrake rose, and headed for the bathroom, gesturing for her to follow. That was one place where they were sure to be left undisturbed even by servants. "I believe you are right," he said, as he slid out of his robe and lowered himself into the bath that had been prepared for him with a little shock at the feel of the cool water against his skin. The tub was sunk into the floor, and Winterhart sat next to the head of the tub to talk to him. These people preferred cool baths over hot; not surprising, given the climate. "Silver Veil told us that the Haighlei both crave and fear changes. I think Palisar is probably the representative of the Haighlei who are most afraid of change—and Leyuet represents those who are somewhere in the middle. The Emperor himself probably represents the Haighlei—the *few* Haighlei—who would welcome changes."

"And Silver Veil?" she asked. "How does she fit into this pattern of change and denying change?"

"Silver Veil is change itself, but hiding within a changeless package." He was rather proud of himself for such a poetic simile, but she made a face and splashed water at him.

He shook the drops out of his eyes, ducked under the surface to rinse his hair, then came up with a new thought.

"I'd like to keep the real identities and purpose of our new 'diplomats' secret even to the Emperor," he continued, combing his clean hair with his fingers. "The only outsider I want to tell is Leyuet—since he's in charge of the Spears, we'll need him to cooperate with Judeth, and he'll have no reason to do that unless we tell him what she is."

Winterhart just shook her head and shrugged helplessly. "Whatever you and Skan decide is fine with me," she told him. "I'm out of my depth with all this skulking-about talk. The best I can do is keep up my part of the deception. You just tell me what you want me to say and do, and I will."

Good gods, am I becoming a leader?
Surely not.

"Exactly as you have been doing." He tilted his head back in open invitation, and she leaned down and planted a warm and lingering kiss, sweet and bitter at the same time, on his lips. "I wonder if you know how remarkable you are," he breathed to her, as her lips left his.

"Oh, I know," she said, with a smile. "But only if you keep telling me."

"In that case," he said, as she reached down to him, ignoring the danger to her robe, and despite the fact that he was soaking wet, "I shall never stop."

They were all together in the gryphons' garden when Leyuet walked in on them with the stiff expression and gray cast around the lips that they had all come to associate with very bad news. This time, at least, he did not bring the Spears with him, but his face betrayed his thoughts, and they were as dark as his skin.

They stared at him in shocked silence for a moment. The sound of falling water seemed unnaturally loud.

Only one thing can have put that particular expression on his face.

"Oh, gods—" Amberdrake exclaimed. "Not *another*—"

He did not have to say anything more. Leyuet nodded grimly, and sat down in a carved wooden seat as if he were exhausted.

He probably is. This is very, very hard on him.

"We discovered it not long ago, but it happened last night, and I'm certain there will be more folk than I who will recall that Skandranon was flying at the time," the Truthsayer said through clenched teeth. "This is the insidious part; whoever is behind this must know where the two of you are at all times now, and makes the murder appear to be the work of the one without an alibi at that time. He must be learning from his mistake the first time."

"I would be surprised if he were not," Amberdrake said, and ran a hand through his hair. "Can I assume that our killer left evidence pointing to Skan?"

"Are marks of a gryphon's claw enough?" Leyuet countered, but now with an odd and ironic air of triumph. "This victim appeared to have been clawed to death by something that came in by way of the open door of the balcony."

He's holding back something, Amberdrake realized—but also realized that he should allow the man to reveal whatever it was in his own good time. *One does not force the conjurer's hand. It isn't polite, and it spoils the trick for everyone, especially the conjurer.*

"And Palisar isn't beating down our door?" Skan said in surprise—obviously the gryphon hadn't seen what Amberdrake had. "I am astonished! How have you kept him muzzled?"

"He kept himself muzzled," Leyuet told them, and fished in the capacious sleeve of his robe for something, the sleeves that every Haighlei seemed to use instead of pockets or pouches.

Ah. Now we have the moment of revelation.

He found whatever it was he was looking for, and held out a silk-wrapped trifle in triumph. Whatever it was, it was about the size of a human finger under the wrapping of black silk.

No one touched it, and Leyuet carefully undid the folds of silk from around it. The last fold fell away, revealing a bit of wood.

Very hard, dark wood from the look of it—and very skillfully carved, into the shape of a gryphon's talon. By the rough bit ending the third "knuckle," there had been a weakness in the wood the carver hadn't noticed, and it had broken off.

"Well!" Amberdrake said, picking the thing up with a bit of silk between it and his fingers, and holding it up to the light. If there were any traces of the carver's identity still on it after contact with so much blood and pain, he didn't want to muddle them by leaving his own traces. "So Palisar is finally convinced?"

Odd. Something about the carving seemed familiar, but he just couldn't place it.

"He couldn't explain *that* away," Leyuet countered, with a grim smile. "He's had temple mages on it, and so far they've found nothing, but he thinks the problem is with them and not the claw; you know how magic is these days. By evening their spells could suddenly go right again."

"Hmm." Amberdrake put the claw back in Leyuet's hand, wrapped again in the insulating silk. "Does anyone else know?"

Leyuet shook his head, and tucked the betraying bit of evidence away again. "Not even the temple mages; Palisar told them nothing. Only the King, the Advisors, and now you know where it was found."

This is important. This might be just what we've been hoping for. "Suppress it," Amberdrake decided instantly. "Let it leak that the victim was clawed to death by something like a huge lion. It isn't going to hurt anything at this stage if Skan goes back on the list of suspects, and if he doesn't—then a rumor just might spread that I'm a mighty mage and can call up demonic creatures to murder my enemies at a distance." He smiled grimly himself. "The latter rumor might help keep me in one piece. If people think I can call up demons, they may think twice about attacking me on their own."

Leyuet nodded; Skan must have told him about the arrow at Morning Court. "The King is coming here to discuss this in a moment, as soon as he can free himself from his guards. Technically, he is coming to have a private moment with Winterhart—"

"Which is an excellent excuse for conferring with all of you," said the King from the door into the gryphons' garden. "No one will dare intrude on the Emperor and his affianced."

Shalaman's baritone voice and steps were full of the vigor and energy of a man many years his junior, and he had donned robes this morning that were a complement, in their color scheme of deep brown, amber, and gold, to Winterhart's. He took a seat beside Amberdrake with the ease of a long-time friend.

"We'd counted on that, Serenity," Amberdrake replied, pleased by the King's casual manner, especially around *him*. It said a great deal— *It tells me also that Shalaman was not exactly in love with Winterhart; he was in love—or at least desired—what she represented. That's rather different from being in love with the person, and easier to get over.* Evidently Shalaman had gotten over both his desire for Winterhart and his disappointment in a remarkably short time. *That is an old lesson of the kestra'chern; often, one can be in love with who they think someone is, while being blinded by their own desires. And just as often, instead of being in love with a lover, one is in love with love.*

"Another murder—" Shalaman shook his head, grimacing, but as if he were discussing the death of a complete stranger. Perhaps he was— his Court was enormous, and there was no reason to assume he knew everyone in it personally. "It is interesting that all of the victims have been rather outspoken people with both powerful and disagreeable personalities. They all had—or had at one time—considerable influence, they all had great wealth and personal power, and they all collected many enemies. And—this is not the sort of thing that one wishes an ally to know, but I fear that assassination has been something of a way of life in the Haighlei Courts of the past. Not in *my* Court, or not until this moment, but it still happens in the Courts of some of the other Emperors. If all the signs did not point so forcefully to you foreigners, it might have been accepted as the result of acquiring too many enemies."

"In the case of at least two, there is very little mourning in the gardens of the women," Leyuet said dryly, regaining some of his composure. "They were hardly popular. If the rumors were that one of their enemies had rid the world of their presence, I think this might have been little more than a matter for quiet investigation. One simply cannot have this sort of thing go on in a civilized Court."

Amberdrake suppressed the urge to laugh at the prim look to Leyuet's mouth as he made that last statement. Shalaman caught his eye at that moment, and the two of them exchanged a look of private amusement that flashed between them like a signal between two mischievous small boys.

"Nevertheless, because the evidence points to the foreigners, it now becomes a case of Haighlei against the wicked outsiders," Shalaman said, as his expression sobered. "How did the last die?"

"Clawed to death, it would seem—but look here!" Once again Leyuet displayed his bit of carved wood. The King bent over his outstretched hand with interest, but did not offer to touch the thing. "This was found in one of the wounds. Now we have proof that someone is trying to force us to take action against the folk of White Gryphon."

"But I want this kept secret," Amberdrake interjected. "For now, at least."

Shalaman straightened, and his mouth twitched with distaste. "I do not like this idea, my friend," he said. "It greatly troubles me. How can I keep you safe when the hand of every person in my court is against you?"

Amberdrake licked his lips and chose his words with care. "We have an enemy, Serenity," he said. "This enemy is very clever, very cunning. He is intelligent enough to learn from his mistakes—so we must not let him know that he has made any. At the moment, the evidence is only that the victim was clawed to death, and any number of supernatural horrors could have been called up or created, or even imported, to have done this thing."

Shalaman pondered Amberdrake's statement, as the sounds of the garden provided an ironically soothing background.

"But magic is no longer functioning—" Leyuet protested. "All men know this."

"Someone could have found a live makaar somewhere," Skandranon pointed out suddenly. "It doesn't take much magic to coerce them. They fly, they're intelligent enough to obey orders, they have claws and fight with them, and they're absolutely vicious. If I hadn't seen that bit of wood, that's the first thing I'd have thought of. In fact, when you bring an accusation against me, that's what I'm going to claim—that Ma'ar must have had an agent with a flock of makaar lurking down here, and now he's using them to make me look like a murderer."

"That will sound contrived," the King replied doubtfully, shaking his head. "Surely you see that."

Skan shrugged, his feathers rustling. "Can't be helped, and it's a good enough suggestion that some people might think about it a little before they jump to any conclusions."

"What I am trying to say, is that it is absolutely vital that we make this enemy of ours think that everything is going well, so he has no reason to alter his methods," Amberdrake said, bringing the discussion back to his original point. "If our enemies are convinced that there are no flaws in their scheme, that we are all falling into their trap, they will have no reason to alter the way they have been working. If we make them overconfident, they may become careless, and make an even bigger mistake than the one that left behind that claw—and a large enough mistake will be fatal for them."

Shalaman leaned forward to concentrate on Amberdrake's words, and he nodded, though reluctantly. "My concern is this; as I pointed out, although there have been no wars-of-assassination within my Court in my reign, the Haighlei are inclined to such things. I do not want your blood on my hands, because relatives wanted vengeance and were not willing to wait for the Spears to bring it to them."

"I understand," Amberdrake said, feeling Shalaman's very real concern and anxiety for him. He was touched by it; Shalaman had made one of those abrupt internal decisions of many men of great passion and high power—he had decided that Amberdrake was his friend in the moment that Amberdrake forgave him. It was not the first time that Amberdrake had seen such a change of heart in a man of this type, but it was always a little startling when it happened to him personally. "I suggested to Skan in jest that perhaps we should encourage the rumors to spread that one of us is doing this by magic—at least people would think twice about trying to attack one of us, then."

"There is another problem," Leyuet interjected, "One that we had not needed to consider until this latest killing, which points so clearly to Skandranon. We are nearing the Eclipse Ceremony, and we simply cannot make a public decision then on your status as allies while there is such a specter of guilt hovering over you!"

The King nodded. "Now that is true. We cannot make a decision</p>

without either declaring your innocence as determined by the Truthsayer, or finding the real killer."

Amberdrake shrugged. "Surely it can wait a little longer than the ceremony—"

"Oh, no," Shalaman said forcefully. "And if we do not make the decision then, we *cannot* do so until the next ceremony. Everything *must* be resolved by the Eclipse itself, or—well, at the very best, you will all have to remain here as virtual prisoners until we catch the real murderer, and then return to your city, and *we* will have to make at least a token effort at evicting you."

Skan sat up straight at that. "What? No one ever said anything about that! How token?" he asked.

Shalaman's expression was not encouraging. "Blood spilled on both sides, to satisfy honor," he said. "Deaths, perhaps. Obviously, I cannot now wed Winterhart to make you my allies without the declaration; that was the only way the question could have been resolved. As you would not be allies, and would be occupying our land without permission, you would have to pay for your presumption in personal currency. I am sorry, but unless we have instituted a change, we must uphold the old ways. If I do not do this, I have no doubt that some of my courtiers will take their own private armies and do it themselves. We are not a peaceful people by nature; it is only our law that makes us so. Every chance to make war within the law is eagerly seized upon."

Amberdrake groaned and buried his head in his hands, his heart sinking. In all of his worst nightmares, he had not thought that the Haighlei would react this way! It wasn't logical!

Then again, our logic and these people seem to have very little in common. Now I understand why Leyuet and Silver Veil kept emphasizing the Ceremony. I hadn't realized that it was quite such an imperative...

Oh, well. I work better under pressure, or at least I can look that way. Calmness in a crisis fosters trust, even if only by contrast.

He raised his head from his hands, and saw that everyone in the garden looked as discouraged as he felt.

He took a deep breath and rearranged his own expression. If Winterhart could pretend convincingly to be estranged from him, he could pretend convincingly to be optimistic.

"We'll worry about that after the Ceremony," he said, firmly. "Unless we concentrate on one thing at a time, we're bound to feel overwhelmed. Right now, the thing to concentrate on is catching this fiend!"

Leyuet's gloomy face brightened as he projected a cheer he did not feel. The King slapped his shoulders heartily, and Skan cocked his head to one side, as if he was holding back a question he'd decided not to ask.

Like whether or not I'm still sane. Or whether I know something I'm not telling all of them.

Perhaps he wasn't sane—but he knew he was right in this. They had to keep their minds focused on catching the murderer, and worrying about the approaching Ceremony would only distract them from that purpose.

"Like any good commander, you see to the heart of the matter and work from there, Amberdrake," Shalaman said, his cheer restored. "So—let us plan our next actions, so as to bring this villain to his knees the sooner!"

Hadanelith leaned forward, threw the wooden claw on the kitchen fire, and chuckled as it burned. Noyoki had mentioned this morning when they all met at breakfast that his magics were coming to him with greater ease now—and perhaps that had been in an effort to compliment Hadanelith for his work in creating as much blood-born power as he had. But the explanation might also be that enough time had passed since the last mage-storm that magic power was resuming some of its old pathways, and if *that* was the case, the Haighlei mages would soon be discovering that fact. While Hadanelith was no mage himself, he had made it his job to find out as much as he could about the spells that "lawkeepers" used to hunt down criminals. No amount of scrubbing would get blood-contamination off a murder weapon; only burning would break the link between it and the last victim.

So that lovely carving must go, consigned to the flames along with every other souvenir that Hadanelith still had in his personal possession. There was that other carving, of course, but that was not his problem. If Kanshin didn't take the proper precautions, that was Kanshin's lookout.

The cheerful bonfire fit in with his feeling of celebration, though, and did not invoke any kind of sense of loss. Everything was going so *well!*

He sat back in the cook's favorite chair and watched the flames crackle merrily. The cook and all of her underlings pointedly ignored him, but he didn't mind. They weren't worth bothering about, and they were all Kanshin's slaves, so they wouldn't go running off to tell someone what he'd done. Even if they told Kanshin, the thief wouldn't care.

But oh, the pure pleasure he got from hearing the latest news from the court, straight from Noyoki's own lips!

Elation made him hungry; he barked an order for fruit into the air, and a slave brought sliced fruit to him directly from the shaking hands of the cook. They might pretend to ignore him, but they didn't dare ignore a direct order. And they feared him, he knew that, and he reveled in it.

He stayed in the kitchen, making the slaves nervous, and eating fruit, until the last of the contaminated objects had been reduced to nothing but ashes in the heat of the bake-oven. Then he stood up and left, overturning the cook's chair with his foot and scattering rinds and cores carelessly before he walked off.

That would teach them not to ignore him!

But the morning's news was too good for a little insubordination to ruin his mood. He strolled back to his rooms, whistling a little, as he contemplated the results of his own genius.

Amberdrake was in the deepest disgrace, of course, and rumor held he was under house arrest. Now most people believed that Amberdrake and Skandranon between them had contrived the murders of their most outspoken foes in the Court, even though the evidence linking them to the deaths was tenuous at best.

So Amberdrake is suffering because he is a murder suspect, and suffering twice because his dear gryphon friend is as much a suspect as he is. He may even be suffering three times over, thinking that the stupid beast might *have decided to do away with some of their opponents in a more direct fashion than simply arguing them down!*

He giggled, for that in itself was a sheer delight. But there was more, much more.

Winterhart had broken off publicly with the kestra'chern, declaring that she could not remain bound to one who was tainted with the suspicion of murder. According to Noyoki, her speech before the Court had been short, but passionate, and had taken everyone by surprise.

It didn't take *him* by surprise; Winterhart was a rigid bitch, and proud to boot. She would never stand for even a hint of impropriety, and her own pride would not tolerate a fall in status. He could have predicted this, although he would have thought it would not happen quite this soon.

But once he learned she had made her break, he knew what Noyoki's next revelation would be. She would either find someone of higher rank than Amberdrake to attach herself to, like any other parasitic, leeching female, or she would turn around and go back to the city.

So he wasn't particularly shocked when Noyoki revealed that the King had declared she had accepted his offer of marriage. It had simply fit in with Winterhart's personality.

It had delighted him, though. Amberdrake must have been shattered; Noyoki didn't know his reaction because he hadn't emerged from his suite. *She* had moved out, though, into private apartments, which put the stamp of finality on the rift between them.

He giggled again, as he flung open the door to his room and glided inside, with a grace even Amberdrake couldn't replicate. Oh, Amberdrake must be reduced to emotional shards, now—for there was nothing he could do to get Winterhart back! Not even if against all odds he proved himself innocent could he get her back! She would never, ever choose to return to someone like *him*, when she was to be the wife of a King!

The greedy little status hunter was probably rolling on her solitary bed right now in an ecstasy of pleasure over her coup and her good fortune.

He would have to find a way to bring her down, too, but without bringing her back to Amberdrake. That would make him suffer even more.

Now—how to go about that? And what to do to her, I wonder?

He sat himself down in *his* favorite chair, the one built into a replica of the little throne he had in his special room back in the settlement. The one with all the delightful surprises built into it...

But before he could settle himself into a good planning session, there was a knock at the door. Frowning, he started to rise, but the door opened before he could get to it, and Noyoki and Kanshin strolled in as though they belonged there.

He glared at them in outrage, and they ignored the glare to appropriate two of the best chairs in the room for themselves. They sat down without even asking if he minded!

Anger held him breathless, which in turn made him speechless.

"You've done exactly as we wanted so far, Hadanelith," Noyoki said, in that supercilious, ever-so-superior tone he always adopted when he spoke to Hadanelith. "The results have been excellent, and Kanshin and I are agreed that you have passed all the tests we set for you."

Tests! Tests! These weren't tests! What is he talking about! The overfed, obnoxious base-born bastard! What does he think he's doing? Who does he think he's dealing with!

"We've selected your next target, Hadanelith," Kanshin said— nervously though. Very nervously. Hadanelith quieted his rage and set it aside. This was odd; he'd never seen the scrawny little thief nervous about any assignment ever before. What could be so difficult about this one?

"Your next victim will be Shalaman," Noyoki said with such careless casualness that it had to be an act.

"Shalaman? The Emperor?" Hadanelith was incredulous, and even angrier than before. He jumped to his feet and faced them both with his fists clenched at his side. "What have you been drinking? You *know* I won't handle a man, I have no interest in them!"

He felt his face flush with fury and outrage. Just who did these two think they were? He'd told them he wouldn't target males—not for *that,* anyway! There was only one man he'd ever be willing to kill, and only after he'd made Amberdrake suffer a great deal more than he had so far! It would take years, decades, to inflict all the misery he'd planned on Amberdrake's soul!

"Now, Hadanelith, we know it's going to be dangerous," Kanshin said in a wheedling voice, as if he were a recalcitrant child. "We're prepared to take care of that. Haven't we always?"

Hadanelith shook his head violently, in disgust, his vision turning red around the edges, he was so angry with them. What was the matter with them? Danger didn't worry him, and they knew it—danger was only a spice!

"I am *not* targeting a male!" he spat. "I told you that before, and I'm not changing my mind just because you think you have a way to kill the Emperor and get away with it!"

"Well, if you're afraid—" Noyoki began.

Hadanelith spat on the floor at his feet in a deliberate insult. "Hardly! Why should I fear one fat old man? I *won't* take him as a target, that's all! That was our bargain—I get targets I like!" He narrowed his eyes, and the red of thwarted rage suffused his entire field of vision. "You're trying to cheat me!"

"Not cheat you—offering you a challenge to your talents!" Noyoki replied, in a coaxing tone of voice. "We know you're brilliant, we planned to give you something with more spice to it than that last target." He gave Hadanelith a sly, sideways look. "How can you resist a chance to assassinate Shalaman at the height of the Eclipse Ceremony?"

Anger vanished, collapsing into itself like a deflated bladder. He gaped at the two of them, certain now that they *had* gone mad—or else that they had been drinking or otherwise ingesting something that had turned their brains to mush in the past few hours.

Assassinate the King! In public!

"You're both mad," he repeated flatly, a chill creeping up his spine.

468

"Completely mad. You only think *I'm* mad; you two ought to be locked away for your own good."

Neither of them changed their expressions, or even said anything. They just watched him.

"What could you possibly tell me that would make me think you weren't mad?" he challenged, beginning to wonder himself. "Killing Shalaman—that's nothing more than suicidal! I'm not stupid, you know! And you're going to have a fine time dragging me up to the Emperor, strapping a knife into my hand, and throwing me at him, because that's the only way it's going to happen!"

In spite of himself, he felt a tiny bit of intrigue as they continued to watch him narrowly but did not reply. They must have *something* up their capacious sleeves to make this idea possible!

Something besides making the sacrificial lamb out of me, anyway.

It was enough to pique even his curiosity. He wanted to know—but he still had no intention of doing anything about it.

Let them *do it, if it's such a good scheme.* And besides, they still hadn't overcome his basic objection. Shalaman was male. They had given him no reason whatsoever for him to target a male. Males were males, they were not inherently tainted like females were. There would be no thrill in it, and without the thrill, why bother?

"We have an absolutely foolproof scheme," Noyoki said with confidence. "We can get you right next to the King, you can kill him, and we can get you away before he drops to the ground."

Fine. There's still no thrill. His mood turned again, back to anger, this time a sullen anger. What did they think he was, some sort of automaton, a killing machine like a makaar, something that could be sent out on a whim and didn't care what it killed?

"No," he said flatly, folding his arms across his chest. "I don't care how well you planned this, or how foolproof it is. Shalaman's male. Our bargains never included males."

"They didn't include Winterhart, either," Noyoki said, offhandedly.

Hadanelith went cold, then hot, then cold again. His groin flared with excitement, and he fought to get himself back under control before there were any visible signs of his interest. "Winterhart?" he said, lightly, and laughed. "And just how does she enter into this?"

If I could take Winterhart—better if I could have her, mold her—but I'll never get her away from Shalaman. Death would be better; I could hold her in death forever. To be the last thing she saw as she died—to fill her mind and soul with my power to bring her down—

That would make her his forever. He would mark her, brand her as his, and take her away from Amberdrake at the same time.

"She'll be at the ceremony at Shalaman's side," Noyoki told him. "And it fits our plans very well for you to get both of them at once. Unless, of course, you don't think you have the strength and skill to kill the King." He frowned. "I wouldn't have thought that of you. Or is it that you haven't the stomach or the courage?"

"I have all of those," Hadanelith snapped. "It's that I'm not—there's no—I'm not interested in men!"

Noyoki's eyes flashed for a moment, as if something had just come clear to him. Hadanelith ignored his expression; this was a quandary, and no mistake about it. Was it worth wasting time on the King to get Winterhart?

I've done it before; gone through men to get to their women. Back in the camp, it was… and here, too. There is *a thrill to that—actually—*

When the women saw their protectors going down under Hadanelith's skilled blade, when they realized that there was no one left to defend them—there was a real thrill in that. Could he possibly manage that in this case?

"We can get you all the time of the full Eclipse to do what you want," Kanshin said persuasively. "Think of it—coming in out of the dark like a demon, striking and bringing fear as well as death! Besides, we haven't told you the best part yet!"

The best part? There's something more!

He felt his interest rising, and gave up trying to pretend otherwise. They had him, at least for the moment. He might just as well hear them out.

But he was going to do so in comfort.

He sat down again, assumed an expression of total boredom, and yawned. "All right," he drawled, picking a tone of voice sure to infuriate both of them. "I can't get rid of you until you get done trying to persuade me that you both aren't fit only to be locked away, so you might just as well speak your piece."

But they were neither infuriated nor offended, at least not openly, and Noyoki leaned forward in his chair with an eagerness that made Hadanelith think of a night-heron about to spear a fish.

"It's very simple—" he began.

And before Noyoki was finished with the explanation, Hadanelith was giggling. This could be more fun than ever.

CHAPTER NINE

Skandranon spread his newly-dyed wings to dry in the hot sun, knowing he looked entirely too much like an oversized cormorant hanging its wings out to dry, and waiting for the inevitable sarcastic comments. Aubri would never be able to resist this opportunity.

"You look like a short-necked, crook-beaked, fisher-bird, old crow," Aubri chuckled from his position atop a pile of pillows in the cool of the shaded garden. "Maybe one that ran into a rock because he wasn't watching where he was going. I can't wait to see the size of the trout *you'll* pull up."

"I am the one with the taste for fresh fish, lazy Aubri," Zhaneel chided. "You are as forgetful as you are slothful." She poked Aubri with a wingtip, then got up and circled Skan, eying him dubiously. "You will be lucky if those feathers dry at all by nightfall, as humid as it is."

"They'll dry," Skan said, with as much dignity as he could muster, given the undignified circumstances. "Drake is good at this feather-painting business. He used every trick there was to make sure I dry out properly. Don't you remember how humid it used to get in the summer, when Ma'ar pounded the camp with thunderstorms?"

Aubri shook his head. "I think you're going about this all wrong. Damned if I know why you want to play the Black Gryphon again. These people already think that you're a murderer—now you're dyeing yourself black and flying around at night? Are you trying to give them more reasons to point fingers at you?"

Skan growled under his breath, while he continued to fluff his body-feathers. Were they sticky? He didn't think so, but until they were dry and he'd had the excess dye rinsed off, he couldn't preen them to find out. "They'll be pointing a lot worse than fingers at me if I'm flying around at night as a *white* gryphon," he pointed out. "I've been shot at once already. If we're going to help catch the real culprits, I've got to find out how they're getting at their victims. Drake thinks they're using magic, but I don't think so, or at least, they're not using magic all the time. I may not be the greatest mage in the world, but I can tell when someone has used magic and there's no trace of it."

"You can tell, when magic is working right, you mean," Aubri countered. "Not even Snowstar is relying on what used to work anymore."

Skan just leveled a look of extreme skepticism at him. "I think they're somehow sneaking onto the Palace grounds, maybe in disguise, lingering for a while to watch several potential victims, then taking the first opportunity they see. Or else they already live in the Palace, and they're either servants or nobles. I think they're outsiders, Drake thinks they're insiders."

He and Amberdrake had hashed out every possible combination of ideas, and they both had their pet theories. Amberdrake thought the murderers were in the Court and using magic to transport themselves from their own rooms to those of the murder victims and back again. It would be a very nice theory, if anyone could find a trace of magic as powerful as a Gate or Pass-through, and if magic was working at all reliably. Skandranon thought they were disguising themselves as servants and sneaking into the Palace complex, then using perfectly ordinary tricks of thieves to climb into the rooms from the outside.

Which is a nice theory if every guard and every servant is conveniently blind and deaf at the time, is what he says. And I must admit there's something rather odd about the idea, because why would a thief who's that good waste his time on something like this! He'd be robbing the Palace bare, then taking the loot off to live in luxury somewhere. Granted, a lot of what he'd take is identifiable, but it's not that hard to melt down gold.

"I don't know, old bird," Aubri said dubiously. "I think you've picked prey too heavy to carry."

Skan only shrugged. "You can think whatever you want," he replied tartly, "but I've made my decisions, and until evidence comes along to make me change my plans, I'm sticking to them."

"You'd stick to anything with feathers that wet," Aubri retorted.

"Except you, you filthy buzzard," Skan snapped back. "You people put me in charge, and that is the way I am going to approach this."

Judeth chuckled sardonically from the deeper shadows under a low-hanging cascade of flowering vines. "I hate to be the one to tell you this, Skan, but you aren't the one in charge. Amberdrake is."

The words hit him like a pailful of cold water in the face. He almost dislocated his neck, whipping his head around to stare at her.

"Amberdrake is better at coordinating things than you are. You're better at anything that requires action. Anyone who knows you both knows that." Judeth shrugged. "Besides, Amberdrake can keep secrets. When have you ever been able to keep a secret?"

Skan just stared at her, unable to formulate a reply.

"And further, when the evidence comes along that shows you're being a foolhardy old feather-brain, risking your life like this, you'll ignore it.

We know you, Skan. We know what you're like. That's the other reason Amberdrake's in charge." She examined the leather trim on her black tunic with care, avoiding his eyes. "On the other hand, right now, stupid as it seems to me, he says you know what you're doing and we might as well let you go ahead with it."

Skandranon thought about pretending he hadn't heard her, but that would only prove her point rather than refute it. *She's taking Drake as the leader here? Does Drake know this! How could he not? But he didn't say anything to me.*

He felt as if he'd been caught in an invisible whirlwind, in the middle of a cloudless sky. Why would Amberdrake do this? And why not even mention it to Skan?

Maybe he didn't think he needed to. Skan had made no secret of the fact that he was tired of being the leader, of making all the decisions. But—it would have been nice if someone had asked him before they arbitrarily decided to give the job to Amberdrake.

"Drake is risking his life as much as I am mine," he said stoutly, as he tried to rearrange his thoughts to cope with the new situation. No point in making an issue of it here and now, but later—

No, first deal with convincing them that I know what I'm doing. At least Drake is with me on this.

He waved his wings to emphasize his point. "Drake's the one these people think is the real mastermind, if not the author of most of the murders. He's in danger from anyone who decides to go back to the old ways of court assassinations. Shalaman told us that much."

"But he's staying mewed up in his quarters like a sensible person, not lurking in the gardens at night, trying to catch someone climbing in a window," Aubri countered.

"That's because he can't," Skan interrupted. "He never *was* a spy or a fighter, and I was both. And I can beat you, broadwinger, at any game you care to mention."

Aubri shook his massive head, and clacked his beak at Skandranon. "You won't catch me in that trap. I'm *not* in shape, and I'll admit you are. That still doesn't make the game you're playing any saner."

Skan sighed. He'd done his best to convey the urgency of their situation to the Silvers who'd arrived in the guise of diplomats. He thought he'd convinced Judeth, and she was really the only one he needed to convince, since the others were all her underlings. But Aubri was stubborn—

Aubri is old, said a small voice inside him, noting the weight at the keelbone, the slightly shabby plumage, the care with which the broadwinger moved. *He's older than you are, and he took a lot of damage in the war. Well, you did, too, but you were young when you took it, and the young heal fast and thoroughly. He's old, and he's as cautious as any old creature would be. He's forgotten how intoxicating danger can be, and all he remembers is the pain of failure.*

Not that Skan had forgotten the pain of failure—but he wasn't willing to let his actions be dictated by it. Not when the safety of all the people in White Gryphon depended on it.

To his way of thinking, "token" warfare all too often became real warfare. If Shalaman's casual description of the restless nature of his young fighters was at all accurate, Skan didn't think that a "token" effort to displace the settlement would remain that way for long. The first time a Haighlei was hurt or killed in their "token" siege, all the rules would change. Shalaman would be far away, and commanders with a grudge to repay would be on the site.

"Just remember the old soldier's rule, Skan," Judeth said, from her couch among the shadows. "Battle plans seldom survive past the first engagement with the enemy. Be flexible, and be prepared to change your mind and your plans."

She was right, and Skan knew it, and she knew that he knew. He didn't have to like it.

"Who knows?" he said instead. "It may turn out that it's so important that I fly night patrols that you dye Aubri and send him out too!"

"Not if I can help it," Aubri growled. "One crook-beaked fisher-bird is enough."

Skan flexed his wings, testing the feathers for lack of anything better to do.

Who decided that Drake was in charge, Judeth! Drake himself! Both of them together!

Amberdrake had been one of the most expert feather-painters in the whole of Urtho's contingent, and he had learned a lot about feather-dyes in that much-different time. He had sworn to Skan that he could take the barrel of black dye the others had brought, thin it with certain chemicals, and produce something that would dry quickly and without stickiness in the oppressive humidity of this place. It would also have the possibly beneficial side effect of coming out glossy.

Well, no use trying to deny to yourself that you're hurt, Skan. Now be reasonable. Does it matter who's in charge? Objectively, it probably didn't; Skan would do whatever he thought was best, and both Amberdrake and Judeth probably knew that. Objectively, it was actually better for everyone if Skan didn't have to worry about coordinating plans and keeping everyone informed while he was flying clandestine missions.

But it was hard to be objective when you thought you were the Gryphon King and you walked in to find someone else sitting on your throne.

Still, he was going to have to think this one through, calmly and rationally. There was no point in getting upset.

I don't want to be calm and rational! I want to be upset about this! But—no, I guess I'm not really upset. I guess I just have hurt feelings because nobody consulted me.

"Where's Drake, anyway?" he growled. "I think Evening Court is about to start; shouldn't he be here?"

"He said he was going to give everyone something to think about besides the murders," Judeth replied, her lips thinned with disapproval. "He wouldn't tell me what it was; he said he wanted Winterhart to react naturally."

Once again, Skan whipped his head around to stare at her fully, but this time it was with dismay.

He wouldn't tell Judeth, and he must not have told Winterhart—oh, no! Oh Drake, what are you getting yourself into this time!

Shalaman sighed and patted Amberdrake on the shoulder in a surprisingly fraternal gesture. "I hope you know what you're doing, my friend," he said heavily. "This all seems very dangerous to me—not to mention unkind to the lady."

Amberdrake half shrugged, then shook his head. "I hope so too, Serenity," he replied with honesty. "I hope Winterhart forgives me for doing this to her—but you know my reasons."

Shalaman nodded and knotted the sash on his tunic a little tighter. As always, he looked magnificent, an imposing figure of a man dressed immaculately (if by Amberdrake's standards rather flamboyantly) in a long tunic and loose, flowing trousers of shimmering saffron silk decorated with heavy red, black, and gold embroidery, with a heavy gold pectoral and armbands in a motif of lions. By contrast, Amberdrake looked dreadful.

This, of course, was precisely the image he wanted to have. He was an innocent man, wrongly accused of hideous crimes, whose lady had abandoned him. Anyone in that situation should look dreadful.

His long hair was unbound and artfully disheveled, his robe looked as if it had been slept in and not changed for days (thanks to an extended romp with his daughter and the two gryphlets), he was unshaven, and he had altered his posture to a defeated slump. Shalaman had been gratifyingly shocked to see him.

Unfortunately, he hadn't needed to resort to cosmetics to create the dark circles under his eyes. He'd earned those naturally.

"I can see why you would want to give my Court something to think and gossip about besides the murders," Shalaman said thoughtfully as he got up to pace the confines of the tiny Private Audience Chamber. "But will this accomplish what you hope?"

"If I'm dramatic enough, and if Winterhart responds the way I think she will, they won't be able to talk about anything else," Amberdrake told him grimly. "I'm very good at creating unpleasant scenes. It comes from needing to know how to prevent them."

Shalaman accepted that without comment. "I'm sure, given time, that Leyuet and Palisar could arrive at something that would accomplish the same thing." His eyes, as he turned to look into Amberdrake's face, were troubled. "I do not like to see Winterhart hurt."

"Neither do I—but I must be honest with you. I don't believe that Palisar is particularly motivated to help us, and Leyuet is not very good at gauging what ordinary people are fascinated by," Amberdrake replied, with complete candor. "Most of all, we don't have time. The Eclipse Ceremony is less than a fortnight away. Idle people want scandal and drama, which I'm about to provide in abundance. This will give the courtiers something to take their minds off the deaths of some rather unpleasant people who were fairly minor fixtures of your court. It will also give me a good reason to appear to be locked away in my suite without being under house arrest. And I think doing both these things will force our enemies to show their hands again."

Shalaman sighed, then motioned to his servant to open the door for him. This servant, like the two bodyguards who were also in on the plot, had been with the Emperor for years, and Shalaman swore they were as trustworthy as himself. Amberdrake had to accept that. After all, one of the possibilities he and the others had discussed was that Shalaman himself was at the heart of this mess, creating a situation in which he could declare a full war on White Gryphon with the heartfelt blessings of everyone with any power in his kingdom. It was an outside possibility, very low on their list, but it *could* be the case.

We have to trust someone, somewhere, or nothing is going to happen.

"Very well," the Emperor said. "I bow to your better judgment, my friend, Thank you for warning me."

Amberdrake smiled wanly as Shalaman left, taking the servant with him. He paced the floor himself, measuring out the proper length of time as dripped out by a waterclock, waiting for Court to get underway and all the participants to be in place. Skan wouldn't be there—he'd insured that fact by choosing the afternoon rest period to dye the gryphon's feathers black again. Judeth and her Silvers wouldn't be there, either; he'd simply told her not to attend.

Her reactions had been odd, though, since the time she'd arrived. She'd held herself back from saluting him more than once; he'd seen the little twitch as she restrained the automatic impulse. Judeth hadn't saluted anyone since Urtho died, not even Skan...

Does this mean she thinks I'm the real leader around here! He wasn't certain he was comfortable with that idea—but he also wasn't comfortable with the notion of Skandranon leading this group in the current circumstances. The old Skan was impulsive, quick to think but also quick to act, and likely to run off and do things without consulting anyone. Skandranon's old ways were coming back with a vengeance. This wasn't the best time or place for someone like that to be the leader.

And you aren't acting impulsively! his conscience chided.

I thought this through completely, he told it sternly. *And I consulted Shalaman. If I'd let anyone else in on the plan, Winterhart would have gotten word of it, and I have to have a real reaction out of her, not something feigned. Leyuet's not the only Truthsayer in the place and besides, she's good at* hiding *emotions. She isn't very good at* creating *them.*

His conscience grumbled that he was underestimating her. Well, he might be, but it was too late now.

He took a deep breath and slumped his shoulders, opened the door of the small room Shalaman used for private appointments, and headed toward the Audience Chamber. If he did his work right, this would be something that the courtiers here would talk about for decades.

If he did it wrong, they would still talk about it for decades, but Winterhart would rightfully never speak to him again.

He waited at the edge of the crowd for the best possible moment to act. At this instant, Winterhart had no idea that she was in the same room with him—but he knew very well that both his appearance and his reputation as a killer would soon clear a path between them. That, and the expectation induced by his appearance that something dramatic was going to happen.

Whispered word spread through the crowd as if by magic, and as if by magic the courtiers parted along the line his eyes followed toward his lady. The gathered Haighlei parted neatly, as if invisible guards were clearing a path for him, and as they moved back they turned to stare avidly at him.

He waited; she suddenly realized by the stares and stir he created that he was standing near the door to the Audience Chamber, at the end of a cleared corridor that divided the courtiers into near-equal groups. She turned, met his eyes, and started. Silence descended, the heavy silence that falls whenever a mob senses drama.

"Oh, *gods!*" he shouted into the silence, clutching his robe melodramatically at his throat. "Oh, gods, it is true! I thought they were lying, I thought—"

He advanced toward her, where she stood at the foot of the platform holding the Emperor's bench. Shalaman might have been a statue; he neither stirred nor spoke. "You bitch!" he snarled. "You faithless dog, running to lick the hand of the first man who offers you a better bone and wallow at his feet! You mongrel cur! You—you—*perchi!*"

She stood staring at him, her eyes round and shocked, her mouth open in disbelief.

"It is not enough that I am accused of vile crimes I know nothing about!" he cried, his voice already hoarse with shouting. "It is not enough that I am a prisoner without a trial! It is not enough that *you* lose faith in me! But to run to fawn at the feet of *him*, to use this as an excuse to make yourself a *queen*—you are lower than a *perchi!* At least a *perchi* gives satisfaction for the money! You give nothing but hollow lies and false smiles, you feign what you cannot feel, and you don't even do it well!"

He went on with an extensive account of her faults, ranting graphically and at length about her failures as a lover. Finally she reddened, lost the look of utter shock, and he knew he was about to get as good as he had just given.

She was a lady—but she had worked in an army. She had worked among soldiers who saw no reason to temper their language around her, and she had tended gryphons, who were the earthiest creatures he knew. She was absolutely outraged and not thinking at all, and all she wanted to do was to strike back.

By the time she was well wound up and in full voice, if he'd *had* a reputation left, it would have been in shreds.

He got caught up in her hysteria, which fed back to her, and only made the performance better. They railed at each other like a pair of gutter-whores, and for several agonizing moments he was afraid that he *had* done his work too well. She wasn't holding back—and she sounded as if she meant it all.

Then, just as his voice began to hold the intimation of *real* heartache, he caught a familiar sparkle in her eyes.

Relief nearly made him faint—which certainly would have been a dramatic ending to the fight, but not the one he'd intended!

End it now, before she starts laughing!

"I cannot bear this!" he cried, pulling out the knife he'd concealed in the breast of his robe. He raised it over his head—making the motion vague enough that it was open to interpretation whether he was going to kill himself or her.

It didn't matter; the King's bodyguards, specifically warned by the King to watch for this particular gesture, rushed at him, seized him and the knife, and bundled him out. He heard the King issuing orders over his screams to lock him in his rooms.

Now he had every reason in the world never to appear in public— *as himself.*

He was a kestra'chern, adept with costume and drama; he was confident that he could look like a dozen people, all very different from each other— and there were an unspecified number of new "diplomats" from White Gryphon who had just arrived. "Poor, mad Amberdrake" could stay locked in his suite. Someone else would join Judeth's people. Someone taller than Amberdrake, with austere tastes, funereal leather clothing, and a forbidding demeanor, whose slicked-back, dark hair (there were more uses for feather-dye than dyeing feathers) never escaped the mathematically-precise tail at the back of his neck. A personal bodyguard appointed for Skandranon—

And he is going to love that!

The King's two guards only manhandled him as long as they were all in sight of the courtiers. The moment that the doors closed on his private rooms, they released him with apologies.

He thanked them—and handed over the knife with a wink. "I'd rather you gentlemen had this—just in case someone asks what you did with it! I'm a dangerous fellow, you know, and you shouldn't leave me in possession of a weapon!"

They both grinned—showing very white, even teeth in extremely black faces; unlike most of the folk of Shalaman's land, their skin tone was a true black, with a bluish cast to it. "Thank you," said the taller of the two. "It *would* be like that idiot of a Chamberlain to ask that, in front of the Court!"

Amberdrake looked from one friendly face to the other, as something occurred to him. "You seem very—accommodating—to someone who's been accused of murder."

The tall one shrugged. "Here is our logic. The Emperor must believe that you are innocent, or why go through all this? If he believes that you are innocent, he must have brought in his Truthsayer, and for some reason, doubtless a reason that seems good to him, he has not made that public. That is enough for me."

The shorter fellow tossed the "confiscated" knife from hand to hand for a moment, before sheathing it in his belt. "Also—we have seen what was done to those women," the man pointed out. "And we have seen the rooms. Now, this might have been done by a mage—but you are not a mage, or you would have gotten rid of them in much subtler ways. It would have been much easier to have them drop over dead with no sign upon them. It might have been done by someone who was both a skilled thief and a skilled torturer, and while as a kestra'chern you have the knowledge to *be* a torturer, it takes a lifetime to learn the craft of the kestra'chern. Therefore, unless you are much, much older than you look, you could not also have become a skilled thief. It might have been done by several people working together—but there has never, during these murders, been a time when three out of the four of you have not had witnesses to prove where you were. I believe in my Emperor, and I believe in the power of the Truthsayer, but I also believe in logic."

Amberdrake had listened to this well-reasoned discourse with astonishment. *This* was a bodyguard?

"You have thought of all that, and you are *only* a bodyguard?" he blurted. "The gods forbid I should encounter a scholar!"

The man laughed aloud.

"Not only a bodyguard, good kestra'chern Amberdrake," he said, with a little bow. "Also the son of King Sulemeth, the Emperor of Ghandai. This is my brother." He indicated the other guard, who bowed also. "This is how Shalaman and every other Haighlei Emperor preserves the peace among us and our lands—they all have sons who are their neighbors' personal bodyguards, as well as daughters who are

Healers, Household Priestesses, Wives, or Consorts."

"But I thought—" Amberdrake began, confused, "I thought Shalaman had no wife, no children."

"Shalaman does not yet have sons and daughters by a Chief Wife and Consort," the man corrected with a smile, "But he does have them by the ten Priestess Year-Wives of the first decade of his reign, and that is sufficient to the purpose. Year-Sons and Year-Daughters can inherit if there is no heir by a Chief Wife."

"It is not wise to contemplate violence when your potential foe's sons are the men guarding your back, but this is neither the best time or place for a discussion of our customs. Now, let us leave you to your rest."

"Indeed." Amberdrake came back to his mission with a start. "Thank you for being so civilized."

The taller guard smiled again. "At first, you were thought to be barbarians. We who are at Shalaman's side are also his voices in matters that would be improper for him to speak of. All I can say is that you are not barbaric—you are civilized, only different. The time of Change is upon us all—even the Emperor."

Winterhart stormed into the bathing room just as he was putting the finishing touches on his disguise.

"You! You beast! You miserable dog!" she said, picking up the first thing that came to hand—which fortunately was a dish of soap and not the feather-dye. "You *bastard!*" She flung it at him; he ducked, and it smashed against the wall.

The single act of destruction seemed to run all of her rage out of her. "How could you?" she wailed, turning from anger to tears in a heartbeat. He froze in dismay; he'd thought she understood back there! "How could you *say* those things? How could—"

"I could say them because I didn't mean them!" he cried, as her distress spilled over into him. "Oh *ke'chara,* how could you think I meant any of that?"

"But the things about—you *know* I'm sensitive about—" she dissolved into sobs, and he dropped everything he was holding to take her in his arms—leaving behind more shards of glass and pottery in his wake.

The moment he touched her, *he* was overcome by the same terrible grief, and for one moment, he could not shut it out. He was so used to leaving himself completely open to her it struck him like a great wave.

Close up, close up now or you never will—

It was a struggle, but he managed to close up his shields before he was overwhelmed and lost.

Think of her as a client, Drake—get her out of this. It's just hysteria and strain, she was close to laughing in the Audience Chamber, and that was as much hysteria as this is. Besides, she's had all this time to brood on it all, and you know how she makes things worse by brooding! Maybe you knew it was just a sham—but she didn't, not for certain, not at the time of the shock. No matter how much she trusts you, it was a shock and she couldn't be positive in her own mind that there wasn't some truth in what you said to her.

He calmed and soothed her with all the resources at his command, now very grateful that their daughter was nowhere nearby. This was the last way he'd want Windsong to see her parents, and as sensitive as she was, she might very well be affected by it all. Such small things as a child built one reaction upon another.

Gentle deflection while appearing to stay on the subject…

"You handled yourself well, lover. You stood in the midst of the Court and spoke your mind without fear. Now, no one will ever think you are hiding your true feelings. I don't see how anyone *could!* The breeze we feel tonight should be from their lips flapping!"

Finally he had her laughing again, mostly at the absurdity of the situation, at the shocked and avid expression he'd seen on the courtiers' faces, at the effect the outburst had invoked in the staid and mannered life of the Haighlei Court.

"They looked as if we'd dropped a muck pile in the middle of the floor," he chuckled. "If this shocked them, I wonder what they would have thought of the tantrums some of Urtho's people used to pull in public?"

"Oh, you've quite driven every thought of the murders out of their minds, beloved," she said as he wiped her face with a damp cloth to remove all traces of tears, then led her back into the bedroom. "You've driven all thoughts of *anything* else out of their minds, at least for the next day or so. It was all they could talk about, and now I know who favors what faction, just by whether or not they came up to sympathize with me or politely gloat at my situation."

"Gloat?" he said. "The ones who don't want you as Consort, do you suppose?"

She nodded as they both sat down on the bed. Sunset had come and gone, and the usual evening breeze had sprung up, driving the stale humidity from the room. "And those very few, mostly women, who really don't believe that you're guilty and who think I'm everything you said about me for deserting you and taking the Necklace." She quirked an eyebrow at him, with just the faintest hint of jealousy. "You have *quite* a devoted following in some quarters. I wouldn't be the least bit surprised if they start showing up at your door, wanting to console you in your deep distress."

"Console me?" he said in dismay. "There are women who feel sorry for me and want to console me?" That was a possibility that hadn't occurred to him and it presented any number of unpleasant and inconvenient possibilities!

"Hadn't counted on that, hmm?" She was smiling smugly now, and didn't bother to hide it—probably in just retribution for what he had just put her through. "Oh, yes, I'm sure they'll be eager to console you, personally and intimately. However, the King's physicians have said you're mad and not to be trusted without a keeper. Theoretically, he has sent one to take charge of you, so no one is going to get in here unless you let him—or her—in."

He heaved a sigh of relief. Trust Shalaman to think of that! He knew his courtiers better than Amberdrake had suspected.

She blinked then and touched his hair as if she had only just that moment noticed it. "What's this?" she asked, startled. "You won't be able to show up in public like that—"

"Not as Amberdrake, but as Hawkwind, Skandranon's bodyguard, there shouldn't be a problem," he told her, and laughed. "Besides, this is a carrier version of the feather-dye. It washes right out again. I won't be able to swim or take a bath in public, but not everyone swims, and these people don't have public baths. I'll just hope it doesn't rain much. Come to think of it, I'd better have a hood with me."

"Why do this at all?" she asked. "We have enough people now. You don't need to go out in public."

"Three reasons." He sat back and stretched his shoulder muscles as he spoke, easing the tension out of them. "Skan should have a bodyguard, and he won't listen to anyone but me. Granted, he doesn't often listen to me either, but at least I have a better chance of getting through to him. Two, if I'm *not* here and an assassin comes calling, I won't be killed, and only the assassin would know I wasn't here. So anyone who would accuse me of sneaking out would be the assassin, or have hired one. Three, no one ever pays any attention to a bodyguard, as I just had brought home to me. I might hear or see something you and Skan don't, since you are Personages and I won't be."

She nodded, and added another reason. "Four, you're going crazy here, cooped up in these rooms."

"I hadn't wanted to mention that," he admitted, "But yes. You're right. It's very lonely here."

He hadn't intended to admit that, but somehow it came out. She blinked thoughtfully, and nodded.

"I can see that," she began, when there was a tapping on the door to the balcony.

Before either of them could answer it, the door opened, and the Black Gryphon stepped in, leaving the door ajar to let in more of the fresh breeze that followed him inside.

"I," he said to both of them, "am one frustrated gryphon."

Skandranon finished the third night of his patrols the way he had finished the first two, with empty talons.

Well, not quite empty—he had already caught three thieves this evening alone. One was not exactly a petty thief, either; he'd managed to scale one of the lesser treasure-towers, and was about to break in through a window hardly big enough to admit a child. Of course, since this man was either a dwarf or of some race that was naturally stunted, the window made a fine entrance. Since the thief was so small, he was able to comfortably snatch the small man from the wall. The Black Gryphon carried the man's tiny, terrified body to the proper authorities, whereupon the thief blurted out a full confession, as they all had. Leyuet's Spears had them all in custody, a neat arrangement so far as Skan was concerned.

He'd assumed that since magic wasn't working properly, their enemies couldn't be using it even to disguise their movement or hide themselves—and that his old night-combat and night-spying skills would be better suited to spotting the culprits from above than even the most experienced Haighlei guard from below. Whoever this was might not think about hiding himself from a watcher above him. Even Ma'ar's people, as accustomed as they were to dealing with gryphons, still occasionally forgot.

All it had netted him, though, was the common and not-so-common thief. No killers. Most of the little rats had not been any kind of threat physically.

Put a bedridden old woman with a cane against any of these clowns, and I would bet on the old woman to beat them senseless.

But he was not going to give up. For one thing, Drake was watching.

The fact that Amberdrake was still considered to be the person in charge of this whole operation still rankled, even though he agreed logically with it. It rankled even though he agreed emotionally—at least in part.

He just hated to think he'd been superseded, and worst of all, no one had *asked* him about it. They'd all just assumed it would be all right with him.

That was what left the really sour taste in his mouth.

As he glided on still-rising thermals, circling with a minimum of wingbeats, it continued to rankle.

Drake is a terrific planner. Drake is a fine organizer. Drake knows what he's doing, and yes, I am a bit too reckless, as long as it's only my own neck I'm baring to the makaar's talon. But still—if they'd just asked me...

He probably would have said yes. He probably would have cheered. Now, it itched like an ingrown feather, and he couldn't stop obsessing on it.

Only a few days to the Eclipse Ceremony, and we still don't have our killer. That was his second ingrown feather. *Shalaman can't marry Winterhart, so he can't ally with us that way. He can't declare us allies while we're still under suspicion. He can't declare us innocent, not without forcing the hand of our enemy in some way we probably won't like. Probably what would happen would be that he would just quit, leaving us with several corpses and no answers, but there are other things he could do—and Drake's histrionics should make him go after another victim before the Ceremony. He'll probably make it look as if I did it, since I'm making myself so conveniently obvious as a potential killer.*

Wait a moment. What's this!

He turned a slow, lazy circle in the sky and peered down at the hint of movement below. There was something or someone climbing up the side of that tower—

Now, it *could* have been a simie, one of those furry little creatures that looked so very human; normally they lived in some of the gardens and made the paintbox-birds miserable with their antics. But the simies often got out of their designated "areas" and went looking for something to do, some new mischief to get into, when they ran out of ways to torment the birds.

I thought the shadow looked too big to be a simie, though—heyla!

There he was...

Skan spiraled down, taking care not to betray himself with the flapping of wings, and drew nearer.

Silence...

The man was scaling the side of the tower, which was odd, because there were a dozen better ways to get into it, all of them involving a whole let less work.

If he was *just* a thief, why bypass all those easier ways in? He moved with a skill that told Skan he knew exactly what he was doing...

In fact, he moved in a way that put Skan's hackles up. Move a little— then freeze in a distorted pose that looked more like an odd shadow than the outline of a human. Move a little more, freezing again, this time in a different, but equally distorted pose. He wasn't going straight to his goal, either, but working his way back and forth along the face of the building to take advantage of all the real shadows.

This has to be the one!

Just as Skan thought that, the man suddenly vanished, and only by accident did Skan see the darker shape of a window inside the irregular shadow-shape he had entered.

Skan folded his wings and dove headfirst for the spot, backwinging at the last moment and thrusting out with all four claws to catch the sides of the window, and hold him there.

He clung there for just a heartbeat, long enough to see that the window was open and that it was big enough for him to enter. Then he plunged forward with a powerful thrust of his hindlegs, wings folded tightly against his body, head down and foreclaws out.

Where i—was his last thought.

He woke all at once, which argued that a spell had knocked him unconscious rather than a blow to the head or an inhaled drug. He was, however, still quite unable to move, he was bound in a dozen ways. No matter how he strained against the bindings, he could not move even a talon-length.

He lay on his side staring at a wall, with a rigid bar or board stretched all along his spine. His neck was bound to this bar, and his tail; his head was tethered to the end of it as well, and he thought he had been bound to it in several places along his chest and stomach. His wings were certainly bound. He counted three straps at least, and there might be more.

He was muzzled, but not blindfolded or hooded. There were more bars, this time of metal, fastened to his ankles, holding all of his legs apart in a rigid pose, and rendering his talons useless. He could flex them, and his legs a little, but it wasn't going to do him any good; the ends of the metal bars were against the wall and floor and weren't going anywhere. A collar around his neck was tied to the muzzle and to the bar between his foreclaws.

A soft footfall behind his back warned him that he was not alone. "Quite an artistic arrangement, don't you think?" said a voice that sounded vaguely familiar. "I thought it up myself."

Skan discovered the muzzle was just large enough to permit him to speak. "Fascinating," he said flatly. "And now that you know you've got a successful arrangement for gryphon trussing, would you like to let me go?"

"No," said the speaker. "I like you this way. It reminds me of home."

Why does he sound familiar? Who is this idiot! He's speaking our language, not Haighlei—could he be one of Judeth's people! No, or how would he have killed all those Haighlei women before Judeth got here!

Something about that combination was teasing at the back of his mind, but he couldn't seem to put the clues together into a whole.

"Haven't you recognized me yet?" The voice sounded disappointed. "Oh, this is really too bad! Either you are becoming a senile old fool, Black Gryphon, or I am simply not notorious enough. I am inclined to believe the former."

"Which means you have outwitted a senile old fool," Skan replied instantly, with a growl. "Hardly impressive."

He hoped to annoy this person enough to get some useful reaction out of him, but he was again disappointed when the man giggled.

"But you aren't the important one, gryphon," the man said smugly. "You're only an annoyance that we had to get out of the way so you couldn't interfere in our real work. We have bigger prey in mind than you."

"We?" Skan asked.

The man giggled again. "Oh, no. You won't catch me in *that* little trap. You have the most remarkable knack for escaping at the last minute— unlike those old bitches I practiced on." The voice took on a sullen quality, rather like an aural pout. "They were hardly good material. All flaws, and nothing really to work on. Very disappointing. Unartistic. Not worth my time, when it came down to that. You have some potential, at least, and I am truly going to enjoy showing him—ah—what you're made of." Another giggle, and this one was definitely not sane. "Now mind you," the man went on, in a belligerent tone, "I don't usually practice my arts on males, but I'm going to make an exception in your case, just to impress Amberdrake."

Skandranon lunged without thinking, succeeding only in throttling himself against the collar. As he choked, he realized how diabolically efficient his captor's bindings truly were, although they gave a little bit more than their creator had intended. *Amberdrake! What's he got to do with this!*

The man wasn't done yet. "I do owe him more than a few favors for what he did to me."

And with that, the last piece clicked into place in Skandranon's mind. *Amberdrake—punishment!—women—tying up—cutting up—*

Hadanelith!

"Hadanelith, you're out of your mind," he said flatly.

"Whatever sanity you had when you lived in White Gryphon coughed once and died when they threw you out on your nose."

"Oh, good—you guessed!" The mocking tone sounded more pleased than anything else. "How nice to be given the recognition one deserves at last! How nice to know one's hard work hasn't been in vain!"

"And just what did you intend to accomplish with all of this nonsense?" Skan asked, making his own voice sound as bored as possible. *Eventually Kechaia is going to test my thoughts—she'll find out I'm in trouble and tell the others.*

The only problem is, I haven't the foggiest notion where I am. Hard to rescue me when they have an entire city or more to cover.

"Well, disposing of those old bats was meant to make you lot look like bad little boys and girls," Hadanelith said. "It worked, too—no one likes you anymore. Even the charming and lovely Winterhart deserted you."

There was *no* doubt about the tone of his voice now; gloating. And he lingered over Winterhart's name in a way that was just enough to make every feather on Skan's body stand straight on end. He practically breathed the name. *Winterhart.*

Oh, Kechaia, I hope you're listening for me now!

On the other hand, Winterhart's apparent defection from the Kaled'a'in had fooled even Hadanelith. Would that be enough to keep her safe?

"My colleagues have continuing plans, however, which I do not particularly feel like discussing with you," Hadanelith continued lightly. "I trust you'll forgive me. And I hope you won't mind waiting until I acquire Amberdrake before I introduce you to the delights of my skill. I want him to watch. He might learn something. I might even let him live afterward; being left alive would be a better revenge than disposing of him."

Hadanelith's voice took on a grating tone. "Before we all went on this mad flight to 'safety' and you morons built White Gryphon, I practiced my hobbies in Urtho's camp, on all the little human hens huddled around his Tower. I used to watch you and all your oh-so-glorious feathered brethren go off to fight Ma'ar, and inside I cheered when fewer of you came back. Urtho the 'artist' created the gryphons, but he quit too early. He made you to be pretty but shallow. The Black Gryphon will die the shallowest of them all."

With another half-hearted struggle and a gasp, Skan replied softly, almost pleadingly, "Don't mock Urtho."

"Mock Urtho?" Hadanelith laughed very near Skan's head, probably hoping for Skan to lash out fruitlessly again. "Uttering Urtho's name is mockery enough. Still, it would be below my honor to mock a lesser artist. If I had any."

Another of his maniacal giggles, this time farther away.

"Ma'ar, at least, came closer to worthy creation than that so-sweet 'Mage of Boredom.' Ma'ar took what Urtho limply tried with the gryphons and created the *makaar*. Now there was something closer to art. Makaar weren't flatulent, preening extravagances made by a pretend leader, they were hunters. They hunted and enslaved with style. And while on the subject of style, let me tell you of how my next carving will go. I believe an amusing end for the failed legend, the 'Black Gryphon,' would be to carve and rebuild him, into a female makaar."

Oh. My. Word. I can't say I like the way this is headed at all.

"Think of it as being remade into a tribute to the departed lesser artist Ma'ar, Skandranon! Like Ma'ar himself, though, the lifespan of the work will be only temporary. A pity, but then again, transforming the 'Black Gryphon' into the 'Bleeding Makaar' is art enough. The knifestrokes begin *here...*"

He went on at some length and in great detail, describing all of the things he had in mind to do to Skandranon, starting with that most private of parts. He tried to push the mental images of what was going to be done to him away from the fore of his thoughts, although it was difficult. The descriptions of the mutilations were bad enough, but Hadanelith gloated over how the agony could be made to linger. Skandranon had never liked pain at all.

Skan could only stare at the wall, listen, and hope that there were no mind-shields around this place, that none of Hadanelith's "colleagues" were aware of the gryphonic ability to Mindspeak, and that Kechara would find him quickly enough for the others to search for him.

Because, in three days' time, it was all going to be too late for

Skandranon's life to make a difference in the relationship between White Gryphon and the Haighlei. Hadanelith, without a shadow of a doubt, had timed his plans to come to fruition before then.

Zhaneel was doing an admirable job of not panicking, but she wasn't far from it. Her ear-tufts were flat to her head, and her entire posture suggested she was restraining herself by pure will alone.

"Where was he supposed to be flying last night?" Amberdrake asked her. It was hard to think; he was very tired, and last night had been a late one for him. He rubbed his temple, trying to will his fatigue headache away.

She shook her head. "Mostly over the Palace, but he also intended to fly some patterns over the city nearest the Palace walls," she told him. Her feathers already showed signs of overgrooming, ragged around the edges and a bit frayed. "Leyuet says that he last heard from Skan at three on the waterclock, when he brought in another trespasser. This one was let go—he was only trying to sneak in to see his lover among the servants."

"Did Leyuet check that out this morning?" Amberdrake asked sharply.

"I don't know—" She shook her head, sadly. "They did not let the boy go until dawn, to frighten him."

"He couldn't have anything to do with it, then." Amberdrake bit his thumbnail and tried to think. "Skan *must* have discovered the murderers, maybe even stopped them before they could strike again—but then what? Why would he disappear?"

"What could they want with him? Where could they have taken him?" Zhaneel echoed, her voice shrill with worry.

"Kechara has not yet found him!" She dropped her head with distress.

"Remember, she has to know *where* to look, what minds to find him among," Amberdrake told her, patting her shoulder to comfort her. "Right now, she's going to have to search through the whole city to find him."

And we have to hope they don't have shields up to cover him. Kechara is good, but I don't know that she's ever broken a shield. Would she know what to look for?

"Does Kechara know anything about mind-shields?" he asked, wanting to give her something she could act on. "All I know is that they exist, and that some kinds of magic shielding acts like a mind-shield. Could she break one if she found it to see if Skan's under it?"

Zhaneel brought her head up, quickly. "I do not know, but I think

I can explain it to her!" the gryfalcon exclaimed. "It would be much faster to search for a shield than to search for Skan! As for breaking one—Amberdrake, there is nothing she has tried with Mindspeech that she cannot do, and she might well be able to break one."

"Talk to her, then, the next time she calls you, and ask her." This was the maddening part; the only time the people here, where Skan was presumably captive, could speak to Kechara was when the little gryphon stopped searching long enough to talk to one of the strong Mindspeakers here. There were only two, with Skan gone—Zhaneel and a Kaled'a'in trondi'irn named Summerhawk. Aubri was a Mindspeaker, but not very strong; Winterhart was on a par with Aubri, and Amberdrake's Gifts were in the sensing of emotions and the healing of the spirit, not in Mindspeaking. It was incredibly frustrating—

But at least Snowstar was in charge of Kechara and her search, and he was interrupting her at regular intervals to get her to talk to one or more of them and to rest and eat. Otherwise, the poor little thing was so frantic to find her "Papa Skan" that she was likely to drive herself until she dropped.

If ever we find her limits, it will probably be now.

He racked his brain, trying to think of any other way they could look for the gryphon. No new murders this morning, and all courtiers accounted for at Morning Court, so if Skan had intercepted the killers, he'd done so before they even got at their potential victim.

And at least he won't be blamed for another killing.

So what else could they do? Ask for a room-by-room search of the Palace? What would that accomplish, besides getting people more annoyed with the Kaled'a'in than they already were?

And besides, if they know there is a search going on, they could and would move him.

"You stay here, just in case he comes flying in with his tail singed," he ordered Zhaneel. "I'm going to go talk to Silver Veil. Maybe she can help."

He left Zhaneel consoling herself with her twins, who played on, oblivious to their mother's worries, and left the suite in his "guard" guise. Like most kestra'chern, by the very nature of her work, Silver Veil was usually alone in the mornings and early afternoon, and he found her enjoying a solitary lunch beside the pool in her own garden. She knew immediately that something was very wrong, of course, even though she did not have the level of Empathy he did.

"What is it?" she asked, leaving her lunch forgotten and hurrying across the garden as soon as she spotted him. "What has happened? I heard nothing of another death!"

"No death that we know of, but Skan is missing," he told her, taking the hands she held out to him with gratitude. "We have a Mindspeaker searching for him, but that takes time."

Her eyes went wide when he said that Skandranon was missing, and her hands tightened on his. "Is there anything I can do to help?" she asked quickly.

"I was going to ask you that; can you think of anything?" He tried not to show his disappointment when she shook her head, but his heart fell a little anyway. He hadn't exactly counted on her coming up with a brilliant plan on the spur of the moment, but he'd hoped, just a bit. She was so resourceful, it was hard to realize that she couldn't do everything, solve every problem:

"I cannot solve every problem," she said softly, as if she had read his thoughts. "I cannot even solve my own."

Only then did he see that her eyes were red, as if she had been weeping, and that there were shadows beneath them that told him she had been spending some sleepless nights.

"I can't do anything more to look for Skan," he told her quietly, drawing her back over to her seat under the trees. "Why don't you tell me about your troubles? I may not be able to help, but at least I can provide a sympathetic ear."

She let him lead her there passively, and sat down again with a sigh. "It is nothing I had not known about when I came here," she said wearily. "It is just that I had not known how it would affect me until I saw Winterhart with the Necklace."

"Winterhart?" he said, puzzled. "What—" But the question was answered by her woeful expression before she could even say a word. "Oh, my very dear! You have gone and fallen in love with Shalaman, haven't you!"

She nodded, a tinge of color creeping over her cheeks. "A dreadful confession for a kestra'chern, to say she has fallen in love with her chief client."

"I did with mine—" he objected, but she waved the objection away.

"Winterhart was not the King," she pointed out. "And you were not in Haighlei lands. It is assumed here, among the Haighlei, that a true kestra'chern is a precious thing, too precious for any one person to have to himself. Yet the King's Consort obviously could not—well. I am caught in a double bind, you see."

"And it would be bad enough that you love him, but he is also in love with you, I suspect," Amberdrake hazarded. "Ah, now a great deal makes sense. That was why he thought he was in love with Winterhart! It was really a reflection of his true feelings for you!"

She nodded. "Your lady is very like me in many ways, and he had every reason to believe that she was accessible to him. I have not let him know of my feelings, and I suspect that custom has made him deny his. As flexible as my King is, he is surprisingly custom-bound."

He let go of her hands and reached out to hold her instead. She did not resist at all but rested her head on his chest with a sigh that conveyed more heartbreak than all the tears in the world.

"I was able to manage when there was no serious contender for his affection," she said softly into his collar. "But when he offered Winterhart the Necklace—oh, it hurt, it hurt! It stabbed me to the heart, and I could scarcely bear to stand there and smile, and pretend to be glad! And even now, although I know it is all a sham, I cannot bear to stay in the Court for very long and watch her in the place of Consort-To-Be at his side!"

"One way or another, in two days it will all be over," he reminded her, with a stab of pain and fear in his own heart, as he wondered just how it would all end. With laughter and triumph—or in bloody war?

"But the situation will still remain," she replied, every word an unshed tear, a whispered fragment of pain. "One day soon, he must take a real Consort, and I know this now, as does he. I will bear it because I must—but, oh, my friend, I shall walk from that moment upon knifeblades, with spears in my heart until the day I die!"

He stroked her hair, unable to arrive at a satisfactory answer for her. "I wish that I had a magic means of helping you," he said at last. "If there were a kestra'chern of your skill available to take your place, do you think—"

"I do not know," she said, but sadly. "It has never happened before that an Emperor took as his Consort a kestra'chern. I suspect he could order it to be so only at the Eclipse Ceremony."

So *much hinges on that damned Ceremony!* he thought bitterly. *Even the barest hope of happiness for Silver Veil!*

"I cannot promise anything," he said at last, "but I will do what I can to help you, as you have so often helped me. Perhaps—perhaps, if everything works out properly at the Ceremony, there may be a solution for you as well."

"But you must not tell him of my feelings for him!" she insisted. "You must not! It is bad enough now, but it would be worse for both of us if you do! Loving in silence is misery, but loving, knowing the other loves, and remaining parted is twice the misery! I have seen it happen all too often that way."

Sadly, so had he. "I swear it," he pledged her. "Yet I also swear that I will do what I can to remedy the situation, if a remedy can be found." He cupped her face in his hands, kissed her forehead, and smiled into her eyes. "I might even offer my own services to the Emperor," he said, only half in jest. "Then, at least, there would be a substitute for you. You often said that I am the one pupil who is your equal."

"You surpass me, and beware lest I hold you to that," she murmured, but she managed a wan smile. "And meanwhile—I shall consult with Leyuet. There may be something that the Spears can do quietly to help search for Skandranon."

"Thank you." He took her hands again, squeezed them gently, and stood up. "I must go back to Zhaneel before she begins plucking her feathers. I will let you know if we learn anything."

"And I, you." She smiled up into his face, this time with more feeling. "Odd, how we can forget our troubles in the troubles of others."

"Isn't it?" he responded.

She escorted him to the door of her suite herself, and let him out with another embrace.

But the moment he left her presence, all the fears for Skan and for their entire precarious situation came back a hundredfold. He hurried back to the gryphons' quarters, half in hope, and half in fear.

Zhaneel was where he had left her, but her muscles were the tiniest bit less tense. "I have spoken to Kechara," she announced before he could ask anything. "I think she understands the concept of shields, and she is going to look for them. Snowstar is to show her one, and he will teach her to break in if she can. He thinks that she should be able to, especially since these people do not know as much about mind-shields as we."

He heaved a sigh of relief. At least that was one bit of good news in all the bad.

"So now we wait," she finished, with tired and worried resignation.

"Now we wait," he confirmed. "But—we also hope. After all, isn't he the Black Gryphon again? And hasn't the Black Gryphon *always* been able to return, no matter how harsh the odds?"

She nodded. And that seemed to be all the answer she needed, at least for the moment.

CHAPTER TEN

Amberdrake paced the floor of the gryphons' suite, surrounded by the rest of the White Gryphon contingent, who were fretting and worrying each in his own fashion. While he knotted and untied a length of satin rope, Zhaneel preened her feathers with exquisite care for each one—preening to the point where she was doing them damage around the edges. Judeth sharpened a knife, by now, it must be the sharpest knife on the continent. The rest of her Silvers were following their leader's example, including Aubri, who sharpened his claws. And Winterhart braided, unraveled, and rebraided the fringes of her sash.

It had been two days since Skan's disappearance, and in all that time Kechara had not been able to contact him.

What she *had* been able to do was to learn what long-distance mind-shields "tasted" like, and how to break or bypass them. That had taken her a day, and Amberdrake was astonished that she had learned in so little time. He had not thought she had the mental capacity to learn *anything* in so short a time period, much less something fraught with so many sophisticated concepts.

She had been searching for mind-shields since dawn, and systematically getting past them. Most of them, predictably enough, were crude things, masking only the minds of those who were Gifted and had shielded themselves against the outside world. Some had been put in place over temples or the minds of Haighlei priests, which again was not surprising, given how these people felt about Mindspeaking in the first place.

Faithfully, she reported every shield found, and every shield broken, although Snowstar was reportedly growing worried that she was nearing the end of her strength.

But time was growing short as well. The Eclipse Ceremony would take place beginning at dawn and ending later tomorrow. Everyone intending to take part in the Ceremony—which was everyone except Zhaneel and Amberdrake—was supposed to meet with the Haighlei priests for a special cleansing that would take until sunrise. Amberdrake was excused by dint of his insanity, and "Hawkwind" because "he" was supposed to be guarding Amberdrake. The servants were due at any moment to come and fetch them all.

There was a knock at the door in the next room. Gesten went to answer it, coming back with the expected result.

"They're here," he said in a toneless voice. "We'd better get going."

Judeth rose from her seat, and the rest stood up with her. "If we're going to have any hope of pulling our tails out of this fire, we have to play along with this," she said, for at least the twentieth time.

Amberdrake nodded, deciding not to answer because as short as his temper was, he was likely to snap at her. She waited for a few moments, then taking the nod and the silence as her orders, ushered everyone else out, including Gesten. Only Makke remained behind to watch the children. Winterhart was the last to go, casting an anxious glance back at him.

He sensed that she wanted to say something—like "don't do anything stupid while we're gone"—but she wisely kept her own thoughts behind her lips. He smiled at her, and mimed a kiss. She did the same.

Then they were all gone. The silence in the suite was enough to make him shake his head with the feeling that he must somehow have gone deaf.

"Well?" he asked finally, just to hear something, even if it was his own voice.

Zhaneel raised her weary head from her foreclaws; she hadn't slept in all this time, and she looked it. "She has found another shield, and she is working on it. This one tastes magical in nature."

He frowned, rubbing his weary, aching eyes. That was odd. That was *distinctly* odd. The chief effect of every mage-storm so far had been to destabilize or knock down shields, so this one would have to have been put up since the last storm.

And to put up a magical shield right now would take an enormous amount of power. Why bother, especially here?

Unless whoever was beneath that shield had something to hide from the priests...

Like more magic? Like—blood-magic!

He had hoped so many times, and had his hopes dashed, that he was afraid to hope this time. And yet—and yet this time all the parameters fit, all of them, and not just some of them.

He waited, and Zhaneel waited, as the water-clock dripped toward three.

Zhaneel suddenly jumped to her feet, uttering a cry that made his ears ring and every hair on his head stand straight up.

"Drake!" she shouted as his heart lurched into a gallop. "Drake, she found him! He is alive!"

Alive, but not necessarily well... according to Zhaneel, Skan was trussed up like a bird for the spit, had been cut on a bit, and had not eaten or drunk since his capture. With his high energy needs, he was not in very good shape at the moment, and he was light-headed with exhaustion. Getting details from a tipsy gryphon through a gryphon with the mind of a child to a gryphon who was giddy with lack of sleep was a lesson in patience.

"Little Kechara is worried about her Papa Skan. I can feel it. She hasn't yet admitted to herself that Skandranon's in trouble, but she can tell something isn't quite right. Skan's been trying to soothe her, but he isn't in very good shape, Drake."

"All right, I want every single detail that she can get from him," Amberdrake said wearily. "I want her to describe everything he's hearing, smelling, and seeing. If he's anywhere in the Palace complex, I might be able to identify the place. The gods know I've walked over every inch of it, looking for clues."

Zhaneel nodded, her eyes closed. "There is the smell of peppers, and of night-trumpet," she said, slowly. "The stone of the wall is a pale yellow, and—it is marble." She lapsed back into silence for a moment. "She looks in his memory, and there are fine furnishings, like the ones in our rooms."

"Could be anywhere," he muttered, mostly to himself. "Could even be out in the city. Damn!"

"Sounds, though. There is no sound of people or traffic, and there are always those sounds in the city," she said, and his heart rose a little. If Skan was somewhere, *anywhere*, within the complex, it would make things much easier.

"The sound of falling water," Zhaneel continued. "And windchimes, wooden ones. Oh, there are night-singers, nearby, perhaps in a garden!"

That narrowed it down a little, to one of the less-desirable, older sections of the complex. Night-singers, which were a type of singing insect, had fallen out of favor a century or so ago, but no one had bothered to eradicate them from the gardens of those who themselves were not particularly in favor. The fashion now was for birds that sang at night, or no singers at all—or, more accurately, the fashion three generations ago was thus, and nothing had changed.

"Anything else?" he asked, in desperation, as his back and neck clenched with tension. She spasmed her talons in her pillows, her eyes squeezed tightly shut.

"No—yes!" she said, and her eyes flew open. "There is a sentry, calling the hour, within hearing distance of the room!"

He leaped to his feet, every nerve alive with excitement, his heart racing again. There was only one place where one could hear the hours called as sentries made their rounds, and that was near the outer walls of the huge complex. And because most people did not care to have their sleep disturbed, there was only one building near enough to the walls to hear that—

"He's in the Hall of Fragrant Joy!" Amberdrake said, fiercely. "He has to be!" He thought quickly. "Zhaneel, try to get the priests to let you in to the others. I'll go after him now, while we still have a chance of getting to him before they really hurt him."

"You?" she said incredulously. "You? You are not a fighter! How could you—"

I will not think about this, or I will not have the courage.

"Zhaneel, it is a moonless night and you *know* you don't fly well at night! Skan has enhanced night-vision, but you don't, and if you can't see to fly, you'd have to walk. That puts you on the ground, where you are terribly vulnerable, and that's in the open. Inside—well, I may not be a fighter, but the hallways in that old section of the Palace are narrow, and you would hardly be able to move, much less fight!" He took her head between his hands and looked deeply into her eyes. "And I do *not* intend to fight! I intend to slip in, find him, turn him loose, and get *out* of there! If I go now, I can probably manage so that no one notices me. You couldn't be inconspicuous no matter how hard you try."

She made a growling sound but nodded in agreement.

"Go get the others; badger the priests until they let you in," he urged. "Send them after me. Now, I've got to go!"

He was already wearing the best possible clothing for night prowling; his guise of Hawkwind, black-on-black. She clicked her beak in anxiety for a moment, then appeared to make up her mind, and rushed out the door.

He didn't bother with the door; perhaps he wasn't a fighter, but he hadn't been spending all these years helping to build White Gryphon without learning some rather odd skills for a kestra'chern.

I will not think about this, only do it.

He had a balcony, and it was a lot faster to get to the ground by sliding down the spiral support poles.

And what was more—if their enemies were watching the door, they'd never see him leave.

He went over the balcony railing and hung by his fingertips for a moment, as he felt for the support pole with his feet. In a moment, he had it; he wrapped his legs around it and let go of the railing, sliding down the pole like a naughty boy fleeing confinement to his room.

Except that, unlike the boy, he had no sense of exhilaration. His muscles all shivered, and his heart beat double-time with fear and tension. He was only too aware that he was one man, alone, and that this course was madness.

A moment later, he was crouched in the shadow of the bushes at the foot of the pole, listening for the sounds of anyone else out in the garden. *I suppose I could have dropped straight down; one story isn't too far to fall. Yes, but if I'd broken an ankle, I wouldn't be able to do Skan much good now, would I?*

He felt the stir of the night breeze against his skin with unnatural clarity. As far as he could tell, there wasn't anyone nearby on the grounds. That was the way it should be; everyone of any consequence was in the various cleansing ceremonies, and the only people who were excused from the ceremonies were the sick, the injured, the mad (like Amberdrake), and those whose duties forced them to work, like the guards and some of the servants, and probably less than a third of those. This was the quietest the Palace had ever been. Lights were going out in every direction he looked, as servants went from room to deserted room, extinguishing them, in preparation for the Ceremony.

In this case, the best way to be inconspicuous—if a man with a face as pale as his ever *would* be inconspicuous here—would be to act as if he was going somewhere on orders. So once he made certain there was no one in the immediate area watching him, he stood up, straightened his tunic, and set off for the Hall of Fragrant Joy at a fast walk.

He felt as if there were hundreds of eyes on him, and the skin of his back prickled, as if anticipating an arrow.

He wanted to run, but that was hardly the way to remain inconspicuous. No one ran, here. It simply wasn't done.

He couldn't have run in any case; the path was visible only because it was white gravel in the midst of dark green grass. If he tried to run, he'd probably fall and break his neck.

Oh, this is blight, Drake. You're going off by yourself, without any reinforcements. You've assumed that Skan will be alone and relatively unguarded, but you can't be sure of that, now, can you! So you're going off to play the hero, and you aren't exactly suited to the role, you know! And what are you going to do when you get there and find out that Skan isn't alone, hmm! Try and talk your way out of it! I don't think anyone is going to believe you just went out for a stroll and happened to show up where he's being held! And with a pale face like yours, you aren't going to pass for Haighlei!

The internal voice did nothing to still the fear; not even clenching his hands into fists kept them from shaking.

Buildings loomed all around him, poking up above the carefully sculptured foliage of the grounds, dark and lifeless. There wasn't a hint of the sounds that usually filled the night here; no music, no conversation, nothing. Just lightless buildings, with the star-filled sky up ahead, and the white of the path barely discernible in the heavy, flower-scented dark. He couldn't even make out much beyond the bare shape of the bushes and trees beside the path.

Thank you so much, Skan, for running off and not taking anyone to back you up. Even leaving Aubri up on a rooftop while you played mighty warrior would have been enough! Now you're in trouble and I'm running to your rescue like the fool I am. In the dark. Alone. Oh, brilliant, Amberdrake.

This was as close to being blind as he cared to go, and it took all of his concentration to keep from stumbling over uneven places in the dark.

Which was precisely why, when a shadow separated itself from the trunk of a tree overhanging the path and flung itself at him, he didn't have any time to react.

And he didn't even feel the blow to his head that sent him into unconsciousness; there was only a sense of timelessness where awareness should have been.

His head hurt—

It throbbed, horribly, with every beat of his heart. His stomach turned over and there was a taste of blood and something bitter in his mouth. His lower lip stung; he tested it with his tongue, finding more blood, finding it swollen-and cut.

His arms were twisted under him and behind his back in an awfully odd pose. He groaned, and tried to roll over. What had he done last night that—

A tugging at his neck stopped him. He couldn't roll over. In fact, he couldn't move at all.

Amberdrake's eyes opened, but slowly, slowly, for they were sticky and felt swollen, and hurt too, though not as much as his head. He didn't learn much of anything, however, for there was nothing more enlightening than a yellow marble wall in front of him. He was lying on his side, but someone had "considerately" propped him up and padded him with cushions placed beneath him in a primitive mattress.

Why does this not comfort me? Possibly because I have obviously been bludgeoned and am now tied hand and foot!

Moving even a little woke pain in his arms and neck, but also told him that much. His arms were pinned together by a restraint at the elbows, behind his back, although they had not been tied so tightly as to be uncomfortable.

Yet. Of course, I'm a kestra'chern, and I can force my muscles to relax, which might help.

His wrists were also strapped together, and there was a collar around his neck that was fastened to something behind him; that was what had kept him from rolling over.

So much for rescuing Skan. Whoever has him must have been watching our rooms. Gods, I hope they didn't get Zhaneel!

Blinding pain washed a red haze over everything for a moment; when it subsided, he continued to take inventory of his situation. Curiously, though, he began to realize that he wasn't afraid any longer. *Maybe because the worst has already happened, so why be afraid!*

His ankles were tied together, and his knees, although he could bend both. He craned his neck a little and bent at the waist as much as the collar would allow, to get a peek at the bindings on his legs. His head throbbed, but there was enough slack in his bindings for him to think about getting himself loose.

If I didn't know better—

"Awake?" Skan rumbled.

"Yes," he said shortly. "What time is it?"

"Mid-morning I think. Well after dawn. Which means the Ceremony is already underway." Skan sighed gustily. "Which completes this disaster, as far as we're concerned."

Mid-morning! Oh, sketi. *That means Zhaneel couldn't get the priests to let her in—or else that they let her in, but wouldn't let her see the others and started her on her own purification rites. Oh, hell. Oh, bloody hell. She's the only one who knows where we are! Or where I thought we'd be—but we may not even be there.*

Not just fear rose up in him—but a hint of panic. This was not just a disaster, this was catastrophe!

He rolled, this time in the direction of the pull on his collar, and managed to get himself faced away from the wall. There was a leash fastened to a ring in the floor to which he'd been tethered, which answered that question, at least.

Skandranon was indeed trussed up like a bird waiting for the spit. He looked very much the worse for wear, but not really visibly damaged—certainly not as damaged as Amberdrake himself was. Another moment of blinding pain held him breathless for a few heartbeats. Then Amberdrake sat up, but slowly, for he had to inch his way over to the tether point of his leash before he could get the slack to sit.

His head protested every move with throbs of pain, reminding him sharply of why it had been a very stupid idea to go rushing off to Skan's rescue without additional help. As if he needed reminding.

"I suppose you rushed off to my rescue without any additional help, right?" Skan said with resignation. "Of course—everyone was being prepared for the Ceremony, but you're supposed to be mad *and* guarding yourself in the persona of Hawkwind, so you were excused as Amberdrake and Hawkwind both."

"So that's where the extra Kaled'a'in came from!" said a delighted voice. "I wondered. There were ten new bodies from White Gryphon, but *eleven* new bodies parading about!"

Amberdrake looked up at the grinning madman in the doorway, and his stomach turned over again, sending sour bile into the back of his throat. "Hadanelith," he said tonelessly, his head echoing painfully. "I won't say it's a pleasure to see you again. I suppose you've come to gloat? That's trite enough to be in your style."

Hadanelith strolled over to Amberdrake in a leisurely fashion, and stood just out of range of a kick, frowning down at him. "You know, Amberdrake, you should never have dyed your hair. It's just not a good look for you."

Amberdrake raised an eyebrow at Hadanelith, and his battered mind finally took in the lunatic's costume. He blinked, certain he was seeing things. Why would Hadanelith be wearing a copy of one of Amberdrake's formal outfits?

"At least you've gotten some sense of fashion," he replied, his mind searching frantically for some guess at what the madman was about to do. His stomach lurched again, and his skin crawled. He'd *seen* Hadanelith's handiwork...

"Oh, this little thing?" Hadanelith smoothed down the beaded placket at the neck of his tunic. "It's part of the plan, you see."

"Which you are going to tell us in excruciating detail," Skan moaned, as if he at least was not the slightest bit afraid of Hadanelith's plans, as if being bored was the worst of all possible tortures. "Oh *spare* us, will you? Good gods, does every half-baked villain have to boast about what he's going to do before he does it? Can't you just kill us so we don't have to endure your boring speech?"

Hadanelith turned to glare at the gryphon, and crossed his arms angrily over his chest. "Yes I *do* 'have to boast about it.' I want you to know how and why and the means. I want you to know everything, because there isn't anything you can do to stop it all, and I want you to lie there in agony because you're both helpless."

Skan groaned, but it was the groan of someone who was in dread of having to endure an after-dinner speech, not someone in fear of death. "You haven't come up with anything new, you know," he complained. "Whatever you think you've invented, some other idiot has tried before you. And Ma'ar was better and more imaginative at gloating than you. Trust me, I know."

Amberdrake clenched his muscles to keep from trembling; he knew exactly what the gryphon was up to, and he feigned an equal boredom as Hadanelith turned his back to the gryphon, his spine straight with indignation.

Listen to what he says, pretend to be interested, and he'll shut up. Tell him to get lost and take his little speech elsewhere, and he'll babble like a brook.

"You and all your friends are finished, kestra'chern," Hadanelith spat, turning back to Amberdrake.

Amberdrake yawned stiffly. His lip split and bled a little more. "Yes?" he replied indifferently. "And?"

Hadanelith's face grew red with rage. "You think you're all so clever," he snarled, flecks of spittle forming at the corners of his mouth. "You think you have everything taken care of. But you hadn't planned on magic, had you? *We* have magic, magic that works, *blood*-magic from those foolish women, and a few slaves and scum we took off the streets. We have magic enough to overcome anything; even if a mage-storm came right this moment, we have power enough to push through whatever we want."

Oh, gods. That explains everything. Amberdrake went very, very cold, and struggled not to show it. That was indeed one of the things no one had counted on—that someone was using the power of blood-born magic to push through spells that no longer worked in ordinary circumstances. He began to shake.

"We have a little surprise planned for the Eclipse Ceremony," Hadanelith continued, smiling now. "My friends here have a job they want me to do. Now normally, I wouldn't handle a job like this, but we're such good friends I thought I'd do them the favor." He raised an eyebrow archly. "Don't you want to know what it is?"

"Find the mind you lost?" Skan suggested. "Or could it be the virility you misplaced?"

Hadanelith flushed again, and ground his teeth together with rage. Amberdrake was fascinated, despite his screaming nerves. He'd never actually seen anyone grind his teeth with rage before. It was something you could actually *hear*—and all this time he'd thought it was just a cliché. "We are going to kill the King," Hadanelith got out from between his clenched jaws. "Publicly. At the height of the Ceremony."

He got himself back under control again, with a speed that would have been impressive if he hadn't been insane. He smiled sweetly at Amberdrake, a smile that struck the kestra'chern like a blow and stopped even his shivering. "And as a little present to you, dear Amberdrake," he said in a caressing tone, "we are going to kill Winterhart as well."

Amberdrake felt his face and body freezing into stone, along with his mind. His vision misted, and there was a roaring in his ears.

Hadanelith saw his reaction, and his smile widened. "My friends have more than enough power to whisk me away as soon as I finish the job," he continued with satisfaction. "Everyone will blame you Kaled'a'in, of course. The Black Gryphon will be proclaimed a coward and traitor to his own people, since he disappeared before the King's disposal. One of my friends has positioned himself to take advantage of all this, since the King hasn't yet declared an heir. He'll see to it that the rest of your contingent is rounded up and executed, and that war is declared on White Gryphon. At the end of it all, he'll be the great hero, and they'll probably demand that he take the Lion Throne before he can even claim it himself."

Amberdrake closed his eyes, fighting off a faint. *Winterhart—oh, gods*—He had to think, had to keep Hadanelith talking so he could get the *time* to think.

"Why should the Kaled'a'in take the blame?" he asked thickly, opening his eyes again. "The Haighlei aren't fools, you know—they don't think all Outlanders look alike! You aren't going to fool them by dressing up in one of my outfits."

"Oh, my very dear Amberdrake," Hadanelith said with a laugh that sent chills down his spine. "My dear, dear kestra'chern! They won't see *me* when they see the murderer!"

His features blurred, and for a moment Amberdrake wondered frantically if the blow to his head had done something to his eyes as well. But nothing else was blurring, and in a moment, Hadanelith's face sharpened into focus again.

Except that now it wasn't *Hadanelith's* face.

It was a face Amberdrake knew only too well, for he looked at it in mirrors several times every day. It was the face that Winterhart knew as her own beloved's.

"You see?" said Hadanelith. "These people so abhor magic that they'll never dream someone might be wearing an illusion! That is the gift I have given these people—my originality. They would never have thought of this. They won't see me when they see a Kaled'a'in murdering their King and his Consort-To-Be. They'll see you."

He laughed—or rather, giggled—a high-pitched whining sound that set Amberdrake even further on edge. *I'd have banished him for that laugh alone,* he thought irrelevantly.

"And the last thing, the very last thing that your dear, faithless lady will see," Hadanelith continued gleefully, "is her former lover gutting her with a smile on his face. *No one* will doubt that you are completely capable of killing her and her betrothed; you made that perfectly clear with your dramatic scene in front of the entire Court."

With a sickening wrench, Amberdrake realized that he himself had set the pattern for all of this. And it wasn't the King that Hadanelith wanted—it was Winterhart. He was murdering the King because that was the only way he could get at Winterhart.

"She should have been mine," Hadanelith said softly, as if he didn't realize that he was speaking aloud. Amberdrake sensed the depth of obsession there, and shuddered. How long had Hadanelith been like this? How long had he wanted Winterhart? He must have known he could never have her!

All those women back at White Gryphon—they were in Winterhart's pattern. Lean, elegant, strong-willed until he broke their will—why didn't I see that before!

"If I cannot have her for my own, then I shall make sure no one else has a chance to carve her into another image," Hadanelith whispered, confirming what Amberdrake had been thinking. Then he shook himself, and looked down at Amberdrake again with that odd, foam-flecked smile.

"A gut-stroke, I think," he said meditatively. "In at the navel, to the left, and up. She will linger quite agonizingly, but not long enough for a Healer to get to her in time to save her. Treasure that image in your mind, Amberdrake. Hold it until I come back. Then Skandranon and I will play some charming little games, until I decide whether I'm going to teach you some of my arts, or let you go."

"Let me go?" Amberdrake said, blinking stupidly, struggling against the multiple blows to his soul.

"Of course!" Hadanelith giggled again. "Why not? No one would ever believe you, and it would be such a major help to my friends if they were the ones to 'capture' you and bring you to justice! I understand that Haighlei executions are terribly entertaining."

As Amberdrake stared at him, Hadanelith raised his right hand and wiggled the fingers at him in a childish gesture of leavetaking. "Fare, but not well, dear Amberdrake."

Amberdrake expected him to walk out of the room in a normal fashion, but evidently that was not dramatic enough for him. He pirouetted in place—stepped to one side—and vanished.

"Kechara has all of this," Skan said hoarsely as soon as he disappeared. "That's why I wasn't talking much. She's relaying it to the others now."

Which was, of course, one thing that *Hadanelith* hadn't counted on.

"The problem is that everyone except Winterhart is too far back in the crowd to do any good," Skan continued desperately. "And Winterhart isn't a Mindspeaker, so they can't warn her. They've decked Aubri out with a ceremonial drape that's strapped down over his wings—he can't fly—"

"Never mind," Amberdrake said fiercely, as he willed his muscles to relax *here* and contract down hard *there*, and wriggled carefully in place. Got to *get the strap around my elbows down first*—His muscles protested sharply as he tried to squeeze his elbows together even tighter. *Got to get some slack in the ropes*—"There's something else Hadanelith forgot—"

They were silk ropes, very impressive to look at and very strong, but also very slick. If you knew what you were doing, silk was the worst of all possible bindings, though the most ostentatious.

The elbow ties dropped past the joints. Now he could ease them further down.

By squirming and shaking, he managed to inch the bindings around his elbows down to his wrists.

Thank the gods he didn't tether the elbow bindings to the back of the collar. Inexperienced binders work along the spine only, without thinking diagonally. The way he bound me, it looks nice, but isn't very hard to get out of—something a real kestra'chern would know.

He curled over backward until he got his wrists passed under his buttocks, then curled over forward and passed his legs through the arch of his arms. A moment later, he had his wrists in front of him and was untying the bindings on them with his teeth.

"I'm—a kestra'chern—Skan," he said, around the mouthful of slick cord. "A *real*—kestra'chern. I've probably—forgotten—more about knots—and restraints—than that impostor—ever learned. There!"

The cords fell away from his wrists, and the ones that had held his elbows followed them. He unfastened the collar—which was looped through but not even locked!—and crawled over to Skandranon. He could get his legs free later. *Now* it was important to get Skandranon out of here and into the air!

Skan's restraints were artistic, but not particularly clever or difficult to undo, either. "Dilettante!" he muttered, as he untied more silk cords and undid buckles. He had to mutter, to keep the fear at bay a little longer, or else it would paralyze him. "Rank amateur!"

Damn knots! Damn Hadanelith! Damn all these people to the coldest hells! I swear, if I had a knife—if Winterhart—oh, gods, if Winterhart—

Knife—Winterhart—

He blinked, and shook his head as the light took on a thin quality. "Is it me, or is the light fading—"

"It's not you," Skan said, his own voice rasping and frantic. "It's the Eclipse! That idiot Hadanelith *has* to be dramatic, he would never strike at any time but the height of the Eclipse! Hurry!"

"I'm *hurrying,*" Amberdrake snarled, doubtful if the red haze he saw was due to the Eclipse. "I'm *hurrying!*"

Shalaman stood tall and proud beneath his heavy weight of fine ceremonial robes, and surveyed his people.

They were gathered below him in a vast sea of faces, as many as could fit into the largest open section of Palace grounds. The Palace gates had been opened today to the public, as they were only opened on the most important of ceremonial occasions, and citizens of the city had been lined up for days to enter, squeezed in together on the other side of a barrier of guards, to view the Eclipse Ceremony with the Court. They were jammed together so tightly that none of them could move. The sheer numbers were overwhelming. Colors warred with each other, and the glare of sunlight on jewelry threw rainbow-hued flashes up into his eyes at unpredictable moments.

The heat down there must have been unbearable, but no one complained or showed any sign of it. This was the Eclipse Ceremony, and time for changes, and no one here wanted to miss a single word.

They were all silent, as his people seldom were. It was entirely possible to hear birds singing evening songs above the faint murmur of breathing and whispers. The light had been thinning for some time now—triggering the birds to go into their sunset melodies—and although it could not be said that the air was getting colder, the sunlight on his skin burned less with every passing moment.

To his right stood Winterhart, and to his left his three Advisors; otherwise, he was alone on the platform of three steps raising up above the level of the crowd. In his mind, he *was* alone, for he and he alone could make the decision about the people of White Gryphon. He was the King; they would listen. They loved him; they knew his loyalty to their interests.

He turned his troubled attention, though not his eyes, on the pale-skinned people from the north. They stood in a group, held away from the platform by an intervening phalanx of his personal bodyguards. He had not wanted to show them any particular favor until he had made up his mind.

He had to recalculate everything he had planned last night. All along, although he had permitted them to remain in doubt, he had planned to bring them into the "changes to come" portion of the ceremony, whether or not the actual murderers were found in time. It would have been better if they had been, of course, but that wasn't strictly necessary. Any words spoken by a Truthsayer during the latter half of the Ceremony had special import, and only today Shalaman had decided to call upon Leyuet to impart publicly all he had learned from the minds of Amberdrake and Winterhart. Having a Bound Couple in the Court would bring special blessings from the gods, and having Leyuet declare Amberdrake's innocence at that point in the Ceremony would give his words all the force of the Gods' Voices.

But he would need the Gryphon King to do that, to speak for his friend—and the Gryphon King was not in evidence. Amberdrake could not be there to speak for himself—officially, he was supposedly mad, and the mad were specifically excluded from the Ceremony.

Without either of the two principals, there was nothing he *could* do about the settlement and the people in it, not with murder charges hanging over them and no one to receive Leyuet's blessing and declaration of innocence.

He'd sent his men for the kestra'chern a few moments ago anyway, out of pure desperation. The priests wouldn't like the fact that Amberdrake hadn't been cleansed, but that was too bad. If Leyuet declared him sane, his presence wouldn't taint the Ceremony, and once that innocence was made public, the White Gryphon folk could be made allies. But his men weren't back yet, either, and he had taken up as much time with prayer and chanting as he could.

The one thing he could not delay was the Eclipse itself, and it was about to move into its final phase.

He looked down at the image of the sun's face, cleverly duplicated in the middle of a square of shadow at his feet. The shadow itself was cast by a thin plate of stone with a round hole in it, which allowed a single round beam of light to shine directly in front of the King. What happened to that round dot of sunlight was replicated in the heavens above, and there was a substantial bite in the circle, a bite of darkness that was visibly increasing. Out there in the gardens, the beams of light that filtered through the tree branches to fall on the ground also had bites of shadow taken out of them, forming dapples of crescents, and those who were wise were watching them instead of squinting up impotently at the sun-disk itself.

Still no sign of the Gryphon King or of Amberdrake.

This must be as the gods have willed it; we have certainly tried for another solution. With a heavy heart, he raised the staff of his office high over his head and began to intone the Words of Change.

And at that precise moment, as if the gesture had called him there, Amberdrake appeared on the second step of the platform out of thin air.

Shalaman stared at him, mouth agape. *What—the men must have found him—the priests must have built him a magical Portal and sent him directly here so that he would be in time!* He felt giddy with relief. Things were going to be fine after all.

But in the next instant, his relief turned to confusion. There was shouting and pushing down among the Kaled'a'in, and instead of rushing to greet her beloved, Winterhart gasped and recoiled from him.

And there was something very odd, and very *wrong*, with the hungry expression on Amberdrake's face. No sane human wore an expression like that!

Shalaman backed up a pace himself, a cold chill falling over his heart as he looked into Amberdrake's eyes. There was *no* sign of sanity there, and he wondered wildly if this were the real Amberdrake after all—if the man was demon-ridden, and this demonic side of him had been the one responsible for the murders! Certainly this man looked capable of any kind of evil!

The guards were not responding. *Of course they aren't! I told them myself to let him through when he arrived, and they can't see his face, so they don't know anything is wrong!*

Shalaman opened his mouth to call for help—

And could not get any sound to come out.

Nor could he move. He was held in place as securely as if someone had bound him in chains and stood him there. He struggled against his invisible bonds to no avail; they held him fast in the position he had last taken, staff held above his head and free arm outstretched, to the sun.

And the last of the sun slipped behind the moon, throwing them all into darkness.

Amberdrake laughed, a horrible, high-pitched giggling; he pulled a knife out of the breast of his tunic, and lunged up the stairs toward Shalaman while the folk of White Gryphon struggled against the guards, shouting incoherently.

Amberdrake screamed and lunged forward with the knife in a vicious series of slashes, cutting the darkness with the glitter of his blade, displaying a knife-fighter's threat show, weaving a pattern of death in the air.

The space of a single breath passed, and a slim figure in silver interposed itself between Shalaman and his assassin.

It was *not* Winterhart—who was dressed in gold, and who was backing away from the assailant with her face frozen in a silent scream.

It was Silver Veil.

Every kestra'chern is taught self-defense, for every kestra'chern may one day require it, she had said once, when he'd expressed worry over her safety. *Every kestra'chern knows the body of man and woman, and knows where to strike if need be.* He had smiled indulgently, then, and with a hint of disbelief. Those were the sort of things a warrior-trainer said to impress his Captain, and were usually of dubious worth. *Now* he believed!

The lovely kestra'chern whirled in a flurry of skirts, and kicked at the assassin's legs, connecting with them expertly and bringing him down on his knees.

But the man was faster than Shalaman could have believed possible; he scrambled to his feet again, and as she tried a second kick, he caught her foot in one hand, then twisted in place and whirled, sending her crashing, gasping, to the ground in a tangle of silver fabric.

And once again, the assassin lunged toward Shalaman, this time unopposed.

Shalaman closed his eyes, the only parts of him that he could still move, and commended his soul to the gods.

At least I shall perish bravely, though I shall not perish as a warrior. Silver Veil, I shall never forget you—

The gods, however, decided that they did not want his soul—at least not right then.

A battle-screech rang out from overhead, and all heads searched the dim sky for its source. Even the assassin jumped, turned, and stared.

Out of the black sun-disk, out of the midnight-at-noon, the Gryphon King plunged with a scream of defiance that shattered the confusion and pierced the spell holding Shalaman captive.

Shalaman flung himself away from the assassin—and toward Silver Veil. The assassin frantically found the right direction—just in time to fling his paltry knife up in puny defense against ten razor-talons and the unstoppable force of stooping predator.

Skandranon, the Black Gryphon, drove the assassin into the stone with a great crunch of breaking bone, sending the blade skittering away—

Just as the sun appeared again from behind the moon, frosting the great gryphon's wings and glinting off his eyes.

The guards at last realized what was happening and started to rush up to the platform, but the Black Gryphon was not yet finished with his wonder-working. He gripped the assassin's face with one clawed hand, made a savage gesture in the air with one talon of the other hand—

And the face of Amberdrake melted away, leaving an entirely unfamiliar—and rapidly bruising—stranger beneath the claws of the gryphon.

Shalaman straightened, still keeping himself between the assassin and Silver Veil. The stranger squealed and struggled, then shrieked with pain as his many freshly broken bones announced themselves to him.

Winterhart took a single look at the man and gasped in recognition.

She started to babble something at Shalaman, but in her distress she was speaking in her own tongue and he couldn't make out a single hysterical word, so he waved at her to be silent. Skandranon mantled at the stranger, all but killing him with his glare. The crushed man soiled himself, unable to stop moving in his sobs of terror.

"Here is your murderer, King Shalaman," Skandranon rumbled angrily. "Here is the man who slew your courtiers in ways not even a mad beast would contemplate, for the sake of collecting the magic power of death and blood, and who held both myself and Amberdrake captive so that his plan to murder you could be completed. He is an exile from among our own people, and I regret that we cast him out instead of finishing him then. We left it to the forest to dispose of a mad beast that we should have dealt with ourselves. He is the one who used his skill in killing to counterfeit the effects of magic, mimicking death-spells with death-skill. *That* was why it looked as if a mage had done the deeds."

"If he is yours——" Shalaman began doubtfully.

Skandranon shook his head. "He is no more 'ours' than the garbage that we bury in the clean earth," the gryphon replied. "We repudiated him and cast him out before we ever met your people. He is not ours, if you are offering him up to our judgment. He is as much yours as any mankilling beast who murders the innocent. He has committed crimes against you and yours, and you may do with him what you will."

Shalaman took a long, steadying breath. "Then you turn him over to us, to be dealt with by our laws?"

Skandranon narrowed his eyes at the whimpering Hadanelith. "He should live so long."

"Lies!" shrieked the captive suddenly. "It is all lies! They cast me out because I would not use my skills for their plans! They——"

"Silence!" Skandranon boomed, tightening his claws on the man's throat until only a faint wheeze could be heard. Sweat stood out on the assassin's pale forehead, and Shalaman might have been tempted to feel sorry for him, if the accusations against him had not been so terrible, and his guilt so sure.

But just to be certain, Shalaman looked to Leyuet, who shook his head. "I need not even trance, Serenity," he said clearly, but with

immense dignity. "It is this man who lies. His soul—I dare not touch it."
The Truthsayer was gray, and he shivered as if with a fever. "It is vile,
filthy—as fully unclean as yours is pure."

There were murmurs of fear and anger from those in the crowd who
were near enough to hear, but no doubt—and those in the first ranks
turned to spread the word back to the ones behind. The word passed
rapidly as Shalaman waved to his guards to come forward.

The man began screaming again, but his words made no sense.
"Noyoki, you bastard!" he howled. "Get me away! You promised! Get
me away! Help me! *Help me!*"

Was there some rescue that was supposed to have taken place? If so,
it appeared that this assassin had colleagues. But "Noyoki?" No one?
What kind of a name was that?

"Your conspirators have deserted you, fool," Shalaman said sternly to
the struggling, screaming man. "Think of this, as you wait my justice."

Where is Amberdrake? Could he be the reason that no one had rescued
the assassin?

No time to think of that now. The guards dragged the assassin away,
followed by two priests, hastily waved there by Palisar, who presumably
would prevent any escapes by magic means. The assassin was screaming
at the top of his lungs, but his words were no longer coherent.

Shalaman could and would deal with him later. What was important
was the completion of the Ceremony.

Silver Veil had gathered herself back up again, although evidencing
a limp, and was back in her place. The Gryphon King remained beside
Winterhart on the platform. Shalaman turned again to face his people,
resolutely putting Amberdrake and his fate out of his mind.

"By the grace of the gods and the strength of my friends, I have
been spared to serve you!" he called out in a voice that would carry
to the edges of the courtyard. "Here is the omen for changes—that
Skandranon, the Gryphon King, once as White as his city, has come to
my aid in the shape of a Black Gryphon King, and has struck down the
murderer of our nobles with his own hands! What say you, my people?
Shall we ally ourselves with these honorable folk of the north? Shall we
add another Black King to the ranks of the Haighlei?"

The roar of assent was more than enough to drown out any few
dissenters. Shalaman bowed slightly in acknowledgment, and turned
to Winterhart. He pitched his voice deeply, so as to be heard over the
crowd noise.

"Would you give me back the Necklace, my dear?" he asked, looking into her strange, foreign eyes.

She smiled and pulled it off over her head, handing it to him with relief that she did not even try to conceal.

She is soul-bonded to Amberdrake. Surely if something had happened to him, she would know. Wouldn't she?

He took the Necklace, and walked to Silver Veil's side of the platform, where she stood flanked by Palisar and Leyuet. One thing at a time, and the first thing *must* be Silver Veil. She looked shaken, but otherwise unhurt.

Unhurt—except for the fear she had felt for *his* sake, the shadows of which still lingered in her eyes. That was enough; it gave him all the insight that he needed to see into his own heart.

I never wanted Winterhart. I will find a solution for the problems this will make, later. I will not let this opportunity escape.

"You would have died for me," he said, as the crowd quieted, sensing more drama to come. He felt their presence at his back, heavy, uncomprehending—but in the joy of the moment, willing to accept anything he decreed. He was the King, and this was the time of changes.

She nodded; Leyuet held his breath. But Palisar, grim, dour Palisar, was—was he smiling? And would he remain smiling when he saw what Shalaman meant to do?

"You would have died for me. Would you live for me as well?" he asked. "Would you live for me only?"

He held out the Necklace to her, keeping his eyes on her face and nothing else.

She did not feign surprise, nor did she affect a coy shyness. She was too complex for the former and too honest for the latter. But her eyes lit up with a joy that told *him* everything he needed to know.

His heart's desire had matched hers, and she had kept hers hidden all this time to avoid putting pressure on him. He knew that as if he had been a Truthsayer, to read her soul.

Her joy was doubled by the fact that she had never truly expected to have that heart's desire fulfilled.

"I would, my King," she said simply, "If you will have me."

He raised the Necklace high overhead, then lowered it to place it around her neck as she bent her head to receive it.

Shalaman spared a glance to his other two Advisors. Leyuet's hands were clasped in front of him and *his* face was alive with pleasure—but oddly enough, so was Palisar's!

"You have Year-Sons enough to choose an heir, Serenity," Palisar said, very softly. "Marry now for joy."

That had been the final real obstacle; Palisar's supposed disapproval had fallen like a card balanced upon one edge, and with as little fuss.

He took Silver Veil's hand and led her to the edge of the platform. Once again, a complete silence fell over the crowd.

"To help flush out the murderer, Lady Winterhart posed as my bride-to-be, and honorable Amberdrake feigned madness in a plan to lure the true madman. Let it be known that the honorable leaders of White Gryphon risked their lives and reputations to save Haighlei from murder. Let it be known that the gods themselves have blessed this Palace with a Soul-bonded pair—Lady Winterhart and Kestra'chern Amberdrake."

The people were clearly stunned, even after mentally preparing themselves for the Eclipse Ceremony and all that it entailed. "This is the season of changes," he said into that silence. "And let it begin with the King wedding his beloved Silver Veil!"

The crowd went insane, cheering and bouncing in place, waving scarves in the air where there was room to move. Even the guards were smiling!

He had not realized that Silver Veil was so popular with the people— all the more reason to wed her! A King could not do better with his people, if his Consort proved to be a popular Advisor, popular with the people as well as the nobles.

She moved to the position that Winterhart had held during the first half of the ceremony. Winterhart had already fallen modestly back to a new place beside the weary Gryphon King.

Shalaman surveyed his cheering, joyous people, as the sun brightened with every passing moment, and his heart filled with a content he had never expected to experience.

He held up the staff, and they fell silent again, this time in pleasurable expectation.

"Hear, all ye people, the changes that are to come!" he boomed into the stillness. "We shall ally with the people of White Gryphon, who bring us new arts and new beasts, a touch of the new to every part of our land and life. We add another King to the Haighlei, Skandranon, the Black Gryphon. I take as my bride, my Consort, and my Advisor, the Silver Veil. From this day, it will be allowable that a King may choose to wed his kestra'chern."

He continued, enumerating all the changes, great and small, that he and his Advisors had determined would be reasonable and acceptable for the next years. The litany went on, but his real thoughts were elsewhere.

I have been given my life by these strangers, he thought, *And—I have been given awareness of my true love. What more could they have given me? I will be in debt to them for the rest of my life, but it is a debt I will joyfully strive to repay.*

Shalaman felt the supporting presence of his beloved and his friends at his back, and smiled at the crowd. He even smiled at Skandranon's grumbling.

"I hope this is over soon. I'm scheduled to fall down and twitch," the gryphon murmured. "Then I'm due to eat everything in sight and sleep for two days, and then—"

Shalaman stifled a laugh at the explicit description of what the Gryphon King would be doing with his mate Zhaneel. These people of White Gryphon would shock and delight his Court for a long time.

Only one shadow still darkened his joy.

Where was Amberdrake?

CHAPTER ELEVEN

Amberdrake worked the last of his bonds loose, and stood up, hands and feet still tingling. He wished he could ignore the sensation; the best he could do was to keep from making too much noise about it.

Now—find those others Hadanelith mentioned. There are probably two; maybe more, but he talked as if there were only two.

If anyone had ever described Amberdrake to his face as a courageous man, he would have laughed. He had never considered bravery to be one of his chief attributes; that was for others, not for him. He was able to recognize bravery when he saw it, but it was never a quality he would have granted to himself. He was often afraid, and knew it, and did not scruple to show it. Not that brave people weren't afraid, but they were able to get beyond their fear to act. Amberdrake knew, in his heart, that fear often paralyzed him.

Thinking on it, he would not have granted himself *physical* bravery, the kind of bravery that made Skan and Zhaneel fly off and risk their lives, over and over, as if such risk was no worse than a cold bath on a winter morning.

And right now, he felt as if he were the biggest coward in this whole shattered world. As Skan vanished out of sight, all Amberdrake wanted to do was find somewhere to hide until the whole mess was over. He wished he could find a nice, secure room and lock the door so that no one could get at him. That *would* be the sensible course, really—what could he expect to accomplish?

There's no way I can just hide when the most powerful and dangerous of our enemies are both here, somewhere, wherever that is. Something has to be done about them. They may be engrossed with whatever magic they're controlling, or they may be confident they've already won, or—

With no real Mindspeaking ability of his own, he would not know whether Skan arrived in time to save the King and Winterhart until long after the fact. The light grew dimmer with every passing heartbeat—and Hadanelith was due to strike at the darkest part of the Eclipse. No one knew he was here except Skandranon and Kechara. Assuming that Kechara wasn't watching Skan, *she* would know what was happening on his side of this little battle, but otherwise he was on his own.

And somehow I doubt she'll be able to tear her mind away from her "Papa Skan."

Was this how Skan felt when he went off on one of those famous solitary missions? Lonely—and deserted—and completely terrified?

Not terrified, not Skan. He's been scared, but always confident in himself.

Kechara might be able to call for help if things went wrong and she *was* watching him, but that also assumed that she had enough understanding of what she saw to tell the others if Amberdrake was in trouble. She had shown a surprising grasp of abstracts lately, but—well, she was tired, and stressed, and under a great deal of pressure, more than she ever should have had to bear. Little Kechara was more toddler than warrior.

No. I'm on my own here. His insides knotted up as he acknowledged that. *I have to find those so-called "friends" of Hadanelith's, and I have to neutralize them before they can rescue him. If all that means is that I occupy their attention until he's secured against magic, then that's what I'll do.*

That certainly sounded brave enough. He only wished that it was going to be as easy as it sounded.

But they were all running out of time; he'd better find Hadanelith's co-conspirators before the full Eclipse fell!

He gathered up what "weapons" he could find—the ropes he'd been bound with, and a length of metal bar. He picked them all up so quietly that there wasn't even a scrape of metal against the floor, even though he knew objectively that the noise was negligible. At least while he was concentrating on keeping quiet, he could convince his body to move, and not freeze like a frightened tree-hare. He crept toward the door, listening with all his concentration after he made each step. His hands shook so hard he nearly dropped the bar. He closed his eyes and swallowed, willing his hands to stop shaking, but they wouldn't. Finally he reached the doorway; he plastered himself flat against the wall next to the door, and listened again, this time holding his breath.

Nothing. Not even a distant murmur of voices. No matter how thick the walls were, this close to the door he'd surely hear something if there was anyone out there! Wouldn't he?

Carefully, he reached out to the door handle, and eased the door open a crack, his teeth clenched as he waited for the hinges to groan. *That would be just my luck.* But the hinges were silent, and he heard nothing, and there was no sign of a guard on the other side.

Meanwhile, the logical part of his mind was still worrying away at the problem of who Hadanelith's co-conspirators were. *This is—probably—a suite in the Palace, which means that one of Hadanelith's friends must belong to the Court. But who could it be?* Unfortunately, Amberdrake had no idea who was quartered where; probably only the Chamberlain would know that. He'd been under the impression that this section of the Palace was about empty. The rooms were not very desirable; they were all too near the outer walls, and the sentries and far-off noise of the city disturbed the nights. There were only a few gardens shared among the suites here, and the entire section was a little too damp during the winter. The only people who lived here, so *he'd* thought, were those too lowly in status to complain about the rooms they were granted. That seemed to fit with someone of low rank, perhaps exacting revenge for being overlooked and slighted, and finding a shortcut to exalted status as well.

But that didn't mean that someone who was quite *high* in status couldn't commandeer a suite or two, especially if they were empty. The conspirators' knowledge of the movements of the courtiers seemed to be that of someone familiar with the ebb and flow of the court.

Then there was Hadanelith's assertion that one of his "friends" could take the Lion Throne, which also argued for a high status. Yet, all the King's Year-Sons were in the guard of his fellow rulers, which would make it rather difficult for one of them to be there and here at the same time.

Unless a Year-Son is using magic to transport himself! Oh, surely that would have been noticed! Or—could he have found someone to impersonate him, and crept back here! That's even more far-fetched a notion than the use of magic to transport him. Impersonators are less reliable than magic—

Or were they? He clenched his eyes closed as he thought about Hadanelith impersonating him, closing in on Winterhart, cutting once to the side, again, up—

Pull yourself together, Amberdrake. Think. Think about what you have learned. Lifebonded pairs can feel each other. If she was hurt, you'd feel—

He'd feel sick, he realized with a lurch of his stomach. What if it wasn't fear for himself that was making his hands shake so? What if this was the side effect of feeling his beloved Winterhart die, somewhere far away?

And what if it isn't! Think, Amberdrake—alive or dead or dying, would Winterhart admire you for shaking and hiding! You have to act. No matter what happens to Winterhart or you, you have to act for the good of White Gryphon.

Amberdrake eased the door open a little more; there was still no reaction indicating someone out in the hallway. He turned his intellect back to narrowing down or eliminate possible suspects; he had a particular suspicion of his own, and he devoutly hoped it was wrong.

But the doubt kept recurring—*could it be Palisar!*

It was a horrible suspicion, no matter how you looked at it.

It was an unworthy suspicion, because he knew very well he would never have entertained it if Palisar hadn't been so openly hostile to the foreigners. But if the Haighlei had customs and rituals for everything, perhaps the Speaker was prohibited from hiding his true feelings, even if it would mean giving himself away to those he plotted against.

But he kept wondering... for certainly there was no one better placed than Palisar to know everything about the movements of every courtier in the Palace. Who better to know exactly what was going on, and who better to know which courtier was vulnerable and which was not?

Add to that the fact that Palisar was a priest, a trusted priest. Who better to *ensure* that the chosen victim was alone? If Palisar sent messages to each of the women who'd been murdered, telling them he needed to talk to them alone, wouldn't they have made sure to send every servant off on errands to obey him? He was the King's Advisor, and it might be presumed that the King had a message he wished to send discreetly. He was a priest, and it might be thought that as a priest he had something of a spiritual nature to discuss. Both of those would require absolute privacy.

And he's a mage—there's another thing. If he's anything like our mages, he's been frantic with frustration at the way magic has been rendered unreliable. Our people have tried every way short of blood-magic to bring things back under control, and even Snowstar admitted to me that the temptation to resort to that is a great one after you've had your spells abort one too many times. What if Palisar has gotten his hands burnt too many times by the storms! What if he didn't resist that temptation to resort to blood-bought power!

Granted, every single one of those arguments could be applied to every single priest-mage among the Haighlei, but still—Palisar disapproved of the foreigners, of change in general, and possessed everything required to be the one holding Hadanelith's leash.

I don't know how the succession goes around here, but as a powerful Advisor, he could have some blood-ties to the King. If he has royal blood, he could see a chance at the throne he wouldn't otherwise get.

Amberdrake touched the door again, easing it open still more. Now it was held ajar enough he could squeeze through it if he wanted to.

I don't want to, but I don't have a choice. He shivered, and clenched his trembling fingers tightly around the iron bar he carried. Even if Skan made it to the Ceremony in time to stop Hadanelith, if Hadanelith got away somehow, things would be worse than they had been before the Ceremony. It would still *look* as if Amberdrake had been the one trying to kill the King.

They're going to want to kill me on sight! The King is going to have orders out to strike first and bring back the body, and I doubt he's going to listen to anything Skan has to say!

Not that Amberdrake could blame him, in the abstract.

What am I doing, just standing here! I have to do something to keep the conspirators from rescuing Hadanelith. Good answer, Drake—and as soon as you magically transform into a squad of mercenaries, it will be no worry at all.

The room began to darken visibly. The last part of the Eclipse must be starting. His time was running out; Hadanelith would strike any moment now! And what if the mages—or mage—wasn't *here*, but was somewhere else entirely?

For a moment, he panicked, then logic asserted itself. *Hadanelith's not predictable enough to be left unsupervised. He was gloating, so he wouldn't see a need to lie. He is insane, but he was never known to lie. He implied they were here, so they have to be here, probably scrying the Ceremony to see when to snatch their assassin back again.*

That made good sense. It also meant that he'd better do something *now.*

Something physical? Against two or more people? Not a good idea. *I'm not a fighter. I do know self-defense, but that isn't going to help me attack someone. What do I have left!*

Bluff!

Well, why not! It couldn't hurt. It could buy time, and as soon as everything is over, Skan can send me help. While I'm bluffing them, they aren't going to be doing anything but watching me. If Skan can catch Hadanelith, the time I buy could give the King's people a chance to shield him against rescue.

Assuming one of them isn't Palisar—

He shook his head angrily, with cold fear a great lump of ice lodged just below his heart. If he kept on arguing with himself, he wouldn't *get* a chance to do anything! Time was slipping away, and the Eclipse wasn't going to delay for anyone or anything.

He pushed the door open, to find himself, not in a hallway, but on the top of a set of stairs. This must be one of the corner towers of Fragrant Joy, where the "suite" was a series of rooms on a private staircase. Very handy, if one was expecting to send an accomplice out over the rooftops at night. And very convenient, if you wanted to isolate a madman in a place he'd find it hard to escape from.

He stalked noiselessly down the staircase as the light grew dimmer and dimmer, listening for the sound of voices. The hand holding the iron bar was beginning to go numb, he was squeezing it so hard. He passed one room without hearing anything, but halfway down to the ground floor he picked up a distant, uneven hum that might have been conversation. A few steps downward, around the turn, and he knew it was voices. A few more, and he distinctly caught the word, "Hadanelith."

He clenched his free hand on the stair-rail, grimly, as his knees went to jelly. It was the other conspirators, all right. Two of them, just as he'd thought, from the sound of the voices. Unless there were others there who weren't speaking.

He pushed the thought that he might be struck down the moment he crossed the threshold resolutely out of his mind. If he thought about it, he'd faint or bolt right back up the stairs again. His throat was tight, and his breath came short; every muscle in his back and neck was knotted up. Every sound was terribly loud, and his eyes felt hot. He forced himself onward. One step. Another. He reached the bottom; there were no more stairs now. He faced a hallway, with several doors along it. He knew which one he wanted, though. It was the first one; the one that was open just a crack, enough to let light from inside shine out into the hall.

The staircase was lit by a skylight with frosted glass at the top; it grew darker and darker in the stairwell, until by the time he reached the door he wanted, it was as dark as early dusk. The voices on the other side of the door were very clear, and it was with a feeling of relief that left him light-headed that he realized neither of the two speakers was Palisar.

It didn't sound as if there was anyone else there; he took a chance, braced himself, and kicked the door open.

It crashed into the wall on the other side; hit so hard that the entire wall shook, and the two men sitting at a small, round table looked up at him with wide and startled eyes.

Bluff, Drake!

The room was well-lit by three lanterns, a smallish chamber without windows, it held the round table in the middle, some bookcases against the walls, and not much else. There were more things on the shelves than books, though he didn't have the time to identify anything. The men had something between them on the tabletop—a ceramic scrying-bowl, he thought. So his guess had been right!

"Put your hands flat on the table, both of you!" he boomed, using his voice as he'd been taught, so long ago, to control a crowd. He hadn't used command-voice much until the journey west; now it came easily, second nature. "I am a special agent for Leyuet and the Spears of the Law! You are to surrender!"

The two men obeyed, warily and not instantly. That was a bad sign…

"We know everything," he continued, stepping boldly into the room. "We have Hadanelith in custody, and he is being *quite* cooperative. You might as well save all of us time and trouble, and do the same. We know he was working for you; we also know that he was the only one who committed those murders. Since you didn't actually commit the crimes themselves, His Serenity the Emperor might be lenient enough to grant you your lives if you show remorse and confess."

Was that a good enough bluff! Do they believe me! They still looked shocked and a bit surprised, but the signs of both reactions were vanishing rapidly. Too rapidly.

At that moment, the last of the light faded behind him. Hadanelith was about to strike! He had to keep their attention off that bowl and on him! Or, eliminate the bowl itself—

Oh, gods. What do I do if they try something? He repeated himself, nearly word for word, taking another step forward every few seconds. And meanwhile, he kept straining his senses, hoping for some warning if either of them moved, hoping to have an instant or two in which to act.

And do what!

* * *

Skandranon felt a deep-in-the-flesh pain he hadn't felt in a decade, and it radiated out from him badly enough to make Winterhart, Silver Veil, and anyone else sensitive wince. He had been starved and dehydrated, trapped in an unforgiving position for many hours—days!—regardless of his bodily needs, and then forced to fly and fight at a moment's notice. His wingtips shivered with the strain of burning off his body's last reserves.

I am useless now, physically—I'll be lucky to reach our quarters without collapsing. So all I have left is my mind and words.

So he muttered about this and that while the last of the Eclipse Ceremony went on, purposely keeping his voice omnipresent. When at last it felt right, and Palisar was speaking to the assembled sea of people, the Black Gryphon caught Shalaman's attention.

"Amberdrake freed me to save you, before freeing himself," he rumbled. "He may still be in great danger from Hadanelith's accomplices."

Shalaman's countenance took on a new expression, one that the gryphon instinctively knew as that of the King on one of his famous Hunts. To Skandranon's amazement, he unclasped his ceremonial robes and let them fall, leaving only his loose Court robe, then snatched a spear from one of Leyuet's men. "You tell me where," Shalaman said, steely-eyed and commanding, while his personal bodyguards fell in behind him.

The Black Gryphon nodded, then closed his eyes, reaching out with hope. *:Kechara, Kechara, love—please hear me.: :Papa Skan!:*

The voice was there as clear as always, with only a little more than usual of the odd echo that usually accompanied fatigued Mindspeaking. *:Papa! Are you having fun!:*

Skandranon couldn't resist a huge mental smile. Kechara wouldn't understand what was going on if he spent two lifetimes trying to explain it to her. What was important to her was "fun" or "not-as-much-fun."

:Papa! Are you hurt! You feel like you have an "ow.":

:Yes, dear heart, I got hurt a little. I'm very tired. Kechara, love, I need you to look for Amberdrake. Find Amberdrake and help him. Can you do that for me!:

There was a pause, and then, *:All right! I miss you!:* Then Kechara was gone from his mind. King Shalaman straightened up and repeated himself. "You tell me where."

Skandranon met the King's eyes and understood. It was The Haighlei Way. He opened his beak to say, "Follow me," then stopped himself. No. That was not what a King would say to another on his own ground.

Skandranon took a deep breath, refolded his wings, and summoned his last bit of endurance. "Run beside me, King Shalaman, as you rim in your great lion hunts, and I will guide you. But we must make haste."

Amberdrake knew, as he flexed his grip on the silk rope and the bar, that his words and acting had failed him. The novelty of his speech was gone. Bluff or not, his status as just one man would catch up with him. Despite what history would show, for better or worse, now was the time for him to throw himself on fate's mercy.

He flung the coil of rope at the table, then pulled, twisting his body sideways with all the strength he could muster. There was a splash and a scrape, and a moment later, a resounding thunk as the scrying-bowl struck the floor. Amberdrake continued his twist and brought the iron bar down on the bowl to shatter it into a dozen pieces.

That was it, Drake—your one move.

He came to rest on one knee, looking up at the two.

But at that moment, he heard—well, it wasn't precisely a *voice* in his mind, and he didn't quite *hear* it—

It was a sense of presence, not words, just feelings, and the aura of boundless cheer and playfulness overlaid with weariness, but bolstered by endless curiosity.

Kechara! he thought, hard, trying to project the image of herself back to her.

Feeling of assent. Before he could respond, she sent him a new sensation; intensified curiosity. It didn't take a genius to figure out what she was asking, either. "What are you doing?" was as clear in feelings as in words.

He was breathless with relief—dizzy with the feeling that he was, at last, no longer alone.

But how had she figured out how to reach him? She was using his *strongest* Gift, that of Empathy, to speak with him without Mindspeech! Where had she gotten *that* idea?

Fear rose screaming inside him. He didn't have any way to explain what he was doing—not without words!

Do what Skandranon would do, Drake—do without words—without focused intellect—let her feel it—let her in!

He had never, ever, lowered his barriers completely with anyone but Winterhart, for an Empath always has to fear being lost in another's emotions—but how could he ever fear little Kechara? There wasn't an unkind bone in her body! He dropped every barrier he had to her, and let her come directly into his mind, just as the light began to creep back and the Eclipse to pass off.

He felt his body slip away from him—felt his back and arms go limp—

One of the two men at the table slid noiselessly out of his chair and seized something from a bookcase against the wall. As the man turned, he came fully into the lamplight, making what was in his hand gruesomely plain.

Amberdrake's stomach lurched, and he sensed Kechara recoiling as well, mimicking his reaction, though she couldn't have any idea what they were both looking at.

It was a wand, crudely fashioned from bone. It *could* have been made of animal bone, but somehow Amberdrake knew that it wasn't. No, this was not just *any* bone, but a human bone, the large bone from the thigh. From one of the earlier victims? *Probably. Probably the first. We'll never know who, I suspect.* Somehow that just made it worse.

This grisly relic must be the mage's primary power-focus, the place where he was storing all the power stolen from those Hadanelith had murdered for him, and all the people he had murdered on his own.

Amberdrake stared at it, his gorge rising and bile collecting at the back of his throat. He couldn't move; he couldn't even think. He could only stare at the nauseating thing, as the mage took in his shock and paralysis, and smiled, slightly. The light strengthened, and the mage moved the wand in front of him, holding it between his palms, and his smile deepened. The other man leaned back in his chair and chuckled. That was when Amberdrake realized that neither of these two had been fooled for an instant. His heart and courage plummeted. They knew he was alone.

This mage was about to level a magical blow at him—and he didn't even have the defenses of a mouse.

He tried to move, and discovered that he couldn't; the bar dropped from his numb fingers and clattered on the floor. This was no spell. It was nothing but pure, overwhelming fear.

I am going to die.

It wasn't even a guess. It was a fact.

:BAD MANS!: Kechara screamed into his mind.

He reeled and dropped to both knees beside his iron bar, momentarily "blinded" and "deafened" by her mental shout, so strong it was clear even to someone who was not a Mindspeaker. Both of the men facing him went stiff with surprise, as if they "heard" it too. Instinctively, he threw up his shields again—which was what she had been waiting for.

:Bad, bad mans!: she screeched again, this time accompanying her angry scream with a building mental shriek, aimed at the two facing him. It came like a windstorm that would not stop building, filling his ears.

The two conspirators were *not* expecting anything of the sort. Neither was Amberdrake, for that matter. He was so used to thinking of Kechara as a child, as a complete and total innocent, that he had underestimated her entirely. He had forgotten that she had more than enough experience to recognize a "bad man" when she saw one.

Both of Amberdrake's opponents collapsed on the spot.

:Ow,: said Kechara, with a mental wince—and her presence vanished from his mind.

Ow, indeed. For one moment, he took the time to shiver in awe at her power—and to be very glad that she had the guidance of all of her friends who loved and cared for her. *Now* he understood why Urtho had kept her locked up in his Tower for so very long. Her range in Mindspeaking was impressive enough to have made her valuable, but this demonstration of her full potential had been considerably more than impressive. With that kind of mental power, she could have been so dangerous—

Danger. He hadn't been mindblasted by Kechara, but he couldn't move either. He had just experienced, with certainty, imminent death, and he could only sit among the pieces of broken pottery and stare at the still bodies of the two conspirators.

"*Drake!*" a voice called from above, after an indeterminate amount of time. All he could tell, when such matters came to mind through the shock, was that it was fully light again outside. "*Drake! Are you all right! Where are you!*"

"Down here, at the bottom of the stairs!" he croaked back. A few moments later, Skan, Aubri, *and* Zhaneel came tumbling breathlessly down the staircase, following the sounds of a great many hard-shod feet from the presumed direction of the outer door.

"*Drake!*" Skan bellowed, as soon as he caught sight of Amberdrake, making him wince and shake his head as his ears rang. The gryphon grabbed him with both foreclaws, seizing him and staring at him as if he was afraid that Amberdrake would vanish or crumble into dust in the next instant. "Drake—Kechara said you were in trouble, then she just—just blanked out on us. We thought something had happened to both of you! We thought you were—"

"Kechara was right, I was in trouble," Amberdrake interrupted, before Skan could work himself up into hysterics.

Not that he hasn't earned a few hysterics. For that matter, so have I!

With a dazed look he was certain made him look very silly—as if vanity could matter at a moment like this—he peered around at the people filling the area. That was when he recognized King Shalaman.

"This one—" he pointed at the larger man "—is your bloodmage. He was just about to level me with a magical attack, when—I broke their scrying-bowl and they fell down." Amberdrake shrugged. He and the gryphons exchanged hasty warning glances; they all knew Kechara was somehow involved, and they also knew about the prohibition on Mindspeaking. It would be a great deal better for all concerned if the Haighlei never learned about Kechara.

Shalaman said nothing, staring unflinchingly through slitted eyes at one of the motionless—but still living—bodies.

"Gods save us!" one of Shalaman's bodyguards stammered. "That is the Disgraced One. The Nameless One."

"Who?" Skan said, "What? What are you talking about?"

"This is the One With No Honor," Shalaman said levelly. "My brother."

The "Nameless One" was bundled up like so much trash, put under as many magical bindings and coercions as the priests could get to work, and then hustled off to some unknown destination. His compatriot was not even treated with the respect one gives sewage. Somehow, Amberdrake had the feeling that this was going to be the most pleasant portion of their experiences with the priests…

Neither Amberdrake nor Skandranon were permitted to leave, although Aubri and Zhaneel were told politely to return to the main part of the Palace with Shalaman and his bodyguard, and wait for them. Amberdrake wasn't particularly worried; actually, he was *wearied*, not worried. In many ways, he and Skan were the heroes of the moment; you don't mistreat your heroes, not even when they've learned something politically delicate, so he didn't have any fear that the "escort" was a thinly veiled guard. In the meantime, he leaned against Skandranon, resting in the glossy black feathers.

Eventually, Leyuet himself arrived, and with him, Palisar.

Skan pulled himself up to his full height as they came through the door, and leveled a stern eye on both of them. "All right," he said. "I assume that we are still here because we now know something that is delicate. So you wanted to speak to us in relative privacy, with no other ears about but those of the Spears. So—speak. You can start with this so-called Nameless One, and what he did to get that way. The sooner we know, the sooner we can eat and bathe and sleep and climb our mates, in whatever order feels right at the time."

"I understand. I would rather not speak of this one," Palisar said with distaste as he took a seat. "Hadanelith has already revealed to us that this piece of trash called himself Noyoki, which means No One, and we would all wish he had *been* no one." Palisar's brows knitted together as he frowned. "He is a blot upon the honor of his family. Still, you have earned the right to know all, and Shalaman has ordered us to reveal it to you. I will not swear you to an oath, but I would ask that what we tell you goes no farther than your respective mates. The fewer who know the whole of this, the better."

He looked pointedly at the two Spears still in the room. They took the hint, and left, closing the door behind him firmly. Amberdrake leaned forward, expectantly.

"The 'Nameless One' is Shalaman's brother," Leyuet began, but Palisar interrupted him with a wave of his hand.

"Half-brother," the priest corrected. "Shalaman's mother was King Ibram's First Consort, and—let us continue to call him Noyoki—this man Noyoki was the last son of the Third Consort, who would be ashamed to have given birth to him were she still alive."

"She was a good woman," Leyuet agreed. He rubbed his temples wearily; by now he must have a headache that matched Amberdrake's. "There is no blame to her for giving birth to a creature without honor. Perhaps if others had the rearing of him—well, it may be that we shall never know. Perhaps he was without honor from the beginning. Perhaps he was born with some lack of understanding of honor."

Palisar raised a skeptical eyebrow but did not comment upon that observation. "Noyoki was selected as a child as one who had many powers," Palisar continued. "He was sent to the priest-school, just as others of his kind have been and will be. He then misused his magical powers and supposedly was rendered magically impotent. Somehow this did not take place, and you may be certain we will find out what it was that prevented the removal of his powers, and why it was not discovered that he had been left potent."

"I should warn you, out of my experience with northern-style magic," Skan rumbled, "Even if your priests had done their job, it is still possible that with enough will and focus, Noyoki *might* have been able to use the power released by blood-magic to work some kinds of spells."

Palisar sat up in alarm. "Tell me that this is not true!" he exclaimed.

Amberdrake shook his head. "I wish I could, but that is something that is well known in the north. Even with minimal talent or none, *some* people can focus their will enough to make use of powers that they cannot now or could never sense, or could sense only dimly. With more refugees coming down from the north, eventually this knowledge will come to the Haighlei. This is one of the many things we would have told you, if circumstances had not gotten so tangled. Sooner or later, an unTalented blood-mage *will* enter your Empires, and he *will* teach others."

"We cannot stop it." Palisar nodded grimly. "Very well. Then we must work to deal with it when it comes. Together. That will be one of the first items on our agenda."

"Noyoki," Skan prompted. "I want to hear all of this."

"What made this man all the more dangerous was that he had not only possessed the ability to work magic, he also had one other, even rarer ability," Leyuet said gravely. "One we had not seen in decades, even centuries, in this city."

"Which the priests were *supposed* to have blocked before they took away his magic," Palisar continued. "I recall the day that I saw him demonstrate this very clearly. He was able to move things from one end of the city to the other with the power of his will alone."

Amberdrake nodded; now he had the whole picture. "I heard something about Noyoki's story, although my informant would not tell me anything about him, when we were warned that the Haighlei do not permit the use of magic by anyone but the priests. But I would never have guessed this other ability of his. Was that what he had been using to cheat with?"

Palisar nodded grimly. "That was why we priests were so terrified of the idea of a dishonorable man loose with that kind of power. That was why we were to have burnt out that ability first, before we ever blocked away his magic."

"And of course, that was how he got Hadanelith in and out of at least one locked room without a trace, not even a trace of magic," Skan put in, with a decisive nod of his own. "And of course, how he was to put

Hadanelith in place to kill Shalaman, and get him away again. It begins to make sense, now."

"We didn't know at the time that he could move anything larger than—say—a water jug, not for any real distance," Palisar replied, grimacing with chagrin, as Leyuet toyed with the carving on the arm of his chair. "He didn't openly use it often, of course. We didn't know such an ability could be strengthened with practice."

Amberdrake looked at Skan. "You and Urtho talked about such things, do you remember talking about anything like this ability?"

Skan flexed his talons and flared his nostrils as he thought. "Such things can be strengthened up to a point. I suspect he couldn't move an object the size of a human very often or for a great distance. That would be why he needed to bring his confederates here, and why he only used it when there was no other way to get at a chosen victim. If it's any comfort to you, it's as rare among our people as it is among yours."

Palisar shrugged. "We'll find it all out for certain in short order," he replied, his eyes focused on some point beyond Amberdrake. "We do not lightly use those whose abilities grant them the means to see the thoughts of others, but when we do call upon them, they are dealing with those whose guilt is known, and they employ their skills without mercy or regard for the consequences."

Amberdrake blinked. Was the priest saying what he *thought! Are they prepared to use coercive force to strip their minds away!*

"Their minds will be broken like eggs before we meet with Shalaman again," Leyuet confirmed grimly. "And like eggs, the contents will be extracted, and the empty shells left behind. We will not slay them. We will not need to. They will, all three, live out their lives in a public place as examples of what the ultimate penalties may be. And in sifting through their minds, we may, perhaps, learn what made them what they are and prevent such a monster from appearing among us again."

Amberdrake shuddered at the ruthlessness in the slender Advisor's words. He knew what a powerful Mindspeaker could do to someone just by accident, having been on the receiving end of Kechara's first "shout," and the edge of the second. He could only imagine the sensation of having one's mind scraped away, layer by layer, until there was nothing left. On the whole—death might have been more merciful.

Did they warrant mercy! Especially after the way they tortured and murdered people! I—I don't know, and I'm glad I'm not the one making the decision. The sounds of birds singing in the gardens outside seemed unnaturally loud and cheerful.

"That, I think is all that needs be said for now." Palisar stood up, then, and gestured to them, a wordless invitation to leave this room and return to the main section of the Palace. Amberdrake was not loath to leave.

I think the strength of fear is wearing off. His joints hurt, his muscles ached with the need to lie down. His mind was in a fog. Later, he would have the strength to think about all of this, but right now—

Right now, he just wanted to fall into Winterhart's arms and rest.

It's over. It's finally over.

The walk back was a long one, and it was accomplished mainly in silence. Both Palisar and Leyuet brooded over their own thoughts, Amberdrake was too tired at the moment to really think of anything to say, and Skan moved haltingly, in no mood to talk. It was only when they reached the door of the Emperor's portion of the Palace that Palisar stopped them all with a lifted hand.

Hot, brilliant white sunlight beat down on them all, but Palisar seemed immune to its effects. "I have some things I must say. I do not favor change," he said, still frowning, "And I did not want you foreigners here among us. I was certain when the murders began that you had brought the contamination of your people here, and that you were the cause, witting or unwitting, of all our current troubles. But I am not a fool, or blind; the *cause* was already here, and your people merely gave birth to the tool. Sooner or later, Noyoki would have found another way to reach for his brother—a man does not recruit a notorious thief to his cause if he is planning to build temples. You tried to be rid of Hadanelith without making the punishment greater than the crimes he committed called for. It was not your fault that he fell into the hands of one who readily used him."

Amberdrake nodded, and waited for Palisar to continue. *He's about to make a concession. I wonder just how large a concession it will be!*

"I said that I do not favor change," Palisar went on. "That is my role, my purpose as the Emperor's Advisor. I do not intend to alter that. But I do not oppose change when it is obvious that it is inevitable. And I do not place blame where there is none." He held out his hand to Amberdrake; not grudgingly, but not with warmth, either. It was very obvious that he was not ready to be the friend of the Kaled'a'in, but at least he was no longer their enemy.

Amberdrake clasped his hand with the same reserve. Palisar nodded, with brusque satisfaction, and they all resumed the walk to the Audience Chamber, the one place where all their answers—or at least, the answers they would get for now—would be waiting.

Two weeks later, Skandranon and Amberdrake watched as Makke packed up the last of the myriad of gifts that the Haighlei had presented to Skan and Zhaneel. The Black Gryphon would never again lack for personal ornaments, he had enough jewelry especially crafted for gryphons to allow him to deck himself like a veritable kestra'chern!

"They're going to make me vain," Skin remarked, as yet another casket of jeweled collars and ear-tuft cuffs went into the packing crate. The curtains at the window and the doors of the balcony billowed in a soft, soporific breeze.

Amberdrake laughed, as he reclined on the only couch in this room. "No they won't. You already are."

Skandranon stared at him with mock effrontery. "I am *not* vain," he protested. "I am merely aware of my considerable attributes and talents. There is such a thing as false modesty, you know."

Amberdrake snorted with derision, and took another sip from the cool drink he held. Skan was pleased to see that the dark circles under his eyes, and the gray cast to his skin, were both gone. The first week after the Ceremony had been rather bad for his friend; all the horrors of what might have been came home to him as soon as he got a little rest. According to Winterhart, he'd had four solid nights of nightmares from which he would wake up screaming.

"I'll be glad to see you back at White Gryphon," Skan continued wistfully. "It's going to be very quiet there without you around."

Amberdrake gazed thoughtfully out the balcony door for a moment before replying. "I don't want to go home for a while," he said, very quietly. "There are things I need to think about before I get back, and this is a good place to be working while I do that." He returned his gaze to meet Skandranon's eyes. "Snowstar sent word that he doesn't want to run White Gryphon."

"Then what I told you a few days ago still applies," Skan told him, wondering tensely if he was going to *have* to return only to shoulder responsibilities that he now knew he was ill-suited to handle. "I had to give him the first chance, since he's been handling everything for me since we arrived here, but—"

"But that's one of the things I need to think about." Amberdrake turned the cup in his hands. "Being the leader of White Gryphon is not something I'd take on without thinking about it."

"I wouldn't want you to," Skan said hastily. "But you'd be good at it, Drake! Listen, I'm already a symbol, and I can't get away from that. I'm an example, and I can't avoid that, either. But if I've learned one thing, it's that I'm not a leader—or at least, I'm not the kind of leader that Urtho was."

"You're a different kind of leader," Amberdrake said, nodding. "When people need a focus and someone to make a quick decision, you're good at that. I've seen you act in that capacity far too often for you to deny it, Skan. You have a knack for making people want to follow you, and the instinct for making the right choices."

"That's all very well, but a *real* leader needs to be more than that." Skan sighed as he watched Makke pack away more gifts, this time of priceless fabrics. "I admire those leaders, but I can't emulate them." His nares flushed hot with embarrassment. "I get bored, Drake, handling the day-to-day snarls and messes that people get into. I get bored and I lose track of things. I get bored and I go stale and I get fat. I make up crisis after crisis to solve, when there aren't any. I turn ordinary problems into a crisis, just so I feel as if I'm doing something. You, though—you're *good* at that kind of thing. I think it's just an extension of what you were trained for."

"What, as a kestra'chern?" Amberdrake raised an eyebrow. "Well, you may be right. There's a certain amount of organizational skill we have to learn—how to handle people, of course—how to delegate authority and when to take it back. Huh. I hadn't thought of it that way."

"And you *won't* get bored and fat." Skan nodded his head decisively. "Judeth says I can have my old job back, so to speak. She'll put me in charge of the gryphon wing of the Silvers. Provided I can find someone to take over my administrative jobs."

"Oh, really?" Amberdrake looked as if he might be suppressing a smile. "Fascinating. I wonder how you talked her into that."

Privately, Skandranon wondered, too. Judeth had been entirely too accommodating.

Then again—leading a gryphon wing took some special talents, and they were talents a mere human wasn't likely to have.

Sometimes getting them to work together feels like herding grasshoppers. It's hard to get them to understand that teamwork is necessary off the battlefield.

"We aren't the only people emigrating out of the battle zone, just the first. She thinks that we're going to need to help the Haighlei deal with more refugees, and they're as likely to be from Ma'ar's army as ours," he said by way of reply. "She wants to have the wing set up and ready to move the first time there's trouble. We're a lot more mobile than you two-leggers, we'll make a good strike and run force."

I just hope that all of those damned makaar died with their master.

"And the more cooperative we show ourselves, the easier it will be to get the diehards like Palisar to fully accept us," Amberdrake acknowledged. "Well, she's right, and you're right, and I have the feeling that we aren't out of the woods yet." His expression turned thoughtful. "You know, the mage-storms are settling down to squalls and dying out altogether, and one of these days magic will go back to being what it used to be. Ma'ar and Urtho weren't the only powerful Adepts up there, just the two *most* powerful. And right now, there probably aren't too many places that are pleasant to live in the North."

Skandranon thought about that for a moment, and he didn't much like the taste of it. Amberdrake was right; there had been plenty of mages up there, and not all of them died or were burned out in that last conflagration. Most mages had either joined forces with Urtho or with Ma'ar; there was no point in worrying too much about those who had been with Urtho, but those who had been with Ma'ar couldn't *all* have been eliminated.

And there had been a few mages, Adepts all, who had opted to sit out the conflict between Urtho and Ma'ar—to wait and watch from within hiding, and see precisely who won before making moves of their own. And where were they?

No one knew. No one would know, unless they came out of hiding. *When a wizard chooses to go into hiding, there isn't much that can pry him out until he's good and ready to come out.*

But no other mage had ever had anything like the gryphons. They had proved to be Ma'ar's downfall.

We could surprise someone else, too.

Well, that didn't matter at this very moment. What *did* matter was that there were two tasks facing the people of White Gryphon that needed to be finished. They needed to complete their city and learn how to run it—and they needed to learn how to live in this new situation and society.

I can take care of contingency battle plans for dealing with possible enemies, if

Drake can take over the city. Skan chuckled to himself. *The old team, just like before. With Gesten putting us both in our place.*

"Well, right now, what if we agree to wait until I have the permanent delegation here set up and running smoothly?" Amberdrake asked. "If I manage that—well, perhaps my skills might be up to administering a city."

"I'll agree to that!" Skan said readily.

People are already deferring to him. Judeth does, and so do the rest of the Silvers. The Haighlei are—I think they're rather in awe of the way he could play so many roles, too.

"Besides, I need to be here to help Silver Veil interview her replacement," Amberdrake continued, but this time with an amused sparkle in his eye. "We both agreed that, on the whole, I am not particularly suited to the position since Leyuet would never be able to unburden himself to someone he thinks of as being god-touched, but she's willing to talk to anyone from White Gryphon that I send for. I have a candidate or two. Jessamine, for one. She's competent, and she would be a complete change of pace from Silver Veil—which would make it impossible for anyone to ever compare the two."

Skan sighed with relief when he realized that Amberdrake was not even thinking about taking the job himself. That *had* been a private worry of his; that Amberdrake would decide to stay here as Silver Veil's successor, with Winterhart in charge of the actual ambassadorial delegation. In many ways, it would be a good positioning of resources. Winterhart was admirably suited to such a task—and if Amberdrake was in the position of Imperial Kestra'chern, his people would be very well appraised of whatever situation currently prevailed in Shalaman's land.

But I want him home, Skan thought stubbornly. *We're a good team, and I need him back home where he belongs.*

Besides, he needs to take over from Lionwind, as well as taking over the city. The Kaled'a'in are more than they were before, and Lionwind is still acting as if they were just one of the Clans, with no outsiders among them to change things. I think he realizes that, too.

In fact—Hmm. There were some stirrings in that direction, before we left. It seemed to me that Lionwind was spending an awful lot of time with the shaman. Maybe he's thinking that he ought to move on to something else, too.

Change or stagnate. Keep moving or die. That always seemed to be the choices facing Urtho's folk.

But if we change, we grow. If Drake takes all this leader business on, it will *make him grow. He's been stagnating, too.*

This was going to wake him up, and that would be good, not only for him, but for Winterhart. *She'll be his partner, just like always—Now that's interesting. She really wasn't suited—or trained—to be his partner when all he was doing was speaking for the kestra'chern. But as the full administrator! Oh, they'll handle that job together like two trained horses in harness!*

"Winterhart would probably enjoy sharing the administrative things out with me," Amberdrake mused aloud, in an unconscious echo of Skandranon's thoughts. "She'd been wasting her talents, really, until we got here. She *was* trained to rule, not only a household, but a full estate with a substantial number of retainers. It would be a shame to let that kind of training and skill go to waste."

"You're going to do it, then." Skan could hardly conceal his glee.

Amberdrake gave him a wry smile. "Sounds as though I've talked myself into it, haven't I? Well—yes. *We* will do it. Provided we don't make total fools of ourselves, setting things up here."

"Good!" Skan settled back to watch Makke pack with a much lighter heart. Everything was settled—and exactly as he wanted!

And now *he* would be able to get back to doing what he did best—being the Black Gryphon, and all that entailed!

I won't be stagnating, either. We'll have to figure out how to work with the Haighlei forces; we have no idea what may be coming down out of the north. We gryphons really should put some thought into organizing ourselves in some way—

He gryphon-grinned at Amberdrake, and the kestra'chern's wry smile softened into a real one.

And Skandranon Rashkae sat back on his haunches and pulled himself straight up in a deliberately statuesque pose against the sunlit sky, content with himself and the world. Life was good.

THE SILVER GRYPHON

A VALDEMAR OMNIBUS

BOOK THREE
OF THE MAGE WARS

Dedicated to 'Dusty' Rhoades, Mike Hackett, Scott Rodgers, and all the rest of those who know the Infobahn is a tool and not a religion.

CHAPTER ONE

*F*reedom!

Tadrith Skandrakae extended his broad gray wings, stretching out his muscles to their fullest extent to take best advantage of the warm wind beneath him. *Freedom at last! I thought I'd never get away from that Section meeting.* He banked just slightly to his left, slipping sideways for the best line. *I know it wasn't my good looks or charm that were putting me under that old crow's watch! I swear, Aubri must get a special pleasure out of keeping people around him who desperately want to he somewhere else.* He half-closed his eyes against the glare of the sun on the water beneath him. He was conscious of two pressures, one tangible and one fanciful; the warm imagined push of the sun on his back, and the strong uplift of the thermal beneath him. Then again, maybe there were three pressures, or four; the warm air below, the hot sun above, and the twin desires to be away from the boredom of yet another Section meeting and the wish to be headed for something exciting.

The thermal tasted of salt and seaweed, and it gave him some welcome relief from rowing his wings against the breeze. Beneath and beyond his left wing, the great Western Sea shone green-blue and vast, the horizon a sharp line where the brilliant turquoise of the sky met the deep emerald green of the water farther out. To his right, the cliff-built city of White Gryphon sent back the rays of the sun in a dazzling display of snowy stone laced with growing things, drifts of trailing vines, and falling water. As had been planned a generation ago, the city itself was laid out in the shape of a stylized gryphon with his wings spread proudly against the mossy uncut stone of the cliff. By day, it glowed; by night, it glimmered, lit with candle, lantern and mage-light. Tadrith loved it; a proud, promising, beckoning city, home to thousands.

Beneath him, the olive-green waters of the cove rolled calmly against the base of the cliff and gurgled around the pillars of the dock, a delicate lacework of foam atop the swells. The moorings there were all empty except for light utility craft, for the fishing fleet of White Gryphon would be out at sea until sunset. Tadrith himself had served with the fleet in his first year as a Silver Gryphon; young gryphons acted as aerial scouts, spotting schools of fish from above, and then worked as catch haulers later in the day.

The only time that nets were used was when the catch haulers were taking the catch in to the shore. In their first years here, the fleet had fished with drag- and gill-nets, but did so no more. Their Haighlei allies had been horrified at the wastage caused by net fishing, for inedible sea life had been caught and wantonly destroyed along with the edible fish. They had rightfully pointed out that the Kaled'a'in would not have countenanced such wastage in *hunting*, so why should they allow it in fishing? Fishing was another form of hunting, after all; you did not kill creatures that were of no threat or use to you in the forest, so why do so in the sea? So now the fleets used only baited lines, allowing for the release of fish that were too young or unwanted. It took longer, and was more work, but that was a small matter compared with the fact that it ensured feeding the next generation, and the ten after that.

Ten generations to come. That's always the concern—the generations to come. Plan and work for ten generations' benefit, Amberdrake says. Even if we wear ourselves to wingsails and bones doing it!

Such thoughts tended to come to everyone at White Gryphon from time to time. Among the young, like him, they came to mind at least once an hour; in times of even harder work, they arose every few minutes. It was only natural, after all, that a day of bright sun and promise would hold a virile young gryphon's attention better than going over Patrol charts and Watch rosters with an elder gryphon, even one as likable as old Aubri.

I have places to go, things to do. I'm almost positive of it.

The landing platform that Tadrith had chosen was not untenanted, a factor that had played some little part in his choice. Not that he was *vain*, oh no! At least, not much. But there were three perfectly handsome young gryphon ladies spreading their wings to catch some sun on that platform, with their mothers in oh-so-casual attendance on the off-chance that a young bachelor might show some interest. He knew all three of them, of course; Dharra was a year older than he and a mage, Kylleen a year younger and still serving with the fleet, and Jerrinni a fellow Silver. *She* was already working with a partner on unsupervised assignments, and he particularly wanted to impress her if he could. She was by far the most attractive of the three, being of the same goshawk type that he was. But that was not the only reason for his interest in her; she was also his senior in the Silvers and her comments to her superiors might edge him up a little toward his long-delayed promotion to unsupervised assignments.

I wear the badge, but I am not yet allowed to bear the responsibilities the badge represents. He did not have to glance down at his harness to see that badge, made in the form of a stylized gryphon.

The Silver Gryphons, so named for that silver badge they wore, served in every kind of military and policing capacity that fighters, guards, scouts, and constables had in the old days. And in addition to those tasks, the gryphons in the Silvers—especially the young ones still in training—made themselves useful in a variety of other tasks.

Or to be more precise, their leaders *assigned* them to those so-useful tasks. Like hauling cargo, or carry-nets full of fish, or hoisting supplies, meat from the herds, and the fruits of the fields down from the top of the cliff, for instance.

Or sitting through boring meetings.

I have a hundred things that need to be done. Or as Father would say, "places to go, people to be." He makes a joke of it, but I live it, more than he ever did even after all of his adventures and missions and roles. Even more than he did at the Eclipse Ceremony.

He sideslipped and caught another thermal, one that would place him precisely where he wanted to be.

The thought of his father, as always, made him flinch internally. Not that Skandranon was a *bad* father—oh, no! He was an excellent teacher, provider, and friend. He was a fine father, but he was a very difficult person to *have as* a father. Trying to live up to the image of the Black Gryphon was… difficult and vexing. *He may be a living legend, but it makes being his son a living hell.*

But the platform and its attractive occupants loomed up before and beneath him, and Tadrith allowed himself a touch of smug satisfaction. He prided himself on his aerobatics, and most especially on his control. His mother Zhaneel was the gryphon who had been most revered for her flying finesse, and he had studied her techniques more than his father's. *At least the Great Skandranon can't do this as well as I can…*

Tadrith banked in over the platform and pulled up, to stall in midair and then fall, wings cupped, to land standing on one foot, then two, and from then to all fours without any sound louder than the creak of the platform accepting his weight. The gryphon ladies all gazed on in approval, impressed by his display of control and dexterity, and Kylleen cooed aloud and smiled in his direction.

Yes! That worked out just the way I wanted. Tadrith stood rock steady and struck a momentary pose, wings folded crisply, crest up and gently ruffled by the breeze. *Just right. That will show them what I'm made of. Father never flew like that! He'd have powered straight in and knocked them half off their feet with the backwash of his wingbeats. I have finesse and style!*

Tadrith's self-congratulatory reverie was shattered a moment later when one mother said to another, "Did you see that? Why, he's the very image of his father, with aerobatics like that."

Crushed, Tadrith drooped his head and crest and stepped off the platform.

I'm doomed.

At least the younger ladies seemed oblivious to the effect that the casual remark had on him. They continued to bestow coy and admiring glances on him as he made as unhurried and graceful an exit as he could manage under the circumstances.

The platform jutted out over the cove below, and led directly to one of the balustraded "streets" that ran along the edge of the terrace. The Kaled'a'in who comprised the greater part of the population of White Gryphon were accustomed to being surrounded by greenery, and even in a city carved and built completely of cliff-stone had managed to bring that greenery here. Built into the balustrades were stone boxes filled with earth brought down a sackful at a time from the fields above; those boxes now held luxuriant vines that trailed down to the next terraced level. More stone boxes each held a single tree or bush, with flowering herbs planted at its base. There was water enough coming down from above to allow for the occasional tiny waterfall to trail artfully from terrace to terrace and end in a long fall to the sea. The greenery had been planned so that it actually formed feather-patterns, adding texture to the pure white of the stone gryphon. Part of the philosophy of White Gryphon, when the city was planned, had been "recovery with dignity." The leaders of the people—Skandranon included—used the survivors' artistry and style as a point of pride and unification. If a simple box would do, an ornamented box was better. This strategy of increased self-esteem, guided by the kestra'chern, worked in making the people feel less like beaten refugees and more like proud homesteaders.

The philosophy was simple. If an object could be made beautiful—

whether it was a street, doorway, or garden—it was.

Homes were carved directly into the cliff behind the avenue, some going twenty or thirty gryphon-lengths back into the stone. The size of a family home or a gryphon aerie was limited only to the willingness of family members to dig (or pay for someone else to dig)—and to live in the windowless spaces beyond the main rooms. Gryphons tended to find such spaces disturbing and confining and preferred not to carve more than two rooms'-worth deep, but *hertasi* and *kyree* and even some humans actually liked the idea of such burrows, and sent their dwellings quite far back indeed. There were entire complexes of man-made caverns back in those cliffs, and Tadrith had to admit that the one advantage they had was that weather made little or no difference to the folk living in those rooms.

Amberdrake was one such. He and Winterhart had buried their personal chambers so far back into the living stone that no natural light ever reached there to disturb late sleepers. Tadrith shuddered at the very thought of so much rock on every side, cutting him off from the air and light. He had no idea how his partner Blade ever tolerated it, for she was another such as her parents.

Not that a gryphon ever needs to worry about being forced to live in such a place. Not while there are hertasi *and* kyree *vying for such mausoleums and eager to give up cliff-side residences to have one.* In the early days, when simply getting a dwelling carved out quickly had been of paramount importance, it had been faster and easier just to sculpt rooms side-by-side, often simply enlarging and improving existing caves. Mage-lights to aid in working deeper into the stone had been at a premium, and there were long stretches of time when magic could not be used to help work the stone at all, so that it all had to be done by hand. Workers tended to carve to a standard that happened to be preferred by most humans and all gryphons and *tervardi*. The *dyheli*, of course, needed the barest of shelters to be contented and all lived above, among the farms, but the *hertasi* and *kyree* who really were not comfortable with views of endless sky and long drops were forced to make do until there was time and the resources to create dwellings more to their liking. That meant there were always those who would happily trade an older, "precarious perch" for a newly chiseled burrow. There were wider terraces, of course, that permitted real buildings and even small gardens, but those were all in the "body" of White Gryphon and most building space was reserved for public use. It was probably fair to say that three-quarters of the population of

White Gryphon lived in glorified cave dwellings.

That was how Tadrith and his twin, Keenath, had gotten their own aerie, which allowed them to move out of their parents' home; they'd found a narrow stretch of unexcavated terrace down at the bottom of White Gryphon's "tail" and had claimed it for themselves, then hired a team of masons to carve out a long set of six rooms, one after the other, deep into the living rock. This sort of residence was precisely the kind preferred by den-living *kyree* and burrowing *hertasi*. Once the dwelling had been roughed in and the twins made it known that they were willing to trade, there was a bidding War going on even before it was completed.

The result was that Tadrith and Keenath had their own bachelor suite of one main room, a food storage chamber, and two light and airy bedrooms on either side of the main room. Both bedchambers had windows overlooking the cliff, as had the main room. The *kyree* family that had gratefully traded this aerie for the dark tunnel-like series of rooms pronounced themselves overjoyed to be leaving such a drafty, windswept perch, and had wondered why their parents had ever chosen it!

Which only proves that one creature's cozy nest is another creature's draft-ridden mess of sticks.

As Tadrith neared his home, which was out on what would be the first primary of the White Gryphon's right wing, the "avenue" narrowed to a simple pathway, and the balustrade to a knee-high, narrow ledge of stone. Perhaps that had something to do with the *kyree*'s reluctance to live there—certainly such an arrangement would be dangerous for young, clumsy cubs. Tadrith and Keenath had been raised in an aerie virtually identical to this one, but on the first primary of the White Gryphon's *left* wing; that distance between them and their beloved parents had played no small part in their final decision as to which family would win the bidding war.

Tadrith could, if he had chosen to do so, actually have landed on the balustrade right outside his own door—but landing anywhere other than the public landing platforms was considered a breech of safety, for it encouraged the just-fledged youngsters, who were by no means as coordinated as they *thought* they were, to reckless behavior. No lives had been lost, but several limbs had been broken, when younglings had missed their landings and slipped off the edge or tumbled into a group of passersby. After a number of hysterical mothers demanded that the Council do something about the problem, the landing platforms were installed and gryphons and *tervardi* were "strongly encouraged" to use them. Tadrith and Keenath, with every eye in White Gryphon always on them, had been scrupulous in their use of the public landing platforms.

By daylight, anyway. And no fledge is allowed to fly after dark, so they'll never see us when we cheat.

In glorious weather like this, the doors and windows always stood wide open, so Tadrith simply strolled inside his shared dwelling, his claws clicking on the bare stone of the floor. The room they used for company was airy and full of light, with the rock of the outer wall carved into several tall panels with thin shafts of wood between them. Translucent panes of the tough material the Kaled'a'in used for windows were set into wooden frames on hinges, which in turn were set into the stone. The room itself was furnished only with cushions of various sizes, all covered in fabric in the colors of sandstone and granite, slate and shale. In the winter, thick sheepskins and wool rugs would cover that cold white floor, and the doors and windows would be shut tight against the gales, but in the summer all those coverings were whisked away into storage so that an overheated gryphon could lie belly-down on the cool rock floor and dump some of that body heat quickly. And, in fact, Keenath was doing just that, spread out on the floor, with wings fanned, panting slightly.

"I was just thinking about dinner," his twin greeted him. "I might have known that thoughts of food would bring you home."

Tadrith snorted. "Just because *you're* obsessed with eating it doesn't follow that I am! I'll have you know that I only just now escaped from yet another yawnsome Section meeting. Food was the very last thing on my mind, and escaping Aubri was the first!"

Keenath laughed silently, beak parted, as his tongue flicked in and out while his sides heaved. "That must have been a first, then," he bantered. "So who was she? The pretty young thing that your mind was *really* on, I mean. Kylleen, perhaps?"

Tadrith was not going to get caught in *that* trap. "I haven't made up my mind," he said loftily. "I have so many to choose from, after all, it hardly seems reasonable to narrow the field this early in the race. It wouldn't be fair to the ladies, either, to deny my company to any of them. It is only polite to distribute my attentions over as wide a selection as possible."

Keenath reached out a claw and snagged a pillow, spun it twice as he raised up, and expertly hurled it at his brother's head. Tadrith ducked, and it shot across the room to thud against the wall on the other side.

"You should be careful doing that," he warned, flopping down on the cool stone himself. "We've lost too many pillows over the cliff that way. So what were you studying that has you panting so hard?"

"Field treatment and rescues under combat conditions, and specifically, blood stanching and wound binding," Keenath replied. "Why? Don't ask me; we haven't seen a state of combat since before you and I were born. Winterhart's idea. Probably because I take after Mother."

Tadrith nodded; Keenath *was* very similar in size and build to their mother, Zhaneel. Like her, he was technically a *gryfalcon* rather than a gryphon. He was small and light, most of his musculature in his chest and shoulders. His coloring and body type were that of a peregrine, his wings long and narrow, but most importantly, he had inherited Zhaneel's stub-taloned, dexterous claw-hands.

This was important, for Keenath was learning the craft of the *trondi'irn* from Winterhart herself, and he needed "hands" as clever as a human's. Before his apprenticeship was complete, he would be able to do anything a Healer with no Gift could do. The difference between him and an herb-, fire-, or knife-Healer was that, like all *trondi'irn*, his training was tailored to the needs and physiology of gryphons and other nonhumans.

Zhaneel had been trained as a fighter—and others had come to the realization that her small size and lack of fighting talons could be put to other uses too late for her to learn a new trade. At that point, she had opted to adapt her style of fighting to her body type rather than try to fit the accepted mold, and with Skandranon's help she had made the best of her situation with brilliant results. But when Keenath had shown early signs that he would resemble her physically, he was encouraged to think of a career in something other than the Silvers.

Nevertheless, it had surprised everyone when he had declared he wanted to train as a *trondi'irn*. Up until now, that had been an occupation reserved for humans and *hertasi*.

Tadrith stretched and yawned, turning his head so that the breeze coming in from the open door could ruffle his crest-feathers. "At least you were doing something!" he complained. "I sat there until I thought my hindquarters were, going to turn to stone, and if any part of me is going to grow stiff on a day like this, that is *not* my primary choice. I couldn't even take a nap; as usual, old Aubri had me conspicuously up front. Have to maintain the tradition of the Black Gryphon, of course; have to pretend every Section meeting is as important as a wartime conference. Have to act as if every detail could mean life or death." He stretched again, enjoying the fact that he could always vent his frustration to his twin. "You should be glad you look the way you do, Keeth. It's bad enough being Skandranon's son, but the fact that I *look* like him doesn't even remotely help! You try living up to the legend, sometime! It's enough to make anyone want to bite something!"

And to display the strength of his own frustration, he snagged the poor, mistreated pillow Keenath had lately lobbed at him, and bit at it savagely. It was a good thing they had the cushions covered in tough linen-canvas, for the pillows had to take a great deal of punishment.

"Well, if you think it's hard living up to the legend, just try breaking away from it!" Keenath retorted, as he always did. Tadrith's twin groaned as he followed Tadrith's example, stretching. "Half the time I'm left wondering if Winterhart isn't pushing me so hard *expecting* me to fail, and half the time I think she's doing it because everyone knows Skandranon never failed at anything he tried."

Tadrith snorted and mock-scraped his hindfeet, as if burying something particularly noxious from a previous meal. "He never let it be known how often he failed, which is the same thing to legend-builders."

His brother snorted right back and continued. "And if it isn't Winterhart, it's everyone else, watching, waiting to see if the old Black Gryphon magic is strong enough in Keenath to enable the youngling to pull off another miracle." He parted his beak in a sardonic grin. "At least you have a path to follow—I'm going through new skies in the fog, and I have no idea if I'm going to run up against a cliff-face."

Naturally, Tadrith had his own set of retorts, already primed, proving how much more difficult it was to have to follow in the wake of the Black Gryphon. It was an old set of complaints, worn familiar by much handling, and much enjoyed by both of them.

Who can I complain to, if not to my twin! For all that they were unalike in form and temper, they were bound by the twin-bond, and knew each other with the twin's intimacy. There were other twins among the gryphons, and one or two sets among the humans, and all the twin-sets agreed; there was a bond between them that was unlike any other sibling tie. Tadrith often thought that he'd never have been able to cope with the pressure if Keenath hadn't been around, and Keenath had said the same thing about his sibling.

Finally the litany of complaints wound to its inevitable conclusion— which was, of course, that there was no conclusion possible. They ran through the sequence at least once every day, having long ago decided that if they could not change their circumstances, at least they could enjoy complaining about them.

"So what has your tail in a knot this time?" Keenath asked. "It wasn't just the meeting."

Tadrith rolled over on his back to let the breeze cool his belly. "Sometimes I think I'm going to do something drastic if Blade and I don't get assigned soon!" he replied, discontentedly. "What are they waiting for? We've earned our freedom by now!"

"They could be waiting for you to finally demonstrate a little patience, featherhead," Keenath said, and had to duck as the pillow made a return trip in his direction.

There might have been more pillows than just the one flying, if Silverblade herself, Tadrith's partner, hadn't chosen that moment to walk in their open door.

She stood in the doorway, posing unconsciously, with the sun making a dark silhouette of her against the brilliant sky. Tadrith knew it was not a conscious pose; it was totally out of her nature to do anything to draw attention to herself unless it was necessary. Blade was the name the gryphons knew her by, though her childhood name hadn't been the use-name she wore now; it had been "Windsong," so dubbed by her fond parents in the hopes, no doubt, that she would grow up to resemble one or the other of them. "Windsong" was a perfectly good name for a *tiondi'iin* or even a *kestra'chern* or a Kaled'a'in Healer or mage. But "Windsong" hadn't had the inclination for any of those things.

The young woman who broke her pose and strode into the aerie with the soundless tread of a hunter was small by Kaled'a'in standards, although there was no mistaking her lineage. Her short black hair, cut in a way that suggested an aggressive bird of prey, framed a face that could only have graced the head of one of the Clan k'Leshya, and her beak of a nose continued the impression of a hunting hawk. Her golden skin proclaimed the lineage further, as did her brilliantly blue eyes. There was nothing of her mother about her—and very little of her father.

She fit in very well with those members of Clan k'Leshya descended from warrior stock, however. Despite her small size, she was definitely molded in their image. There was nothing to suggest softness or yielding; she was hard, lithe, and every bit a warrior, all muscle and whipcord.

Tadrith well recalled the first time he had seen her stand that way. The day she showed her real personality, one month after her twelfth birthday, a month during which she had suddenly turned overnight from a lively if undistinguished child to a rough and unpolished version of what she now was. Amberdrake had been holding a gathering of some sort, which had included the children, and of course Tadrith and Keenath had been in attendance. Winterhart had addressed her daughter as "Windsong" during the course of the meal, and the little girl had unexpectedly stood up and announced to the room in a firm and penetrating voice that she was *not* to be called by that name anymore.

"I am going to be a Silver," she had said, loudly and with total conviction. "I want to be called Silverblade from now on."

Silverblade had then sat down, flushed but proud, amidst gasps and murmurs. It was a rather dramatic move even for someone with an outgoing personality like Tadrith; for one as self-effacing as Blade, it must have taken an enormous effort of will—or assertion of the truth, as the k'Leshya believed. The willpower to do anything would come, the songs and writings said, if the motive was pure.

Nothing her parents could say or do would persuade her otherwise— not that Amberdrake and Winterhart had been so selfish as to attempt to thwart her in what she so clearly wanted. From that day on, she would respond to no other name than Silverblade, or "Blade" for short, and now even both her parents referred to her by that name.

It certainly fits her better than "Windsong." She can't carry a tune any better than I could carry a boulder!

"Keeth! I hear you didn't kill too many patients today, congratulations!" she said as she invited herself into the room and sat down on one of the remaining cushions.

"Thank you," Keenath said dryly. "And do come in, won't you?"

She ignored his attempt at sarcasm. "I've got some good news, bird," she said, turning to Tadrith and grinning broadly as he rolled over. "I didn't think it could wait, and besides, I wanted to be the one to break it to you."

"News?" Tadrith sat up. "What kind of news?" There was only one piece of news that he really cared about—and only one he thought Blade would want to deliver to him herself.

Her grin broadened. "You should have stayed after the meeting; there was a reason why Aubri wanted you up front. If you were half as diligent as you pretend to be, you'd know for yourself by now." She eyed him teasingly. "I'm tempted to string this out, just to make you squirm."

"What!" he burst out, leaping to his feet. "Tell me! Tell me this

instant! Or—I'll—" He gave up, unable to think of a threat she couldn't counter, and just ground his beak loudly.

Now she laughed, seeing that she had gotten him aroused. "Well, since it looks as if you might burst, if I don't—it's what we've been hoping for. We've gotten our first unsupervised assignment, and it's a good one."

Only the low ceiling prevented him from leaping into the air in excitement, although he did spring up high enough to brush his crest-feathers and wingtips against the ceiling. "When? Where? How long till we can get in action?" He shuffled his taloned feet, his tail lashing with exuberance, all but dancing in place.

She laughed at his reaction, and gestured to him to sit down. "Just as quickly as you and I would like, bird. We leave in six days, and we'll be gone for six moons. We're going to take charge of Outpost Five."

Now his joy knew no bounds. "Five? Truly?" he squealed, sounding like a fledgling and not caring. "*Five?*"

Outpost Five was the most remote outpost in all of the territory jointly claimed by White Gryphon and their Haighlei allies. When this particular band of refugees had fled here, as they escaped the final Cataclysm of the Mage of Silence's war with Ma'ar the would-be conqueror of the continent, they had been unaware that the land they took for a new home was already claimed. They'd had no idea that it was part of the land ruled by one of the Haighlei Emperors (whom the Kaled'a'in knew as the Black Kings), King Shalaman. A clash with them had been narrowly averted, thanks to the work of Amberdrake and Skandranon, Blade's father and Tadrith's. Now White Gryphon jointly held these lands in trust with the Emperor, and its citizens were charged with the responsibility of guarding the border in return for King Shalaman's grant of the White Gryphon lands.

It was a border of hundreds of leagues of wilderness, and the Emperor himself had not been able to "guard" it; he had relied on the wilderness itself to do the guarding. This was not as insurmountable a task as it might have seemed; with gryphons to fly patrol, it was possible to cover vast stretches, of countryside with minimal effort. Outpost Five was the most remote and isolated of all of the border posts. Because of that, it was hardly the most desirable position so far as the Silvers were concerned.

For *most* Silvers, perhaps, but not for Blade and Tadrith. This meant three whole months in a place so far away from White Gryphon that not even a hint of what transpired there would reach the city unless he or Blade sent it by teleson. There would be no watching eyes, waiting to see if he could replicate his legendary father. There would be no tongues wagging about his exploits, imagined or real.

Of course, there would also be no delicious gryphon ladies for three months, but that was a small price to pay. Three months of chastity would be good for him; it would give him a rest. He would be able to use the leisure time to invent new and clever things to do and say to impress them. He would have all that time to perfect his panache. By the time he returned, as a veteran of the border, he should be able to charm any lady he chose.

Outpost duty was a long assignment, in no small part because it was so difficult to get people *to* the outposts. Even though magic was now working reliably, and had been for several years, no one really wanted to trust his body to a Gate just yet. Too many things could go wrong with a Gate at the best of times, and at the moment the only-purpose anyone was willing to put them to was to transport unliving supplies. The consumables and their mail and special requests would be supplied to their outpost that way; a mage at White Gryphon who was familiar with the place would set up a Gate to the outpost. Workers would then pitch bundles through, and the mage would drop the Gate as soon as he could.

No one wants to leave a Gate up very long either. You never know what might go wrong, or what might stroll through it while it's up.

"You know, of course, that there's a great deal of uninhabited and poorly-surveyed territory in between Five and home," Blade went on with relish. "We're going to be completely on our own from the time we leave to the time we return."

"What, no lovely gryphon ladies and human stallions to wile away your time of exile?" jibed Keenath, and shuddered realistically. "Well, never mind. I can guarantee that in the case of the ladies, I can make certain that they will not notice your absence, twin."

"They are more likely to cry out in pain at your poor attempts at gallantry, Keeth," Tadrith told him, and turned back to Blade. *"You* realize that this shows a great deal of trust in our abilities, don't you? I mean, the usual first assignment is something like—"

"Like guarding the farms, I know," she replied smugly. "That must have been why they kept us behind the others, training and overtraining us. They wanted to be sure we were ready, and I bet they decided to send us out there because we're the only people who really *want* to go. In fact, I would bet my favorite armband that Aubri plans to send us out on long outpost duty every chance he can get!"

They grinned at each other with relish, for there was another aspect to outpost duty they both anticipated with pleasure. Those so posted were expected to do a certain amount of exploring, and sometimes the explorers found something valuable. The Emperor Shalaman got a share, of course, as did the treasury of White Gryphon, but the generous portion remaining went to the intrepid explorers who made the discovery. Not that Tadrith was *greedy*, of course, but he did have a certain love of ornamentation, a pronounced interest in the finer things of life, and finding something extremely valuable would make it possible for him to indulge his interests. And it didn't hurt to have the wherewithal to impress the ladies, either, and ornament them a bit now and then.

"Just how much exploring has been done up there?" he asked.

Blade's eyes widened knowingly. "Not all that much," she replied. "And there are more ways to explore than sailing over the tree-canopy, hoping something on the ground will show itself."

He nodded, following her thoughts. Probably most of the Silvers assigned to Outpost Five in the past had been gryphon teams; that made sense, although it probably wore them down terribly, not having humans and *hertasi* to tend to them. A human on station, though, could make a detailed survey of a particular area, including the smaller animals and plants living there, and take mineral samples. That was something a gryphon was ill-suited or, for that matter, ill-inclined, to do.

"There's been no trouble from that sector for years," she mused. "We should have plenty of time for surveys."

"But most of all, you'll be on your own," Keenath said enviously. "I wish I could find some way to escape for a few months."

Blade patted his shoulder sympathetically. "And miss all the benefits of *trondi'irn, hertasi and kestra'chern* fawning on you every spare moment? The horror! You could ask to be taken on by the Silvers once you've finished training under Winterhart," she suggested. "Then you'd get some assignments elsewhere. Down with the embassy at Khimbata, maybe; you could go as the *trondi'irn* taking care of the Emperor's gryphon-guards."

Keenath's eyes lit up at the idea, and Tadrith knew how he felt. For a chance to get out of White Gryphon he would have put up with just about anything.

The problem was that there was literally nothing that he said or did that Skandranon didn't eventually find out about. It wasn't that Skan was purposefully spying on his sons, or even deliberately overseeing them—

Well, not much, anyway. And not overtly.

—it was just that everyone told the Black Gryphon everything that went on in this city. A mouse couldn't sneeze without Skandranon finding out about it eventually.

Neither can we—except that it's guaranteed that if we sneeze, someone will go running to Father with the news. Not only that, but the report would be detailed as to how, when, and how well we sneezed.

It wasn't exactly tale-bearing, for people made certain to bring Skan the most flattering reports possible. Skan was a very proud father.

He can't get enough of hearing about all the marvelous things Keeth and I are doing, especially now that we aren't in the family aerie to bully into making reports on ourselves. The trouble is, he is fully capable of blowing the most minor accomplishment up into the equivalent of a brilliant piece of wartime strategy or heroism.

It was embarrassing, to say the least.

And, of course, anyone who wanted to curry favor with the Black Gryphon knew the fastest way to his heart was to praise his sons. Skan would go out of his way to see that someone who flattered the twins got a full hearing and careful consideration. That was *all* he would do, but often enough, that was sufficient.

As Keeth continued to look envious and a little pained, Tadrith preened his short eartufts in sympathy. "I wish there was a way to send you out of the city for *trondi'irn* training, Twin," he murmured.

Keenath sighed. "So do I. When we were all choosing the subject we wanted to study, I *tried* to think of some discipline I could enjoy that would also get me out of the city at the same time, but I couldn't. I think I'm going to be good at this, and it certainly feels right, but it means I'm stuck here."

Blade wore as sympathetic an expression as Tadrith.

"There is this, Keeth," the gryphon said to his twin. "You can just go on doing what you are doing and you will have earned every right to be considered unique and special. You're writing your own definition of a *trondi'irn*. You don't have to stand there, blushing at the nares with embarrassment when someone comes in acting as if running the obstacle course was the equivalent of stealing one of Ma'ar's magical weapons."

But Keeriath ruffled his neck-feathers and clicked his beak. "That's true up to a point, but there is another problem. Father literally does not understand me. We have absolutely nothing in common. When I talk about what I'm doing, he gets this strange look on his face, as if I were speaking a foreign tongue." He laughed weakly. "I suppose I am, really. Well, I'll get my chance eventually."

"You will," Blade promised, but she made no move to rise to her feet. "I'm going to have to break the news to *my* parents, assuming that they don't already know, which is more than likely. Tad, you'd better figure out how to tell yours."

"They'll know," Tadrith replied with resignation. "Father is probably already telling everyone he thinks will listen how there's never been anyone as young as l am posted so far away on his first assignment."

Blade laughed ruefully. "You're probably right. And mine is probably doing the same—except—"

She didn't complete the sentence, but Tadrith knew her well enough not to pressure her. They each had their own set of problems, and talking about them wasn't going to solve them.

Only time would do that.

Or so he hoped.

Silverblade sat back on her heels when the twins began to argue over what Tadrith should pack. She was in no real hurry to get back home; since she was still living with her parents, she did not even have the illusion of privacy that her own aerie would have provided. The moment she walked in the door, the questions and congratulations—bracketed by thinly-veiled worry—would begin, and at the moment she did not feel up to fielding them.

She breathed in the scent of salt air and sunbaked rock, half closing her eyes. *I love this place. The only neighbors are other gryphons, quiet enough that the sound of the surf covers any noise they might make. And I love the fact that there are no other humans nearby, only* tervardi, *gryphons, and a few* kyree.

How she envied Tad his freedom! He really had no notion just how easy a parent Skandranon was to deal with. The Black Gryphon had a sound, if instinctive and not entirely reliable, knowledge of just when to shut his beak and let Tad go his own way. He also attempted to restrain his enthusiasm for the accomplishments of his twins, although it was difficult for him. But at least he showed that he approved; Amberdrake had never been happy with the path-choice his daughter had made, and although he tried not to let his disapproval color their relationship, it leaked through anyway. How could it not?

Perhaps "disapproval" was too strong a word. Amberdrake understood warriors; he had worked with them for most of his life. He respected them most profoundly. He liked them, and he even understood all of the drives that fueled their actions.

He simply did not understand why his child and Winterhart's would want to be a warrior. *He can't fathom how he and Mother produced someone like me. By all rights, with everything that they taught me, I should never have been attracted to this life.*

That was a gap of understanding that probably would never be bridged, and Blade had yet to come up with a way of explaining herself that would explain the riddle to him. "Blade, would you play secretary and write the list for me?" Tadrith pleaded, interrupting her reverie. "Otherwise I know I'm going to forget something important."

"If you do, you can always have it Gated to us," she pointed out, and laughed when he lowered his eartufts.

"*That* would be so humiliating I would rather do without!" he exclaimed. "I'd never hear the last of it! Please, just go get a silver-stick and paper from the box and help me, would you?"

"What else are gryphon-partners for, except doing paperwork?" she responded, as she rose and sauntered across the room to the small chest that held a variety of oddments the twins found occasionally useful, each in its appointed place. The chest, carved of a fragrant wood that the Haighlei called *sadar,* held a series of compartmentalized trays holding all manner of helpful things. Among them were a box of soft, silver sticks and a block of tough reed-paper, both manufactured by the Haighlei. She extracted both, and returned to her seat beside Tad. She leaned up against him, bracing herself against his warm bulk, using her knees as an impromptu writing desk.

As the twins argued over each item before agreeing to add it to the list or leave it out, she waited patiently. Only once did she speak up during the course of the argument, as Keenath insisted that Tad include a particular type of healer's kit and Tad argued against it on the grounds of weight.

She slapped his shoulder to get him to be quiet. "Who is the *trondi'irn* here?" she demanded. "You, or Keeth?" Tad turned his head abruptly, as if he had forgotten that she was there. "You mean, since he's the expert, I ought to listen to him."

"Precisely," she said crisply. "What's the point of asking his opinion on this if you won't take it when you know he's the authority?"

"But the likelihood that we'd need a bone-setting kit is so small it's infinitesimal!" he protested. "And the weight! I'm the one who's going to be carrying all this, you know!"

"But if we need it, we'll need exactly those supplies, and nothing else will substitute," she pointed out. "We don't know for certain that there's a bone-setting kit at the Outpost, and I prefer not to take the chance that the last few teams have been as certain of their invulnerability as you." Keenath looked smug as she added it to the list, unbidden. "I'm going to insist on it. And if it isn't in that basket when we leave, I'll *send* for one. We may be in a position of needing one and being unable to ask for one to be Gated to us."

Tad flattened his ears in defeat as he looked from one implacable face to the other. "You win. I can't argue against both of you."

Gryphons could not smirk like humans could, but there was enough muscular control of the beak edges at the join of the lower mandible that one could be approximated. More than a touch of such an expression showed on Keeth as they continued on to the next item. Part of the reason why Blade felt so comfortable in the Silvers and with the gryphons in particular was that their motives and thoughts were relatively simple and easy to understand. In particular, they made poor liars; gryphons were just too expressive to hold a bluff effectively once you knew how to read their physical cues, such as the lay of their facial feathers and the angle of their ears. Although they were complex creatures and often stubborn, gryphons were also exactly what they appeared to be. The *kestra'chern*, her father in particular, were anything but.

Their job was to manipulate, when it came right down to it. The whole point of what they did was to manipulate a client into feeling better, to give him a little more insight into himself. But she wasn't at all comfortable with the idea of manipulating anyone for any reason, no matter how pure the motive and how praiseworthy the outcome.

Oh, I know things simply aren't that black-and-white, but—

Ah, things were just simpler with the Silvers. Issues often *were* a matter of extremes rather than degrees. When you had only a single moment to make up your mind what you were going to do, you had to be able to pare a situation down to the basics. Subtleties, as Judeth often said, were for times of leisure.

She noted down another item, and let her thoughts drift.

I can't wait until we're away from here. I wish we could go without having to talk to my parents.

Once they were away from White Gryphon, she would finally be able to relax for the first time in several years. And once again, it was her father who was indirectly responsible for her unease of spirit.

He knows too much, that's the problem. When she had been a child, she had taken it for granted that Amberdrake would know everyone of any importance at all in White Gryphon. She hadn't known any reason why he *shouldn't*. But as she gradually became aware just what her father's avocation really entailed, she gained a dim understanding that the knowledge Amberdrake possessed was extraordinarily intimate.

Finally, one day it all fell together. She put the man together with the definition of *kestra'chern* and had a moment of blinding and appalling revelation.

Not only did her father know everyone of any importance, he also knew the tiniest details about them—every motive, every desire, every dream and indecision. Details like that, she felt deep in her heart, no person should ever know about another. Such secrets gave the one who held them too much power over the other, and that would weigh as an unimaginable responsibility.

Not that Father would ever use that power...

Or would he? If he had a chance to manipulate someone for a cause he thought was right, wouldn't he be tempted to do just that? And wouldn't the fear of having such secrets revealed to others be enough to make almost anyone agree to something that Amberdrake wanted?

She had never once seen any indications that Amberdrake had given in to the temptation to use his tacit power—but he was her father, and she knew that she was prejudiced on his behalf. For that matter, she was not certain she would know what to look for if he had misused his powers.

Oh, it's not likely. Father would never do anything to harm anyone, if only because he is an Empath and would feel their emotional distress.

She ought to know; she was something of an Empath herself, although in her case, she got nothing unless she was touching the person in question.

That was one of the reasons why Amberdrake was so confounded by the idea that she wanted to be a Silver. How could an Empath ever choose to go into a profession where she might have to kill or injure someone?

Easily enough. It's to prevent the people I must take care of from killing or injuring others.

He would never accept that, just as he would never accept the idea that she would not want to use her Empathic ability.

She shuddered at the very idea. *He knows every nasty little secret, every hidden fear, every deep need, every longing and every desire of every client he has ever dealt with. How he manages to hold all those things inside without going mad—I cannot fathom it. And that he actually* wants *to know these things—! I could never do that, never. It makes my skin crawl. I don't want to know* anyone *that intimately. It would be like having every layer of my skin peeled off—or doing it to someone else over and over.*

She loved her father and mother, she knew they were wonderful, admirable people, and yet sometimes the things that they did made her a little sick inside. All a Silver ever had to do was stop a fight, or break some bones once in a while, and apply force when words didn't work. That was just flesh, and flesh would heal even if it was shredded and bleeding—it wasn't as serious as getting into someone's heart and digging around.

From that moment of understanding of who and what her father was, she had been terrified that people would simply assume that she was like him—that she *wanted* to be like him. Her greatest fear had been that they would take it for granted that she would cheerfully listen while they bared their souls to her—

Gods. No. Anything but that.

For a while, until the Healers taught her how to control her Empathic ability, she had even shied away from touching other people, lest she learn more than she wished to. Even after she had learned to block out what she did not want to know, she had been absolutely fanatic about her own privacy.

At least as much as I can be while I still live with my parents.

She kept her thoughts strictly to herself just as much as she could; never confided anything about the things she considered *hers* alone. Even affairs of love or desire.

Especially matters of love and desire.

By now she wondered if both her parents thought she was a changeling. Here were two people who knew everything there was to know about the physical, and yet their daughter appeared to be as sexless as a vowed virgin.

She had made up her mind that she was not even going to give her father and mother the faintest of hints that she *might* have an interest in partnering anyone or anything. Unfortunately, they would not have been taken aback by *any* liaison she cared to make. They were, in fact, all too assiduous at suggesting possible partners, and would have been cheerfully pleased to offer volumes of advice on approach and technique once she even hinted at a choice!

And it would be advice of a kind she blushed even to contemplate. There was such a thing as too much information.

Why can't they be like other parents! she thought, rebelliously. *Why couldn't they have been surprised that I was no longer an innocent little girl, horrified by the idea that I might one day bed someone, and attempt to guard my virtue as if it were the gold mines of King Shalaman! Any of those would be so much easier to deal with!*

She had found out personally that it was much harder to deal with sunny cooperation than with outright opposition.

It's a great deal like the hand-to-hand combat styles we Silvers learn, she thought in frustration, noting down yet another item for Tadrith. *When your opponent moves against you, there are any number of ways you can counter him. You can block him, parry him, evade him, or use his attack against him. When he attacks, he gives you options, to counter him. But when he does nothing—when he actually flows with your moves, it is impossible to do anything to extract yourself from the situation.*

Ironic, to think of her outwardly serene life with her parents as a combat situation.

The only real escape from this ridiculous situation was to move away from White Gryphon altogether. As she had advised Keenath, there *were* positions available for Silvers in the Haighlei Empire. The ambassadors from White Gryphon needed a token guard of honor in order to convey the proper presence at the court of the Emperor; that guard was comprised mostly of humans, but always had at least four gryphons and two each of the *kyree* and *dyheli*. The *tervardi* preferred not to live in such a warm climate, and the *hertasi* took sly enjoyment in their roles of servants, ferreting out intelligence that would otherwise never have come to the attention of the ambassadors. The Emperor also had two gryphon-guards assigned to him, serving alongside the younger sons of the other Haighlei Kings.

I could ask to be posted there… I think I would enjoy the solitude of the outposts, but there are more things to consider here.

Tad would never be able to tolerate assignment after assignment to the lonely wilderness. He would go absolutely, stark, staring lunatic after a while. He was a very social creature, and their partnership would not last very long if she was the only other being around to talk to.

Not to mention what would happen to him without female gryphons about. He only thinks *he's nothing like his father. He has as wild a reputation among the fair flyers as his father ever had, if not more so. I had better check in on him to make sure he gets some sleep before we leave.*

She chuckled to herself, and Tad looked back at her for a moment in curiosity.

And as far as that went, *she* was no chaste virgin, untouched and unawakened. *She* might well go quietly insane if she lived too long away from civilization.

For one thing, after too long out there, some very disturbing things might begin to look attractive. Tension can do that. When I find myself eying snakes and fondling branches, I'll know I've been away too long. Still, that's only one thing to miss, and easy enough to simulate—it is far more difficult to replace a lover's concern. For another complication—well—there is Ikala.

She sighed. Ikala was important to Blade, and she had kept her parents from finding out about him only through plotting and planning that would have done a spymaster proud.

Haighlei Kings with more than one son—and most of them, ceremonially wedded to a new priestess-bride each year, had many children—sent those sons off to be the personal guards of other Kings. This ensured that there would be no warfare and no assassination attempts, for every King had hostages from every other King. Furthermore, every King had the opportunity to win the loyalty of the sons of his fellow Kings, giving him an ally in the courts of his neighbors. It was a good system, and in the highly structured and rigid culture of the Haighlei, it worked well.

Ikala was one of those younger sons, twentieth in succession behind the actual Crown Prince of Nbubi. But instead of being sent to serve in one of the other Courts, he had elected to come to White Gryphon instead, to be trained by Aubri and Judeth and serve in the Silvers.

The culture of the Haighlei was a strange one by Kaled'a'in standards. Every action was tightly bound up in protocol; every moment cemented with custom. The Haighlei lived in the most rigid society that the Kaled'a'in had ever seen or heard of; change was only permitted when decreed by the Emperor and his chief priests and then only at the Eclipse Ceremony...

How anything gets changed at all is a mystery. There was a hierarchy for everything, from the gods to the poorest beggar, and no one was ever allowed to leave his place in that hierarchy except at approved times, under rigid circumstances. And that was why Ikala, son of a King, was here in White Gryphon.

Ikala cannot bear the constraints of his people any more than I can. Ikala had found relief here, as she hoped to find it in the wilderness. Perhaps that was why she had felt so drawn to him from the first. They were both trying to escape from lives that others wished them to lead.

Ikala was not the only Haighlei here; many found an escape in White Gryphon from the intolerable rigidity of their own culture. Although there were not as many as Blade would have expected, they were generally young, for the old were content to wait for their next lives to improve their lot. They were also more often female than male, even though there was no real difference in the way that men and women were treated by Haighlei law and custom. This was just as well, since there were more Kaled'a'in men in White Gryphon than women—an accident that Snowstar and Cinnabar thought might be due to one of the more subtle effects of the mage-storms following the Cataclysm that destroyed Ka'venusho. Perhaps that was the reason why so many more young Haighlei women came here than men; the perfectly ordinary reason of husband hunting!

The Kaled'a'in had been nearer the source of the blast than the lands of the Black Kings, and nearest when the storms were at their worst. Many other subtle changes had taken place during their migration here, not all of them as obvious as a superfluity of male children.

There were changes that affected the mages, for instance. We had more than half of the mages associated with Urtho's army. You'd never know that now.

The mage-storms had made it very difficult to practice magic, for the strength of spells literally varied from storm to storm. But once the last of the storms had passed, it became evident that they had not only affected magic, they had affected the mages as well. Some, formerly powerful, had lost much of their ability. One or two who had only been at the level of hedge-wizard before the storms were able to aspire to the rank of Master. Some had undergone personality changes so subtle that the effects did not come to light for months or years, growing slowly odder and less social, until at last they would gather their belongings and vanish into the wilderness alone. One had caused a great deal of damage before he left, both physical and emotional.

That one was *not* Hadanelith, though Hadanelith had caused a fair share of emotional damage himself. It was generally granted, however, that Hadanelith had *not* been warped into what he was by the mage-storms. All evidence seemed to indicate he had always been quite mad, and quite dangerous.

Only the mages of k'Leshya were so affected, at least, as far as anyone knew.

Then again, perhaps Shalaman's Nameless Brother was turned into what he became by the storms as well. We'll probably never know for certain.

At any rate, since now the rate of birth for boys and girls was about equal again, the next generation would not have the trouble finding mates that this one had until Haighlei women started coming in by curious ones and twos.

Ikala had intrigued Blade, however, because he was very much different from the other Haighlei that had drifted into the city. He had kept to himself and simply observed for several weeks, after accepting hospitality at the hostel set up for visitors. He had not made any secret of his lineage, but he had not attempted to trade on it either. He had gone about the city quietly watching everything and everyone—while the Silvers were watching him, as they watched all newcomers. Then, one day, he presented himself to Judeth and asked to be taken into the Silvers as a trainee.

Had he been making up his mind if he wanted to stay? Had he already known he intended to remain and was only looking for a place where he could earn his way? Not even Blade knew—unless he had told Judeth, which was possible—and he had spent more time talking to her than to anyone else.

This was a fact that she had taken great pains to conceal from her loving family, as was her growing affection for him. She wasn't certain what she was going to do about that yet. As with many things, it would have to wait until she returned from this assignment.

But having a Silver well acquainted with another court than Shalaman's would mean that White Gryphon could open up a second embassy in Nbubi. Ikala could prove invaluable there, as an expert in the background, able to advise the ambassador as Silver Veil had advised Amberdrake in Shalaman's court. And that would be a fine place for Blade and Tadrith to be posted—and perhaps even Keeth.

Unless, of course, Amberdrake managed to get himself appointed as Ambassador there—or Winterhart did—

No. No, that couldn't possibly happen, she reassured herself hastily. *Father's needed too much here. Mother wouldn't go without him, not after the mess that almost happened the last time. And he knows that there's no one here that could replace him.*

Of course he could always train someone as his replacement.

Oh, why am I making up these stupid scenarios when I don't even know where

I'm going after this, or whether Ikala and I would ever be more than close friends, or even if Judeth would consider Tad and me for posts with the Embassy! She realized that she was making up trouble for herself out of nebulous plans that weren't even a possibility yet!

Things must be going too well if I'm planning for opposition that doesn't exist and problems that would take a thousand variables to come up!

Just about then, Tad spoke to her. "I can't think of anything else," he said. "What about you?"

"I haven't had any great inspirations for the supply list, but then I haven't been really thinking about it," she confessed, and frowned at the scrawled document in her hands. "I'll tell you what; let's go talk to Judeth or Aubri, and see if either of them have any suggestions."

Tad clicked his beak thoughtfully. "Is that wise?" he asked. "Will it look as if we aren't capable of thinking for ourselves?"

"It will look as if we are not too full of ourselves to accept advice from those older and wiser than us, and if we tell them that, they'll adore us for it," she responded, and got to her feet, stamping a little to ease a bit of numbness. "Come on, bird. Let's go show the old dogs that the puppies aren't totally idiots."

"Not totally," Tadrith muttered, although he did get to his feet as well. "Only mostly."

CHAPTER TWO

"Outpost Five, heh?" Aubri stretched both his forelegs one at a time, regarding the blunted, ebony talons on the end of each claw with a jaundiced eye. Wind rattled the wooden wind chimes harmoniously in the open window behind him, and Tad watched golden dust motes dance in the beam of clear sunlight lancing down to puddle on the floor beside the old gryphon. "Let me see if I remember anything about Outpost Five."

Tad sighed as Aubri went through the whole of his dry, impish, "absentminded" routine, first scratching his rusty-brown headfeathers meditatively (which made more dust-motes dance into the light), then staring up at the ceiling of the dwelling he shared with Judeth. His head moved again after a long moment, and Tad hoped he was finally going to say something. But no—he looked down at the shining terrazzo floor, inlaid in a geometric pattern of cream and brown that to all outward appearances fascinated him. That is, he seemed to be staring at those places; like any raptor, a gryphon's peripheral vision was as good as his straight-on sight, and Tad knew very well that Aubri was watching them—well—like a hawk.

"Outpost Five," the elder gryphon muttered, shaking his head so that the fragments of feather-sheath dislodged by his earlier scratch flew in all directions. A single headfeather, striped in brown and cream and as large as a human's palm, drifted down to lie in the pool of sunlight beside him. Its edges were outlined in light, and the white fluff at the base glowed with a nimbus of reflected sunshine. "Outpost Five... now why does that sound familiar?"

This could go on for some time if Tad didn't put a stop to it. He fixed Aubri with a look that said wordlessly, *I know just what you're doing and I'm not falling for it.* In tones of deepest respect, he told his superior "You and Commander Judeth took Outpost Five three years ago, sir, when we first took responsibility for it from the Haighlei. You said the tour of duty was a vacation from trainees who couldn't molt without explicit written instructions."

Aubri blinked mildly, but his great golden eyes were twinkling with hidden amusement. "Did I say that? I'm cleverer than I thought. Well, yes, I think I remember Outpost Five, now that you mention it. Pretty remote; it's hard to find volunteers to man it. Good place for a vacation if what you want is thunderstorms every evening, fog every morning, and just enough of the sun to taunt you about its existence. There's a reason why the Haighlei call that kind of territory a 'rain forest.' It is wetter than a swimming kyree."

Well, good. That's one thing that wasn't in our lessons on manning outposts. And there's nothing in the briefing Blade read me that says anything about the weather there. "Would you say the weather is difficult enough to become a hindrance to our duties, sir?" he responded politely.

"Hindrance? I suppose if you're the kind that thinks he's going to melt if he has to fly in the rain." Aubri's mild manner turned just a trifle sharp, as if giving Tad subtle warning, that he'd better *not* be thinking any such thing. His pupils dilated and constricted rapidly, another sign of warning. "No one promised sunny beaches and half-day duty when you volunteered for the Silvers."

"It *is* dangerous to fly during thunderstorms, sir," Blade put in politely, verbally maneuvering Tad from under Aubri's talons. "And it can be dangerous to take off during heavy fog. We won't be doing White

Gryphon any favors if we get ourselves bunged up doing something stupid and they have to send in replacements and a rescue party. If the weather can become difficult enough to be dangerous, we ought to know about it in advance and know what warning signs to watch for. We can always ground ourselves and wait out a dangerous storm."

"Well, now, that's true enough." Aubri was back to being the bumbling, genial old "uncle." "But I don't think I said anything to give either of you the impression that the weather was going to make it impossible to fly your regular patrols. You'll just have to be careful, the way you were taught, and be diligent in watching for developing problems, that's all. The thunderstorms aren't violent, just briefly torrential, and the fog is always gone an hour after dawn."

Both of which would have made his bones ache, if he's having the same problems as my father. Aubri might be the oldest surviving gryphon from Urtho's forces; he was certainly older than Skandranon. He looked it, too; his feathers were not as sleek or as perfectly preened as Tad's were; in fact, they were a bit ragged, a trifle faded from what must have been his original colors of dark, warm brown and tan. Now he was rusty-brown and cream, and even feathers just grown in looked a bit shabby. Like Skandranon, he was of the broadwing variety, hawklike rather than falconiform, but he was huskier than Skandranon. His raptoral prototype was probably the umber-tailed hawkeagle, rather than the goshawk. There were signs of age in the delicate skin around his beak and eyes, a webwork of faint wrinkles, though those wrinkles were not as pronounced as the ones that humans got with increasing age. There was *no* sign of age in the mind, although you could not have told that from the way he was acting now.

"Acting," indeed. It's all an act, first, to last, the old fraud. He never forgets anything; I'll bet he remembers the order in which every trainee finished the last run on the obstacle course two weeks ago.

Aubri and Judeth were adept at playing the ally–antagonist game, with Aubri playing the absentminded and easily-fooled ally and Judeth the sharp-edged antagonist. Tad had caught onto the game in his first day of training, but then he had seen both Aubri and Judeth all the time when he was growing up. In particular, he had watched "absentminded" and "bumbling" Aubri best Skandranon time and time again over a game of stones, so it wasn't likely that he would ever be fooled into thinking that Aubri wasn't as sharp as his human partner.

Not that Father would ever admit to losing a game to Aubri except on purpose.

"Where is Commander Judeth, by the way?" he asked, for the white-haired human co-Commander of the Silver Gryphons had not been in evidence when the two of them arrived a few moments ago. Aubri jerked his beak toward the door, still standing open, as it had been when they arrived. On warm, pleasant days like this, most of the inhabitants, of White Gryphon preferred to keep all doors and windows open to the sea breezes, and Aubri was no exception.

"Meeting with the Haighlei; they're picking out the next set of Silvers to be in Shalaman's personal guard when Sella and Vorn come back." He preened a talon thoughtfully, chewing on the very end of it, his beak making little clicking sounds as he did so. "They'll probably take Kally and Reesk," he added. "They can't resist matched sets."

"You think so?" Blade asked skeptically; like Tad, she was aware that there were several pairs available for the duty whose skills were greater than the partners named.

Aubri snorted his contempt for anyone who would choose the looks of a set of guards over their ability. Not that Kally and Reesk were *bad;* no one was offered for Shalaman's guards who was bad. For that matter, anyone who wasn't up to Aubri's standards was generally asked to find some other vocation long before they got out of training—and exceptions had better prove themselves within six months or they would have to return that coveted silver badge. But by the yardstick of those that Judeth and her partner picked to represent White Gryphon in the service of the Haighlei Emperor, these two were just average.

Nevertheless, they were showy, their plumage of ruddy gold and bronze would complement the gold and lionskins of Shalaman's Grand Court, and they could stand at perfect attention for hours without moving a feather. Tadrith pointed out all of those attributes.

"The Emperor's Chief Advisor has other things to consider, sir," he finished politely. "It is very important, protocol-wise, for the Emperor's guards to be as still as carvings all during Court. That stillness implies *his* power and control."

"It's not as if they're ever going to have to *do* anything, sir," Blade said injudiciously. "Even assuming an assassin or madman got as far as the Emperor's Guard, he'd take one look at a pair of gryphons in full battle rage and pass out." Tad winced. *That* was not a bright thing to say—not to a veteran of the Great Wars and the Migration. There was a slight grating as Aubri's talons reflexively scratched the terrazzo.

"Maybe," Aubri replied with a narrow-eyed glare in her direction that

thoroughly cowed her. *"Maybe.* Never assume anything, young Silver. Assumptions get you killed. Either you know, or you make your plans for the worst-case contingency. Always. Never count on the best happening. I thought we taught you better than that."

The ice behind his words would have done his partner Judeth proud, and his tone was so sharp that even an idiot would have known he had made a mistake.

Blade flushed at the rebuke, and snapped stiffly to attention. Aubri waited a moment, to make certain that his words had taken effect, then waved a talon at her, and she relaxed, but warily.

That's one mistake she won't make again.

"Now, what was I saying? Outpost Five…" He yawned, all trace of the Commander gone from his demeanor again. He could have been any lazy old gryphon, without a single interest beyond a place in the sun to rest, a bit of good gossip, and the quality (and timely delivery) of his next meal. "Standard outpost, all the comforts of home if you happen to be a hermit, good hunting, always pretty damp, the nights are a bit chilly. Oh, and the area is largely unexplored." He gryph-grinned at Tad's ill-suppressed look of eagerness. "Figured that out, did you? If I were to guess, and it's *only* a guess, I'd say your best bet might be gold. Quartz pebbles in the river and streambeds that match the kind I've seen in the past where gold can be panned and separated out. We didn't bother looking when Judeth and I were there, we're too old to go wading around in cold water sloshing pans about. Since you've got a two-legger with you, it wouldn't hurt to do a little panning, just to see if there's anything there."

"No, it wouldn't," Tad agreed, as Blade grimaced, but nodded. That *would* be the easiest way to find gold, if Aubri was right and the area was sitting atop a vein or even a lode. Chances were, if they did find gold, panning would be the only way any of it would be taken out of the place for a long time. The Haighlei would first have to perform a divination to see if the gods approved of mining there, then they would have to wait for approval from Shalaman himself, *then* the priesthood and the Emperor would make a joint declaration that mining would be permitted. Even then, there would be no rush to sink mines; Shalaman himself would choose *one* person from among the handful born into the trade of mining expert to determine (with the help of the priesthood) where and when the first shaft should be sunk. That person, with the aid of his hereditary miners, would dig the first shaft while a member of the priesthood watched to be certain it was all done as the gods deemed fit and appropriate. If he struck the vein, the whole process might be gone through again, to see if the gods would allow a second mine in the forest. If not, it would be taken as a sign that the gods did not approve despite the earlier indications, and the whole concern would be packed up and moved home. Protocol.

And meanwhile, those citizens of White Gryphon willing to endure primitive conditions for the sake of the possibility of a fortune, would be industriously panning gold out of the streams, with Shalaman's blessing and his tax collectors monitoring. Panning involved nothing that would change the forest, the stream, or the earth beneath both, and so did not require the approval of the gods.

"What else?" he asked, and got the *figure it out for yourself, brat* look from Aubri. "I meant, what supplies would you suggest we take," he amended hastily. Blade took the hint and passed their list over to Aubri, who spread it out on the floor in front of him; "Other than the usual kit, I mean, the one we learned in training. This is what we'd thought of adding so far."

He was rather proud of the fact that he'd already put *prospecting pans* down; after all, if they didn't find any gold, they could always bake pies in them.

Aubri perused the list slowly, rumbling a little to himself. Finally, he looked up.

"This is all very well thought out," he said, "but it doesn't go far enough. That's not your fault," he added hastily, as both Tad and Blade's faces fell: "We train you fledges about *regular* outpost duty; but Five is almost twice as far away as any of the others. That was why Judeth and I went out there. If *we* couldn't handle it, we certainly didn't want to send any of you."

Aubri and Judeth shared the leadership of the Silvers as co-Commanders under Skandranon. Tad's father had turned over the actual working position to Aubri not long after the affair of the Eclipse Ceremony, more than twelve years ago. Skandranon had decided by then that he didn't *want* to be a leader, not unless it was a leader in name only. He much preferred to be the Black Gryphon (or White Gryphon, depending on whether he was at Khimbata and Shalaman's court or at home) with his talons into everything. The day-to-day trivia of leadership bored him; *doing* things made him happy.

Aubri, on the other hand, found himself, much to his surprise, to be quite good at the day-to-day trivia. Furthermore, it amused him. He said once to Skandranon that after all that he had been through during the Wars, dealing with requisitions and stupid recruits was a positive pleasure. The real truth was that he had long ago mastered the art of delegation and knew just who to saddle with the part of the job that he didn't care for. And now, with the able tutelage of his partner, and co-Commander Judeth, he very, much enjoyed being a leader. For the last three years or so, both of them had been claiming that they were going to retire "soon," but not one creature in the Silvers believed them. Neither of them was ever likely to enjoy retirement half so much as active duty.

It was Tad's opinion that what would probably happen was that a third co-Commander would be appointed, one in charge of the more physical aspect of the daily activities of the Silvers, and the minor decisions that didn't require an expert of the quality of either Aubri or Judeth. Judeth would remain in place as the overall Commander in charge of major decisions, and Aubri in charge of training, with which Judeth would assist him.

Now that, I can see happening. Judeth doesn't much like climbing all over the city all day, but they're both so experienced that it would be stupid to turn over complete control of the Silvers to someone younger—at least, not until they are comfortable with his competence. And Aubri loves bamboozling the trainees. Yes, that would make altogether too much sense, which is probably why that's what they'll do. They're the two creatures in the whole world that I can trust to act sensibly.

Tad couldn't imagine the Silvers without Aubri and Judeth in charge. It would have to happen someday, but he couldn't imagine what that day would be like when it came.

"Now look, you two," Aubri was saying. "You are going to be a long, long way from the city; it might be hard to get things to you if something wears out or breaks. Just because something minor like your water pump goes out, that doesn't mean we're going to rip open a Gate to send one to you. Gates are expensive, and *you* have perfectly sound limbs for carrying water in buckets."

Tad was taken aback, and so was Blades. *That* simply hadn't occurred to him; living among mages had made him think of Gates being put up quite casually. Gryphons flew, mages made Gates, it was that simple.

But now he realized that although a Gate went up just about every two or three days, they didn't stay up for very long, and what was more, they didn't even go up to the same place more often than once every month or two. There were just a lot of outposts and other far-flung ventures to supply, and that was what had made it seem as if Gating was commonplace and simple.

Aubri's eyes twinkled. "Your Gates will be opened at the scheduled times, not one moment earlier unless it's a *real* emergency of a life-threatening nature. They will remain open for *only* the scheduled times, so if there's more stuff you've asked for than can be chucked through in a hurry, that's too bad. You may have to wait through *several* resupply opportunities for your water pump. So what does that mean, Silvers?"

"Manuals," Blade said with resignation, adding them to the list. "We'll need repair manuals. All the repair tools we'd need will be there already, right?"

"And the manuals, too, don't worry; that outpost's been open a long time, and remember that Judeth and I were there first. *We* had the rank to order whatever we thought should be in place out there. Try again."

Blade chewed a nail and frowned as she thought. Her brows furrowed, and her eyes darkened until they were nearly blue-black. "Um. You said it's really damp. Humid?"

He nodded. "There's fog there, isn't there? Every morning. And rain every evening."

She brightened. "Bladders. Seals. Anything made of leather or wood—or metal that might rust. Repair parts that can get ruined by damp! That would be for—the water pump, the stove, the plumbing—" She began to scribble.

"Good!" Aubri turned to Tad, who fortunately had an answer waiting, because he already knew Aubri's prejudices. He'd heard the litany often enough, when he was still living at home.

"The kind of equipment that might go missing or get spoiled by damp that doesn't rely on magic to work," he said promptly. "Things like firestrikers, tinder boxes, trace sextant and compass for surveying... ah..." He pummeled his brain. Aubri nodded.

"Don't strain yourself; since you've just shown me that you know the principle, I'll give you a list. It's basically a few common replacement parts and some old army gear; won't add that much to your load, but there isn't much you can't do with it if you put your mind to the problem."

He didn't even move; he just stretched out a claw and stabbed a piece of paper already waiting on the top of the goldenwood desk that stood just within snatching distance. He must have been ready for them, once again proving that he wasn't nearly as absentminded as he seemed.

Blade took it from him, and Tad noticed that she seemed a bit bemused. Probably because she had a tendency to take everything and everyone at face value, and every time Aubri went into his "senile old featherhead" act, she fell for it.

Well, she can't help it. This was her big weakness, and Tad had a good idea why she wasn't likely to cure it any time soon. Part of the problem was that she just didn't *want* to look past the surface masks that everyone wore, no matter how honest and genuine they were. Tad's partner just didn't want to know what surprises might lie beneath those polite masks; that Empathy thing of hers bothered her, and if she could have had it surgically removed, Tad had it figured that she would have done so no matter what the risk. And there were reasons behind that as well; she had realized a long time ago that she would never, ever be as good as her father at delving into people's hearts and souls. She was the kind of person who, if she couldn't excel at something, didn't want to try.

Silly. Not every mage can be a Snowstar, but the hedge-wizards can do plenty of things he hasn't got the time for, or even do subtle things he can't do at all. Well, it'd be flogging pointlessly to take that *up with her, at least now. Maybe after we've been out there a while, and we've had a lot of peace and privacy.* That particular twitch of hers bothered him, though, and he wanted to have it straightened out before too very long. Any amount of mind-magic was useful, the more so in someone who might well be supposed to boast nothing of the sort. *Father always says that if you've got an ability, it's stupid not to train and use it, even if it isn't something that you'd use very often.*

Blade compared the two lists, and added several items to theirs before she handed the one Aubri had given her back to him. Tad was pleased to note that she had *not* needed to copy the whole thing down. So they hadn't done so badly on their own.

I wonder if there was a bonesetting kit on Aubri's list, though. It certainly fits his criteria of "nonmagical" and "spoiled by damp." But, oh, the weight! If only someone could come up with better splints and casting material! It seems so stupid to be hauling wood and powdered rock!

Aubri crossed his forelegs in front of him, and regarded both of them with a benign, almost paternal expression on his face. "Well. Two more of my fledges go out to prove their wings. I think you'll like the post; neither of you are the kind to pine after a city when you can thrash around in the forest and see things no one else ever has before." He sighed. "Adventures are for the young, who haven't got bone aches. Now me—I'm happy to be here in White Gryphon where I can sunbathe every day. But there should be enough new discoveries there to make even two youngsters like you happy."

He did not mention that he knew *their* personal prime reason for being so happy with this assignment; getting away from their beloved families. He had never acted as if he recognized them as Skandranon's and Amberdrake's offspring—

Well, he wouldn't; not while we were in training. But he's never even mentioned our parents casually. Maybe he is a little absentminded in that direction; maybe he doesn't recognize us now that we're grown.

"We're looking forward to it, sir," he said honestly. "And it'll be nice to be away from home for the first time."

Aubri nodded, then grinned. "Oh, you aren't the only ones who've been interested in long assignments outside the city, believe it or not. I told Judeth that she should never assign anyone to Five who didn't have a good reason for being there as well as a good reason for getting away from home. I've never seen anyone who fit those qualifications better than you two. And to tell you the truth, I had a third reason to want you out there—you're a two-and-four team. That's a good combination for an outpost."

That was a gryphon paired with a human. That particular team was not all that usual among the Silvers; people tended to team up with members of their own species. Usually the two-and-fours were default teams, made up of those who couldn't find a compatible partner among their own kind. Quite often they broke up after training, when a senior Silver could take a junior out of training as a partner. Those who were in default two-and-fours generally did just that.

"I like a two-and-four for these remote postings," Aubri continued, then got that twinkle back in his eye. "The teams are more flexible, more versatile. Even if some people think there's something wrong with a gryphon who doesn't team up with one of his own."

Tad stared back at his superior with his head held high and challenge in his gaze. He'd heard that one before, and it didn't ruffle his feathers. "Oh? Does that include you, too, sir?"

Aubri laughed. "Of course it does! Everyone *knows* I'm a twisted personality! All of us war veterans are warped, it comes with combat! What's your excuse?"

Tad grinned back as the perfect answer came to him. "Family tradition, sir," he responded immediately, prompting Aubri into another bray of laughter.

"Well said! And I can't wait to tell the Black Boy what you just told me; if that doesn't make his nares redden, nothing will." He shook his head, and the feathers rustled. "Now, you two run along. Give that list to the supply officer; he'll see to getting your basket packed up. All you need to worry about is your own kit."

They both stood and snapped to attention. Aubri chuckled, and rose slowly to his feet to let them out—old, maybe, but not dead yet.

As Tad had expected, his father already knew about the posting, and was outwardly (and loudly) enthusiastic. If he had beaten every contender and been appointed as Judeth's sub-Commander, Skandranon could not have been more thrilled. It was positively embarrassing. As they gathered for the evening meal in the main room of the family aerie, with the sky a dark velvet studded with jewel-like stars beyond the window, Tad wondered if he shouldn't have opted for a quiet bite alone—or perhaps have gone hungry.

"Outpost duty! And you fresh out of training!" he kept saying, all through dinner. "I can't ever remember any Silver as young as you are being put on remote duty!"

His tone was forced, though, and he hadn't eaten more than half his meal. At the least, this sudden change in his son's status had put him off his feed. Was he worried?

Why should he be worried! What's there to be worried about!

Zhaneel, Skandranon's mate, cuffed him lightly. "Let the boys eat," she admonished him. "You won't be doing Tadrith any favor by giving him no time to have a proper meal."

But her look of rebuke followed by a glance at Keeth made Skandranon's nares flush red with embarrassment. He *had* been neglecting Keeth the whole time, although Keeth didn't seem too terribly unhappy about that. "I hear fine reports about you from Winterhart," he said hastily to his other son. "You're training in things your mother and I dreamed of doing, but were never able to achieve."

Tad winced. Now, if *that* didn't sound forced, he'd eat grass instead of good meat!

"Well, if there hadn't been that annoying war, Father, you two would probably have invented the gryphon *tiondi'irn*, the gryphon *kestra'chern*, and the gryphon secretary," Keeth said, with a sly grin at his brother. "And probably the gryphon seamstress, mason, and carpenter as well!"

Trust Keeth to know how to turn it into a joke, bless him.

Skandranon laughed, and this time it sounded genuine and a bit more relaxed. "And maybe we would have!" he replied, rousing his feathers. "Too bad that war interfered with our budding genius, heh?"

Tad kept silent and tore neat bites from his dinner, the leg of a huge flightless bird the size of a cow and with the brains of a mud-turtle. One of these creatures fed the whole family; the Haighlei raised them for their feathers, herding them on land that cattle or sheep would damage with overgrazing. The gryphons found these creatures a tasty alternative to beef and venison.

Tad was perfectly pleased to let clever Keeth banter with their father. He couldn't think of anything to say, not when beneath the Black Gryphon's pride lurked a tangle of emotions that he couldn't even begin to unravel. But he was more and more certain that one of them was a fear that Skandranon would never admit to.

Of course not. He doesn't want to cripple me with indecision or even fear of my own before I go out there with Blade. He knows that if he shows he's unhappy with this, I might be tempted to back out of it. And he knows that there's nothing to worry about; we're hardly the first team to ever take this outpost. We're just the first team that included one of his sons, and he's been thinking about all the accidents that could happen to us ever since he heard of the posting.

He was worrying too much; Tad knew that, and he knew that his father knew it as well. This was not wartime, and they were not going to encounter hostile troops.

But this is the first time I'm "leaving the nest." I suppose it's perfectly normal for parents to worry. I worry, too, but I know that it can be done. I wonder why parents can say they trust their young so much, yet still fear for them! He supposed that a parent's imagination could conjure up a myriad of other dangers, from illness to accident, and play them out in the space of a heartbeat. Parents had to be that way; they had to anticipate all the trouble youngsters could get into and be prepared to pluck them out of danger before they got too deeply into it.

But I'm an adult, and I can take care of myself! Isn't he ever going to figure that out! He has been an adult for ages longer than I have, and he has had to be rescued before—so why is it that adults regard trouble as the sole territory of the young! Do we remind them of their vulnerability that much!

Between bites, he cast a glance at his mother, surprising her in an openly concerned and maternal gaze at him. She started to look away, then evidently thought better of it, and nodded slightly.

Mother's worried, but she admits it. Father won't, which will make it worse on him. And there's no reason for either of them to worry at all! Maybe the more intelligent a parent is, the more they worry, because then they are able to see more of what could go wrong. The Kaled'a'in Quarters know that they could concentrate just as much on what could go right, but when it comes to children—or young adults—it could be smartest to have only grudging optimism. Still...

He spared a thought for Blade, who was probably undergoing the same scrutiny at the hands of her parents, and sighed. He didn't know how Amberdrake and Winterhart would be reacting to this, but Blade had threatened to spend the night with friends rather than go home to face them. Tad had managed to persuade her to change her mind.

It could be much worse, he told himself. *They could be so overprotective that they refuse to let me take the post, Or, worse than that, they could be indifferent.*

A couple of his classmates had parents like that; Tad had heard mages speculating that the raptor instinct ran so strongly in them that it eclipsed what Urtho had intended. Those parents were loving enough as long as their young were "in the nest." They began to lose interest in them when they fledged, just exactly as raptor parents did. Eventually, when the young gryphons reached late adolescence and independence, their parents did their best to *drive* them away, if they had not already left. Such pairs were more prolific than those who were more nurturing, raising as many as six or eight young in a reproductive lifetime.

But those offspring were, as Aubri would say, "glorified gamehawks;" they lived mostly for the hunt and, while extremely athletic, were not very long in the intelligence department. Most of the gryphonic fatalities at White Gryphon had occurred among this group, which for the most part *were* assigned to hunting to supplement the meat supply of the city. They were very much like goshawks in focus and temper; they would fly into the ground or a cliff during a chase and break their foolish necks, or go out in wretched weather and become a victim of exposure. Some simply vanished without anyone ever knowing what happened to them.

Aubri had said once in Tad's hearing that a majority of the fatalities in gryphon-troops of the war—other than those attributable to human commanders who saw all nonhumans as expendable and deployed them that way—were also among this type of gryphon. Needless to say, the type had been in the minority among those that had reached safe haven here, and were not likely to persist into a third generation. Not at the rate that they were eliminating themselves, at least!

When they weren't hunting, they could usually be found lounging about on the sunning platform with others of their kind, either attempting to impress like-minded females or comparing wing-muscles. Granted, there was always a bit of that going on among young gryphons, but this lot acted like that *all the time!*

Very attractive, to look at perhaps. But as trysting mates or play-fighters, I don't think I could stand them.

So while Skandranon was probably thinking over how many young gryphons of Tadrith's generation had been lost, it was not occurring to him what those unfortunate fatalities had in common.

Say—an absolute dearth of brains. A squandering of what they had. And most importantly, a lack of decent parenting. Keeping a young one's body alive was one thing, but it only created more breeders to do the same with the next generation they bred. Even a charming young idiot can succeed with good parenting. I'm proof of that, aren't I?

His father had lost some of his self-consciousness and was now speaking normally to Keeth and Zhaneel about some modification Winterhart had made to the standard obstacle course in order to train *trondi'irn*. Tad took full advantage of their absorption to get some more of his meal down in peace.

Skandranon was an odd sight just now; halfway into a molt, he was piebald black and white. The white feathers were his natural color—now—and the black were dyed. He dyed himself whenever he was due to visit Khimbata in his capacity as special representative of White Gryphon. Ever since the Eclipse Ceremony, when he had come diving dramatically down out of the vanishing sun to strike down an assassin who would have murdered Emperor Shalaman, Winterhart, and probably several more people as well, he'd been virtually forced to wear his Black Gryphon "guise" whenever he visited. He had rescued Shalaman, the Black King, as the Black Gryphon—and in a culture that set a high value on things that never changed, he was mentally set in that persona whenever he returned to the site of his triumph.

The Gryphon King, beloved where e'er he goes. That was what Aubri had said to his face, mockingly.

But the real irony of the statement was that it was true: He never left Khimbata without being loaded down with gifts of all sorts. His jewelry collection was astonishing; if he and Zhaneel wore all of it at one time, they'd never get off the ground.

Between us, if we're lucky, Keeth and I might manage to be a quarter as famous as he is—and then most of it will be due to the fact that we're his sons.

That could have been a depressing thought, if Tad had any real ambition. But to be frank, he didn't. He'd seen the negative effects of all that adulation—how it was always necessary for Skandranon to be charming, witty, and unfailingly polite no matter what he personally felt like. How when the family visited Khimbata, Skandranon had barely a moment to himself and none to spare for them. And how even at home, there was always *someone* who wanted something from him. He was always getting gifts, and a great many of those gifts came with requests attached. Even when they didn't, there was always the chance that a demand, phrased as a request, would come later, perhaps when he wasn't expecting it and was off his guard.

There was no way for Skandranon to know whether someone wanted his friendship because of *what* he was or because of *who* he was—and the difference was critical.

No, thank you. I am very fond of obscurity, all things considered.

It would be no bad thing to be an obscure Silver, always assigned to the Outposts, hopefully collecting enough extra from his discoveries to finance a comfortable style of living. Let Keeth collect all the notoriety of being the first gryphon *trondi'irn;* Tad would be happy to donate whatever measure of "fame" fate had in store for him to his brother! Just as he had finished that thought, he noticed that the others were looking at him. Evidently Keeth had run out of things to say, and it was his turn again.

Oh, bother.

Skandranon cleared his throat. As always, the sound, an affectation acquired from living so much with humans, sounded very odd coming from a gryphon.

It sounds as if he's trying to cough up a hairball, actually.

"Well!" Skandranon said heartily. "Your mother and I are very interested in hearing about this outpost you're being sent to. What do you know about it?"

Tad sighed with resignation, and submitted himself to the unrelenting pressure of parental love.

Blade couldn't bring herself to sit, although she managed to keep from pacing along the edge of the cliff. The stone here was a bit precarious for pacing—how ignoble if she should slip and fall, breaking something, and force Judeth and Aubri to send someone else to the outpost after all! *Tad would never, ever forgive me. Or else—he'd take a new partner and go, and I would be left behind to endure parental commiserations.*

Ikala sat on a rock and watched the sunset rather than her. He'd asked her to meet him here for a private farewell; her emotions were so mixed now that she honestly didn't know what to say to him. So far, he hadn't said anything to her, and she waited for him to begin.

He cleared his throat, still without looking at her. "So, you leave tomorrow. For several months, I'm told?" Of course, he knew her assignment, everyone in the Silvers did; he was just using the question as a way to start the conversation.

The sun ventured near to the ocean; soon it would plunge down below the line of the horizon. Her throat and tongue felt as if they belonged to someone else. "Yes," she finally replied. Now she knew why people spoke of being "tongue-tied." It had been incredibly difficult just to get that single word out.

She wanted to say more, to ask if he would miss her, if he was angry that she was leaving just as their friendship looked to become something more. She wanted to know if he was hurt that she hadn't consulted him, or chosen him as her partner instead of Tad. Above all, she wanted to know what he was thinking.

Instead, she couldn't say anything.

"Come and sit," he said, gesturing at the rocks beside him. "You do not look comfortable."

I'm not, she said silently. *I'm as twitchy as a nervous cat.*

But she sat down anyway, warily, gingerly. The sun-warmed rock felt smooth beneath her hand, worn to satin-softness by hundreds of years of wind and water. She concentrated on the rock, mentally holding to its solidity and letting it anchor her heart.

"I am both happy for you and sad, Blade," Ikala said, as if he was carefully weighing and choosing each word. "I am happy for you, because you are finally being granted—what you have earned. It is a good thing. But I am sad because you will be gone for months."

He sighed, although he did not stir. Blade held herself tensely, waiting for him to continue, but he said nothing more. She finally turned toward him. "I wanted an assignment like this one very much," she agreed. "I'm not certain I can explain why, though—"

But unexpectedly, as he half-turned to meet her eyes, he smiled. "Let me try," he suggested, and there was even a suggestion of self-deprecating humor. "You feel smothered by your honored parents and, perversely, wish for their approval of a life so different from theirs. Additionally, you fear that their influence will either purchase you an easier assignment than you warrant, or will insure that you are never placed in any sort of danger. You wish to see what you can do with only the powers of your own mind and your own skills, and if you are not far away from them, you are certain you will never learn the answer to that question."

"Yes!" she exclaimed, startled by his insight. "But how did you—" Then she read the message behind that rueful smile, the shrug of the dark-skinned shoulders. "You came here for the same reason, didn't you?"

He nodded once, and his deep brown eyes showed that same self-deprecating humor that had first attracted her. "The same. And that is why, although I wish that you were not going so far or for so long—or that we were going to the same place—I wanted you to know that I am content to wait upon your return. We will see what you have learned, and what that learning has made of you."

"And you think I will be different?" She licked her lips with a dry tongue.

"At least in part," he offered. "You may return a much different person than the one you are now; not that I believe that I will no longer care much for that different person! But that person and I may prove to be no more than the best of friends and comrades-in-arms. And that will not be a bad thing, though it is not the outcome I would prefer."

She let out her breath and relaxed. He was being so reasonable about this that she could hardly believe her ears! "I don't know," she admitted. "I think I've spent so much time proving who I'm not that I don't know who I am."

"So go and find out," he told her, and laughed, now reaching out to touch her hand briefly: The touch sent a shivery chill up her arm. "You see, I had to come here to do the same thing. So I have some understanding of the process."

"Are you glad that you came here?" she asked, wondering if the question was too personal, and wishing he would do more than just touch her hand.

Now it was his turn to look away, into the sunset, for a moment. "On the whole—yes," he told her. "Although in doing so, it became impossible to follow the alternate path I might have taken. There was a maiden, back in my father's court—but she was impatient, and did not like it that I chose to go somewhere other than to the court of another emperor. She saw my choice as a lessening of my status, and my leaving as a desertion of her. I have heard that she wedded elsewhere, one of my more traditional half-brothers."

"Oh—I'm sorry—" she said quickly, awkwardly.

But he turned back to her, and did not seem particularly unhappy as he ran his hand across his stiff black curls. "There is not a great deal to be sorry about," he pointed out. "If she saw it as desertion, she did not know me; if I could not predict that she would, I did not know her. So…" He shrugged. "Since it was not long before my sorrow was gone, I suspect my own feelings were not as deep as she would have liked, nor as I had assumed."

"It's not as if you were lacking in people willing to console you here!" she pointed out recklessly, with a feeling of breathlessness that she couldn't explain. She laughed to cover it.

"And that is also true." His smile broadened. "And it was not long before I felt no real need of such consolation, as I had another interest to concentrate on."

Her feeling of breathlessness intensified; this was the nearest he had come to flirting with her, and yet behind the playfulness, there was more than a hint of seriousness. Did she *want* that? She didn't know. And now—she was very glad that she was going to have three months to think about it.

"Well, I think, on the whole, it will be a good thing for you to have six months to learn what it is that Blade is made of," he said, in a lighter tone. "And I shall have the benefit of knowing that there will be no other young men at this outpost that may convince you to turn your attentions elsewhere. So any decisions you make—concerning our friendship—will be decisions made by you, only."

She snorted. "As if any young man could 'make me change my mind' about anything important!" she replied, just a little sharply.

"Which only proves that I cannot claim to know you any better than any other friend!" he countered. "You see? This much I do understand; you have a strong sense of duty, and that will always be the first in your heart. I would like to think that I am the same. So, whatever, we must reconcile ourselves to that before we make any other commitments."

It was her turn to shrug. "That seems reasonable… but it isn't exactly… romantic." That last came out much more plaintively than she had expected, or intended.

"Well, if it is a romantic parting that you wish—" He grinned. "I can be both practical and romantic, as, I suspect, can you." He took one of her hands, but only one, and looked directly into her eyes. "Silverblade, I crossed an empire, I left my land and all I have ever known. I did not expect to find someone like you here, and yet—I do not follow some of my people's reasoning that all is foredestined, but it sometimes seems as if I was drawn here because you were here. Now I know something of what I am. I believe that there is in you a spirit that would make a match for my own. If, in the end, a few months more will bring us together, such a wait will be no hardship." He patted her hand. "I trust that is romance enough for your practical soul?"

She laughed giddily. "I think so," she said, feeling as lightheaded as if she had just drunk an entire bottle of wine. "I—I'm not nearly that eloquent—"

"Neither is the falcon," he said, releasing her hand. "But she is admirable for her grace without need of eloquence. Go become a passage bird, Silverblade. When you return, we shall try out hunting in a cast of two."

Blade hadn't needed to do all that much packing last night, but she had pretended that she did—and as soon as she was done, she blew out her candle and willed herself to sleep. The need for rest was real, and if she had not torn herself away from her overly-concerned parents, she would not have gotten any. They would have kept her up all night with questions, most of which she didn't have any answers to, since all of them were fairly philosophical rather than practical.

She dressed quickly and quietly, and without relighting her candle. With any luck, only her mother would be awake; Winterhart, for some reason, seemed to be handling this better than her spouse. *Don't people usually complain that their* mothers *never, see them as grown up!* she thought, as she pulled on a pair of light boots, then fastened the silver gryphon badge to the breast of her tunic. The Silvers had no regular uniform; Judeth thought it better that they wear the same clothing as those around them. Uniforms might remind people too much of the regular troops, and war, and even the most battle-hardened wanted to put warfare far behind them.

Now—if I can just walk quietly enough, I might be able to get out of here without another discussion of my life-view.

Her father Amberdrake was notorious for sleeping late —to be fair, it was usually because he'd been up late the night before, working—and she hoped by rising with the first light, she might avoid him at breakfast.

But no. When she carried her two small packs out to leave beside the door, she saw that there were candles burning in the rest of the house. Amberdrake was already up.

In fact, as soon as she turned toward the rear of the dwelling, she saw him; dressed, alert, and in the little nook at the back of the main room that they used for meals, waiting for her. But so was her mother, which might temper things a bit.

She sighed, while her face was still in shadow and he couldn't see her expression. Breakfast with Amberdrake was always a bit strained at the best of times, and this was not going to be "the best" of times.

He keeps remembering when he was the chief kestra'chern and it was his habit to find out about his fellows when they all drifted in for breakfast. He keeps trying to do the same thing with me.

"Good morning, Father," she said, feeling terribly awkward, as she approached the tiny table. "You're not usually up so early."

She wondered if Amberdrake's smile was strained; he was too good at keeping a serene mask for her to tell. However, it was obvious that he had taken special pains with his appearance. *Silk tunic and trews, raw-silk coat, some of his Haighlei gift-jewelry, and Zhaneel's feather in his hair. You'd think he was having an audience with Shalaman.*

She regarded him objectively for a moment. He was still a strikingly handsome man. Despite the white streaks in his hair, her father scarcely looked his age in the low mage-light above the table, and the warm browns and ambers of his clothing disguised in part the fact that there were dark circles under his eyes.

Caused by worrying, no doubt.

"I didn't want to miss saying good-bye to you, Silverblade," he said, his voice quite calm and controlled. "If I slept until a decent hour, I knew that I would. You dawn risers are enough to make a normal person's eyes cross."

She knew that her answering laugh was a bit strained, but there was no help for it. "And you night prowlers are enough to make people like me scream when we think of all the perfectly good daylight you waste sleeping!" She slid into the seat opposite him, and helped herself to fresh bread and preserves. *He* reached across the table and added thinly-sliced cold meat to the plate quite firmly. She didn't really want anything that substantial first thing in the morning, but she knew better than to say so. Why start an argument? That would be a poor way to leave her parents.

What can it hurt to nibble a piece to please him! It can't, of course. Not that long ago, she would have protested; now she knew there was no point in doing so. She'd only hurt his feelings. He was only trying to help.

And after today he won't be able to be so meddlingly helpful for six whole months!

I should be pitying the people, gryphon and human and hertasi alike, who will wind up as my surrogates for his concern.

She ate one slice of the meat, which was dry and tasted like a mouthful of salty old leather, and went back to her bread. Amberdrake pushed a cup of hot tea toward her, then made a move as if he was about to serve her a bowl of hot porridge from the pot waiting beside him.

"Oh no!" she exclaimed. Not for *anything* would she eat porridge, not even for the sake of pleasing her father! "None of that! Not when I'm flying! I do not want to decorate the landscape underneath me!"

Amberdrake flushed faintly and pulled his hand back. "Sorry. I forgot that you didn't inherit my impervious stomach."

"No, she inherited my questionable one. Stop badgering the child, dear." Winterhart emerged at last from the rear of the dwelling, putting the last touches on her hair. Blade admired the way she moved with a twinge of envy. Winterhart managed to combine a subtle sensuality with absolute confidence and a no-nonsense competence that Blade despaired of emulating.

Now if I looked like that… Ah, well. Too bad I inherited Mother's interior instead of her exterior!

Unlike her mate, Winterhart had not dressed for a special occasion, which much relieved Blade. Her costume of a long linen split skirt, tunic, and knee-length, many-pocketed vest, was similar to anything she would wear on any other day. The only concession she had made to Amberdrake's sartorial splendor was to harmonize with his browns and ambers with her own browns and creams.

"I hope we won't be unwelcome, but we would like to see you and Tadrith leaving, Blade," Winterhart said, quite casually, as if they were only leaving for a few days, not six months. "We *do* know how to stay out from underfoot, after all. Yours is not the first expedition we've seen on its way."

Now it was her turn to flush. "Well, of course I want you there to see us off! Of course you won't be in the way!" she replied, acutely embarrassed. "I would never think that!"

The only trouble was, deep down inside, she had been thinking precisely that.

She gulped down her cooling tea to cover her embarrassment and guilty conscience, as Amberdrake toyed with a piece of bread, reducing it to a pile of crumbs.

He's trying to pretend that he isn't worried; trying to put on a brave face when I know he's feeling anything but brave. Why! Why is he so worried! If he's transparent enough for me to see through, he must be all of a knot inside.

Finally Amberdrake looked up at her, slowly chewing on his lower lip. "I know I probably seem as if I am overreacting to this situation, ke'chara," he said quietly, "I shouldn't be so worked up over the simple fact that you and your partner are going off on a normal, peaceful assignment. I realize that I am being quite foolish about this, and I can't even pretend that I have some mysterious presentiment of doom. It's all due to old—well, I suppose you'd have to call them habits, habits of feeling, perhaps."

Winterhart stood behind him and put her hands on his shoulders, gently massaging muscles that must have been terribly tense. Outside, seabirds cried, greeting the dawn and the winds that would carry them out to their fishing grounds.

Amberdrake reached up and covered one of his mate's hands with his own. "I have two problems with this assignment, really, and neither of them is rational. The first is that it is you, my daughter, who is going off for six months to a place that is unsettlingly far away. And you'll be all alone there, except for a single gryphon. If it were someone else, I would see him or her off with a cheerful heart, and go about my business."

"But it isn't," she stated.

"No." He sighed, and patted Winterhart's hand. "Your mother is handling this better than I."

"I have perfect confidence in Aubri and Judeth," Winterhart said serenely. "They wouldn't send anyone that far away who wasn't prepared for any contingency." Her tone turned just a little sharp as she looked down at him. "If you won't trust Blade, dearheart, at least trust *them.*"

"Intellectually, I *do,*" Amberdrake protested. "It's just—it's just that it's hard to convince the emotions."

He turned back to Blade, who was even more embarrassed at her parent's decision to bare his soul to her. She struggled not to show it. And underneath the embarrassment was exasperation.

Can't he learn that I am grown now, and don't need him to come haul me out of difficulties! Can't he just let me go?

"The other problem I have is very old, older than you, by far," he told her earnestly. "And it has absolutely nothing to do with your abilities; it's something I would still feel even if you were a warrior out of legend with magical weapons at your side. It doesn't matter to my heart that this is peace time, that you are simply going off to man a wilderness outpost.

The point to my reaction is that you are going *out*. When——" momentary pain ghosted over his expressive features. "—when people used to go out, back in the days of the wars, they didn't always come back." She opened her mouth to protest; he forestalled her.

"I *know* this is peacetime, I *know* you are not going forth to combat an enemy, I *know* that there is no enemy but storms and accident. But I still have the emotional reaction to seeing people going out on a quasi-military mission, and that fact that it is my daughter that is doing so only makes the reaction worse." He smiled thinly. "You cannot reason with an old emotional problem, I am afraid."

She looked down at the polished wood of the tabletop, and made little patterns with her forefinger, tracing the grain of the wood. What on earth did he expect her to say? What *could* she say? *That was years and years ago, before I was even born. Can't he have gotten over it by now! He's supposed to be the great magician of the emotions, so why can't he keep his own trained to heel! What could possibly go wrong with this assignment! We'll have a teleson with us, we'll be reporting in, and if there* is *a life-threatening emergency and they can't get help to us quickly, they'll take the risk and Gate us back!*

But that wasn't what he wanted to hear, and it wouldn't help anything to say it. "I can understand. At least, I think I can. I'll try," she finished lamely.

True, it is nothing but wilderness between here and there—but when we get "there," we'll be in a fortified outpost built to withstand storm, siege, or earthquake. And, granted, no one has even tried to explore all the rain forest in between, but we'll be flying, not walking! What could possibly knock us out of the sky that our people or the Haighlei wouldn't have encountered a long, long time ago!

It was—barely—possible that some mage-made creatures of Ma'ar's survived from the Cataclysm. It was less likely that any of them could have made it this far south. And even if they did, there had never been *that* many of them that could threaten a gryphon. *The last makaar died* ages *ago, and there never was anything else that could take a flying gryphon down. We'll be flying too high for any projectile to hurt us, and even if we weren't, there'll be the mass of the carry-basket and all our supplies between us and a marksman.*

"Father, I promise you, we'll be fine," she only said, choking down a last dry mouthful of bread. "Makaar are extinct, and nothing less could even ruffle Tadrith's feathers. *You've* seen him; he's one of the biggest, strongest gryphons in the Silvers!"

But Amberdrake shook his head. "Blade, it's not that I don't trust or believe in you, but there is far more in this world than you or Tadrith have ever seen. There were more mages involved in the Mage Wars than just Urtho and Ma'ar; plenty of them created some very dangerous creatures, too, and not all of them were as short-lived as makaar. I will admit that we are a long distance from the war zones, but *we* got this far, so who's to say that other things couldn't?"

He's not going to listen to me, she realized. *He's determined to be afraid for me, no matter what I say.* There was more likelihood of moving the population of the city up to the rim of the canyon than there was of getting Amberdrake to change his mind when it was made up.

"What's more, as you very well know, the mage-storms that followed the Cataclysm altered many, many otherwise harmless creatures, and conjured up more." His jaw firmed stubbornly. "You ask Snowstar if you don't believe me; some of the territory we passed through was unbelievable, and that was only after a year or so of mage-storms battering at it! We were very, very lucky that most of the things we encountered were minimally intelligent."

"Sports and change-children die out in less than a generation," she retorted, letting her impatience get the better of her. "That's simple fact, Father. There're just too many things wrong with most, magic-made creatures for them to live very long, if they've been created by accident."

He raised an elegant eyebrow at her, and the expression on his face told her she'd been caught in a mistake.

"Urtho was not infallible," he said quietly. "He had many accidents in the course of creating some of his new creatures. *One* of those accidents was responsible for the creation of intelligence in *kyree*, and another for intelligence in *hertasi*. And neither race has 'died out within a generation.'"

She had already spotted the flaw in his argument. "An accident may have been responsible for the intelligence of the creature, but not the creature itself," she countered. "Creature creation takes great thought, planning, and skill. An accident is simply not going to be able to duplicate that!"

He looked as if he were going to say something, but subsided instead.

"Besides," Blade continued, taking her advantage while she still had it, "people have been going to this outpost for years, and no one has seen anything—either there or on the way. Don't you think by now if there was going to be any trouble, someone would have encountered it?"

Amberdrake dropped his eyes in defeat and shook his head. "There you have me," he admitted. "Except for one thing. We don't know what lies beyond that outpost and its immediate area. The Haighlei have never been there, and neither have we. For all we know, there's an army of refugees from the wars about to swarm over you, or a renegade wizard about to take a force of his own across the land—"

"And *that*," Blade said with finality, "is precisely why we will be there in the first place. It is our duty to be vigilant."

He couldn't refute that, and he didn't try.

Blade extracted herself from her parents with the promise that she and Tad would not take off until they arrived. With one pack slung over her back and the other suspended from her shoulder, she hurried up the six levels of staircase that led in turn to the narrow path which would take her to the top of the cliff. She was so used to running up and down the ladderlike staircases and the switchback path that she wasn't even breathing heavily when she reached the top. She had spent almost all of her life here, after all, and verticality was a fact of life at White Gryphon.

Below, on the westward-facing cliff the city was built from, she had been in cool shadow; she ascended as the invisible sun rose, and both she and the sun broke free of the clinging vestiges of night at the same time. Golden fingers of light met and caressed her as she took the last few steps on the path. It would be a perfect morning; there were no clouds marring the horizon to presage storms to the east. Red skies were lovely—but red skies required clouds ... *If I am going to be traveling, I prefer a morning like this one; not a cloud in the sky and the air dry, cool, and quiet.*

At the top of the cliff a great expanse of meadow and farmland composed of gently rolling hills stretched out before her. It was completely indefensible, of course; like Ka'venusho, Urtho's stronghold, there was no decent "high ground" to defend. This was why the city itself had been built into the cliff, with the only access being a single, narrow path. You couldn't even rain boulders down on White Gryphon from above, for the path had been cut into the cliff so cleverly that it channeled objects falling down from the edge away from the city entirely.

Judeth's idea, but it took some very clever stonecrafters, to put her idea into solid form.

At the edge were large constructions of wooden frames and pulleys that could lower huge amounts of material down to the first level of the city; that was how food was brought down from the farms up here. Those could be dismantled or destroyed in mere moments by a very few people. Nothing that was up here would be left to be used by an enemy if there ever was an attack.

The farmers used to live in White Gryphon and travel up each day to tend their flocks and fields; now they didn't bother with the trip. There was a second village up here on the rim, a village of farmhouses and barns, a few warehouses and workshops, and the pens where herds were brought during the few days of each year that the weather was too bad to keep the herds in the fields. If severe winter storms came from the sea instead of the landward side, the herds could be driven into the shelter of the forest, and those who were not sent to watch over them could take shelter within the rock walls of White Gryphon.

The stockade and supply warehouse of the Silvers was up here as well. Space was too precious in the city for any to be wasted on bulk stores except in an emergency. And as for the stockade, most punishment involved physical labor in the fields with the proceeds going to pay back those who had been wronged. Since most crime in the city involved theft or minor damage, that was usually acceptable to the victims. There *had* been those—a few—who were more dangerous. Those were either imprisoned up here, under bindings, or—dealt with, out of the sight of the city. After Hadanelith, no one was ever exiled again. The possibility that another dangerous criminal might survive exile was too great to risk.

Just outside the stockade was a landing platform. Sitting squarely in the middle of it was what appeared to be a large basket, about the size of a six-person expedition-tent. There was a complicated webbing of ropes attached to it, and standing nearby was Tadrith, with a *hertasi* helping him into a heavy leather harness. As usual, he was carrying on a running dialogue with his helper, trying to get his harness adjusted perfectly. She knew better than to interrupt; her life would depend on that harness and whether or not he was comfortable in it.

This was the carry-basket that would take her and all their supplies to the Outpost. It looked far, far too heavy for Tadrith to fly with, and it was. Even the strongest of gryphons would not have been able to lift *her* alone in it unaided.

But magic was working reliably enough these days, and there would be a mage somewhere around who had made certain that the basket and anything that might be in it would "weigh" nothing, with a reserve for changes in momentum and speed. He would essentially have made the basket into a variant of one of the Kaled'a'in floating-barges. Tadrith would not be "lifting" the basket, only guiding it.

The spell was a complicated one that Blade couldn't even begin to understand. Anything *inside* the basket—like herself—would still have its apparent weight. If that wasn't the case, everything not tied down would be in danger of drifting off on a stiff breeze. But to Tad, although the basket had no up-and-down weight, it would still have a certain amount of side-to-side mass and momentum. He would not be lifting it, but he *would* have to exert some strength in pulling it, just as teams of *dyheli* and horses pulled the floating barges.

Blade hurried up to check the supplies lashed down inside the basket. As Aubri had promised, the supply sergeant had taken care of everything she and Tad would need except for their own personal gear. Most of the supplies they had requisitioned—the ones for after they reached the outpost—had already been sent on via Gate. So only what they would need for the trip, what there had not been time to send by the Gate, and what she had brought with her would actually travel with them.

That's certainly going to relieve Tad.

It had also relieved Tad when she told him that she was nothing like her father when it came to wardrobe. *She* could manage very simply, actually; but Aubri had once described Amberdrake's floating-barge and if gryphons could have blanched, Tad would have, at the thought of having to help move all that mass of clothing, gear, and furniture.

She tossed her two bags into the basket, and waited quietly beside the platform for the last of the adjustments to be made. The *hertasi* in charge was Gesten's daughter Chana; as thorough and meticulous as her father, she would not leave Tadrith's side until they were *both* satisfied with the fit of every strap. Blade knew that every buckle would be checked and rechecked, every rivet and every ring subjected to the most exacting scrutiny. Chana would leave nothing to chance, and there was no possible compromise with safety in her view.

Finally, she stepped back. "It'll do," she said, in her hissing *hertasi* voice. "Try to bring the rig back in one piece."

Blade suppressed a laugh, for the remark was so like Gesten that it could have been *he* who was standing there. Like her father, Chana would never admit to concern for the trainees she served, only to concern that the equipment return intact. But of course, it went without saying that if the equipment came back to the warehouse in pristine condition, the trainee would certainly have arrived at the landing platform in like shape.

Tad waved her over, as Chana began hooking up his harness to the basket itself. "We're waiting for the parents, I presume?" he said casually.

She sighed. "Much as I would like to simply slip away, if we leave without allowing them their fanfare, they may not let us come back."

"Or we may not want to," he groaned, and flexed his claws restlessly. "Because when we did, they'd make our lives sheer misery with guilt."

She laughed, and patted him on the shoulder. "Parents always know how to pull your strings," she advised him. "After all, they attached those strings in the first place."

"Do I hear someone borrowing my words?" The newcomer to the conversation was as elegant as Amberdrake in dress and demeanor, though far less flamboyant. Blade knew him too well to blush.

"Of course, Uncle Snowstar," she retorted. "You weren't using them, so why shouldn't I?"

He chuckled at her impertinence; next to Skandranon, she was the only person likely to take that tone with him. It was not wise to risk the anger of an Adept-level mage as powerful as Snowstar, as others, even his own underlings, had found out to their sorrow.

"I don't think you'll have any trouble with the basket-spells, Tadrith," he said, turning to the young gryphon. "They are as tight as any I've ever set."

Blade had assumed her "adoptive uncle" had come to see them off, along with her parents; she was astonished to hear him say that he himself had placed the magics on their carry-basket that would make it possible to fly with it. *"You* set them, uncle?" she said, making no secret of her surprise. "Isn't that—well—?"

"Rather beneath me?" He laughed. "First of all, it is always a good idea for a mage to keep in practice on anything he might be asked to do, and secondly, if something were to fail, magically, on *your* basket—" He shrugged suggestively. "Suffice it to say, it was easier and safer to do the work myself, than have to explain to your parents why I let some 'inferior mage' do it."

Blade nodded ruefully. "Only too true," she told him. She would have said more, but at that moment she caught the sound of familiar voices from below the edge of the cliff.

At nearly the same moment, Tad pointed warningly with his beak at a trio of rapidly approaching gryphons, who could only be his parents and sibling.

"All we need now are Judeth and Aubri to make this show complete," Blade groaned, resigning herself to a long and complicated farewell that would shave precious time off the amount of daylight they *could* have used for traveling.

"Is that a complaint or a request?"

Commander Judeth stalked out of the door to the Silvers' clifftop headquarters, but she was smiling rather than frowning. She was not Kaled'a'in; her hair, before it turned to snowy white, had been a dark blonde, and her eyes a clear gray-green. Nevertheless she had been one of Urtho's generals who understood the value of her nonhuman troops and deployed them with care and consideration, and no one had been unhappy to find her among the k'Leshya when the last Gate came down. She had proved her worth over and over, both during their retreat from lands racked by mage-storms and at White Gryphon. With her partner Aubri, she had organized the first beginnings of the Silvers, and the Silvers in their turn bore the stamp of her personality. She alone of all of them wore anything like a uniform; a black tunic and trews modeled from the tattered originals of her old dress uniforms. The gryphon-badge stood out proudly against such an elegant background.

She stopped just short of the platform and looked sardonically from Tad to Blade and back again. "Can I take it from that remark that you think I might be a hindrance to a timely departure?" she continued.

Blade flushed, and the old woman allowed a hint of a smile to steal across her lips.

"I assure you, Aubri and I came here solely to make certain that your loving relatives did *not* do any such thing," she said crisply, and cleared her throat.

"*All* right, troops!" she called out in a voice that had once commanded thousands, just as Amberdrake and Winterhart appeared at the end of the trail. "Let's get up here and get your good-byes said and over with! This isn't a holiday trip, this is a military departure! *Move your rumps!*"

"Thank the gods," Blade breathed, as her parents and Tad's scrambled to obey. "We just might actually get out of here before noon!"

"In a quarter-mark," Judeth replied sternly. "Or every one of you will be on obstacle-course runs before midmorning."

Blade chuckled; not because Judeth wouldn't make good on that promise—but because she *would*.

What had promised to be a difficult departure was already looking better, even with emotionally-charged families approaching. After this, things could only start looking up.

* * *

CHAPTER THREE

Skandranon continued to peer off into the blue, cloudless sky for a long time after Tadrith and Silverblade were out of even his extraordinary range of vision. Even after fooling himself several times that some speck or other was them, he gazed on, feeling his eyes gradually go out of focus as his thoughts wandered.

He was torn now between pride and anxiety. Their takeoff had been a very good one by anyone's standards; stylish, crisp, and professional. There had been no exhibitions of fancy flying, but not a single mistake in maneuvering either. With so many people watching, *he* would have been tempted to indulge in some theatrics, when he was Tad's age.

And the odds were fairly good that I could have pulled them off, too. But on the other hand, I did have my share of foul ups. With the rising sun in his eyes, though, it didn't make any sense to keep staring off after them. He suppressed a sigh, and told his knotting stomach to behave itself; a gryphon's bowels were irritable enough without encouraging cramps through worry.

Well, they're gone. My nestling really has fledged, gone past the brancher stage, and now—well, now he's on his way to have his own adventures. Real adventures, not just high scores on the obstacle course. He'll be making a name for himself now, just like I did.

He dropped his eyes to meet Zhaneel's, and saw the same pride and worry in her gaze that he felt. She wouldn't show it in front of the boy and, in fact, had kept up a brave and cheerful front, but he knew this sudden departure had her upset.

He tried to look completely confident for her, but it was a struggle that he wasn't certain he had won. *Adventures. Huh.* Now that *he* wasn't the one having the "adventures," he wasn't so sure whether or not looking for adventures was such a good idea. Was Tad ready? With the war, there had been no choice but to go and face the dangers—whether one was ready or not—but this wasn't war, and it seemed to him that they could all afford to be more careful of their young.

His wings twitched a little as the temptation to follow them rose before him. *I could use some exercise. Lady Cinnabar is always telling me to get more flying time in. And if I happened to parallel their course—*

"You promised *not* to fly as the children's wingman all the way to the outpost," Zhaneel whispered, quietly enough that no one else could have overheard her. "Remember. You did promise."

Drat. He had. And *she* could read him like a child's primer. He twitched his wings again, ostentatiously settling them. "I'm glad I'm not making that trip," he said, not precisely as a reply, but to reassure her and to show her that he had heard her and he remembered his promise. Granted, she had caught him in a moment of extreme weakness and vulnerability last night when she extracted that promise, but that did not negate the fact that he had made the promise in the first place. If the Black Gryphon's word to his mate wasn't good, how could anyone trust him?

Aubri sniffed derisively. "You *couldn't* make that trip, old bird," he retorted. "They're a lot younger than you, and in better shape on top of that."

Skan bristled and started to retort, but paused for a moment to rethink his position. Aubri was not going to get him going this time. "Oh; in theory I could," he replied, as mild as a well-bred matron. "*You* did, and I'm in better shape than you—what's more, Tad's towing that carry-basket, and that will slow him down to a pace even *you* could hold. But what would the point be? What would I have to prove? That I'm stupid enough to make a pointless journey to show I'm still the equal of a youngster? It would be a complete waste of time, and I don't have enough time to waste."

Aubri looked surprised and chagrined that he hadn't managed to egg Skan on to rash words or a rasher boast.

Zhaneel cast him a look of gratitude which promised another interesting evening, and more than made up for the faint blow to his pride administered by Aubri's taunts.

Judeth had listened to the conversation with a wry half-smile, and now put her own opinion. "So, now the next generation goes off hunting adventures," she said, combing her fingers through her hair, "while we stay home and see to it that when they come back, they won't find anything much changed. Personally, I don't envy them in the least."

"Nor I," Skan said firmly. "Adventures always seemed to involve impact with the ground at a high rate of speed, and ended in a lot of pain. Maybe my memory is faulty sometimes, but I haven't forgotten *that* part."

Amberdrake finally came out of his own reverie and sighed. "Your memory isn't faulty, old bird. I remember picking quite a few pieces of broken foliage and *not a few* rocks out of your hide, and more than once." He patted Skan's shoulder. "I don't know why you couldn't have picked a gentler way of collecting souvenirs."

Skan winced, and Aubri grinned at his discomfiture. From the look in his eyes, Aubri was about to make another stab at puncturing Skan's pride.

But Aubri had reckoned without Winterhart, who had been listening just as intently to the conversation as Judeth had.

"And I recall that rather than collecting souvenirs of enemy territory, Aubri specialized in attracting enemy fire," she said, with a little smirk and a wink at Judeth that was so fast

Aubri didn't catch it. "In fact, he did it so often that his wing used to refer to getting hit by flamestrike as 'being Aubri'ed.' As in, 'Well, I've been Aubri'ed out until my primaries grow back.' Or, 'Well, *you* certainly got Aubri'ed back there!'"

Aubri met this piece of intelligence with his beak open in a gape. "They did *not!*" he gasped indignantly.

Of course they didn't. Skan, who had known every piece of gossip there was to know back then, would have heard of this long before Winterhart ever had. In fact, Winterhart would probably not have heard any such thing, since before she was Amberdrake's lover, she had tended to treat the gryphons of her wing as little more than intelligent animals. Such an attitude was not likely to make anyone tell her *anything.*

But Aubri's reaction was so delightful that everyone fell in with the joke. For once, someone besides Skan was going to come in for a share of abuse.

Is it my birthday! Or has the Kaled'a'in Lady decided to bless me, however momentarily!

Judeth rubbed the side of her nose with her finger. "I'm afraid they did," she confirmed impishly, and then elaborated on it. "When I deployed your wing, they always liked to fly formation with you on the end since it just about guaranteed that no one else would get hit with lightning or mage-fire. Once or twice I heard them talking about 'Old Charcoal,' and I think they meant you."

Aubri's beak worked, but nothing came out; the muscles of his throat were moving, too, but he didn't even utter as much as a squeak.

"It could have been worse," Winterhart continued, delivering the final blow. "I did succeed in discouraging the nickname of 'Fried Chicken.'"

Aubri's eyes widened; his head came up and his beak continued to move, but all he could manage to say was, "Well!" over and over. Since he sounded exactly like a highly-offended old matron, he only managed to cause the entire gathering to break up into laughter. And if the laughter was somewhat nervous, well, there were four nervous parents there who drastically needed the release of laughter.

They laughed long enough to bring tears to the eyes of the humans and make Aubri's nares flush bright red. Before Aubri managed to have an apoplectic fit, though, Winterhart confessed that she had made it all up. "Not that you didn't deserve the nickname, after all the times you came back singed," she added. "But no one ever suggested pinning it on you."

Aubri growled, his hackles still up. "They wouldn't have dared," was all he said, and Judeth led him off to ease his ruffled feelings and ruffled feathers.

"I don't think he liked being on the receiving end of the teasing," Amberdrake remarked mildly.

"Then perhaps he will stop treating Skandranon to so much of it after this," Zhaneel responded, her voice quite tart. "A little is amusing, but he makes a habit of sharpening his tongue on Skandranon, and I am weary of hearing it! Skandranon does not deserve it; and if Aubri continues in this way, there may be trouble with younger gryphons believing in his so-called teasing. They will think that anything Skan says he has done is only wind and empty boast!"

Skan turned to her in surprise; she didn't often spring to his defense this way. "Aubri doesn't mean anything by it," he said on his old friend's behalf. "He's getting old and cranky, and he just likes to tease. And I don't think I'm going to lose any respect from the youngsters just because he tries to raise my ire now and again."

Zhaneel sniffed and twitched her tail with annoyance. "That might be, and I will not be rude by chiding him in public, but I have had enough of it, and he can expect to get as good as he has given from now on."

"I agree," Winterhart put in firmly, crossing her arms over her chest. "Skan deserves a great deal of respect, after all. Maybe not as much as you'd *like*, you vain creature, but more than Aubri gives you."

Skan cast a look at Amberdrake, who only shrugged. "Don't get me involved in this," he said. "I don't think Aubri means anything of what he says, and I don't think anyone else takes him seriously either—but I think I'm outnumbered here."

Winterhart made a little face, and put her arm over Zhaneel's gray-feathered shoulders. "Come along, my dear," she said to the female gryphon. "I think we should discuss this at length, just the two of us, since the men don't seem to take this situation with the gravity we think it merits."

"I concur," Zhaneel said agreeably, and the two of them sauntered off toward the cliff rim and several pleasant lookouts that had been constructed there.

Skandranon turned a face full of astonishment on Amberdrake—who was gazing after the two females with equal puzzlement.

"What prompted all that?" he asked, trying very hard to get his thoughts back on track. Amberdrake shook his head.

"I haven't any more idea than you do," he confessed. "Maybe with their chicks gone from the nest, they both feel they have to defend *something*. I might be considered something of an authority on human emotions, but I have to admit to you that sometimes my lady Winterhart baffles me." He nodded with his chin toward the head of the trail. "Care to walk down with me so we can both worry about the youngsters together?"

Skan let out a deep breath; so Drake *was* just as troubled about Tad and Blade as he was! "Yes, I would," he admitted mournfully. "Zhaneel made me promise not to go with them, not to follow them, and not to talk about them with her unless she brings the subject up. I wish I had her confidence that everything is going to be all right, but I keep thinking of all the things that can go wrong."

Amberdrake followed his mate's example by draping an arm over Skan's shoulders. It felt very good there; the support of an old and trusted friend, even if the friend was just as much in need of support himself. Tradition spoke of an elegant half-arch being only a fallen pile of stones without its counterpart to make it whole.

"So much can go wrong, even in the most peaceful of times. I fear the worst, too," Amberdrake told him. "But as Blade very rightfully reminded me, their job is not to confront danger directly. They're only scouts, of a sort. If something dangerous appears, they are *supposed* to send a warning by way of the teleson, then keep themselves intact so that they can get home and brief us in detail."

Skandranon took care not to step on Amberdrake's feet, and snorted in reply to his statement. "And just how likely do you think that is to happen?" he demanded. "They're our children! Do you think there's even half a chance that they wouldn't see themselves as the front line of the White Gryphon defenses and go confront something dangerous if it appeared?"

He maneuvered Amberdrake into the inside position, between himself and the cliff, as they started back down toward the city. Drake needed to walk on the protected inside, since if one of them was to slip on the trail, it had better be Skan; he could fly and Drake obviously couldn't.

"I honestly don't know," Amberdrake admitted. "My daughter baffles me more often than my mate does. I sometimes wonder if the midwife switched babies with someone else when she was born. She doesn't seem anything like either of us, and believe me, I have *tried* to find common ground with her."

"I know what you mean," Skan replied with chagrin. "Although Keenath affects me more that way than Tadrith does. Still. Just because we've never seen either of them act the way *we* did at their age, it doesn't follow that they wouldn't. If you understand what I'm trying to say."

"I think so." Amberdrake picked his way over a rough spot in the trail before continuing. "Children tend to act differently around their parents than when they're on their own. At least, that's what I've observed, both professionally and nonprofessionally."

Of course he wouldn't remember himself being that way; he lost his own parents and all his family when he was hardly fledged. But he's right; I went out of my way to be the opposite of mine. They never wanted to be anything but followers, and I wanted to be the one others looked to for leadership. Sometimes I wonder if they weren't smarter than I was. "I wish we had some other way besides the teleson to keep track of them," he fretted. "It's very tempting to wish that Urtho was here to give us another Kechara…"

He couldn't finish the sentence; the pang of loss he felt even when mentioning the name of the creator of his adoptive "daughter" was enough to still his voice for a moment.

"It's more than tempting to wish she was the way she used to be," Amberdrake sighed, "and not just because she'd be useful now. I'd gladly continue all the evasion and diplomatic garbage we had to concoct for the Haighlei if it meant she was still such a powerful Mindspeaker. She is such a cheerful little soul, though; I don't miss her powers at all if it means we get to see her alive and happy."

Kechara had been one of Urtho's rare "mistakes," although Skan had never discovered what his leader, mentor, and friend had intended when he created her. Had she simply been a first attempt at the "gryfalcon" type, of which Zhaneel was the outstanding example? Was it possible that she had been a deliberate attempt to create a gryphon with tremendous ability at mind-magic? Or had she simply been a "sport," something Urtho had not intended at all, an accident that Urtho saw and carried through, then hid away for her own protection?

Whichever the case had been, little Kechara had been what the other gryphons referred to as a "misborn." Severely stunted, slightly misshapen, with wings far too long for her dwarfed body, her mind had been frozen in an eternally childlike state. But her pure strength at mind-magic had been without equal. Adorable little Kechara had been able to reach her mind-voice as far away as the Haighlei capital of Khimbata, which was how she had discovered where Amberdrake and Skandranon had been made prisoners long ago. The madman Hadanelith and his two Haighlei allies had captured them in the last stage before the attempted assassination of Emperor Shalaman during the Eclipse Ceremony. Without Kechara, Skandranon would never have been able to get away in time to save him, and Amberdrake most certainly would not even be alive at this moment. Impelled by danger to him that even she had been able to perceive, her mental "shout" had sundered magical shields and incapacitated Hadanelith's two allies across all that distance.

Urtho had known just how powerful her abilities were, and had kept her close-confined in his Tower for safekeeping. He had known that she might be viewed as a prize to be captured or a weapon to be used, and had thought to protect her from that fate. But in confining her, he had assumed that she would not live very long, an assumption that had proved incorrect.

Skan shook his head. "I agree. And I also know that I would never want to take the chance that another one with worse problems than hers might be born—we just don't have the skill and judgment that Urtho did. We all love her, but Kechara's flaws were too high a price to pay for her gifts, objectively speaking. Quite frankly, I think that it is only because she still doesn't understand most of what she saw in other people's minds that she hasn't been driven mad by it all."

He had done his best to make certain she never lost her trusting nature—and so had Judeth, Aubri, and anyone else in White Gryphon who ever came into contact with her. In her turn, she served the city and its people faithfully and joyously. She carefully relayed messages she barely, if ever, understood to and from all of the Silvers with even a touch of mind-magic of their own. It was a task they had all tried to ensure was never a chore for her, and she had loved the attention and approval.

Skan reflected that it was odd, the way the Haighlei had acted concerning her. For them, a creature with the mind of a child and the ability to read *anyone's* thoughts would have been a blasphemy. For a year or two after the Eclipse Ceremony, Skan was fairly certain the Kaled'a'in had been able to keep Kechara's existence secret from their allies—but eventually they *surely* had discovered just what she was. There had been many, many circumspect little hints, diplomatic tail-chases and discreet suggestions. Finally an official communique from High King Shalaman had come, advising the "permanent elimination of the long-range communicator of White Gryphon"—referring to Kechara—making it clear by its phrasing that it was not an idle request, and that not doing so would have grave consequences. Skandranon, Zhaneel, and Amberdrake went to Khimbata to appeal to Shalaman in private, and returned to White Gryphon with a delegation of mages led by Advisor Leyuet. Between various nervous ceremonies of state, "Papa Skan" explained to Kechara that it was time for her to rest from her work, and that they were going to make sure nobody was ever scared of her. Kechara trusted Skandranon completely, of course, and gleefully greeted the delegation. The grim-faced Haighlei, who were steeling themselves to meet a monster and fight against its horrible soul-invading power, instead faced a little creature who only thought they were very funny and demanded their absurdly elaborate and colorful hats to play with.

Well, that's the Haighlei for you. I suspect one could probably get away with just about anything, so long as it was wrapped in the proper historical protocol. Come to think of it, the reason Shalaman was so incensed about those murders in his Court was because the assassinations hadn't *been done with the proper protocol! Perhaps if we could have found a way for Kechara to be put into Shalaman's service under their religion, she could have kept her powers—but that wouldn't really have been true to her, either, and it would only have made her into the tool, the bargaining chip that Urtho feared she'd be used as. It would have destroyed her loving innocence if she were used against one of us and realized it. At least this way she could stay at home and play. At least she can still talk to all the gryphons, as long as they're within the city limits.*

"Well, what are we going to do, old friend?" the aging gryphon asked, as they picked their way steadily down to the topmost level of the city. This level was the receiving platform for everything lowered down from the cliffs above, or sent up from the city to the cliffs. Work crews were already unloading pallets of food from the farms, and would continue to do so all day. "What do we do about the children, I mean?"

"What *can* we do?" Amberdrake asked, with only the faintest hint of irritation. He led the way to the broad white-painted stairs that formed the back slope of the White Gryphon's "head." "Nothing. This is their job; the job they chose. They've been assigned to it by their superiors, who have judged them capable. Like it or not, they have grown up, and

I'm afraid we had better start getting used to that."

Skan ground his beak and prowled after him, talons clicking on the stone ramp alongside the stairs, which was easier for a gryphon to handle than steps. "I don't like it," he said finally. "But I can't tell you why."

Amberdrake stopped suddenly, turned, and faced him, looking down at his friend with a troubled expression as the gryphon stopped a step later and looked up. "I don't either, and I haven't any real reason to feel this way. I wish I could say that I have a premonition about this—because this feeling that there is something *wrong* makes me look like a nervous old aunty—"

"But?" Skan prompted. "You're worried you don't have the correct dress to play aunty?"

Amberdrake chuckled, then sighed. *"But* I am afraid I haven't had anything of the sort, and there hasn't been a solid sign from anyone who does have Foresight that something is going to go wrong with Blade and Tad. I know what I would say to any of my clients who felt this way."

Skan looked into his friend's eyes, and shook his head. "Let me guess. What we are feeling is a combination of old war reactions, and unhappiness because this fledging of our youngsters is a sure sign that we are getting old."

"Too true. And who wants to know that he is getting old? Not I, I can promise you." Amberdrake's expression was as honest as it was rueful. "I've been keeping my body limber and capable for decades now, through all kinds of strain, as loose as a downfeather and as tight as whipcord as needed, but—it's all been to last as long as possible during the pace of time. One never bothers to think about growing old as one is *growing* older. Then suddenly it is *there,* looming in your face. Your bones and joints ache, youngsters are expressing concern that you are over-exerting yourself, and when you try to insist that your experience means you know more than they do, you find them exchanging knowing looks-when they think you don't notice."

"Alas. It is life's cruelty, I say. One moment we are fretting because we are not considered old enough to do anything interesting, then we turn around and younglings barely fledged are flying off to do the interesting things we can't do anymore!" Skan shook his head, and looked out over the ocean. "And we are supposed to accept this gracefully! It is hardly fair. I protest! I believe that I shall become a curmudgeon: Then at least I can complain, and it will be expected of me."

"Too late for that."

Skandranon snorted, "Then I shall be an exceptional curmudgeon. I've earned the title. The Curmudgeon King."

"Endured Where E'er He Goes. May I join you, then? We can drive the youngsters to distraction together." Amberdrake seemed to have thrown off some of his anxiety and, to his surprise, Skan realized that he had relaxed a bit as well.

"Certainly," the Black Gryphon replied with dignity. "Let's go down to the obstacle course, and make loud comments about how we used to run it better and in half the time."

"And with more style," Amberdrake suggested. "Finesse and grace, not brutal power."

"Naturally," Skan agreed. "It couldn't have happened any other way—as far as they know."

"So, just how worried are *you*?" Winterhart asked Zhaneel as soon as they were out of the range of Skandranon's hearing. As a *trondi'irn* she had a very good notion of just how sensitive any given gryphon's senses were, but she knew Skan's abilities in excruciating detail. For all that he was suffering the onset of the ailments of age, he was a magnificent specimen with outstanding physical abilities, not just for his age, but for *any* gryphon male.

"About Skan, or about the children?" Zhaneel asked, with a sidelong glance at her companion.

"Hmm. Both, of course," she replied, returning Zhaneel's glance. *She's just as observant as I thought.* "Skan, first. He's the one we have to live with."

"As we must live with Amberdrake, heyla?" Zhaneel nodded shrewdly. "Well. Come and sit beside me here, where the wind will carry away the words we do not wish overheard, and we will discuss our mates." She nodded her beak at a fine wooden bench made of wave- and wind-sculpted driftwood, and sat down beside it on the cool stone rimming the cliff.

Winterhart sank gracefully down into a welcoming curve of the bench, and laid one arm along the back of it. "Drake is very unhappy about all this. I think he expected Judeth and Aubri to assign Blade to something like bodyguard duty, or city-patrol. I don't think it ever occurred to him that they might send her out of the city, much less so far away."

It didn't occur to me, either, but it should have. I've known that Blade wanted to get away from the city—and us—for the past year. Maybe if Drake hadn't been so adamant about her living with us until she was a full Silver...

Keeth and Tad had been able to move out in part because Skan had lent them his resources to excavate a new home to trade for an existing one. Sensing Blade's restlessness, Winterhart had tried to persuade Drake to do the same for Blade, but he wouldn't hear of it.

"Why should she need to move out!" he'd asked at the time. *"It's not as if she has any need for a place of her own. We give her all the privacy she would have anywhere else, and it's not as if she could feel embarrassed to bring a lover here!"* Then he had sighed dramatically. *"Not that there's any interest in that quarter. The way she's been acting, a vow of celibacy would be an improvement in her love life. Where could we have gone wrong! It's almost like she doesn't want to listen to her body."*

Winterhart could have told him—that children were always embarrassed by the proximity of their parents when trying out the first tentative steps in the dance of amorous life, and inhibited by their parents when learning for the first time what kind of adults they would become—but she knew he wouldn't believe her. He would have, if Blade had been anyone else's child, but not when he was her father. *A parent can sometimes be too close to his child to think about her objectively.* When it came to seeing someone else's children, a parent could see a larger canvas, but with their own—all they would see were the close daily details, and not grasp the broad strokes. Amberdrake, brilliant as he was, couldn't grasp things like Blade not wanting to be around parents as she learned her body's passions. And if Blade had actually come out and *asked* him for a place of her own, he would probably have given in and made it possible. But she was too shy and too proud, and now, in retrospect, Winterhart could see that requesting assignment to outpost duty had probably seemed the only way she could get that longed-for privacy.

"Skandranon is fretting, but not to pieces, I think," Zhaneel said, after a long pause during which she gazed out seaward. She might have been watching the fishing fleet; her eyes were certainly sharp enough to make out details in things that were only moving dots to Winterhart. "I hope that as he realizes the children *are* capable, he will fret less. Part of it is inaction. Part of it is that he wishes to do everything, and even when he was young, he could not do half of what he would like to do now."

That observation surprised a faint chuckle out of Winterhart. "It is odd how our youthful abilities grow larger as we age, isn't it?" she replied. "I am absolutely sure that I *remember* being able to work for two days and nights without a rest, and that I could ride like a Kaled'a'in and shoot like a highly-paid mercenary, as well as perform all my duties as a *trondi'irn*. I couldn't, of course, but I remember doing so."

"Even so," Zhaneel agreed. "It will not be so bad with Skandranon as with Amberdrake; our children are male, and one is still left to us. Your little falcon was the only chick in the nest, and female. Men wish to protect their females; it is bred in the blood."

"And as much as Amberdrake would deny it, he is more worried because Blade is female, you are right." Winterhart stared out to sea, wondering how she could ever convince her spouse that their "delicate little girl" was as fragile as tempered steel. "Perhaps if I keep comparing her to Judeth?" she wondered aloud. "I don't think Blade is doing it consciously, but I can see that she has been copying Judeth's manner and mannerisms."

"He admires and respects Judeth, and what is more, he *has* seen her in action; he knows that Judeth took special care in training your Blade, and perhaps he will take comfort from that," Zhaneel observed, then tossed her head in a gryphonic shrug. "I can think of nothing else you could do. Now, what am I to do with Skan? Concentrate on Keenath, perhaps?"

"Could we get him involved in Keeth's physical training?" Winterhart asked her. "I'm a bit out of my depth there—and you and Skan *did* invent obstacle-course training. I've started all the *trondi'irn* on working-under-fire training, but the Silvers' gryphon-course is set up for combat, not field-treatment. It isn't really appropriate, and I'm not sure how to adapt it."

"Ye-esss. I believe that might do. It will give him action, and something to think about. Or at least more action besides climbing my back to give him exercise." Zhaneel cocked her head to one side. "Now, what of Winterhart? And what of Zhaneel? What do we do to take our minds from our absent children?"

Winterhart shook her head. "You have me at a loss. I honestly don't know. And I'll probably wake up with nightmares every few days for the next six months. I suppose we should concentrate on our mates' worries instead?"

"That will certainly give *us* something to do, and give them the job of dealing with how we comfort them."

Zhaneel nodded, then turned, and reached out to touch Winterhart's shoulder with a gentle talon. She smiled, and her eyes grew softer as she met Winterhart's gaze. "And perhaps we can give each other the comfort of a sympathetic ear, now and again, sister-in-spirit."

* * *

One small problem with finally being on duty. Rising at unholy hours. Tadrith sighed, but inaudibly, his partner sometimes seemed to have ears as sharp as a gryphon's. As usual on this journey, Blade was up at the first hint of light. Tad heard her stirring around outside the tent they shared; building up the fire, puttering with, breakfast, fetching water. She was delightfully fastidious about her person, bathing at night before she went to bed, and washing again in the morning. It would have been distinctly unpleasant to share a tent with anyone whose hygiene was faulty, especially now that they were away from the coast and into the wet forest. It was very humid here, and occasionally oppressively hot. Blade was not just being carried like living baggage; the basket shifted in every change of wind, and she had to shift her weight with it to keep it from throwing him off. This was work, hard work, and she was usually damp with sweat; by the time he landed for a rest, she was usually ready for one, too.

He, of course, was not burdened by the need to wash in order to get clean, and most humans expressed pleasure in a gryphon's naturally spicy musky scent. He couldn't fly with wet wings, and there usually wasn't time to bathe before night fell when they stopped. He had decided to forgo anything but dust-baths until they arrived at their outpost. So he felt perfectly justified in lying in warm and sheltered comfort while she went through her bathing ritual and tended to the camp chores.

There wasn't anything he could do to help her anyway. He couldn't fetch water; raptoral beaks were not well suited to carrying bucket handles. He shouldn't have anything to do with the campfire; gryphons were feathered and feathers were flammable.

He had done the larger share of work last night, when it came to chores. He had brought up enough wood to feed the fire until this morning, and provided part of his kill to feed them both at breakfast. He would take the tent down, just as he had put it up; the fast way of erecting it required magic, and although he was no match for his father in that area, he *was* a minor mage in simple object-moving spells. So he had done his share of the camp chores; this was not lazing about, it was the just reward of hard work.

He closed his eyes, and listened to water splashing and Blade swearing at how cold it was, and smiled. All was well.

Because they were already working so hard, he was bending a personal rule and using magic to hunt with. He used it to find a suitable animal, and to hold that animal in place once he found it. They couldn't afford energy wasted in prolonged hunting, not now; he had to have the tent up, the wood in camp, and his kill made before dark. Back at White Gryphon, he could afford to be a "sportsman;" there were plenty of herd beasts and fish to feed the gryphons, and wild game was rightfully considered a delicacy. Once he arrived at Outpost Five, there would be time enough on each scouting patrol to hunt "properly." But he would consume more food than they could carry on this trip, and that meant hunting with absolute efficiency, using every trick at his disposal.

Finally, the sounds of fat sizzling into the fire made him open his eyes and bestir himself again. That was breakfast, and although he personally preferred his meat raw, there were other things to eat besides meat. Though primarily carnivores, gryphons did enjoy other delicacies, and Blade had found some marvelous shelf-fungi last night when he had been bringing in wood. A quick test had proven, them to be nonpoisonous, and a quick taste showed that they were delicious. They had saved half for breakfast, still attached to its log just in case detaching it might make it decay.

Fresh venison and fresh mushrooms. A good night's sleep and a fine day of flying ahead of us. Life is good.

"If you don't come out of there, sluggard," Blade's voice warned from beyond the canvas, "I'm going to have all of this for myself."

"I was simply granting you privacy for your bath," he replied with dignity, standing up and poking his beak out of the tent flap. "Unlike some other people I could mention, I am a gentleman, and a gentleman always allows a lady her privacy."

Perhaps it was technically morning, but out there under the trees it was gloomy as deepest twilight. Blade was slicing bits of fungus into a pan greased with fat; he saw that she had already set aside half of the remainder for him. It sat on top of his deer-quarter, from which she had sliced her breakfast steak.

She had dressed for the heat and humidity, in a sleeveless tunic and trews of Haighlei weave—though not of Haighlei colors. The Haighlei were quick to exploit the new market that White Gryphon provided, weaving their cool, absorbent fabrics in beiges, grays, and lighter colors, as well as black and white. The people of k'Leshya could then ornament these fabrics to suit their own cultural preferences. The results varied as much as the root-culture of the wearer. Those of Kaled'a'in descent embroidered, belled, and beaded their garments in a riot of shades;

those who had been adopted into the clan, those outsiders who had ended up with k'Leshya and the gryphons, were usually more restrained in their garments. Blade, consciously or unconsciously, had chosen garments cut in the style of the Kaled'a'in, but in the colors of her mother's people. In this case, she wore a subdued beige, with woven borders in cream and pale brown. As always, even though there was no one to see it, the Silver Gryphon badge glinted on her tunic.

Around them, but mostly *above* them, the birds and animals of this forest foraged for their own breakfasts. After three days of travel, they were finally into the territory that the Haighlei called a "rain forest," and it was vastly different from any place he had ever visited before. The trees were huge, incredibly tall, rising like the bare columns of a sylvan temple for what seemed like hundreds of lengths until they finally spread their branches out to compete with each other for sun. And compete they did; the foliage was so thick and dense that the forest floor was perpetually shrouded in mysterious shadow. When they plunged down out of the sunlight and into the cover of the trees, it took some time for their eyes to adjust.

Despite that lack of direct sunlight, the undergrowth was surprisingly thick. As was to be expected, all kinds of fungi thrived, but there were bushes and even smaller plants growing in the thick leaf litter, and ropelike vines that wreathed the trees and climbed up into the light. Anywhere that a tree had fallen or the course of a stream cut a path through the trees, the undergrowth ran riot, with competition for the light so fierce that Blade swore she could actually see the plants growing larger as she watched them.

She was the team "expert" on plants, and half of the ones she had examined at their campsites were new to her. And they hadn't even done any exploring; the only plants she saw were the ones she found in the course of setting up camp! Tad couldn't even begin to imagine what she'd find when she began looking in earnest—and he began taking her up into the canopy.

He couldn't identify half of the calls they heard from above them. He couldn't even have told her if those hoots and whistles were coming from the throats of furred animals, birds, or reptiles. It was all just a further reminder of how little had been explored here. *Now* he understood why the Haighlei were so careful about what they did here; not only were there scores of completely unknown hazards in this forest, but careless handling of the woodlands could destroy a priceless medicinal herb or some other resource without ever knowing that it was there.

That's all very well, he reminded himself, as he eased himself out of the tent and ambled over to fall on his breakfast with famished pleasure. *But it is difficult to be philosophical on an empty stomach. Later, perhaps…* He devoted himself single-mindedly to his meal. This would be the light one; he would eat heavily when they camped and he could digest while resting. A full gryphon could not fly very well.

A hungry gryphon did not take long to finish a meal, and Tad was famished. He polished off the last of his kill in short order, saving the tasty fungus for last. While he ate, Blade put out the fire, buried their trash in the wet ashes so that it would decay properly, and packed up the gear they had taken out as well as everything inside the tent. Tadrith would leave the bones of his meal for the forest scavengers, who would no doubt be glad of the windfall. When they took off, the only signs that they had been here would be ephemeral; the firepit, the bones, and the pressed-down foliage where they had walked and set the tent. In two days, three at the most, the forest would begin to reclaim the site. In a month, it would be gone. Not even the bones would remain.

No vultures, not in a place like this. Probably rodents, or perhaps some type of swine or canine. He preened his talons fastidiously, and stropped his beak on the log that had played host to their fungi. *Well, I believe it is time to do my part again.*

He strode over to the tent, concentrated for a moment, then extended his power with a deft touch. He let the mage-energy reach for the trigger point of the tent-spell where it lay just under the center of the canvas roof. Obediently, the canvas tent folded in on itself, starting from the top. The sturdy, flexible poles, once holding the canvas rigidly in place, now became the slightly stiffened ropes they really were. Without a hand to aid it, the tent folded, and refolded, as if it was a living creature. Within a few moments, where the tent had been, a boxy package of canvas sat ready to be put in the basket.

Now, as it happened, in accordance with Aubri's advice, the tent *could* be erected without magic, although new poles would have to be cut for it, since the rope supports obviously required magic to become "poles." Clearly, this was a great deal easier, however. Once the spell was triggered, the supports, which were nothing more than magically-bespelled pieces of thick rope sewn into special channels along the seams of the tent, stiffened in a particular order, unfolding the tent and setting it up at the same time. Since the shape of the supports was dictated by the shape of the channel, it was possible to have a tent that did not require a center-pole or guy-ropes, and only needed to be staked down in seven places to keep it from blowing away in a wind.

Of course, if there had been no mage about to trigger the spell, the tent *would* have required a center-pole as well as corner-poles, and guy-ropes at each corner.

This was standard issue among the Silvers now. Tad could never have set the spell himself; that required the hand of a Master. But even an Apprentice could trigger it, so any expedition coming out of White Gryphon that would be camping always had at least one mage along.

The spell that made the tent collapse and fold itself up was a more complicated one, but again, it only needed an Apprentice to trigger and feed it. Tad could handle that sort of spell easily, and enjoyed doing so. Perhaps it was analogous to the way that a human felt when whittling or chip-carving wood. There was an odd, suffused warmth of satisfaction at having created something by use of a tool, which was a different sensation from the visceral feelings of hunting by claw or flying by wings. Perhaps it was the ability to affect things outside one's own momentary grasp that made one feel civilized?

Tad picked up the neat bundle of canvas and rope and deposited it in the carry-basket. Blade was already stretching out and untangling the ropes of his harness. No matter how carefully they stowed the ropes the night before, in the morning they *always* seemed to have gotten tangled. How that could be was another of those mysteries he was certain he would never be able to solve. There were times when he suspected a supernatural explanation.

The harness had to be stowed out of reach of rodents or other creatures that might like to gnaw on leather—and it had to go somewhere where dampness would not get into it. There was only one place that answered that description, and that was the tent itself, so although the ceiling of their temporary dwelling was fairly high, enough of it was taken up with the harness resting in a net suspended from the corners of the roof that Blade could barely stand upright inside.

But if that minor discomfort meant that they could trust the harness not to have suffered damage in the night, it was a small price to pay. Both of them were agreed on that. "I'll share my bed with it if necessary," Blade had said firmly.

"I thought that sort of thing was your father's specialty," he'd jibed back, only to be flattened by a swung harness-girth. Apparently Blade was *not* amused!

Blade finally got the ropes sorted out; now she stood dangling the harness from one hand, beckoning with the other. It was time for Tadrith to go to work.

The harness took some time to get into, and Blade made certain that it was comfortable for him. This was not the token harness of soft deerskin every gryphon in the Silvers wore, displaying his or her badge, and carrying the pouch in which they kept small necessities. Every strap must fit snugly, but without chafing. Large feathers must be moved so that they lay on top of the leather, or they would be broken off. Tadrith could do none of this for himself; instead, he must stand as patiently as a donkey while Blade rigged him up.

The air warmed marginally, and now the usual morning fog began to wreathe among the trees. First, a few wisps formed and wafted through the forest of columns, disappearing and reforming again, like the ghosts of floating snakes. Then the ropes and swaths of fog thickened and joined together, until Tad and Blade were surrounded on all sides by it. Then, lastly, it began to thicken, until they could not see the trunks of trees more than two or three gryphon-lengths away.

Up above, the sounds of birds, animals, and insects continued unabated. Down below, under the cover of the fog, animal sounds increased. *Perhaps, now that they are concealed, they feel bold enough to call,* Tad thought. *I perhaps they are calling to one another* because *they cannot see each other. It is an interesting question.*

Neither the fog nor the heavy overcast that had shadowed them for the past two days had given them any great amount of trouble, but Tad felt a difference in the air today. Gryphons were supremely sensitive to changes in the weather, and he knew by the feeling behind his nares and the way his feathers felt against his skin that they were going to have a real storm today. Storms around here seemed to stretch for leagues, so there would be no moving out of its path unless they were very lucky. If he had been alone, he might have taken a chance and tried to climb above the clouds—but he dared not with the basket in tow. Unpredictable winds could catch it and send it and him tumbling; lightning could incinerate either him or Blade, or both, in a heartbeat.

No, if the storm threatened, they would have to go to ground quickly, before deadly updrafts or windshear caught them unaware. Then they would have to make a quick camp and get shelter before they were drenched. If the storm was over quickly and he was still dry, they could take to the air again to make a little more distance before nightfall; but if he was drenched, he would have to wait until his wings were dry, which would probably take all night.

He said nothing to Blade, but she must have felt the same urgency. Perhaps long association with him had made her weather-sensitive, too; at any rate, without skimping on her checks, she hurried through the preparations. Sooner than he had expected, she was done. She made a quick final check of the campsite as he shook himself, checking the harness for loose spots.

While she continued to police the campsite, he stretched and did wing-exercises, carefully loosening and warming up every muscle, even those he didn't normally use in flying. He faced away from the campsite, sunk his talons deeply into the ground, and energetically beat his wings as if he was trying to lift the earth itself. He twisted, writhed, and stretched, in a series of dancer-like movements designed to make sure every muscle was ready to do what he had asked it to. Then, when he finally felt no sense of strain no matter which way he moved, he looked at Blade.

"Ready?" she called, as she made her way back through the fog toward the basket.

He nodded. "Let's get in the air," he replied. "There's a storm coming."

"I thought so." She removed the stakes holding the basket firmly to the ground and tossed them in, then vaulted into the basket herself. She shifted a few things with a deft sensitivity to the weight and balance within it, then settled into place with both hands clutching the front of the basket.

That was his signal. With powerful wingstrokes, he rose slowly into the air. Leaves and dust scattered across the forest floor in the wind of his creation, and Blade narrowed her eyes against it.

He rose about three lengths into the air before encountering the momentary resistance of the basket beneath him. But the spell was still holding firm, and the pull against the harness was no more than if he had been hauling a deer-carcass instead of the massive basket.

Immediately, he felt something mildly wrong. The basket felt heavier, and now he noticed a stiffness in his muscles that had not been there when he finished his warm-ups.

Is it the damp and chill?

No matter; he was committed now, and he dared not abort the takeoff. He simply worked a little harder, made his wingbeats a little deeper, strained a little more against the harness.

Blade' hung on as the basket lurched up off the ground; this was the moment when it was possible to overset the basket, or novice riders tumbled out. He and the basket rose together through the trees in a series of jerks, propelled by the powerful downthrust of his wings.

He was breathing harder than he should have. *What is the matter with me? Did I get less sleep than I thought? Or did I eat too much!* The thought of the mushrooms hung uneasily in his mind; they were not poisonous, but what if they had some subtle weakening effect on him?

But if they had, wouldn't he have noticed it last night? Wouldn't he have noticed as he was warming up?

Not necessarily...

In the next moment, they were above the layer of fog that clung to the earth and shrouded the leaf-littered ground, hiding it. He looked up, and the spreading branches of the canopy rushed to meet them.

He willed strength into his muscles, strained toward the light. A thousand birds screamed alarm to see them, then fell silent with shock, as the laden gryphon labored up through the branches. He threaded his way through the hole left in the canopy after the death of some millennium-old forest giant, while below him, Blade shifted and released her holds to fend off reaching branches that threatened to foul the ropes or catch on the basket itself. She used a long pole with a crosspiece tied to the far end, cut last night for this specific purpose. As they burst through the last of the branches into the open air, she dropped the pole. They would not need it for the next descent, and it was too long to carry with them without causing problems.

The contrast between the gloom below the trees and the overcast brightness above dazzled Tad until his eyes adjusted; he did not pause, however, for he needed more height. He might not be able to see clearly, but there was no doubt which way he had to go. "Down" was the direction of the dragging on his harness; he rowed his wings in great heaves in answer to that steady pull, and by the time his eyes cleared, he was as far above the canopy as the branches were above the forest floor.

That was enough. He angled out into level flight, taking his direction from his own inner senses, and now the basket hung true beneath him, no longer bobbing with every wingbeat. Blade did not release her hold on the edges, for she might have to shift her weight to compensate for sudden changes in the wind, but she did allow herself some relaxation.

As soon as they leveled out and he was certain that there were no strange winds to contend with, Tad took a survey of the weather. His weather-sense had not betrayed him; the clouds hung low, fat-bellied and gray with unshed water. He could not scent rain on the air yet, but it was just a matter of time. These were not yet storm clouds; the storm, when it came, would roar down at them out of clouds that would tower thousands of lengths above their slate-blue bottoms.

If they were extraordinarily lucky, they might manage to fly out from under this weather system before it developed into a storm, but he was not going to count on it. From the wind, they were flying in the same direction that this storm was going, which made it very likely that they would actually be flying into the teeth of it rather than away from it.

I'll have plenty of warning before we get into trouble. In fact, I'll see activity in plenty of time to land.

He might even feel it long before he saw it. *We aren't making the best time right now,* he noted ruefully. In spite of the careful warmup, he still felt—not stiff, not strained, but vaguely *achy.*

Am I coming down with something? Or did I just eat too much this morning? He drove westward, moving as quickly as he could, watching the horizon for the telltale flickers of the lightning that would herald the storm front. He hoped he was not coming down with a fever; although gryphons were not prone to such infections, they were not completely unknown. This would be a bad time and place to get sick—although, if it proved to be a real emergency, Blade could use the light teleson set they carried with them to call for help. Now that magic was working again, even rudimentary mind-magic like hers could be amplified by the teleson to carry all the way back to White Gryphon. It would be *work,* but she could get help.

It's probably just from sleeping in the damp. I've never had to sleep in a tent on damp ground before. Now, for the first time, he had a hint of how he might feel in years to come, when his joints began to ache and stiffen. No wonder his father moved so deliberately! And he had thought it was just an affectation, to increase his appearance of dignity!

I don't think I'm going to like getting old.

He flew on for some distance—and was very glad that they were not making this journey afoot. He had just traversed territory it would probably take *days* to cross on the ground, and all within a few marks. It wasn't even noon yet!

Now he scented water, and the air felt heavy and thick, and another explanation for his flying difficulties occurred to him. *This is not good air for flying. It may not be me at all; it may only be the atmosphere that is weighing us down.* It was as difficult to fly in thick air as in thin, though in different ways, and the extra exertion necessary would certainly be enough reason for the ache in his joints!

There was still no sign of the coming storm, but it could not be far off now. He strained his eyes, hunting for that elusive flicker of blue-white light among the clouds—

Tadrith had no real warning, just a sudden lurching sensation in the pit of his stomach, as if he had been caught in a burst of wind and been hurled up, then dropped. His head spun with disorientation for a moment, and he gasped.

Then—the magic on the basket was broken, like water draining out of a broken pot, all in the blink of an eye.

And the moment it vanished, the basket regained its real weight—the full weight of Blade, all their supplies, and the basket itself.

With nothing more holding it up than one very shocked gryphon.

It dropped like a stone, and pulled him, shrieking in strangled surprise, with it.

The harness cut into his shoulders; the sudden jerk drove the breath from his lungs and all thoughts from his mind. He pumped his wings frantically and with complete futility against the weight that hauled him down; below him, Blade shouted and sawed at the basket-ropes, trying to cut him free.

He had to slow their fall! She was *never* going to get him loose—even if the ropes were cut, *she* would still plummet to her death! He wouldn't leave her!

There was no time to try magic, no chance to concentrate enough for a spell, and what could he do, anyway? With his heart pounding in his ears, and his vision clouded with the strain, he tried to make his wings move faster, harder, scoop in more air. Surely, if he just tried hard enough, he could at least slow the basket! Fear sent him more energy, fueling the frantic wingbeats.

His wing-muscles howled in agony, burning with pain, as if a million tiny demons were sticking him with red-hot daggers. His foreclaws scrabbled uselessly at the empty air, as if some part of him thought he might be able to catch and hold something.

His mind jabbered as they plummeted down toward the forest canopy.

He did not even have enough control to pick where they were going to hit.

Below him, he thought Blade was screaming; he couldn't hear her through the pounding in his ears. His vision went red with the strain…

Then they hit the trees.

That slowed them. As they crashed through the treetops, he felt the basket lighten a little; and for a moment he had hope that the springy boughs might actually catch and hold them.

But the basket was too heavy, and the branches not strong nor thick enough. As the basket dragged him down into the gloom, he realized belatedly that hitting trees with wings spread wide was not a good idea for a flying creature.

He was jerked a little sideways as the basket encountered more branches, which was not good for him; instead of dropping through the hole the basket made, he hit undamaged tree limbs with an open wing.

Pain shot through him like a bolt of lightning.

Then, there was only darkness.

CHAPTER FOUR

For some reason, Blade had never been the kind who sat frozen with shock when something dreadful happened. She had always acted; there was an even chance that whatever she did in an emergency, it would be the right thing. Without even thinking about it, Blade had her crossdraw knife out in an attempt to cut Tad free as they all plummeted toward the tree canopy below. She sawed frantically at the ropes holding him a helpless prisoner of gravity, but it was obviously of no use; they were falling too fast and there were too many ropes to cut.

We're dead, she thought absently, but her body wasn't convinced of that, and just before they hit the treetops, she dropped into the bottom of the basket, curled into a protective ball.

The basket lurched about as they hit tree limbs and broke through them. As wood crashed and splintered all around her, she was thrown around in the basket among all the lashed-down equipment like another loose piece of junk. Something hit her shoulder hard and she heard herself scream. The pain was like an explosion of stars in her head.

Then, mercifully, she blacked out.

Her head hurt. Her head hurt a *lot.* And her shoulder hurt even more; with every beat of her heart it throbbed black agony, and every time she took a breath or made the tiniest movement, it lanced red fire down her arm and side. She concentrated on that pain without opening her eyes; if she couldn't get that under control, she wouldn't be able to move. If she couldn't move, she, and probably Tad, would lie here until something came to eat them.

Surround the pain and isolate it. Then accept it. Stop fighting it. Don't fear it. Pain is only information, it is up to you how you wish to interpret it. You control it. Her father's lessons came back as she controlled her breathing; she hadn't ever used them on anything worse than a sprained wrist before, but to her surprise, they worked just as well on this serious injury.

Make it a part of you. An unimportant part. Now let the body numb it, let the body flood it with its own defenses. Blade knew the body could produce its own painkillers; the trick was to convince it to produce enough of them. And to convince it that at the moment, pain was getting in the way of survival...

Slowly—too slowly—it worked. She opened her eyes.

The basket was on its side, a couple of wagon-lengths away from her. It looked as if she had been tossed free when, or just before, it hit the ground. Fortunately her lashings holding the cargo in place had held, or she probably would have been killed by her own equipment.

The basket lay in a mess of broken branches, wilting leaves draped everywhere. It didn't look like it was ever going to be useful for anything again.

Probably a fair share of the equipment is worthless now, too, she thought dispassionately. It was easy to be dispassionate; she was still in shock. *I'm alive. That's more than I thought a few moments ago.*

She sat up slowly, being very careful of whatever injury made her shoulder hurt so badly. With her good hand, her left, she probed delicately at her shoulder and bit her lip, drawing blood, when her fingers touched loose bone that grated.

Broken collarbone. I'll have to immobilize the right arm. No wonder it hurts like the Haighlei hells! Well, so much for doing any lifting or wielding any weapons.

Her questing fingers ran over her face and head without encountering anything worse than a goose-egg knot on her skull and more spatters of congealing blood. With the same care as before, she stretched out her right leg, then her left.

Bruises. Lots and lots of bruises, which just at the moment she couldn't feel at all.

I must be black and blue from head to toe. That could be bad; she'd start to stiffen up soon, and in the morning it would be worse.

She cradled her right arm in her left hand, and worked her legs until they were under her and she was in a kneeling position. She couldn't see anything but the basket at the moment, but from the direction that the ropes went, Tad should be right behind her.

She was almost afraid to look. If he were dead—

She turned, slowly and carefully, and let out a sob of relief as she saw him—and saw his sides heaving. He wasn't dead! He wasn't in good shape, but he was still breathing!

He lay sprawled atop a tangle of crushed bushes, still unconscious. His left wing was doubled up underneath him at an angle that was not natural, with his primary feathers pointing forward instead of back, most of them shredded and snapped. So he had one broken wing for certain, and that meant that he would not be flying off anywhere for help.

As she shifted again, trying to get to her feet, his eyes opened, and his beak parted. A thin moan came from him, and he blinked dazedly.

"Don't move," she called sharply. "Let me get over there and help you first."

"*Wing*—" That came out in a harsh whisper, and he panted with pain.

"I know, I can see it. Just hold still and let me get to you." Gritting her teeth, she worked her right arm inside her tunic and belted the garment tightly, using only her left hand. That would do for immobilizing the shoulder for now.

She stood up with the aid of the debris around her, and worked her way over to Tad. Once there, she stared at him for a moment, deciding where to begin. The rain forest was unnervingly quiet.

"Can you wiggle the toes on your left hind foot?" she asked.

He did so, then repeated the gesture with his right, then his foreclaws. "The right rear hurts when I move, but not as if something is broken," he offered, and she heaved a sigh of relief.

"All right, your back isn't broken, and neither are your legs; that's better than we had any right to expect." The knife she had been trying to use to get him free was gone, but now she could reach all the snap-hooks holding the ropes to his harness. Hissing with pain every time her shoulder was jarred in the least, she knelt down in the debris of crushed branches and scratchy twigs and began unsnapping him.

"I think I'm one big bruise," he said, as she worked her hand under him to free as many of the ropes as she could without having him move.

"That makes two of us," she told him, straining to reach one last set of snap-hooks. He knew better than to stir until she told him to; any movement at all might tear fragile blood vessels in the wings where the skin was thinnest, and he would bleed to death before she could do anything to help him.

Finally, she had to give up on that last set. She moved back to his head, and studied his pupils. Was one a little smaller than the other? Without a light to make them react, she couldn't tell. "You might have a concussion," she said doubtfully.

"You might, too," he offered, which she really could have done without hearing. *I can't wait for the concussion-headache to set in.*

"Just lie there," she advised him. "I'm going after the medical gear." *If I can find the medical gear. If it's still worth anything.*

It *had* been packed on top of the supplies, even though that meant it had to be offloaded and set aside every time they stopped for the night. Now she was glad that she had retained the packing order that the supply sergeant had ordained for the basket; they would have been in *worse* shape if she'd had to move foodstuffs, camping gear, and the tent to get at it!

The only question is, did everything fall on top of it!

She worked her way over to the basket again, to find to her great relief that the medical supplies were still "on top"—or rather, since the basket was on its side, they were still the things easiest to reach.

Although "easiest to reach" was only in a relative sense…

She studied the situation before she did anything. The basket was lying in a heap of broken branches; the supplies had tumbled out sideways and now were strewn in an arc through that same tangle of branches. The medical supplies were apparently caught in a forked sapling at about shoulder height, but there was a lot of debris around that sapling. It would be very easy to take a wrong step and wind up twisting or even breaking an ankle—and she only had one hand to use to catch herself. And then, the fall could knock her out again, or damage her collarbone even worse—or both.

But they *needed* those supplies; they needed them before they could do anything else.

I'll just have to be very, very careful. She couldn't see any other way of reaching the package.

"Tad? Tad, can you concentrate enough to use a moving spell?"

All she got back was a croaked "No…" and a moan of pain.

Well… it wasn't a very good idea anyway. A delirious gryphon casting a spell nearby is more risky for me than if I tried running up that tree!

It looked like she would have to make it by foot. It was an agonizing journey; she studied each step before she took it, and she made certain that her footing was absolutely secure before she made the next move. She was sweating like a foundered horse before she reached the sapling, both with the strain and with the pain. It took everything she had to reach up, pull the package loose, then numbly toss it in the direction of the clear space beside Tad. It was heavier than it looked—because of the bonesetting kit, of course. She nearly passed out again from the pain when she did so—but it landed very nearly where she wanted it to, well out of the way of any more debris.

She clung to the sapling, breathing shallowly, until the pain subsided enough that she thought she could venture back the way she had come. Her sweat had turned cold by now, or at least that was how it felt, and some of it ran underneath the crusting scabs of dried blood and added a stinging counterpoint to her heartbeat.

When she reached the spot beside her precious package, she simply collapsed beside it, resting her head on it as she shuddered all over with pain and exertion. But every time she shook, her shoulder awoke to new pain, so it was not so much a moment of respite as it was merely a chance to catch her breath.

With the aid of teeth and her short boot knife she wrestled the package open, and the first thing she seized was one of the vials of pain-killing yellow-orchid extract. She swallowed the bitter potion down without a grimace, and waited for it to take effect.

She'd only had it once before, when she'd broken a toe, and in a much lighter dose. This time, however, it did not send her into light-headed giddiness. It numbed the pain to the point where it was bearable, but no more than that. Another relief; the pain must be bad enough to counteract most of the euphoric effect of the drug.

There was another drug that did the same service for gryphons; she dragged the pack of supplies nearer to Tad, fumbled out a larger vial, and handed it to him. He tilted his head back just enough that he would be able to swallow, and poured the contents into his beak, clamping it shut instantly so as not to waste a single bitter drop.

She knew the moment it took effect; his limbs all relaxed, and his breathing eased. "Now what?" he asked. "You can see what's wrong better than I can."

"First you are going to have to help me," she told him. "I can't try to move you until this collarbone is set and immobilized. If I try, I think I might pass out again—"

"A bad idea, you shouldn't do that," he agreed, and flexed his forelimbs experimentally. "I think I can do that. Sit *there*, and we'll try."

He was deft and gentle, and she *still* blacked out twice before he was finished amidst his jabbered apologies for each mistake. When he was done, though, her arm and shoulder were bound up in a tight, ugly but effective package, and the collarbone had been set. Hopefully, it would remain set; they had no way to put a rigid cast on a collarbone. Only a mage could do that; the Healers hadn't even figured out a way to do so.

Then it was his turn.

It could not have been any easier for him, although he did not lose consciousness as she rolled him off the broken wing, set it, and bound it in place. This time she did use the bonesetting kit; the splints and bandages that hardened into rigid forms when first soaked, then dried. She was no *trondi'irn*, but she had learned as much as she could from her mother, once it became obvious to her that her old playmate Tad was going to be her permanent partner. Besides that, though, she guessed. She didn't know enough of the finer points of gryphon physiology to know if what she did now would cause lifelong crippling. Thin moans escaped Tad's clenched beak from time to time, however, and he did ask her to pause three times during the operation.

Finally they both staggered free of the ruins, collapsed on the thick leaf mold of the forest floor, and waited for the pain to subside beneath the ministrations of their potions.

It felt like forever before she was able to think of anything except the fiery throbbing of her shoulder, but gradually the potion took greater hold, or else the binding eased some of the strain. The forest canopy was still preternaturally silent; their plunge through it had frightened away most of the inhabitants, and the birds and animals had not yet regained their courage. She was intermittently aware of odd things, as different senses sharpened for an instant, and her mind overloaded with scent or sound. The sharp, sour smell of broken wood—the call of one insect stupid enough to be oblivious to them—the unexpected note of vivid red of a single, wilting flower they had brought down with them—

"What happened?" she asked quietly, into the strange stillness. It was an obvious question; one moment, they were flying along and all was well, and the next moment, they were plummeting like arrowshot ducks.

His eyes clouded, and the nictitating membrane came down over them for a moment, giving him a wall-eyed look. "I don't know," he said, slowly, haltingly. "Honestly. I can't tell you anything except what's obvious, that the magic keeping the basket at a manageable weight just—dissolved, disappeared. I don't know why, or how."

She felt her stomach turn over. *Not the most comforting answer in the world.* Up until now, she had not been afraid, but now...

I can't let this eat at me. We don't know what happened, remember? It could still all be an accident. "Could there have been a mage-storm?" she persisted. "A small one, or a localized one perhaps?"

He flattened his ear-tufts and shook his head emphatically. "No. No, I'm sure of it. Gryphons are sensitive to mage-storms, the way that anyone with joint swellings is sensitive to damp or real, physical storms. No, there was no mage-storm; I would *know* if one struck."

Her heart thudded painfully, and her stomach twisted again. If it wasn't a "natural" event... "An attack?" she began—but he shook his head again.

But he looked more puzzled than fearful. "It wasn't an *attack* either," he insisted. "At least, it wasn't anything I'd recognize as an attack. It wasn't anything offensive that I'd recognize." He gazed past her shoulder as if he was searching for words to describe what he had felt. "It was more like—like suddenly having your bucket spring a leak. The magic just *drained* out, but suddenly. And I don't know how or why. All the magic just—just went away."

All the magic just went away.... Suddenly, the chill hand of panic that she had been fighting seized the back of her neck, and she lurched to her feet. If the magic in the *basket* had drained away, what about all the other magic?

"What's wrong?" he asked, as she stumbled toward the wreckage of the basket and the tumbled piles of supplies.

"Nothing—I hope!" she called back, with an edge in her voice. *What's closest? The firestarter! Yes—there it is!* The firestarter was something every Apprentice mage made by the dozen; they were easy to create, once the disciplines of creating an object had been mastered. It was good practice, making them. They were also useful, and since their average life was about six months, you could always barter them to anyone in the city once you'd made them. Anyone could use one; you didn't have to be a mage to activate it—most were always ready, and to use one you simply used whatever simple trigger the mage had built in. The one in their supplies was fresh; Tad had just made it himself before they left.

It didn't look like much; just a long metal tube with a wick protruding from one end. You were supposed to squeeze a little polished piece of stone set into the other end with your thumb, and the wick would light.

You *could* manipulate it with one hand if you had to, and of course, she had to. Hoping that her hunch had been wrong, she fumbled the now-dented tube out of a tangle of ropes and cooking gear, and thumbed the end.

Nothing happened.

She tried it again, several times, then brought it back to

Tad. "This isn't working," she said tightly. "What's wrong with it?"

He took it from her and examined it, his eyes almost crossing as he peered at it closely. "The—the magic's gone," he said hesitantly. "It's not a firestarter anymore, just a tube of metal with a wick in it."

"I was afraid you'd say that." Grimly she returned to the tumbled supplies, and pawed through them, looking for anything that had once been magical in nature. Every movement rewoke the pain in her shoulder, but she forced herself to ignore it. The way that the supplies had tumbled out aided her; the last things into the basket had been on top, and that meant they were still accessible.

The mage-light in the lantern was no longer glowing. The tent—well, she couldn't test that herself, she couldn't even unfold it herself, but the canvas felt oddly limp under her hand, without a hint of the resistance it used to possess. The teleson—

That, she carried back to Tad, and placed it wordlessly before him. It wasn't much to look at, but then, it never had been; just a contoured headband of plain silver metal, with a couple of coils of copper that could be adjusted to fit over the temples of any of the varied inhabitants of White Gryphon. It was used to magically amplify the range of those even marginally equipped with mind-magic. All the gryphons, *kyree*, and *heitasi* had that power, and most of the *tervardi* as well.

Tad should have been able to use it to call for help. A shiver ran down her body and she suppressed the urge to babble, cry, or curl up in a ball and give up. She realized that she had been unconsciously *counting* on that fact. If they couldn't call for help—

He touched one talon to the device, and shook his head. "I don't even have to put it on," he said, his voice shaking. "It's—empty. It's useless." Unspoken words passed between them as he looked up mutely at her. *We're in trouble.*

"It wasn't just the basket, then," she said, sitting down hard, her own voice trembling as well. *How could this happen! Why now! Why us!* "Everything that had any spells on it is inert. The mage-lights, the firestarter, the tent, probably the weather-proof shelter-cloaks——"

"And the teleson." He looked up at her, his eyes wide and frightened, pupils contracted to pinpoints. "We can't call for help."

We're out here, on our own. We're both hurt. No one at White Gryphon knows where we are; they won't even know we're missing until we don't show up at the rendezvous point where we were supposed to meet the last team that manned the outpost. That'll be days from now.

"It's a long way to walk," he faltered. "Longer, since we're hurt."

And there's something nearby that eats magic. Is it a natural effect, or a creature? If it eats magic, would it care to snack on us! It might; it might seek out Tad, at least. Gryphons were, by their very nature, magical creatures.

Don't think about it! Over and over, the Silvers had been taught that in an emergency, the first thing to think about was the problem at hand and not to get themselves tied into knots of helplessness by trying to think of too many things at once. *Deal with what we can handle; solve the immediate problems, then worry about the next thing.* She got unsteadily to her feet. "There's a storm coming. That's our first problem. We have to get shelter, then—water, warmth, and weapons. I think we'd better salvage what we can *while* we can before the rain comes and ruins it."

He got shakily to his feet, nodding. "Right. The tent—even if we could cut poles for it, I'm not sure we could get it up properly with both of us hurt. I don't think the basket will be good for much in the way of shelter——"

"Not by itself, but two of the sides and part of the bottom are still intact," she pointed out. "We can spread the canvas of the tent out over that by hand, and use the remains to start a fire." She stared at it for a moment. So did he.

"It looks as if it's supported fairly well by those two saplings," he pointed out. "The open side isn't facing the direction I'd prefer, but maybe this is better than trying to wrestle it around?"

She nodded. "We'll leave it where it is, maybe reinforce the supports. Then we'll clear away the wreckage and the supplies, cut away what's broken and tie in more support for the foundation by tying in those saplings——"

She pointed with her good hand, and he nodded.

"Look there, and there," he said, pointing himself. "If we pile up enough stuff, we'll have a three-sided shelter instead of just a lean-to."

That, she agreed, would be much better than her original idea. In a moment, the two of them were laboring as best they could, her with one hand, and him with one wing encased and a sprained hind-leg, both of them a mass of bruises.

He did most of the work of spreading out the canvas over the remaining sound walls of the basket; he had more reach than she did. She improvised tent stakes, or used ones she uncovered in the course of moving supplies, and tied the canvas down as securely as she could manage with only one hand. One thing about growing up in the household of a *kestra'chern;* she had already known more kinds of knots and lashings than even her survival instructor.

She wasn't certain how Tad felt, but every movement made her shoulder ache viciously. *There's no choice,* she told herself each time she caught her breath with pain. *Rest once it starts to rain; work now.*

She wasn't sure what time it was. They hadn't gone very far before they had come crashing down, and they hadn't been unconscious for long, or else they would have awakened to find insects trying to see if they were dead yet. Scavengers didn't wait long in this kind of forest. That meant it was probably still early morning. If the rain threatened by those clouds held off, they had until late afternoon before the inevitable afternoon thunderstorm struck. *If our luck hasn't gone totally sour, that is...*

Eventually, they had their three-sided shelter; the limp tent canvas stretched tightly over the remains of the basket and the three young trees that had caught it. There were some loose flaps of canvas that she didn't quite know what to do with yet; she might think of something later, but this was the best they could do for now.

They both turned to the tumbled heaps of supplies; sorting out what was ruined, what could still be useful even though it was broken, and what was still all right. Eventually, they might have to sort out a version of what could be carried away in two packs, but that would be later. She would fight to remain here, and so would Tad. Walking off should not become an option until they were certain no one was going to come looking for them.

Always stay with a wreck, if you can. That much she also remembered very well from their survival course. *The wreck makes the best target for searchers to find and the first place they'll look for you when they spot it.*

If they could stay here, they had a shelter they could improve more each day, plus what was left of the supplies. Even things that were ruined might be useful, if they had long enough to think of a use for them. If they were forced to leave, there was a lot of potentially useful and *immediately* useful gear they would be forced to leave behind.

If. That was the trick. She could not for a moment forget that something out there had drained away their magic without any warning at all. If the wreck made a good target for searchers to find, it also made a good target for other things to find—including whatever knocked them out of the sky. *Assume it's an enemy, and assume he attacked.* That was the wisest course of reasoning and the one she had to begin planning for.

For that matter, there was no telling what prowled the forest floor. Just because they hadn't *yet* run into any major predators, that didn't mean there weren't any. The longer they stayed in one place, the easier it would be for predators to locate them.

"Thank goodness for Aubri," came a muffled sigh from her right, and Tad came up out of his pile of seeming-rubbish at the same moment. He held in his talon a nonmagical fire-striker, and Blade put aside the pile she'd been sorting to take it from him. Now she could make a fire with the dry, shellac-coated splinters of the basket and pile damp, green wood around that fire so that it could dry out enough to burn.

Tad remained with his pile; evidently he'd found the box that had held all of the nonmagical gear that Aubri had insisted they take with them. She eyed the improvised shelter for a moment. *Think first, plan, then move. If you ruin something, there's no one around to help with repairs. And not much to make repairs with.*

She wanted a way to shelter the fire from the rain, without getting too much smoke into the shelter. And she *didn't* want to take a chance on ruining the shelter they already had.

Right. There's the tent flap. I bend those two saplings over and tie them to the basket, then unfold the tent flap and tie it down—there. And I think I can do that with one hand. Then maybe we can create a wind barrier with long branches and some of those big leaves. Plan now firmly in mind, she one-arm manhandled the saplings into place, then pulled the flap of canvas out over the arch they formed to protect the area where she wanted to put the fire. Carefully she tied the end of the tent flap to another broken tree, fumbling the knot several times; if it wasn't caught by a big gust of wind, it would hold. At least they wouldn't be lacking in wood, even though it was very green. They'd brought down a two or three days' supply with them when they fell and they also had spare clothing to use for kindling. *Build the fire first, then see about that barrier.*

She scraped the leaf-litter away from the ground until she had a patch of bare earth, then carefully laid a fire of basket-bits, broken boxes, and some of the leaves she found that were actually dry. With the striker came a supply of tinder in the form of a roll of bone-dry lint lightly pressed together with tiny paper-scraps. She pulled off a generous pinch and put the rest carefully away, resealing the tinder box. The firestriker was a pure nuisance to operate, especially one-handed. She finally wound up squatting down and bracing the box with one foot, and finally she got a spark to catch in the tinder and coaxed the glowing ember into a tiny flame. Frowning with concentration, she bent over her fragile creation and fed the flame carefully, building it up, little by little, until at long last she had a respectable fire, with the smoke channeling nicely away from the shelter. At that point, *everything* ached with strain.

Breathing a painful sigh, she straightened, and looked over at Tad to see what he'd found. The thing that caught her eye first was the ax. That, she was incredibly glad to see! It was small enough to use one-handed, sharp enough to hack through just about anything. And right now, they needed firewood.

She got painfully to her feet and helped herself to the implement, then began reducing the debris around their improvised camp into something a bit more useful to them.

She tossed branches too small to be useful as firewood into a pile at one side. If they had time before darkness fell or the rain came— whichever was first—she'd make a brush-palisade around the camp with them. It wouldn't actually keep anything out that really wanted to get at them, but animals were usually wary of anything new, and they might be deterred by this strange "fence" in their path.

And anything pushing through it is going to make noise, which should give us some warning. Now just as long as nothing jumps over it. When Tad needs to urinate, we'll collect it and spread it around the perimeter, the scent of any large predator should scare most foragers and nuisance animals away. And other than that, it is a perfect day, my lord.

The branches holding huge leaves she treated differently, carefully separating the leaves from the fibrous, pithy branches and setting them aside. When she had enough of them, and some straight poles, she'd put up that sheltering wall.

Every time she swung the ax, her body protested, but it wasn't bad enough to stop her now that she had some momentum going. *If I stop, I won't be able to move for hours, so I'd better get everything I can done while I'm still mobile.*

Evidently Tad had the same idea; he was sorting through the supplies with the same single-minded determination she was feeling. He'd found her two packs of personal supplies, and his own as well and put all of them in the shelter; laid out next to them was the primitive "Aubri gear." In between swings of the ax she made out candles and a candle-lantern, a tiny folded cook-stove, canteens, two shovels, and three leather water bottles. Two enormous knives good for hacking one's way through a jungle lay beside that, also a neat packet of insect netting, fishing line and hooks, and a compass. He'd gotten to the weapons they'd carried with them as a matter of course, and she grimaced to look at them. They were largely useless in their present circumstances. Her favorite bow was broken; the smaller one was intact, but she couldn't pull it now. Nor could she use the sword Tad was placing beside the oiled-canvas quivers of arrows. Beside that he laid his set of fighting-claws—which might be useful, except that he couldn't walk while wearing them.

And what are we going to do if we're driven away from here and something attacks us on the trail. Ask it politely to wait while he gets his claws on!

But her heart rose in the next moment, because he had found a sling! He placed it beside his claws, and two full pouches of heavy lead shot beside it. Now *that* she could use, and use it well, even with only one hand!

That gave her a little more energy to swing, and his next find added to that energy, for it was a short spear with a crosspiece on it, like a boar-spear. It had broken, but mostly lengthwise with the grain of the haft, and what remained was short enough to use one-handed. *I can keep us fed with the sling; with the knife and the spear I can fight things off. He has his beak and talons, which are not exactly petty weapons. And he has some magic.*

All gryphons had at least a small command of magic; Tad didn't have a *lot*, not compared to his father, but it might be useful…

But she shivered again, thinking about what Tad's magic might attract, and decided that she had chopped enough wood. She ringed the fire with the green logs, stacked the rest at the back of the lean-to, and piled the remains of the basket that she had chopped up wherever she could under shelter. *I don't think I want him using any magic until we know for certain that whatever sucked the magic out of the basket isn't going to bother us.*

She joined Tad in his sorting, sadly putting aside some once-magical weapons that were now so much scrap. Unfortunately, they were shaped too oddly to be of any immediate use. The best purpose they could be put to now was as weights to hold pieces of canvas down to protect more useful items—like wood—from the rain.

She found the bedding at the bottom of the spill and took it all into the lean-to to spread on the ground, over mattresses of leaves and springy boughs. She made another trip with more assorted items and the weapons and gear she could actually use now. The rest, including some broken items, she laid under a piece of canvas; she might think of something to do with them later.

Most of the equipment was just plain ruined, and so was a great part of their food. The rations that survived the smash were, predictably, the kind a mercenary army normally carried; dried meat and a hard ten-grain ration-biscuit made with dried vegetables and fruit. This was not exactly a feast, but the dried meat would sustain Tad, and the hard ration-bread was something that a person could actually live on for one or two months at a time.

He wouldn't *enjoy* living on it, but it was possible to do so without suffering any ill consequences.

She paused, and took a closer look at the smashed and ruined food. At the moment, some of it *was* still edible, though it wouldn't stay that way for long.

Better save the rations for tonight, and eat what we can of this. She gathered together enough of the food to make a very hearty meal, and placed it by the fire, then laboriously took the rest out into the forest and deposited it a goodly way away from the camp. Better *not* let the local fauna associate the camp with food. They could set snares another time, for the curious, to supplement the dried-meat ration.

Time for that windbreak-wall beside the fire. She stuck the ends of four of the long, whippy branches into the soil and tied the tops to whatever she could reach along the supported tent flap, using her teeth and her one good hand. Then she threaded the leaves on another of the long branches, overlapping them like shingles. When she came to the end of the branch, she tied *that* along the base of the four wall supports, about a hand's length from the ground, once again using teeth as well as her hand. Then she went back to threading leaves on another branch, and tied that one so that it overlapped the one below it. It didn't take very long, and when she finished, she thought that the result, like the shelter, would hold up fairly well as long as no violent winds came up, which wasn't too likely under the canopy.

When she left her completed wall, Tad was already sticking brush into the soft loam of the forest floor to make that brush-fence she had considered. She joined him, just as thunder rumbled threateningly in the distance. She took a quick glance over her shoulder, saw that everything worth saving was under some form of shelter and that the fire still burned well. *It'll survive, I hope. We'll just have to hope our luck has turned.* She joined Tad in constructing the "fence." Their new home wasn't much of one, but it was, after all, better than nothing. The work went quickly; the earth was so soft here that it didn't take much effort to thrust the thin branches down well enough to anchor them securely.

Thunder rumbled right above them; she glanced up just in time to catch one of the first fat drops right in her eye.

A heartbeat later, as they were scrambling back to the shelter of the tent, the sky opened up. Together they huddled under the canvas, it was a very close fit, but no closer than it had been when the tent was still a tent.

Water poured out of the sky at a fantastic rate. *Now* she was glad that she had brought everything under the lean-to that she could, as she found it; she'd seen waterfalls with less water cascading down them! It all came straight down, too, without a sign of any wind to blow it sideways. There must have been some high winds *at* treetop level, though; the trunks of trees nearest her swayed a little as she watched them. The trees acted as a buffer between them and whatever wind the storm brought with it.

There was no moment when lightning was not illuminating some part of the sky, and there were times when she saw the fat raindrops seemingly hanging in the air due to a trick of the flickering light.

The rain knocked loose what branches hadn't come down with them, one or two thudded against the shelter, and she was glad that there was canvas *and* the basket between them and the debris. Canvas alone would have caved in or torn.

She wondered if she should clear the fallen branches away later. *If it isn't hurting anything, I'll leave it. If we look like a pile of debris to animals, they might leave us alone. No—what am I thinking! The native animals will know what is right or wrong for their own area. I must be delirious.*

Tad gazed out at the powerful storm with his eyes wide and his feathers roused against the cool damp. She wondered what he was thinking. Every time one of the really big lightning-bolts flashed across the sky, the back of his eyes glowed greenly.

Her shoulder began to stab at her again, throbbing in time to the thunder; the drugs she had taken must have worn off a bit. If she was in serious pain, Tad probably was, too, and there was no reason why they should endure it if they didn't have to. The medical kit contained enough pain-relieving drugs to last two people for two weeks—by then, they would either be found or be in such serious trouble that a little pain would be the least of their worries. She felt for the bag of medicines and fished in it for two more vials of painkiller, handing him his. He took it, pierced the seal with a talon, and swallowed it down before she even had hers open. He took hers away from her and punctured the wax seal for her in the same way; she took it back gratefully, and downed it.

"Should we set a watch?" he asked. "I think we should. I think we should really try to stay awake even if we're taking painkillers. I don't like the idea of lying here helpless. It was different when we could set mage-wards, but now…"

She thought about the question for a moment. *We probably ought to, even though it's not likely we could do much against a real enemy. Then again; if all that comes to plague us is scavengers and wild beasts, if we set a watch, whoever is awake can probably fend off any trouble.*

"I agree. If you can sleep now, go ahead," she said finally. "I can't, not even with this demon's brew in me. If you're rested by the time I can't stay awake any longer, then you can take second watch."

He nodded, and she draped some of the bedding over him to keep him warm. "I'll have something for you to eat when you wake up," she promised. "I think it's going to rain until well after dark; I'll wake you up when I can't keep my eyes open anymore." She had no idea how he did it, but he was actually asleep shortly after she finished speaking. *Must be exhausted,* she decided. *He was trying so hard to slow our fall; that must have taken an awful lot out of him. I ought to be surprised that he didn't just collapse completely after his wing was set.*

She ought to feel a great deal more than she did; it was hard to sustain anything, even fear, for very long. *That's shock, and maybe it's just as well. As long as I plan everything and concentrate, I can carry it out.*

Later, perhaps, she would be able to feel and react; now she was oddly grateful for the peculiar numbness.

Since the supplies she had salvaged were pretty much mixed up together already, she used the hodgepodge of foodstuffs to make a kind of giant pancake with meat, vegetables, and spices all baked into it. She made as many of these cakes as she had supplies for; ate one herself, and saved the rest for Tad. After that, she just stared out into the rain. It was growing darker by the moment, although that, simply could have been thickening clouds and not oncoming nightfall. A dull lethargy settled over her, and the rain lulled her into a state of wary weariness.

There was no sign that the rain was going to collapse the roof, and no sign that it was going to stop any time soon. Belatedly, she realized that *here* was a good source of fresh water for them, and she began to rummage through the supplies again. As she found things that could hold water, she stuck every container she could find into the streams of run-off along the front edge of the canvas. Before long, she had all their canteens and storage-bottles full, and had refilled the rest of their containers a second time, *and* she'd washed and rinsed the dishes.

I can get a wash! That revived her somewhat; she felt sweaty, grimy, and the mere idea of being able to wash herself revived her a little. She put a potful of water beside the fire to warm up; if she didn't have to wash herself in cold water, she wasn't going to! They might not have magic, but they still had other resources.

Besides, there were some remedies for bruises in that medical gear that had to be steeped in warm water. When she finished washing, she could do something about her minor injuries. They probably wouldn't feel so minor when she tried to sleep.

Poor Tad; I don't think my remedies will work on his bruises; he hasn't got bare flesh to use them on. No point in soaking his feathers either; that would only chill him and make him feel worse.

Rain continued to pound the canvas; the falling rain was the only sound in the whole forest, at least to her limited ears. She sat with her knees drawn up to her chest and her good arm wrapped around them, watching the silver water continue to pour out of the sky, sent into a trancelike state by the steady, dull roaring. The flash of lightning and the pounding of thunder were the only things that kept her from completely succumbing and falling asleep a time or two. She caught herself with a sudden shock and a pounding heart, jerking herself awake.

When her water warmed, she clumsily stripped off her tunic, fished out a scrap of ruined cloth and bathed her bruises with gratitude in lieu of soap. How good a simple thing like a warm, damp cloth on her aches felt! And how good it felt to be clean! Her sense of being grimy had not been wrong.

Oh, how I wish I had one of those hot pools to soak in… Well, while I'm at it, why don't I wish for rescue, a soft bed in a deep cave, and enough painkiller to keep me asleep until this shoulder is healed! More such thoughts would only depress her or make her frantic with worry; she should concentrate on *now*, and on doing the best she could with what she had.

Just being clean again made her feel a great deal better; time to put on clothing that was equally clean. The air had cooled considerably since the rain began; now it was getting positively chill as well as damp. She pulled out a tunic with long sleeves—and realized as she started to put it on that it would be impossibly painful to get her arm into the sleeve without ruining the tunic.

Well, who was there to see her? No one.

She slit the front of the tunic with her knife; she could belt it closed again. But before she put on any clothing, she wrapped a blanket around her shoulders, and went back to the medical kit. She should treat the bruises first, then get dressed.

She found the herbs she needed in the kit, and put them into the pot of remaining warm water to steep. Now the rain did show some signs of slacking off, but it was also getting much darker out there. This wasn't just thickening cloud cover; it must be just past sunset.

She reached for the shortened spear, and pulled out a selection of knives that could be thrown in a pinch, then considered her next move.

Do I build the fire up to discourage night prowlers, or bank it so as not to attract attention?

After some consideration, she opted for the former. Most animals were afraid of fire; if they smelled the smoke, they might avoid this area altogether. She had to burn green wood, but that was all right, since the smoke it made drifted away from the lean-to and not into it. A bigger fire warmed the interior of their shelter nicely, and beside her, Tad muttered drowsily and settled into deeper sleep.

When the herb-water was a deep, murky brown, she stripped off her blanket; soaking bandages in the potion until the bowl was empty, she wrapped the soaked cloth around the areas most bruised, curling up in the blanket until they dried.

The heat felt wonderful—and the medicines actually began to ease the dull throbbing ache wherever some of the worst bruises were. The scent of the potion arose, bitter and pungent, to her nose.

Good. At least I don't smell like anything edible. I wouldn't want to eat anything that smelled like me. Even the bugs won't bite me how. Maybe.

It wasn't long before the bandages were dry enough to take off; she pulled on her breeches with one hand, then got her tunic on over her good arm and pulled it closed. Fortunately the belt fastener was a buckle with a hook instead of a tonguc; she belted the slit tunic so that it would stay closed, more or less.

The rain stopped altogether; insects called out of the gloom in all directions. As the last of the light faded, odd whoops and strange, haunted cries joined the buzzing and metallic chirping of insects. Bird, animal, reptile? She had no way of knowing. Most of the calls echoed down from high above and could come from any throat.

It was very damp, cold, and very dark out there. The only other spots of light were foxfire off in the distance (probably from a decaying stump), and the mating lights of wandering insects. No moon, no stars; she couldn't see either right now. Maybe the cloud cover was still too thick. Maybe the cover of the leaves was too heavy.

At least they had a fire; the remains of the basket were burning very well, and the green wood burning better than she had expected.

Perhaps the most frustrating thing of all about their situation was that neither she nor Tad had done a single thing wrong. They hadn't been showing off, nor had they been in the least careless. Even experienced campaigners like Aubri and Judeth would have been caught unaware by this situation, and probably would have found themselves in the same fix.

It wasn't their fault.

Unfortunately, their situation was still a fact, and fault didn't matter to corpses.

Once Blade had immobilized Tad's wing, it hadn't hurt nearly as much as he had expected. That might have been shock, but it probably wasn't; the break was simple, and with luck, it was already knitting. Gryphon bones healed quickly, with or without the services of a Healer.

It probably didn't hurt nearly as much as his partner's collarbone either; his wing was not going to move no matter what he did, but if she had to move and work, she *was* going to be jarring her shoulder over and over again.

I wish the teleson wasn't gone. I wish I could fix it! He could fix the firestarter and the mage-light, and probably would after he slept, but the teleson was beyond him, as was the tent and the cook pot. If they had the teleson, help could be here in two days, or three at the most. Now it might be two or three days before anyone even knew they were in trouble.

He had volunteered for the second watch because he knew that she was going to have to be *very* tired before she could sleep—but once she was, those painkillers were going to hit her hard. Once she fell asleep, it was going to be difficult to wake her until she woke by herself.

For his part, although the painkiller helped, Keeth had taught him a fair amount about taking care of himself; he could self-trance pretty easily, and he knew several pain-reduction and relaxation techniques.

Lucky I have a trondi'irn *for a brother.*

He made himself comfortable, and once Blade draped a blanket over him so that he was warm, he fell asleep quickly.

Strange images, too fleeting to be called "dreams," drifted with him. Visions of himself, visiting a trading fair in Khimbata, but as an adult rather than a child trailing after his Haighlei nurse, Makke; moments of flying so high above the earth that even with his keen eyesight, humans below him were no more than specks. There were visions that were less rational. He thought, once, that the trees were talking to him, but in a language he didn't recognize, and that they grew frustrated and angry with him because he didn't understand what they were trying to tell him.

None of this was enough to actually disturb his rest; he roused just enough to dismiss the dreams that were unpleasant without actually breaking his sleep, then drifted back into darkness.

He was just about on the verge of waking all by himself—half-dreaming that he ought to wake, but unable to really get the energy to rouse himself—when Blade shook him slightly, enough to jar him completely out of his half-sleep.

He blinked up at her; her face was a bizarre mask of purpling bruises and dancing golden firelight. If it had been a little more symmetrical and less obviously painful, it would have been oddly attractive. He tasted bitter herbs in the air as she yawned, and guessed that she had bandaged herself with some of her human medicines.

"I took more painkillers, and I can't stay awake anymore," she confessed, yawning again. "I haven't seen or heard anything that I can confirm, although my imagination has been working away nicely."

"Fine, then get some sleep," he said, a little thickly, and blinked to clear his eyes. "I'll take over until dawn."

She settled herself between the wall of the tent and him, lying against him. He let her curl up in such a way as to take the most advantage of his warmth; she needed it. *And she probably needs the comfort just as much,* he thought, as she tried to arrange herself in a way that would cause the least pain to her broken collarbone. *It can't have been easy, sitting here, staring into the dark, and wondering what was out there, with your partner a great snoring lump beside you.*

Granted, he wouldn't have stayed a great snoring lump for long if there'd been trouble, but that was no comfort when you were straining your ears trying to tell if that was a nightbird, a bug, or a maneating whatever out there.

Gryphons were not noted for having powerful night vision, but both Skandranon and his two offspring were better than the norm at seeing in the dark. They weren't owls—but they weren't half-blind, either, and they *were* better than humans. He let his eyes adjust to the darkness, and mentally marked the shadows so that he knew where everything was. Some, he could even identify, by matching the general shape with his memory of the objects surrounding the camp; the place that looked like a crouching bear was really a stump overgrown with inedible fungi. And the bush that seemed to have a deeper shadow at the heart of it really *did*; it had grown around what remained of a snag, which could have passed for another crouching creature. Deep in the distance, a phosphorescent shape was a rotting tree with a patch of foxfire fungus in it—and it wasn't really moving, that was an illusion brought on by eyestrain. Things that might have been pairs of eyes reflecting the firelight were nothing of the kind; if he watched them until they moved, it was clear that they moved independently of one another, which meant they were only a couple of light-bearing insects, probably flying in pairs because they were in the middle of a mating dance. A swift and silent shape passing from branch to branch above his head was an owl; one that flew with a faint fluttering just out of range of the firelight was a bat.

Once he identified things in his range of vision, he began cataloging sounds. The obvious buzzes and whirs were insect calls; likewise there were croaks and cheeps he knew were frogs. There were some calls he recognized from around White Gryphon; not *all* the creatures here were new to him. The occasional sleepy twitter or mutter from high above meant that something had mildly disturbed a bird's rest—nothing to worry about, birds bumped into each other while they slept all the time.

Then there were the howls, barks, and growls. He took note of all of them, keeping track of where they were coming from and under what circumstances. Most of them originated from up in the tree canopy; that meant that, barring something completely strange, whatever made them wasn't going to bother the two down below. The things living in the trees would, for the most part, be prey rather than predator; life in the tree tops was difficult, with the most difficult task of all being how to get to water. Anything living up there had a reason not to want to live on the ground. Any creature up there would probably be relatively small, no bigger than Blade at the most, with a disproportionately loud call, because in the thick leaf cover up there, it would be hard to keep track of herd- or flock-mates. And if you yelled loudly enough when something grabbed you, there was a chance that you might startle it into letting go.

Predators in the tree canopy would either be snakes or winged; four-footed predators would hunt on the ground. While it was certainly possible that there could be a snake up there large enough to swallow Blade or even Tad, it would not be able to seize both of them at once, and it would not be very fast except when it struck. That left winged predators, and Tad was confident that he would be a match for anything that flew, even grounded.

No, what they had to worry about was what lay down here, so sounds up above could be dismissed unless and until they erupted in warning or alarm calls.

While his vision was incredibly keen by human standards, it was even more suited to picking up tiny movements. So once he had identified everything that lay in front of the shelter, he did not need to sit and stare into the darkness as Blade did. He need only relax and let his eyes tell him when something out there had changed its position. No matter how clever a predator was at skulking, sooner or later it would have to cross a place where he would spot it moving through the shadows, even on a night with no moon.

His hearing was just as good, and now that he knew what the normal noises were, he could listen through them for the sound of a grunt, a growl, or the hiss of breath—or for the rustle of a branch—or the crack of a twig snapped beneath a foot.

That was the other reason why he didn't mind taking second watch. When all was said and done, he was much better suited to it than Blade was.

Now, if anything decided to come up *behind* them, he wouldn't see it, and he might not hear it either. But it wouldn't get through the canvas and basketry of their shelter quickly, and they should have time to defend themselves.

Or so I tell myself.

He stared out into the darkness, watching winking insect lights, and finally acknowledged to himself that, far from feeling competent, he was feeling rather helpless.

We're both crippled and in pain, we can't use most of the weapons we have left, we aren't entirely certain where we are, and we're too far from home to get back, and that's the honest truth. I don't like it at all.

They had to hope that in three days or so, when they didn't make the appointed rendezvous, they'd be missed, and that White Gryphon would send out a search party looking for them. They had to hope that they could survive long enough to be found!

Oh, stop feeling sorry for yourself and eat! he scolded himself. *You aren't going to get a chance at a better meal for a while, and starving yourself is hardly going to do any good. Whatever Blade fixed, it probably won't keep past morning.*

Slowly, to make them last, he ate the meat-and-vegetable cakes that Blade had concocted. They weren't bad, considering how awful they could have been. Blade was not noted for being anything other than an indifferent cook, and these had actually been one of her best efforts. The two of them would probably joke about the incongruity of cooking a gourmet meal in the middle of a disaster, after they had escaped this stranding and healed. *Of course, to hear the stories about Father, you would think he was so dashing that he would fight off two hundred makaar, seduce his wingleader, arrange a tryst, fight off another hundred makaar, and then pause for tea from a silver cup.*

Blade had placed the odd cakes close enough to the fire that they kept warm without burning or drying out much. They would probably stay with him for a while, which was a good thing, since he wasn't going to be doing much hunting for the next couple of days. And even then, in order to take down the size of prey he was used to, he'd have to somehow surprise it on the ground.

Father's claims about being able to slip through enemy lines unseen might be true, but deer have keener noses and ears than human soldiers. I'm going to have to be very lucky to catch anything larger than a squirrel.

He was satisfied before finishing the cakes, so he covered the last four of them with a leaf followed by a layer of hot ashes, burying them next to the fire. He would leave them for breakfast; they should keep that long. Then he rested his chin on his foreclaws and resumed his interrupted thoughts.

The trouble is, I have no idea just what it was that knocked us out of the sky.

Obviously, he had several options. It *could* have been a purely natural phenomenon—or, if not natural, simply an anomalous and accidental creation of the mage-storms.

The trouble with that theory is that there have been a number of folk through here, Haighlei included. So that precludes it being stationary or ground bound. If it was something natural or accidental, it had *to be stationary, it seemed, so why didn't anyone discover it before this?* The Haighlei in particular, suspicious as they were of anything magical that was not under the direct control of one of their Priest-Mages, made a point of looking for such "wild" magic, using broad, far-ranging sweeps. They had established the outpost; they would have come this way, though perhaps not this exact route. They should have found something this powerful.

Granted, we were a bit off the regular route. I wasn't watching the ground that closely for landmarks, I was watching the sky for weather. I think I was even veering off a bit to avoid the worst of the storm.

Still, a "bad spot," even a null area, should show up to any skilled mage who was looking for it. It should be obvious to any mage looking for oddities.

I wasn't looking; I have to think about using mage-sight in order to see things. I'm not like Snowstar, who has to remind himself not to use it.

That left the next possibility; it was something new, or else something that was outside his knowledge. He inexorably moved his thoughts toward the uneasy concept that something had brought them down intentionally, either in an attack or as a measure of preventive defense.

But if it was a defensive measure, how did they ever see us from the ground! The attack couldn't have come from the air; there hadn't been anything in the air except birds and themselves. It hadn't come from the tree canopy, or he would have seen something directly below. It *had* to have come from ground level, below the tree canopy, so how had "they" seen the basket, Blade, and Tad?

Still, so far, whatever brought them down hadn't come after them; that argued in favor of it being a defensive, perhaps even a reflexive, answer to a perceived threat.

But it happened so quickly! Unless "they" had a spell actually ready to do something like that, I can't see how "they" could have done this before we got out of range!

That argued for an attack; argued for attackers who might actually have trailed them some time before they landed last night, and waited for them to get into the sky again before launching a spell that would send them crashing to the ground.

So why didn't they come see if they'd killed us! Could they have been that sure of themselves? Could they simply not have cared?

Or could they be better at hiding themselves than he was at spotting them?

Could they be out there right now!

It was certainly possible that the attackers had struck from some distance away, and had not reached the site of the crash before he and Blade were up, alert, and able to defend themselves. The *kind* of attack certainly argued for a cowardly opponent, one who would want to wait until his prey was helpless or in an inescapable position before striking.

Unless, of course, he is simply a slow opponent; one who was making certain of every inch of ground between himself and us before he initiated a confrontation.

He sighed quietly. There was only one problem; this was all speculation. None of this gave him any hard evidence for or against anything. He just didn't have any facts beyond the simplest—that they *had* been the victim of something that destroyed their holds on magic and brought them tumbling helplessly down out of the sky.

So, for the rest of the night, he continued to scan the forest and keep his ears wide open, starting at every tiny sound, and cursing his unending headache.

Dawn was heralded by nothing more obvious than a gradual lightening of the darkness under the trees. Tad knew that his partner was about to waken when her breathing speeded up and her heart rate increased—both of which he could hear quite easily. At his side, Blade yawned, stirred, started to stretch, and swore under her breath at the pain, that movement caused her.

Tad hooked a talon around the strap of the medical supply bag and dragged it over to her so she could rummage in it without moving much. She heard him, and shoved her hand in and pulled out one of the little vials; without being asked, he pierced the wax seal with his talon, and she drank it down.

Blade lay quietly for many long moments before her painkillers took effect. "I assume nothing happened last night?" She made it an inquiry.

"Nothing worth talking about—except that I think there was some squabbling over the remains of the foodstuffs." He hadn't heard anything in particular except a few grunts and the sound of an impact, as if one of the scavengers had cuffed another. "We ought to consider putting out snares, especially whip-snares that would take a catch out of reach of the ground. It would be very frustrating to discover we'd trapped something, but a scavenger beat us to it."

She sat up slowly, rubbing her eyes with her good hand. "I should have thought of that last night," she said ruefully.

"They wouldn't have worked last night," he pointed out. "It was raining until well after dark. Chances are, the lines would have been ruined, or stakes pulled out of the mud. If it doesn't rain that badly today, we can put them out *after* the afternoon rains are over."

She yawned again, then grimaced and gingerly rubbed her bruised jaw. "Good idea," she agreed. "Snares are a more efficient means of getting us supplemental rations than hunting. We'll trap the area where I dumped the ruined food. Even if there's nothing left, animals still might come back hoping there will be. Oh, *gods,* I am stiff and sore!"

"I know precisely how you feel. I saved us some breakfast." He scraped away the ashes and revealed the cakes, now a bit crisper than they had been, and a bit grimier, but still edible. *I wish I had some bruise medicine that would work as well on me as hers does on her.*

"Did you!" She brightened, and scratched the back of her neck with her good hand. "Well, that puts a better complexion on things! And my bruise remedy seems to have the additional value of keeping away bugs; for once I haven't got any new bites. Do you think you want another dose of your painkillers?"

He shook his head. "I took one as soon as it was light enough to see which vial was which." He handed her a cake, and ate the remaining three, neatly but quickly. One cake seemed to be substantial enough to satisfy her, though he noted that she did devour every crumb and licked her fingers clean afterward. Thanks to the fact that she had filled and refilled every container they had, he had even been able to get a drink without her assistance from a wide pot.

He waited until she ate, washed her face and hands, and looked a bit more alert. "Now what do we do?" he asked, as she dried off her face on her ruined tunic of yesterday. He made a mental note to have her set that out when the rains started, to give it a primitive wash.

She sat back on her heels, wincing as she jarred her shoulder. "Now— we discuss options," she said slowly. "What we do next, and where we go."

He stretched, taking care with his bandaged wing, and settled back again. "Options," he repeated after her. "Well, we both know that the best thing we can do is stay here. Right?"

"And build a beacon." She squinted past the canvas up through the treetops, at the tiny patches of sky visible, now and again, winking through the greenery like bright white eyes. "A very smoky beacon. It's going to take a lot of smoke to trickle up through that cover."

"It's going to take two or three days before they know we're missing," he said aloud, just to make certain he had all of his reasoning straight. "We have a shelter, and we can make it better and stronger, just by using available wood and leaves. I saw what you did with that windbreak, and we could certainly add layers of 'wall' that way over the canvas and wicker. If you look at the fallen leaves, you'll see that the ones you used dry up a lot like light leather; they'll hold up as shelter material."

She nodded, although she made a face. "It won't be easy, one-handed," she warned. "And I'm still the only decent knot tier in this team. You can bite holes, I can tie cord through them, but it is still tedious."

"So we take it slowly. I can do quite a bit, I just have to be careful." He paused for a moment, and went on. "We're injured, but I'm *still* a full-grown gryphon, and there aren't too many things that care to take on something my size, hurt or not."

"In that two or three days, whatever brought us down can find us, study us, and make its own plans," she countered, falling easily into the role of opposition—just as he would, when she proposed a plan. "We have to assume we were attacked and plan accordingly to defend ourselves. This place isn't exactly defensible."

He nodded; that was obvious enough. There was cover on all sides, and they didn't have the means to clear it all away, not even by burning it down.

Assuming they could. He wasn't willing to place bets on anything. Chances were, if they tried, nothing would happen after all, they had no way to take down trees with trunks big enough for two and three men to put their arms around. But there was always the chance that they would succeed "better" than they anticipated—and set fire to the whole forest, trapping themselves in an inferno. He had not forgotten that the green wood around the fire last night had certainly burned more efficiently than he had anticipated. No, setting fire to this place to get a defensible clearing was not a good idea.

"We ought to be someplace where our beacon has a chance of being seen at night," she went on. "I don't think we made *that* big a hole in the tree cover when we went through it."

"We didn't; I checked." Too bad, but she was right. Half the use of the beacon was at night, but there wasn't a chance that a night flyer would see a fire on the ground unless it was much larger than one that two people could build and tend alone.

"The last problem is that there's no source of water here," she concluded, and held up her good hand. "I *know* we've had plenty of rain every afternoon ever since we entered this area, but we don't dare count on that. So—we're in an undistinguished spot with no landmarks, under the tree canopy, with nothing to put our backs against, and no source of water."

He grimaced. "When you put it that way, staying here doesn't seem like much of an option."

"We only have to go far enough to find a stream or a pond," she pointed out. "With luck, that might not be too far away. We'll get our break in the cover, and our water source, and we can worry about making it defensible when we see what kind of territory we're dealing with. But I think we ought to at least consider moving."

"Maybe," he said, doubtfully, "but—"

What he was going to reply was lost in the rumble of thunder overhead and the spatter of rain on leaves.

"—not today," he breathed, as the rain came down again, as torrential as yesterday, but much earlier in the day.

Blade swore and stuck her head out to get a good look at the rain—a little too far, as she managed to jiggle the canvas and wicker of their roof just enough to send a cascade of cold water down the back of her neck. She jerked back, and turned white with pain.

The stream of oaths she uttered would have done a hardened trooper proud, but Tad didn't say anything. The cold water was insult enough, but when she lurched back, she must have really jarred her bad shoulder.

"I'll get wood," he offered hastily, and crawled slowly out of the shelter, trying not to disturb it any more.

Getting soaked was infinitely preferable to staying beside Blade when several things had gone wrong at once. She was his partner and his best friend—but he knew her and her temper very, very well.

And given the choice—I'd rather take a thunderstorm.

CHAPTER FIVE

"Wet gryphon," Blade announced, wrinkling her nose, "is definitely *not* in the same aromatic category as a bouquet of lilies."

"Neither is medicine-slathered human," Tad pointed out mildly. "I'll dry—but in the morning, you'll still be covered with that smelly soup."

Since he had just finished helping her wrap her limbs and torso in wet, brown bandages, he thought he had as much right to his observation as she had to hers.

In fact, he had shaken as much off his feathers as he could before he got into the tent, and he was not *wet* anymore, just damp. "And it could be worse. You could be sharing this shelter with a wet *kyree,*" he added.

She made a face. "I've been stuck in a small space with a wet *kyree* before, and you are a bundle of fragrant herbs, if not a bouquet of lilies, compared to that experience."

Supper for her had been one of the pieces of travel-bread, which she had gnawed on rather like a *kyree* with a bone. They had been unbelievably lucky; Blade had spotted a curious climbing beast venturing down out of the canopy to look them over, and she had gotten it with her sling. It made a respectable meal, especially since Tad hadn't done much to exert himself and burn off breakfast.

He *had* gone out to get more wood, searching for windfall and dragging it back to the camp. Then he had done the reverse, taking what wreckage they were both certain was utterly useless and dropping it on the other side of their brush-palisade where they wouldn't always be falling over it.

Blade had gone out in the late afternoon to chop some of the wood Tad had found, and bathe herself all over in the rain. He had been a gentleman and kept his eyes averted, even though she wasn't his species. She was unusually body-shy for a Kaled'a'in—or perhaps it was simply that she guarded every bit of her privacy that she had any control over.

At any rate, she had gathered up her courage and taken a cold rain bath, dashing back in under the shelter to huddle in a blanket afterward. She claimed that she felt much better, but he wondered how much of that was bravado, or wishful thinking. She was a human and not built for forceful—or bad—landings. Although the basket had given her some protection, he had no real idea how badly hurt she was in comparison with him. Nor was she likely to tell him if she was hurt deeper than the skin-obvious. To his growing worry, he suspected that her silence might hide her emotional wounds as well.

After she was dry, she had asked his help with her bruise-medicines. There was no doubt of how effective they were; after the treatment yesterday, the bruises were fading, going from purple, dark blue, and black, to yellow, green and purple. While this was not the most attractive color-combination, it did indicate that she was healing faster than she would have without the treatments.

He finished the last scrap of meat, and offered her the bones. "You could put these in the fire and roast them," he said, as she hesitated. "Then you could eat the marrow. Marrow is rich in a lot of good things.

This beast wasn't bad; the marrow has to have more taste than that chunk of bread you've been chewing."

"Straw would have more taste," she replied, and accepted the larger bones.

"I can bite the bones open later, if they don't split, and you can carve out the cooked marrow. We can use the long bone splinters as stakes. They might be useful," Tad offered.

Blade nodded, while trying unsuccessfully to stretch her arms. "You try and crunch up as much of those smaller bones as you can; they'll help your wing heal." She buried the bones in the ashes and watched them carefully as he obeyed her instructions and snapped off bits of the smaller bones to swallow. She *was* right; every gryphon knew that it took bone to build bone.

When one of the roasting bones split with an audible *crack*, she fished it quickly out of the fire. Scraping the soft, roasted marrow out of the bones with the tip of her knife, she spread it on her bread and ate it that way.

"This is better. It's almost good," she said, around a mouthful. "Thanks, Tad."

"My pleasure," he replied, pleased to see her mood slowly lifting. "Shall we set the same watches as last night?" He yawned hugely. "It's always easier for me to sleep on a full stomach."

"It's impossible to keep you awake when your belly's full, you mean," she retorted, but now she wore a ghost of a smile. "It's the best plan we have."

His wing did hurt less, or at least he thought it did. Gryphon bones tended to knit very quickly, like the bones of the birds that they were modeled after. Just at the moment, he was grateful that this was so; he preferred not to think about the consequences if somehow Blade had set his wing badly. Not that his days of fancy aerobatics would be over, but having his wing-bones re-broken and reset would be very unpleasant.

He peered up at the tree canopy, and as usual, saw nothing more than leaves. And rain, lots of it.

"I'm afraid we're in for another long rain like last night," he said ruefully. "So much for putting out snares."

"We can't have everything our way." She shrugged. "So far, we're doing all right. We could survive a week this way, with no problem—as long as nothing changes."

As long as nothing changes. Perhaps she had meant that to sound encouraging, but as he willed himself to sleep, he couldn't feel any encouragement. *Everything changes eventually. Only a fool would think otherwise. We might think we know what we're doing, but it only takes one serious mistake out here and we're dead. Even a minor mistake would mean that everything changes.*

The thought followed him down into his sleep, where it woke uneasy echoes among his dreams.

He slept so lightly that Blade did not need to shake him awake. He roused to the sound of water dripping steadily from the leaves above, the crackling and popping of the fire, and the calls of insects and frogs. That was *all.* It was very nearly silent out there, and it was a silence that was unnerving.

The forest that he knew fell silent in this way when a large and dangerous predator—such as a gryphon—was aprowl. He doubted that the denizens of this forest knew the two of them well enough to think that they were dangerous. That could only mean that something the local creatures *knew* was dangerous was out there.

Somewhere.

"Anything?" he whispered. She shook her head slightly without taking her eyes off the forest, and he noticed that she had banked the fire down so that it didn't dazzle her eyes.

He strained both eyes and ears, testing the night even as she did, and found nothing.

"It isn't that everything went quiet, it was that nothing much started making night-sounds after dark," she whispered back. "I suppose we might have driven all the local animals off—"

"Even the things that live up in the canopy? I doubt it," he replied. "Why would anything up there be afraid of us?"

She shrugged. "All I know is, I haven't heard or seen anything, but I have that unsettling feeling that something is watching us. Somewhere."

And whatever it is, the local creatures don't like it either. He had the same feeling, a crawling sensation at the back of his neck, and an itch in his talons. There were unfriendly eyes out there in the night, and Tad and Blade were at a disadvantage. *It* knew where they were and what they were. They had no idea what *it* was.

But if it hadn't attacked while he was asleep, hopefully it wouldn't while Blade took her rest. "Get to sleep," he told her. "If there's anything out there except our imaginations, it isn't likely to do anything now that I'm on watch. I look more formidable than you do, and I intend to reinforce that."

Under the packs holding Blade's clothing were his fighting-claws. He picked up her packs with his beak and fished them out. The bright steel winked cruelly in the subdued firelight, and he made a great show of fitting them on. Once Blade had fastened the straps, he settled back in, but with a more watchful stance than the previous night.

If there's nothing out there, I'm going to feel awfully stupid in the morning, for putting on all this show.

Well, better to feel stupid than be taken unaware by an attacker. Even if it was just an animal watching them, body language was something an animal could read very well. Hopefully, in the shiny claws and the alert stance, it would read the fact that attacking them would be a big mistake.

Blade pulled blankets around herself as she had the night before, but he noticed that she had a fighting-knife near at hand and her crossdraw knife under her pillow.

I just hope she can make herself sleep, he fretted a little. *She's going to be of no use if she's exhausted in the morning. If there was the slightest chance of convincing her to drink it, I'd offer her a sleeping tea.*

He waited all night, but nothing happened. Drops of water continued to *splat* down out of the trees, and frogs and insects sang, although nothing else moved of made a sound. He began to wonder, toward dawn, if perhaps they *had* frightened away everything but the bugs and reptiles.

It wasn't likely, but it was possible…

By the time the forest began to lighten with the coming of dawn, every muscle in his body ached with tension. His eyes twitched and burned with fatigue, and he could hardly wait for Blade to wake up. But he wouldn't awaken her himself. She needed her rest as much as he needed his.

Finally, when dawn had given way to full daylight, she stirred and came awake, all at once.

"Nothing," he said, answering her unspoken question. "Except that nothing larger than a gamebird made a sound all night, either, near the camp."

Now he moved, removing the fighting-claws, getting stiffly to his feet, and prowling out into the rising fog. He wanted to see what he could before the fog moved in and made it impossible to see again, shrouding in whiteness what the night had shrouded in black.

He was looking for foot- or paw-prints, places where the leaves had been pressed down by a body resting there for some time.

This was the area of which he was most proud. He wasn't just a *good* tracker, he was a great one. Blade was good, but he was a magnitude better than she.

Why a gryphon, who spent his life furlongs above the ground, should prove to be such a natural tracker was a total mystery to him. If Skandranon had boasted a similar ability, no one had ever mentioned it. He only knew that he had been the best in his group, and that he had impressed the best of the Kaled'a'in scouts. That was no small feat, since it was said of them that they could follow the track of the wind.

He suspected he would need every bit of that skill now.

He worked his way outward from the brush-fence, and found nothing, not the least sign that there had been anything out in the darkness last night except his imagination. He worked his way out far enough that he was certain no one and nothing could have seen a bit of the camp. By this time, he was laughing at himself.

I should have known better. Exhaustion, pain, and too many drugs. That's a combination guaranteed to make a person think he's being watched when he's alone in his own aerie.

He debated turning and going back to the camp; the fog was thickening with every moment, and he wouldn't be able to see much anyway. In fact, he had turned in his tracks, mentally rehearsing how he was going to make fun of himself to Blade, when he happened to glance over to the side at the spot where he had left the wreckage he had hauled out of the camp yesterday.

He froze in place, for that spot was not as he had left it. Nor did it look as if scavengers had simply been rummaging through it.

Every bit of trash had been meticulously taken apart, examined, and set aside in a series of piles. Here were the impressions he had looked for in vain, the marks of something, several somethings, that had lain in the leaf mold and pawed over every bit of useless debris.

His intuition, and Blade's, had been correct. It had not been weariness, pain, and the medicines. There *had* been something out here last night, and before it had set to watch the camp it had been right here. Some of the larger pieces of wreckage were missing, and there were no drag marks to show where they had been taken. That meant that whatever had been here had lifted the pieces and carried them off rather than dragging them.

And except for this one place, there was no trace of whatever had been here. The creature or creatures that had done this had eeled their way through the forest leaving nothing of themselves behind.

This couldn't be coincidence. It *had* to be the work of whatever had brought them crashing down out of the sky. Now their mysterious enemies, whatever they were, had spent the night studying him, Blade, and as much of the things belonging to them as had been left within their reach. They now had the advantage, for he and Blade knew nothing of them, not even if they ran on four legs, six, eight, two, or something else. All that he knew was that the creature—or creatures—they faced were intelligent enough to examine things minutely—and cunning enough to do so without clear detection.

He turned and ran back to the camp, despite the added pain it brought him. It was not simple fear that galvanized him, it was abject terror, for nothing can be worse to a gryphon than an opponent who is completely unknown.

As Tad spoke, Blade shivered, although the sun was high enough now that it had driven off the fog and replaced the cool damp with the usual heat and humidity. The pain, weariness, the drugs—all of them were taking their toll on her endurance. Her hands shook; her pale face told him that it wasn't fear that was making her shake, it was strain. This just might be the event that broke her nerve.

Tad had tried to be completely objective; he had tried only to report what he had seen, not what he had felt. Out there, faced with the evidence of their watchers, he had sensed a malignant purpose behind it all that he had no rational way of justifying. But Blade evidently felt the same way that he did, and rather than break, this new stress made her rally her resources. Her face remained pale, but her hands steadied, and so did her voice.

"We haven't a choice now," she said flatly. "We have to get out of here. We can't defend this place against creatures that can come and go without a sign that they were there. If we're lucky, they're territorial, and if we get far enough out of their territory, they'll be satisfied."

Once again, the wildlife of this place was mysteriously absent from their immediate vicinity; only a few birds called and cried in the canopy. Did they know something that the two below them did not?

"And if we're not, we'll be on the run with *no* secure place to hole up," he argued. His focus sharpened, and he felt the feathers along his cheeks and jaws ripple. "If they can come and go without our seeing them, they can track us without our knowing they're behind us! I don't want some unseen enemy crawling up my tail. I want to see whoever I am against." That unnerved him, and he was not ashamed to show it.

The idea that something could follow them, or get ahead of them and set an ambush, and he would never know it until it was too late... It just made his guts bind and crawl.

Blade was quiet for a moment, chewing on her lower lip. All around them, water dripped slowly from the leaves, making the long fall to splash into puddles below, and the air was thick with the perfumes of strange flowers. "Look," she said, finally. "We didn't fly all that far before we were brought down. Twenty, maybe thirty leagues at most. We can go back in the direction of our previous campsite. *That* was defensible; remember, there was a cliff nearby? And remember the river that ran alongside it?"

Nervously, Tad flexed his talons into the loam. New scents rose to his nostrils, of earth and old leaves, dampness and the sharp aroma of a torn fungus. "You have a point." He thought about her suggestion, mentally trying to figure out how long it would take two injured people to walk the distance that two uninjured people had flown. *It isn't so much the distance, as what we have to cross to get there.* "It might take us as much as four days," he pointed out. "We don't have any real way of getting good directions other than the north-needle, and we're going to be crawling through leagues of this—" He waved his claw at the tangled undergrowth. "We're going to be carrying packs, we'll have to guard our backtrail and watch ahead for ambushes, and we're both injured. All of that will delay us; in fact, we probably ought to assume that we're going to be creeping through the forest, not hiking through it."

If we're, going to do this, I want to creep. I want to go from bit of cover to bit of cover; I want to walk so that we leave no sign and little scent. I want to leave traps behind.

"But when we get there—we'll be at a cliff face, Tad. That means caves, probably at least one waterfall; even if we don't find the river at first, we can work our way along the cliff until we do find the river. We'll at least have something we can put our backs against!" She looked unbelievably tense, and Tad didn't blame her. Of the two of them, she was the most vulnerable, physically, and the least able to defend herself, knife skill or not.

Not that either of us will be particularly good at it. In terrain like this, I'm at a distinct disadvantage. If anything gets in front of me, I can probably shred it, but at my sides and rear I'm badly vulnerable at close quarters.

If they left this camp, their choice of how to proceed was simple; pack out what they could, or try to live off the land with very little to aid them. Take the chance that they could improvise, or—

Or find out that we can't. We're hurt; we are going to need every edge we can get. That means tools, weapons, food, protection.

"The one advantage that we have is that whatever these creatures are, they don't know us, so they can't predict us," she persisted. "If we move now, we may confuse them. They may linger to look over what we left. We aren't going to lose them unless they lose interest in us, but we may leave them far enough behind that it will take them a while to catch up."

If only they had some idea of what kind of creature they were up against! The very fact that they would be trying to slip quietly through the forest rather than running might confuse their foes.

Or it might tempt them into an attack. They might read that as an admission of weakness. There was just no way of knowing.

He nodded, grinding his beak a bit. "Meanwhile, if we stay, they can study us at their leisure," he admitted. "And that makes us easy targets."

Go or stay? Remain where they were or try to find some place easier to defend?

Either way, they were targets. The only question was whether they made themselves moving targets or entrenched targets.

Aubri and Father always agreed on that; it's better to be a moving target than a stationary one. "All right, I agree," he conceded. "Let's make up two packs and get out of here. You might as well load me down; it isn't going to make a great deal of difference since I can't fly anyway."

She nodded, and wordlessly turned to rummage through the supplies cached in the tent. In a few moments, she handed him a pack to fill.

He joined her in picking through all the supplies they had salvaged. It was obvious what they were going to leave behind just about everything they had saved. They would have to abandon everything that wasn't absolutely essential.

Their discards went everywhere, now that there was no point in sheltering them. If their foes *did* come to rummage through what they left behind, the confusion of belongings might gain them a little more time.

Clothing, personal items, those joined the rejected items; it was easier to decide what to leave than what to take. The piles of discards grew larger, with very few items making it into the packs. The medicine kit *had* to come along; so did the weapons, even though the pouches of lead shot were heavy. So far, there hadn't been anything around that Blade could use in the sling instead of lead shot. This was the wrong time of the year for fallen nuts; the soil here wasn't particularly rocky, and they couldn't count on a cairn of pebbles turning up at a convenient moment. The only distance-weapon she could use one-handed was the sling, so the shot had to come, too.

The food had to come with them, and some of the tools, and just enough bedding and canvas to keep them warm and dry at night. All of that cloth was bulky and heavy, but if they got soaked, they could easily die of cold-shock, even with a fire to keep them warm and dry them out. Then again—if they got soaked in another long rainstorm and they were caught without shelter, there would be no way to build a fire to warm them. No, the canvas half-shelter and a blanket apiece had to come along.

They were leaving a great deal for their opponents to look over, and Tad hoped that it would keep them very, very busy. *And if only I knew something, anything about "them," I'd be able to think of a way to keep them even busier!*

Part of their training included this sort of selection process, and they had learned just what was truly essential to survive. It didn't take long before they had two packs put together, one large, and one small. Blade would carry two spears and use them as walking sticks; that way she would have both aid and weapon in one. It had taken some ingenuity to rig her pack so that it would stay on with a minimum of pain—there couldn't have been a worse injury than a broken collarbone when it came to carrying a pack. Much of the weight was going to fall on her hips, now, and would probably cause bruises and abrasions. Both Tad and Blade had come to accept that pain was going to be an omnipresent part of their immediate future, and their concern regarding it was more a case of figuring out ways to lessen its immediate impact, since eliminating it was impossible. "Endure now, heal later" was the philosophy that would serve them best.

The morning fog was just beginning to lift when they took a bearing with the north-needle and headed into the west. Blade led in more open areas. She was small—they both had the feeling that if an attack came, it would come from the rear. *He* was better suited to bearing the brunt of an attack from the front than she, and in open areas he could turn around quickly to help Blade. In close quarters, he led, with Blade guarding his tail. They were still vulnerable from the sides, but it was better than a completely unguarded rear. They had discussed booby-trapping the camp, but decided against it. If their foes were kept nicely busy with what remained, that was good, but if one of their number was hurt or killed by a booby-trap, it might make them angry and send them hot on the trail, after revenge. Also, discovery of one trap might make whatever it was give up on a search of the camp entirely and go straight into tracking them, which would lose them valuable distance.

As they left the area, Tad paused once for a look back at the camp, wondering if they were making a dreadful mistake. They were leaving so much behind, so much that they might need desperately in the next few days! But their pathetic little shelter looked even more vulnerable now, and rationally, he knew that it couldn't withstand a single determined blow, much less a coordinated attack by several creatures at once. In fact, with its canvas-over-wicker construction, it *could* become a trap for both of them. It wouldn't take much to drive the supporting saplings through the wicker-work.

A shiver ran along his spine at that thought, for it was all too easy to picture something slamming the cup of wicker down on top of them, trapping them inside, where they would be helpless to defend themselves...

With a shudder, he turned away, and followed after Blade as she picked her way through the tangled growth of the forest floor.

There was still fog in the treetops, just high enough that there was no real way for them to tell precisely where the sun was. In a little while, the last of the fog would burn off completely, and then they might be able to cross-check their bearings with the angle of the sun—although so far, they hadn't been able to manage that yet.

We'll know where we are exactly, but only if we can find a hole big enough to see the sun through. And then it will only be possible if the sun is high enough to shine down through the hole at the time we find it.

Living in this forest was like living inside an enormous, thick-aired cave. How could anything that lived here know where it was? It was very disorienting for Tad not to be able to see the sky, and somewhat claustrophobic; he wondered if Blade felt the same as he.

She seemed determined to concentrate on the forest ahead, slipping carefully through the underbrush in such a way that she disturbed as little as possible? The kind of leaf litter that served as the forest floor didn't hold tracks very well, and if their enemies could just hold off following until the afternoon rains started, it wouldn't hold a scent very well either. If she found their surroundings claustrophobic, she wasn't letting the feeling interfere with what she was doing.

But he kept swiveling his head in all directions every time they paused to pick a good route. Those frequent pauses as she pondered her route to the next bit of cover gave him ample opportunity to feel the forest closing in on him. His nerves were afire with tension; he couldn't imagine why she wouldn't feel the same.

But maybe she doesn't; maybe this doesn't bother her. Maybe she doesn't even need to feel sky and wind. He had always known that humans weren't like gryphons, and that thought made her seem positively alien for a moment.

But, then again, she lived in a veritable burrow back in White Gryphon, so maybe this landscape felt cozy to her, rather than constricting. But oh, how he longed for enough room to spread his wings wide, even if that longing reminded him pointedly that he *couldn't* spread them at the moment!

As Blade eeled her way between two bushes that were barely far enough apart to let him through, he realized something else that was very strange. There weren't any game trails here.

That realization was just as disconcerting to him as not being able to see the sky. He *knew* there were some large animals that lived down here on the forest floor, so why didn't they leave regular trails? There should be deer trails, going to and from water. Deer couldn't collect rainwater in vessels to drink, obviously; they had to have a water source. He had never in all of his life encountered a deer herd that didn't make paths through their territory just by virtue of the fact that there were a lot of them going in the same direction.

Was there something living down here that was so dangerous that it was suicidal to *have* a regular trail, foolhardy to move in groups large enough to make one?

Could that something be what had brought them down, and what had been examining their ruined belongings?

That's altogether too logical, and is not a comforting thought. I know there are large cats like lions here, and bears, because the Haighlei told us there were—yet I have never seen deer and wild pigs afraid to make game trails in lion or bear country. If there is something else living here that makes creatures who regularly face lions afraid to leave a game trail...

The answer could be that whatever this putative creature was happened to be so fierce, so bloodthirsty, that it wasn't safe for herbivores to travel in herds. That it was the kind of creature that slaughtered everything within its reach, whether or not it was hungry. He swallowed, his throat feeling tight and dry.

But he might be overreacting again. He didn't *like* this place; perhaps his imagination was getting the better of him. *Maybe we just are in a bad place in the forest. Maybe there's nothing here worth foraging for to bring deer and other browsers into this area. There certainly doesn't seem to be anything tasty for a plant eater to feed on; all these bushes are extraordinarily tough and we've seen precious little grass. Maybe that's why there aren't any trails through here; it simply isn't worth a deer's time to come here.*

And perhaps that was the reason for the unnatural silence all about them.

There might be an even better explanation for the silence—they were dreadfully *obvious* to anything watching and listening. Despite the fact that they were trying very hard to be quiet, the inevitable sounds they were making were an unholy racket in contrast with the silence surrounding them. Try as they might, as they passed from one spot of cover to the next, they rattled vines and rustled bushes, and none of those noises sounded natural.

And anything living up in the trees is going to have a fine view of us down below. I doubt that Blade looks harmless to what's up there, and I know I don't. I look like a very large, if oddly shaped, eagle.

Tree dwellers might not recognize Blade as a predator, but they would certainly recognize Tad. There were eagles here, they knew that for a fact, for he had seen them flying below him, hunting in and above the forest canopy. Anything that looked like an eagle was going make a canopy dweller nervous.

And yet… there hadn't been a silence this wary and profound since they had felt as if they were being watched. For that matter, the tree dwellers hadn't been particularly quiet in any of the other places that they had camped before they had crashed.

This is exactly like the silence that falls when an eagle-owl is hunting, and everything stays absolutely quiet and motionless until the moment it makes a kill, hoping that whatever it is hunting, it will not find one of them.

There weren't even the sounds made when other animals hunted… *but when a greater predator prowls, the lesser remains silent and hidden. Are we the greater predators, or is something else?*

Perhaps he should put his mind to thinking of ways to delay pursuit.

If whatever-it-is does come after us, it wouldn't matter now if I laid booby-traps behind us. Would it? How much worse could I make things, if I hurt something that was following us?

Well, the answer to that could well be— much worse. Why anger something that was following only out of curiosity?

Perhaps not booby-traps then, at least not yet. Perhaps just things to confuse the trail. The first thing to confuse would be scent, because that was of primary importance to a ground-dwelling predator in an environment like this one. There wasn't much of a line-of-sight, but scent would hold and cling until the next rain washed it away. And by then, a trail would more than likely be too cold to follow anyway.

He began watching for a vine with leaves veined with purple and red; it had a pungent, peppery smell. He'd noticed that they were fairly common, and when he finally spotted one, he hissed at Blade to stop for a moment.

When they next moved on, it was with the thick juice from those leaves rubbed all over their feet and hands—and they were going to have to remember not to rub their eyes until they washed it off, for it burned just like real pepper! There were other plants, less common, that had equally distinctive odors, and as he came across them he intended to gather generous samples. Every time the current scent was about to wear off, he'd change it. If anything came hunting them depending on its nose, he'd have handed it a surprise. And maybe one of these plants would have the effect of numbing a sensitive nose.

He had to hope this ploy would work, for they were certainly proceeding at a crawl to begin with, and their progress only slowed as the day progressed. His pack was awkward, heavy, and made his bad wing and all his bruises ache; he wasn't suited to walking in the first place, and his injuries combined with the pack only made it worse. Fortunately for his own feelings, Blade wasn't doing any better, so he wasn't in the position of knowing that he was the one impeding their progress.

The longer they walked, the worse it got. Eventually the fog burned off, and the temperature rose, so that he was overheated as well as in pain. Blade's shirt stuck to her, dark with sweat. He couldn't sweat, so he panted. Neither sweating nor panting brought any relief in the humid air; it must have been nearly as sultry as a Kaled'a'in steambath. There wasn't a breath of breeze down here to stir the heavy air. If he had been left to his own devices, he'd have called a halt and flung himself to the ground for a rest.

As he had predicted, their progress was measured in furlongs, not leagues, with no discernible differences in the territory that they crossed. He could only be certain that they were not walking in circles by virtue of the fact that Blade kept checking the north-needle every time they stopped moving. They stopped for a brief break and something to eat. The sun actually penetrated the canopy in a few places eventually, but it was not much help in showing them where they were. There wasn't enough of it visible to help them get a bearing from it, either by using a measuring stick or by taking the angle of it.

In fact, the sunlight proved to be something of a new hazard. The beams of sunlight lancing down through the dark green leaves *were* very pretty, very picturesque, but they were also to be avoided at all costs. Pinned even for a moment in such a bright light, they would be extremely obvious as something that didn't belong there.

There were still no signs of any watercourses, either, which probably meant that this forest depended on rain rather than ground water for the trees to thrive. That was not precisely a surprise, given the daily thunderstorms.

But a creek or a small stream would have given them a path to a river, and a way to break their trail completely. If they were ever able to wade for some distance along the path of a creek bed, they would completely lose anything that hunted by scent. He had been hoping for a stream, in fact, for that very reason.

That, and stream water would certainly be cooler than the water in my water skin. The tepid liquid he was carrying had not been particularly refreshing, although he had drunk his ration dutifully. *And it would taste better. Much better.*

But there was no sign of any sort of a stream, and eventually the beams of sunlight faded, the light all about them dimmed, and a distant rumble heralded the afternoon storm approaching. At that point, despite their lack of progress, he was almost grateful to hear it. Now they would have to stop and rig a shelter for the night, because it wouldn't be long before the rain started to fall and made it impossible to get anything constructed.

Blade stopped, held up her hand, then motioned him up beside her.

"We've got to stop and get our canvas up," she said, weariness in every syllable. He felt instantly sorry for her; she sounded even more tired than he was.

She pointed ahead, to one of the few distinctive places he'd seen in this forest. There was a break in the cover, through which the fat, gray bellies of the clouds were clearly visible; at some point in the past few years one of the forest giants had toppled here. They edged forward to a place where the hollowed-out carcass of an ancient snag stood, half-covered with vines, the remains of the rest of the tree lying on the ground beside it, smothered in vines and plants. "That snag is big enough to hold both of us. We'll use that for the base of our shelter; it's the closest thing I've seen today to something that we can count on to protect us overnight."

And she doesn't mean from the rain. He nodded. Abandoning any pretext at moving quietly, they thrashed their way through the undergrowth to the giant snag. It stood a little taller than Blade's head, and as she had stated, was just large enough to hold both of them in its hollow interior. There was no room for a fire, but in confines that close, they would keep each other warm with the heat of their bodies.

And I'm not certain that I want a fire to advertise our presence tonight.

They *were* going to need one initially, though—otherwise they were going to be sharing this shelter with a wide variety of multi-legged guests. Rotten wood meant insects, and some of them could be noxious or even poisonous.

They didn't have much time before the storm broke, though; perhaps not enough time for Blade to use the fire-striker to start a fire in the hollow. But he *was* a mage, and the easiest spell in the lexicon was to call fire.

Dare I? It could have been the mere presence of magic that got us attacked... Well, if I don't, she might not get a torch going before the rain comes. And the fire-spell is so very small, so limited in scope and duration—I'd better chance it. "Move back," he ordered her; as soon as she had obeyed, he closed his eyes, concentrated—and called fire into the midst of the hollowed-out trunk.

There was enough in the way of dry leaves and dry, half-rotted woodchips on the floor of the snag to start an enthusiastic and very smoky fire. The smoke had the immediate effect of driving out everything that could leap or fly; Blade bundled other burnables together into two torches and they lit both at the fire and proceeded to char the interior. Smoke rose all about them in a thick fog; he coughed and backed out to get a breath of cleaner air more than once. Half-rotten wood did not give off the kind of pleasant smoke that made sitting beside a campfire a pleasure. It was a pity they hadn't come upon this place earlier; some of the grubs might have been very tasty, especially cooked. Now their only concern was to rid the tree of all other inhabitants before the rains came.

He coughed again, as a new and more acrid set of odors joined the heavy smoke. *We must have hit a nest of something nasty. Ugh. Or maybe we've just incinerated a crop of unpleasant fungi.* He hoped that whatever they burned off didn't give off poisonous fumes. *A little late to worry about that now.*

They didn't quite beat the downpour completely. They were in the process of roofing the snag with their canvas and tying it down when the first cloudburst descended, wetting them both to the skin.

At that point, Blade gave in to the inevitable and stood in the downpour until she and her clothing had been flushed clean, and he let the rain wash all of the soot and dirt from his own feathers before shaking himself partially dry under the shelter of a nearby tree. It was too bad that Blade's clothing didn't sluice clean so easily, nor could she shake herself dry. He made a dash to the snag and squeezed himself into the downed tree with the supplies. She had already gotten out blankets and bread and dried meat. He tucked the packs up in a way that she could sleep on them, and put her blanket on top of the pile. He had to put the dried meat out into the stream of water pouring off the canvas and soak it until he could eat it. Meanwhile, Blade emptied and refilled their water skins, then joined him in their shelter.

Their combined body heat did do something to warm the interior; with blankets over each of them, they weren't completely miserable, and Blade's clothing actually began to dry out. And the strong smell of smoke wasn't too bad after a while—though they must not have gotten all of the bugs out of their shelter, since periodically he would feel a small one taking a trip under his feathers, or Blade would slap at something. Once again, the rain persisted until after nightfall, though once it stopped, it was—again uncannily silent beneath the trees.

"Damn," Blade whispered. "I was hoping…"

"That we'd left them behind?" Tad was altogether glad of the thick wood at his back, and of the deep shadow of the interior of their shelter. Not even an owl would be able to see them in here. "It might not be *them* that's making everything so quiet. It might just be the smell of smoke; you know how most wild things fear fire."

"And I might be the Haighlei Emperor. No, they're out there. They followed us, I'm sure of it." She stared out into the darkness fiercely, as if willing her eyes to be better than they actually were.

"Well, they can't get us in here," he said, and meant it. "It's safe enough for you to sleep if you want to take second watch this time."

"You can't sleep?" she asked. He shook his head.

It was true, he *wasn't* going to be able to sleep for a while; he was horribly tired, but not sleepy. His muscles kept twitching and jumping with accumulated fatigue. His nerves all felt strung as tightly as a Kaled'a'in horse-bow, and every tiny sound out there had him peering into the darkness as fiercely as she. It was going to be some time before he relaxed enough to fall asleep.

"Well, I think I've reached the limit on my nerves," she replied, punctuating the sentence with a yawn. "Believe it or not, I'm going numb. Right now, I hurt so much that all I want to do is drink my medicine and drop off as soon as the pain stops. In fact, right now, *they* could come kill me as long as they did it while I was asleep; I just can't get up the energy to care."

"I know how you feel." Awkwardly, he managed to pat her leg in sympathy. "You go ahead. I'll take the first watch as long as I can."

She sounded fatalistic; he wasn't quite ready to share that emotion, but there was something else to consider. *I'm not sure it would matter if we both fell asleep tonight. So far, we haven't any evidence beyond the fact that something probably dangerous is probably following us.* They *haven't actually done anything. Even assuming that they intend to attack us, as cautious as* they *have been, I don't think they're ready to try and pry us out of some place like this.* "I think we're as safe as we can be under the circumstances. Get some sleep while you can."

She didn't need a second invitation. In an instant, she had downed her vial of medicine and curled up against his side in her blanket, propped up by the packs to save her shoulder. Provided she didn't get a kink in her neck from sleeping this way, or stiff muscles from a chill, she ought to be more comfortable tonight than she had been since the accident.

He stared out into the darkness until his eyes burned—and just as he was contemplating waking her to take her watch, the forest itself woke. But not with sounds of alarm—to his intense relief, these were *normal* night sounds, the same they had heard every other night of this journey.

The *whoop* of something up above startled Blade awake. She came alive with a jerk and a thin gasp of pain. "What?" she demanded, then relaxed as she recognized the noises outside their shelter for what they were.

The sudden onset of normal night sounds had been the trigger that let all of his own fatigue catch up with him. Suddenly, he could not keep his eyes open, no matter how hard he tried. He was actually nodding off even as he stared into the dark.

"Can you take over?" he whispered, and felt her nod. That was all he needed; a moment later, not even the scream of a makaar would have awakened him.

For the second time that morning, Blade motioned to Tad to freeze. Obedient to her hand gesture, he went rigid, and for something as huge as he was, he blended into the forest surprisingly well. His eyes were fixed on her, not on the forest around him; that was because she hadn't used the gesture that meant *danger*, just the one that meant *wait*.

In fact, there was no danger, only an opportunity. She had spotted another of the long-limbed tree dwellers climbing cautiously down out of the canopy, in pursuit of something it had dropped. This must be a young one; the elders never were so foolish as to risk coming down into the danger zone just because they wanted something they had lost. If she was lucky, this one would not survive a lesson in *why* they did not.

Although this hunting was delaying them, it was a necessary delay.

Her quarry dropped down off the tree trunk and took two cautious steps on the forest floor, reaching for the bright object it had lost. It had four long limbs, a pointed snout, and large eyes set on the sides of its head. If it had been up in the canopy, she would never have been able to spot it, for its brown fur blended in beautifully with the bark of the tree. Not that she could have reached it with her puny weapon, either. Nothing short of a very powerful bow would put a missile up into the canopy with force great enough to kill.

She whirled her sling twice and let fly.

The beast barely had time to register the movement and start to turn his head. Then the lead shot struck it squarely on the skull with a wet *crack*, and it dropped to the ground, instantly dead.

Grinning with elation, she ran forward anyway, just to make certain of it with her knife; fresh meat was too precious a commodity for her to take any chances that it might simply be stunned. When she finished, she stood up and motioned Tad to come up and join her.

She straightened and walked over to see what it had dropped. The brightly colored object that had exerted a fatal attraction for this tree dweller proved to be absolutely unidentifiable. It was bladder-like, and a bright blue and red. It could have been, a flower, a seed pod, a fruit, even an insect carapace or a portion of some other unfortunate animal. She ignored it at that point; perhaps it was edible, but this was not the time nor the place to experiment.

Tad, meanwhile, had made short work of her prey. It hadn't been very large, and he had dismembered it and eaten it almost whole. This was the second such catch she'd made this morning for him, and he looked much the better for the fresh meat. The first had been a rodent, both rabbit-like and rat-like; bigger than a rat, but small for a rabbit. This one was about the size of a large rabbit, though the long limbs had made it look bigger. If her luck kept up, she'd be able to keep *him* in fresh-killed prey, mouthful by mouthful. That would take one worry away from her; how to keep him from starving. Gryphons weren't big eaters just by choice.

Although the forest sounds had by no means returned to normal, there were more signs of other living things now, which made her feel a bit better. Maybe they were outdistancing their invisible trackers. Or maybe those trackers were just waiting until nightfall to move in on them.

At least this meant that she could actually *see* some game to take down.

I can probably get enough small animals and birds over the course of the day to keep Tad in good shape, she decided, retrieving the bit of lead shot and pocketing it before checking her north-needle. Tad had cautiously taken the downed creature into the shelter of a bush to eat it; she pressed herself against the bole of the tree and picked the next landmark they would head for. That was how she was navigating, in line-of-sight increments; checking her north-needle, picking a particular bit of distant cover that was farther west, and moving in toward it. Not only were they—hopefully—avoiding being spotted by their foe, they were not frightening the game.

She made two more such moves when she spotted another one of the rat-rabbits, nosing about on the forest floor in search of something edible. She warned Tad to freeze and potted it, too. That made three pieces of small game in about three marks, or one piece per mark, and she was beginning to feel very proud of herself. That was not at all bad for someone hampered by a bad shoulder, with a primitive weapon, in unfamiliar territory. *If I remember my gryphon-rations correctly, he should actually prosper on that amount of food. Granted, it's like feeding a hawk by tidbitting it, but beggars can't be choosers. If he isn't exactly full at any one time, he isn't going hungry, either.*

He looked faintly annoyed at being asked to swallow another bit of game every mark or so, but he didn't say anything. He was used to eating once lightly, and once hugely, then sleeping on that larger meal. He probably wondered why they were stopping so frequently just so he could eat.

But if she carried the game until they had enough for him to have that single large meal, she'd be weighing herself down for no good purpose. Let the game ride in the most efficient way possible; inside Tad.

If he hasn't figured out what I'm doing, he will soon, she decided, moving on ahead.

She was worried about him; in spite of the fact that she was the one with the worse injury—as her shoulder reminded her sharply of just how badly hurt she was, every time she moved a bit too quickly—in some ways he was the more vulnerable of the two of them.

She knew, only too well, just how vulnerable he was. Trapped on the ground as he was, he had as many weaknesses as she did. Unless he could get his back up against something to protect it, he could not only be attacked from the rear, but from below. Most of what he had learned about fighting was meant for aerial, combat, not ground fighting. Granted, he could improvise, and granted, he had four sets of very nasty "knives" on the end of each limb, not to mention the weapon in the middle of his face, but he was made for another element. Faced with the need to fight on terms and terrain he was not suited to, he was vulnerable in ways even he probably didn't realize.

His other weakness was the sheer volume of food he had to consume in order to stay in decent physical shape. If she couldn't get that into him—well, too many days of rain-soaked dried meat, and he wouldn't be in good condition at all.

Too many days of that kind of ration, and we'll have to find a permanent place to hole up, because he won't even be able to travel.

Walking was much harder on him than flying; he wasn't built for it. Intellectually, of course, she had known that; watching him try to move through the underbrush had driven it home to her in a more concrete form.

He was *not* clumsy; he was a great deal more graceful at this sort of travel than his classmates had ever been. He was, in fact, as adept at it as some humans—but he tired easily, and occasionally his wings got caught up on some obstacle or other. It would be some time before his legs strengthened and gained the endurance for steady walking, and until then, he was handicapped.

If they ever ran across a large browser like a deer, he *should* be able to bring it down so long as they surprised it, but until then she was the better ground hunter. He was going to be depending on her for something he was normally self-sufficient at.

She was just grateful that he was as good a tracker as he was. He'd done a fair amount to confuse their scent and backtrail, and that could only help right now.

That might be one of the reasons I'm spotting game today; that muck he had us rub all over ourselves is probably hiding our scent and confusing the tree dwellers. Scent rose, especially in *this* heat; a wary canopy beast would not come anywhere near the ground with the scent of a large predator coming up to meet his nose, but at the moment all that they smelled like was crushed plants.

And that might very well be the explanation of why they had been surrounded by silence until lately. Quite frankly, Tad was damp, and he smelled like—well—damp raptor, a combination of wet feathers and the heavy musk that was peculiar to gryphons and birds of prey. He hadn't been able to dry out properly since the accident, and that made his scent more obvious. *Could be that when we first camped, not only was he not as fragrant, but we simply weren't on the ground long enough for the scent to rise into the canopy. Now we are.*

That speculation made her feel a little better; and the current state of affairs did seem to offer support for that speculation. Tad didn't smell like raptor, wet *or* dry, at the moment. The juicy plant he had her rub all over both of them imparted a peculiar, sharp, mossy scent to their respective hides. It made a hideous mess of her clothing, streaking it a mottled green, but she wasn't particularly worried about stains.

Besides, the stains make a fairly good impromptu camouflage.

She ought to start looking for a good place to go to ground for the night. As she kept an eye out, she tried to mentally reckon up the time it would take for them to be missed. They ought to start putting up some sort of signal if there was any chance that the White Gryphon people might be looking for it.

We should have made our rendezvous today or tomorrow, so by tomorrow or the day after, the Silvers we're relieving will know there's something wrong. They have a teleson; they'll let Judeth know, but it would take a team of rescuers coming at full speed another two or three days to reach here. So—what does that make it? Another two or three days before help will have a chance of being here at best. More likely a week.

So there was no point in looking for a shelter *and* a place where they could set up a good signal fire. Shelter alone would do for today and tomorrow.

Nothing presented itself for another mark—except the first signs she had seen yet of large animals on the forest floor. She came across a place where a pig had clearly been rooting at the base of a tree, searching for underground fungi, and with regret she saw that the trail went off into the north and not the west. A pig would have been very welcome to both her and Tad.

But she was not going to risk going off in a different direction on just the chance that they might be able to bring one down.

The heat was oppressive; when the rains came again, she had every intention of soaking herself and her clothing. If she didn't, by tomorrow morning her tunic and trews would be able to stand by themselves, they were so saturated with sweat. She was grateful to Tad for his subterfuge with the plant scent for more reasons than the obvious; without the pungent aroma of crushed leaf hanging around her, she would be smelling herself by now.

On the other hand, maybe if I smelled bad enough, our trackers would be offended and leave us alone. Hah!

Sweat trickled steadily down the back of her neck, and her hair itched unbearably. For that matter, so did her feet, shins, armpits... any number of tiny forest insects were finding her tasty fare, and she was covered with itching, red welts. Something she had forgotten was that their original tent not only set itself up and took itself down, the spells on it protected them from insects. Without that protection, she seemed to be the only source of food for every bloodsucker for furlongs about, except for the ones buzzing about poor Tad's eyes and ears. Her bruise-medicine eased the itching enough for her to sleep, but she would have given a great deal to discover a plant that rendered her inedible to bugs. Every time she paused, she found herself reaching inside her clothing to scratch at another itch.

She kept reminding her herself to *rub*, not scratch. If she broke the skin, she opened herself up to infection—if she bled, she added a particularly tasty scent to her own, and one the plant juice would not cover.

Something near her ear buzzed, landed, and bit. She slapped and swore, as Tad crept into cover beside her.

We *may not need stalking beasts to finish us off. The insects may nibble us to death.*

"Ants," Tad muttered in her ear.

"Is that what just got me?" she asked without turning her head.

"No. That had wings and a long nose. I am reminding myself to lie on an anthill, if we can find some of the small brown ones. It will be irritating, but they will rid me of any passengers I may be carrying. Their secretions, when the ants are angered, drive away mites and other small pests."

She felt a twinge of raw envy; if only it could be that easy for her! But lying on an anthill would do her no good since most of the bugs that plagued her were winged, and the subsequent ant bites would be just as irritating as her current crop of bites and stings.

She couldn't wait for the afternoon rain; sweat made the bites itch worse, and standing in the pouring cold water gave her the few moments of complete relief she got from the incessant itching.

Time to move. Maybe we'll find a stream today, and I can go to sleep lying in it! Then again, given our current luck, if we found a stream it would be infested with leeches.

Never mind. The one thing they had to do was keep moving, and cope with whatever came up. It couldn't be more than a week until help came.

All they had to do was to survive that long.

CHAPTER SIX

Uh, hells. This isn't easy, one-handed. A bit off-balance because of her injured shoulder, Blade threw her final bundle of branches over the canvas of tonight's shelter just as the first rumbles of thunder began in the distance.

Ah, damn! That hurt!

Blade doubled over despite herself. Her chest felt constricted, as if cinched tight with rope. Thunder rumbled again, nearer. She'd finished just in time, though not too soon so far as she was concerned; she was ready for the rain, more than ready by now. As she straightened up, she had no doubts that she was ready for rest as well.

This shelter was both superior and inferior to the last one; like last night's, it was also based on the remains of a fallen tree, but this tree had fallen quite recently. The splintered wood of the trunk shone fresh and pale against the greenery, which was how she had spotted it in the first place. Although there were no hollow places in the trunk or snag to shelter in, the tree had taken down another right next to it in its fall, and there was an intersection of the two trunks, providing a triangular area with two man-high "walls" of wood. Stretching the canvas over the top of this place made a roof; piling branches on top of the canvas disguised their presence. A further barricade of brush hid the entrance, and they would even have the luxury of a small fire tonight, screened from view by the brush. More branchlets over a pile of big leaves made a springy floor, giving them more comfort tonight than they had enjoyed since the accident.

Now if only she could find something in her medicines to numb these damned insect bites!

Thunder rumbled again, overhead this time. In the course of gathering their branches, she had stirred up many tiny animals; mice, lizards, snakes, and frogs. She had caught and killed as many of those as she could, and tonight she and Tad would supplement their dinner with these tidbits. Individually, they weren't impressive, but she had collected an entire sack of them, enough to give Tad much-needed supplements. She'd probably appropriate a couple of snakes to roast and give some flavor to her flavorless bread, but the rest would go to Tad.

She would be adding insects to her ration, for she had found grubs of a wood-borer that she recognized, ant pupae, and crickets, all of which she could choke down so long as they were toasted. When she had been going through survival training, she had never *really* pictured herself putting any of her training into practice!

Well, I have this much revenge; if the bugs, are eating me, I'm eating the bugs! Insects were really too small to do Tad any good, so by default they went to her.

Tad was inside the shelter arranging things and getting the fire going, and she thanked the Star-Eyed that he had enough magic to light fires again. With the help of magic, even the greenest, wettest wood could be coaxed to burn. Without it—they'd have a poor fire, or none, and she could not bear the thought of eating untoasted bugs.

I'd rather go hungry a bit. I might get hungry enough to consider it, but not now.

Their shelter lay underneath a long slit of sky, cleared by the falling tree. It had shown gray when they first arrived here, gray with those fat, round-bellied clouds, and had been growing steadily darker ever since, as the inevitable afternoon storm gathered strength. Was it her imagination, or were those storms coming earlier every afternoon?

She remained standing where she was, watching the clouds overhead, while the dark gray went bright white periodically and thunder followed the lightning. As the sky darkened steadily, the ambient light dimmed, stealing the color from the leaves, softening the edges of the shadows, and painting the clearing in shades of indigo blue. White light suddenly flooded the entire area, not just the clouds. Lightning lanced across the raw sky and thunder cracked right overhead, making her jump and yelp involuntarily—and jolting her shoulder again, which made her swear.

She forced herself to hold still, to wait for the pain to ebb. *I ought to be used to this by now*—But she wasn't; every time she jerked her shoulder, the pain lanced down her arm and up her neck. It wasn't getting any better. She could only hope that she was just being impatient, and that this didn't mean that it wasn't healing.

Two breaths after the lightning came the rain. As always, it poured down in a torrent. She held out her good arm and tilted her head up, letting the sweet, cool water wash away all the sweat and grime she had accumulated, opening her mouth and drinking the fresh, clean liquid. It actually eased her thirst and did not taste of warm leather. As sweat washed away and her skin cooled down, her insect bites stopped itching.

With walls of trunk on either side of her, she felt secure enough to stand out in the open and indulge herself; the only thing that would have improved the situation would have been a bar of soap! But even with nothing but water, she was getting reasonably clean, and that always made her temper improve. She stood out in the downpour until the dark green stains on her tunic faded to match the others already there, until she was as chilled as she had been overheated the moment before, until the swollen welts of her insect bites stood out against her cold, pallid arms and the bites themselves no longer bothered her at all. There was something very exhilarating and elemental about standing out in a storm like this one; powerful storms back home had always been too cold and dangerous to "play" in, something that had disappointed her ever since she was a child. But here—there wasn't much chance that she would be struck by lightning when everything else around her was so very much taller than she, and to be able to stand out in rain so heavy that it literally stole the breath was an intoxicating experience. It was enough to make her forget her pain, almost enough to make her forget their danger.

Is this what Tad feels when he flies! If so, I envy him. Is this the way it feels to not face people, not be in a building or cave, and be encompassed by the elements! To stand alone and alive as a living creature only, and not as Someone's Offspring? Is this the moment that makes all the pettiness of everyday living worthwhile!

Only when she was so chilled she had begun to shiver did she duck her head and scuttle back to the heap of branches that covered their shelter.

She pushed past the brush and almost went back out into the rain when she encountered a thick cloud of eye-watering smoke.

"What—what *is* this?" she demanded as, coughing, she fanned her hand in front of her face and dropped to the ground where the air was marginally clearer.

"Sorry," Tad said apologetically. "I'm trying to get rid of the bugs, both in here and on me. It's working; I certainly got rid of my little plague."

"You almost got rid of me," she grumbled, crawling all the way inside to settle beside him. More thunder punctuated her statement. "I suppose it'll be worth it if this smoke-weapon of yours allows us to get a good night's sleep." Then she laughed. "But if I'd known that this was how you were going to interpret my wish for an herb to repel insects, I might have been more careful in what I asked for!"

He gryph-grinned at her, his beak gaping wide. "You didn't remember Drake's favorite proverb—'Be careful what you ask for'—"

"I know, I know," she groaned.

Tad had been snacking, and the bag was almost empty, but he had saved her two of the biggest snakes—though they weren't very big, being no longer than her forearm. One was brown, one was green, and both looked vaguely orange in the uncertain light. Tad carefully scraped some hot coals to one side with a stick, then added drier wood to the rest of the fire.

She skinned out the snakes with Tad's help, then arranged her snakes, along with her harvest of crickets, grubs, and pupae, on the blade of their shovel and placed that on top of the glowing coals: There wasn't much aroma, but her bugs did toast quickly, and she was very hungry by now. She picked them gingerly off the hot metal and ate them, trying not to think too hard about what she was doing. They weren't too bad, though; she could almost imagine that she was eating toasted grain if she didn't pay too close attention to the shapes.

The snake was better, and made it possible to finish her ration-bread. Tad, meanwhile, had placed his dried meat out in the rain to soak; he wolfed it down with no expression of pleasure when it was soft enough to eat.

"Do you take first watch, or shall I?" he asked. She put a pan of water on the fire to steep her bruise-remedy in, then made up her potion with the addition of a couple of recognizable, foraged herbs known to numb sore throats. If they soothed a sore throat, perhaps they would make her bites stop bothering her.

"I'd appreciate it if you would," she replied. "I'm hoping this stuff will let me fall asleep without clawing my skin off, but it's bound to wear off before daybreak. If I'm going to be itching, I might as well be awake so I can control myself."

He nodded. "The smoke worked as well as an ant hill, and my passengers are no longer with me to bother either of us. At the moment, I'm feeling fairly lively. You might as well get to sleep while you still can."

By now her clothing and her hair were both dry, though only her gryphon-badge was as pristine as it had been when they set out. Besides being stained, her tunic and trews were torn in several places, and the hems were beginning to fray. *I look like a tramp,* she thought ruefully. *I hope Ikala is not with a search party… oh, that's ridiculous. He would hardly expect me to look like a court lady, and I would be so happy to see a rescuer that the last thing I would be thinking of would be my clothing!*

Tad helped her wrap her herb-steeped bandages around the worst of her bruises, and to dab the remainder of the mixture on her insect bites, as best as his large, taloned hands would allow. At first, she thought she was going to be disappointed again in her attempt to heal her bites, but as the mixture dried, she noticed that her itching had ebbed, at least temporarily. The tenderness of her flesh was perhaps in some way eased by the tenderness of the gryphon's care of her, as well.

Tad looked at her, disheveled feathers slightly spiked from the moisture, with inquiry in his expression.

She sighed with relief. "It's working," she said. "I'll have to make more of this up and keep it with me in one of the waterskins. If I keep putting it on, I might find it easier to freeze in place without being driven mad."

Tad chuckled. "Good. Now we just need to find something that will keep the bugs off us in the first place—without driving *us crazy* with the smell!"

With her mind off her itching, she turned a critical eye on Tad, and without warning him what she was about to do, reached over to feel his keelbone, the prominent breastbone that both gryphon and bird anatomy shared. That was the first place that a bird showed health or illness, as muscle-mass was consumed by a gryphon or bird that was not eating enough.

It was a bit sharper, the muscles on either side of it just a little shrunken. Not something an ordinary person would notice, but Tad was her partner, and it was her job to do as much for him as she could. "You've lost some weight," she said thoughtfully. "Not a lot, but it has to be either the short rations or the fact that you're using up energy in healing. Or both."

"Or that I'm building leg-muscle and losing wing-muscle because I'm not using it," he pointed out. "I don't remember walking this much before in my life. Much more of this and I'm going to look more like a plowhorse than a hawk."

She granted him a skeptical look, and crossed her legs and rested her chin on her good hand. "I wish we'd find the river," she replied fretfully.

"No matter *what* is following us, if we just had the river, we could fish; I'd get some decent food into you. Even if there's something following us and scaring off the game, I doubt that fish would be frightened off by a land predator." The river, the promise of the river, it now seemed to embody the promise of everything—food, shelter and rescue as well. Perhaps she was placing too much hope on a strip of water, but at the moment it was a good goal to concentrate on.

He heaved a huge sigh and scratched at one bug-bitten ear. "I really have no idea where we are in relation to the cliff and the river," he confessed. "And this kind of forest is very strange to me. If this place were more like home, I could probably find a river, but I can't see the sky and the ground cover is ten or twelve layers thick here…"

"I know, and I'm not blaming you," she assured him hastily. "How could you know anything about this kind of forest? We never trained here. We expected we'd be going to an established outpost, with shelter, a garden, food stores, and weapons."

"Emphasis on the food stores," Tad said hoarsely, as if the momentary thought of all the food he was used to eating made him homesick. He rubbed at his throat a moment and then swallowed. He'd been gulping more air for days than was healthy for him.

She frowned with frustration. "I'm sure there are plenty of things to eat growing all around us, if only I knew what they were! Roots, stalks, leaves—even some things you might be able to eat, too!" She waved her hand, helplessly. "We haven't the luxury of experimenting, since we don't dare make ourselves sick, so we're stuck. Only a native would know how to find his way around a place like this."

"A native like Ikala?" Tad replied shrewdly, and chuckled when she blushed involuntarily. "Well, I wish he was with us."

"I do, too—" she began, intending to change the subject, quickly.

"And probably for more reasons than one!" he teased, not giving her a chance to change the subject, and sounding more like his old self than he had in days. "I can't blame you; he's a handsome fellow, and he certainly accounted well for himself in training. It wouldn't be a bad thing to get to know him better."

"I suppose," she said, suddenly wary. There was nothing that Tad liked better than to meddle in other peoples' love lives. "If we'd had a chance to ask him more about forests like these, we might be faring better now."

He saw what she was trying to do. "Oh, come on, Blade!" he coaxed.

"Stop being coy with me! Am I your partner, or not? Shouldn't your partner know who you're attracted to?" He gave her a sly, sideways look. "I know *he's* attracted to *you*. It's obvious, if you're watching."

"And you were watching, I suppose," she grumbled, giving up on her attempt to distract him to something more serious. He laughed.

"I'm supposed to watch out for you, aren't I? You'd be happier with a male friend to share some—hmm—pleasant moments with, and I know it would be easier dealing with you if you were happier." He tilted his head comically to the side.

"Oh, thank you," she said sarcastically. "Now you sound like both my parents. They can't wait to get me—attached."

Into bed with someone, you mean, she thought sourly. *And Tad knows it. He should know better than to echo them! He knows how I feel about that!*

"They're obsessed with it, and have built much of their lives around pleasures of flesh. They think of it as a means to all happiness, even if it is by a strange, obscure path! Seeing you bedded with someone is not my goal. I simply want to see you content in all areas of your life," Tad said persuasively. "He's certainly a fine prospect. Good-looking, intelligent, and open-minded enough that you wouldn't get all tangled up in Haighlei custom with him. Good sense of humor, too, and that's important. And being trained as a prince, he knows that you have to be able to concentrate on your duty, you can't just devote yourself slavishly to a man. Hmm?"

Blade fixed her partner with a stern and fierce gaze, neither agreeing nor denying any of it. "You're matchmaking," she accused. "Don't try to deny it; I've seen you matchmake before, you're as bad as an old woman about it! You want to see everyone paired off and living—well, if not happily ever after, at least having a good time while the affair lasts!"

"Of course!" Tad replied smugly. "And why not?"

She growled at him. "Because—because it's invasive, that's why not! I repeat—I get enough of that kind of nonsense from my parents! Why should I put up with it from you?"

He only snorted. "I'm your partner, I have to know these things, and I have to try to help you get what you want and need, whether or not you know what it is! I'd tell *you*, and I'd expect you to help me. We both have to know if there's something that is going to have us emotionally off-balance, because that's going to affect how we do our job. Right? Admit it!"

She growled again, but nodded with extreme reluctance. He was right, of course. A Silver's partnership was as close as many marriages, and partners *were* supposed to confide in each other, cooperate with each other, in and out of the duty times.

And for some reason, what seemed so invasive from her parents didn't seem so bad, coming from Tad. Perhaps it was because Tad was a gryphon, and not human. Despite the gryphons' abilities to see things like a human did, Tad would always be one step removed from complete empathy with Blade, and that gave her a barrier of safety.

"So tell your partner how you feel about it." He settled his head down on his foreclaws. "What *do* you think of Ikala, then?"

Rain drummed down outside their shelter and pattered through the branches they had piled on the roof. Lightning made patterns of the branches screening the front of the shelter, reflecting whitely off Tad's eyes and the silver gryphon-badge on her tunic. As usual, rain and thunder were the only sounds that *could* be heard outside.

Inside—the smoke had finally cleared away and the fire burned brightly. She was dry, full, and warm. Her shoulder didn't hurt too much, and she was in a well-camouflaged shelter with two very solid walls on either side of her and a cushioning of springy boughs between her and the cold, damp ground. In short, there was nothing to distract her from her thoughts, which were confused to say the least.

"I suppose I don't really know," she said slowly, as Tad's dark eyes watched her with that intensity that only a raptor could display. "He *is* very handsome, he's very charming, he's quite intelligent... but I just don't know. Part of the time I think I like him for himself, part of the time I think I'm attracted to him just because he's so exotic, and part of the time I think it's because he's the only person in White Gryphon that my father *doesn't* know everything about!"

Tad chuckled heartlessly. "There is that. I've noticed that Ikala has never once had the occasion to patronize a *kestra'chern*. Amberdrake should find him more of an enigma than you do."

"That would certainly be an improvement," she said acidly. "It would be very nice for once to have a conversation with someone without the person wondering if Father was going to tell me all the things he'd really rather I didn't know."

"And it would be very nice for you," Tad commented, "to talk to your father without wondering if he *was* going to tell you things you'd rather not know." Blade nodded, and Tad shrewdly added, "I don't go to *kestra'chern*, so you are doubly safe talking to me about how you feel;

word will not reach your father. May I give up all my hedonism if I lie."

Blade smiled despite herself. Depend upon a gryphon male to count *that* as the ultimate oath.

"He's under control," she added. "He's a very controlled person. I like that."

I like it a great deal more than unbridled passion, truth to tell.

Tad coughed. "Still," he prompted helpfully. "Some might say that argues for a certain coldness of spirit?"

She snorted. "You know better than that, you've worked with him. He loses his temper about as often as anyone else, he just doesn't let it get away from him. And—so far as not visiting a *kestra'chern*—"

"And?" Tad's eyes sparkled with humor.

She blushed again. "And he hasn't exactly been—well—chaste. He's had female friends while he's been here. They just weren't *kestra'chern*. Even if they were casual. Recreational."

And I could almost envy Karelee. I wish she hadn't been so enthusiastic about his bed abilities.

"Oh?" Tad said archly. "He hasn't been chaste? I suppose you were interested enough to find out about this."

She coughed and tried to adopt a casual tone. "Well, one *does*, you know. People talk. I didn't have to be *interested*, people gossip about that sort of thing all the time. I only had to be nearby and listen." She favored him with a raised eyebrow, grateful to feel her hot face cooling. "Winds know that *you* do enough talking, so you ought to know!"

"Me? Gossip?" His beak parted in silent laughter and he squinted his eyes. "I prefer to call it the 'gathering of interpersonal information,' for 'management of sources and receivers of pleasure.'"

"Well, I call it gossip, and you're as bad as any old woman," she retorted. "You are just as bad when it comes to matchmaking. And as for Ikala—he is attractive, and I don't deny it, but I think you're getting way ahead of yourself to tie the two of us together in any way. I don't even know how

I feel, so how could I even speculate about how *he* feels? And anyway, you and I have our missions to run, and when we get out of here, we have a long tour of duty at a remote outpost to take care of. If we don't die of embarrassment at having to be rescued."

If we are rescued, if we do get out of here… The unspoken thought put a chill in the air of the tent that the fire could not drive away. All frivolous thoughts faded; this was the change in subject she had tried to make, but not the new subject she would have preferred. Reflexively she glanced out through the screening branches. It was getting darker out there, and it looked as if—once again—the rain was going to continue past nightfall.

That might not be so bad, if it keeps our unseen "friends" away.

"Well," she said, as lightly as possible, which was not very, "now you've got my brain going, and I'm never going to be able to get to sleep. I'll just lie awake thinking."

He yawned hugely. "And I am warm and sleepy. I always get worn out listening to people's reasons why they won't be happy. Shall we switch watches?"

He didn't wait for her to answer, settling his head back down on his foreclaws. She shrugged. "We might as well," she replied, and edged over until she was in a position where she could see through a gap between two of the branches hiding the front of their shelter. She memorized the positions of everything in sight while the light was still good enough to identify what was visible through the curtain of rain. The flashes of lightning helped; if she concentrated on a single spot, she could wait until the next lightning bolt hit to give her a quick, brightly-lit glimpse of what was there, and study the afterimage burned into her eyes.

Tad hadn't been lying about his fatigue; within a few moments, she heard his breathing deepen and slow, and when she turned to look behind her, she saw that his eyes were closed. She turned back to her vigil, trying to mentally review what she had done when she constructed the shelter.

She had tried not to take too many branches away from any one place. She had tried to pile the ones she brought to the shelter in such a way that they looked as if they were all from a single smaller tree brought down by the larger. *With all this rain, every trace of our being here should have been washed away. No scent, no debris...*

Smoke, though—the smoke Tad had used to drive out insects had been very dense and odoriferous, and she wondered if the rain had washed all of it out of the air. If not—how common would smoke be in a forest that experienced thunderstorms every day? Common enough, she would think. Surely lightning started small fires all the time, and surely they burned long enough to put a fair amount of smoke into the air before the rain extinguished them.

Well, there wasn't anything she could do about the smoke—or the shelter itself—now. If there was anything looking for them, she could only hope that she had done everything she needed to in order to cover their presence. Last night it would have been difficult for their possible followers to find them; she hoped tonight it would be impossible.

The rain turned from a torrent to a shower, and slowed from a shower to a mere patter. Then it wasn't rain at all, but simply the melodic drip of water from the canopy above, and the sounds of the night resumed.

She breathed a sigh of relief, and checked the fire. No point in letting it burn too high now; the inside of the shelter was at a good temperature, and with two walls being the trunks of trees, it should sustain that level without too much work. She rebuilt the fire, listening to the hoots and calls from above, tenting the flames with sticks of green fuel and banking the coals to help conceal the glow. This should let the fire burn through the night without needing too much more fuel or tending. It would burn slowly now, producing a bed of deep red, smokeless coals instead of flame. That was precisely the way she wanted it.

With the level of light in the shelter down to the point where Tad was nothing more than a large, dark shape, she turned her attention back to the outside.

Nothing had changed; the creatures of the canopy continued to go about their business with the accompanying noise, and now the luminescent insects she had noted before began to flit about the foliage. She allowed herself to relax a little further. It just might be that whatever had been following them had decided to leave them alone.

But don't count on it, she cautioned herself. *Assume the worst. Assume that they're still—*

Something moved out in the darkness.

Just a shape, a shifting of shadow, but she knew that there should not have been a shadow in that place, much less a moving one. Instantly she was on the alert.

Whatever it was, it was big. Bigger than the tame lion she'd seen in Shalaman's menagerie. She knew to within a thumb's breadth just how wide a distance lay between each bush, how tall a young tree was. The head of the shadow would rise a little above hers, she thought, though she had the impression of a very long, slender neck; the chest briefly obscured one bush while its hindquarters still lay behind another. Altogether, that would make it about the size of a horse, perhaps a little smaller. She couldn't quite tell how bulky it was, but the fluid way in which it moved and the fact that it melted in with the other shadows so well suggested that it had a slender build.

Her view was a narrow one, limited to the wedge of forest between the two long walls of log—yet in a moment, as she concentrated further, she knew that there was more than one of those creatures out there. One shadow flitted as another froze; further flickering in the distance suggested that either they were incredibly fast, or there might be a third.

Two, at least, for certain. But they don't seem to know we're here.

The first of the shadows darted suddenly out of sight; a heartbeat later, and a bloodcurdling scream rang out into the night.

Blade's heart leaped into her throat, and she felt as if she had been plunged into ice water. Tad only wheezed in his sleep. It took all of her control to remain frozen in place. She had an impression that those shadows possessed extremely sharp senses, and that if she moved, even obscured by branches as she was, they might spot the movement, or hear it.

Silence descended, as Blade tried to get her heartbeat started again. It was a good thing that she had heard the death scream of a rabbit before, or she would have thought that one of those *somethings* had just killed a child.

Now, as if the canopy dwellers had only just noticed the shadows' presence, the silence extended up into the tree-tops. Only the insects and frogs remained unaffected, chirping and trilling as calmly as they had a moment before.

She blinked—and in the time it took her to do so, the shadows vanished, at least from her view.

She did not breathe easier, however. From the silence, she knew that *they* were still out there, and she had no intention of letting them know her location.

I can only hope that they haven't had the bright idea to come take a walk on top of the sheltering logs.

The very idea made her want to shiver. The back of her neck crawled as she imagined one of those creatures sniffing around the brush piled above her head. There was nothing between her and these hunters stronger than a layer of canvas and a pile of flimsy branches and leaves. Surely if one of the hunters got close, no amount of brush and herb juice would obscure their scent. Surely the scent of the fire alone would tell the creature that they were here—

But I'm assuming that the thing is intelligent, that it would associate a fire with us. I'm assuming that it's hunting us—it could simply be here, we could have wandered into its territory. We haven't seen any large predators nor any sign of them; this could simply be the local equivalent of a lion.

And yet... something about the way it had moved had suggested intelligence and purpose. That could be her imagination, but it might be the truth. It was wary; it moved carefully, but when it did move, it was quick and certain. That was an indication of something that either had incredible reflexes, or something that decided very precisely what it was going to do before it acted.

In any case, there was no reason to take any chances, and every reason to be painfully cautious. No matter what else, these creatures were hunters, predators. The behavior of the canopy dwellers showed that, and demonstrated that the animals that lived in the treetops recognized these beasts and feared them.

Even if those things are just the local equivalent of a lion, they're still big, they're still carnivorous, and they're hunting. There's no reason to put myself on their menu.

A new thought occurred to her; what if they were not dealing with one enemy, but two? One that had brought them down, and a second that was hunting them? In that case, there were two possibilities; the shadows were either wild hunters that had nothing to do with what brought them down—or they were allied with it. In the second case, the shadow shapes out there could be the equivalent of a pack of hunting hounds, trailing them for some unknown master.

It was not something that was unheard of; that was the problem. *Urtho wasn't the only mage that created living things. Ma'ar did, and so did others who never participated in the wars. The ability to create a new species was a mark of prestige or a symbol of ability above and beyond the status of being an Adept. Among the higher mages there were a handful that had created new creatures for centuries before the war with Ma'ar.*

That gave her yet another possible scenario; a mage who hunted other intelligent creatures, and had chosen them for his next prey. Their chasers were his dog pack—

Ma'ar had been one such, and she'd heard tales of others, both from her own people and from the Haighlei. That, in fact, was one of the reasons why the Haighlei restricted magic use to the priests; they had a tale of a sadistic, powerful mage who captured men and brought them to his estate to hunt them like beasts. A brave young priest had suspected what was happening and allowed himself to be taken, thus giving his fellows an agent within the spell-protected walls through which they could channel their own power to destroy the mage.

That was how the story went anyway.

She grew cold all over again, and restrained herself from running her hand through her hair nervously. Her imagination went wild again, taking off all on its own. She had never had any difficulty coming up with scenarios for trouble. *So—suppose that one of the neutral mages came down here to hide before the Cataclysm. Even if he wasn't Urtho's equal, he could have guard-beasts and birds to warn him when anything was in the area. The Haighlei never travel through the wilderness in groups of less than ten, and that includes a priest, but all he'd have to do would be to stay quiet while they passed by. Unless they actually stumbled over him, they wouldn't find him. Then he could hunt individuals at his leisure.*

There was just one problem with that hypothesis; no one had ever been reported missing from here. Unless a Haighlei was so antisocial as to sever all familial and clan ties and go off wandering the wilderness, *someone* would have raised a fuss by now if anyone had vanished, wouldn't they? Woodcutters, explorers, trappers, hunters—they all told friends, neighbors, and fellow workers *where* they were going, what route they intended to take, and when they should be back. They did so especially if they were going off into poorly-explored lands; if something happened, they would want others to mount a rescue as soon as possible.

Perhaps there had been a few Haighlei hermits who had wandered in here only to vanish—but not enough to provide sport for a maniacal manhunting mage.

Well, all right, then—what if he came here to escape all the conflict. What if he wants to be left alone, and he brought us down to keep us from revealing his presence!

But that didn't make any more sense than the first hypothesis. There had been others through here; they had all flown overhead on the same route. Why hadn't *they* been brought down?

Because we were the only gryphon-human pair!

But there had been Aubri and Judeth...

Oh, winds. I should be a storyteller.

She gave it up as a bad notion. It was getting too complicated, and usually, the more complicated a hypothesis was, the more likely it was that it was incorrect.

Stick to the two possibilities that work best. Simple answers work best and are more likely. First: we hit some kind of accidental—thing—that brought us down, and now we're having to guard ourselves from the local predators which are following us because we're hurt and look like easy prey. Second: something down here brought us down for reasons of its own and now is hunting us. And the first is more likely than the second.

That didn't mean they were in any less danger. Wolves and lions had been known to trail wounded prey for days, waiting for it to die. And if her guess about the size of the shadow-creatures was right, they were a match for Tad, which would make them formidable opponents indeed. If the shadows knew that she and Tad were hurt, that might well put them in the category of "wounded prey."

A bird called; another answered. And as if that tentative call had been meant to test the safety of the area, or to tell other creatures that the menace had gone for the moment, the canopy above began to come to life again.

She sighed, and let her shoulders relax. She cast a wry glance at her slumbering companion.

Somehow, Tad had managed to sleep through it all.

Tad yawned, and stretched as best he could, blinking in what passed for light in their shelter. When Blade woke him for his watch, she had looked tired, but that was to be expected. She also looked nervous, but how could she not be? He would be nervous on his watch, too. Nervous sentries remained living sentries; relaxed ones had short epitaphs.

"I saw something out there that might account for the way everything goes silent every so often," she offered. "It was pretty big, and I think there were two or more of them. I didn't see anything more than a shadow, though. One of them caught a rabbit, and every bird and beast in the canopy shut up and stayed that way for a long time."

Well, that accounts for the nerves, and for the fact that she looks tired. Nerves wear you out and she didn't have much of a reserve when she began her watch.

"Huh." He glanced out into the darkness, but didn't see anything— and some of the local creatures were acting as if they were in the middle of a singing competition. "Well, if silence means that there's something out there we should be worried about, I'd say you can sleep in peace until dawn. I'm surprised I slept through it. I must have been more tired than I thought—or my medicine is stronger than I supposed."

She managed a ghost of a chuckle. "It got my hackles up, I can tell you that much. It's quick, very quick; and I didn't hear a rustle of leaves or a single broken twig. I'd say the one I saw was about the size of a horse, which would make it a formidable predator in a fight. It might have been my imagination, but I thought that it acted fairly intelligent."

"So do the big cats, hunting," he reminded her. "Everything acts intelligent in its own realm. Drink your painkillers, get some sleep. We'll see what's out there in the morning. I set some snares before the rain—"

She chuckled again. "Don't count on there being anything left. I think you were robbed. That may have been where our shadows found their rabbit."

He sighed. "Probably, but it was worth doing. And we'll know how intelligent they are by how the snares were robbed. If it was just snatch-and-eat, then they won't be any more intelligent than the average lion."

"Good point." She settled herself down at the back of the shelter; he was certain she was going to get a good rest for the rest of the night, so long as things stayed noisy up in the canopy. The mattress of boughs and leaves he'd made was very comfortable, and she should be able to lie cradled in a way that permitted her to sleep soundly, rather than fitfully. With her shoulder supported so that pressure was off her collarbone, she should be in less pain.

He had not wanted to mention it before this, but he had already seen signs on their backtrail that something was following them. It could have been anything, and he hadn't seen any signs that their follower was particularly intelligent—just alert and incredibly wary. The trouble with telling her now was that there was nothing to prove whether or not the shadowy creature that was following them was something they had just picked up today, or if it had been following them all along and only now was feeling bold enough to move in where he might catch a glimpse of it. It could certainly match the description that Blade had given him of the creature she saw tonight.

That basically was all that he *knew* as a fact. This, of course, had nothing to do with what his own imagination could conjure up.

In his imagination, the sighting confirmed the fear that he'd had all along, that they were being followed for some specific purpose. The only question in his mind now was if the purpose was a simple one—kill and eat the prey—or something more complicated than that. If it was simple, then these creatures were simple predators, and relatively "easy" to deal with. If, however, there was a larger purpose in their minds—if his imagination was right, and in fact these creatures had something to do with their accident—then he and Blade were in very deep trouble.

Such extreme caution combined with curiosity as these "shadows" had exhibited was very unlike most predators he was familiar with. In general, large predators tended to shy completely away from anything that was not familiar, at the most watching it from a distance. Only if the unfamiliar object continued to remain in a predator's territory would it gradually move in closer to investigate it.

Predators are very nervous, very jumpy. They have a lot of competition, and normally they can only take down large creatures if their prey is old, sick, very young, or wounded. Prey that fights back is to be avoided, because the predator can't afford to be injured in the struggle. Being a carnivore is an expensive business, as I well know. When your dinner can run away from you, you're going to spend a lot of energy hunting and killing it. Vegetarians have it easy. Their dinner can't move, and they don't have to do anything other than walk up and open their mouths.

That meant that the predators following them were not following "normal" behavior; the gryphon and the human were strange, they might be dangerous, hence there was no reason to follow them. In fact, there was every reason to *avoid* them—unless he and Blade were giving off signals that fit the profile of "sick, old, very young, or wounded," or had become familiar enough for their pursuers to investigate.

Either the territory these shadows claimed was so very large that he and Blade had been within its boundaries all along, or these creatures were something out of the ordinary.

The fact that one of them had killed and eaten a rabbit did not tend to make him believe that they would not attack him or Blade. Wolves made very good meals of mice, yet did not hesitate to pull down deer. For that matter, *he* was eating mice this very night! No, a predator's prey on a given night did not necessarily define what it *could* take. Something as big as a horse could very easily consider something as big as a gryphon to be reasonable prey. Top predators often pulled down animals very much larger than they themselves were; the only exceptions were birds of prey, who would ideally not kill anything larger than they could fly off with— generally much less than half the bird's own body weight. The only eagles that had ever carried off lambs were Kaled'a'in-bred bondbirds, who had the required wingspread and muscle mass, and carried them off at the behest of their bondmates.

I think we are going to have to set traps around our camps at night, he decided reluctantly. *Even if these creatures manage to escape from a trap, there is a chance that we will make them hesitant to attack us by frightening or even injuring one or more. If they are nothing more than animals, the mere fact that one of them is hurt should make them give up on making us into dinner.*

They would just have to also take the chance that in frightening or injuring one of those shadows, they would not make an attack more likely.

Well, if we anger them at least we'll know that they have the intelligence to connect a trap outside the camp with the people inside it—and the intelligence to want revenge for an injury.

There was one point on which he felt Blade was incorrect; he was fairly certain that the creatures she saw had been very well aware of the presence of the camp, and its precise location. They had also probably thought that they would not be seen where they were. They must have very keen senses to hunt at night, and their sense of smell, at least, had clearly not been deceived by his subterfuges with the plant juices. They must have been able to scent the fire. Where the fire was, there the camp would also be. And no matter how well-banked the fire had been, some hint of it was surely visible out there in the darkened forest. No, those creatures knew exactly where the camp was; the only encouraging part was that they had not felt it necessary to surround the camp and place it in a state of siege. Nor had they decided to rush the camp to try and take the occupants by surprise.

So they don't feel ready to try and confront us yet. I hope that their interest is only curiosity.

Noise was priceless; an indicator that the shadows had gone elsewhere to hunt for food.

At least, I hope that's the case. I hope the canopy dwellers are better at spotting these creatures than we are.

All this was enough to give a gryphon a headache.

Wait until morning, and I'll see to it that we're more careful. And I'll try and make the best time afoot that I can, since I'm the slower of the two of us. Maybe we can lose them. Maybe, we'll find a river and really be able to hide our scent and our trail. And tomorrow night, if they follow us again, maybe we can find a way to discourage them from continuing to do so.

And maybe horses would fly, and maybe they would stumble upon a lost enclave of amorous female gryphons, and maybe this was all just a bad dream.

Tad surveyed the remains of his snare—pulled up out of the ground, and left carelessly tangled, but all in a heap, as if it had been examined closely, then dropped. It looked very much the same as the debris back at the crash site that had been so carefully examined.

"Well, as I warned you, this is where our friends found their rabbit last night," Blade said with resignation. "See over there?"

He'd already noticed the few bits of fur and the drops of blood on a dead leaf. "I should have known better than to expect that anything would leave a snared rabbit alone," he sighed. "It doesn't look as if they found any of the other snares—but neither did any rabbits. Then again, if any rabbits *had*, they'd probably have gone the way of this one."

At least the shadows hadn't gone *looking* for other snares. Or had they? They'd examined this one that had been sprung; had they gone looking for others, found them, and left them alone once they saw how the snares were set?

Or was he ascribing far too much in the way of intelligence to them?

He regarded the scraps of fur ruefully. *Hardly fair to stalk me and then eat my breakfast.* He thought wistfully of how nice that rabbit would have tasted, and resigned himself to a tasteless meal of dried meat, but Blade had been out and prowling before he was, and had a surprise for him.

"Maybe your snares didn't work, but my sling did," she said, with a tiny smile. She pulled a decent-sized rabbit out of the game bag at her side, and his mouth watered at the mere sight of it.

"Thank you," he said, doing his best not to snatch it out of her hand. He took it politely, but his hunger was too great for more than that. Fortunately she was quite used to watching him eat, for his growling stomach made it impossible for him to wait long enough for her to go elsewhere while he dined. Nor was he able to do anything other than devour his meal in a few gulps.

"What about you?" he asked belatedly, a moment later, when the rabbit was a mere memory and a comfortable feeling in his crop.

At least I managed to resume civilized behavior without a rabbit leg still sticking out of my mouth.

"I'm appropriating a bit of your dried meat," she replied, "And I can eat that as we move. Let's get the packs on and get out of here; I don't want to stay here a moment longer than we have to."

"Agreed," he said firmly. "Especially after last night. Luck permitting, we *should* find the river today or tomorrow."

The canopy dwellers had gone silent once more on his watch, although he had not seen anything. That had given him a very strange feeling; his hackles had come up, as he wondered if the shadowy hunters had decided to take a walk on the great tree trunk and come at them from the rear. He'd never know until the moment that they came crashing down through the branches and canvas...

But they hadn't, and the noises had resumed within a very short time, remaining at a constant level until dawn. Blade had made another batch of her herb concoction and had poured it into one of her waterskins after dabbing her itching bites liberally with it. He hoped it worked as well for her in the heat, of the day as it had last night.

He put some effort into confusing their backtrail, while Blade set the course. This time he laid some false, dead-end trails, even taking one up a tree. That made him think; if they had trouble finding a place to shelter tonight, perhaps *they* ought to go up a tree—

Oh, no. Blade can't climb with only one hand. Well, so much for that good idea. I could perhaps pull her up by rope, if it came to that, but the risk of hurting her further would be too great.

Once again, however, they were in luck. This time, in late afternoon, they came upon another good site to hole up. It was another fallen tree, but this time it was one with a large den dug out underneath it. Whatever had dug it originally wasn't home, and from the look of things, hadn't been resident for some time. It *did* have some current occupants, far too small to have dug the den originally, and between them, he and Blade bagged the entire family of five. He wasn't certain quite what they were; something like a beaver with no tail, and about the same size. He didn't even know what species they were, and it really didn't matter. They had rodent teeth, and that was enough for him. Rodents were always edible.

This bit of good fortune more than made up for the fact that Blade had not been as lucky with her sling; the rabbit she had gotten for his breakfast was the only kill she'd made all day. She'd had targets, but had missed her throws. She was so crestfallen about it that he had done his best to reassure her that it was all right.

Well, tonight he would have a truly full stomach for the first time since the crash. The fresh meat had made a great deal of difference to him; he felt much more energetic and lively after having it.

With his help she made a fire outside their den. While she built it up into something respectable, he excavated the den quite a bit more. His talons weren't well suited to digging, but he did have determination, and the earth was soft. When he finished, he knew that it would be a tight fit for both of them, but that they would manage. To keep them off the raw earth, he lined it with branches and packed the dirt he'd dug out into a little dam to prevent water from coming in during the rain. He took a torch and charred the underside of the log to prevent "visitors," then went out to collect a tangle of vines to conceal the entrance. Blade roasted her share of the catch, made up her medicine, then put out the fire and buried the ashes, doing her best to obliterate any traces of their presence that might persist through the afternoon downpour. Like the hollow snag, there would be no room in this den for a fire tonight. As long as the den stayed dry, he didn't think they'd need one.

Need and want, why are they so far apart sometimes!

By the time Blade was done tidying things, he was ready to eat; she took over, clumsily weaving the vines with one hand and both feet into a rough mat that they could pull over the hole. Last of all, she collected a lot of leaves from that peppery plant and tucked them into the mat to kill their scent.

As soon as the rain started, they would climb into this hole and pull the mat over the entrance. There they would remain until dawn. In his opinion, this was their most vulnerable camp yet, but he had an answer to that.

Although she couldn't climb, *he* could, and since the den was barely big enough for the two of them without their packs, he had an idea.

"Help me with this," he said, as soon as he'd finished gulping down his meal. "I want to make some decoys." He dragged in some more vines and began making them into bundles that resembled a human and something with four feet. She was puzzled, but gave him a hand, as the clouds began to gather for the afternoon rain.

"What are you planning on doing with these?" she asked, as the bundles began to take shape. "They aren't going to fool anything for long."

"Not if they're on the ground—but what if they're up there?" He nodded up at the canopy. "I'm thinking of taking the packs and these up to a good branch and tying them there. Maybe our trackers will see 'us' up there, and decide we're becoming too much work to pursue. Provided, of course, that they can't climb."

Somehow, I don't think they can, even though the canopy creatures are afraid of them. I think they're too big; there's a maximum size that a tree-climbing predator can be and still hunt successfully, and I think they're bigger than that maximum size.

"If you really want to, it's worth trying." She didn't look convinced, but at least she wasn't too negative. He was just as glad that she didn't object to him taking the packs elsewhere to store; although the tree he had in mind was a dwarf by the standards of the ones around him, he was not looking forward to the climb, and that was giving him enough qualms without having to argue with her.

He accomplished the feat by clamping all four sets of talons into the bark and hitching himself up like an inch-worm. This used an entirely new set of muscles, as well as awakening a new set of pains in his broken wing, and by the time he reached a suitable place to cache the packs and the two decoys, he wished with a strength beyond telling that. he would have been able to glide down instead of climbing. He was *not* looking forward to retrieving the packs in the morning!

He had taken a rope with him, rather than the packs and the decoys themselves. Once he got himself securely in place, he dropped the end down, and Blade tied it to the first pack as best she could with one hand. When he had hauled that up and tied it successfully in place, he dropped the end back down. The second pack came up next, and following that, the two decoys.

And now, if there is a disaster, Blade will at least have a rope she can try to escape by. If there is any time to escape, I can come back up here and pull her up. Maybe.

It did not take long to secure the items in place, but this was not the best of perches, nor was it a place where he would have wanted to spend the night. The packs would remain dry through the storm, but not the decoys. If they had been up here instead of the decoys, it would have been a soggy and most uncomfortable night for them.

He lowered himself down, inching backward and no doubt giving Blade an interesting view all the while. He dropped off the trunk the moment he thought that he'd be able to land safely. "There!" he said, more briskly and brightly than he actually felt. "Now, we have just enough time to rig a deadfall and a couple of other traps before the rain starts!"

Blade groaned at the idea of so much work, but nodded: They both knew that the more distractions they could offer the hunters, the better.

And the more challenge we give to their intelligence, the more we'll learn about them.

He let her lead, though, so that she wouldn't see how tenderly he was walking. His fear was rising again.

By the time the rain started, their traps were in place and concealed, placed in hiding around the tree rather than around their real den, to lend verisimilitude to the decoys in the tree. He and Blade scrambled for their shelter as the first drops started falling, but as was her custom, she stayed outside long enough to get a good sluicing down by the rain before coming in.

She was soaking wet when she came in, but since he had lined the den with branches, they weren't lying directly on the soil; the water she brought in dripped through their bedding and from there into the earth. There wasn't a lot of room to move, and by the time he had snaked out a claw and pulled the mat of vines over the entrance, there was even less. By dint of much squirming, she managed to anoint both herself and him with her bruise-cum-bug-bite medicine. He squinted his eyes at the bitter scent, but decided that he could live with it. With any luck, they *had* to be getting near the river, and he could wash it all off rather than attempting to preen it off tomorrow.

They had deliberately made the entrance as small as possible, just barely large enough for him to squeeze inside. That meant that there wasn't enough room for anyone to stand watch except Blade, because she was the one near the entrance, and he was crammed so far back that he really couldn't see anything. As thunder roared and the rain fell down mere hand-lengths away from their noses, they looked at one another in the semidarkness.

"There's no point in really standing watch," he ventured. "I mean, one of us should try and stay awake, just in case one of us can *hear* something, but there's no point in trying to look out. We made that mat too well; I can't see anything from where I am."

"I can't see that much," she admitted. "Are you sleepy? Your ears are better than mine; if you could take second shift, I can take first."

"I have a full stomach, of course I'm sleepy," he retorted, forbearing to mention the fact that he was afraid that if he didn't try to sleep *now*, his stiffening muscles would make sleep impossible. In fact, he fully expected to wake up about the time she was ready to sleep. His sore legs and back would see to it that he didn't oversleep.

That was precisely what happened. By that time, she was ready for sleep, warm and relatively cushioned, with him curled around her. She dropped off almost immediately, while he concentrated on keeping his muscles relaxed so that they didn't go into cramps. That was *quite* enough to keep him awake all by itself, but the position he was in did not agree with his broken wing either. It probably wasn't, causing any damage, but the wing twinged persistently. He caught himself nearly whining in pain once, reducing it to a long wheeze and shiver.

So he was fully awake and wary when the usual silence descended outside in the canopy, signaling the arrival of the shadowy hunters.

Of all of the nights so far, this one was perhaps the most maddening and the most frightening. He was essentially blind, and he and Blade were curled in an all-too-accessible hole in the ground. If anything found them and really was determined to dig them out, it could.

But as he strained his ears, he heard nothing in the way of movement outside the mat of vines. He hoped that if anything heard them, their breathing and tiny movements might be taken for those of small animals that were too much effort to dig out, and which might have a rear entrance to this den through which they could escape.

I wish I'd thought of that and dug one. That might have been a smarter thing to do than rig those traps.

As the moments stretched out unbearably, he became acutely sensitive to every sound, more so than he ever remembered being before. So when he heard the deadfall "go," it sounded as loud as a peal of thunder.

And what was more, he clearly heard the very peculiar cry of pain that followed.

It wasn't a yelp, and it certainly wasn't a shout. There were elements of both a hiss and a howl in it, and it was not a cry he had ever heard before in his life. It startled him, for he could not for a moment imagine what kind of animal could have made such a sound. It cut off rather quickly, so quickly that he wondered if he had managed to actually kill something with his trap.

Possible, but not likely, not unless our "friend" out there was extraordinarily unlucky.

Then he heard more sounds; another thud, tearing and breaking noises, something being dragged briefly, another hiss. Then nothing. His skin crawled under his feathers.

More silence, while his beak ached from being held clamped shut so tightly that his jaw muscles locked, and then, when he least expected it, the canopy sounds returned.

He waited, on fire with tension, as the faint light of dawn began to appear in the tiny gaps in their covering. When he couldn't bear it any longer, he nudged Blade with his beak.

She came awake instantly, her good hand going to her knife.

"I heard the deadfall go," he whispered. "I think we got *something.* Whether it was one of them, whether it's still there—I can't tell. If it *is* still there, I don't think it's still alive, though."

She nodded, and cocked her head to listen to the sounds of the forest. "I'd say we're safe to come out," she said. "Are you ready?"

"As ready as I'm likely to be." They'd discussed this last night; she was going to come out in a rushing attack, just in case there was something lying in wait for them, and he was supposed to follow. It had all seemed perfectly reasonable and appropriate last night. Now, with his muscles so sore, stiff, and cramped, he wasn't certain he was going to be able to crawl out, much less rush out.

She drew her knife and wriggled around until she was crouched in place. With a yell, she threw off the mat and leaped out—inadvertently kicking him in the stomach as she did so.

His attack-cry was considerably spoiled by this. Instead of a fierce scream of defiance, all he could emit was a pitiful grunt, remarkably similar to a belch. But he managed to follow her out, if not in a rush, at least in a hurry.

There wasn't anything there, which, although an anticlimax, was also a relief. "Sorry," she said, apologetically. "My foot slipped."

What could he say? "It happens," he managed, as graciously as possible—not very, but he doubted that she blamed him at the moment for not speaking with an Ambassador's tact and dissimulation. "Let's go check that deadfall."

When they got close to where the trap had been, it was quite clear that it was going to be empty, for the remains of the vegetation they had used to conceal it were scattered all over the area. The trap itself was quite empty—though there *was* a trace of blood on the bark of one of the logs.

"We marked him," Blade said, squatting down beside it to examine it further. "How badly—well, probably not too badly. Maybe a scrape, or a minor cut. Possibly a broken bone. But we did hurt him a little."

She stood up and looked toward the tree where the decoys were hidden. "We'd better go see how they reacted."

When they reached the base of the tree, they finally saw something of what their trackers could do, and some clues as to their nature.

Persistent. And... possibly angry. But not foolishly persistent.

There *were* scratches, deep ones, in the bark of the tree, about twice as high up on the trunk as Blade was tall. So the decoys had worked, at least for a while, and the hunters had been unable to resist trying to get at the quarry when it was openly in sight.

Or else they were so angry when one of their number got caught in the deadfall that they tried to get to us no matter how difficult it was going to be.

Now they knew this much: the hunters could leap respectable distances, but they *couldn't* climb the tree trunk, which at least meant that they were not great cats. The ground at the foot of the tree was torn by claws, either as the hunters tore at the ground in frustration, or when they tried to leap up to drag their prey down out of the tree.

On the other hand, there wasn't a lot of damage to the tree trunk itself; the hunters had made several attempts, but it didn't look as if they had tried mindlessly, over and over, until they were exhausted.

That meant that they were intelligent enough to know when their task was impossible.

Or intelligent enough to recognize that the decoys were just that. In that case, they might well have reasoned that we would have to come back to get the packs before we left, no matter where we hid ourselves overnight.

And if it had been anger that motivated their attack, their anger did not overcome them for long.

Blade looked around, shivering, as if some of the same thoughts had occurred to her. "Let's, get the packs and get out of here," she urged. "Fast. They haven't shown themselves by day before, but that doesn't mean they won't now. We might have given them a reason to."

He swarmed up the tree far more quickly than he had thought possible a few moments before, and this time he didn't notice his sore muscles. There was no need to concern himself with ropes on the way up, which made things simpler. He untied the packs when he got there, and dropped them and the rope that held them in place down to the ground, leaving the decoys stuck in the forks of the branches. If the shadow-lurkers were still deceived by the decoys, they might linger, giving him and Blade that much more of a head start.

He went down the tree twice as fast as he had gone up. Every nerve in his body jumped whenever an unexpected sound occurred, and the quicker they left, the happier he would be. There was just a moment more of delay during which they stowed the rope and donned the packs, and then they were on their way without even a pause for a meal.

He wasn't hungry, and he suspected that Blade wasn't either. His insides were all knotted up with tension, and he kept hearing old gryphon proverbs in the back of his mind, about well-fed gryphons and the inability to fly out of danger.

Not that I can fly out of danger now—but it's better to run or fight on an empty stomach than a full one!

It was barely dawn by the light, and the morning fog had not yet lifted. The entire world was painted in dim grays and blues, vague gray shapes and columns appearing and vanishing in white mist. In a way, that was all to the good, for rather than using the trees as cover, they counted on the fog itself for primary concealment. They were able to make much better time that way, and since they were taking their bearings from the north-needle rather than the sun, it didn't matter that everything was obscured and enshrouded.

The fog itself had an odd, bitter aftertaste to it, nothing at all like the sea mists Tad was used to. The air felt heavier and thicker, although that was probably his imagination. The fog condensed on his feathers, and he kept shaking himself so that it didn't soak in. Poor Blade had no such ability; her hair was damp, and she would probably be shivering if they weren't trotting along fast enough to stay warm from exertion.

He found himself trying to think what kind of creature the hunters could be. *Those stories about Ma'ar and all the creatures he made—what sort of things did he do? Father said that most of what he did was to make copies of the creatures that Urtho developed...*

The makaar had been analogs of gryphons; had there been analogs of *hertasi* and *kyreel* The *tervardi* and *dyheli* were natural creatures, surely Ma'ar had not bothered to make analogous creatures to them; why would he? But then again, why not? Ma'ar had never hesitated to do or try anything he considered might give him an edge.

He made cold-drakes and basilisks, but those weren't analogs of anything Urtho made, so there goes Father's theory. There were smaller creatures, but I can't remember anything that might correspond in size to the hunters. Did he do flightless makaar! But why would he, when a makaar on the ground would be more helpless than I am! The shadow-hunters can't be analogs of hertasi, *because I'm certain that what we've been seeing is four-footed, not two-footed.*

Had anyone else involved in the Mage Wars made a four-footed hunter the size of a horse?

I just can't remember anyone ever going into a lot of detail about the mage-made creatures. Maybe Snowstar would know, but he's rather effectively out of reach at the moment.

He kept his ears trained on the trail behind them, and his eyes on Blade's back. She was a ghost in the fog, and it was up to him to keep track of her and not lose her. Her pale beige clothing blended in beautifully with the fog—but so would his own gray plumage. For once, it would probably be harder for the hunters to see *them* than vice versa.

Whatever is behind us is clever, very clever. They weren't deceived by my false trails, and they either gave up on the decoys or recognized them as false, and if they gave up temporarily, there's no guarantee that they won't realize what's going on when they come back. They didn't find us, but they might not have bothered to look. Or they might have needed to hunt and feed, and they couldn't take the extra time to figure out where we were. Why should they! They knew we'd come out in the morning, and all they have to do is wait for us to come out and get on our way and they could trail us again. They could even be hoping we will stay put in that campsite, since it has been proven to protect us once.

He wanted rock walls around him; a secure place that these shadow-hunters couldn't dig into. He wanted a steady food source that the shadows couldn't frighten away. Once they had both, they could figure out ways to signal the help that must be coming.

And he wanted to *see* them. He wanted to know exactly what was hunting them. Traps might give him more of a chance to see one, provided that any injured or dead hunters remained in the trap. And there was no guarantee of that, either.

They freed the injured one from the deadfall. That was what I heard last night; they were freeing him.

That meant cooperation, which meant more intelligence. Wolves might sniff around a trapped fellow, might even try to help him gnaw himself loose, but they would not have been able to remove parts of a deadfall trap except by purest accident, and then only after a great deal of trial and error effort.

He had *heard* them last night. It had not taken them long at all to free the trapped one. And they had done so without too many missteps, if there were any at all.

The snare—they didn't just chew the leg or head off the rabbit it caught and then eat the rest. The noose of the snare was opened. They killed the rabbit, pulled the snare open and removed it, then pulled up the snare and looked it over.

That was evidence of more intelligence, and certainly the ability to manipulate objects. What that evidence meant to their survival, he couldn't yet tell.

But he had his fears, and plenty of them. He could only wonder right now if Blade shared those fears. Maybe it was time to stop trying to shelter her and start discussing things. Maybe it had been time to do that a couple of days ago.

Blade stopped in the shelter of a vine-covered bush.

Is that what I think it is!

She frowned with concentration, and motioned to Tad to remain where he was so she could hear without distraction. There was something in the distance, underneath the chatter of the four-legged canopy creatures, and the steady patter of debris from a tree where some of the birds were eating green fruit—a sound—

Tad shifted his weight impatiently. "Shouldn't we—" he began.

"Hush a moment," she interrupted, and closed her eyes to concentrate better. Was that really what she thought it was? She began to isolate it mentally from the rain of bits of leaf, twig, and half-eaten fruit.

"I think I hear running water," she said at last. "Come on!"

She abandoned all attempts at secrecy, trotting as quickly as she could through the tangle, of underbrush, with Tad hot on her heels. If that *was* the long-sought river she heard, then their safety lay more surely in reaching it than in trying to hide themselves or their trail. Above them, a few canopy creatures barked or chattered a warning, but most of them seemed to regard her and Tad as harmless.

Well, they would. Now we're running openly, not stalking. We can't be hunting, so we're not a danger to them directly. The sounds above kept on, and the fruit eaters didn't even pause in their gluttony. That was comforting; it meant there was nothing else around that aroused, the tree dwellers' alarm. If there *had* been something trailing them closely, when they broke cover, it would have had to do the same to a certain extent, just to keep up with them. And if that had happened, the treetops should have erupted with alarm or once again gone silent, or both.

There was sunlight pouring down through a huge gap in the trees, off in the distance; it shone green-gold through the leaves, white between the trunks of the trees. The closer they got, the clearer the sound of water running rapidly over rocks became.

They literally burst through the luxuriant curtain of brush at the river's edge, teetering on the rocks lining the banks. She wanted to cheer, but confined herself to pounding on Tad's shoulder enthusiastically.

The river at their feet was wide, but so far as she could tell, it was deep only in the middle. More to the point, across the river lay the cliff they had been looking for, with a wide beach made of rocks and mud lying between the rock cliff face and the river.

Caves, waterfalls—even a crevice that we can fortify. Any of those will do very nicely just now!

"Let's get across," Tad urged. "If they're following us, we'll be able to see them, and there's going to be water between them and us."

Water between them and us. Right now, that was the best protection she could imagine. Tad was right; with an open space of water between their enemy and themselves, they would certainly be able to see the mysterious hunters coming. *We can look for a cave as soon as we're across.*

For the first time in four days, they should be able to find... a safe and secure place to wait for rescue, a place too difficult to dig them out of, with walls of rock instead of flimsy canvas.

And they might be able to actually *see* the creatures that were following them—assuming that the shadow-hunters were bold enough to go this far. They might give up. She wasn't going to count on it, but they might. This was certainly more trouble than most predators wanted to go through for a meal.

Now she grinned, and it was heartfelt. "Let's go get wet," she said. "We both need a bath anyway!"

CHAPTER SEVEN

Blade peered through the curtain of rain, looking a few lengths ahead to see if there was anything like a cave in sight, then looking back down at her feet to pick out her footing among the slippery mud and river rocks. Here, out in the open, the rain came down in sheets, making footing doubly treacherous. More rain sluiced down the cliff face, washing across the rocks at her feet. This time, they hadn't gone to ground when the rains came; they didn't even look for a shelter. Instead, they continued to make their way along the cliff-side bank of the river. For one thing, the only shelter from the rain lay back on the other side of the river, and she didn't really want to take her chances back there. For another, every moment they spent in huddling away from the rain was a moment that they could not spend in looking for *real* cover, the protection of a place from which they could not be extracted by force.

By now poor Tad was a wet, sodden mess, and after this, she was certainly going to have to figure out what they could spare to make him a new bandage for his wing. The bandages he wore were soaked and coming loose, and wouldn't be any good until after they had been rinsed clean and dried. *Sacrifice some clothing, maybe, if we don't have enough bandages. I could shorten the legs of my trews for cloth, since they don't seem to be much protection against the bugs. That and some rope might make a decent sling.*

She was going to have to get him dried out before they slept; allowing a gryphon to go to sleep wet was a sure prescription for illness.

We need a cave, or at worst, a cleft. This rain is going to go on until nightfall, and we won't be able to see anything then.

The water level in the river didn't seem to be rising much, if any, which suggested that it was probably as high now as it ever got, except in the occasional flood. *And I hope we don't happen to be in the midst of flood season!* There was evidence aplenty for a flood, in the form of flotsam, mostly wood, washed up and wedged among the rocks. It would make admirable firewood, if they could ever find a place where they could build a fire!

It would be just our luck to have pinned our hopes on finding this cliff only to discover that there is less shelter here than there was in the forest. If they didn't find a place to hole up before dark, they might have to spend the night exposed on this rocky shore, where they would have the grim choice of lighting a fire and attracting attention or shivering, cold and damp, wrapped up in wet blankets all night.

The gods, or fate, were not to be so unkind, however. After a few more furlongs of picking their way across the rocks and sliding through the mud, the cliff receded somewhat to her left and the river opened up before her. A white, roaring wall loomed up out of the rain, as if someone had torn a hole in the clouds and let all the water out at once. After a moment of blinking and trying to get her dripping hair out of her eyes, she realized that she was not staring at a torrent in the midst of the downpour, she was looking at a waterfall, and just on their side of the waterfall, there was a series of darker holes in the cliff wall that must be caves.

Tad spotted them at the same time, and shouted into her ear. "If any of these are deep enough, this is where we should stop! We may not be able to hear anything coming, but whatever tries to come at us from ahead won't be able to get past the falls! We'll only have to guard in one direction!"

She winced at the bellowing, since she was right beside the excited gryphon, but saw at once that he was right. That overcame her misgiving at camping in a place where the sound of an enemy approaching would be covered by the roar of the water; And as if to emphasize just what a good spot this was, a stunned fish came floating to their very feet to lodge among the rocks, flapping feebly. It had obviously been knocked silly by going over the falls, and Tad, who was probably starving, was on it in a heartbeat. Two gulps, and it was gone, and Tad had a very satisfied look on his face.

"See what else you can forage!" she shouted at him. "I'll check out these caves!"

"Wait a moment!" he shouted back. Picking up a milky-white, smooth pebble from the rocks at his feet, Tad stared at it in concentration that she found very familiar. Then he handed it to her, gryph-grinning with open beak. The pebble glowed with mage-light.

She accepted it with relief; at least he had enough magic back now that he could make a mage-light again!

She didn't have to go far to find their new shelter; the very first cave she entered proved to be perfect. It went back a long way, slanting upward all the time. For a few lengths, the floor was covered with soft, dry sand. Then there was a pile of driftwood marking the high-water line that past floods had also left behind; that was where the sand ended and dirt and rock began. A thin stream of water ran down the center of the cave, coming from somewhere near the back, cutting a channel through the sand and rock alike.

She made her way past it, holding the blue-glowing rock over her head to cast the best possible light ahead of her without dazzling her eyes. The cave narrowed, the farther she went back, then abruptly made a ninety-degree turn upward. This was where the stream of water originated. She put her head inside the hole and looked up. Besides getting a faceful of rain, she clearly saw the cloud-filled sky a great distance above. At one time, a real stream of water, perhaps a branchlet of the river that tumbled down the cliff further on, had cut a channel through here, forming the cave. Now, except perhaps during rain, that channel was dry. But it formed precisely what *they* needed; a natural chimney to carry the smoke away from their fire. Provided that nothing acted to funnel more water down that ancient outlet, this would be a perfect shelter. She could not have asked for anything better. Even the chimney was too small for anything threatening to climb down it, except perhaps snakes and the like. There were signs that other creatures had found this place just as congenial, a collection of small bones from fish and other creatures, and a cluster of bats toward the rear of the cave. She did not mind sharing this cave with bats; after her constant battles with insects, she was altogether happy to see them. They didn't seem disturbed to see her.

"Blade?" Tad called from behind her, and she realized that although the sound of the waterfall did penetrate in here, it was much muted by the rock walls.

"Coming!" she responded, turning her back on the chimney and climbing back down to the driftwood pile. She smelled smoke, and indeed, a plume of it, ghostlike in the blue light of the bespelled pebble, drifted toward her and the chimney outlet. A warmer light up ahead greeted her; Tad had already started a fire with the driftwood, and she joined him there.

"The fish around here must not be terribly bright," he said cheerfully. "Quite a lot of them ended up on the rocks a few moments ago. I got you some." He pointed with his beak at a pair of sleek shapes at his feet.

"After you ate your fill, I hope?" she admonished. "You need the food more than I do; I manage quite well on that travel-bread."

His nares flushed, and she judged by that and the bulging state of his crop that he had been perfectly greedy. Not that she blamed him, especially not after going on short rations for so many days. "You might as well put this under something, so we can sleep," she said, handing him the pebble and shrugging painfully out of her pack. "If I'd ordered up a cave, I couldn't have gotten a better one than this. We can even make a really smoky fire back there—" she pointed to the rear of the cave, "—there's a natural chimney that'll send it up without smoking us out. The only thing we don't have is a nighttime signal. We need to talk about that."

He ground his beak as he thought, his good wing half-spread in the firelight to dry. "I can't imagine them flying at night—" he began, then laughed. "Well, on the other hand, since it's me and you who are lost—"

"Skandranon will have night flights out if he has to fly them himself," she finished for him, with a wry chuckle. Then her humor faded. She could not forget, even for a moment, that they were still being hunted. Until they knew by what, and for what reason, they should not assume they would be here to rescue when rescue came. Yes, they had good shelter now, and it would be very difficult to dig them out of it. But not impossible; not for—say—a renegade mage and his followers, human or created.

Tad, however, was going to take the moment as it came; he shrugged out of his pack and nudged a fish over to her with one talon. "You eat," he said. "There's enough wood in here already to easily last the night. While you cook and eat that, I'll go back out and see what I can see."

She hesitated a moment, then gave a mental shrug and bent to pick up the fish. *I might as well eat and make myself comfortable. He's right about that.* While the rain fell, it was unlikely that anything would try to find them. If the creatures trailing them were semi-intelligent, they would assume that the two castaways had followed their usual pattern, and had taken shelter *before* the rain started. The hunters would probably be looking for them on the other side of the river first, especially if the hunters had not traced them as far as the river when the rain began. Any trail would end short of the river itself, and the mud and rock of the riverbank would not hold any scent or footprint through the rain. The trail on the other side of the river would be completely obliterated, and if they could keep their fire out of sight, it was possible that they could keep their presence in this cave a secret for a day or more. By the time smoke got up the rock chimney and exited above them, it would be very difficult for anything scenting it to tell where it originated.

After that, of course, it would become increasingly harder to stay hidden. Every time they left the cave, which they would have to do to catch fish, wash, and get firewood, they stood a chance of being seen. Watchers on the other side of the river could spot them without being seen themselves.

But I'll worry about that after I eat, when I can think better, she decided. It was wonderful to be able to have enough space to properly open the packs and spread everything out. Once again though, she found herself attempting a task one-handed that was difficult enough using two; scaling and gutting a fish. She wound up slipping off her boot and using a foot as a clumsy "hand" on the tail to hold it down.

She saved the head and the guts for later use as bait; they could not count on having the kind of luck that sent a harvest of fish down over the cliff to their feet every day. That was all right; they had fishing line and hooks with them, and if the fish guts didn't work, she could try a bug, a breadball, or a bit of dried meat. Once again, her shovel came into play as an impromptu grill; it probably would have been better if she'd had something to grease it with, but at the moment, she was too hungry for trifles like that.

The fish burned a little and stuck to the shovel, but that didn't matter in the least—she could scrape the fish meat off and eat, and some blackened fish meat stuck to it wouldn't adversely affect the use of the shovel as a shovel. She was hungry enough, in fact, that she very nearly burned her fingers, picking flaky bits of meat off the hot carcass before it had properly cooled. She alternately swore softly and ate, making a happy pig of herself.

Tad reappeared, dripping wet again, and regarded her thoughtfully. "Clay," he said. "Next time, wrap it up in clay and bake the whole thing. When you break the clay open, the skin comes off with it, but the rest of the fish is fine."

"Where did you learn that one?" she asked, looking up at him in surprise.

"Mother. She loves fish, and even though she likes it best fresh, she's been known to accept baked fish if it wasn't straight out of the sea." He gryph-grinned at her again, and cocked his head to one side. "You know how she is—unlike father, she'll wish for the ideal, but *not* complain when it isn't given! What do you want to do about the firelight? Move the fire back farther into the cave? The cave bends enough that I think that will make it harder to see from across the river. Or does it matter?"

So, he *had* been thinking about their stalkers. "I'm not sure it matters; sooner or later they're going to see us, or see signs of where we are. I'd rather put some thought into defenses."

"I've set up some simple line snares on the path, so watch out for them," he said. "Not much, there's not much I can do in the rain, but some. It should help, I would think. I can do better tomorrow."

"So that's why you're wet!" She signed to him to sit beside the fire, as she devoured the cooked fish. It didn't taste like much, a bit bland, which in itself made it an improvement over the dried meat, which tasted like old boots. It was hot and satisfying and *cooked*, which made all the difference, and she ate every scrap, using her knife to scrape the burned bits off the shovel and eat them too. Then she settled back on her heels, sucking her slightly-burnt fingers to get the last of the juices, and gave him all of her attention.

"Right, then. Let's settle the short-term first, then the long-term. First watch?" she asked.

"Yours," he said promptly. "As full as I am, I'm going to doze off no matter what. I can't help it; it's the way I'm built. And I have marginally better night-vision than you do. I also have better hearing," he added, "but with that waterfall out there, that isn't going to matter. I can run our fishing line from one of the snares into here, and stack some stones over the light pebble to make a sort of alarm."

Well, that seems pretty reasonable to me. "Good enough. If I see anything tonight, should I take a shot at it? Across the river is in the range of my sling, and with all these rocks around I can afford to miss now, and we won't have to go after my ammunition to get it back." That was another source of easing tensions. Now she was no longer limited to the pouches of lead shot for ammunition. The rocks might not fly as true, but she could lob as many of them around as she needed to. "My vote is that we not provoke anything tonight," he said instantly. "Let's not give them the answer to the question of where we went. If they can't find us tonight, we *might* get lucky and they'll go away."

"Probably not, but it's worth giving ourselves the chance. Agreed. Do we trap the other side of the river?" That was another good question. It might well be worth it to try—or it might make them targets when they crossed the river to check the traps. The river wasn't all *that* deep even at its deepest; barely chin-high on Blade. Anything energetic enough could cross it easily. After all, *they* had, and neither of them was in the best of shape. A stealthy swimmer could cross it and never betray himself by sound, what with the waterfall out there pounding away.

He shook his head. "No; we trap this side of the river, but not the other. We'd be too vulnerable on that side, and why bother? We really don't *want* to catch these things, do we?" He didn't look as if *he* did, and she agreed with him. After all, what could they do with one if they did catch it, alive or dead? All that would do would be to tell them what the hunters looked like, and there were easier ways to do that.

"Not unless we have to start whittling down their numbers," she murmured, thinking that this cave was both a good and a bad place to be. They could defend it—but it would be hard for rescuers to spot, and it would be very easy to place them in a state of siege from which there was no escape. The narrowness of the chimney that made it impossible for anything to climb down also rendered it impossible for them to climb up.

"Right. Then tomorrow, if it looks clear, we go get some green wood and leaves from across the way to make a smoke signal with. We get all the dry driftwood we can and stock it in here." He cocked his head to one side, and waited for her contribution.

"Water we have, finally; I might just as well start fishing and as long as we're running a smoke-signal fire, it can do double duty and I can smoke what we don't eat." *That way if we're trapped in here we'll have something to eat.* "We ought to go back down the way we came in and decide what kind of traps we can lay."

"At least one rockfall, right at the entrance, with a release one of us can trigger from in here," he said promptly, and yawned. "With a lot of work and cleverness we can even barricade the opening of the cave with wood and rocks; we're certainly clever enough, so all we need is the work. And that is about all of the thinking that I'm good for. I have *got* to get some sleep. I don't need a blanket; it's plenty warm enough in here next to the fire." He winked at her. "I can even lie down on this nice, soft sand so that I'm between the fire and the entrance, and screen it with my body. I shall sacrifice staying near the cold and water to do this duty."

"Big of you. Help me spread out the bedding so it can dry," she responded dryly. "Then you can sleep all you like—at least until it's your turn on watch!"

And may there be nothing to watch for—except a search party, and that soon, she thought, as he chuckled and moved to help her with the damp blankets. *By now they'll have missed us back home. We didn't make the rendezvous, and the other patrol should have sent word back with their teleson. How long until we're missing instead of overdue! And will they look for us when they think we're only late! I wish I knew.*

I only know one thing. Father's going to go out of his mind when he hears of this. I'm glad I'm not the one to tell him!

Amberdrake stared at Commander Judeth; for a moment her words made no sense.

Then suddenly, they made all too much sense.

"They're *what!*" All of Amberdrake's hard-won equanimity deserted him. He rose out of the chair in his office as if he'd sat on a hot coal. Indeed, that was very much the way he felt.

"Calm down, Drake, the youngsters are only overdue by a day," Judeth told him. She looked outwardly calm, but he knew more than enough about her and the tiny telltale signals her body showed to know that she was seriously worried. And yet, that was simply *not good enough.* "The patrol they were relieving got to the rendezvous point expecting them to be there yesterday, and they weren't there."

She's worried. She's only *worried. And she still hasn't done anything.* "And they haven't shown up yet." He held both the arms of his chair in a strangle grip, and stared at her with unveiled accusation in his eyes. "So why aren't you doing anything? You *know* those two are as by-the-book as any trainees you've ever had! They have never, *ever* violated orders. If they had a reason to be late, if they knew they were going to be delayed, they'd have sent a teleson message! If they haven't, it's because they can't, because something happened to them!"

His voice was rising, and he knew it, and what was more, he didn't care that he was making a blatant display of his emotions. For once in his life he *wanted* someone to know how upset he was. Judeth made soothing motions, as if she thought he could somehow be propitiated by a few words. As if she thought he could be "reasoned out of his hysteria."

She was certainly going to try. "We *are* doing something, Drake; the patrol has left the rendezvous and they are going on out to see if they can't find some sign of Blade and Tad. It's too early to get in a panic about this—"

Too early to get in a panic! Who does she think she's talking to! He held himself back from exploding at her only by great effort of will. "You tell me that when it's *your* child that's missing!" he snapped at her. "Or have you gotten so wrapped up in being a *commander* that you've forgotten this isn't wartime? Instead of telling me not to panic, I suggest you tell me what else you're doing *right now.* And if you aren't doing anything right now, I am not interested in hearing why you can't! I'll pull in every resource I have to see that something *does* get done, and without any nonsense about *not getting into a panic* because one person thinks it's *too early!*"

That was the closest he had ever come in his life to saying that he was actually going to use all the power and influence he held and had never used before, for any reason. *And I will, I'll do it, if I have to blackmail everyone in this city. Even her.* It was a threat, a real one, and he was not bluffing. But he felt he owed it to Judeth to warn her that lightning was going to fall on her before it came. If he used all his influence, it would be worse than lightning, and Judeth's position as commander might not survive the storm.

Her eyes darkened dangerously at his words, but her voice remained calm and even, which was something of a testament to her own control. Judeth did not like threats, but she was a realist, and she must know that he was not bluffing. "Right at this moment, the original patrol is flying out about a day in the right direction to see if they can find anything. If they don't, they'll go north of the track, then south, to see if they somehow went off course. Meanwhile, we're working on it. We're not just sitting around, waiting to see what happens. We're trying to find some way of locating them from here, and—*and*—" she finally raised her own voice as he got ready to explode again. "—*and* we are putting together search parties. Those will leave in the morning, since we can't *possibly* get one together before then. There is no point in grabbing unprepared people and sending them out at random. Now, if you can think of anything I might have missed, I'd like to hear it."

The truth was, he couldn't, but that didn't stop him from wanting some action right that very moment, something besides merely "readying a search party." "I can't think of anything, but I'm—this is difficult. It's hard to think," he admitted grudgingly. "Does Skan know yet?"

"Aubri's telling him." *Poor Aubri,* her tone said, but *Poor Skan,* was what *he* was thinking.

He was afraid of this. He didn't want Tad to go off on this assignment any more than I wanted Blade to. I know he thought about going to Judeth and asking them to be reassigned to something else, and didn't do it. And now he must be wondering if he is to blame for them being missing.

"I'll tell Winterhart—" he began, his throat tightening at the thought. *Gods, how do I tell her? This was my fault, if it all comes down to it; something I said or did made Blade want to be in the Silvers in the first place, all my interference made her want to be assigned somewhere far away from here—if I hadn't tried to meddle in her life so much, she would still be here—maybe even doing something else with her life. And Tad would have a different partner, one that wouldn't have urged him to ask for assignment out of the city.* He desperately wanted someone else to take on the burden of telling her, so that he did not have to face her accusing eyes. Cowardly, yes, but—

"No, I'll tell her," Judeth said firmly. "I already know where she is, and I'm Silverblade's commander; that's part of my job. You go to Skan; I'll send her to you there."

There, as everyone in White Gryphon knew, was "Kechara's nursery" this time of the day. Skandranon spent at least an hour with her and the other children, human and otherwise, every afternoon. He loved to spend time with them, telling stories, playing games. Once again, Amberdrake got to his feet and headed for the door; this time Judeth didn't stop him.

As soon as the White Gryphon Council Hall was finished, the spouses of every city official had demanded the addition of real offices to it—Winterhart included. "We're tired of you people bringing work home, and we're tired of having work *follow* you home," she had said, both in her capacity as "spokes-spouse" and in her capacity as a city official herself. "Home is where you go to get away from idiots who couldn't find the public latrine without a map and a guide! And *every* official gets an office, even if it's no bigger than a closet!" she had added. "I don't care if the post of k'Leshya Clan chief has never had a physical office before, the k'Leshya Clan chief has also never lived in anything other than a tent before, and if he can break tradition by living in a cave, he can break it a little more by having an office and regular hours, and he can bar the door when his office hours are over!" She had glared at Amberdrake, and her eyes had said, *And that goes twice as much for you, my dear and over-obliging spouse!*

Since Lionwind's wife had been standing behind Winterhart, nodding her head at every word and with one hand on her knife, he and every other city official had readily agreed.

The offices were all built into the cliff behind the Council Hall, small and private, and close to the other public buildings. The administrative building for the Silvers was not that far away from Amberdrake's office, and in that building was the nursery they had made for Kechara when she was still acting as the communication center for the Silvers. She shared it with the youngsters of anyone else in the Silvers or in city administration who needed to have someone tend their little ones while they worked. It was a good arrangement for everyone, and it gave Kechara a never-ending stream of playmates who were all her mental age, even if she was chronologically six or more times older.

Even though Kechara's powers were severely limited, she could still "talk" to any gryphon within the city territory. That alone was useful to the Silvers, and a very good reason to keep her right where she always had been.

As Amberdrake hurried toward the building, every muscle and nerve writhing with anxiety, he couldn't even begin to imagine how Judeth had thought that Aubri could break something like this gently to Skan. She must have been so upset by the news that her ability to reason had flown right out the door! *Aubri hasn't the tact of a brick. When Skan—"DRAKE!"* The bellow of a gryphon enraged could probably be heard all the way up to the farms, and the gryphon that burst out of the door of the Silvers' headquarters looked perfectly ready to chew up iron and spit out nails. *Burst* was indeed the correct term; the white-and-black gryphon erupted from the door flying, his head swiveling in all directions, presumably looking for his friend as he gained altitude. *"Drake!"* Skan bellowed again, from a height of about three lengths above him. "These *idiots!* They've lost—"

"I know, I know," Amberdrake shouted back, waving his hands frantically. "That's why I'm—"

Skan folded his wings and landed heavily, as if he were pouncing on something, every feather on end. "I want every mage in this city working on a way to find them!" he said wrathfully. "I don't care what they're doing! This is an emergency! I want everybody pulled in off of whatever they're doing, and I want search parties out there *now!* I want messengers sent to Shalaman! I want every man the Haighlei can spare out there looking, too! I want—"

We have to work this together, or they're not going to listen to us. Amberdrake seized his friend's head in both hands, hooking his fingertips into the gryphon's nares. He pulled Skan's beak down so that the gryphon was looking directly into his eyes. "I *know,*" he said forcefully. "Believe me, I feel the same! We have to call the Council to authorize this, Skan, but I don't think anybody on it is going to disagree with us, and if they do—"

Skan growled wordlessly at the very idea. "If they do, we—we both know things they wish we didn't," he pointed out.

"We do. And I'll use that." There it was, Skan agreed with him. It wasn't *right*, but it was better than arguing with shard-counters until it was too late to do anything.

"But there's no point in scattering everybody like a covey of frightened quail," Drake persisted, trying to convince himself as much as Skandranon. "All right? Let's get things coordinated. Judeth told the original patrol to look for them; right now that's all that anyone can do *out there*. We have to organize, and get people out there, talk people into using Gates again if we have to. We have to get Council backing for all that before anything else can be done, and that isn't going to happen if we're both standing here and wasting precious time screaming like outraged parents!"

"We *are* outraged parents!" The gryphon kicked clods of dirt in flurries of rage. "I don't want to have to follow procedure!"

Amberdrake put his fists on his hips and leaned toward Skandranon. "We will get Council approval, by whatever means necessary."

I hate it, but that's the case. If we want to have more than just "the usual effort" from the Silvers, we have to get Council authorization. And that's where the threats of blackmail come in.

Skan growled again, but without as much force behind it. "Damn it, Drake, why do you have to be so right?" he snarled. "All right then, I'll go back in there and have Kechara call in the Council members so we can authorize all of this."

Amberdrake wanted to add *don't frighten her*, but he held his tongue. Of all of them, Skan knew best how not to do anything that would make Kechara unhappy. He was her "Papa Skan," and she loved him with all of her heart—which was as large as her poor brain was small. He would no more do anything to frighten her than he would allow Blade and Tad to languish in the wilderness, unsought-for and unrescued.

He headed back toward the Council Hall, certain that if Winterhart and Zhaneel were not already on the way there, after Kechara's call, they would be.

Skan came stalking in shortly after Drake, and within moments after that, the rest of the Council members came hurrying in. Judeth was one of the first, looking very surprised and taken aback, and just a little annoyed; and although Skan leveled an icy glare at her, his tone was civil enough.

"I've called this meeting," he said. "Since this *is* an emergency situation."

He waited only until there were enough Council members present to constitute a quorum, and until everyone was seated before nodding to Judeth.

"You're the commander of the Silvers, so I think it best that you explain the emergency to the rest of the Council," he said crisply. Judeth looked as if she wanted to say something scathing to him, but held her tongue, which was probably wise.

Amberdrake had a good idea of what she was thinking, however. She was, first and foremost, a military commander, and under any other circumstances, the fact that two of the most junior members of the Silvers were missing—or overdue—should not have been considered an emergency the Council should be concerned with. Only an hysterical— but powerful—parent could have thought that it was.

And Amberdrake would have cheerfully throttled her for suggesting any such thing, if she dared.

Throttled her, then revived her so I could throttle her again. Part of him was appalled at this capacity for violence within himself; the rest of him nodded in gleeful agreement at the idea. *Then I'd revive her so that Skan could have a turn.*

But she evidently knew better—or the threat of his influence made her think twice about suggesting any such thing. Judeth explained the situation, coolly and calmly, while the other members of the Council listened without making any comments. Skan kept glaring around the table as if daring any of them to say that this was not the sort of emergency for which the Council should be called.

No one did, but Snowstar did have something to say that put the entire situation into a perspective that Amberdrake greatly appreciated.

"Has anyone ever gone missing this way before?" he asked, without looking either at Skan or at Amberdrake. "I know that there have been a handful of accidents among the Silvers, but I don't ever recall any of our Silvers on Outpost Duty ever *disappearing* before. Judeth, you haven't even had any fatalities in the Silvers since we encountered the Haighlei, and all of *those* were on the trek to find the coast. If this is a new development, I think it is a very serious one."

Aubri opened his beak, then looked at Judeth, startled. She was the one who replied.

"Actually—you're right," she said, sounding just as surprised as Aubri looked. "The fatalities among young gryphons since we founded the city have all been among the hunters, *not* the Silvers, and the accidents

705

causing injuries among the Silvers have all been just that—accidents, usually caused by weather, and not a single death from something like a drunkard or fight. To date we haven't had a single case of Outpost Patrols going missing. They've broken limbs, they've gotten sick, we've had to send help out to them, and one set of humans even got lost once— but they had a teleson and we knew they were all right, we just couldn't find them for a while. We've never had anyone just vanish before..."

Her eyes were the only part of her that showed how alarmed this new observation made her, but Amberdrake was savagely pleased at the way that her eyes went blank and steely. He knew that look. That was General Judeth, suddenly encountering a deadly enemy where she had been told there was open ground with no threats.

"I kept thinking this was—sort of one of the hazards of duty—but that was under war conditions or while we were making our way here," Aubri muttered, so shamefaced that his nares flushed a brilliant red. "Snowstar, you're right! We've *never* lost a Silver since—since we allied with the Haighlei!"

You two have been making the mistake of thinking that the Silvers were the extension of the old army—but they aren't and our situation is completely different than it was before the wars. And how could I have been so blind not to have seen your blindness!

"Then I believe this does qualify as a full-scale emergency," Snowstar said firmly. "When two highly-trained individuals drop completely out of sight, for no reason and with no warning, it seems to me that the danger is not only to them alone, but possibly to the entire city. What if they were removed so that they could not alert us to some enemy who is moving against us? How can we know that if we don't mount a rescue, in strength and numbers?"

Heads nodded all around the table, and Amberdrake exchanged stricken glances with Winterhart, who had come in just in time to hear that. He felt cold all over, and she had paled. He could have done without hearing that. He was perversely glad that Snowstar had thought of it, for it certainly swayed even the veterans on the Council to their cause, but he could have done without hearing it.

Either Snowstar really believes that, or the self-proclaimed non-diplomat Snowstar just made a shrewd play in our support. Or both.

A heavy and ominous silence filled the Council Hall, and no one seemed prepared to break it. Skan was as frozen as a statue, and beside him, Zhaneel simply looked to be in too much shock to be able to think.

Winterhart stood beside her Council seat, unable to sit, clutching the back of it; her knuckles were as white as her namesake. Amberdrake himself felt unable to move, every limb leaden and inert.

Judeth cleared her throat, making all of them jump. "Right," she said briskly, silence broken. "We have the original pair flying a search pattern; we're putting together more search teams. Does anyone have any further suggestions?"

Skan opened his beak, but Snowstar beat him to it. "I'll organize the mages and start distance-scrying," he said immediately. "We're probably too far away, but those who *can* scry for them should at least try. We'll look for the traces of the magic, on all the items they had with them; even if something made them crash, those traces will still be there. I'll also pick out mages for the search parties."

Once again, Skan opened his beak—then glared around the table, to make certain that he wasn't interrupted this time. "We should send a message to Shalaman," he said belligerently. "His people know that forest better than we do. We should make him—I mean, *ask* him—to send out parties of his hunters."

"That's good," Judeth approved, making a note of it. "I can put anyone who's been posted to that area on search parties, but if we can field Haighlei who are trained to hunt the forest in addition to our own people, that will be even better. Anything else?"

Search parties, magic, the Haighlei… Thoughts flitted through Drake's head, but he couldn't make any of them hold still long enough to be examined. Judeth looked around the table to meet shaking heads, and nodded.

"Good. We've got a plan," she said firmly. "We should assume that whatever has happened to these Silvers could endanger the city, and make finding them a top priority. Let's get to it."

She stood up and was halfway to the door before anyone else was even out of his chair. He didn't blame her. If the situation was reversed, *he* wouldn't want to be in the same room with four frantic parents either.

And he wouldn't want to face two people who had just threatened to blackmail him for not taking the loss of their children seriously enough.

Everyone else deserted the hall as quickly. Only Aubri paused at the door, looking back with uncertainty in his gaze. He opened his beak, then swallowed hard, shook his head, and followed the others.

Skandranon wanted nothing more than to rush off to the rescue of his son. Failing that, he wanted to tear the gizzard out of those who were responsible for his disappearance. Right now, so far as his heart was concerned, the ones responsible were right here in White Gryphon.

Judeth and Aubri. It was all *their* fault. If they hadn't assigned the children to this far-flung outpost, both his beloved son and his dear friend Amberdrake's daughter would still be here.

"I *knew* that this was a mistake all along!" he seethed at Zhaneel as he paced the length and breadth of the Council Hall. "I knew they were too young to be sent off on Outpost Duty! No one that young has ever been sent off alone like that before! They should have been posted here, like everyone else was! Judeth's getting senile, and Aubri was already there to show her the way—and—"

"*Please!*" Zhaneel suddenly exploded. "*Stop!*"

He stared at her, his mouth still open, one foot raised.

"Stop it, Skan," she said, in a more normal tone. "It is not their fault. It is not the fault of anyone. And if you would stop trying to find someone to blame, we would get something done." She looked up at him, with fear and anxiety in her eyes. "You are a mage; I am not. You go to work with Snowstar and the others, and I shall go to the messenger-mage and send a message in your name to Shalaman, asking for his help. At least I can do that much. And Skandranon—he is *my* son as well as yours, and *I* am able to act without rages and threats."

With that, she turned away from him and left him still standing with his foot upraised and his beak open, staring after her in shock.

Alone, for Amberdrake and Winterhart had already left.

Stupid, stupid gryphon. She's right, you know. Blaming Aubri and Judeth won't get you anywhere, and if you take things out on them, you're only going to make them mad at you. The Black Gryphon would be remembered as an angry, overprotective, vengeful parent. And what good would that do? None, of course.

What good would it do?

All at once, his energy ran out of him. He sat down on the floor of the Council Hall, feeling—old.

Old, tired, defeated, and utterly helpless, shaking with fear and in the grip of his own weakness. He squinted his eyes tightly closed, ground his beak, and shivered from anything but cold.

Somewhere out there, his son was lost, possibly hurt, certainly in trouble. And there was nothing, *nothing* that he could do about it. This was one predicament that the Black Gryphon wasn't going to be able to swoop in and salvage.

I couldn't swoop in on anything these days even if I could salvage it. I'm an anachronism; I've outlived my usefulness. It is happening all over again, except this time there can't be a rebirth of the Black Gryphon from the White Gryphon. The body wears out, the hips grow stiff and the muscles strain. I'm the one that's useless and senile, not Judeth and Aubri. They were doing the best they could; I was the one flapping my beak and making stupid threats. That is all that is left for a failed warrior to do.

For a moment, he shook with the need to throw back his head and keen his grief and helplessness to the sky, in the faint hope that perhaps some god somewhere might hear him. His throat constricted terribly. With the weight of intolerable grief and pain on his shoulders, he slowly raised his head.

As his eyes fell on the door through which Zhaneel had departed, his mind unfroze, gradually coming out of its shock.

What am I? What am I thinking?

I may be old now, but I am still a legend to these people. Heroes don't ever live as long as they want to, and most die young. I've lasted. That's all experience. *I'm a mage, and more skilled than when I was younger—and if I'm not the fighter I used to be, I'm also a lot smarter than I used to be! And what I'm feeling—I know what it is. I know. It was what Urtho felt every time I left, every time one of his gryphons wound up missing. I loved him so dearly, and I breathe each breath honoring his memory— but he was a great man because he accepted his entire being, and dealt with it. I am not Urtho—but I am* his *son in spirit, and what I honor I can also emulate. There's plenty I can do, starting with seeing to it that Snowstar hasn't overlooked anything!*

He shook himself all over, as if he was shaking off some dark, cold shadow that was unpleasantly clinging to his back, and strode out of the Council Hall as fast as his legs would carry him.

What I honor in Urtho's deeds, others have also honored in me. Urtho could embrace every facet of a situation and handle all of them with all of his intellect, whether it angered him personally or not. That was why he was a leader and not a panicked target. He could act when others would be overwhelmed by emotion. If I think of this disappearance in terms only of how I feel about it, then I will miss details that could be critical while I fill my vision with myself, and that could cost lives. Let the historians argue over whether I was enraged or determined or panicked on this day! I can still be effective *to my last breath!*

It was not clear at first where the Adept had run off to, and by the time Skan tracked him down, Snowstar had managed to gather all of the most powerful mages together in his own dwelling and workshop. Skan was impressed in spite of himself at how quickly the Kaled'a'in mage had moved. It was notoriously difficult to organize mages, but Snowstar seemed to have accomplished the task in a very limited amount of time.

There were seven mages at work including Snowstar. They had been divided into pairs, seated at individual tables so that they didn't interfere with each other, each pair of them scrying for something in particular. One pair looked for the teleson, one for the tent, one for the basket. Snowstar was working by himself, but the moment that Skan came near him, he looked up and beckoned.

"I'm looking for Tadrith myself," he said without preamble, "I was waiting for you to help me; the blood-tie he has with you is going to make it possible to find him, if it's at all possible. You will both feel similar magically, as you know."

"If?" Skan said, growing cold all over. *Is he saying that he thinks Tad is—dead!* "You mean you feel he is already dead—"

Snowstar made a soothing gesture. "No, actually, I don't. Even if Tadrith was unconscious or worse, we'd still *find* him under normal circumstances. The problem is that I'm fairly certain that they're quite out of our range." The white-haired Kaled'a'in Adept shook his head. "But 'fairly' isn't 'completely,' and under the impetus of powerful emotions, people have been known to do extraordinary things before this. As you should know, better than any of us! I'm more than willing to try, if you are."

Skan grunted in extreme irritation, but reined it in. "Stupid question, Snowstar. I'd try until I fell over."

Snowstar grimaced. "I know it was a stupid question; forgive me. Fortunately, that won't matter to the spell or the stone." He gestured at a small table, and the half-dome of volcanic glass atop it. "Would you?"

Skan took his place opposite the chair behind the table; he'd done scrying himself before, once or twice, but always with another mage and never with Snowstar. Each mage had his own chosen vehicle for scrying, but most used either a clear or black stone or a mirror. He put his foreclaws up on the table, surrounding his half of the stone with them. Snowstar placed his own hands on the table, touching fingertip to talon-tip with Skan.

After that, it was a matter of Skan concentrating on his son and supplying mage-energy to Snowstar while Snowstar created and loosed the actual spell. Some mages had a visual component to this work, but Snowstar didn't. It took someone who was not only able to see mage-energy but one who was sensitive to its movement—like a gryphon—to sense what he was doing.

Skan felt the energy gathering all around, them and condensing into the form of the spell, like a warm wind encircling them and then cooling. He felt it strain and tug at the restraints Snowstar held on it. And he felt Snowstar finally let it go.

Then—nothing. It leaped out—and dissipated. It wasn't *gone*, as if it had gone off to look for something. It was *gone* as if it had stretched itself out so thin that a mere breeze had made it fragment into a million uncoordinated bits.

Snowstar jerked as if a string holding him upright had snapped, then sagged down, his hands clutching the stone. *"Damn,"* he swore softly, as harsh an oath as Skan had ever heard him give voice to. "It's no good. It's just too far."

Skan sagged himself, his throat locked up in grief, his chest so tight it was hard to take a breath. *Tad...*

A few moments later the others had all uttered the same words, in the same tones of anger and defeat—all except the pair trying to reach the teleson.

They simply looked baffled and defeated, and they hadn't said anything. Finally Snowstar stopped waiting for them to speak up for themselves and went over to them. "Well?" he said, as Skan followed on his heels.

Skan knew both of them; one was a young Kaled'a'in called Redoak, the other a mercenary mage from Urtho's following named Gielle. The latter was an uncannily lucky fellow; he had been a mere Journeyman at the beginning of the mage-storms following the Cataclysm, but when they were over, he was an Adept. He was more than a bit bewildered by the transition, but had handled it gracefully—far more gracefully than some would have.

"I can't explain it, sir," he said, obviously working to suppress an automatic reaction to authority of snapping to attention and saluting. "When I couldn't reach Tadrith's device, I tried others, just to make certain that there wasn't something wrong with me. I've been able to call up every teleson we've ever created, including the one out there with the patrol looking for the missing Silvers. I got the one we left with the garrison at Khimbata, which is farther away than Tadrith is. I got all of them—except the one we sent out with Tadrith and Silverblade. It's—" he shook his head. "It's just gone, it's as if it was never there! It hasn't even been retuned or broken, that would leave a telltale. I've been working with telesons most of my life as a mage, and I've only seen something like this happen once before."

"Was that during the Wars?" Snowstar asked instantly.

Gielle nodded. "Yes, sir. And it was just a freak accident, something you'd have to have been an Adept to pull off, though. Some senile old fart who should never have been put in charge of anything was given an unfamiliar teleson to recharge and reversed the whole spell. Basically, he sucked all the magic out of it, made it just so much unmagical junk." Gielle shrugged. "The only reason he *could* do that was because he was an Adept. Senile, but still an Adept. We make those telesons foolproof for a good reason. Tadrith couldn't have done that, even by accident and a thousand tries a day, and even if someone actually smashed the teleson, I'd still be able to activate it and get a damaged echo-back. If it had been shattered by spell, the telltale would still mark the area magically. I don't know what to think about this."

Snowstar pursed his lips, his forehead creasing as he frowned. "Neither do I. This is very peculiar…"

Skan looked from one mage to the other, and back again. He caught Redoak's eye; the Kaled'a'in just held up his hands in a gesture of puzzlement.

"The signature of an Adept is fairly obvious," Redoak said slowly. "All Adepts have a distinctive style to even a moderately-trained eye. Urtho's was his ability to make enchantments undetectable—his mark was that there was no mark, but as far as I know, he could only veil spells he himself had crafted. The Haighlei would have seen something like this situation, I wager, by now. An Adept usually doesn't refrain from doing magic any time he can, especially not one of the old Neutrals. They were positively flamboyant about it. That was one of the quarrels that Urtho had with them."

"I have an idea," Snowstar finally said. "Listen, all of you, I'll need all your help on this. We're going to do something very primitive, much more primitive than scrying." He looked around the room. "Redoak, you and Gielle and Joffer put all the small worktables together. Rides-alone, you know where my shaman implements are; go get them. Lora, Green wing, come with me." He looked at Skan. *"You* go to the Silvers' headquarters and get me the biggest map of the area the children were headed into that you can find or bully out of them. They might give me an argument; you, they won't dare."

"They'd lose a limb," Skan growled, and he went straight for the door. He did his best not to stagger; he hadn't used that much mage-energy in a long time, and it took more out of him than he had expected.

All right, gryphon. Remember what you told yourself earlier. You have experience. You may fall on your beak from fatigue and tear something trying to fly in and save the day, but you have experience. Rely on experience when your resources are low, and rely on others when you can—not when you want to, vain gryphon. Work smarter. Think. Use what you have. And don't break yourself, stupid gryphon, because you are running out of spare parts!

He saw to his surprise that it was already dark outside; he hadn't realized that he had spent so long with the mages, trying to find the children. No wonder he was tired and a bit weak!

The Silvers' headquarters was lit up as if they were holding high festival inside, which made him feel a bit more placated. At least, they were *doing* something, taking this seriously now. *Too bad Snowstar had to convince them there was a threat to their own hides before they were willing to move. They should have just moved on it. Wasn't that the way we operated in the old days!* He barged in the front door, readied a foreclaw and grabbed the first person wearing a Silver Gryphon badge that he saw, explaining what he wanted in a tone that implied he would macerate anyone who denied it to him. The young human did not even make a token protest as the talons caught in his tunic and the huge beak came dangerously near his face.

"S-stay here, s-sir," he stammered, backing up as soon as Skan let go of him. "I'll f-find what you w-want and b-bring it right here!"

Somehow, tonight Skan had the feeling that he was *not* "beloved where e're he went." That was fine. In his current black mood, he would much rather be feared than beloved.

People have been thinking of me as the jolly old fraud, the uncle who gives all the children pony rides, he thought, grating his beak, his talons scoring the floor as he seethed. *They forgot what I was, forgot the warrior who used to tear makaar apart with his bare talons.*

Well, tonight they were getting a reminder.

The boy came back very quickly with the rolled-up map. Skan unrolled it just long enough to make certain that they weren't trying to fob something useless off on him to make him go away, then gruffly thanked the boy and launched himself out the door.

Despite the darkness, he flew back with his prize. When he marched through Snowstar's door, he saw at once that the workroom had already been transformed. Everything not needed for the task at hand had been cleared away against the wall. Other projects had been piled atop one another with no thought for coherence. It was going to take days to put the workroom back into some semblance of order, but Skan doubted that Snowstar was going to be thinking about anything *but* Blade and Tad until they were found.

At least we have one friend who took all this seriously without having to be persuaded.

The several small tables were now one large one, waiting for the map he held in his beak. The moment he showed his face at the door, eager hands took—snatched!—the map away from him and spread it out on the table. Redoak lit a pungent incense, filling the room with smoke that just stopped short of being eye-watering. The mage that Snowstar had called Rides-alone, who came from one of the many odd tribes that Urtho had won to his cause, had a drum in his hands. Evidently he was going to be playing it during—whatever it was they were going to do.

"Right." Snowstar stood over the table, the only one who was standing, and held a long chain terminating in a teardrop-shaped, rough-polished piece of some dark stone. "Redoak, you watch what the pendulum does, and mark what I told you out on the map. Rides-alone, give me a heartbeat rhythm. The rest of you, concentrate; I'll need your combined energies along with anything else I can pull up out of the local node. Skan, that goes for you, too. Come sit opposite me, but *don't* think of Tad or Blade, think of me. Got that?"

He was not about to argue; this looked rather like one of those bizarre shamanistic rituals that Urtho used to try, now and again, when classical spellcasting failed. He simply did as he was told, watching as Snowstar carefully suspended the pendulum over the map at the location where the youngsters had last been heard from. Rides-alone began a steady drum pattern, hypnotic without inducing slumber—somehow it enhanced concentration. How *that* was managed, Skan could not begin to imagine.

For a long time, nothing happened. The stone remained quite steady, and Skan was afraid that whatever Snowstar had planned wasn't working after all. But Snowstar remained impassive, and little by little, he began to move the pendulum along a route going north and east of the point of the youngsters' last camp.

And abruptly, without any warning at all, the pendulum *did* move.

It swung, violently and abruptly *away* from the spot Snowstar had been trying to move it toward. And in total defiance of gravity, it hung at an angle, as if it were being repelled by something there.

Snowstar gave a grunt, although Skan could not tell if it was satisfaction or not, and Redoak made a mark on the map with a stick of charcoal. Snowstar moved his hand a trifle.

The pendulum came back down, as if it had never exhibited its bizarre behavior.

Snowstar moved it again, a little at a time, and once again came to a point where the pendulum repeated its action. The strange scene was repeated over and over, as Redoak kept marking places on the map and Snowstar moved the pendulum back.

It took uncounted drumbeats, and sweat was pouring down the faces of every mage around the table, when Snowstar finally dropped the pendulum and signaled to Rides-alone to stop drumming. There was an irregular area marked out in charcoal dots on the map, an area that the pendulum avoided, and which the youngsters' flight would have bisected. Redoak connected the dots, outlining a weirdly-shaped blotch.

"I would lay odds that they are in there, somewhere," Snowstar said wearily. "It's an area in which there is *no* magic; no magic and no magical energy. Whatever is given off in the normal course of things by animals and plants is immediately lost, somehow, and I suspect magic brought into that area is drained away as well. I can only guess that is what happened to their basket when they flew over it."

"So the basket became heavier, and they couldn't fly with it?" Redoak hazarded, and whistled when Snowstar nodded. "That's not good. But how did you know what to use to find all this?"

Snowstar shrugged modestly. "It was Gielle that gave me the idea to look for a negative, and I remembered shamanic dowsing; you can look for something that is there, like metal, or something that is *not* there, like water. Urtho taught it to me; we used to use it to make certain that we weren't planting our outposts atop unstable ground." He looked across the table at Skan, who was trying very hard to tell himself that it wasn't likely for all the magic-infused into the basket to drain off at once. He did not want to think about what that would have meant for poor Tadrith if the basket regained its normal weight in a single moment while aflight.

"Take that map with you, and tell Judeth what we've found," the Adept told Skan. "I'll work with the mages I'm sending out with the search teams. There's probably something about the area itself that we can shield against. I doubt that a mage caused this. It might just be a freak of nature, and the Haighlei would never have seen it, because they were looking *for* magic, not for its absence."

Skan nodded, and Redoak brushed a quick-drying varnish on the map to set the charcoal. The fumes warred unpleasantly with the lingering scent of the incense, but the moment the map was dry, the younger mage rolled it up and handed it to the Black Gryphon. Skan did not wait around to see what the rest of the mages were going to do; he took the map and fled out the door for the second time that evening.

This time he went straight to the planning room—which Judeth still referred to as the "War Room" out of habit. And it looked very much as if they were planning for a wartime situation. Judeth had a map spread out over the table, there were aides darting everywhere, Aubri was up on his hindquarters tracing out a line with one talon when Skan came in through the door.

"Snowstar thinks he has a general area," Skan said, as silence descended and all heads but Judeth's swiveled around at his entrance. "That's what he wanted the map for. *Here.*"

He handed the map to the nearest aide, who spread it out on the table over the existing one at Judeth's nod.

"What's that?" she asked, pointing at the blobby outline on the map.

"It's an area where there isn't magic," Skan replied. He repeated what Snowstar had told him, without the details about shamanic dowsing. "That would be why we can't raise the teleson. Snowstar thinks that anything that's magical gets all the mage-energy sucked out of it when it enters that area."

"And if the spell making the basket into something Tad could tow lost its power—" Judeth sucked in her lower lip, as one of the aides coughed. "Well, no matter how they landed, they're stuck now. No teleson, no magic—they'd have to hole up and hope for rescue."

Aubri studied the map for a moment. "The only teams we've sent out there were gryphon pairs; with one exception," he pointed out. "You and me, Judeth. We used a basket, and our flight path took us over that area. Nothing happened to *us,* so where did this come from?"

"Maybe it's been growing," offered one of the aides. "Maybe the more it eats, the bigger it grows."

"Well, that's certainly cheerful," Judeth said dryly, and patted the girl on the shoulder when she flushed a painful red. "No, you have a point, and we're going to have to find out what's causing this if you're right. If it's growing, sooner or later it's going to reach us. I did without working magic long enough and I'm not in the mood to do it again."

"That's a lot of area to cover," Aubri pointed out. "They could be anywhere in there, depending on how far they got before they had to land."

Land. Or crash. Skan's imagination was all too clever at providing him with an image of the basket plummeting down out of the sky...

"We can probably cover it with four teams including a base camp," Judeth said, at last. "But I think we're going to have to do a ground search, in a sweep pattern. Those trees are bigger than anything most of us here have ever seen before, and you could drop Urtho's Tower in there and not see most of it. Gryphons may not do us a lot of good."

"They can look for signal smoke," Aubri objected.

Judeth did not say anything, but Skan knew what she was thinking, since it was something that he was already trying *not* to think about. The youngsters might be too badly hurt to put up a signal fire.

"Right, then the two already in the area can look for signal smoke," she said. "I'll fly in a mage *here*, to set up a match-Gate terminus, and I'll call for volunteers for four teams who are willing to trust their hides to a Gate—"

"I shall go," said a deep voice from the doorway.

Skan swiveled his head, as Ikala moved silently into the room. "With all respect, Commander, I must go. I know this forest; your people do not. Forget my rank and my breeding; my father would say that you should, in a case like this. These two are my friends and my sworn comrades, and it is my honor and duty to help them."

"You are more than welcome, then. I'm going, you can count on it," Skan said instantly. "Drake will probably want to go, too. Judeth, that'll give you one mage and a field-Healer, along with a fighter."

Judeth sighed, but made no objections, probably because she knew they would be futile. "All right, but these are going to be *big* teams. I don't want tiny little patrols running around in unknown territory. I want two mages, so you have one for each night watch on each team, and I want at least as many fighters. Ikala, you go call for volunteers among the hunters and the Silvers. Skan, go back to Snowstar and explain the situation and what we need." She glared at both of them. "Don't just stand there, *go!*"

Skan went, but he was a fraction slower than Ikala and reached the door in second place. By the time he was outside, Ikala was nowhere in sight.

But he was overjoyed that Ikala was still willing to volunteer, even with the need to trust to a Gate for transport. The young Haighlei was precisely what they needed; someone who knew the ordinary hazards of such a forest, and how to meet them.

Snowstar had already anticipated Judeth's decision about a Gate. "As if any of us would be afraid to trust our own Gates!" he replied scornfully. "We've been perfectly willing to use them for the last five years, it's been the rest of you who were so overly cautious about them!"

"Not *me!*" Skan protested, but Snowstar was already on to other things. "Gielle will fly out with a gryphon as soon as it's light; I'll have Redoak head one of the other three teams after you all get through the Gate," the Adept was saying. "I have more mages willing to volunteer than Judeth needs, but not all of them are suited to this kind of mission. Tell her I'll be choosing combat experience over sheer power; we can't take the chance that this dead zone is a freak of nature. No matter what she thinks, it might have a traceable cause, and that cause might be one of the mages who escaped the Wars."

Skan nodded; he was certain that Judeth had already thought of that.

"I'll go find Drake," he said. It was going to be a long night, and one he was certain none of them would be able to sleep through. They might as well start getting ready for deployment.

At least *that was* something useful.

Aging and hedonistic you may be, stupid gryphon, but you're also effective.

CHAPTER EIGHT

Amberdrake did not sleep that night. Despite the feeling that he was working at a fever pitch, he got precious little accomplished. Most of what he did was to go over the same scenarios, in his mind, on paper, in fevered conversation with whoever, would listen—usually the long-suffering Gesten. But no matter how tired he became, the weariness was never enough to overcome him, not even for a moment.

Insomnia was only one of the physical effects he suffered. He simply could not be still; he would sit or lie down, only to leap to his feet again as another urgent thought struck him. The muscles of his neck and back were so tense that no amount of soaking would relax him—not that he stayed long enough in a hot pool to do any good. He had not eaten since the news. His throat was too tight to swallow, his stomach a tight, cold knot, and as for his nerves—if he'd had a client as wrought up as he was, he would have recommended immediate tranquilization by a Healer. But if he had submitted himself to a Healer, he would be in no condition to accomplish anything thereafter. He could not do that.

Amberdrake recalled Zhaneel's words of so long ago, as if they were an annoyance.

Who heals the healer!

Skan and Snowstar had not commandeered all of the mages in the city—there was always one whose sole duty was to oversee magical communications. Those communications were between both White Gryphon and the Silvers posted outside the city—in Shalaman's bodyguard, for instance—and with Shalaman himself, via his priests. There could be no speaking with Shalaman directly, of course. There was no such thing in Haighlei society as a direct link to anyone important. The messages would have to go through the priests, who were the only people permitted the use of magic, then to Shalaman's Chief Priest Leyuet, and only then to Shalaman. Amberdrake tracked down the mage in question and had him send his own personal plea for help to the Haighlei in addition to Skan's—but after that, he was at loose ends.

There was only so much he could do. He was no mage, he could not possibly help Skan in trying to locate the children. He could pack, and did, for a trek across rough, primitive country, but that did not exactly take much time, even with Gesten coming along behind him and repacking it more efficiently. He certainly couldn't do anything to help the rescue parties of Silvers that Judeth and Aubri were organizing.

Even if he could have, it might only have made things worse. He suspected that after his threats, overt and covert, Judeth would not appreciate seeing his face just now. Aubri would be more forgiving, but Judeth had lived long under the comfortable delusion that she no longer had to cope with the vagaries of "politics." As with most true military leaders, she had always hated politics, even while she used political games to further her own causes. She had thought that without a King, a court, or a single titular leader among them, she was at last free to do what she wanted with a policing branch. She tried to keep the Silvers autonomous from the governing branch, and that was largely what she had accomplished.

Now Amberdrake had made it very clear to her that there was no such thing as an environment that was free of politics, that under duress, even friends would muster any and all weapons at their disposal. And she had just learned in the harshest possible way that no one is ever free of the politics and machinations that arise when people live together as a group.

No one likes to have their illusions shattered, least of all someone who holds so few.

Judeth would be very difficult to live with for some time. He only hoped that her good sense would overcome her anger with him, and that she would see and understand his point of view. Hopefully Judeth would see Amberdrake as having used a long-withheld weapon at a strategic time, rather than seeing him as a friend who betrayed an unspoken trust to get what he wanted. If not—he had made an enemy, and there was nothing he could do about that now. Nor, if he'd had the chance to reverse time and go back to that moment of threat, would he have unsaid a single word. He had meant every bit of it, and Judeth had better get used to the idea that people—even the senior *kestra'chern*—would do anything to protect their children. That was one thing she had never had to deal with as a military commander before, because a military structure allowed replacement or reassignment of possible mutineers. Parental protectiveness was a factor that was going to be increasingly important as the children of the original settlers of White Gryphon entered the Silvers. Perhaps it was for the best that the precedent had been set in this way.

And no matter what happens, knowing myself, I will have simultaneous feelings of justification as a concerned and desperate parent, as well as guilt over not having done better and had more forethought.

So there was nothing more he could do, really, except to wait. Wait for morning, wait for word from Shalaman and from the mages, wait, wait, wait...

Just as it was when he had served in Urtho's ranks, waiting was the hardest job he had ever held. He had been in control of at least part of the life of this city for so long that, like Judeth, he had gotten accustomed to being able to fix problems as soon as they arose without anyone offering opposing force. Now, as the number of emergencies died down and new people came into authority, his control was gone. All of his old positions of influence were in the hands of others, and he was back to the old game of waiting.

Finally he returned home, since it was the first place where anyone with news would look for him. As he paced the walkway outside the house, unable to enter the place that now seemed too confining and held far too many memories of his lost daughter, his mind circled endlessly without ever coming up with anything new. Only the circling; anger and fear, fear and anger. Anger at himself, at Judeth, at Blade—it wasn't productive, but it was inevitable, and anger kept his imagination at bay. It was all too easy to imagine Blade hurt, Blade helpless, Blade menaced by predatory animals or more nebulous enemies.

And once again, he would be one of the last to know what others had long since uncovered. He was *only* Blade's father, as he had *only* been a *kestra'chern.* Yet hanging about in the hope that someone would take pity on him and tell him something was an exercise in futility. So he alternately paced and sat, staring out into the darkness, listening to the roar of the waves beneath him. In the light falling gently down onto the harbor from the city, the foam on the top of the waves glowed as if it was faintly luminescent. A wooden wind-chime swung in the evening breeze to his right, and a glass one sang softly to his left. How often had he sat here on a summer evening, listening to those chimes?

Caught between glass and wood, that which breaks and that which bends, that which sings and that which survives. So our lives go.

Winterhart joined him long after the moon had come out. He turned at her familiar footstep, to see her approaching from the direction of the Council Hall, the moonlight silvering her hair. In the soft light there was no sign of her true age; she could have been the *trondi'irn* of Urtho's forces, or the first ambassador to the Haighlei so many years ago. Only when she drew close were the signs of anxiety and tension apparent in her face, her eyes, the set of her mouth.

"They're putting together the last of the supplies," she said, before he could ask. "Skan and the mages haven't come out of Snowstar's work area yet, and Shalaman hasn't replied. Don't worry, he will before the night is over; remember how long his court runs at night."

He did remember; in the tropical heat of the climate around Khimbata, Shalaman's people all took long naps in the afternoon, and then continued their court ceremonies, entertainments, and duties until well after midnight. And he had no fear that Shalaman would refuse help; the Emperor could send off a hundred hunters or more from his forces, and they would never be missed. No, the only question was how soon the hunters could be somewhere that they could do some good. First the priests would have to approve the departure, then they would have to travel across many leagues of forest before they were anywhere near the place where the children had vanished. All that would take time, precious time…

Blindly, he held out his arms and Winterhart came into them. They held each other, seeking comfort in one another's warmth and presence. There was no point in talking; they would only echo one another, each saying what the other was thinking. They both knew that, and knew that talking would ease nothing, soothe nothing.

So they simply sat down on the smooth, cool stone bench outside their home, and held each other, and waited beneath the stars. Neither of them were strangers to waiting.

That did not make waiting any easier—except that it removed the additional pain of loneliness.

Judeth must have gotten over her own anger by dawn, for she showed no signs of it when a messenger summoned both Amberdrake and Winterhart to what the young Silver called a "planning session." The two of them had bathed and changed clothing, hoping that clean bodies would restore their minds a little. Amberdrake had shunned his usual finery in favor of something very like Winterhart's practical working garb, hoping that there might *possibly* be something he could *do* once the sun rose. When the summons came, both of them had been sitting over a breakfast neither of them had been able to touch, and it was a relief to rise and follow the youngster back to the Council hall.

Skan and Zhaneel and their other son Keenath were already there, showing just as much strain as Amberdrake felt, although only someone who knew gryphons well would have recognized the signs of strain in overpreened feathers, plumage lying flat against the body, posture that showed their muscles were as tense and knotted as Amberdrake's. He doubted that they had slept, but the sight of Keenath made a moment of intense anger flash through Amberdrake's heart.

He still has *a child. And if his other had not been so intent on leaving the city, mine might not have gone either!*

But that was irrational and entirely incorrect, and he knew it. He suppressed it immediately, and he and Winterhart maneuvered through the group crowded in here so that they could form a united block with the other set of parents.

Judeth did not look as if she had slept either. Deep shadows touched the swollen pouches under her eyes, and she looked twice her real age. Aubri didn't even pretend to be calm; he chewed incessantly on one of his old, shed feathers, presumably to keep from shredding his current plumage.

There were thirty or forty people in the group; Amberdrake noticed that at least six of them were mages and he, Winterhart, Skan, Keenath and Zhaneel were the only non-Silvers. Ikala was among the Silvers gathered here, and Amberdrake was irrationally pleased to see him, as if the tall young man represented more than just a local expert on the rain forest.

The Council Hall was the only room large enough to hold all of them, and Judeth had completely taken it over, strewing maps and other documents all over the table. It looked as if she had been here for some time. "Snowstar and the mages have uncovered something damned peculiar," she said, when they had all gathered around the map-covered table. She tapped a darkened, irregularly shaped blob on the map in front of her. "This area here has no signs of magic. *None*, and they tell me that's practically impossible. The missing patrol was due to pass along this line—" She drew a swift mark with a piece of charcoal which crossed the southern end of the irregular-shaped area. "—and if there's something in there that's negating mage-energy, you can imagine for yourself what that would mean for both their carry-basket and their teleson."

Amberdrake was all too able to imagine what that would do to a carry-basket; and from the way Winterhart suddenly clutched his arm, her fingers digging into the muscle, so was she. In his mind, he saw the two figures he had watched fly off into the distance suddenly stricken for a moment, then plummeting to their deaths on the unforgiving ground below.

"That means we're going to have to come in somewhere near the edge and walk in," Judeth continued, without any hint that *she* had envisioned the same disaster that had played itself out behind Amberdrake's eyes. "Our Gate probably won't work inside this area, and we'll have to suppose for now that nothing else magical in nature will work either. We'll have to operate by the old rules of working without magic, although yes, we *will* be taking mages, just in case magic does work after all. Though—if there's no local mage-power available, Snowstar tells me that the mages will be just like Journeymen and Apprentices, and limited to their own personal power. That's going to put a serious crimp in their activities, and any mages that go along had better start thinking in terms of budgeting themselves before they act."

She leveled a sharp glance across the table, to the point where the mages of the Silvers had bunched together.

"What about the gryphons?" someone wanted to know. "Can't they just fly overhead and scout the way they always do?"

She closed her eyes for a moment, and sighed. "If I wanted a sign that our luck has turned truly wretched, I could not have conjured up one more certain. This *is* the rainy season for that part of the world— and the weather-mages tell me that storms will be unceasing over this particular area for the next several days to a week. Thunderstorms have already grounded the original pair that was out looking for our missing Silvers; they are on the ground and we know where they are. It might well be a side effect of the loss of magic over the area; we just don't know for certain. But what that means is that there won't be any flying going on. I'm not going to ban any gryphons from the search-parties, but they'll be strictly on foot unless the weather improves drastically."

"I'm still going, and so are Zhaneel and Keeth," Skan spoke up firmly. Judeth nodded, as if she had expected as much. "In that case, since I'm going to divide the searchers into three parties, each gryphon can go with one. I've already sent out a gryphon with a Gate-mage; but he'll be coming straight back, and so will the two still out there while weather cooperates." Judeth cocked an eyebrow at Skan as if she expected him to object to this, but he didn't. Amberdrake could certainly understand why. A gryphon on the ground was severely handicapped; Skan, Zhaneel, and Keenath would be as much a hindrance as they were a help. The two who had been on patrol would be exhausted, and the one who had ferried the Gate-mage even more so.

Judeth continued. "Now, here's the current plan. We'll Gate in here—that's the closest I want to get to this area with anything that depends upon magic."

She stabbed down with her index finger. *Here*, the point where her finger indicated, was on the line that Blade and Tad had been expected to fly.

"The Gate-mage and a small party will stay here, at a base camp, holding the area for the rest of you. We'll divide up; the party with Skan and Drake in it will go north, up to the top of the area, and then in. The one with Ikala leading it, including Keenath, will go straight in. The one with Winterhart and Zhaneel will go south, then in. That way we'll cover the maximum area in the shortest possible time." Judeth straightened, and looked straight at Skan again. "And in case you're wondering why I haven't put you two in on the expected line, it's because the two gryphons out there already flew that line and didn't see anything before weather forced them down. So either the missing patrol *didn't* fly that line, or it's going to take an expert in that kind of territory to find signs of them. That's Ikala, not you; he'll be leading a party of people all used to moving quickly, and after he scouts the line on the ground, he'll be covering the areas north and south of that line. I'm putting you two on the likeliest alternate track; Tad always had a tendency in training to stay on the northern side of a given flight line. My guess is, if they're anywhere off the line, it's in the north."

"But that's just a guess," Skan stated. "They could be south."

She nodded. "And the gods know I've guessed wrong before; that's why the third party. The parties are going to number eight; one gryphon, one Healer or *trondi'irn*, or whatever comes close—that's you, Drake—two mages, and five fighters, all *experienced* Silvers. Any smaller is dangerous, any larger is unwieldy. Don't bother to pack at all; you'll be taking standard Silver kits including medical supplies, and you aren't going to have time to change clothing. Besides, by the time you make a camp at night, you and your clothing should be sluiced clean."

Her stare at Amberdrake said, as clearly as words, *And if you don't like that, you don't have to go.*

He stared right back at her. *Try and keep me from going and you'll have a fight.*

She waited for him to say something, staring into his gaze with challenge in her stance, but it was she who finally dropped her eyes. "This is an in-and-out mission, the faster the better. As of this moment, consider yourself facing a real enemy, a powerful one, if he can drain all the mage-energy out of a place. I don't *know* what's caused magic to leach out of that area, but I have to assume it's a hostile, and it isn't going to like having twenty-four people traipsing all over its territory. As soon as the mage gets to the Gate-point, we'll be bringing it up, and I don't want it up for longer than it takes to pitch all of you through it. Is that understood?"

Once again, she stared at him as if her words were meant for him alone. Her tone of voice implied that, given the opportunity, she *would* "pitch" Amberdrake through the Gate. He simply nodded, as did everyone else.

"Good. From now until you leave, you are all sleeping, eating, and everything else right here." She smiled thinly at their surprise. "That'll be quicker than trying to gather all of you up once the mage gets into place. I don't intend to waste a single minute on any dallying. I'll have sleeping arrangements brought in; the mage I sent out is being carried by Darzie, so I expect to hear that they've made their landing within the next full day."

Amberdrake was impressed, as much by the identity of the gryphon as by the speed with which the duo expected to reach their destination. He wondered what Judeth had promised to get Darzie to fly a carry-basket at all, much less try to do so breaking a record and in bad weather.

Darzie was *not* a Silver; he was one of a new class of gryphons who were primarily athletes. Whether as aerobats, fast couriers, or actual racers, these gryphons earned a very fine, even luxurious, living by serving the Haighlei appetite for speed and spectacle. Darzie was *the* best of the fast couriers and one of the fastest racers—he was a more consistent flyer than gryphons who actually clocked the occasional faster time. It was hard to imagine what hold Judeth could have over him to induce him to risk injury and strain in this way.

But maybe he was being uncharitable; maybe Darzie had actually volunteered…

Not without blackmail…

It didn't matter, so long as Judeth had gotten him, whether it was through bribery or blackmail, or a combination of both.

Maybe she's following my example. The gods know she has enough power of her own to leverage just about anyone in this city into doing her bidding at least once.

"Any questions?" Judeth asked, and looked around the room. "No? Right. Fall out, and for those of you who haven't slept, I'm calling Tamsin in to make you sleep." There was no doubt who she was targeting with the daggers of her gaze, and both Amberdrake and Skan flinched; but she wasn't finished. "That includes me; we won't be any good to anyone if we aren't rested when the call comes. Right, Drake?"

Her question came as a surprise, and he was doubly surprised to sense the compassion and sympathy—and worry of her own—behind the words. It penetrated even his defensiveness.

"Ah, right," he admitted sheepishly, relaxing just a trifle. *So she does understand, and she's forgiven us…* He had not hoped for it so soon, but he welcomed it as a tiny bright spot of hope in the midst of too much grief.

"Good. Glad you agree, because you're going to be one of the first to go to sleep." A commotion at the door proved to be bedding, food, and Tamsin all arriving simultaneously. "Now, stand down, all of you, and get yourselves taken care of. I'll be watching to see that you do."

And she did; standing over them all like a slavemaster, to see that every member of the three search parties ate, drank, and submitted to Tamsin's touch. As Judeth had warned, Amberdrake was one of the first, and after one look at Judeth's expression, he knew better than to protest.

So he crammed down a few mouthfuls of food as dry and tasteless as paper, drank what was given him, and laid himself down on a standard, military-style sleeping roll. He closed his eyes as Tamsin leaned over him, and that was the last thing he knew until the rally-call awakened him.

* * *

Rain. Why did it have to be rain! Even snakes would be better. Skandranon tried to keep his thoughts on his purely physical discomfort, but try as he might, he couldn't. His skin crawled, and the rain had nothing to do with it. If Skan's feathers hadn't been plastered flat to his body, they'd have been standing up in instinctive alarm.

He did not like this place, and his dislike was not connected in any way whatsoever with the miserable weather!

It could have been that this bizarre, claustrophobic forest had swallowed Blade and Tad without a trace, but that wasn't the reason his soggy hackles were trying to rise either. The other mage of the party felt the same, and if there had been any choice in the matter, he'd have gone back to the base camp because it just plain felt *wrong* here.

The two of them, after some discussion last night before the human took the first sleep shift, had decided that the problem was that lack of mage-energy in this place. Presumably an Apprentice-level mage or Journeyman would not be affected in this way; they were not used to sensing and using energies outside themselves, unless those energies were fed to them by a mage of greater ability. But a Master (as Skan and the human Silver, Filix, were) was as accustomed to the all-pervasive currents of mage-energy as a gryphon was to the currents of the air. Skan could not remember a time in his adult life that he had not been aware of those currents. Even when the mage-storms had caused such disruptions in magic, the energy had never *vanished,* it just hadn't worked or felt quite the same. But having no mage-energy about—it felt wrong, very wrong. It had him disoriented and off-balance, constantly looking for something that simply wasn't there.

It feels as if I've suddenly lost a sense; something subtle, like smell.

Nevertheless, a quick trial had proved to his satisfaction that magic still *worked* here, and furthermore, those magical items that they had brought in with them were still empowered. Further checks proved that, at the moment at least, there was no ongoing drain of mage-energy. The power that built up in any area naturally was slowly rising back up. So whatever was wrong in this forest, whatever had caused this anomaly, it had not completely negated magic, just removed it. Whether that drainage had been gradual or all at once was anyone's guess. And there must be something coming along to drain mage-energy again as it built up, or there would be some areas that had at least a *little* power available.

As for what *that* could be, he had no idea. He did not care to think about what must have happened if the basket had also had all of its empowering mage-energy drained—all at once.

Skandranon mentally worked on a few new phrases to use when he finally complained about it all to someone whom he could corral into listening sympathetically. He had a reputation for—colorful—language to maintain after all. He would much rather concentrate on that, than how miserable his soggy feathers felt, how cold he was, how sore his muscles were after two days of walking. *That* was something he simply hadn't considered, and it was galling to realize that Drake was in better physical shape than he was! Drake had been climbing the stairs and ladders of White Gryphon for almost twenty years; *he* had only been flying. He could not think of more than a handful of times that he had actually climbed *up* rather than down, and none of those times had been in the last three years. At least Keeth had been working out on the obstacle course lately, and Winterhart had made certain that all muscles were exercised. Poor Zhaneel must be as miserable as he.

But she has the best trondi'irn *in the city to tend her. Keeth* is *a* trondi'irn. *I only have Drake, who does his best, but still... he's preoccupied.*

Rain dripped into his nares and he sneezed to clear them, shaking his head fiercely. He and Drake were at the rear of the party; with his keener sense of hearing than the humans possessed, it seemed a good idea to have him at the back where he might be able to detect something following them. Now he wished he had thought to ask Judeth for a couple of *kyree* scouts for each party; they would have been much more effective than any of the humans.

Rain poured down out of the sky, as it had since the fog lifted that morning. This was a truly lovely climate; fog from before dawn to just after, followed by rain until well past darkness, followed by damp chill until the fog came again in the morning. Judeth had been absolutely right in grounding them, and he would have grounded himself once he saw the weather; there was no way for a gryphon to fly safely in this muck, even if he could get his wings dry long enough to take off. Darzie had managed to bring his mage in safely only because he was insanely self-confident and lucky enough for four gryphons, and because the weather changed abruptly to something more like a "normal" rainy season outside of the "no-magic" area.

That, and Darzie is young enough to think he's immortal, and good enough to fly as if he were. Like another stupid, stupid gryphon I used to know. In spite of the fact that the rainy season was normal back at the base-camp, "normal" still meant a raging thunderstorm every afternoon. Darzie had flown *and landed* in one of those thunderstorms, blithely asserting that it was all a matter of timing and watching where the bolts hit. His passenger had been white-lipped, but remarkably reticent about discussing the flight.

Drake had found out what had tempted Darzie into making the trip; a challenge. Judeth had asked the young gryphon if hc knew of anyone who might be persuaded, and had hinted broadly that she didn't think *he* could do it. That had been enough for Darzie, who had insisted that he and only he could manage the trip. And he had, in record-breaking time, and without damaging himself or his passenger. For sheer speed, audacity, and insane courage, that flight had surpassed even some of the Black Gryphon's legendary accomplishments.

Some, but not all. Darzie will just have to take his own time to become a legend, and if he is wise, he will do it in his own way, and not try to emulate me. I think that my life must have used up the luck of twenty gryphons.

Skan, the base-camp crew, and the other twenty-three rescuers had piled through the Gate in a record-setting time of their own. Although no people had been "pitched" through, all the supplies had been; hurled in a mass by a small army of Judeth's support crew. Not even during a resupply had Skan ever seen a Gate go up and down again so quickly.

Darzie flew home to receive his justly-earned accolades and the admiration of every unattached female in the city; the results of that would likely be more exhausting for him than the great deed itself. The Gate-mage and his helpers and guards remained to set up a base camp; the rest of them had shouldered packs and moved out under the beginnings of a rainstorm. No one had told them, however, that they were going to have to climb down a cliff to get into the forest where the children were lost. The three gryphons had shaken themselves dry and flown themselves down, but the humans had been forced to get to the bottom the hard way. That experience, in a worsening thunderstorm, had been exciting enough to age even the most hardened veteran in the lot. Absolutely everything they touched was slippery, either with mud, water, or substances they were probably better off not knowing about.

Once at the bottom, the three parties had formed up and gone their separate ways—and Skan had been amazed at how quickly the forest had swallowed the other two search parties. In an amazingly short period of time, he couldn't even hear the faintest *sound* of the others; only the steady drumming of the rain, and the whistles, chirps, and calls of creatures up in the tops of the trees.

Each day had been much like the one before it; only the navigator knew for certain that they were going in the right direction and not in circles. The only time that Skan was ever dry was just before he slept; the moment he poked his beak out of the tent he shared with Drake and the other mage, he was wet. Either fog condensed on his feathers and soaked into them, or he got soaked directly by the usual downpour.

Just at the moment, the downpour had him wet to the skin.

And he was depressed, though he would have been depressed without the rain.

How can we ever hope to find any sign of them! he asked himself, staring up at the endless sea of dripping leaves, and around at the dizzying procession of tree trunks on all sides, tangled with vines or shrouded with brush. There wasn't a sign of a game trail, and as for game itself—well, he'd had to feed himself by surprising some of the climbing creatures in the mornings, while he could still fly. *They could be within shouting distance of us, and we would never know it!* This forest was not only claustrophobic, it was uncannily enveloping. One of the fighters swore that he could actually *see* the plants growing, and Skan could find it in his heart to believe him.

How long would it take until vines and bushes covered anything left after a crash! A few days! A week! It had been a week since the children went missing, maybe more than a week; he lost track of time in here.

And they could have been down for three or four days before that. Gloomy thoughts; as gloomy as their surroundings. And yet he could not give up; as long as there was any chance, however minuscule, that they would find the children, he would search on. No matter what, he had to *know* what had happened to them. The uncertainty of not knowing was the worst part.

Drake looked like Skan felt; the *kestra'chern* was a grim-faced, taciturn, sodden, muddy mess most of the time. He spoke only when spoken to; tended to the minor injuries of the party without being asked, but offered nothing other than physical aid, which was utterly unlike him. He hiked with the rest of them, or dealt with camp chores, but it was obvious that his mind was not on what he was doing. It was out *there*, somewhere, and Skan wondered if Drake was trying to use his limited empathic ability as a different kind of north-needle, searching for the pole star of pain and distress hidden among the trunks and vines. With the blood tie between himself and his daughter, he should be especially sensitive to her. If she were alive, he might be able to find her where conventional methods were failing.

More power to him, he's never tried using it that way, but that doesn't mean it won't work. Skan only wished he had a similar ability he could exercise. As it was, he was mostly a beast of burden, and otherwise not much help. He couldn't track, he couldn't use much magic without depleting himself, and as for anything else—well, his other talents all involved flying. And he could only fly for a short time in the mornings.

Regin, the leader in their party, held up a hand, halting them, as he had done several times already that day. There didn't seem to be any reason for this behavior, and Skan was getting tired of it. Why stop and stand in the rain for no cause? The more ground they covered, the better chance they had of finding something. He nudged past Filix, and splashed his way up to the weather-beaten Silver Judeth had placed in charge.

"Regin, just what, exactly, are we waiting for?" he asked, none too politely.

Fortunately, the man ignored the sarcastic tone of his voice, and answered the question by pointing upward. Skan looked, just in time to see their scout Bern sliding down the trunk of a tree ahead of them with a speed that made Skan wince. "Bern's been looking for breaks in the trees ahead," Regin said, as Bern made a hand signal and strode off into the trees. "We figure, if the basket came down it had to make a hole; that hole'll still be there. He gets up into a tall tree and looks for holes all around, especially if he can see they're fresh. You might not believe it with all these clouds around, but if there's a break in the trees more light gets in, and you can see it from high enough in the canopy. That's what we're waiting on."

Bern reappeared a moment later, and rejoined the party, shaking his head. Skan didn't have to know the Silver's signals to read that one; *no holes.* He and Regin had a quick conference with the navigator, and the scout headed back off into the forest on a new bearing. The rest of the party followed in Bern's wake.

So far, there had been no sign of anything following or watching them, much less any attacks. Skan was beginning to think that Judeth's insistence on assuming there was a hostile entity in here was overreaction on her part. There hadn't been any signs that *anything* lived in here but wild animals; surely whatever had drained off all the mage-energy here must be a freak phenomenon. Maybe that was what had caught the two children...

Skan dropped back to his former place beside Amberdrake, but with a feeling of a little more hope, brought on by the knowledge that at least they weren't totally without a guide or a plan.

Drake still seemed sunk into himself, but he revived a bit when Skan returned and explained what the lead members were up to. "I've heard worse ideas," he said thoughtfully, wiping strands of sodden hair out of his eyes, and blinking away the rain. "It's not a gryphon eye view, but it's better than nothing."

Once again, the leader signaled a stop. Skan peered out and up through the curtains of rain, but he couldn't see anything. Wherever the scout was this time, not even Skan's excellent eyes could pick him out. "I have no idea how Bern is managing to climb in this weather, much less how he's doing it so quickly." Skan moved up a few feet and ducked around a tangle of vines, but the view was no better from the new vantage. "He must be as limber as one of those little furry climbers that Shalaman keeps at his Palace as pets. For all we know, this sort of place is where those come from."

Drake shrugged dismissively, as if the subject held no interest for him. "I—"

"*Hoy!*"

Skan looked up again, startled, and just caught sight of the tiny figure above, waving frantically. He seemed to be balanced on a thick tree limb, and clung to the trunk with only one hand. The other hand waved wildly, and then pointed.

"*Hoy!*" the call came again. "*Fresh break, that way!*"

Fresh break! The same thought occurred to all of them, but the Silvers were quicker to react than Skan or Drake. They broke into a trot, shoving their way through the vegetation, leaving the other two to belatedly stumble along in their wake.

Skan's heart raced, and not from the exertion. He longed to gallop on ahead, and probably *would* have, except that it was all he could do to keep up with the Silvers. And much to his embarrassment, just as he developed a sudden stitch in his side, Bern, the scout who had been up in the tree, burst through the underbrush behind them, overtook them, and plunged on to the head of the column.

Show-off.

Another shout echoed back through the trees, muffled by the falling rain. The words weren't distinguishable, but the tone said all Skan needed to know. There was excitement; but no grief, no shock.

They've found something. Something and not *someone*—or worse, bodies...

From some reserve he didn't know he had, he dredged up more

strength and speed, and turned his trot into a series of leaps that carried him through the underbrush until he broke through into the clearing beneath the break in the trees. He stumbled across the remains of a crude palisade of brush and onto clear ground.

A camp! That was his first elated thought; if the children had been able to build a camp, they could not have been too badly hurt. Then he looked at the *kind* of camp it was, and felt suddenly faint. This was no orderly camp; this was something patched together from the remains of wreckage and whatever could be scavenged. Regin looked up from his examination of the soggy remains of the basket as Skan halted inside the periphery of the clearing.

"They crashed here, all right." He pointed upward at the ragged gap in the canopy. "They're gone now, but they did hit here, hard enough to smash two sides of the basket. They both survived it, though I can't guess how. Maybe there was enough in the way of branches on the way down to slow their fall. The medical kit's gone, there's signs they both used it."

They were here. They were hurt. Now they're gone. But why! "Why aren't they still here?" he asked, speaking his bewilderment aloud.

"Now *that* is a good question." Regin poked through a confusion of articles that looked as if they had just been tossed there and left. "Standard advice is to stay with your wrecked craft if you have an accident. I'd guess they started to do that, were here for maybe two days, then something made them leave. It looks to me as if they left in a hurry, and yet I don't see any signs of a fight."

"They could have been frightened away," Amberdrake ventured. "Or—well, this isn't a very *good* camp—"

"It's a disaster of a camp, that's what it is," Regin corrected bluntly. "But if all I had was wreckage, *and* I was badly hurt, I probably wouldn't have been able to do much better. It's shelter, though, and that isn't quite enough. I wish I knew how much of their supplies got ruined, and how much they took with them." He straightened, and looked around, frowning. "There's no sign of a struggle, but no sign of game around here either. They might have run out of food, and it would be hard to hunt if they were hurt. There's no steady water source—"

Amberdrake coughed politely. "We're *under* a steady water-source," he pointed out.

Regin just shrugged. "We're taught not to count on rain. So—no game, no water, and an indefensible camp. Gryphons eat a lot; if their supplies were all trashed, they'd be good for about two days before they were garbage, unfit to eat. After that, they've *got* to find game, for Tadrith alone. My guess is, they stayed here just long enough to get back some strength, and headed back in the direction of home. They're probably putting up signals now." He grimaced. "I just hope their trail isn't too cold to follow—but on the other hand, if they headed directly west, we should stay pretty much on their trail. That's where I'd go, back to the river. It's a lot easier to fish if you're hurt than to hunt."

Skan groaned. "You mean we could have just followed the river and we probably would have found them?"

Regin grinned sourly. "That's exactly what I mean. But look on the bright side; now we *know* they're alive and they're probably all right."

Skan nodded; as Regin signaled to Bern to start hunting for a trail. But as Bern searched for signs, Skan couldn't help noticing a few things.

For one thing, the piles of discarded material had a curiously ordered-disordered look about them, as if they had been tossed everywhere, then gathered up and crudely examined, then sorted.

For another, there were *no* messages, notes, or anything of the sort to give a direction to any rescuers. Granted, the children might not have known whether anyone would find the camp, but shouldn't they have left *something?*

And last of all, there was no magic, none at all, left in any of the discarded equipment. So the surmise had been correct, something had drained all of the magic out of their gear, and from the signs of the crash, it had happened all at once. And yet none of the search-party gear had been affected—yet.

So what had done this in the first place? What had sorted through the remains of the camp?

And what had made the children flee into the unknown and trackless forest without even leaving a sign for searchers to follow?

Was the answer to the third question the same as the answer to the other two?

Tad entered the cave, sloshing through ankle-deep water at the entrance, carefully avoiding Blade's three fishing lines. Blade held up some of her catch, neatly strung, and he nodded appreciatively.

"Water's higher," he told her. "In places it covers the trail here."

That was to be expected, considering how much is falling out of the sky. "Well," Blade said with resignation. "At least we have a steady water supply—

and we don't have to leave the cave to fish anymore."

It had not stopped raining for more than a few marks in the middle of the night ever since they had arrived here. She'd wondered what the rainy season would be like; well, now she knew. The stream of water running down the middle of the cave had remained at about the same size, only its pace had quickened. The river had risen, and now it was perfectly possible for them to throw lines into the river itself without going past the mouth of the cave, with a reasonable expectation of catching something.

That was just as well, since they were now under siege, although they still had not seen their hunters clearly. The flitting shadows espied in the undergrowth had made it very clear that there was no getting back across the river without confronting them.

Tad nodded, spreading his good wing to dry it in front of the fire. He had gone out long enough to drag in every bit of driftwood he could find, and there was now a sizable store of it in the cave. He'd also hauled in things that would make a thick, black smoke, and they had a second, extremely nasty fire going now. It stood just to one side of the stream at the rear of the cave, putting a heavy smoke up the natural "chimney." Whether or not there was anyone likely to *see* it was a good question; this was not the kind of weather anything but a desperate or suicidal gryphon would fly in.

On the other hand—how desperate would Skandranon or Tad's twin be by now? Desperate enough to try?

Blade both hoped so and hoped that they would have more sense; their pursuers were getting bolder, and she hadn't particularly wanted Tad to go out this afternoon. The stalkers were still nothing more than menacing shadows, *but* she had seen them skulking through the underbrush on the other side of the river even by day, yesterday and this morning.

"I think *they* might try something tonight," Tad said, far too casually. "I know I was being watched all the time, and I just had that feeling, as if there was something out there that was frustrated and losing patience."

"I got the same feeling," Blade confessed. She hadn't enjoyed taking her shields down and making a tentative try at assessing what lay beyond the river, but it had felt necessary. In part, she had been hoping to sense a rescue party, but the cold and very alien wave of frustrated anger that met her tentative probe had made her shut herself up behind her shields and sit there shivering for a moment. "I—tried using that Empathic sense, and I got the same impression you did. They would like very much to get a chance at us."

She hoped that Tad wouldn't make too big a fuss about that confession; he'd been at her often enough to use *everything* she had. Now she'd finally given in to his urgings, she was not in the mood for an "I told you that was a good idea." She wasn't certain that it *was* a good idea; what if those things out there had been able to sense her just as she sensed them?

Then again, what would they learn? That she was hurt, and scared spitless of them? They already knew that.

Fortunately for him, Tad just nodded. "It's good to know that it's not just my own worry talking to me," he said, and sighed. "Now I don't feel so badly about setting all those traps."

"What—" she began. At that moment, one of her fishing lines went tight, and she turned her attention to it long enough to haul in her catch. But after re-baiting the hook and setting the line again, she returned to the subject.

"What other traps do you think would work?" she asked. "On our side of the river, that is. Where could we set more?"

Thus far, they hadn't had any luck with deadfalls like the one that had marked one of the shadows before. It was as if, having seen that particular sort of trap, the hunters now knew how to avoid it. Large snares hadn't worked either, but she hadn't really expected them to, since there was no way to conceal them. But perhaps now, with water over the trail, trip-wires *could* be hidden under the water.

"I tended to that during my 'walk' earlier. There's only one good place, really," he told her. "The river's gotten so deep and fast that there's only one place where I think they might try to cross—that's downstream, past where we crossed it when we first got here. I didn't set a trap right there, though—what I did was rig something that's harmless but looks just like the rockfall I rigged later on." He gryph-grinned at his own cleverness, and she could hardly blame him.

"So they'll see the harmless decoy, and then walk right into the rockfall?"

He nodded, looking very proud of himself. "It's a good big one, too. If they actually try coming after us, at least one of them is going to be seriously hurt or killed, unless they've got lightning reflexes and more luck than any one creature deserves to have."

"Just as long as you don't hurt someone coming to rescue us!" she warned. Yesterday she might have argued with him about the merits of setting something meant to kill rather than discourage—but that was before she had opened herself to the creatures across the river. She still might not know what they looked like, but now she knew what they were. Killers, plainly and simply, with a kind of cold intelligence about them that made her wish for one good bow, two good arms, and three dozen arrows. She would debate the merits of permitting such creatures the free run of their own territory some other time; and if they gave up and left her alone, she would be perfectly happy to leave *them* alone. But if they came after her or Tad, she would strike as efficiently and with the same deadly force as they would.

There was still the question of whether or not these creatures were the "hunting pack" of someone or something else; she did not have the ability to read thoughts, even if these creatures had anything like a thought. But she hadn't sensed anything else out there with them; all of the creatures had been of the same type, with a definite feeling of *pack* about them.

Which could simply mean that their master was off, lounging about at his ease somewhere, watching all of this in a scrying-mirror. That would certainly fit the profile of a sadistic Adept; she couldn't picture Ma'ar, for instance, subjecting himself to mud and pouring rain.

If that was so, if there was an Adept behind all this, and she ever got her hands on him…

"That wasn't the only trap I built," Tad continued proudly, oblivious to her dark thoughts. "I have trip-tangles under the water that will throw them into the stream, I balanced boulders to roll at a touch and trap feet and legs, and I put up some more snares. Between all that and the rock barricade we have across the front of the cave, I think we can feel a little safer."

"Just as long as we can continue fishing from in here," she corrected. "And as long as *you* can stand to live on fish."

"All I have to do is think about eating any more of that dried meat, and fish takes on a whole new spectrum of delight," he countered. "I'm learning to tell the difference between one fish and another, raw. Some are sweeter, one has more fat—"

And they all taste the same to me. "Fine, I believe you!" she interrupted hastily. "Listen, I wonder if we could rig some kind of a net or something to haul in driftwood as it comes down over the falls. There's a lot of stuff getting by us that we could really use."

There was nothing that Tad liked better than trying to invent a new way to do something, and the idea of a driftwood-net kept him happily occupied for some time. And more importantly, it kept him *zestfully* occupied; no matter how cheerful and energetic he seemed—or tried to appear—he was tired, and so was she. The ever-present roar of the falls would cover the sounds of anything approaching them, and most especially would cover the sounds of anything bold enough to try swimming across the river at this point. They both knew that, and she suspected that *he* was staying half-awake even through her watch, as she was staying through his. Not especially bright of either of them, but neither of them were able to help themselves. Their imaginations supplied the creatures out there with every kind of supernatural attribute, especially in the dark of the night. It was easier to dismiss such fears by daylight, except that she kept reminding herself that just because their hunters hadn't done something *yet*, that didn't mean they weren't capable of a particular action. It was hard to strike a balance between seeing threats that didn't exist and not being wary enough, especially when you didn't know everything the enemy could do.

"Not long until dark," Tad observed, after a long discussion of nets and draglines and other ways of catching runaway driftwood. He pointed his beak toward the river. She nodded; although it was difficult to keep track of time without the sun being visible, the light did seem to be fading. Another one of her lines went taut; this fish was a fighter, which probably meant that it was one of the kinds Tad liked best. *Any* fish seemed pretty tasteless to her, wrapped in wet clay to bake and without any herbs to season it with. She'd thought about using some of the peppery leaves just to give her food some spice, then thought better of the idea. Although they had not had any deleterious effect rubbed on the skin, there was no telling if they were poisonous if eaten. You could rub your skin all day with shadow-berries and not get anything worse than a purple stain, but eat a few and you would find yourself retching up your toenails...

She fought the fish to exhaustion and reeled it in, hand over hand, taking care not to tangle the line. That was enough for tonight; she pulled in the other lines, and by the time she was done, there was no doubt; it *was* darker out on the river.

She took the fish back behind the rock barrier to the fire, where Tad still basked. Each day they added a few more rocks, but they were rapidly approaching the point where they wouldn't be able to use river clay as mortar anymore. It just wasn't strong enough.

There was another advantage to this cave; no bugs. Enough smoke hung in the air from their signal-fire to discourage insects of all sorts. Her bites had finally begun to heal and didn't bother her too much anymore. In fact, if it hadn't been for those watchers out there, she would be feeling pretty pleased with the state of things. They had fire, excellent shelter, and plenty to eat, and sooner or later *someone* from White Gryphon or even Khimbata would see or smell the signal-fire, and they could go home. And in the meantime, while they were not comfortable, they were secure.

She took one of the big, sluggish bottom feeders from her string, gutted it, wrapped it in wet clay, put it in the firepit and raked coals and ashes over it. The rest she handed to Tad as they were.

No longer as famished as he was when they first got here; he ate them with gusto. And if he lacked fine table manners, she was not going to complain about the company. *I can think of worse people to be stranded with.*

"How's the wing?" she asked, as she did at least once a day.

"It doesn't hurt as much as it did yesterday, but I still don't want to unwrap it," he replied. "Whenever I move in an unusual way, it hurts."

In Tad-language, that meant "it hurts enough that my knees buckle and I almost pass out." She knew; she'd seen it happen. Tad was so stoic. He tried very hard to be cheerful, and it was likely for her benefit alone. By moving very carefully, she had managed to keep the same thing from happening to her, but that meant a lot of restriction on her movement.

If *only* she had two good hands—or he had two good wings! If either of them could manage to get to the top of the cliff, she was sure they could think of a way to bring the other up afterward. Up there, they wouldn't have to worry about pursuit anymore; if the hunters couldn't climb a tree, they sure as stars couldn't climb a cliff!

Might as well wish for three or four experienced Silvers with long-range bows, she thought grimly. *I have the feeling that there is something about all of this that I'm missing completely, something that should be obvious, but isn't. I just wish I had a clue to what it is.*

"Do you really think they're going to try something tonight?" she asked, more to fill the silence than because she thought he'd changed his mind.

For an answer, he nodded toward the cave entrance. "Rain's slackening early. The current isn't bad in that one wide, shallow spot. Not that hard to wade across, if you've got claws to hang onto the rock with. And we already know they do have claws."

She wondered if she ought to try opening herself up to them a second time, then decided against it. They could be waiting for her to do exactly that.

Silence fell between them again, and she just didn't feel right about breaking it with small talk. She checked her fish instead, and found the clay rock hard; that was a good indication that the fish inside was done, so she went ahead, raked it out of the coals, and broke it open. The skin and scales came away with the clay, leaving the steaming white flesh ready to eat without all the labor of skinning or scaling. She made fairly short work of it. As usual, it tasted like—not much of anything. Visceral memories of hot, fresh bread smothered in sweet butter, spicy meat and bean soup, and that incredible garlic and onion-laced fish stew that Jewel made taunted her until she drove them from her mind.

After that, they let the fire die down to coals and banked them with ashes to reduce the amount of light in the cave. If the hunters *were* going to try something tonight, there was no point in giving them the advantage of being able to see their targets clearly silhouetted.

She moved toward the barricade by edging along the side of the cave to keep herself in the shadows as much as possible. Tad did the same on the other side. The rain had indeed slackened off early for once; instead of illuminating a solid sheet of water in front of her nose, the intermittent flashes of lightning showed the other side of the river, with the churning, rolling water between.

There was no sign of anything *on* the other side of the river, and that wasn't good. Up until now, there had always been at least one lurking shadow in the bushes over there; now there was nothing. That was just one more indication that Tad's instincts and her reading of the hunters' impatience were both correct. They were going to try something tonight.

She glanced over at Tad; when lightning flickered, she could see his head and neck clearly, although he was so still he could have passed for a carving. He kept his eyelids lowered, so that not even a flicker of reflection would betray his presence to anything watching. His natural coloration blended beautifully with the stone behind him, and the lines of his feathers passed for rock-striations. It was amazing just how well camouflaged he was.

His ear-tufts lay flat along his head, but she knew better than to assume that meant he wasn't *listening;* the ear-tufts were largely decorative tufts of feathers that had nothing to do with his hearing. No, he was listening, all right. She wondered how much he could hear over the roar of the waterfall beside them.

But when the noise of his trap coming down thundered across the river, it was not at all subtle; in fact, it was loud enough that even the rock of the cave mouth vibrated for a moment. She jumped, her nerves stretched so tight that she went off-balance for a moment, and had to twist to catch herself with her good hand. She regained her balance quickly and moved to go outside. He shot out a claw, catching her good wrist and holding her where she was.

"Wait until morning," he advised, in a voice just loud enough for her to hear it over the roaring water. "That killed something. And they aren't going to be able to move the body."

"How much rock did you pile up?" she asked incredulously. How had he been able to pile up *anything* with only a pair of talons instead of hands, and with one bad wing?

"Enough," he replied, then chuckled with pardonable pride. "I didn't want to boast until I knew it had worked—but I used a little magic to undermine part of the cliff-face that was ready to go. I honestly didn't know how much was going to come down, I only knew it would be more than I could manage by stacking rocks."

"From the sound of it, a *lot* came down," she answered in awe. *What a brilliant application of a very tiny amount of magic!* "Did you feel it through the rock?"

He nodded. "There could be a problem, though," he added. "I might have given them a bridge, or half a bridge, across the river. There was that chance that the rock would fall that way."

But she shrugged philosophically. If he had, he had; it might well be worth it to find out just what, precisely, had been stalking them all this time.

"And the cliff could have come down by itself, doing the same thing," she answered. "There's no point in getting upset until we know. I doubt that we're going to see any further trouble out of them for tonight, anyway."

She was quite right; the rest of the night was as quiet as anyone could have wished, and with the first light they both went out to see what, if anything, Tad's trap had caught.

When they got to the rock-fall, they both saw that it had indeed come sliding down into the river, providing a bridge about halfway across, though some of it had already washed farther downstream. But as they neared it, and saw that the trap had caught a victim, Blade was just as puzzled by what was trapped there as she had been by the shadows.

There had been some effort made to free the creature; that much showed in the signs of digging and the obvious places where rubble and even large stones had been moved off the carcass. But it was not a carcass of any animal she recognized.

If a mage had taken a greyhound, crossed it with a serpent, and magnified it up to the size of a horse, he would have had something like this creature. A deep black in color, with shiny scaled skin just like a snake or a lizard, and a long neck, it had teeth sharper and more dagger-like than a dog's. Its head and those of its limbs not crushed by the fallen rock were also dog-like. They couldn't tell what color its eyes were; the exposed slit only showed an opaque white. She stared at it, trying to think if there was anything in all of the stories she'd heard that matched it.

But Tad had no such trouble putting a name to it.

"Wyrsa," Tad muttered, "But the color's all wrong…"

She turned her head to see that he was staring down at the thing, and he seemed certain of his identification. "What's a *wyrsa*?" she asked sharply.

He nudged the head with one cautious talon. "One of the old Adepts, before Ma'ar, made things like this to mimic *kyree* and called them *wyrsa*. He meant them for a more formidable guard dog or hunting pack. But they couldn't be controlled, and got loose from him—oh, a long time ago. Long before Ma'ar and the War. Aubri told me about hunting them; said that they ran wild in packs in some places." His eyes narrowed as he concentrated. "But the ones he talked about were smaller than this. They were white, and they had poison fangs and poison talons."

She bent down, carefully, and examined the mouth and the one exposed foot for poison sacs, checking to see if either talons or teeth were hollow. She finally got a couple of rocks and carefully broke off a long canine tooth and a talon, to examine them more closely. Finally she stood up with a grunt.

"I don't know what else is different on these beasts, but they aren't carrying anything poisonous," she told him, as he watched her actions dubiously. "Neither the teeth nor the claws are hollow, they have no channel to carry venom, and no venom sacs at the root to produce poison in the first place. Venom has to come from somewhere, Tad, and it has to get into the victim somehow, so unless this creature has poisonous saliva…"

"Aubri distinctly said that they were just like a poisonous snake," Tad insisted. "But the color is different on these things, and the size. *Something* must have changed them."

They exchanged a look. "A mage?" she asked. "Or the storms?" She might know venom, but *he* knew magic.

"The mage-storms, if anything at all," Tad said flatly. "If a mage had changed *wyrsa* deliberately, he wouldn't have taken out the venom, he'd have made it worse. I'll bet it was the mage-storms."

"I wouldn't bet against it." Blade knelt again to examine the head in detail; it was as long as her forearm, and most of it was jaw. "Tad, these things don't *need* venom to hurt you," she pointed out. "Look at those canines! They're as long as my finger, and the rest of the teeth are in proportion. What else do you know about *wyrsa*?"

He swallowed audibly. "Aubri said that the bigger the pack was, the smarter they acted, as if part of their intelligence was shared with every other one in the pack. He also said that they were unbelievably tenacious; if they got your scent, they'd track you for days—and if you killed or hurt one, they would track you forever. You'd never get rid of them until they killed you, or you killed them all."

"How comforting," she said dryly, standing up again. "And we've hurt one *and* killed one. I wish we'd known this before."

Tad just shuffled his feet, looking sheepish. "They might not connect us with the rockfall," he offered tentatively.

"Well, it's done and can't be undone." She caught something, a hint of movement out of the corner of her eye, and turned her head.

And froze. As if, now that she and Tad knew what the things were and the *wyrsa* saw no reason to hide, a group of six stood on the bank across from them. Snarling silently. Tad let out his breath in a hiss of surprise and dismay.

Then, before she could even blink or draw, a breath, they were gone. She hadn't even seen them move, but the only thing across from them now was a stand of bushes, the branches still quivering as the only sign that something had passed through them.

"I think we can safely assume that they *do* connect us with the rockfall," she replied, a chill climbing up her spine. "And I think we had better get back to the cave before they decide to try to cross the river again."

"Don't run," Tad cautioned, turning slowly and deliberately, and watching where he placed his feet. "Aubri said that would make them chase you, even if they hadn't been chasing you before."

She tried to hide how frightened she was, but the idea of six or more of those creatures coming at her in the dark was terrifying. "What charming and delightful creations," she replied sarcastically. "Anything else you'd like to tell me?"

He shook his head, spraying her with rain. "That's all I remember right now."

She concentrated on being very careful where she walked, for the rain was getting heavier and the rocks slicker. It would do no one any good if she slipped on these rocks and broke something else.

Well, no one but the wyrsa.

"Has *anyone* ever been able to control these things?" she asked. "Just out of curiosity."

The navigable part of the track narrowed. He gestured to her to precede him, which she did. If the *wyrsa* decided to cross the river, he did make a better rear guard than she did as soon as he got turned around. "Not that I've ever heard," he said from behind her. "I suppose that a really good mage could hold a coercion-spell on a few and make them attack a target he chose, but that would be about the limit of 'controlling' them. He wouldn't be able to stop them once they started, and he wouldn't be able to make them turn aside if they went after something he didn't choose. I certainly wouldn't count on controlling them."

"So at least we probably don't have to worry about some mage setting this pack on our trail after bringing us down?" she persisted, and stole a glance, over her shoulder at him. His feathers were plastered flat to his head, making his eyes look enormous.

"Well… not that I know of," he said hesitantly. "But these aren't the same *wyrsa* I know. They've been changed—maybe they are more tractable than the old kind. Maybe the poison was removed as a trade-off for some other powers, or it contributed to their uncontrollability. And a mage could have brought us down in their territory for amusement without *needing* to control them, just letting them do what they do."

"You're just full of good news today, aren't you?" she growled, then repented. *I shouldn't be taking our bad luck out on him.* "Never mind. I'm sorry. I'm just not exactly in a good frame of mind right now."

"Neither am I," he said softly, in a voice in which she could clearly hear his fear. "Neither am I."

Tad kept a watch all day as Blade concentrated on fishing. Once or twice a single, *wyrsa* showed itself, but the creatures made no move to cross the river to get at them.

Of course not. Night has always been their chosen hunting-time, and that should be especially true of wyrsa *with this new coloration.* Swift, silent, and incredibly fierce, he would not have wanted to face *one* of this new type, much less an entire pack.

I wonder how big the pack is, anyway! Six! Ten! More!

Were they the sport-offspring of a single female? *Wyrsa* were only supposed to litter once every two years, and they didn't whelp more than a couple at a time. *If these are all from twin offspring of a single litter, back when the storms changed them—how many could the pair have produced! Four years to maturity, then two pups every two years...*

There could be as few as the seven that they had seen, and as many as thirty or forty. The true answer was probably somewhere in between.

He and Blade ate in silence, then she banked the fire down to almost nothing while he took the first watch. As soon as it was fully dark, he eased several rocks into place to disguise his outline, then pressed himself up against the stone of the floor as flat as he could. He hoped he could convince them that he wasn't there, that nothing was watching them from the mouth of the cave. If he could lure one out into the open, out on the slippery rocks of the riverbank, he might be able to get off a very simple bit of magic. If he could stun one long enough to knock it into the river—well, here below the falls it *would* get sucked under to drown. Nothing but a fish could survive the swirling currents right at the foot of the falls. That would be one less *wyrsa* to contend with.

He didn't hear Blade so much as sense her; after a moment's hesitation, she touched his foot, then eased on up beside him.

"Couldn't sleep," she mouthed into his ear. He nodded. Stupid, maybe, but she had good cause for insomnia.

She pressed herself even farther down against the stone than he had; anything that spotted her from across the river would have to have better eyesight than an owl.

The rain is slacking off. That was both good and bad news; he had an idea that the *wyrsa* didn't much care for rain, and that they were averse to climbing around on rain-slick rocks. Like him, they had talons, but he didn't think that their feet were as flexible as his. Those talons could make walking on rock difficult.

On the other hand, as the rain thinned, that made visibility across the river better, especially if the lightning kept up without any rain falling.

Something moved on the bank across from his position. He froze, and he felt Blade hold her breath.

Lightning flickered, and the light fell on a sleek, black form, poised at the very edge of the bank, peering intently in their direction. And now he saw that the white glazing of the dead one's eyes had been the *real* color; the *wyrsa's* eyes were a dead, opaque corpse-white. The very look of them, as the creature peered across the river in their direction, made his skin crawl.

He readied his spell, hoarding his energies. No point in striking unless everything was perfect…

He willed the creature to remain, to lean forward more. Lightning flickered again; it was still there, still craning its neck, peering.

Stay… stay…

Now!

He unleashed the energy; saw the *wyrsa* start, its eyes widening—

But instead of dropping over, stunned, it *glowed* for a moment. Blade gasped, so Tad knew that she had seen it, too, as a feeling of faintness and disorientation that he had experienced once before came over him. He wheezed and blinked a few times, dazzled, refocusing on the *wyrsa.*

The *wyrsa* gaped its mouth, then, as if recharged, the creature made a tremendous leap into the underbrush that nothing wholly natural could have duplicated, and was gone.

And with it went the energy of the spell. If the *wyrsa* had deflected it, the energy would still *be* there, dissipating. It hadn't. The spell hadn't hit shields, and it hadn't been reflected.

It had been inhaled, absorbed completely. And what was more—an additional fraction of Tad's personal mage-energy had gotten pulled along behind it as if swept in a current.

"Oh. My. Gods," he breathed, feeling utterly stunned. *Now* he knew what had hit them, out there over the forest. And now he knew why the *wyrsa* had begun following them in the first place.

The *wyrsa* were the magic-thieves, not some renegade magic, not some natural phenomena. They ate magic, or absorbed it, and it made them stronger.

Blade shook him urgently. "What happened?" she hissed in his ear. "What's the matter? What's going on?"

He shook off his paralysis to explain it to her; she knew enough about magic and how it worked that he didn't have to explain things twice.

"Goddess." She lay there, just as stunned for a moment as he was. And then, in typical fashion, she summed up their entire position in a two sentences. "They have, our scent, they want our blood, and now they know that *you* produce magic on top of all that." She stared at him, aghast, her eyes wide. "We're going to have to kill them *all*, or we'll never get away from here!"

CHAPTER NINE

Tad hissed at the cluster of *wyrsa* across the river. The *wyrsa* all bared their formidable teeth and snarled back. They made no move to vanish this time, and Tad got the distinct impression that they were taunting him, daring him to throw something magical at them.

Well, of course they were. They had no reason to believe he had anything that could reach across the river except magic, and they *wanted* him to throw that.

Throw us more food, stupid gryphon! Throw us the very thing that makes us stronger, and make it tasty!

He'd already checked a couple of things in their supplies. The stone he had made into a mage-light and the firestarter he had reenergized were both inert again; if he'd needed any confirmation of the fact that these were the creatures that had sucked all of the mage-energy out of the carry-basket and everything in it—well, he had it.

I wonder what Father would do in a situation like this! But Skan would not likely have ever found himself in a situation like this one. Nor would his solution necessarily have been a good one... since it likely would have involved a great deal of semi-suicidal straight-on combat and high-energy physical action, which he was not in the least in any shape to perform. Skandranon was more known for his physicality than his raw inventiveness, when it came right down to facts.

Oh, Tad, not you, too—now you are even comparing yourself to your father. The real question is not what my father would do, the real question is, what am I going to do in this situation!

He raised himself up as high on his hindquarters as he could get, and gave a battle-scream, presenting the *wyrsa* with an open beak and a good view of his foreclaws. They stopped snarling and eyed him warily; with a little more respect, he thought. He hoped.

"I wish you wouldn't do that." Blade emerged from the back of the cave where she'd been napping, hair tousled and expression sour. "It's a bad way to wake up, thinking that your partner is about to engage in mortal combat."

"They don't seem to like the look of my claws," he replied, trying to sound apologetic without actually apologizing. "I was hoping I could intimidate them a little more."

He studied the knot of *wyrsa*, which never seemed to be still for more than an eyeblink. They were constantly moving, leaping, bending, twining in, around, over and under each other. He'd never seen creatures with so much energy and so much determination to use it. It was almost as if they physically couldn't stay still for more than a heartbeat.

They had come out of the underbrush about the time that the fog lifted and the rains began; if the rain bothered them now, it certainly wasn't possible to tell.

Then again, why should it bother them? That it did had been an assumption on his part, not a reflection of what was really going on in those narrow snake-like heads. They had neither fur nor feathers to get wet and matted down. The only effect that rain had on their scales was to make them shiny.

"On first blush, I'd say they don't look very intimidated," Blade pointed out. But her brows knitted as she watched the *wyrsa* move, and her eyes narrowed in concentration. "On the other hand—that's a very effective defensive strategy, isn't it?"

Tad gazed at the stalkers' glistening hides, the way it moved and flashed. The patterns they moved in knotted and reknotted, like a decorative interlace. "Is it? But it bunches them up all in one place; shouldn't that make it easier to hit one?" He watched them carefully, then suddenly shook himself as he realized that the creatures' constant movement was making him go into a trance! He glanced over at Blade. She lifted an eyebrow and nodded.

"Not bad if you can put your attacker to sleep, hmm?" she asked, then smiled slyly, which put Tad instantly on the alert. He'd seen that smile before, and he knew what it meant. Trouble, usually for someone else. "Well, let's see if we can take advantage of their bit of cleverness, shall we? Stay there and look impressive, why don't you? I need something to keep them distracted."

She retreated into the cave. The *wyrsa* continued their hypnotic weaving as Tad watched them, this time prepared to keep from falling under their spell, glancing away at every mental count of ten.

"Duck," came the calm order from behind him.

He dropped to the floor, and a heavy lead shot *zinged* over him, through the space where his head had been. Across the stream, one of the *wyrsa* squalled and bit the one nearest it. The second retaliated, and Tad had the impression that it looked both surprised and offended at the "unprovoked" attack. The weaving knot was becoming unraveled as the two offended parties snapped and hissed at one another.

Another lead shot followed quickly, and a third *wyrsa* hissed and joined what was becoming a melee. That seemed to be more provocation than the others could resist, and the knot became a tumbling tangle of quarreling *wyrsa*, with nothing graceful, coordinated, or hypnotic about it. Now most of the knot was involved in the fight, except for a loner who extricated itself from the snarling, hissing pack. This creature backed up slowly, eying the others with what was clearly surprise, and Blade's third shot *thudded* right into its head. It dropped in its tracks, stunned, while the rest of the group continued to squabble, squall, and bite.

Blade stepped back into the front of the cave and watched the *wyrsa* with satisfaction. "I wondered just how cohesive that pack was. I also wonder how long it's going to take them to associate a distance-weapon with us; I doubt that they've ever seen or experienced one before."

At just that moment, another one of the creatures emerged from the bushes, and uttered a cry that was part hiss, part deep-throated growl. The reaction to this was remarkable and immediate; the others stopped fighting, instantly, and dropped to the ground, groveling in submission. The new *wyrsa* ignored them, going instead to the one that Blade had brought down, sniffing at it, then nipping its hindquarters to bring it groggily to its feet.

"I'd say the pack-leader just arrived," Tad said.

The new *wyrsa* swung its head around as he spoke, and glared at him from across the river. The dead-white eyes skewered him, holding him in place entirely against his will, while the *wyrsa's* lip lifted in a silent snarl. The eyes glowed faintly, and his thoughts slowed to a sluggish crawl.

Tad felt exactly like a bird caught within striking distance of a snake; unable to move even to save his own life. It was a horrible feeling of cold dread, one that made his extremities feel icy. At just that moment, Blade stepped between them, and leveled a malevolent glare of her own at the pack-leader. In a calm, clear voice, she suggested that the *wyrsa* in question could do several highly improbable, athletically difficult, and possibly biologically impractical things involving its own mother, a few household implements, and a dead fish.

Tad blinked as his mind came back to life again when the *wyrsa* took its eyes off him. He'd had no idea Blade's education had been *that* liberal!

The *wyrsa* might not have understood the words, but the tone was unmistakable. It reared back as if it were going to accept the implied challenge by leaping across the river—or leaping into it and swimming across—and Blade let another stone fly from her sling.

This one cracked the pack-leader across the muzzle, breaking a tooth with a wet *snap*. The creature made that strange noise of hiss and yelp that Tad had heard the night one got caught in his deadfall. It whirled and turned on the others, driving them away in front of it with a ragged squeal, and a heartbeat later, the riverbank was empty.

Blade tucked her sling back into her pocket, and rubbed her bad shoulder thoughtfully. "I don't know if that was a good idea, or a bad one. We aren't going to be able to turn them against each other again. But at least they know now that we have something that can hit them from a distance besides magic."

"And you certainly made an impression on the leader," Tad observed, cocking his head to one side.

She smiled faintly. "Just making it clear which of us is the meanest bitch in the valley," she replied lightly. "Or hadn't you noticed the leader was female?"

"Uh, actually, no. I hadn't." He felt his nares flush with chagrin at being so caught in the creature's spell that he had completely missed something so obvious. "She's really not my type."

Her grin widened. "Makes me wonder if the reason she's keeping the pack here has less to do with the fact that we killed one of her pups, than it does with her infatuation with you. Or rather, with your magnificent... physique." Her eyes twinkled wickedly.

Whether or not she realizes it, she's definitely recovering. But I wonder if I ought to break something else, just for the sake of a little peace!

He coughed. "I think not," he replied, flushing further with embarrassment.

"Oh, no?" But Blade let it drop; this was hardly the time and place to skewer him with further wit, although when they got out of this, he had the feeling that she would *not* have forgotten this incident or her own implications. "You know," she continued, "if we had even a chance of picking her off, the pack might lose its cohesiveness. At the very least, they'd be spending as much time squabbling over the leadership position as stalking us."

He scratched the side of his head thoughtfully. She had a good point. "We have to be able to see them to pick one particular *wyrsa*," he pointed out. "And traps and rockfalls are likely to get the least experienced, not the most. But it does account for why they're being so persistent and tenacious."

"Uh-huh. We got one of her babies, probably." Blade sank down on the stone floor of the cave, and watched the underbrush across the river. He turned his attention in that direction himself, and was rewarded by the slight movement of a bit of brush. Since there wasn't a breeze at the moment, he concentrated on that spot, and was able to make out a flash of dark, shiny hide before the creature moved again.

"Interesting." Blade chewed on a nail, and regarded the brush with narrowed eyes. "I don't think we're going to see them out in the open again. They learn quickly."

That quickly! That was impressive; but he called to mind what Aubri had told him about the pack's collective intelligence. If there were many more than just the knot that he'd seen, it would mean that as a group, the pack might be as smart as a makaar, and that was pretty smart.

Regardless of what Father claims.

The bushes moved again, and he caught another glimpse of slick black hide. *A cross of greyhound and snake… I can't imagine anything more bizarre. But then, Blade would tell me that my imagination isn't very good. I wonder what kind of vision they get out of those strange eyes! Can they see in the dark! Could that white film be a screen they pull across their eyes to protect them from daylight! Can they actually "see" magic! Or scent it!*

"I wonder what we look like to them," he said, musing aloud. Blade shot him a sharp glance.

"I suppose I looked fairly harmless until I whipped out my sling," she replied. "But I suspect that *you* look like a movable feast. After all, you *are* burdened with a magical nature, and it might be rather obvious to them."

"You mean—they might be more interested in me than you as prey?" he choked. She nodded.

"Probably as someone they'd want to keep alive a while, so they could continue to feed on your magic as it rebuilt. They're probably bright enough for that."

He hadn't thought about that.

It did not make him feel any better.

Amberdrake stood beside the leader of their party and wrung more water out of a braid of hair. He waited for the fellow to say something enlightening. Fog wreathed around them both, and shrouded everything more than a few paces away in impenetrable whiteness.

"I wish I knew what was going on here," Regin muttered, staring at the pair of soggy decoys wedged up in the fork of a tree. "There's no trail from the camp, which looks as if the Silvers were trying to conceal their backtrail. But there isn't a sign of anything hunting them, either. And now—we find this." The ground beneath the tree was torn up, as was the bark of the lower trunk, but there was no blood. There *was* a deadfall rigged of wood that had been tripped, but there was no sign that anything had been caught in it. They might have passed the site by, thinking that it was just a place where some large forest creature had been marking his territory.

Except that there was a human-shaped decoy and a gryphon-shaped decoy wedged high in a tree.

That isn't very enlightening.

"They might have run into some sort of large predator," Drake pointed out. "Just because we didn't see any sign of a hunter, that doesn't mean they weren't being trailed. That would account for why they tried not to leave a trail. Maybe that's even the reason why they left their camp in the first place."

This was the first sign of the children that any of them had come across in their trek toward the river. Amberdrake took it as a good omen; it certainly showed that the duo had gotten this far, so their own party was certainly on the right track. And it showed that they were in good enough health to rig something like this.

"Maybe. But why decoys?" Regin paced carefully around the trunk of the tree, examining it on all sides. "Most forest predators hunt with their noses, and even in this rain, the trail from here to wherever they *did* spend the night would be fresh enough to follow. I wonder what we can learn from this."

"I don't know; I'm not a hunter," Amberdrake admitted, and let it go at that.

Skan didn't, however. "Whatever tore this place up is an animal—or at least, it doesn't use weapons or tools," he pointed out. "It might just be that the—that Blade and Tad wandered into its territory, and they built the decoys to keep it occupied while *they* went on their way."

"Maybe." Regin shook his head. "Whatever it was, I don't recognize the marks, but that doesn't surprise me. I haven't recognized much in this benighted forest since we got into it. And I'm beginning to wonder how anything survives here without gills."

With that, he shrugged, heading off into the forest in the direction of the river. Amberdrake followed him, but Skan lingered a moment before hurrying to catch up lest he get left behind and lost in the fog.

"I don't like it," he muttered fretfully as he reached Drake's side. "I just don't like it. It didn't look right back there, but I can't put my finger on why."

"I don't know enough about hunting animals to be of any help," Drake replied bluntly. He kept telling himself that the children were— must be—still fine. That no matter how impressive the signs these unknown creatures had left were, the children had obviously escaped their jaws. "All I know is that whatever made those marks must be the size of a horse, and if I were being chased by something that size, I probably wouldn't be on the ground at night. Maybe they put the decoys up one tree and then climbed over to another to spend the night."

Unless, of course, they're too hurt to climb trees. But in that case, how did the decoys get up in one?

"Illusion!" Skan said suddenly, his head coming up with a jerk. "That's it! There's no illusion and no traces of one on those decoys. Tad's not a powerful mage, but he's good enough to cast an illusion, and if I were building a decoy I'd want to make it look as much like me as possible! So why didn't he put an illusion on it?"

"Because he couldn't," Drake said flatly. "If mage-energy got sucked out of the basket and everything else, it could have gotten sucked out of him, and it might not have built up enough yet for him to do anything."

"Oh." Skan was taken a bit aback, but finally nodded his acceptance of Drake's explanation. Amberdrake was just as glad, because he could think of another.

Tad can't work a simple magic like an illusion because he's hurt too badly.

On the other hand, those decoys were soggy enough to have been here for a couple of days, so that meant that the children made fairly good progress for two people trying to hide their backtrail, So that in turn meant that they couldn't have been hurt too badly. Didn't it?

He also didn't want to think about how having mage-energy drained from him might affect Tad in other, more subtle ways. Would it be like a slowly-draining wound? Would it affect his ability to work magic at all? What if he simply was no longer a mage anymore? Gryphons were inherently magical for good reasons, and Urtho would not have designed them so otherwise. Although the Mage of Silence had made many mistakes, the gryphons were considered his masterpieces. Magic collected in their bodies with every breath and with every stroke of the wings. It stabilized their life systems, cleaned their organs, helped them fly. Amberdrake had never heard of what would happen if a gryphon were deprived of mage-energy completely for an extended amount of time; would it be like fatigue poisoning, or gout, or something even more insidious, like a mental imbalance?

The rescue party was moving along in a tightly-bunched group to keep from getting separated in the mist. *We're on the right track at least; the children certainly came this way,* Amberdrake reminded himself. *They're moving right along, thinking, planning. If they're in trouble, the best place for them is the river. There's food there that's easy to catch, and maybe caves in the cliffs. They're doing all the right things, especially if they're having to deal with large predators.*

Maybe this was why the rescuers hadn't found much in the way of large game. They'd tried to send on their findings by teleson, so that the other two parties out searching knew to turn back to the river. The mage Filix *thought* he'd gotten everything through clearly, but without local mage-energy to draw on, he couldn't be certain that all the details had made it over. Still, whether the children went north or south when they encountered the river, *someone* should run into them now. Their own party was going to try to the north, mostly because they did know for certain that Ikala's would be coming up from below them, also heading north.

This damned fog. It makes me more nervous than the rain! If—when—we all get out of this, I am never leaving the city again, I swear it. Not unless it's to visit another city. So far as I'm concerned, you can take the "wilderness experience" and bury it in a hole. He'd never forgotten the hardships of the trek to White Gryphon, and he had been all too well aware of what this mission would involve. He thought he'd been prepared for it. *Except for one thing; I'd forgotten that now I'm not as limber as I used to be for this sort of thing. Judeth and Aubri certainly didn't volunteer to traipse through the woods, and now I see why. They probably think I'm a fool, forcing myself to go along on this rescue, trying to do a young man's job. Maybe letting me go was Judeth's way of getting revenge upon me for threatening her!*

But Blade wasn't Judeth's daughter, nor was Tad Aubri's son.

No, I'd rather be out here. At least I know that I'm doing something this way. Zhaneel and Winterhart must feel the same, or they wouldn't have insisted on coming either.

But the fog was doing more than just getting on his nerves; he kept thinking that he was seeing shadows flitting alongside them, out there. He kept feeling eyes on him, and getting glimpses of skulking shapes out of the corner of his eye. It was all nonsense, of course, and just his nerves getting the better of him, but—

"Drake," Skan whispered carefully, "we're being paced. I don't know by what, but there's something out there. I can taste it in the fog, and I've seen a couple of shadows moving."

"You're sure?" That was Regin, who had signaled for a halt and dropped back when he heard Skan whispering. "Bern thought he might be seeing something, too—"

"Then count me as three, because I saw large shadows moving out there and behind us," Drake said firmly. "Could it be whatever tore up the ground back there?"

"If it is, I don't want to goad it into attacking us in this fog," Regin replied. "Though I doubt it will as long as we look confident."

"Most big hunters won't mess with a group," Bern confirmed, nodding. "They like single prey, not a pack."

Drake must have looked skeptical, because Regin thumped him on the back in what was probably supposed to be an expression of hearty reassurance. It drove the breath out of him and staggered him a pace.

"There's too many of us for it to want to contend with—" Regin pointed out with confidence, "And *we* aren't hurt. I don't care if it paces us, as long as it doesn't come after us, and it won't. I'm sure of it."

Amberdrake got his breath again, and shrugged. "You're the leader," he said, keeping his uncertainty to himself.

Regin grinned, as if to say, "That's right, I am," but wisely kept his response to a grin and waved them on again.

Drake continued to feel the eyes on his back, and kept thinking about beings the size of a horse with talons to match—the kinds of claws that had torn up the earth to the depth of his hand. Would a party of seven humans and one gryphon look all *that* formidable to something like that? And what if there was more than one of those things out there? The way the ground had been dug up certainly suggested that there were several.

"You won't like this," Skan gryphon-whispered, which was as subtle and quiet as a human's normal speaking voice. The gryphon glanced from side to side apprehensively. "Drake, I think we've been surrounded."

All the muscles in Amberdrake's neck went tight, and he shivered reflexively. He no longer trusted Regin's self-confidence in the least.

At just that moment, Regin signaled another halt, and Bern took him aside to whisper something into his ear.

The leader looked straight at Skan. "Bern says we're surrounded. Are we?"

"I think so," Skan said flatly. "And I don't think whatever it is out there is just curious. I also don't think it's going to let us get much farther without a fight."

Regin's face darkened, as if Skan had challenged him, but he turned his eyes to the shrouding fog before replying. "The General always says the best defense is a good offense," he replied in a growl. "But there's no point in lobbing arrows against things we can't see. We'll lose ammunition without impressing them."

"The rains are going to begin as soon as the fog lifts, sir," Bern pointed out. "We *still* won't be able to see what's out there, and you can't shoot with a wet bowstring."

Regin leveled his gaze on Filix next. "Is there something you can do to find out what's following us? Maybe scare it away? I don't want to waste time better spent looking for Silverblade and Tadrith."

The mage shrugged. "Maybe. I can try. The best thing would be to try to stun one so that we can see what it looks like. I don't have to see something to stun it, I just have to know in general where it is."

The leader spread his hands, indicating his full permission. "You're the mage. Try it, see what happens."

Amberdrake opened his mouth to object, but closed it again; after all, what did he know? Nothing about hunting, predators, or being stalked. If their stalkers were only curious after all, stunning one wouldn't hurt them; if they were thinking about making a meal of the rescuers, well, having one of their lot fall over without a mark on him should make them back off for a while. At least, it certainly seemed to him that it should work out that way. And by the time the hunters regained their courage, the rescue party would probably be long gone.

Skan opened his beak, and Amberdrake thought he was going to object as well, but it was too late. Filix had already spotted something, or thought he had, and had unleashed the spell.

The result was not what any of them had expected.

A dark shadow in the fog glowed suddenly—Amberdrake got an odd, unsettling feeling in the pit of his stomach—and Filix and Skan cursed together with heartfelt fluency.

"What?" Regin snapped, looking from one to the other: *"What!"*

"It ate my spell—" Filix began, but Skan interrupted him waving the teleson he'd been carrying around his neck.

"It ate the teleson!" the gryphon roared. "Damn! Whatever's out there is what pulled Blade and Tad down, and you just fed it everything it wanted!"

* * *

Skan was just glad that they had alerted the other parties that they had finally found signs of the missing children *before* the teleson became a pretty piece of junk. By the time they camped that night, it was evident that, not only had the creatures out there "eaten" the teleson—or rather, drained away all of its mage-energy—but they'd "eaten" the energy from every other magical device the party had.

Why they'd waited so long to do so was a matter of conjecture at this point. Maybe they'd been screwing up their courage to do so; maybe they just been biding their time until they had a certain number of their lot in place. Maybe the things were staying in hiding until something was thrown at them, as a form of cover.

"It wasn't my fault!" Filix kept protesting. "How was I going to know?"

He couldn't have known that some bizarre animals were the cause of the trouble, of course, but since they *had* known there was something out here that ate magic, it seemed to Skan that lobbing spells around indiscriminately was obviously a bad idea. He had been about to say just that when Filix had lobbed the first one.

Well, what the search party had to deal with now were the results. In the short term, that meant the tents had to be put up by hand, and using freshly-cut poles and ropes; fires had to be started with the old-fashioned firestriker, and any number of other problems, both inconvenient and possibly hazardous, suddenly arose to confront them.

In the long term—having gotten a taste, the strange and possibly hostile creatures that had stalked them through the fog and rain might now be looking for a meal.

The tents were keeping the rain out, but were not precisely dry anymore. They weren't keeping bugs out, either. Skan wondered how long it would take until it occurred to Regin that the waterproofing and bug-protections on their rations might also have been magical. Serve him right if he had to eat soggy, weevil-ridden ration-bread!

The two tents shared a canvas "porch;" it lacked a canvas floor and one wall, but gave protection to their fire. They gathered in the two tents on either side of the fire, with the flaps tied back. Regin called them for a conference as the light began to dim in the forest outside. Rain drummed down on the canvas, but Regin had pitched his voice to carry over it.

"We're doing fine," Regin decreed, as they sat, crowded into the two tents meant for a total of four, not eight; at least this way they all had space to get in out of the wet, even if it was not completely dry beneath the canvas. "We have nothing to worry about. Canvas still keeps out rain, wood still burns, and we still have the north-needle, which is, thank the gods, *not* magical. We've found the river, and it's only a matter of time before we either run into the missing Silvers or one of the other parties does. If they do, they'll try and notify us, realize what happened when they don't get our teleson, and come fetch us. If we find them first, we'll just backtrack along the river until we meet one of the other parties, then get back to the base camp. Not a problem."

Skan was hardly in agreement with that sentiment, but Regin *was* the leader, and it was poor form to undermine confidence in your leader when it was most needed by others.

This is not a wartime situation. And now we know that the magic stealers are just some kind of strange wild animal, not an enemy force. If we're just careful, we should get out of this intact and with the children. At least, that was what he was trying to tell himself.

"For tonight, I want a double watch set; four and four, split the night, a mage in each of the two watches." Regin looked around for volunteers for the first watch, and got his four without Skan or Drake needing to put up a hand.

Skan did not intend to volunteer, but Filix seemed so eager to make up for the mistake that cost them all their magic, that it looked as if the younger mage had beaten the gryphon to volunteering. Skan wondered what the young man thought he was volunteering *for;* he was hardly a fighter, and the idea of throwing magic at something that *ate* magic did not appeal to the gryphon.

I am not lobbing a single spell around until we lose these menaces, he resolved. *If these things eat magic, it stands to reason that magic makes them stronger. And the stronger they are, the more likely they are to attack us physically.*

Well, Filix could use a bow, at least, even if he didn't possess a gryphon's natural weaponry.

He might do all right at that—provided he thinks before he acts. He wanted to take Filix aside and caution him, but an earlier attempt had not been very successful. Filix clearly thought that Skan was overreacting to the situation. One of the biggest problems with the younger mages— youngsters who had come along after the Cataclysm—was that they thought magic could fix everything. They had yet to learn that magic was nothing more than another tool, and one that you *could* do without if you had to. Maybe things wouldn't be as convenient without it, but so what? *Snowstar ought to force them to spend a year* not *using magic.*

Regin nodded with satisfaction at his volunteers. "Right. Close up the watch right around the camp; there's no point in guarding a big perimeter tonight. If you get a clear shot, take it; maybe if we make things unpleasant enough for whatever is out there, it'll get discouraged and leave us alone."

And maybe you'll provoke them into an attack! Skan reminded himself that he was *not* the leader and kept his beak clamped tightly shut on his own objections. But he resolved to sleep with himself between Drake and the tent wall, and to do so lightly.

Somehow he managed to invoke most of the old battle reflexes, get himself charged up to the point where nerves would do instead of sleep, and laid himself warily down to rest with one eye and ear open. In his opinion, Regin was taking this all far too casually, and was far too certain that they were "only" dealing with a peculiar form of wild animal. And he was so smug about the fact that he had brought nonmagical backups to virtually every magical piece of equipment except the teleson that Skan wanted to smack him into good sense again.

Bringing backups isn't the point! he seethed, as he positioned himself to best protect Drake in an attack. *The fact that there is something out here that can eat magic and is clearly hostile*—that's *the point! What good are our backups going to do if these things decide that they want more than just a taste of us from a distance?*

The rains slowed, then stopped. The fire died, leaving them with nothing but glowing coals for a source of light. Just as the camp quieted down for the night, the "wild animals" proved that they were not intimidated by a party of eight.

Skan came awake all at once with the sound of someone falling to the ground, followed by cursing and a bowstring snapping practically in his ear. But it wasn't Filix taking the shot—the mage was lying on the ground, just outside the canvas wall nearest Skan, gasping for breath.

The other three humans not on watch scrambled up, but Skan was already on his feet, ready for trouble. A moment later, Regin hauled the half-conscious mage into the tent. "What happened?" Skan asked harshly, as the other two fighters scrambled outside, leaving himself, Regin, and Drake alone with the disabled mage. Amberdrake went to the young mage's side immediately and began examining him.

The leader shook his head. "I don't know," the young man admitted, looking pale and confused in the light from the single lamp that Drake had lit. "He saw something out there, and I think he was going to work some magic on it—he muttered something about his shields—and then he just fell over. I took a shot at something moving, but I don't think I hit it."

"He's been drained," Amberdrake said flatly, looking up, with his hand still on Filix's forehead. "I saw this once or twice in the war, when mages overextended themselves."

I remember that; it was on the orders of an incompetent commander.

"The only difference is that this time, Filix didn't over-extend himself, he was drained to nothing by means of the spell he cast," Drake continued. "My guess is that those creatures out there were able to use his previous magic to get into his shield-castings, and then just pulled everything he had out of him, the way they pulled the mage-energy out of the teleson. And probably Tadrith and Silverblade's basket as well."

"Stupid son of—" Regin bit off what he was going to say. "Is he going to be all right?"

"Maybe. Probably. As long as he doesn't give whatever is out there another chance to drain him." Drake looked angry and a little disgusted, and Skan didn't blame him. "I'll do what I can for him, but you should be aware that it isn't much. Lady Cinnabar herself couldn't do much for something like this. What he needs is rest, rest, and more rest. We're going to have to carry him for the next few days. He probably won't even regain consciousness until tomorrow, and his head will hurt worse than it ever has in his life for several days."

"Well, we'll go short one this shift." Regin shook his head again. "Stupid—" He glanced at Skan, who drew himself up with dignity.

"I know better than to try anything magical," he retorted to the unspoken rebuke. "I'll use a more direct method of defending this camp, if I have to use anything."

Stupid fool thought that if he cast shields, he'd he safe against this, Skan fumed. *Never bothered to remember that magical shields are themselves magical, did he! And since shields are spun out from your own power, they are traceable directly back into your own mage-energies. He probably didn't think it was necessary to cast anything more complicated, and figured his shields would block anything coming in…*

The result had clearly been immediate, and had certainly been predictable.

He pulled Drake back into the tent they had been trying to sleep in. "We'll stay here," he told Amberdrake. "Leave him in the other tent with Regin."

"With just one man to watch him?" Amberdrake asked. Skan shook his head.

"Does it matter?" he replied. "There's nothing you can do for him, and if something comes charging in here, we're going to have more important things to think about than defending an unconscious mage."

There it was; hard, cruel, war-truths. This *was* a war, whether or not Regin realized it yet.

Evidently Drake did; he grimaced, but didn't protest any further. He remembered. He knew that the two of them must make their priority that of finding the children. And he knew all about cutting losses.

Which was just as well, because a few moments later, the second attack came.

There was no warning. They hadn't even blown out the lantern or tried to lie down again. The rain must have covered any sounds of approach, for there certainly was nothing outside the tent walls to indicate anything was wrong. All that Skan knew was that Bern shouted, then screamed, and something dark came ripping through the canvas of the tent, knocking over the lantern in the process, plunging them into darkness until the spilled oil flared up. He knocked Drake to the ground and stood over him, slashing at whatever came near in the darkness.

He ignored anything outside the tent to the point where it simply didn't exist for him, concentrating fiercely on tiny currents of air, sounds, movement, and what little he could see reflecting from the burning spilled oil. His talons connected several times with something that felt like snakeskin, tearing through it to the flesh beneath, and he clenched any time he was able to, so that he might rend away a chunk of meat. But his opponents uttered nothing more than a hiss, and they dashed away through the double rents in the tent canvas as if his fierce opposition surprised them. The fight couldn't have lasted for very long, for not only was he not tired, he hadn't even warmed up to full fighting speed when the attacks ceased, and the attackers vanished, silent shadows sliding between the raindrops.

He stood over Drake a while longer; the *kestra'chern* had the good sense to stay put and not move the entire time. When Amberdrake finally moved, it was to pat the flame out with the edge of a bedroll and then right the lantern.

"Are they gone?" came the voice from between his feet.

"I think so," Skan replied, shaking his head to refocus himself. Only then did he hear the moans of wounded, and the sound of Bern calling his name.

"We're here!" Drake answered for him as he relit the lantern with a smoldering corner of the bedroll. "We're all right, I think."

"That's more than the rest of us can say," the scout replied grimly, wheezing and coughing. "Can you get out here and help me? If I let go of this rag around my leg, I'm going to bleed myself out."

Drake swore, scrambled for the medical kit in the darkness, and pushed through the ruined tent wall. Skan followed slowly.

When the lantern had been relit so that Drake could see to treat wounds, and everyone had been accounted for, they discovered that Regin and Filix had been killed by more of the things. They had probably died instantly, or nearly so. Amberdrake reached for the bodies, and could only locate so many pieces. *At the very least, they got the mercy of a quick death.* There wasn't much left of them. Blood was spattered everywhere, and it was difficult to tell what part belonged to whom.

He left the tent quickly, reminded all too forcefully of some of Hadanelith's victims.

And of Ma'ar's.

I'm supposed to be hardened to this sort of thing, but maybe I've just seen too much death, too much suffering. Maybe I am not as tough as I thought I was, or wish I could be, even after all this time. It was one thing to think about cutting losses— another thing to lose people like this. We were caught unprepared, despite my hoped-for lessons of experience.

Amberdrake remained for a few moments longer, and when he came out, he surprised Skan by the thoughtful look of concentration he wore. Finally, as the other men bundled the two bodies hastily in the remains of the tent, he drew Skan aside.

"Are these things animals, or not?" he asked.

Skan blinked. "They certainly fought like it," he replied cautiously. "*Extremely* efficient predators. They didn't have weapons, just talons and teeth, and... and speed. I don't think I've ever seen anything that fast since the last makaar died. *Fierce* predators; no wonder we haven't seen much game, and all of it small. They must have emptied out the forest around here, of ground-based game at least." He shook his head. "We should have figured that out, and assumed they'd attack us for food. They must be half-mad with hunger by now; they can't live long on rabbits, snakes and bugs, not as big as they are."

Drake nodded, as if he had expected Skan to say that. "In that case, tell me this; why didn't they drag their prey off with them to eat? Why didn't they try and kill more of us?"

Skan opened his beak to reply, and shut it with a *click*.

Why didn't they, if they're just *big hunters with an incidental ability to eat mage-energy!*

"Maybe we don't taste good?" he suggested lamely.

"Maybe. But that hasn't stopped lions from becoming maneaters when they're famished. Shalaman showed us that, remember." Amberdrake chewed on his lower lip a moment. "I have a feeling... that these things are planning something. And that they don't intend to let us get away. Skan, they're a lot worse than they seem."

"They seem bad enough already to me," Skan grumbled, "But I see your point."

He didn't have time to think much more about it, however, for Bern, as acting leader, decreed that there would be no more rest that night.

They spent the rest of the dark hours in the open, sitting in a circle with their backs together, facing the forest with weapons in hand.

It was a long, cold, and terrifying night. Every time a drop of water fell from a leaf, someone started. Every time a shadow seemed to move, they all got ready to defend their lives. Skan had never spent a night as frightening as this one, not even during the war, and he prayed no one else would ever have to, either. Stelvi Pass had been a summer day compared to this unending, wet, cold waiting. He didn't know how Amberdrake was managing to bear up; it was bad enough to endure this knowing that he *could,* if there was no other choice, escape by flying into the treetops. Even in a fight, he could defend himself against fairly stiff odds. But Drake couldn't escape and he wasn't a fighter, and in his place, Skan knew he'd have been babbling with fear.

As soon as there was any light at all beneath the trees, Bern ordered them to move out, down to the river that they had heard all night long. The flood-swollen river, which roared at their feet, with nothing on the other side but a rocky cliff-face and a scrap of path.

"You two aren't fighters, so you get across the river and hold it for us so we can cross," he ordered Drake and Skan. Skan took one look at the swollen, raging waters, and seriously considered mutiny.

But Amberdrake just picked up a coil of rope from the wreckage of the camp, and gestured to him to follow down to the rocks at the edge. There he rigged a harness of rope for himself, while Bern and the rest stood nervously with their backs to the water, facing the forest, bows and swords ready. Soon enough, the fog would rise, and when the shadow-creatures came back, the besieged rescuers wouldn't be able to see them until it was far too late.

Drake, the expert in ropes and knots, moved far more quickly than Skan would have thought possible under the circumstances. His fingers fairly flew as he put together a harness it would be impossible to get out of without undoing at least half of the knots. It must have seemed to the four injured fighters that he was taking a ridiculous amount of time, however. He was even making sure that it would fit over his pack—the precious pack that had what was left of their medical kit, and the oil and oil lamp.

"Hurry up!" Bern shouted, his voice pitched higher with strain and nerves.

Drake ignored them, and turned to Skan. "You can't carry me over, but you can tow me through the water," he pointed out. "There's no way I'm going to slip out of this."

He fastened the loose end of the rope to a tree at the water's edge, without elaborating anything, but his plan was obvious to Skan. The harness was rigged so that Drake *could* swim freely, but could also be towed along easily, which is what he meant Skan to do, flying above the river. Once he got Drake to the other side, the *kestra'chern* could fasten his rope to a boulder or spike of rock, and the others could plunge in and drag themselves across.

Providing, of course, there weren't more of those things on the other side, waiting somewhere.

If that last thought occurred to Amberdrake, he didn't hesitate for a second; once he had the end of the rope tied off, he plunged immediately into the river, almost before Skan had hold of the end fastened to his harness. Caught off-balance for a moment, Skan held on against the tug of the current, then launched himself into the air.

Amberdrake sputtered and submerged once, then steadied. He called out, "It's drier in here than in the forest!"

Once there, he was utterly grateful that Drake was a good swimmer, and he allowed himself a brief, tension-relieving smile at Amberdrake's quip. His friend was able to keep his own head above water, so that Skan's only task was to pull him onward.

Only! This is like playing tug-of-war against five teams of draft horses!

It was obvious within a few moments that this was going to be a great deal more difficult than it looked. They weren't even a single length from the shore, and Skan wanted to quit.

The gryphon's wings beat laboriously, the muscles in his back and chest burning with pain, as he pulled against the current and the weight of Drake's body. Below him, Amberdrake labored against the current trying to pull him under, and occasionally lost the battle. But he had honed his swimming ability in the powerful surf below White Gryphon; between his own strength and Skan's, his head always popped back above the surface again, long enough for him to get another lungful of air. Ten heartbeats later, they were out of time.

"Hurry!" Bern shouted again, his voice spiraling upward in fear. "They're coming!"

Skan ignored him as best he could, concentrating every fiber on getting a little more strength out of his wings. Drake was not doing well down there; the treacherous currents kept pulling him under, and each time he rose to the surface it took a little longer.

They were about halfway across when the sounds of battle erupted behind him; short screams and cries that echoed above the roaring river. He ignored those, too, as best he could.

His world narrowed to the face of his friend in the water below, the rope in his front talons, the pain of his laboring body, and the farther shore.

His lungs were on fire; his forelimbs ached with all the tortures of the damned from the strain of holding Drake and pulling him onward. His vision fogged with red, as it had only a few times in the past, when he had driven himself past his limits.

The bank was only a few lengths away—but he was out of energy, running out of strength, and just about out of endurance.

He wasn't going to make it. He could drop the rope and save himself, or they would both be dragged under.

No! He was *not* going to surrender with the goal so close! *Come on, gryphon. If he can do this, so can you. You're a team, remember! He's counting on you not to let him drown.*

Think of what Winterhart would do to you if you did! Think of what Gesten would do!

Amberdrake has been with you all your life, gryphon, all your life. He's had his hands in your guts and your blood in your hair, putting you back together from pieces. He didn't leave you then, he wouldn't leave you.

From somewhere came another burst of strength, and with a cry that was half a scream of defiance and half a moan of agony, he drove himself at the bank.

He made it by mere talon-lengths, dropping down on it with all the grace of a shot duck, and landing half on the bank, half in the water. With a groan, he grabbed the rope in his beak and dragged himself and Drake, talon over talon, onto the bank and safety.

He wanted to just lie there, panting, but there were still four more people on the other side. Somehow he pulled himself up to a standing position on shaking legs, just as Drake got to his hands and knees, and both of them turned toward the far bank at the same time.

All they saw was torn foliage, the slashed end of the rope hanging off the tree Drake had tied it to, splashes of red that weren't likely flowers—and the empty shore. They watched, panting and slumping down against each other until the fog closed in, leaving them staring at blank whiteness.

They were alone.

It could not be much longer before whatever it was that had attacked them found a way to cross, unless it took a long time—to eat.

For a moment, he felt stricken, numb, frozen with shock. But he had been in too many fights, and lost too many comrades, for this to paralyze him now.

Mourn later, find safety now!

Drake looked at him from beneath a mat of hair that had become a tangled, dripping mess, his clothing half torn from his body by the fight of last night, and a strange look of hope in his eyes. For one stark moment, Skan was afraid that he'd gone mad.

"Blade—" he began hoarsely, then coughed, huge racking coughs that brought up half a lungful of river water. Skan balled his talons into fists and pounded his back until he stopped coughing and waved Skan off.

"Blade—" he began again, his voice a ruin. He looked up and pointed north along the riverbank. "She's that way. I can feel her. I swear it, Skan!"

With one accord, they dragged themselves to their feet and stumbled northward over the slippery rocks and wet clay of the bank below the cliff face. North—where their children *must* be.

Tad inspected the last of the traps with no real hope that he would find anything at this one that differed from all the rest. The first *wyrsa* they had killed had been the last; none of the traps worked a second time. In fact, the *wyrsa* seemed to take a fiendish delight in triggering the damned things and leaving them empty.

So far, they had not dared the last one, another rockfall that he or Blade could trigger from inside the cave. He suspected, though, that it was only a matter of time before they did. On the other hand, they would not be able to disarm it without triggering it, so perhaps they were all even.

As he had expected, this snare lay empty, too. He decided that the rope could be better used elsewhere, and salvaged it. It certainly would have been nice if *this* one had worked, though. His nerves were wearing thin, and he was afraid that the *wyrsa* might be able to drain mage-energy from him constantly now, since they were so close. He didn't dare try shielding against them; shields were magical too, and they could surely be eaten like anything else magical.

When they had first found the cave, he had thought that the noise of the river and the waterfall would cover the sounds anything approaching made, but over the past few days he had discovered to his surprise that he had been wrong. To a limited extent, he had actually gotten used to the steady roaring, and was able to pick out other noises beyond it.

But the very last sound he had been expecting was the noise of someone—a two-legged someone—scrambling over the rocks at a speed designed to break his neck. And panting.

Especially not coming *toward* him.

Those were not *wyrsa* sounds, either, not unless the *wyrsa* had acquired a pair of hunting-boots and put them on!

He had barely time to register and recognize the sounds before the makers of the noise burst through the fog right in his face. He hadn't heard the second one, because *he* had been flying, and his wingbeats had *not* carried over the sound of the falls. Tadrith looked up to find his vision filled with the fierce, glorious silhouette of the Black Gryphon.

"*Father!*" he exclaimed, in mingled relief and shock. "Amberdrake—"

"*No time!*" Skandranon panted, as Amberdrake scrabbled right past him without pausing. "Run! We're being chased!"

No need to ask what was chasing them. Skan landed heavily, then turned to stand at bay to guard Amberdrake's retreat. Tad leaped up beside him, despite his handicap. With two gryphons guarding the narrow trail, there wasn't a chance in the world that the *wyrsa* would get past!

But they certainly tried.

The fog was as thick as curdled milk, and the *wyrsa* nothing more than shadows and slashing claws and fangs reaching for them through the curtain. But they couldn't get more than two of their number up to face Skan and Tad at any one time, and without the whole pack able to attack together, their tactics were limited. They *were* fast, but Tad and Skan were retreating, step by careful step, and that generally got them out of range before a talon or a bite connected.

Step by step. And watch it. Slip, and you end up under those claws. Thank Urtho for giving us four legs. They retreated all the way to the shelf of rock in front of the cave, and that was where their own reinforcements stepped in.

"Duck!" came the familiar order, and this time when he and his father dropped to the ground, not only did rocks hurl over their heads, but a pair of daggers hummed past Tad's ear like angry wasps. They both connected, too, and one was fatal. The *wyrsa* nearest the water got it in the throat, made a gurgle, and fell over, to be swept away by the rushing torrent. The second was lucky; he was only hit in the shoulder, but gave that familiar hiss-yelp, and vanished into the fog. Skan and Tad took advantage of the respite to turn their backs in turn and scramble into the cave itself.

There they turned again, prepared for another onslaught, but the *wyrsa* had evidently had enough for one day.

Tad sat down right where he was, breathing heavily, heart pounding; his father was less graceful and more tired than that, and dropped down into the sand as if he'd been shot himself, panting with his beak wide open.

"I always knew those throwing-knives were going to come in handy some day," Amberdrake observed.

He looked nothing like the Amberdrake that Tad had known all his life. His long hair was a draggling, tangled, water-soaked mess; his clothing stained, torn, muddy, and also sodden. He wore a pack that was just as much of a mess, at least externally. At his waist was a belt holding one long knife, a pouch, and an odd sheath that held many smaller, flat knives, exactly of the kind that had just whizzed over Tad's head.

"Yes, but—you had to—learn how—to throw them—first," Skan replied, panting. "You and your—bargains!"

"They *were* a bargain!" Amberdrake said indignantly. "A dozen of them for the price of that one single fighting-knife that you wanted me to get!"

"But you—knew how to—*use* the—fighting-knife!"

Blade brought her father and Skan a skin of water each, and they drank thirstily. She looked from one to the other of them, and carefully assessed their condition. "I don't think I'm going to ask where the rest of your group is," she said quietly. "I'm pretty certain I already know."

* * *

A tiny oil lamp cast warm light down on Amberdrake and his patient. Blade sat at her father's feet while he examined her shoulder, as Skan and Tad kept watch at the mouth of the cave. "You did a fine job on Tadrith's wing," Amberdrake murmured. "I only wish he had done as good a job on your shoulderblade."

Well, that certainly explained why it wouldn't stop hurting. "You're not going to have to rebreak it, are you?" she asked, trying not to wince. He patted her unhurt shoulder comfortingly, and it was amazing just how good that simple gesture felt.

"Not hardly, since it was never set in the first place. Immobilized, yes, but not set. I'm astonished that you've managed as much as you have." He placed the tips of his fingers delicately over the offending bone. "It's possible that it was only cracked at first, and not broken, and that somewhere along the line you simply completed the break. Hold very still for a moment, and this *will* hurt."

She tried not to brace herself, since that would only make things worse. She felt his fingers tighten, sensed a *snap*, and literally saw stars for a moment, it hurt so much.

When she could see again, *she* was still sitting upright, and *he* still had his hands on her shoulders, so she must have managed not to move. She sagged gratefully against the rock he was sitting on, and wiped tears from her eyes, weakly.

"Now, stay still a moment more," he urged. "I haven't done this for a long time, and I'm rather out of practice."

She obeyed, and a moment later, felt the area above the break warming. The pain there vanished, all but a faint throbbing in time with her pulse.

I'd forgotten he still has some Healing ability... not enough that he ever acts as a Healer anymore, but enough that he could in the war. In fact, he was first sent by his family off to train as a Healer, but his Empathic senses got in the way. In the war he was supposed to have been very good, even on gryphons.

Amberdrake finally lifted his hands from her shoulder and sighed. "I'm sorry, dearheart, I can't do as much as I'd like."

It was far more than she'd had any hope of before they arrived!

"You did a great deal, Father, believe me. I hope you saved plenty of yourself for Tad," she said. "Especially since you did specialize in gryphon-trauma during the war!"

"I did," he replied as she twisted around to look up at him. He combed his hair out of his eyes with one hand, and grimaced. "I'll keep working on you two as I recuperate, too. But I never was as competent at Healing as I'd like, and accelerating bone growth—well, it's hard, and I never did learn to do it well. Maybe if I'd gotten the right training when I was younger..."

"Then *you'd* have been a Healer, Lady Cinnabar would have been *your* lady and apprentice instead of Tamsin's, and I wouldn't be here," she interrupted. "I love you just the way you are, Father. I wouldn't change a thing."

And suddenly she realized that she meant exactly that, probably for the first time since she had been a small child.

She knew that he had needed to extend his empathic sense in order to Heal, and he still hadn't barricaded himself; he felt that, and his eyes filled with tears.

He wanted to hear that from me as much as I wanted his approval! she thought with astonishment. *How could I have been so blind all this time! Thinking only the child could want approval from the parent—how stupid of me—the parent wants approval from the child just as much.*

"Blade—" he said. She didn't let him finish. She reached up for him as he reached down for her, and they held each other while his tears fell on her cheeks and mingled with hers.

It was he who pulled away first, not she; rubbing his nose inelegantly on the back of his hand as he sniffed, and managing a weak smile for her. "Well, aren't we a pair of sentimental idiots," he began.

"No, you're a pair of *sensible* idiots, if that isn't contradictory," Skandranon interrupted. "You two were overdue for that, if you ask me. And, if you don't ask me, I'll tell you anyway, and I am right, as usual. Drake, what can she do now, if anything?"

"I've strengthened and knitted the bone a bit," Amberdrake replied, looking at her although he answered Skan. "And I've done something about the pain. I wouldn't engage in hand-to-hand, but you can certainly throw a spear, use a sling, or do some very *limited* swordplay. No shields, sorry; it won't take that kind of strain."

"We don't have any shields with us, so that hardly matters," she replied dryly. "Nor bows, either; we had to concentrate on bringing things we could use."

"Well... I know how to make a throwing-stick and the spears to go with it, if you know how to use one," Amberdrake admitted. "That should increase your range. There ought to be *some* wood in here straight enough for spears."

He knows how to make *a weapon!* She throttled down her surprise, and just nodded. "Yes to both—now let me go replace Tad at the front and you can work your will on him."

She almost said *magic*, but stopped herself just in time. Since the *wyrsa* hadn't come calling when her father began his Healing, evidently they did not eat Healing-energy. Which was just as well, under the circumstances. Perhaps it was too localized, or too finely-tuned to be sucked in from afar.

She stood up, hefted a spear in both hands, marveling at her new freedom from pain, and smiled with grim pleasure at the feel of a good weapon. Tad retreated to the back of the cave, and she took her place beside his father.

"So, what exactly are those nightmares?" Skan asked: "Have you any idea?"

She stared out into the rain—the rain had begun early, which meant that the fog had lifted early. That was to their advantage; with four enemies in the cave, she didn't think that the *wyrsa* would venture an attack in broad daylight.

"Tad thinks they're some kind of *wyrsa*, maybe changed by the mage-storms," she told him. "They're about the size of a horse, and they're black, and I suppose you already know that they eat magic."

"Only too well," Skan groaned.

"Well, to counter that advantage, they seem to have lost their poison fangs and claws," she said. "I don't think they're going to try entrancing us again after the first time, but if they start weaving in and around each other, they can hypnotize you if you aren't careful."

"The *wyrsa* I used to hunt were better at it than that," Skan observed, watching the bushes across the river tremble. "So they've lost a couple of attributes and gained one. Could be worse. One touch of those claws, and you were in poor shape, and that was with the hound-sized ones. A horse-sized one would probably kill you just by scratching you lightly."

"I suppose that counts as good news, then." She sighed. "I think this is a pack of youngsters led by one older female, probably their mother. We don't know how many there are; two less than when they started, though. I don't know if you saw it, but Father got one; Tad got one a couple of days ago, with a rockfall. The problem is, no trap works twice on them."

"*Wyrsa*, the size of a horse," Skan muttered, and shook his head. "Terrible. I'd rather have makaar. I wonder what other pleasant surprises the mage-storms left out here for us to find?"

She shrugged. "Right now, this is the only one that matters, It's pretty obvious that the things breed, and breed true, so if we don't get rid of them, one of these days they'll come looking for more magic-meals closer to our home." She turned her gaze on Skandranon for a moment. "And what *did* happen to your party, other than what I can guess?"

Skandranon told her, as tersely as she could have wished. She hadn't known any of the Silvers well, except Bern, who had been her tracking teacher, but it struck her that they had all acted with enormous stupidity and arrogance. Was it only because when they didn't meet with any immediate trouble that they assumed there wasn't anything to worry about?

"Between you and me, my dear," Skandranon said in an undertone, "I'm afraid the late Regin was an idiot. I suspect that he assumed that since you were a green graduate, probably hurt, and female to boot, you got into difficulties with what to him would have been minor opponents. He was wary at first, but when no armies and no renegade mages appeared, he started acting as if this was a training exercise."

She tried not to think too uncharitably of the dead Silver. "Well, we *don't* have much experience, and it would be reasonable to think that we might have panicked and overreacted," she said judiciously. "Still. I'd have thumped that Filix over the head and tied him up once I found the wreck and *knew* there was something that ate magic about. Why attract attention to yourself?"

"Good question," Skan replied. "I wish now I'd done just that." His mournful expression filled in the rest; she could read his thoughts in his eyes. Or was that *her* empathic sense operating? *If I had, they might still be alive. I should have pulled rank on them.*

She turned her attention back to the outside, for she felt distinctly uneasy having the Black Gryphon confess weakness, even tacitly, to her. And yet, she felt oddly proud. He would not have let her see that, if he were not treating her as an adult and an equal.

"Well, what it all comes down to is this," she said grimly. "No one is going to get us out of this except ourselves. We have no way to warn anyone, and what happened to you is entirely likely to happen to them', unless they're smarter than Regin was."

"Oh, that goes without saying—the closest team to us is led by Ikala," Skan said—rather slyly, she thought.

And she clutched her hands on the shaft of the spear as her heart raced a little. *Ikala—if I was going to be rescued by anyone.*

She shook her head; this was not some fanciful Haighlei romance tale. "They're still in danger, and we can't warn them," she repeated. "Remember, these damned things get smarter every time we do something! I think they may even get smarter every time they eat more magic. I doubt that they're native, so Ikala won't know about them. The best chance we all have to survive is if we four can eliminate these creatures before anyone else runs afoul of them. If they *do* get nastier every time they eat something, everyone out there could become victims. For all we know—if they share intelligence as Aubri said—they may share their power among each other as they die off. The fewer there are, the more powerful the individuals might become."

She was afraid that Skan might think she was an idiot for even *thinking* the four of them could take on the *wyrsa* pack, as ill-equipped as they were, but he nodded. "Are you listening to this, Drake?" he called back into the cave.

"To every word, and I agree," came the reply. "It's insane, of course, to think that we can do that, but we're used to handling insanely risky business, aren't we, old bird?"

"We are!" Skan had actually mustered up a grin.

But Amberdrake wasn't finished yet. "And what's more, I'm afraid that trait runs in both families. Right, Tad?"

A gusty sigh answered his question. "I'm afraid so," the young gryphon replied with resignation. "Like father, like son."

Skan winked at her. "The basic point is, we have four excellent minds and four bodies to work on this. Well, between your broken bones and our aching ones, we probably have the equivalent of *two* healthy bodies, rather than four, but that's not so bad! It could be worse!"

Blade thought about just a few of the many, many ways in which it *could* be worse, and nodded agreement. *Of course, there are many, many ways in which it could be better, too.*

"So, while those two are back there involved in patching and mending, let me get my sneaky old mind together with your resilient young one, and let's see if we can't produce some more, cleverer tactics." He gryph-grinned at her, and to her surprise, she found herself grinning back.

"That's it, sir," Tad said, from back in the cave. "That's all the weapons we have."

"Blade?" There was surprise in her father's voice. "I thought you said that you didn't have a bow."

"I did!" She left Skan for a moment and trotted back to the fire, to stare at the short bow and quiver of arrows in surprise. "Where did *that* come from?"

"I brought it in my pack," Tad said sheepishly. "I know you said not to bring one because you couldn't use it, but—I don't know, I thought maybe you might be able to pull it with your feet or something, and if nothing else, you could start a fire with it."

"Well, she still can't use it, but I *can*," Amberdrake said, appropriating it. He looked up at Skan and his son. "You two get out there and start setting those traps before the sun goes down; we'll get ready for the siege."

There would be a siege; Blade only hoped that the traps that the other two were about to set would whittle down the numbers so that the inevitable siege would be survivable. If the mother *wyrsa* had been angry over the loss of a single young, what would she be like when she lost several?

Tad and Skan were going out to set some very special single traps—and do it now, while the *wyrsa* were at a distance. They knew that the *wyrsa* had withdrawn—probably to hunt—because Blade and her father had used their empathic abilities to locate the creatures.

It had been gut-wrenching to do so, but it had at least worked. They hoped that the *wyrsa* would be out of sensing range of small magics, because that was what they intended to use.

The bait and the trigger both would be a tiny bit of magic holding the whole thing together. That was why it needed Skan and Tad to do the work; they were physically stronger than Blade and her father. When the *wyrsa* "ate" the magic holding everything in place—

Deadfalls would crush them, sharpened wooden stakes would plunge through them, nooses would snap around their legs and the rocks poised at the edge of the torrent would tumble in, pulling them under the water. And for the really charming trap, another huge rockfall would obliterate the path and anything that was on it.

They would have to be very, very clever; the magic had to be so small that the *wyrsa* would have to be on top of it to sense it. Otherwise it would "eat" the magic from a distance, triggering the trap without its killing anything.

Meanwhile, Blade and her father gathered together every weapon in their limited arsenal for a last stand.

It has to be now, she kept telling herself. *The* wyrsa *are nibbling away at Tad and they'll do the same to Skan. The more they eat, the stronger they get. We have to goad them into attacking before they're ready, and keep them so angry that they rely on their instincts and hunting skills instead of thinking things over. If we wait, there's a chance the next party will bumble right into them...*

That would be Ikala and Keenath—and the idea that either of those two could be in danger made a fierce rage rise inside her, along with determination to see that nothing of the kind happened.

Spears; the long ones, and the short, crude throwing-spears that Amberdrake was making, with points of sharpened, fire-hardened wood. Those were hers, those, and her fighting-knife, which was just a trifle shorter than a small sword. Amberdrake would take the bow, his own fighting-knife, and his throwing-knives. She still had her sling, and that could be useful at the right time.

There wasn't much, but it was all useful enough. When she had divided it into two piles, hers and her father's, she sat down beside him at the fire to help him with the spears. He made the points, she fire-hardened them, until the pile of straight wooden stakes was all used up. Then she took a single brand from the fire, and he put it out.

She went all the way to the back of the cave and started a *huge* new fire there, one of the objects being to make the *wyrsa* believe that they were farther back there than they actually were. She piled about half of their wood, the wettest lot, around it. This wood was going to have to dry out before it caught—and she thought she had that timed about right.

It's too bad this cave is stable, she thought wistfully. *It would be nice to arrange to get them inside, then drop the ceiling on them.*

Well, in a way, they were going to do that anyway.

She helped her father drag all of the rest of the driftwood that they had collected to the front of the cave and arrange it along the barricade. There was quite a lot of it, more than she remembered. Tad had certainly been busy!

And this had better work, because we are using up all of our resources in one attempt. What was it that Judeth always told us! "Never throw your weapon at the enemy!" I hope we aren't doing that now.

But being cautious certainly hadn't gotten them anywhere.

Strange how it was the younger pair that was so cautious, and the older willing to bet everything on one blow.

Periodically, she or her father would stop, close their eyes, and open themselves to the *wyrsa* to check on their whereabouts. It was Amberdrake's turn to check when he cut his "search" short, and put his fingers to his mouth to utter the ear-piercing whistle they had agreed would be the "call in" signal. Skan came flying back low over the river, with Tad running on the trail a little behind him.

At that point, the gloom of daylight had begun to thicken to the darkness of night, and they were all ready to take their positions. Blade sent up a petition to the Star-Eyed One that this would all work...

The Star-Eyed only helps those who help themselves, and those who have planned well don't need the Star-Eyed's help. Always remember that, Blade. If you haven't done your best, you have no reason to hope for the Star-Eyed's help if it still goes bad.

She crouched down behind a screen of rock and dead brush, away from their safe haven of nights past and waited, her spear-thrower in one hand, three spears in the other. She hadn't had time to practice, and she only hoped that she could hit somewhere in her targets, instead of off to one side of them. From where she crouched, she wouldn't have to make a fatal hit, just a solid one, and they would probably go into the river. There was nowhere for them to hide, even in the darkness, because it wasn't going to *be* dark, not completely. Skan had made a quick sortie across the river before they went off to set traps and had returned with rotten wood riddled with foxfire. Any time she saw one of the chunks of foxfire vanish, she was supposed to throw.

They had planned as well as they could. Now it was just a matter of waiting...

And I never was very good at waiting!

She kept quiet, tried not to fidget, and listened for sounds up the trail.

Skan had an advantage over all of the others; he knew where each trap was, because he felt the mage-energy. And he would know as they were triggered; because he would sense that, too. Under any other circumstances, the tiny bits of energy he and Tad had invested in the triggers would have vanished in the overall flows of energies, but with *nothing* around to mask them, they "glowed" to him like tiny fires in the distance.

And he tensed, as he felt the first of them "go out."

That was the strangling-noose...

He wished he had Drake's empathic ability as well. It would be nice to know if their trap had gotten anything.

They had been careful to set things that worked differently—though hopefully the pups would venture over here slowly, and would be so greedy to get at the bits of magic that none of them would realize that the magic-bits and the traps had anything to do with each other.

The next one is the set of javelins, and if there's a group, it should take out several.

And they'll be cautious after they spring that one.

The javelins, hidden under brush, were far enough away from the trigger that he was fairly certain that the pups would make no connection between the two.

And there it goes! In his mind's eye, another little glowing "fire" went out.

Two down, two to go.

One trap working from above, one from in front. One takes out a single pup, one takes out several. No pattern there, and nothing in the way of a physical trigger to spot.

The next trap would take out a single pup again and it worked from the ground. That would be the foot-noose. He felt his chest muscles tighten all over as he "watched" that little spark of energy, and waited for the pups to regain their courage. He knew that at least he and Tad were safe from detection tonight; they'd used up all but a fraction of their personal energies making the traps. There was nothing to distract the pups from the bait.

Time crawled by with legs of lead, and he began to wonder if he and Tad had done their work a little too well. Had he discouraged the pups? Or would the loss of several more goad them into enough rage to make them continue?

Only Blade and Amberdrake knew the answer to that question, and only if they had opened themselves up empathically again.

Just when he was about to give up—when, in fact, he had started to stand, taking himself out of hiding—the third "spark" died.

He crouched back down again, quickly.

They all heard—or rather, felt—the fourth trap go. It was the one that had originally been set with a crude string-trigger that went into the cave. When it went, it would not only take several *wyrsa* with it—hopefully—but it would have the unfortunate side-effect of spreading rock out into the river, widening the shelf in front of the cave. But that couldn't be helped...

The rocks under him shook as the *wyrsa* triggered the last trap—and he didn't need to be empathic to know that this final trap totally enraged them. Unlike the cries that they had uttered until now, their ear-piercing shrieks of pure rage as the remaining members of the pack poured over the rocks were clearly audible over the pounding water.

More than four—But it was too late to do anything other than follow through on their plan. With a scream of his own, he dove off the cliff, right down on the last one's back.

The head whipped around and the fangs sank into his shoulder, just below where the wing joined his body. He muffled his own screech of pain by sinking his own beak into the join of the creature's head and neck.

The thing wouldn't let go, but neither would he. It tried to dislodge him, but he had all four sets of talons bound firmly into its shoulders and hindquarters. In desperation, it writhed, and rolled, and sank its fangs in up to the gumline. He saw red in his vision again, but clamped his beak down harder, sawing at the thing's flesh as he did so. He jerked his head toward his own keel, digging the hook of his powerful beak even further through hide, then muscle, then cartilage.

The spine… he had to sever the spine…

Amberdrake stood up on his tiny shelf of rock and fired off arrow after arrow into the one *wyrsa* that had been unfortunate enough to cross *his* blob of foxfire. The arrows themselves had been rubbed with phosphorescent fungus, so once the first one lodged, he had a real target. He'd throttled down any number of emotions as the *wyrsa* came closer and closer, but—strangely enough, now that he was fighting, he felt a curious, detached calm. His concentration narrowed to the dark shape with an increasing number of glowing sticks in it; his world constricted to placing his next arrow somewhere near the rest of those spots of dim light. Sooner or later, he would hit something fatal.

He knew that he had, when the shape bearing the sticks wobbled to the edge of the water, wavered there for a moment, then tumbled in.

He chose another as it crossed a blob of foxfire, and began again.

Tad was close enough to his father that he saw the difficulties Skan was in. At that point, it didn't matter that it was not in the plan—he surged out of hiding and pounced, sinking *his* beak into the *wyrsa's* throat, and his foreclaws into its forelimbs. A gush of something hot and foul-tasting flooded his mouth, and the *wyrsa* collapsed under Skan's weight.

He let go, spitting to rid himself of the taste of the *wyrsa's* blood, as Skan shook himself free of the creature's head and staggered off to one side. Tad guarded him as he collected himself, keeping the other *wyrsa* at bay with slashing talons.

Then he wasn't alone anymore; his father was fighting beside him. "Good job," Skan called; "I owe you one."

"Then take the one on the left!" Tad called back, feeling a surge of pleasure that brought new energy with it.

"Only if you take the one on the right!" Skan called back, and launched himself at his next target.

Tad followed in the same instant, as if they had rehearsed the maneuver a thousand times together.

Blade's weapon was not as suited to rapid firing as her father's, and she had to choose her targets more carefully than he. He had a great many arrows; she had a handful of spears, and not all of them flew cleanly.

But when she *did* connect, her weapon was highly effective. She sent three *wyrsa* tumbling into the river, and wounded two more, making them easier targets for Skan and Tad.

Just as she ran out of short spears, she saw—and sensed—the moment that they had all been waiting for. The bitch *wyrsa* was herding her remaining pups before her into the cave the two humans and two gryphons had abandoned. She obviously intended to reverse the situation on her attackers, by going to ground in what should have been *their* bolt-hole.

"She's going in!" Blade shouted. She seized the longer of her two spears and jumped down to the ground. A moment later, her father joined her, and with Tad and Skan they formed a half-circle that cut off the *wyrsa* from escape.

The pups had clearly had enough; now that they were all in the cave, they were silhouetted clearly against the fire at the rear. The pups, about three of them, milled about their mother. They didn't like the fire, but they didn't want to face the humans and gryphons either.

The wyrsa-bitch, however, was not ready to quit yet. She surged from side to side in the cave, never presenting a clear target, and snarled at her pups. It looked to Blade as if she were trying to herd them into something. She and Amberdrake edged up farther into the cave, following the plan. In theory, with the two weakest members of the party in plain sight, the bitch should do what they wanted her to.

"She's trying to goad them into a charge!" Amberdrake shouted. "Get ready!"

Blade grounded the butt of her spear against the rock, hoping against hope that she wouldn't have to use it—

"*Now!*" Drake shouted, as the bitch herded her pups up onto the brush and rock barrier.

And at that signal, Skan and Tad used the last of their mage-energy, and ignited the oil-soaked wood of the barricade with a simple, small fire-spell.

With the fire already going at the back of the cave, there was a good draft going up the chimney. The flames swept back, and merged with the second fire at the rear. The cave was an oven, and the *wyrsa* were trapped inside.

The wyrsa-bitch turned and heaved herself at the barricade nearest Blade. Her dead-white eyes blazed rage as she stared at the human, and Blade felt her hatred burning, even without being open empathically.

Amberdrake dropped his spear; it clattered to the ground as he seized his head in both hands. His knees buckled and he fell in a convulsing heap.

Without hesitation, Blade picked up her own spear, aimed, and threw.

The bitch-wyrsa took it full in the chest and continued forward, screaming defiance. She heaved up into the air, towering above all of them for a moment—and Blade was certain she was going to come over the barricade anyway. Blade's heart pounded in her ears—only that sound, and the sound of the *wyrsa's* scream, louder than anything she had felt before.

The *wyrsa* fell forward, but didn't leap. The spear jutted from her chest, only a quarter of its length in. She stumbled forward in shock. Her forelegs crumpled—and the butt of the crude spear struck the ground and drove itself in deeper.

Blade fell into a crouch without hesitation and groped for her fighting-knife, but she could not take her eyes off the vision of the black *wyrsa* pitching backwards, to be consumed in flame.

"We won," Tad said, for the hundredth time. As the rain washed *wyrsa* blood from the rocks, he locked his talons into another body and dragged it to the river, to roll it in. Blade hoped that something in there would eat *wyrsa*, and that the blasted things wouldn't poison the fish.

After the flames had died down, they had all moved back into the cave to see what was left. Not much was recognizable compared to the bodies outside the cave, but the skulls of the charred *wyrsa* were easily broken off for later cleaning. The families of those people the creatures had killed were entitled to them, perhaps for a revenge ceremony during mourning, so the grisly task was done with solemn efficiency. Inside, the rock was nicely warmed, and the two exhausted fathers, had a good, comfortable place to lie down and get some rest.

Meanwhile she and Tad dragged their own weary bodies out into the rain again, to clean up the mess.

"This is the last one, thank the gods," Blade said, as she hauled the last of the beheaded bodies to the river's edge. Together, she and Tad shoved it in, and together they turned and walked back to the cave.

"Drake is burning some fish for you, Blade," Skan greeted them as they climbed over the rock barricade. "Zhaneel would not approve. By the way, *both* the other rescue-parties are near enough for Mindspeech with me, so we won't have to eat fish much longer."

Blade's heart surged with joy—and then her throat tightened, as she realized just *how* close the others must have been last night.

They could have walked right into the same kind of trap that my father did, she thought soberly. She had been wondering ever since yesterday evening if they were doing the right thing by trying an all-or-nothing last-stand. Now she knew they *had* been.

"When will they get here?" Tad asked eagerly, as Blade accepted fish from her father with a smile of thanks.

"Tomorrow, probably. Your mother is thrilled, Blade. Tad, your mother and brother would be flying in here now if it weren't raining." Skan gryph-grinned at all of them. "I promised them that we would do our best not to melt before they got here."

"That was probably safe," Blade agreed. "Did you tell them anything other than that we were all safe?"

Skan ground his beak and dropped his head. "I confess, I told them everything while they were still far enough away that your mothers couldn't flay us alive for risking all our necks last night." He coughed. "I know my Zhaneel, and I suspect Winterhart will react the same. Weary by the time they reach us, they will be so grateful that we are all right that they will probably have forgotten that we took on all those *wyrsa* by ourselves."

Amberdrake winced. "Maybe Zhaneel will—but Winterhart won't," he said guiltily. "And she'll *never* forgive me for acting like a hotheaded young fighter and standing on a ledge in the dark, firing arrows into the damned things! And if I actually admit that I—well—I was *good* at it—"

Blade patted his knee, and smiled as a rush of love filled her heart.

"Don't worry, Father," she said fondly. "I'll protect you."

For the first time in days, if not weeks, Tad lay on a ledge in the open, sunning himself. Finally, *finally*, the rains had lessened last night, and although the fog had appeared on schedule, the rain had not chased it away. It looked as if the weather was getting back to "normal."

Tad whooped, and leaped off his ledge to gallop toward his brother. Keeth arrowed in for a landing down on the recently-added stretch of rock-and-gravel beach in front of the cave. A moment later, as Tad and his brother closed on each other for the gryphonic equivalent of a back-slapping reunion, the "mothers' party" appeared around the curve of the trail.

Now it was Blade's turn to launch herself off her ledge and run straight into the arms of her mother, while Amberdrake brought up the rear. Tad grinned to his twin as they watched his Silver partner hugging her mother and even shedding a few tears. She was acting just as any normal human would in the same situation, and about time, too!

Things settled down a little, and Winterhart paused to wipe a couple of happy tears, as the second party rounded the bend. With a gasp, Blade broke off her conversation with her mother to run straight for the leader of the party.

Ikala looked surprised, but extremely pleased, when she threw her arms around him—and it would have taken an expert to determine if she kissed him first, or he kissed her.

Tad took a quick look at Amberdrake and Winterhart; they looked stunned, but gradually the surprise was being replaced by—glee?

Probably. Now they're finally going to get their *wish, after all!*

"What is *that* all about?" Keeth gurgled. "She's never done *that* before!"

Tad laughed. "Oh, it has been a complicated mess, but I think I can explain it. Drake sees her as a real person now—not just as his daughter, his child. They've fought alongside each other. Now she's—well, now she knows who *she* is; that she's not a reflection of Drake or her mother, and that she doesn't have to work so hard at being their opposite. It's—well, she's free, free to be herself."

"And you?" Keeth asked shrewdly.

Tad laughed. "After seeing Father in action, I can't say I mind being the son of the Black Gryphon anymore: And now he has fought beside me, and he knows there is more to me than obstacle courses and fatherly pride. Word will get around, and then he will have to cope with being referred to as 'the father of that brave Silver.' I guess that's justice."

Keeth grinned and leaned against his brother. "That should give us all some rest and freedom."

Freedom, he thought with content. *That's what it is all right. Freedom.*

ABOUT THE AUTHORS

Mercedes Lackey is a full-time writer and has published numerous novels and works of short fiction, including the bestselling *Heralds of Valdemar* series. She is also a professional lyricist and licensed wild bird rehabilitator. She lives in Oklahoma with her husband and collaborator, artist Larry Dixon, and their flock of parrots.

www.**mercedeslackey**.com

Larry Dixon is a writer and fantasy illustrator. Dixon has contributed work to Wizards of the Coast's *Dungeons and Dragons* source books, including *Oriental Adventures*, *Epic Level Handbook* and *Fiend Folio*. He has collaborated with his wife, Mercedes Lackey, on a number of books, including *The Mage War* trilogy, *The SERRAted Edge* novels and *The Owl* trilogy.